A SHILLING ON GOOD FRIDAY

To Dear Ros,

In memory of my good friend, Michael, who was there when the seeds of this yarn were being sown in 1960's Portsmouth.

Enjoy the read.

Adrian

Back cover:

Image showing HMS *Excellent* Gunnery School at Portsmouth. Taken from *HMS Excellent 1830-1930: A History of the RN Gunnery School at Whale Island, Portsmouth & Stories of the Old Wooden Line of Battleships on board which the school was originally formed.*

Charpentier Ltd., Portsmouth 1930.

George Atzerodt photographed onboard the monitor USS *Montauk* following his apprehension.

A SHILLING ON GOOD FRIDAY

VOLUME ONE

A Lesson Learnt

Adrian John Hoare

Man of Kent Publishing

Distributed by Lightning Source

British Library Cataloguing in Publication Data
A catalogue record for this book is available from the British Library

ISBN 978-09933369-0-4

Typeset by Amolibros, Milverton, Somerset
www.amolibros.com
This book production has been managed by Amolibros
Printed and bound by Lightning Source

Hark! 'tis the voice of angels,
Borne in a song to me,
Over the fields of glory,
Over the jasper sea.

From the hymn by F. J. Crosby (1820 – 1915)

Photograph of Mina Reynolds by Trasks of Philadelphia: sent by William Reynolds to his mother in the autumn of 1865.

DEDICATION

To my wife, Theresa Eily Hoare.

In appreciation of her considerable forbearance on those occasions, since 1970, when I may have appeared unduly pre-occupied as I ventured in the footsteps – both at home and abroad – of my collateral ancestor, William Reynolds.

Foreword

The history of the United States is tightly stitched to that of England. After all, the American "Tree of Liberty" was grown from English seed. And so, it is not unusual to find a young English boy begin his career in Queen Victoria's Royal Navy, only to wind up a soldier in Abraham Lincoln's army. Of the two million-plus soldiers that made up the Union army nearly half were of British ancestry and, of those, over 50,000 were British subjects (Canada added another 10,000 men in the Union ranks). Such is the story of William Reynolds as told through the engaging writing of Adrian Hoare.

I first met William Reynolds, the English seaman and Union soldier who found himself an unsuspecting player in the hunt for Abraham Lincoln's murderers, in the summer of 1993. At the time I had spent well over two decades researching and writing on the events surrounding John Wilkes Booth and his murderous act. That summer, I received a phone call from a good friend and fellow historian, Charles Jacobs. While my interests centered mostly on Lincoln, Charles was interested in the exploits of a local Marylander named Elijah White who served as a colonel in the Confederate army. We often shared our research and knowledge, swapping stories about the Civil War and its interesting people.

Charles told me he had been contacted by an Englishman who had a relative who served in the Union army. The soldier had kept up a regular correspondence with his mother back in England, apprising her of his exploits in America. The letters survived, eventually winding up in the hands of a descendant. As so often happens with historical documents, the letters took on a life of their own and soon consumed the interests of his descendant. He was, of course, the author of this remarkable narrative, Adrian Hoare.

Reynolds' letters detailed his unusual story as a fifteen-year-old boy who enlisted in the Royal Navy in 1857. After five years in Her Majesty's service and, aggrieved with his treatment, he jumped ship during a layover in Halifax, Nova Scotia. Making his way to Baltimore, Reynolds enlisted in the Union army where he saw service in Louisiana during the Red River Campaign under General Nathaniel Preston Banks. Wounded during the battle of Pleasant Hill, he was invalided out of the army and found work as a coal miner in Pennsylvania. However, when he became restless with life in the mines, Reynolds re-enlisted in the 213th Pennsylvania Volunteers in 1865. Assigned to protect the Baltimore and Ohio Railroad near Relay, west of Baltimore, he was chosen to lead a small unit of soldiers in search of the assassin of President Lincoln and any conspirators attempting to escape north.

It was while leading his patrol one miserable, cold, wet night in April 1865, that Reynolds stumbled into history. Roaming the Maryland countryside in search of George Atzerodt – one of Wilkes Booth's fellow conspirators – he ran into another patrol charged with the same duty. Invited to join forces, Reynolds agreed and soon found himself at a farmhouse near Germantown, where Atzerodt was hiding in the belief that he was safe from arrest.

Reynolds' letter home to his mother, describing his rendezvous with history, took hold of Adrian's imagination and wouldn't let go. Delving into every aspect of his remarkable life as a seaman and soldier, Adrian developed a strong desire to visit the site where Reynolds became a part of American history.

The phone call from my friend, Charles Jacobs, was in the form of a request. He told me Adrian was planning a trip to the United States and a visit to Germantown and the site of Atzerodt's capture. Charles knew I had researched Atzerodt's capture and written on the subject. Would I be willing, Charles asked, to take Adrian under my wing and show him around the area and tell him what I knew about the story? Of course, my answer was yes, both out of friendship to Charles and because I had my own motive in meeting Adrian.

In the course of our conversation Charles mentioned that Adrian lived in the village of Hildenborough, in Kent, England. It was from Grafty Green, a small village in Kent, not far from Hildenborough, that my great-great-great grandfather had gathered up his wife and four children and emigrated to America in 1835. Two of his children, along with a son-in-law, enlisted in the Union army, serving in the same theater of operations as William Reynolds. It was exciting to think that the four men may have crossed paths at some point in their historic venture. I had spent a great deal of time researching my family genealogy and wanted to know more about the place where my ancestor had lived. Perhaps, I thought, Adrian might just be able to help me with my research while I helped him with his. We proved to be a perfect match.

It was a fresh morning following a night of rain, much like that which occurred when George Atzerodt awoke on April 20th 1865 to find a Colt revolver thrust in his face, when I met up with Adrian and his family. With Adrian and myself in the front seat of a rented car and Theresa, his wife, and sons, Richard and Philip, we began our day tracing the footsteps of Atzerodt as he fled Washington and the scene of Lincoln's murder. We began in Germantown in the District of Columbia, close on the heels of Atzerodt as he made his way through the military pickets surrounding the city to the small village of Germantown in Montgomery County, Maryland.

Atzerodt, assigned by Booth to assassinate Vice President Andrew Johnson, lost courage at the last minute and fled from the hotel where Johnson was staying. After a few hours of fitful sleep, he decided to leave the city for rural Maryland. His destination was his father's old homestead, now owned by his cousin, Hartman Richter. The dull Atzerodt had visited his cousin on several occasions during the war and had found solace away from the bustling city overrun with Union soldiers. Confused and frightened at first by Booth's act, Atzerodt felt sure that Germantown was well beyond the military's reach. He was mistaken; a mistake that cost him his life. Captured by a military posse, Atzerodt was taken to Washington where he was soon tried as an accessory in Lincoln's murder, found guilty, and hanged along with Mary Surratt, Lewis Powell and David Herold.

While official records make no mention of William Reynolds or his part in Atzerodt's capture, there is little doubt that he participated, as he claimed in his letters. Like so many soldiers who found themselves caught up in America's great Civil War, Reynolds was a prolific letter writer. Far from home and loved ones, he kept in touch with his family through his mother, writing her about his great adventure in America. Although he was not well educated by his own country's standards, Reynolds had a keen eye for the smaller as well as the larger events of his own life and those around him. And, like so many of his peers, he was capable of writing lucid and interesting letters to loved ones back home; and, as with the letters of many of those peers, these important documents were cherished and carefully preserved, being passed from generation to generation for us today. Because of William Reynolds and his letters, we have the good fortune to travel by his side through some of the more exciting times in history; to witness, through his eyes, everyday events, both small and large, that still interest us today.

William Reynolds' letters are, of course, only one part of our good fortune today. Without Adrian Hoare's dedication and beautiful prose the letters might well remain carefully stored away in a family trunk unknown to history. Adrian's research is impeccable and his skill in translating Reynolds' story into an interesting narrative enriches our history. Like Lazarus of old, William Reynolds rises from the dead to live once more through the pages of this novel.

Perhaps this is the true meaning of immortality.

Edward Steers Jr.
Berkeley Springs, WV.

Dr Edward Steers Jr. is a retired microbiologist and former Deputy Director of the National Institutes of Health in Bethesda, Maryland. He lives in the mountains of West Virginia, near Berkeley Springs, with his wife, Pat and is the acclaimed author of Blood on the Moon *(The University Press of Kentucky 2001) and* The Lincoln Assassination Encyclopaedia *(Harper Perennial 2010). In addition, he has written a wealth of other books relating to Lincoln and the conspiracy against him. In his New York Times bestseller,* Manhunt: the 12-Day Chase for Lincoln's Killer, *James L Swanson describes Ed Steers as the premier contemporary historian of the assassination.*

Introduction

The following story is based on the life of William Reynolds who entered this world on the island of Malta in August 1842. It is a poignant yarn and one which I have fashioned from the content of a small collection of letters which came my way during the 1960s. I believe I was eighteen years of age when my late father handed me a bundle of old family missives, four of which had been penned by the said William Reynolds during the year 1865. I recall setting about reading them with some enthusiasm.

It was about this time that my paternal grandmother, then in her late eighties, was becoming increasingly unable to fend for herself. In consequence, she left her home in Copnor, Portsmouth and moved into an elderly persons' residential home. It was in the course of assisting my father in taking care of my grandmother's possessions, that I made something of a discovery. In the front room of her modest terraced house, while in the process of salvaging some picture frames, I uncovered a delicate, Victorian watercolour from beneath a framed and yellowing photograph that had been cut from a newspaper. The subject was a small boy with light brown hair and blue eyes. He was dressed in early Victorian costume and stood beside a loo table, or circular dining table, draped with a blue and white cloth. On his left forearm was perched a parrot, whilst in his right hand he held a sprig of three cherries. The back of the portrait bore the inscription 'W. Mitchell. Miniature and Portrait Painter, July 1849'.

The identity of the young boy was later revealed to me by one of my father's cousins. This, she told me, was William Reynolds, a name I recognised as being the author of four of those letters. She recalled the days, before the outbreak of the Great War, when, as a child, she lived with an aunt and uncle in the village of Southbourne, near Chichester. There, on the wall above her bed, used to hang this same portrait. By all accounts her aunt was well versed in family history and used to tell her stories of her long departed cousin, William Reynolds. Sadly, however, her niece admitted to not paying a great deal of attention, so was unable to impart to me any information of significance. By 1947, on that aunt's death, the portrait of William Reynolds was passed to her younger sister, my grandmother, who, presumably, at this time, also became the custodian of that bundle of letters later given to me by my father.

The content of Reynolds' letters fascinated me and I set about trying to discover more about his life. Those letters were a good starting point and, what with reading between the lines and engaging in a good deal of related research over subsequent years, I was gradually able to put flesh on the bones. Then, in 1983, I met Colin Welland in the wake of his gaining an Oscar for the screenplay of *Chariots of Fire*. The consequence of the meeting was that he expressed an interest in writing a cinema screenplay based on the material that I had amassed at that time. Sadly, however, the necessary financial backing was not forthcoming during Colin's twelve-month option to acquire the copyright. However, moving on and putting that disappointment behind me, I continued to undertake further research and found myself entering my sixties with something I felt could form the basis of a novel. I was encouraged after approaches to the likes of writer Geraldine Brooks (*Year of Wonders* and *March*) – who considered the storyline a truly absorbing tale worthy of creative attention – and the late Anthony Minghella, Chair of the British Film Institute. Minghella, whose directing credits included *The English Patient* and *Cold Mountain*, advised me that, based on his own experience, perseverance furthers. So here is the product of my own perseverance.

Adrian John Hoare,
Hildenborough, Kent, 2014

One

PHILADELPHIA 1865

The young man's gaze seemed transfixed and impassive, cast beyond the sash window that was partly raised in its frame against a greying sky. Outside the October Monday morning went about its business. A grinding of wheels against tracks and a clattering of hooves signalled the passage of the regular ten o'clock horse-car as it slowed, then gathered pace towards its destination in the inner city.

William Reynolds was propped up and cushioned against his harsh, iron bedstead by a yellowing bolster that had seen better days. For the moment his thoughts were introverted and confused. His face was drawn and gaunt, his cheeks pinched and robbed of colour. It was a countenance that, to most, would have suggested his twenty-three years had long since passed him by.

A stiffening breeze began to infiltrate the room and this helped to pull William out of his distant muse. It was a chill air that blew from the direction of the river and carried a faint drizzle out of the north-west and, with its penetration, William drew the coverlet about him. He was not bitter about his ailment, indeed, having been under the misapprehension that it was hereditary, he had to some extent been expecting it. In a sense, therefore, he had conditioned himself accordingly, despite having obtained recent assurances that his illness was less severe. No, he was more in a state of sadness about his lot and sad for Mina. With the doctor's news there was no longer scope for optimism. The prognosis was dire and what lay ahead would be a stern test of his resolve. He had been tested before in his short life, having suffered all manner of strife and hardship which had placed his life in mortal danger. Yet, to the extent that he had been responsible for his own actions in moments of crisis and, being a fit enough fellow in times past, there had usually been a greater than even chance of pulling

3

through. But now he was truly in the hands of his Maker. The turmoil of a life of conflict had been exchanged for the turmoil and inevitability of terminal illness. Now, it seemed, all chance had wasted away: wasted like his own body had begun to recede, his affliction laying claim to its own daily tollage of flesh.

Borne on the gathering breeze off the Schuylkill and out of the street below, William could hear a departing voice on the front threshold. It was the kindly Doctor Jackson who, somewhat ironically, had been the bearer of all but kind news when he had earlier presented himself at William's bedside.

"My dear, you must remain strong. I have been entirely honest with your husband. His case is very distressing. Try to keep him comfortable. Plenty of fresh air for which purpose, incidentally, I have opened the front window in his room. I will come again tomorrow and the next day."

"But sir, we have little in the way of money. If you call again you should receive due payment for your trouble but our funds have…"

Mina's faltering words were interrupted by the doctor.

"Hush, my dear, no talk of money here. You see, I'm an old Union man and a patriot. Your dear husband is to be admired for what he did for the Country. I beg only one indulgence. I will need to call early, as I have today. I will see William before my pre-arranged visits. Good day to you my dear."

"Good day, sir, and thank you. Thank you from both of us…for your kindness, sir."

Doctor Jackson turned away and set his face and grey whiskers into the weather. Yet in swift realisation that this was on the cusp of becoming inclement, the physician turned on his heels and called back to the girl on the threshold.

"Oh, and Missus Reynolds, please close your husband's window. It was not a good idea of mine in the circumstances. The weather is falling damp now and it seems set for the day."

"Yes sir. I will do so immediately. It's Mina, sir. Please call me Mina."

Mina Reynolds watched the doctor walk away, half expecting that he might hail her again with some further instruction. Yet in truth she was in no hurry to confront her husband and reveal her tearful eyes; and so it was not until she had seen the doctor cross the street and clamber into his horse-drawn buggy, and then watched the conveyance depart at a brisk trot, that she chose to gently close the door. That done she lingered awhile in the hallway, into which the mean morning light struggled to find entry.

The wall hangings were of sombre hue, dirtied by the passage of time. In its gloominess the confined space matched Mina's feeling of desolation and, for the moment, she let go her emotions. Slumping to her knees at the foot of the stairs, she rested her forehead upon the third step and wept silently. Her chestnut locks fell about her head onto the threadbare carpet and became wetted by the product of her lament.

Once Mina had closed the front door and several minutes had elapsed, it troubled William that there came no footfall on the stairs. Whilst barely cushioned by its lean carpet it was the creaking stretchers that usually proclaimed an ascent from below, yet all was silent. In response to the absence of that precursor, therefore, William alighted from his bed, reached for his shirt and trousers and proceeded to discard his nightshirt. There was perhaps a hint of contempt in the brusque manner he cast the soiled garment aside. It saddened him that it boldly advertised the two turbulent nights of hoarse coughing that had gone before, stained as it was with dry phlegm, now streaked occasionally with tiny flecks of blood. And thus, clothed now in his day wear, yet devoid of his stockings, William stood on the stair-head and peered below. He leant forward to clasp the pine stair-rail as a crutch to his weary frame; like the wall hangings it was caked with the sweat and grease of past times.

"Mina! Mina! Come here my love, come here. I cannot stand to see you in such a troubled state. Come to me." William's heartfelt words did little to immediately allay his wife's sobbing which now, in the knowledge of his awareness of her distress and, being released from the wish to hide it, no longer came cloaked in silence. Instead her weeping fell into audible sobs of distress that convulsively caught her breath. Yet with time and William's patience, his wife's anguish fell victim to his gentle coaxing, the flow of tears was stemmed and the sobbing dropped to a whimper. As the parlour clock struck the half hour after ten, Mina had joined her husband at the top of the stairs. He pulled her close, rearranged the now tear drenched tufts of hair that fell about her face and tried to mask his own despair with a loving smile. Then, clasping her head to his breast, his eyes fell upon the wall above. Here a framed lithograph depicted a handsome barque. Rounding the Cape of Good Hope, the vessel was all but on her beam ends, as, beneath scudding clouds, she ploughed a frothing sea. William was drawn to ponder that he, too, was now cast adrift and set to founder. The prospect made him shudder as he turned and ushered Mina into the bedroom.

"You must rest. But let me first settle you with a drink," said William, as he led his wife to the comfort of an upholstered chair. That done, he descended to the scullery to prepare a hot milky beverage for them both. He had determined that he would augment his with a generous lacing of some local whisky he had put by, a potent distillation from grain raised in the Pennsylvanian hills where he had dwelt awhile and eked out a living during the previous winter. As for Mina's drink, he would slip a little balsamic concoction into the milk. It was a patent medicine the local pharmacist had been keen to promote as providing a mild sedative effect when Mina had previously shown signs of agitation. A generous spoonful was guaranteed to induce sleep. Once rested they would need to collect their thoughts and, to the extent that they had any future, deliberate on what might lay ahead.

★ ★ ★

As William subsequently reclined on the marital bed, cuddling his wife – who soon succumbed to the soporific influence of her medication – he found himself dwelling upon his short time with Mina. It had been three months since the couple's shameful embarrassment of being caught in flagrante delicto by Mina's mother, Ann Thompson. A balmy evening it had been, during the early days of July and the widow had returned to the family home earlier than expected after visiting a friend.

William and Mina had planned their assignation in Willow Street in the knowledge of Widow Thompson's intended absence for a few hours and of her elder daughter, Josie's plan to stay the night at a cousin's house below Gray's Ferry. Yet, as is so often the case, events did not unfold in the manner envisaged. Ann Thompson had felt unwell during her excursion, excused herself and promptly returned home. Being a woman of maturing years, in her mid-forties, she had begun to enter upon that phase in her life that troubled her with night sweats and a propensity for being beset with varying degrees of irritability. And thus she had been especially ill-conditioned in her mood to deal with what confronted her as she entered the back parlour. Her mouth gaped open, her normally florid cheeks drained of colour, cod-like in hue and pouting appearance. In front of the hearth, lit eerily yellow by candlelight, a man's bare posterior rose and fell in a rhythm of intensity and joy, his trousers about his knees yet not serving to impede the unrelenting progress of his task. Beneath him lay Ann Thompson's younger daughter, her legs spread-eagled, the whiteness of her soft thighs pinked and lustred by the exertion of coitus and the warmth of the night.

The insular noisiness and intensity of their lovemaking and the stealth of the widow's reappearance had rendered the young couple oblivious to the intrusion; and thus their motion had continued for several seconds without interruption, seconds within which Ann Thompson registered – amid shock, anger and embarrassment – the full gravity of the act in which her fourteen year old daughter was participating. It was the widow's sudden shriek of disgust that stunned the young couple into fumbling disengagement.

William Reynolds recoiled in disbelief, embarrassed to the very core that their most intimate of liaisons had been witnessed and by none less than Mina's mother. Pulling his trousers about him and amid utterances of apology, William had retreated from the room, only to be troubled by a fit of coughing and wheezing as, in trepidation, he awaited the mother's wrath. He had withdrawn into the street, having recovered some composure and, leaving the front door ajar, had hoped that Mina might join him there in due course; for he was now desperate to speak to her, to at least make some amends for having defiled her in the eyes of her mother. Yet, in truth, she had been a willing participant and he believed she thought sufficient of him not to cast him as having forced himself upon her in a time of weakness. Such accusation could have dire consequences for a man such as he, an adult rising twenty three having forcibly taken a girl barely out of childhood.

On the other side of the scale rested the girl's reputation, caught by her mother in fornication, sullied like the woman arrayed in purple and scarlet. No, William would offer to marry Mina, for his feelings toward her had grown during their few weeks of acquaintance and to the point of genuine affection. That, he thought, would be the honourable way out of this, a radical accommodation, yet one to which he would be prepared to commit; and, although it was a deliberation that immediately came to mind to help quench his guilt, he was prepared to acknowledge that he was growing to love the girl and that he had come to a crossroads in his life. His own recklessness had deprived him of family he held dear, alienated him from kith and kin, and there was no telling whether he could make amends in the eyes of his own flesh and blood. It was his earnest and greatest wish that he should do so in time, but, in that moment, it occurred to William Reynolds that a settled married life, pursuing his newly acquired clerking job, would suit all concerned and not least, himself.

Since leaving the Jarvis Hospital, where he was told he was consumptive, he had begun to feel better in himself. However, the wheezing and coughing had continued and he had seen two physicians in the city. Both had sent him away telling him it was only bronchitis. So he had cheerfully taken a job as a ledger clerk, in a glove manufactory south-west of the city, and had proceeded to dwell little more upon his health. That apart, he had money put aside in the Government Bank. Matrimony might be the making of him in the eyes of his family beyond the ocean; and were he settled into a married life, with a sound roof above his head, he might yet again resurrect the notion of his mother being prepared to join him in this fine City of Brotherly Love. As for the immediate problem of Widow Thompson's fury, he felt sure that an offer of marriage might quench the flames of ire and quickly soften any resentment of him. These then were William's hurried thoughts, as, contemplating the starry heavens, he had waited in some trepidation on the Willow Street sidewalk, its stones still palpably reflecting the heat of the day.

As it transpired, William Reynolds was to have no further contact with the widow or her daughter that fateful evening. A full half hour passed and, pre-occupied with his thoughts, he had failed to notice that Widow Thompson's front door had been pulled shut. What hint there was of flickering candlelight had transferred to the upper storey of the tiny, brick rowhouse. How had poor Mina fared, pitched alone against her mother's anger? Was she now banished to her room, scorned and ridiculed and left to cry herself to sleep? Nursing muddled views on the matter – yet himself relieved for having been spared exposure to the widow's words at the height of her indignation – William set heel and toe in the direction of his own lodgings across the city. There were no public carriages or horse-cars at this hour, the streets being left to those on foot, or to those well-breeched citizens equipped with private conveyances or the means to take horse.

For William, his mind unsettled, his thoughts in turmoil, the late evening's walk passed soon enough, yet not without incident. Somewhere around Market and 19th Streets, as he ambled south amid poorly lit thoroughfares towards Rittenhouse Square, he had encountered a drunkard high on cheap liquor. In their own preoccupations – and in the bar-crawler's case, his oblivion – they had blundered into each other, William having had cause to suffer the ribald oaths of the other as if the fault lay entirely with him. The middle-aged drunkard had lunged at the younger man, unleashing a fist that fell well short of its intended target. And so, startled at the suddenness of the encounter and concerned to prevent the altercation from developing into something more sanguine, William had hurried away at too speedy a pace for his own good. Breaking sweat by the time he had reached his rooms, the excitement and a hurried gait had combined to cause some uncomfortable chest pain and a shortness of breath. He quickly attended to his nightly ablutions, undeterred by these complications and the onset of a fit of rough coughing.

Since his return to Philadelphia, William had settled his physicians' fees with a smile on his face and with a sense of satisfaction. Whilst viewing it as money well spent, in truth he had been seduced by quackish insistence that he was merely inclined to bouts of chronic bronchitis. If the trigger for these was not excitement and over exertion, it might simply be the city's pollutants, caused to linger as the barometer rose. Essentially, he had been led to believe that he was not a consumptive, contrary to diagnosis at the hospital in Baltimore. And thus, troubled by the events the day had brought – yet with general peace of mind and with earlier fears allayed – William discarded his day clothes in favour of his nightshirt, oblivious to the insidious bacterium that was eating at his vitals. Then, entering his tiny scullery, he uncorked a flask bottle containing some doubtful compound of bryony and horehound. Clearing his throat of wretched mucous, he proceeded to swallow a dose of the vegetal nostrum. This intake of expectorant – to salve cough and help hurry sleep – brought the curtain down on this most defining of days since William Reynolds had returned to the magnificent city of Philadelphia.

★ ★ ★

Three days elapsed and her smile said it all. As soon as William saw her emerge from the gated entrance of the Society of Friends Laundry Company, it lifted his spirits, his relief was palpable. Mina sauntered towards her lover, eager to embrace him yet holding that eagerness in check. William noticed that she held a mildly coy expression, her pearly complexion, blushed sweetly about the cheeks, exuding her intrinsic femininity and early youth.

"Willie! Willie, you remembered! I feared that you were lost to me, that you would turn your back on me and that I would never see you again." She hugged her lover closely as he returned the comforting embrace and lifted her off her feet. The three days had seemed an eternity to them both after what had transpired, it always having been their intention, forged prior to the events in the house on Willow Street, that they would meet at this time.

The day had presented William with an earlier than usual start at the glove factory and thus, released at a younger hour from his bookwork, he had set forth across the city in the earnest hope that Mina would still cherish the appointment.

"I imagined your Mother would have forbidden you to have anything to do with me. I thought that purgatory would descend upon us for our sins and that we would be condemned never to meet again," said William.

Absorbed in their own company and with eyes only for each other, the young couple proceeded along Race Street, in the direction of the Old City and the Delaware waterfront.

"Let's sit down a while. Over there, beneath the trees," said William, pointing to a grassy clearing. Taking Mina's hand, he ushered her across the street in the direction of a little green oasis which, inset from the sidewalk, offered a sylvan retreat from the clamour of the late afternoon's traffic.

Here Mina and William settled themselves within the shade of an ageing maple. The breeze that kissed the overhanging foliage caused some gentle stirring and parting of leafage, sufficient to permit a glinting infiltration of rays to softly dapple and dance upon their space.

"I have brought you a little something to eat," claimed William as he opened a brown paper bag and offered its contents to Mina. The bag emitted an enticing whiff of freshly baked pastry. "A slice of your favourite plum cake and some gingerbread. I was passing Murphy's bakery on Arch Street and, hearing the chink of a few cents in my pocket, thought they could be well spent."

Mina said nothing. She simply uttered some incoherent mewl of delight. The sight and smell of the cakes played havoc with the salivary glands of a youngster who, short of having taken breakfast by the light of wick and oil, had since completed a ten hour toil within the humid air of the laundry.

It did not go unnoticed to William that the hand with which she claimed her piece of plum cake was chafed red by hours of kneading wet linen and by stints of cranking at the box wringers.

"So what of your mother, Mina? How are things between you?"

"Better now. That night, when you had gone, she started to scold me mercilessly, but it was all too much for her. She came over faint. Within fifteen minutes Mother had taken to her bed. I didn't see her again until I returned home from work the following evening."

"How was she?" asked William, waveringly.

"She had calmed down. It was as if nothing had happened. I think it was because Josie had returned from her night away and she didn't want her to know. We had a normal supper together. It was only later, when Josie was out in the backyard filling the coal scuttle, that she started scolding me again."

Mina stopped talking to sample the plum cake and to weigh in her mind how she might continue. She calculated that, however she chose to convey the substance of her mother's words, it risked putting her lover to flight. It was a risk to be faced whether the essence of what she said was delivered with sensitivity or simply put bluntly, such had been the gravity of the widow's pronouncements. Mina swallowed her mouthful of cake as her thoughts drifted back from the recalled sound of her mother's words; and perhaps it was resigned acceptance that, in any event, William's reaction was a matter beyond control, that actually cast a measure of serenity about her demeanour. In continuing, therefore, she surprised herself with the calm and measured way in which she addressed her lover.

"Mother wants me to marry you, Willie. You see, she likes you. She doesn't hate you for what she saw. She had already formed a good opinion of you when she met you before. She thought you a polite young man."

Although William had appeared unmoved by Mina's words, she had been oblivious to his outwardly impassive response, having chosen at this point not to look him in the eye. In truth William had been astonished by what he had heard, yet pleasantly so. He raised himself on one elbow from his recumbent position but made no utterance, feeling more inclined to allow Mina her say. He continued to give no sense of how he might react but listened with rapt attention.

"Mother said that I was a child but that I had been taken as a woman, that I had tasted forbidden fruit. At first she said my childhood had been snatched from me, that I had been violated, but I would not entertain the suggestion that you were to blame Willie. I told her it was as much my wish as yours. She said that since I had forsaken my childhood and chosen the ways of a woman then I should follow those ways within the sanctity of marriage."

As Mina fell silent she stole a sideways glance at William who was in the throes of rising to his feet. He gripped her arm, but gently and lovingly, and from his expression she immediately gauged that he was unflustered by and at ease with her remarks. She had a sense of the young fellow's innermost feelings that had been quickened by what she had said, latent feelings that cheered her before they could be expressed. When William spoke, his words came only as confirmation of this and any trepidation she had harboured melted away in a surge of joy.

"Yes, yes…she's right, Mina, your Mother is right. You are young, some might argue too young for marriage, but this way we can heal the breach that has opened between you," said William.

"Do you really mean…"

"Yes, of course. We have known each other but a few weeks but I love you Mina and I'm sure it would be for the best." Rather than sounding downcast by Mina's disclosure, as she had initially feared, William's words came laced with a tremor of excitement, buoyed by an appreciation that his happiness could at last be realised. They were words in which his own delight could be felt, a companion to Mina's joy.

"Besides," William continued, "I need a wife and I am ready to take on the responsibilities of a married life. I have been all at sea in fending for myself since my return to Philadelphia. Excepting you, dearest Mina, I have no friends. The very thought of having a loving wife, of comfort, routine and regular meals at my own fireside…"

"Oh, Willie, I am so happy to hear you say this," exclaimed Mina, her voice now tremulous with emotion. "I will forever feel ashamed and embarrassed by what we allowed Mother to witness but this will please her and bring us some redemption. Oh, Willie, I am so overjoyed."

"For several years now I have craved 'home sweet home' back in dear old England, but it was beyond my grasp," said William. He loosened his collar since it was causing him discomfort, wetted by the sweat of emotion and the afternoon heat. "Now I can put those thoughts aside and think only of our own home, together…here in Philadelphia. And just perhaps that will prove the tonic to rid me of my accursed cough."

Mina and William had found joy and happiness in the mutual discovery that their relationship was secure. Moreover, it was a relationship that could be nourished through nuptial union promoted at the bidding, if not with the blessing, of Widow Thompson. And thus, with triumviral unanimity of purpose, events moved quickly in the wake of the momentous events on Race Street.

July ran its course and, shortly before the month of August was spent, William and Mina had said their vows before the pastor of the city's Second Baptist Church. A few days later, with the monthly tenancy having terminated on his rooms near the glove manufactory, William moved Mina and himself, together with his in-laws, into fresh lodgings on Christian Street. Here, a few blocks to the south of his place of work, William had negotiated an initial six months' lease on a three storey red-brick rowhouse.

In viewing the accommodation and agreeing terms with the Irish landlord, a wide-eyed, chirpy Wexford man named O'Farrell, the young couple had had to withstand a tedious account of the fellow's life since his leaving of Erin's shores. A steerage passenger aboard a brig bound for New York, back in '47, he had endured over three weeks in the fetid, disease-ridden vapours of the steerage compartments. Once released from that overcrowded, lurching prison, he had found his way to Philadelphia in search of liberty and bread on his table.

"But, I found more than that, Mister Reynolds. I found prosperity too and a good Maryland missus, bless the Lord. Within thirteen years I had laid claim to the legitimate ownership of five houses between here and Broad Street. I attribute my good fortune to hard work, good judgement, and an occasional touch of the blarney. But most of all, Mister Reynolds, I attribute it to the Good Lord having found the time right and long overdue to cast his blessings and direction upon poor Irish Catholics with a resolve to help themselves."

In his promotion of the house on Christian Street, O'Farrell had assured William and Mina that it was "a sound and commodious property in good decoration", although, on subsequent closer inspection – once the prospective tenants were in occupation – this description had appeared a shade wide of the mark.

The house had been let, according to O'Farrell, to a succession of his fellow Irishmen and their families. One chap had gone off to the War and never returned. Two had secured employment building the new Pennsylvanian railroads that increasingly snaked into the city. The last tenants, a large family from County Clare, had proved slatternly and careless and failed to keep up with their rent. In view of this disappointment, O'Farrell had become inclined to let an Englishman or an American take up residence in Christian Street. He drew the line at letting the house to any of the Italian or German immigrants who were beginning to flood South Philadelphia or to the many free Negroes who, since the end of the War, had come north from Virginia and the Carolinas.

"But as for you, Mister Reynolds, you look a tidy enough gentleman to make a good tenant. That apart, my opinion of Englishmen has been elevated on the testimony of my cousin. He fought alongside English boys down in Virginia...reliable, steadfast fellows, he said. Took a bad hit at Fredericksburg did Cousin Joe. They were advancing on Marye's Heights, raked by Rebel canister when his thigh was opened up. He told me that two Englishmen put their own lives on the line to haul him to safe ground."

And so, washed with Cousin Joe's gratitude for the deeds of his countrymen and having thought it advantageous to disclose that his own mother hailed from West Meath, William struck what he felt were good enough terms with his new landlord.

The move to Christian Street was undertaken by the newlyweds in blithe contentment, expectation and a degree of optimism. The clement yet often oppressively warm days of midsummer had done nothing, however, to ease William's chesty ailments, indeed, late August had brought an aggravation of hard coughing and lethargy; and with expectoration came first signs of blood. Unease again began to creep into William's thoughts, stoked by the sobering realisation that he was embarking upon a married life with its own particular and additional responsibilities. Yet he still took comfort from those assurances that sprang from his earlier consultations with two supposedly respected physicians. Bronchitis. Prone to bouts of chronic bronchitis. Restorative treatment would depend upon getting plenty of fresh air, the pursuit of a sensible diet and avoiding both damp conditions and the city's unwholesome emissions. That had been the advice and he had since done his best to adhere to it, as far as this was possible or necessary, during the warm days of a Philadelphian summer. In particular, as time permitted, he had taken to occasional long walks along the far side of the Schuylkill, to the extent that he could access the riverbank in those parts, terminating his perambulations opposite the Fairmount Waterworks and filling his lungs with clear air borne along by the river. Yet of late such deep inhalation had provoked chest pains, lowering William's enthusiasm for these riparian excursions.

The property on Christian Street was of solid, narrow fronted appearance, its red brick front topped with a deep moulded cornice. Its proportions were of classical style yet a little dull and uninspiring, the three floors each punctuated with a pair of sash windows. Callers approached the entrance door via a shallow flight of steps from the sidewalk at which level a small windowed aperture gave scant light to a basement. It was a compact house and, as O'Farrell had intimated, a commodious one. As an established older property, it had an outwardly more presentable appearance than the many rowhouses, which, amid frenzied building, now rose from former farmland down towards the Schuylkill.

Although unfurnished, the house did boast a few remnants that O'Farrell had chosen to leave. One was a rickety iron and brass bedstead, its skeletal frame enhanced by its isolation in what was to become the marital first floor bedroom. In the ground floor dining room stood a vast deal table, of refectory rather than conventional proportion, around which William and Mina imagined the large family from County Clare seated with infinite ease and room to spare. Four bar-backed dining chairs looked forlorn, their upholstered seats threadbare and musty, a further four irretrievably broken and cast into the basement. Completing this assemblage of discarded furniture had been an old Boston rocker and a cherrywood side table, both of which, in earlier times, might have graced a fine parlour or drawing room.

Three days after Mina and William had moved into their new home, these inherited items of furniture had been augmented by the addition of all manner of moveable chattels recovered from the house on Willow Street. Mina's mother and her sister, Josie, had solicited the help of an old friend, an employee at a stabling concern in the city, who was able to arrange the gratuitous loan of a horse and open wagon. And thus the two women had arrived, seated with the stabling attendant on the box-seat, pots and pans a'clinking and looking all the part a collection of New England pedlars. Six weeks earlier Ann Thompson had reacted with apparent nonchalance, almost disinterest, to her younger daughter's disclosure of her forthcoming marriage following the assignation on Race Street.

"That is right and proper and I am pleased to hear it, Mina," was the widow's unhurried response. "But what will I do? I depend on your wages and those of your sister. Without you around, Mina, I will struggle to pay the rent and probably get evicted."

There had been a ring of despair in these words, delivered in such a way as to induce guilt in her young provider who was now bent on fleeing the nest.

"But, Mother, I thought this was what you wanted," pleaded Mina. "I thought you would be delighted that Willie had agreed to make me his wife."

"Yes, my dear," had been the reply. "It's just that…well, with you gone, I could end up in the Blockley Almshouses."

As the instigator and architect of the now impending marriage, Widow Thompson was, in truth, overjoyed at the prospect of her daughter's betrothal. She would never admit it but, in her innermost assessment, she was pleased that she had stumbled upon, and was known to have witnessed, the young couple's illicit lovemaking. For although the initial shock had been hard to bear, Ann Thompson was a woman of innately listless disposition with an eye to improving her lot and securing some comfort in old age; and, through William Reynolds' own display of carnal weakness in her own parlour, she had seen opportunity and marked him as a ticket to betterment. Here was a young man in a steady job of work, with supposedly good prospects and, by all account, according to Mina, with some money in the Government Bank.

To attain her goal and unlock the potential, Widow Thompson hadn't reckoned upon the ease with which William Reynolds would accede to the pressure she would bring to bear upon her daughter, for both to commit to an early marriage. Since she could not have anticipated William's own readiness to embark upon a married life with Mina, she wrongly concluded that his unhesitant yielding to the arrangement was a measure of her own influence. Ipso facto, viewing her future son-in-law as being of a compliant nature, perhaps even intimidated by her, Ann Thompson had continued to tug at her daughter's heart-strings, to play on her deepest emotions, to induce a sense of guilt that her plans might see her mother having to seek the charity of the workhouse. And so, on the eve of the wedding, when Mina had disclosed William's agreement to take his in-laws with them to Christian Street, a smug sense of self-satisfaction had permeated her mother's demeanour in affirmation of a successful strategem.

As a matter of fact, William had not bowed to Ann Thompson's machinations. He had exercised some considerable thought as to whether he and his wife should open their doors to Ann and Josie Thompson. He could appreciate that there was indeed some truth in the contention that, without Mina, her mother might struggle to make ends meet. Josie could not match her younger sister's income. She was a fine seamstress, raised in skills imparted by her paternal grandmother, but it was the girl's brusque manner and irritability that afforded her few commissions. In consequence, her contributions to the family budget were erratic and comparatively meagre. As to the widow's income, there was a very modest annuity which she supplemented with the proceeds from taking in washing and ironing, although these were not substantial. William appreciated that it would be pointless to leave the two women to struggle financially and face an eviction order, for he knew Mina could not stand by and see her mother and sister admitted to the Blockley institution. Neither could he, for William was not a heartless individual and equally would not stand idly by and see them destitute. He had even felt a sense of duty and indebtedness towards his

16

mother-in-law, since it had been through making her acquaintance that he had also met Mina. That had been back in June, on the first Saturday following his arrival in the city.

William had taken a room for the week at Naylor's Hotel on Dock Street, an area of hustle and bustle, its character moulded by long maritime associations. Flanked by Society Hill and the old Quaker city, the Dock Creek area was also tucked in closely behind the Delaware River shore where the waterfront piers and wharves sprouted a myriad of masts and rigging. Here the reek of tanning, of rope and tallow and tobacco storehouses, of all manner of chandlers' wares and of beer, fish and oysters, fused to intoxicate or jar the senses, depending on one's inclination. In William's case the locality and its smells raised fond memories of his boyhood days and those of his youth as he set about his immediate plans to find his feet in the city and to secure a job. As for the hotel itself, it was a comfortable enough establishment, clean, but of ramshackle appearance and possessed of a ground floor tavern as much prized for its oysters as its beer. In his search for employment William had been assured that the good offices of the Union League would most certainly be of assistance but, on that Saturday morning, relaxing in the hotel saloon, he had also chosen to scour the job advertisements in the *Philadelphia Inquirer*. Lost amid the many notices seeking able-bodied men for construction and related work, William had been oblivious to the opening door that squeaked on ungreased hinges and to the creak of warped pine beneath an approaching footfall.

"Coffee sir? Would you care for a mug of coffee?" The words roused William from his newspaper and were uttered by a woman of mature years brandishing a steaming pot of freshly brewed coffee beans. "The landlord's wife thought as you were the only guest to have stayed in this morning, you might like to share this pot with us, since there's more than we need."

The pervading aroma that accompanied the coffee pot proved too enticing and, naturally enough, the young man's response was in the affirmative. Clasping a mug that he had plucked from the top of a nearby sideboard, he proffered it towards the stoneware spout and, as he did so, wondered why he failed to recognise the woman whose conduct suggested she was entirely at home in the establishment.

"Thank you, ma'am, thank you. It smells good." In William's estimation, the woman was on the cusp of being considered elderly although, in truth, she was in her mid-forties. "Tell me," he said, "are you a friend of the hotel owner? Excuse me for enquiring, ma'am, but I cannot recall making your acquaintance or seeing you about the place."

"That's because I'm a Saturday visitor, sir. Only Saturdays," came the reply. "The landlord engages me to help his good lady on a weekly basis to do their personal washing and ironing. It's a service that extends to the guests as well, if they so wish. Not the bedding, of course, that goes elsewhere, but the personal items of clothing, you understand."

The woman became quite talkative. She introduced herself as Ann Thompson from Willow Street who had first accepted these Saturday chores some two years before, having then been recently widowed, and she had scarcely missed a Saturday since. For assistance, and early morning company in traversing the old city, she brought her younger daughter, Mina, who was now a laundry-maid by trade.

"At this very moment, as I rest awhile and revive myself with a cup or two of coffee, Mina is ironing shirts for the landlord and for several of your fellow guests. I'll send her up to talk with you when she's through her stint," declared the washerwoman, without recourse to establishing whether this would be to William's liking. "She'll enjoy that."

No sooner, it seemed, had the widow made her exit and William had once again buried himself in the small print, than there came a few tentative knocks on the door. With senses stimulated by the recent intake of coffee, William was now less preoccupied with his reading and was quick to acknowledge the request from the threshold. Indeed, apart from the gentle taps upon the door panel he was sure he had detected the sound of two pairs of footsteps in the outside corridor. A guiding hand had seemingly delivered Mina Thompson to the saloon door, as if left to her own devices she might have found another niche in which to spend her time away from the wash-room. Yet William, unassumingly and naively, had placed little or no significance upon this at the time.

Mina struck William as being a girl of neat appearance and average height, possessed of a fairly deep forehead but well balanced features. Her dark brown hair, in the fashion of the day, was drawn back to lay flat upon her head, then tidily gathered and twisted at the back. In contrast to her brown eyes and hair colouring, her skin was pale and clear, not in an unhealthy way, but a product of the shade and seclusion of city life. To William the tight fitting bodice of Mina's working dress – its jasper background studded with pink rosebuds – was indicative of an evolving maturity. In a whim, and mistakenly, he calculated her life had run the course of sixteen or seventeen summers.

"So, you're Mina I gather. Come in and sit yourself down," said William as his opening gambit. As Mina entered the room he had risen to his feet, causing the opened *Inquirer* to scatter its pages upon the carpet before him. Scooping to gather the newspaper, amid murmurings of self-scolding and some mild embarrassment, William swiftly regained his composure and retrieved his seat on the bentwood sofa. The girl did as he suggested, perching herself rather awkwardly upon a drawing room chair. "Thank you, sir. Yes, I'm Mina. Well, Mincora actually. I was baptised Mincora, but they all call me Mina."

"Your mother tells me that you both wash and iron linen here every Saturday," continued William.

"Yes, we're usually done by midday but it can take longer. If it's a bright, windy day and the early washing gets its full airing in the yard, then we stay on to finish the job. Otherwise we can be lugging home damp linen and returning it when done," said the girl. "Fact is, sir, I'm laundering all week, laundering on Saturdays and doing my own washing and ironing on the Sabbath. But it's a living, I suppose, it's a living," she sighed. "It puts a few dollars in my mother's purse and a few cents in mine."

William had felt some immediate attraction towards Mina's rather impish, cheery nature, delivered in the face of what must have been extreme workaday monotony. He liked her spirit and warmed to the girl's personality.

Mina continued with her laundering discourse. "I can only recall missing three Saturdays in the hotel wash-room. The first occasion I was ill with measles for two weeks. The last time was a sad occasion. It was two months ago, yes, two months exactly…I remember the date…Saturday, April the twenty second. Our dear President's body was due to arrive on the funeral train from Harrisburg and out of respect everything had closed down for the day."

"Did you go and see the lying-in-state?" asked William.

"No, that was on the Sunday and they say the queue stretched back to the Schulykill River! No, Mother and I and my sister joined the Saturday crowds on the route to Independence Hall. We had to wait hours and it was all very upsetting, hearing the muffled drums and gunfire and seeing ladies fainting and distraught. I even saw grown men weep openly as the ranks and ranks of soldiers in their blue finery marched by ahead of the procession. Mister Lincoln's hearse was a sad but impressive sight…and the horses, yes the horses…eight of them pulled the hearse and all as black as Philadelphia coal." Mina delivered her words with sad enthusiasm, the mournful nature of the occasion having had a profound and lasting effect on her.

William, in turn, did not respond but Mina noticed that he looked pensive and absorbed in his own thoughts.

"Are you alright, sir?" Mina left no time for the question to be answered before continuing. "By the way…your accent…do you come from across the ocean…from Ireland, maybe, or England?"

"I'm an Englishman, Mina, and my name is William Reynolds. Call me William, not sir. That makes me nervous and ill at ease. No, I'm fine. It's just that I became lost for a moment in my own recollections of times past. I apologise, it was not intended," said William. He hesitated awhile, shrugged and raised his eyebrows. A somewhat fanciful yet dismissive smile engaged his features, as if, in recognition of some coincidence, he nevertheless felt disinclined to place much significance upon it. "In truth," he continued, "that Saturday you will remember for the rest of your days and, strange to say, it also marked the end of a week that was a defining week in my own life. And, queer as it may seem, there was also a common thread, the President's death."

"The President's death? The poor man was assassinated by some actor from Maryland, was he not? So what do you know of his death, sir…sorry, William?" enquired Mina. "How could that have impacted on the life of an Englishman?"

"I know little of your President's death, Mina, little more than you, I'm sure," came the reply. "Only what we read in the newspapers. They say the trial of the conspirators is nearing its end and they will be sentenced soon enough. Suffice to say their fate is sealed. As for my own experiences, they would take a time to tell."

"Well, I would be interested to hear them," said Mina.

"Then we shall meet again and I will tell you a little of my life's adventures."

This initial encounter with Mina had been contrived by the girl's mother and although, with hindsight, William was fully sensible of the elder woman's motives, he held no resentment, indeed, he was pleased that she had acted in such a forward and manipulative way. Thus was conjured almost a feeling of gratitude towards Ann Thompson and, come the day of his marriage to Mina, two months later, he had in no sense felt snared, a victim of deception. Instead he had gone willingly to the altar in the knowledge that his love for the girl was complete. In consequence, for that love of his wife and for the sake of her peace of mind, William had been willing to indulge Mina's feelings and fears for her close family when the young couple completed their plans for the move to Christian Street. And when their deliberations had been concluded on the subject of what might or might not become of Ann and Josie Thompson, the doors of their new abode were thrown open to that extended family. It was an action that might have been viewed as a kind hearted and truly benevolent gesture by the new tenant. Some, on the other hand, may have seen it as ill-advised, a move that he might, in time, regret. To Mina her husband's warm-heartedness had thrilled her to the core but it was a kindness that came with stipulations.

Firstly, William resolved that Josie and his mother-in-law were to be accommodated on the top or second floor of the house, where, subject to judicious furnishing, two good-sized bedrooms each had the capacity to double as sleeping and living quarters. This would ensure that both women had facilities capable of affording them privacy and solitude since it set them apart from William and Mina, who were to monopolise the use of the floor below. This aside, William had decided that his mother-in-law had already witnessed enough of their unbridled intimacy, although he had been loath to impart his thoughts on the subject to Mina. He had been careless that night in Willow Street and, not surprisingly, continued to feel sorely piqued and humiliated by having allowed the widow to be privy to their lovemaking. He had been mortified at the time and, although matters had since turned out well enough, William continued to be self-reproachful for allowing himself to be caught red-handed as he deprived the woman's daughter of her virginity in shameful and lustful fornication. In consequence, he was determined that she and Josie would not be afforded the latitude, in his own home, to descend to breakfast fully briefed upon the past night's passionate distractions within the marital bed. Such knowledge, in William's assessment – a calculation perhaps distorted by his paranoia and sensitivity on the issue – would most certainly be communicated by the audible shift of Christian Street's ill-fitting and poorly seasoned floor timbers, stressed by exertions from above.

In conveying this stipulation upon the geography of her mother's billeting within the house, Mina had placed significance upon her husband's disturbed nights and bouts of coughing. His being up and about, and having occasion to move about the house, might prove disruptive to the others' slumbers were they to be accommodated directly below the newly-weds. And to Mina's credit this proved a persuasive and entirely reasonable requisite, accepted without question by her mother, least of all, and...surprisingly perhaps, without utterances about the strain of having to trudge up and down so many stairs.

In contrast to the more fanciful considerations that had shaped William's first stipulation, his second had derived from thoughts of a more tangible nature involving issues of greater import. In essence this concerned and established the role of all within the house in terms of what would be expected of them in contributing to the household's effective functioning, both in the practical sense of domestic economy and in the pecuniary sense of keeping heads above water. It was a stipulation that William had found necessary because of the attitude of his sister-in-law and the resentment that this sullen girl of sixteen appeared to increasingly show towards her younger sister and her husband, despite their offer of a home. William was the breadwinner and head of the household whose pride was such that he would brook no thought of his wife persisting with the drudgery that the laundry had inflicted upon her. Henceforth her work would be in the home. Housewifery would be her lot, with all that this entailed and, in truth, she had relished the prospect of immersing herself in homely pursuits. She was better conditioned to many of the harsher domestic tasks than most girls of her age. Cleaning, blacking and burnishing and the like had been commonplace chores in times past but now Mina was eager to grasp responsibility for such work in a home of her own. For now she felt like a phoenix rising out of the childhood drudgery of Willow Street. As the tenant's wife her mother had no call upon her time and labours. Instead she could put her shoulders to those tasks with renewed vigour for William's sake, a purpose which alone would greatly lighten the load; and with time to spare she would delight in the more feminine and dutiful aspects of homemaking. Mina would strive to ensure that theirs would be a cheerful, welcoming hearth and parlour, a place of love and warmth where she and William – and, for that matter, her mother and sister should they choose – might find consolation and relaxation at the close of day. A parlour into which, at Sunday twilight, Mina might bring forth a tray of hot tea and a plate of freshly baked savoury cakes.

To complement the joy of such womanly self-expression, Mina would continue to assist her mother with the Saturday work at Naylor's, at least in the short-term. This was a decision jointly agreed by the young couple and, happily, Mina's mother did not dissent. For William's part, he was minded that the move across the city would deprive Ann Thompson of the modest income she had secured from taking in dirty linen and the hotel work would at least maintain some momentum while she sought to replenish lost custom within her new surroundings. Mina shared her husband's sentiments on this issue and his thoughts about idleness begetting idleness, for she, likewise, was fully cognisant of her mother's slothful tendencies. She had been the past victim of her indolence and slatternly ways and was only too alert to ensuring that her mother did not presume, with her own personal responsibilities lifted, that she could fall into a comfortable niche in the new home without bearing her part. Happily the widow had been content to continue with the assignment, for she got on well with the landlady. She was a garrulous sort who lightened the day's work with her cheerfulness and insistence that her employee's energies, such as they were, required frequent lubrication from the intake of coffee or the occasional glass of porter. Conveniently, there was a horse-car connection to Society Hill, a short step away from Dock Street, and thus the journey from Christian Street could be undertaken with comparative ease.

As for Josie Thompson, William had detected that she had resented him from the outset, from the moment Mina had disclosed that she was to be wed. It was clear that Josie begrudged the prospect of her younger sister leaving the house on Willow Street since it followed that she, Josie, would at long last have to pull her weight in the family home and be in thrall to her mother. Added to this was an underlying jealousy that Mina, her little sister, had already found herself a husband and was set to secure the approbation, the independence and the self esteem of being a man's wife, something that, for the foreseeable future, was beyond her own grasp. Yet Josie did little to foster her own appearance. She was untidy of habit, had inherited her mother's slovenliness and was inclined to be uncommunicative and irritable. William had had to choose his moment to broach the issue of his sister-in-law's contribution to the household budget, deeming it, in the circumstances, to be a probable cause of irritation and a topic unlikely to bring forth a genial and constructive reply. It had not been something he could leave to Mina, judging that any indignant, sharp worded response could well reduce the younger sibling to tears. Yet for all of William's care in selecting that moment, his words were interrupted and rebuffed in peevish resentment of their substance; and, seemingly, with scant consideration to the fact that, with some little effort on Josie's part, the young couple were fully prepared to accommodate the girl beneath their roof.

The following day brought an apology from Josie for her rudeness. She had thought better of alienating William, for she had clearly come to realise that there was little choice but to accompany her mother to Christian Street. Otherwise she would be homeless, be forced to fend for herself and take separate lodgings. In those circumstances, the need to secure a proper job would be paramount. And so she deferred to William, ate humble pie and agreed to make every effort to procure gainful employment by the time September had run its course. In her sister's preparedness to submit to such humiliation, however, Mina wondered whether her mother had exerted influence and that, beneath the surface, the climb down had been tendered grudgingly and with inward reluctance.

Such were the politics of the household on Christian Street as the new tenant and his charges began adjusting to their fresh surroundings. The stipulations set as a precursor to occupancy were seemingly met without any lasting discord. All in the house ate together and the post-prandial tendency during those early days, for Widow Thompson and Josie to join the newly weds in their sparse parlour, was testimony to the concord that prevailed. Even Josie kept her word. By the second week in September she had proudly announced that she had found employment. By a stroke of luck, while purchasing cotton thread at her usual haberdasher's shop on Market Street, she had been alerted to a vacancy at a nearby milliner's. The haberdasher, being aware of Josie's capabilities, and having been told she was looking for work, mentioned that she knew the milliner was seeking a trimmer or at least a person with skills enough to become one. Thanking the haberdasher, Josie had presented herself at the milliner's shop. Here she expressed her interest in the vacancy, only to return at the proprietor's behest with samples of her workmanship and to be immediately given the job with a starting pay of ten dollars a month. Two weeks into the job, she had been a changed person. Possessed now of some self-esteem and, at times, a conviviality that others in the house found hard to believe, Josie spoke excitedly and with animation of the workroom in which she plied her skills; and with her enthusiasm, talk of bonnets and buckram, of caps and lappets and silk ribbonry, infused a fresh vocabulary into the evening discourse of September days.

However, as the month had entered its twilight and October beckoned, there was no other sense of joy, of optimism, in the house on Christian

Street. Mina had finished at the laundry but circumstances had obstructed such inclination there may have been to engage in any housekeeping beyond the most basic of chores. Indeed, in this respect, Mina had occasion to prevail upon her mother for assistance. The fact was that William's health had deteriorated quite markedly. Following a series of disturbed nights, of harsh coughing and chest pains the last Saturday in September delivered him an improved night's rest and, feeling somewhat better in himself, he had set off to church on the Sunday morning, accompanied by Mina.

Since the beginning of July William had become accustomed to attending the Church of the Mediator at 19th and Lombard Streets, an Episcopal church located close to his previous lodgings. He had decided to continue to worship there since it lay some six or seven blocks from his new abode and he had found the minister, the Reverend Appleton, to be the most congenial and benevolent of clergymen. He also delivered a good sermon. Since William was not of these shores, the incumbent had been inquisitive of his background although the newcomer had not found this an irritant. He was quick to realise that what amounted to a burgeoning congregation was largely drawn from the increasing immigrant population that was flooding South Philadelphia in the aftermath of war; and the Reverend Appleton was naturally keen to obtain at least some rudimentary understanding of the diverse origins from which his congregation was drawn. As far as William was concerned, in return for telling a little of his history, he had been warmly welcomed into the Mediator's fold with the incumbent swift to offer him helpful guidance towards finding his feet in the city.

Unfortunately, however, that Sunday morning was to prove sadly eventful for William Reynolds as he and his young wife took their seats amid the crowded pews of the Church of the Mediator. Perhaps the walk had been too strenuous an outing for him, for lately his constitution had been sorely taxed and a dampness pervaded the morning air. Whatever prompted the upset, it came upon him during early prayers – a fit of heavy coughing that caused some minor commotion and soon rendered him languorous and close to collapse. With the help of two men to take her husband's weight, Mina had hurriedly retreated from the body of the church and settled William into the vestry where they were soon joined by a smartly dressed and distinguished looking gentleman, his face framed by a fine set of greying mutton-chop whiskers. The gentleman explained that he was a physician.

"Who is this young man? Is he inclined to these attacks? Where does he live?" The gentleman's questions came thick and fast. "This may be the House of God but it's damp and musty at the onset of leaf fall and he'd do better to be in his bed."

Mina had explained to the doctor that she was the man's wife, that they lived on Christian Street and that William suffered with bronchial problems that had become aggravated of late.

"Then we must get him home ma'am, and right away. The exertion of walking to church and the dampness has surely tried a delicate constitution. I don't like the sound of his breathing," said the whiskered gentleman who, being familiar with the geography of the room, had opened a tiny cabinet beside the vestment hooks and removed a small phial. Extracting the glass stopper, he had proceeded to draw the open bottle from side to side beneath William's nostrils. He explained that the vestryman kept this restorative aid to hand since occasionally ladies had been known to feel faint while attending church. A touch of smelling salts laced with lavender oil would normally revive them and perhaps it would assist William a little.

"Look, my dear, I think this would be for the best," continued the physician. "My son will be outside in ten minutes or so. We have a runabout in which he brought me to church and he is due to collect me after the service. I will direct him to take your husband home first. Trouble is, my dear, the carriage is only a two-seater so you will need to return on foot. Come to think of it, you may care to start now, so you're home ahead of your husband. Rest assured, I will look after him."

"Thank you for your thoughtfulness, sir," had been the reply. "My mother and sister are at home, but I will take my leave of you now and hurry back, for it will come as a shock to them."

"My son will help him into the house," said the physician. "And be sure to seek some medical advice. It's not an ailment to go unchecked."

The physician's son duly arrived with the open carriage and, under his father's supervision, helped William Reynolds aboard the conveyance and took him home at a gentle trot. There he was put to bed, and, feeling somewhat exhausted by his outing and the events at church, William fell into a prolonged and undisturbed slumber until dusk. On waking he was able to take a little food, for nothing other than fluids had passed his lips since breakfast, and then only a modicum of the widow's watery gruel.

Monday dawned bright and clear after yet another disturbed night and soon after daybreak Mina left the house in the direction of the glove manufactory. It had been a week since William sat at his ledger desk – his pulpit as he called it – and, with no prospect of any immediate return to his bookwork, had prevailed upon Mina to inform his employers that he remained indisposed.

By the time Mina had returned to the house mid-morning it was with the news she had sought out a local physician with the promise that he would attend upon her husband later that afternoon. Yet it was to prove more of the same. The doctor's pronouncements closely resembled those of other medical men who had gone before. Bronchitis. A severe bout of the ailment. Keep the patient in bed and the room airy. Plenty of fluids and the occasional spoonful of a most distasteful pulmonic syrup, which, according to its advocate, was highly effective. To the patient, however, the nature of its bottling and foul taste reminded him of the many country cure-alls that seemed to find favour back in the mining hills of Schulykill County. As he rose to depart the visitor gave his assurance that he would call again later in the week as if he were bestowing some great favour. Had William felt stronger and more collected in himself then he might have discouraged the physician's return. Instead he was left to ponder, with a degree of cynicism, as to whether the fellow's motives were purely financial.

"We will need to do as the snail, my dear, and draw in our horns," said William, with a note of despair. It was the Sabbath again, a week having passed since the events at the Mediator.

"Yes, but mother has found more work. She placed a notice with several local shopkeepers. She's downstairs right now with ironing piled high. And Josie has settled into her job." Mina's reply was upbeat.

"Quite so, Mina, and that's a blessing. Their efforts might just help to keep us going. At least O'Farrell was paid up to the tune of six months' rent. That ties us over until the end of February."

"You'll be on your feet again long before then, Willie."

"Let's hope so," replied William. "Otherwise without you and I bringing in a wage we will have little choice but to live off my savings. They've already half gone since I arrived in Philadelphia and I fear they will have dwindled away entirely, come Christmas. It's the infernal doctors' bills that are so crippling."

Perhaps the Good Lord was privy to these remarks for several streets away, and at about the same hour, a conversation was taking place within the brick and timbered porch of the Church of the Mediator. The morning service had concluded and the congregation all but finally dispersed amid the customary flurry of departing farewells and platitudes. Yet holding back, and seemingly intent on engaging the Reverend Appleton in discussion of a more serious tenor, was the kind physician who had forsaken his prayers to attend to the ailing Englishman. The doctor proceeded to tell the clergyman that the events in the vestry had occupied his mind during the previous week. He was keen to learn more of the young man and what had brought him across the ocean, the episode having stimulated a degree of curiosity about the couple's circumstances; and whatever the physician subsequently gleaned from the minister was to shortly cause him to set routine aside.

Since he had settled back into civilian life, during the previous eighteen months, Doctor Elisha Boyleston Jackson had again become a creature of habit. The comfort and certainty had an appeal after the turmoil, upheaval and horror of the Union field hospitals. There, and for three years, as an assistant surgeon under contract to the army, the doctor had encountered no two days the same. Attached to the Army of the Potomac, he could be called upon at all hours to receive the wounded as they stumbled or were stretchered back from the dressing stations. And then his work would start, often toiling under poor candlelight and in makeshift conditions, his hands and arms slippery with the blood of the stricken, his nostrils assailed by the smell of chloroform and iodine and the sweetness of clotted blood and flesh laid bare. In those dire and desperate times the doctor craved past days of attending the sick in his native Philadelphia, mild and docile days in comparison and ones that held a sense of order and of benign and comforting repetition.

Once back home, as he resumed his career of general physician, he would be out of his bed at an early hour, before sunrise, taking care not to cause his wife and sons to be drawn from their slumbers. He would then partake of his breakfast before settling into a comfy chair. Here he would remain for upward of an hour, a spell of physical inactivity that served a dual purpose. On the one hand it satisfied the doctor that he was allowing his digestive juices to assault and deal appropriately with his first meal of the day. Secondly, it afforded him some quiet time in which he could read his newspapers and journals and stay abreast of current medical thinking and advances. By the time he had finished, the rest of the house was beginning to function. Missus Jackson was up and about, their sons likewise, as they prepared to go about their business, and, on a cloudless day, the sun was up over the Delaware and casting its rays across the city's rooftops.

Such was the start of day in the Jackson household on the bright morning that followed the doctor's conversation with the Reverend Appleton. Beyond this, however, came a departure from routine. Doctor Jackson would normally rise from his chair and take his usual constitutional. Like clockwork the good doctor would head eastwards along Pine and as far as Broad Street whereupon he would turn north, returning home via Walnut or Locust Streets and the greenery of Rittenhouse Square. One neighbour had been known to quip that he could set his pocket watch by the doctor's routine and the punctuality of his return. Once home, Doctor Jackson would spruce himself up, attire himself in a smart enough rig to befit his profession, then set about his business, be it time in surgery, house visits, lecturing students at the University Medical School or such other peripheral engagements that befall a man of medicine.

On this particular Monday morning in early October, Doctor Jackson chose to dress for business before taking to the city streets. On such mornings, when his business affairs entailed a string of house visits, he relied upon a horse and buggy being brought round to his home at eight-thirty precisely. He chose not to use his own animal and the larger runabout for the purpose of his doctoring. Instead he found a hooded two-seater buggy to be more convenient, coming as it did with a hired driver. It was a private arrangement that served the doctor well, since his travelling companion would convey him between the homes of his patients before returning him to his own front door, in time for a light lunch and the likely prospect of an afternoon surgery. On this occasion, however, with a change of routine to start the week, he had sent his younger son to the stabling establishment with word that the buggy be delivered to him, instead, at ten o'clock. That issue sorted, at a quarter to eight the physician gathered up his medical bag and bade farewell to his wife, having explained to her the reason for his changed arrangements. He directed his perambulation southward via 21st Street until, in due course, he came upon Christian Street.

Doctor Jackson's firm use of the knocker had to be repeated before the door was eventually opened by a somewhat flustered Ann Thompson. The widow's damp and spumy forearms showed signs of having been pulled from a hot tub of soap suds as, somewhat bewildered and taken in awe of the finely dressed gentleman before her, she uttered a hasty apology.

"Excuse me, sir, for keeping you waiting, but I was out in the backyard taking advantage of the mild weather. Can we help, sir?"

The physician removed his hat, a silk stovepipe, revealing a balding pate. To Ann Thompson's eye this rendered him far less formidable in appearance.

She relaxed her manner as a friendly smile crossed the gentleman's features, a whiskered face touched florid by the exertions of his walk.

"A very good morning to you ma'am. The apology falls to me for prevailing upon you so early and without notice. Please accept it. Now, tell me, am I correct in believing this to be the home of Mister William Reynolds?" enquired the visitor.

"Yes, sir, but William has yet to get out of his bed. He's not at all well. Who shall I say has called and what is your business, sir?" came the reply.

"My name is Jackson, but that won't mean much to him. I'm a physician...here, take my card. Mister Reynolds has met me...only recently, although he may not remember. Kindly tell him that if he would grant me an audience I would be pleased to help..."

Before the doctor could finish his sentence he was distracted by a girl's emergence in the front passage. He immediately recognised her as Missus Reynolds, the young lady in the vestry, although Mina was not as swift to reciprocate.

"What is it, Mother?" enquired the younger woman.

"This gentleman is Doctor Jackson, my dear. He'd like to speak to William." Suddenly a belated sense of recognition was etched in Mina's features. "Oh, yes sir, you're the kind gentleman who helped us in church. Please come in, sir. My husband's upstairs in bed. If you'd care to wait in the parlour a few minutes, I'll go and tell him you're here. Please follow me."

Doctor Jackson nodded his assent to this suggestion and, in the wake of the two women who retreated before him, he entered the house. He followed Mina into the parlour where she seated him before an unwelcoming hearth, its grate dirtied by a recent fall of soot. As she hurried to draw back the heavy curtains and banish the parlour's gloom with a flood of morning light, Mina apologised for being ill-prepared for his visit.

"No matter my dear," was the doctor's retort. "It is early in the day and you had no notice of my intention. I apologise profusely that I did not send word. It was only yesterday after church that I resolved it necessary to talk with your husband."

"I'll go and tell William you're here, Doctor," said Mina as she made to leave the room.

"Well, if he's willing to see me, don't let him come down. Let him stay rested and warm in his bed. I will come up to him, Missus Reynolds."

Once Mina had made ready the bedroom, plumped William's pillows and assisted him into such angle of recumbency as he deemed comfortable enough to receive a visitor, she descended to the parlour and beckoned Doctor Jackson to ascend the stairs. William was indeed curious as to why the good physician had chosen to pay him a visit, but for his part he was pleased to greet him and have the opportunity to personally express his gratitude for the doctor's past kindness.

"Ah, Mister Reynolds, good day to you sir. We meet again and before I say any more I must beg your pardon for this unannounced intrusion on your day, and at so early an hour." The visitor's face bore the creases of a gentle smile as he advanced towards the bed and offered his outstretched arm to its occupant. "My name, incidentally, is Jackson and I am hoping I may be of some help to you. That is my earnest wish," said the visitor as the two shook hands.

"It is a great pleasure to see you Doctor Jackson and I welcome the chance to thank you for already helping me. Please sit yourself down, sir."

Having led Doctor Jackson up the stairs, Mina had remained in the bedroom doorway, not quite knowing whether she was meant to be party to what might ensue between the two men.

William caught her eye and continued. "Mina, perhaps Doctor Jackson would like a drink and would you mind taking his coat, my love, before he makes himself comfortable?"

Seizing on this comment the doctor was quick to interject. "Excellent. If it's no trouble I would welcome a drink after my walk." He proceeded to place his hat and bag at the end of the bed, then removed his frock coat and handed it to the advancing Mina. "My coat can go there, my dear, on the hook behind the door. Thank you."

"I was just about to prepare some tea for William when you called, sir," said Mina. "Would tea be to your liking, Doctor?"

"That would be fine, Missus Reynolds. Nothing like a hot cup of tea to quench the thirst and restore tranquillity to one's state of mind. Isn't that what the English say?"

It was a rhetorical question to which the physician neither expected nor received an answer. Then, dragging his chair closer to the bed, Doctor Jackson sat down and proceeded to address the younger man. "Now, let me come to the point Mister Reyn...or may I be so presumptuous as to call you William?"

"Of course, Doctor, please do. And you have no cause to chide yourself for presumptuousness. Let's face it, I am a mere working fellow, torn from his roots and trying to make his way in a foreign land. You, on the other hand, sir, are a gentleman of standing, a man of medicine no less."

"You do yourself a disservice, William, the way you speak of yourself. Anyway, the fact is I have found my thoughts returning to the events of last week. Yesterday they drove me to speak to my friend, Sam Appleton, the rector. He knew a great deal about you and what he told me did not fail to impress me, so much so that I have determined to try to help you. That's if you are happy to accept my help."

"Thank you, Doctor, but with respect I have already seen several physicians since I arrived in the city and they all tell me that I'm afflicted with bronchitis. They all give me medicine for the same and have similar advice as to how I should conduct my life. I have even seen a physician this week since the upset in church and because I have felt so bad. He's given me that wretched syrup," said William, pointing to the bottled concoction on the nearby washstand. "That besides, my ailment has currently left me bereft of income and I fear that my employers will prove impatient to replace me before long. I do have savings, sir, but they are fast evaporating and I cannot expose them further to yet more bills."

"William, you misunderstand me. What I am offering is to give my time and medical expertise freely since in my assessment you are a deserving case. Rest assured, my boy, there will be no bills," said Doctor Jackson.

The elder man's response took William by surprise but instilled him with no sense of satisfaction. For William was a proud man and despised the notion of accepting charity.

"Sir, you owe me no favours. I cannot accept your kindness. You don't know me, Doctor, so why should you feel the need to attend me without due reward? Not wishing to be disrespectful or to insult you, sir, but…well, it's not in my nature," pleaded William.

The doctor was not irritated or offended by the young man's remarks. He smiled, reflectively, before reacting. "William, I understand what you're saying. But consider this. Yes, I owe you no favours but I know you have served the country well. You have found a good wife to care for you and you have a roof over your head. But I am aware you have no friends, your livelihood is compromised and your funds are at risk. You know, they call this the City of Brotherly Love but in reality it can be a harsh environment in which to make one's way, especially if afflicted with chronic illness. So treat my offer as just recompense from the country you served so well and me simply the means of its delivery. It is nothing more than that."

It was at this point that Mina returned with the tea, a welcome interruption that somehow – and least of all because of Mina's presence – offered both men reason to stray from a topic that each sensed would benefit from suspension. Instead, and once Mina had departed, the two sipped their tea and their conversation dwelt upon other matters.

Once Doctor Jackson had drained his cup he reached inside the pocket of his grey, brocaded waistcoat and, extracting his watch, decreed that it was half past nine and he needed to be gone. "That apart, my good fellow, you're looking tired now and that cough is troublesome. In short, you need me to be out of the way so you might rest," said Doctor Jackson. He would visit again on Friday morning, but at a more social hour and in between other house calls. In the meanwhile he charged William to dwell upon his proposition. If on Friday, after serious consideration, William was prepared to set his pride aside and accept the offer of help, then the doctor intended that he would proceed to undertake a thorough medical examination. And so, feeling that his early mission was complete, and without further ado, the physician donned his coat, gathered up his hat and bag and bade farewell.

The following Friday came soon enough, although to William Reynolds the interval's component days, and more so, the sleepless nights, seemed for the most part, interminable. If anything his bouts of coughing became more frequent and rasping, his chest more wheezy, his phlegm and spittle the more suffused with blood. The women in the house, Mina excepted, had begun to take to their beds earlier, bent on making good the sleep that had evaded them; for William's fits of noisiness, often in the depth of night, now wreaked such disturbance as to wake the dead, let alone the slumbering. As for poor Mina, it was not sleep deprivation alone that threatened to undermine her own state of health and natural resistance. She would often wake, from what snatches of sleep came her way, to find the sheets drenched by her husband's night sweats. Yes, William would finally lapse into meaningful sleep as dawn beckoned but it was a light and brief sleep; and during this troublesome week he was roused twice on successive mornings by the noise of passing freight trains. Two blocks behind the house on Christian Street, and beyond a cluster of grimy mills and commercial yards, the tracks of one of the railroad companies coursed their way eastwards from the Grays Ferry Bridge. It was a route that often witnessed the passage of early coal trains, their wagons laden with anthracite destined to stock the coaling wharves along the Delaware. If the clanging bell that signalled a locomotive's approach failed to wake a light sleeper, then the subsequent throb and hiss of stack and pistons and the rumble of endless wagons would surely do so.

On the Friday morning, roused in this way from shallow slumber, William found that Mina was already up, dressed and elsewhere. Easing himself up on his elbows, he grasped an old walking stick that rested against the washstand. It was a stick of burred walnut, left there by Mina to enable her husband to beckon her, as occasion required, with taps of its ferrule upon the floorboards; and with this done, William laid back on the bed, the sheets now rank and creased from his night's abnormal perspiration.

The response to his beckoning took a few minutes. Then the tell-tale creaking of stairs beneath Mina's ascending footfall announced her emergence from the kitchen.

"It's Friday, Willie," said Mina, as she placed a laden tray upon the washstand and, without further word, set about organising and propping up her husband in readiness to receive his breakfast.

William knew precisely to what Mina was alluding. Later in the morning Doctor Jackson was due to return and he would need to decide whether he was prepared to submit to the physician's kind offer of gratuitous care.

"Once you've had your breakfast, Willie, I'll fetch you a clean nightshirt. And while you're washing and getting into it, I'll change those sheets. We can't let the Doctor see you in this state."

Mina placed the tray upon the counterpane. It held a bowl of gruel, a plate of buttered bread and a cup of tea. William's appetite was meagre but he began to despatch the gruel as Mina sat at the end of the bed. It was at least more palatable than the liquid oatmeal his mother-in-law was apt to prepare.

When he had partaken of his fill, William pushed the tray aside and wiped his mouth on his sleeve. "Mina, my love," he began, "I have wrestled long in my waking hours with what to do about the Doctor's offer. Trouble is, it's against my nature to accept charity from a stranger, call it pride or arrogance or whatever."

"Yes, Willie, but the Doctor seems to have been moved by your predicament. He has taken the trouble to enquire of your history and would not be prepared to show you such kindness if he felt it was not deserved. He feels you have had a raw deal and deserve better. Mother and Josie feel you would be foolish to decline his offer. To be honest, so do I."

"I think my grandmother is of the same opinion," said William, reflectively.

"What? Your grandmother?" Not surprisingly Mina's reaction had a ring of astonishment.

"It was last night. It must have been well after midnight. I was calm enough, no coughing, just wheezy, and my thoughts were of nothing but Doctor Jackson. I heard Dreer's clock chime the hour twice, then must have fallen into a short but restful spell of sleep. My grandmother came to me in a dream. It was…"

"Did she say anything?" interrupted Mina.

"No, she was just sitting there, as always, in her chair by the hearth, her black cat coiled in her lap. It was Grandma, alright. She was wearing her favourite cap with its lappets of Honiton lace. And there was a fire in the grate for its flickering glow reflected in her smile. It was a meaningful smile that somehow was telling me I was wrong to have doubts. Simply that."

"So there, William," said Mina, in a somewhat patronising tone. "So there's your answer. The Good Lord has surely spoken to you through your Grandma's image."

As Mina rose to find William a fresh nightgown and to gather up clean sheets there came a knock upon the door. Leaving William to change, she made her way downstairs, dismissing the thought that this might be Doctor Jackson; for the parlour clock had just struck nine and the physician had expressly stated he would call at a later hour. On opening the door, and in confirmation of that thought process, Mina immediately recognised the caller as the minister from the Church of the Mediator. The Reverend Appleton raised his brimmed felt hat, in greeting and courteous regard, revealing a head of neatly cut, brown hair and side whiskers trimmed close to his face. His black town coat contrasted sharply with the whiteness of his neckcloth and his features suggested he was a man in his mid-thirties, his looks only marred perhaps by a heavily indented philtrum that gave prominence to his upper lip. Yet to those close to him he would flippantly call it a blessing, draw upon folklore and talk of the kiss of angels or of it being an indent left by the finger of God. Only, in his case, God's finger had tarried longer and, in consequence, his life's work had been forged in his mother's womb.

"Good day to you Missus Reynolds. Please excuse my early call but is your husband well enough for me to have words with him?" enquired the clergyman. Fretful that she had yet to change the bedding and clear away William's breakfast crockery, yet outwardly successful in hiding any trace of irritation, Mina was almost apologetic in her reply. "Well, yes, Reverend,

I'm sure William will be pleased to see you…it's if you don't mind the mess, sir. I was about to change the bed and make things ready to receive the physician. He is expected this side of midday."

"I know. I saw Doctor Jackson earlier this week and he told me of his impending visit."

It transpired that the purpose of the rector's appearance on Christian Street, so early in the day, was to dissuade William from making too hasty a decision and instead to be amenable to Doctor Jackson's proposition. He had learnt from Jackson that the patient appeared to have misgivings about accepting gratuitous care, a stance seemingly driven by pride and the young man's self-esteem. In this knowledge the minister was somewhat circuitous in approaching what to William was a sensitive issue yet, all in all, as their conversation progressed, came the sense that his prudence was paying dividends. He felt that he had at least succeeded in preventing slight to the other by an avoidance of any impression that physician and clergyman had conspired together. Which was the truth of the matter, for Doctor Jackson knew nothing of Appleton's visit ahead of his. It was not something that Jackson had solicited but something the minister thought apposite. After all, he had fired the physician's interest in William in the first place by telling him a little of the fellow's history. And from what Jackson had subsequently told him of the young man's reservations he had felt disposed to try to influence the other's direction and thus salvage matters to William's undoubted advantage. Furthermore, he wished to avoid any rebuff of the kind offer for the giver's case since the doctor had not tendered it lightly, but sincerely, and after some consideration.

William was duly forthcoming about his concerns and confided with Reverend Appleton regarding the views of Mina and her family and of the past night's vision of his grandmother and what that seemed to mean. And as he told of his dream and spoke lovingly of his Grandma, William was for a moment seized with emotion and became tearful and his fit of tears provoked a spell of hoarse coughing. The clergyman was himself saddened that the truly ailing member of his flock who lay recumbent before him, and in the throes of uncontrollable coughing, was more gaunt, pale and hollow-eyed than he had witnessed before. Yet he also detected that his family's views and the construed import of his grandmother's image could, with some encouragement on his own part, induce a weakening in William's stance.

"If it is your worry, William, that in accepting Doctor Jackson's offer your pride will be hurt and you will feel a lesser man for it, then banish such thoughts. It is your health that is important and besides, no one other than myself and your immediate family will be privy to the Doctor's offer and administrations," observed the rector.

"I understand, sir, but it is not easy to set pride aside and accept charity, however well intended."

"Pride has its place, my friend, but for all its worth it displays far greater destructive power and can be a blight on good reasoning and wise forethought. Just look to the Scriptures. Doesn't Proverbs tell us that pride goeth before destruction and that a rod of pride lies in the mouth of the foolish? Be wise, William, not foolish. Pride won't serve you well if you reject the Doctor's kindness out of hand."

"Don't think me ungrateful, I just feel…well, awkward," said William.

"And you speak of charity. But you are not some idler constantly falling upon the beneficence of others. You have made your way in the world and served your fellow citizens well. The Doctor feels you are most deserving of his attentions. If there is any charity here it is not in the sense of alms but in the sense of Christian love for one's fellow man. The Bible talks of faith, of hope and charity and tells us that the greatest of these is charity."

With these comments the Reverend Appleton felt that he had said enough and prepared to bid farewell to William and Mina. He had no wish to out-stay his welcome, feeling that any further deliberation on the subject could be construed by William as an attempt to exert undue influence. Instead he felt he had achieved what he had set out to do and that his remarks had not ventured beyond the scope of words designed to manipulate and coax the other's thought processes. And thus, it was with some degree of satisfaction that he made haste descending the stairs, only to catch a glimpse of the parlour clock as he passed the open door and to realise that he had seriously overlooked the passage of time. In consequence, as he hurriedly jammed on his felt hat and crossed the threshold, his farewell to Mina came amid mutterings that he would be late for a churchwardens' meeting. He would, however, return later the following week to see how the patient was faring.

It was shortly before noon when Doctor Jackson made his appearance. It was a little later than he had planned but at least he had completed his morning house calls and Mina had made full use of the time at her disposal. She had changed William's sheets and assisted him with his toiletry and with the trimming and washing of his hair. She had then cleaned and dusted the bedroom throughout such that, when she ushered the Doctor in at seven minutes to twelve, he was confronted by a neat and tidy room and an equally presentable occupant. Yet neither transformation was of such moment to register with the physician. Doctor Jackson's scrutiny was drawn immediately to William's physical state and the extent of perceptible deterioration. It had similarly shocked the clergyman before him, yet, in Doctor Jackson's case, he had only set eyes on the young man some few days before. Now the Doctor perceived a quite startling change in him, his features seemingly tormented by the rigour of his affliction. Suddenly he seemed more scrawny, his face more hollow-cheeked and his skin a ghastly puttied hue. This and a fortnight's growth of beard – for he had felt too tired to shave – had conspired to age him and leave him looking ravaged and wasted. To Doctor Jackson's eye the signs were ominous and began to confirm his own worst suspicions.

"And how are you today, my boy?" enquired the physician. It was a question not posed with any hint of light heartedness, as might happen in the normal course of events. Doctor Jackson knew the answer and his face carried a seriousness of expression that told of a growing realisation of the gravity of William's condition.

"Wretched sir. I can't say I've felt this queer before. I've not mentioned it to Mina but I'm beginning to wonder whether they were right at the Baltimore hospital…at the Jarvis…that I am consumptive and that now it is beginning to take a hold of me. But I felt better when I came to this city and made a new start. I've had these problems with my breathing and the coughing, but they all say it's bronchitis," said William in a tone of despondency.

The Doctor chose not to offer a view on William's suspicions. "Let me examine you, my dear fellow. I cannot help you unless I take a closer look," he said. "Pray leave matters to me."

Doctor Jackson had fully expected some resistance to this suggestion, given the attitude that prevailed when he last visited the house, but this did not prove to be the case. In the time that had elapsed between the clergyman's departure and the good doctor's arrival, William had not entered upon any further dialogue with Mina regarding his reservations. Instead he sought his own counsel and, within that intervening hour or two, the thoughts of others must have weighed so heavily in his mind as to unhinge previous conviction; for now, having got himself out of bed and seated to receive the doctor, he acceded to the latter's words without question and clambered back into bed in readiness to receive the physician's attentions.

Doctor Jackson released the clasp on his medical bag and withdrew from it a wooden box which he proceeded to open to reveal its contents: a percussion hammer and pleximeter together with a handsome cedar and ivory stethoscope. As he extracted these items he noticed that William's eye was drawn to them, prompting him to volunteer a little information to sate the patient's apparent curiosity.

"A present from the Army Medical Corps in appreciation of my time and contribution when attached to the Army. It's all a bit like music, William – plenty of percussion and good listening. I've always been told I have a keen ear for chest examinations and, indeed, I have. But when I went off to the war I thought that would be an end to it. Fortunately, however, the field hospitals tended to be a few miles behind the battle lines, so my ears were spared the full force of the artillery, if not the screams of the amputees."

The doctor removed his coat and rolled up his shirt sleeves before commencing his investigations. He began by peering into the patient's mouth and looking at his tongue. Then he embarked upon an exhaustive examination of the thorax, back and abdomen, first by the practice of palpation, then by reliance upon the use of his new set of instruments. Throughout the examination Doctor Jackson offered no opinions and, other than on occasions when he directed William to cough, asked that the patient remain quiet to avoid unwelcome distraction. Sometimes, head tilted and alert to the product of his stethoscope's earpieces, the doctor's expression was indicative of his being quite lost to the immediate surroundings. Instead his energies were so focussed and closed to other influences that his trained ear was set free to discern and interpret every nuance of sound, every murmur that rose from William's chest.

In time Doctor Jackson broke free from his assiduous attentions to the patient's upper body, unwound his frame to recover full stature and gently coaxed and eased his now stiffened back muscles into a posture they recognised. Turning to the adjacent washstand, he poured a little water from jug to basin and soaped his hands, now clammy from his explorations. Only when he had dried his hands, and unfurled and secured his shirtsleeves, did he speak.

"O.K, my boy. That's helpful. I'll be back to see you on Monday morning and we'll discuss your condition. I'll tell Missus Reynolds to keep you well supplied with fluids and, if the weather remains mild, to keep those sashes open back and front. It'll help ease your breathing. Oh, and I'll leave this medicine. You can forget that syrup you dislike. This should give you some relief. We swore by it when away with the Army." As he spoke the doctor proceeded to polish his instruments with a piece of white muslin before returning them to their felt lined box. "We'll meet again on Monday, William. Try to get some rest." Then, snapping closed his leather bag, Doctor Jackson strode across the room and was gone, pausing only at the bottom of the stairs to give Mina her instructions.

On the Sunday morning Elisha Boyleston Jackson took his wife to church. He had not relished telling William Reynolds the truth about his illness and leaving him in the knowledge that what life he had left would be lived out in torment and wretchedness. For, in the doctor's assessment, the prognosis was distressing and devoid of hope, his young patient now deeply drawn into the maelstrom of an advanced stage of incipient phthisis. One of his lungs was all but gone, wasted by the disease, and the likelihood was that William would not last beyond Christmas. Christmas 1865. A little over two months away. Destined to be committed to the cold ground of a distant city, far from his homeland and blood-tied kin. That is what troubled the physician so, the fact that with his news would come the realisation and anguish in William's breast that never again would he set eyes upon his own flesh and blood. Of one thing Doctor Jackson was sure. The young man would require plenty of spiritual guidance in the coming weeks and he had no doubt that Samuel Appleton would earnestly set about finding the time to fulfil that need when he came to learn of William's plight.

The physician could have told his patient of the gravity of his condition two days before, but he had refrained from doing so. His listening had been thorough and revealing and he had great self-belief in his percussive and auscultatory skills when it came to thoracic examinations. And so, by the time he had risen to his feet on Friday morning and turned his attentions to washing his hands, he had already established conclusively, in his own mind, what exactly was the nature and progression of William's illness. Yet having reached his conclusions he was inclined not to address the patient extempore but to bide his time. He felt that he needed to choose his words carefully and thus, to the extent that this was remotely possible, to soften the blow as best he could. Monday was to be soon enough, allowing the good doctor an opportunity and expectation that time spent knelt at prayers on Sunday morning would serve him well in discharging a responsibility that rested and weighed upon his shoulders.

★ ★ ★

Ten days had passed since the kindly physician made his Monday return to the house on Christian Street and, through no choice of his own, changed the lives of its occupants forever. The month of October now drew towards its close. With it the march of decline in William Reynolds' physical condition seemed to be out-stripped only by that of the final vestiges of summer days – those last green leaves that resolutely held firm for so long, only to be browned and rimed with October's passage and cast tumbling into the city's streets.

Mina was inconsolable. Her life had been torn apart with the news of her husband's prognosis and the fragility of her emotions was testament to her tender years. Gone were those early womanly aspirations to develop her homemaking skills, gone and crushed in their infancy. Instead she was a child again, showing little or no inclination to assist and care for her husband, but needing to be cosseted and coaxed from self-pity. She would often lie upon the bed and sob herself to sleep. Otherwise she got into the habit of taking to the old Boston rocker, casting her tearful head against the painted top-rail and letting the chair's motion send her to sleep, or at the very least, induce a heavy drowsiness sufficient to quell the sobs and stem their secretion. And when at the twilight hour her mother came into the parlour to light the lamps it was to find her daughter still slumped in her chair, sometimes at sleep, at others open – eyed, yet uncommunicative. The grate would be devoid of coals or kindling, ready to cheer the onset of evening, and in the kitchen the stove would stand idle and cold, left to await the attentions of others if the household was to be blessed with any supper of sorts. Sadly, Mina's indifference and self-absorption seemed to generate a sense of resentment from her mother and sister – resentment that more and more was falling upon their shoulders – and their general lack of compassion was palpable and found wanting in a family relationship. And so, with Mina often prostrated by her own dejection and self-pity, and caring little for her husband's comforting arms and kind words, William would sometimes find himself attending to his every need. It was almost as if it were Mina and not he that death was beckoning.

In these dark days of autumn Doctor Jackson never failed to call at some stage every day, if only to provide a little passing company. Ann Thompson, in fairness to the woman, also chose to sit with William some afternoons when not busy with her washing and ironing. She showed signs of being a good listener as her son-in-law drew solace from reminiscence upon times past and his childhood in England; and always he spoke of his beloved

Grandma and of her cat that was prized for both its accomplishment as a mouser and its affection as a pet. In William's view the animal was worth all of $50. Then there was the Reverend Appleton, who, having been appraised of the gravity of the patient's affliction, fell into the habit of calling on alternate afternoons. He would sit an hour with William and talk of matters temporal and spiritual and allow William to draw comfort from Scripture; and they would begin by repeating together the twenty-third psalm, for that was William's favourite among the Psalms of David, and he found strength and fortitude in its recital. And all the while the rector would ensure that beneath the roof of the Church of the Mediator at 19th and Lombard Streets, prayers and collects were offered up in William's name and a candle burned bright for him.

The clergyman's last visit had been uncommonly fleeting in its duration since other commitments had left him short of time and he had to be gone to prepare a sermon before Evensong. But he left with William a book by the celebrated Mister Dickens, being a story he had recently read and enjoyed immensely. If William could summon interest and concentration enough to get into the book, then rapt pre-occupation with a good yarn might lift him out of life's torment and prove balm to a troubled mind. That was in the forefront of the rector's thoughts, although his reservations were twofold as to whether it was the right book for a young man in such predicament. For in its opening the story was a sombre one and in its title it spoke of expectations – *Great Expectations* – when the reality was that William Reynolds had nothing in the way of expectations left in this World, excepting the belief and comfort that, thereafter, he would forever dwell in the house of the Lord. But the Reverend Appleton detected that William was cheerful enough to accept the loan of this latest of Dickens' novels. He had read and enjoyed a little of the author's work in years past, notably *Nicholas Nickleby* and some of the great man's Christmas stories and articles in *Household Words*, but the turbulence of his life in recent times had not been conducive to such pursuits as reading. And so, true to that cheerfulness sensed by the rector, and on that very evening, William had taken the book with him down to supper, a rather salty meal of stewed beef, greens and dumplings that had tested Josie's patience in its preparation and had equally proved a hurdle for William in its dispatch.

With the dishes cleared away and Mina and her mother busying themselves with the dirty pots and crockery, William sat himself down on a chair by the hearth and determined that he would give Mister Dickens a try. His hope was that a little reading would tire him sufficiently to permit him to climb the stairs, fall into bed, and, with a touch of good fortune, pass a reasonable night's sleep; and so William had come to supper fit for an early return to his bed, wearing a clean cotton nightshirt and with stockinged feet to ward off any evening chill. By the time he stole away from the dining room table and entered the parlour the fire had taken to hissing and flaring and was throwing a cosy warmth about the room.

The radiance of the fire, assisted by the glow of a paraffin lamp, its wick newly drawn, ensured that a good light fell upon the reader's pages as he warmed his feet on the iron fender. He had not felt such comfort for a long time and for once his breathing was easier and he was not unduly troubled by spells of hard coughing; and that comfort was soon enhanced by his mother-in-law when, with work in the kitchen complete, the women joined him in the parlour and Ann Thompson brought with her mugs of hot coffee. Yet William's first thought, as he cast one of the widow's woollen shawls about his shoulders, turned to the title page, and let his eye fall upon the author's name, was of a day's outing with his Grandma to the Portsdown Fair. The outing must have shortly followed the move to the present family home in Portsea. In William's recollection it also took place when the country was at war in the Crimea since he had vivid recollections of the endless columns of foot soldiers, buoyantly marching into the town behind their regimental bands. A column of fusiliers, resplendent in their red tunics, had passed by on their way to the Dockyard Gate as William and his Grandma waited in Queen Street for the large horse-drawn cab that was to convey them to Portsdown.

As to the fair itself, William's abiding memory of the day had not been the fun of the side-shows and the carousels but the view from the crest of Portsdown, a view that had taken his breath away. There below, as if seen by a bird in flight, lay the distant towns of Portsmouth and Gosport, clustered about the harbour's mouth, the haven's shimmering expanse dotted about and here and there, forested, with the masts of countless ships. And then, as William raised his eyes to the horizon, in the tender haze about Spithead, two ships under canvas were making for their anchorage. All of which had little relevance or connection with the writings of Charles Dickens, excepting when it came to the return journey. William remembered looking out across the flat farmland that lay beyond the barracks at Hilsea, of falling into a brief slumber induced by the motion of the conveyance and then being woken by his Grandma as southbound traffic was drawn to a halt.

A farmer's wagon had suffered a broken axle-tree and accordingly lay crippled upon the highway, its load partly shed. The sight of the broken cart was mirrored, as William recalled – and much to his dismay at the time – by the smashed piece of trumpery that lay at his feet. It was a cheap fairing won at a side-show, a bauble which had slipped his grasp as sleep overtook him. Well, it was apparent that they had reached the outskirts of the town when they came upon the accident. The coachman, being a jovial and garrulous sort, launched into a discourse that presumably he felt would instruct or amuse his passengers, who numbered a dozen or so. They had he said, if they were not already aware, been brought to a halt in the district of Mile End. He then directed attention to a well proportioned red brick terraced house that stood back from the west side of the road behind a short garden and proceeded to tell his audience that this had once been the home of a gentleman who worked in the Navy Pay Office. That gentleman and his wife had been blessed, in this very house, and some forty years past, with the birth of a son; and that son was none other than the celebrated novelist, Mister Charles Dickens. It struck William at the time that few of the adult passengers seemed especially impressed with the information, presumably on account of a general indifference or because they were already cognisant of that knowledge. As for the children, who were in the majority, most were too young, tired and fidgety after a day at the fair to have even registered, or for that matter have comprehended, the utterances of the enthusiastic coachman.

Being at the time a child of some twelve years or so, and inclined to curiosity in all manner of topics, the episode was sufficiently cherished to have remained in William's memory. He particularly remembered that once the road had been cleared and they got going again, his Grandma – who enjoyed her books and was a well read woman – confessed she did not know that the house at Mile-End Terrace was the birthplace of Charles Dickens; and thus, it had been a joy to her to learn as much. She then proceeded to tell William about the great man, his achievements as a novelist and of his latest tome, *Hard Times*, a story she had followed through its serialisation in the periodical, *Household Words*. Moreover, he had by all accounts become something of a controversial figure, outspoken politically and a champion of the working man and the common soldier. He had taken the Government to task over their failings in domestic reform and had been damning of their mismanagement of the war in the Crimea and of the plight of the fighting men. Grandma had spoken with animation when she fell upon this issue, for two of her three sons had been with the Fleet in the Black Sea whilst the third was spending a sixth year with his Regiment in the distant East Indies.

And so, as William readied himself to make a start on *Great Expectations*, sitting before the fire in Christian Street, this early introduction to Mister Charles Dickens on the day's outing with his beloved Grandma, came flooding back to him in a wave of nostalgia. He felt homesick and the more so because of his situation; and he felt tears well in his eyes, tears that he quickly stemmed and wiped away for fear of Mina seeing them and upsetting herself in turn. Yet there was no worry on that score, for she had fallen asleep beside him while her mother sat, head bowed, silently pre-occupied with her sewing.

William remembered reading the first two chapters before his concentration upon the text proved soporific and he fell into a deep sleep. By the time he awoke the hour was approaching eleven o'clock and the women had long since retired to their beds They had chosen, no doubt, to let William be, seeing he was at restful sleep, but now, as the embers in the grate had fallen to ash, a chill had crept upon the room and roused him from his slumber. As he prepared to follow Mina to bed, William was again beset with thoughts of home, since his evening reading had again taken him back to yet earlier days. It had been the paludal landscape bordering Pip Pirrip's home that had triggered further nostalgia, the flat wilderness and patchwork of marsh and dykes and alders and of marsh mists obscuring distant prison hulks. William's thoughts returned to the country of his own early boyhood, a land of poor salt marsh lying close to his own village home, sometimes remote in its setting, where novice buglers and drummer boys would practice their rudimentary skills away from habitation. A watery land again, fringed by brackish osier beds, where mists would descend to bleach or hide the string of prison hulks moored head to stern out in the harbour reaches. Excepting that here the noise of great guns was not reserved for escaped convicts but was commonplace and more to do with the Gunnery School going about its business or with the Saluting Battery marking the arrival or departure of some mighty warship.

As William laid his head upon his pillow beside his young wife, his thoughts of hearth and home and of dear old England caused him to spill more tears. Yet, however sad, he was somehow grateful for these thoughts, grateful to Samuel Appleton for triggering them through the loan of his book. He had to face such reflection if he were to write to his mother and open his heart and tell her his news. Doctor Jackson had told him to do so, to write at once and, to his credit, he had tried several times. But the composition had caused such distress and such a weeping, leaving little choice but to put down his pen. That done he had found it difficult to console himself and pick up the thread again. So he had started afresh, only to encounter the same outcome. Now William felt he had to muster sufficient inner resolve to complete the task. That was his final thought of the day. He would try again. Tomorrow.

The morning was slow to cast its burgeoning light for the wind had got up and driven heavy wracks of shower cloud across the city. William had slept well into the early hours, yet now he was awake, drawn from his rest by sharp squalls of wind and rain that, in their ferocity, had set the window panes rattling like empty cans on a rolling ship. He began to cough and, for a time, the coughing gathered in its momentum and intensity before he succeeded in clearing some viscid matter that had built up in his chest overnight. In turn, of course, the commotion roused Mina who was thrown into distress by William's exertions until he settled and she became more collected in herself and for once ventured forth and brought her husband coffee and fresh water.

"Mina, my love, I will try again today to write to my Mother. It must be told. Doctor Jackson has even offered to write the letter for me but I have to do it myself," said William, reflectively.

"What time is he calling today, Willie?" Mina's eyes were tearful as she spoke and the shroud of sadness with which circumstances had now engulfed her was perceptible in her tone.

"It won't be this morning. He's instructing students at the Medical School and seeing his patients this afternoon. He hopes to call in the early evening."

"Then, if you feel up to it, settle yourself down and compose your letter this morning. It'll be quiet and that will aid your concentration. I've jobs to do in the scullery although I haven't the heart for them. Mother's taking the horse-car into the city. She needs some new outdoor boots for the winter."

"My chest is sore, Mina, but I've had some sleep. It'll be a harder task the longer I leave it. I'll come and get myself some milk and oatmeal, then get myself washed and dressed. I can't sit and write a letter in my nightshirt."

Within an hour William had managed some breakfast and attended to his toilet. At least with time's progression and the flight of the early shower clouds that had fettered the advance of dawn, the bedroom was now largely blessed with a good natural light; and, with the passage of the rain, the wind fell markedly and the windows stopped chattering in their frames. William proceeded to re-position a small occasional table to a spot he felt best suited to the task that lay ahead. From a downstairs cupboard he had returned with writing paper, pen and a bottle of black ink, all of which had been brought from the house on Willow Street. Now he felt ready to make a start. He took a few sips of water, for his mouth and tongue had become dry and in texture vied with that of the paper before him; and thus refreshed, William drew up a chair, made himself comfortable and dipped his nib into the ink bottle. He began to write.

Dearest Mother,

How is it that I have written to you twice since the end of June and have had no answer? I have also sent you several papers, some with pictures in them, but with no tidings in reply.

Mother, when you receive this, do answer it immediately. Oh, my poor Mother, I have sad news to break to you but it must be told. I have kept a bold front to many hard, stern tussles and have been blessed with the best of health, but I tried my constitution too far at last, the blow has come, but, Mother, I expected it to come long ago, I knew it would sooner or later. I am in a rapid pulmonary consumption and cannot last but a short time longer but could expect nothing else from such a life, knowing the disease was hereditary from my father. But Oh! Mother! I am so miserably situated. I will repeat my last letter over to you.

When I left Baltimore in June I hardly knew what to do. You had written to me not to come home and be dependent on any of my folks. But Mother, I was too proud for that, do not think that I grew into manhood without your old pride glowing within me. Do you remember, Mother, Old Parson Veck and the shilling on Good Friday? I never forgot it, that pride has always burned within. I took the lesson from you that day. Well, I had over $300, it would cost $90 to come over (as it takes double to leave this country than it does to come in) and when I had turned the rest into gold where would it be, gold being at the rate of $1.39, I should have little more than half my money. I knew that was not sufficient to set me up in business in the Old Country and besides, you saying if I had ever a spare corner in this country you would someday, perhaps, fill it up, I determined to try and set up business in this country. But how did I fail? I must tell you. I decided to start in the magnificent city of Philadelphia. There I visited a doctor; he told me there was nothing the matter but bronchitis. I was glad enough and took medicine for the ailment but, at the same time,

*consumption was eating my vitals out. Yet my constitution was so hard I
did not feel it.*

*Well, Mother, I became acquainted with an old widow woman who had
two daughters. Both worked to keep the old woman but one in particular I
noticed. She worked hard all day and came home and gave her Mother all
her earnings and worked about the house and got supper and such like. I
thought if I had a wife like her, how she would help me. Consequently I fell
in love with her and married her. Shortly I began to find myself failing. I
did not notice it at first, at last I found I was really getting weak and pale.
I sent for a physician, then came the bills, $10, $15 and so on, but I was
never told my danger. My money and strength gradually dwindled, I slowly
sank and at last found myself sick. Then, Mother, I came to my senses
and, to my horror, found how I was situated. I found my mother-in-law to
be dirty and entirely devoid of energy, my sister-in-law to be ill-tempered
and morose and my wife not worth one cent. She is good, Mother, if there
was only someone to cultivate it but her mother has ruined her, she is a
spoilt child. Now, for instance, when I am taken suddenly sick with a fit of
coughing or weakness, she will put her head beside me and cry nearly into
fits, instead of trying to help me. And she has no thought, I have to ask for
every little thing to be done.*

As William wrote these words they seemed to bait and play upon his
emotions to the point of torment. The tears had risen since he began his
missive and now, as he wrote candidly of Mina, they welled heavily in his
eyes, spilled and coursed down his sunken cheeks. He withdrew his pen
from the paper and sat back on his chair, anxious to prevent the product
of his grief from splashing across the unfinished letter.

William wiped his eyes upon his shirtsleeve, being without a handkerchief
at the time, then dried and cleaned his pen with an old fragment of cloth he
had placed nearby. A point had been reached in his letter – having filled both
sides of two sheets of paper – where he was minded to turn those sheets
upon their sides and to employ a technique that might permit its completion
without recourse to additional paper. William was only too aware of the
high cost of postage and, for the purpose of minimising that burden, had
hitherto prevailed upon Josie to call upon the dealer in stationery whose
premises adjoined her workplace. This she had done somewhat grudgingly,
the new-found conviviality that had surfaced during her first few weeks
at the milliner's having since made its exit and left the Josie of old. Yet,

to her credit, she had returned home with a bottle of Thaddeus Davids' steel pen ink and, furthermore, it was of the requested shade of red. And so now William sought out that new bottle of ink, that he recalled having placed in the cabinet beside his bed, and, being somewhat more collected in himself, prepared to resume his efforts at the table. His neat copperplate gave no hint of the illness and distress that afflicted him, lacking none of the precision that had always characterised his hand. And so, as he took up his pen again they were words of a carmine tint that advanced at right angles across the scripted black; words wrought in heartbreak that in their regimentation and contrasting hue, began to cast a checkerboard attractiveness about the page.

But Mother, perhaps it is well enough I have procured one friend to close my eyes and point out where I lay after a hard struggle and there is one comfort I have, that my wife loves me truly. But Oh! Mother!! I am so miserable, to think I have a kind, good Mother so far away and have to die here alone, poor and miserable, without even life's comforts.

I do not know what I should have done only for an old doctor named Jackson who is very patriotic and took me under his charge gratuitously because of my serving the country and having no friends. He came to the house and examined me thoroughly and told me my case. He said, my boy, I am not going to lie to you or tell you that you are well when you are not. Your case, he said, is very distressing, one of your lungs is entirely gone. Write and tell your mother, he said, that you are labouring under rapid consumption. He then promised he would do all he could for me, he calls constant every day.

But, Mother, it is not medicine alone I want, I want good food and nursing, neither of which I can get. Oh, Mother, bitter tears I shed when I think of you and your kind, pitiful face and your Motherly hand to smooth my pillows and to fan me when I lay exhausted from hard coughing and your nice gruels and rice puddings. But oh, bitter thought, I have no one but one without experience who lays on my bed breaking her heart instead of aiding me in any way.

Mother, do write soon or I shall never see your handwriting again. When you receive this do not weep, keep a stout heart and write at once. And Mother, ask Uncle James if he will not forgive me and write me a few lines. Surely he will, he may consider this almost a dying man's request, for I have made three former attempts to write this letter. I should so much like to hear from him, it would let me know he had looked over my faults. You said, Mother, you had his portrait to send me, send it Mother, do, that I may look at you all to the last.

How is Uncle Charley? He is a fine, aristocratic looking gentleman in the picture, everyone admires him, and poor Grandma's picture is the best I have ever seen. How glad I was to see it, it came better than $50. I often look at them now. Oh Mother! Mother! If you were only here for one day, that I would tell you all the ins and outs, you would not think so hard of me. But God's will be done, there is no hope for us, either one. The ocean is between us, so we must be, so we must die, but no ocean separates us hereafter.

Now, Mother dear, keep good spirits and write soon. Give my kindest love to Grandma and Uncle James and also to Uncle Charley. Tell Uncle Charley a few lines from him would be received with infinite pleasure, be sure and send Uncle James' picture and please send a paper occasionally. And Mother, do not wait for an answer to your letter before you write another, write every week and I will do the same as long as I am able. I am getting exhausted now, dear Mother, sitting so long, and I am beginning to cough. I will conclude with kind love to all from your ever loving and affectionate son,
William Reynolds.

N.B. I send my wife's portrait. I cut it small because of the extra paper. Goodbye, Mother. God bless you, Willie.

As William drew his letter to a close he was oblivious to events below where Mina had been going about her several chores. Being but fourteen years of age, it had only been the previous spring that she had fully blossomed into womanhood. Now, in the scullery at Christian Street, she was beset with nausea, but, in her naivety and inexperience, thought little of it. To Mina it was another symptom of the pain of grief and melancholy that had cast its dark shroud upon her home.

Upstairs William put aside his pen and returned to his bed, exhausted by the emotional trauma that accompanied his achievement. As sleep embraced him, his mind was wistfully drifting back in time. His adult life had fallen away and he was a boy again.

Two

Gozo, Malta: Montgomery Co., Maryland
April 1847

The ferryman's tanned and sun-crimped features shaped a broad and toothless grin. It reflected his appreciation for payment above the normal reckoning from the family that stepped ashore from his boat in the pretty port of Mgarr. Yet their generosity was prudent investment as it brought forth immediate dividends. His vessel secured, the boatman hailed a fellow islander who presented himself at the quayside, appeared to receive instruction, then hastily scurried away as if his life depended upon it.

The new arrivals numbered four in total. A woman of about fifty, her daughter, the daughter's husband and a child approaching five years of age. They had travelled from their home in Valletta and had spent the previous night at a lodging house on the Maltese shore, close to the ferry-boat jetty. With the exception of the child, of course, it was their clear understanding that, for the time being at least, it would be their last visit to the island. Soon they would depart for England. Fate would decree that none would ever return to Gozo. For the moment they spent a few minutes in fine adjustment of their attire and in recovering their composure after crossing the Comino Channel. The stretch of water had been generally calm, yet less gracious in its middle reaches, where, for a short time, a low swell had caused the elder woman and the child to feel nauseous.

The young Gozitan who had been summoned and instructed by the ferryman was soon to reappear, now leading a brace of donkeys that were harnessed with a cart in tow. It was a primitive conveyance and rudimentary in its seating arrangements, yet for the travellers it offered a most acceptable and welcome alternative to facing the arduous climb up the hill of Migiarro. In past times they had been left to tackle the ascent on foot and were only too aware of its gruelling nature. Now, to aid their comfort, a flagon of fresh drinking water was brought forth by the young man, together with a bag of dried figs and prickly-pear. The water was well received since the late morning heat was beginning to rival that of a summer's day. The fruit, on the other hand, proved less popular, yet it was declined in a manner that appeared not to cause offence. And thus, with thirsts sated, the islander helped the strangers aboard his conveyance, seated them as comfortably as possible, then goaded the donkeys into action.

The ascent to the fort was achieved in the space of ten minutes or so. The road out of Mgarr fell away on either side into gullies filled with olive and carob. Far below the view of the little port receded and, in its recession, the harbour appeared increasingly idyllic, its crystal clear water dappled in hues of a turquoise blue under the cloudless sky. Its surface shimmered in the April sunshine and was dotted with luzzu, the colourful local fishing boats that bore the painted eye of Osiris. Shortly, as the road levelled off, a track to the left took the party through some outworks, which, in turn, led to a bridge that crossed a dry ditch. Beyond the bridge stood the impressive main gate to Fort Chambray.

After initial formalities the family entered the fortress and were escorted by a soldier from one of the local Fencible regiments to a far corner of its confines. The soldier clutched a bunch of huge keys and led the visitors to an old timber door set low into a stone wall. The child, who had become sleepy during the ascent of the hill, had by now recovered his senses and, in the escorted passage, was distracted and impressed by the finery of the soldiers who went about their business. He caught a glimpse of open ground where a detachment from a British infantry regiment was being drilled and drummer boys were being put through their paces. The tunics, plumed helmets and glints of steel caught his eye. The resonance of drum roll was sweet to his ear.

The visitors took shelter for a few minutes out of the glare of the sun as the soldier fumbled with the many keys, choosing to step inside a tiny one-roomed chapel that stood nearby. Initially the interior appeared dark to eyes accustomed to bright sunlight. It was an unpretentious little structure, with largely plain walls and a few frescoes, a chamber that would sometimes serve as the penultimate resting place for the bodies of deceased soldiers awaiting interment beyond the timber door.

A sigh of achievement fell from the lips of the soldier as he finally came upon the key that succeeded in accessing the little garrison cemetery. He beckoned the family to follow him which they did. It was now the best time to visit this sun-drenched, secluded burial ground set high in a far corner of the fort and in the lee of its now crumbling ramparts. That thought was in the mind of Margaret Black when she planned what she knew would be her final pilgrimage to her husband's grave. Perhaps the others would have the opportunity to come again, especially her grandson, who was seeing his grandfather's resting place for the first time; and today he was seeing it in its fairest garb, before the summer sun scorched the earth brown and laid it bare. For now, as they approached the late sergeant's tombstone, it rose from a green sea of spring grasses studded with wild flowers, a profusion of growth that partially obscured the stone's inscription. Behind, hugging the base of the ramparts and as affirmation of the Mediterranean climate, the huge terminal inflorescences of two agaves thrust skywards from their spiny rosettes and stood silhouetted against the blue.

The widow shed a few tears but said little, keeping her own counsel. Her daughter, Charlotte, and son-in-law, John, sought to interest their young son in the fact that this was his grandfather's grave. Yet, given his tender years, they readily appreciated that any impact was likely to be short-lived and beyond recall in later life.

Sacred to the memory of the late Colour Sergeant William James Black of the 94th Regiment who departed this life on the 7th January 1833 aged 35 years leaving a widow and four children to deplore the death of a tender and affectionate parent. This stone was erected by his brother sergeants as a testimony of their esteem.

As William Reynolds grew up he would retain vague memory of seeing the grave on this April day, a sight occasionally rekindled in his mind's eye when his mother spoke lovingly of her father and of the respect in which he was held. Yet William's overwhelming recollection of the occasion would be the fine sight of the soldiers and their accoutrements and it was to soldiering he would in time aspire. And with that aspiration he would come to wish he had known his kind and esteemed grandfather who lay at rest under the sun in the little garrison cemetery at Chambray.

★ ★ ★

The two boys lounged on the deck of the side porch, their backs poorly cushioned against a timber upright that helped support the overhang. Nothing in the way of conversation had passed between them since they slipped away after supper. For once they thought they had evaded their mothers' watchful eyes and by guile rather than luck had avoided recruitment for clean-up chores. That in itself gave them some meagre satisfaction. Little else seemed to cheer them. In truth, seeing their melancholy mood at the dinner table and being alert to their stratagem, their mothers had felt sorry for the boys and had chosen to turn a blind eye. And so they had been permitted to slink away and were left unhindered to watch the sun go down beyond the line of trees that followed the Little Seneca Creek. Then, as the sunset faded and the twilight deepened and became nightfall, their attentions fell upon the flicker of several moths drawn to the light of the paraffin lamp that hung beyond the kitchen door; and still they remained tight-lipped.

The farmstead, a rambling, two-storey frame house encased in white clapboard and shingles, occupied a plateau that rose above the general level of the surrounding countryside, a mile or so to the south of the Germantown crossroads. It was approached from the south-east by a dirt track that climbed up through the cornfields from the Darnestown road and it had been home to the two twelve year olds who had watched the sun go down for close on three years. George Andreas Atzerodt and Ernest Hartman Richter were cousins. They had been brought here with their siblings when the two families chose to leave their native Prussia. They had stepped ashore at Baltimore, from the brig *Apollo,* in June 1844, and had made their home within the gently undulating countryside of Montgomery County in the State of Maryland. This was good agricultural country, the land worked by farmers who were largely of English and German stock and it was in the small community of Germantown that Heinrich Atzerodt and his brother-in-law Johann Richter purchased a run-down tobacco farm. The prospect that these laymen confronted was not an easy one, particularly during that first winter. The living was hard in the face of competition from the established farming community and especially the slave owning planters. Yet theirs was an optimistic outlook and, with local hired help, they toiled hard at their enterprise, razed to the ground the old house and the former slave quarters, built a good-sized farmstead and put their hand to raising corn and root vegetables; and all this with moderate success for men unaccustomed to building and working the land. And not surprisingly, as they were seen to keep their heads above water and to push on from there, they came to be held in good opinion by both their compatriots and by the wider Germantown community.

In the winter of 1846, however, a major decision had been reached by Heinrich Atzerodt and his wife Victore, a decision that heralded something of a return to the old way of life. Heinrich, for all his commitment and willingness to work the family acres, had never felt that he had truly adapted to farming in the same way as his brother-in-law. He was a blacksmith by trade and in truth yearned to return to working with hammer and tongs. Not for him was the loneliness of working the fields and the sowing and nurturing of spring crops. Instead he longed to run a village smithy again. Heinrich wanted to be a man of iron once more, to put his brawny arms to hot-shoeing and wielding his ball-peen hammer upon the anvil; he craved to hear the hiss of hot tools being quenched in the water bosh. And so, when he learned of an opportunity that would quench his own desire, that would release, not steam, but his own frustration, he resolved to seize it.

The decision to leave Germantown was least well received by George Atzerodt and by his cousin Hartman Richter. Being of similar age, the boys were close and the comradeship they had forged was now on the eve of being severed. Heinrich Atzerodt had sold his interest in the farm to his brother-in-law, Johann. The transaction was signed and sealed and early the next day the doors of the old tobacco shed would be flung open revealing the large four-wheeled wagon that stood within. Made ready for the journey through the recent attentions of the local wheelwright, it was now laden high with the Atzerodts' chattels and worldly goods, fit to carry the family south to Virginia and to the watery land that sits between the lower Potomac and the Rappahannock. By sunrise, with the horses already harnessed, the family would have clambered aboard the wagon and they'd take the dirt track down to the Darnestown road. It would be a time for tears.

George rose to his feet and jumped down from the porch. He gathered up some stones and hurled them against the old tobacco shed. It was an expression of his dismay and discontent over what awaited him on the morrow.

"George, hurry in now, time for bed and you must say farewell to your cousins." Victore Atzerodt had emerged onto the porch where she stood wiping her hands on her apron in the light of the paraffin lamp. The boys jumped as her words broke the restored silence that had followed the clatter of stones upon the tobacco shed. "Komm jetzt, Georg, du mußt früh ins Bett, weil wir bei Sonnenaufgang unterwegs sein müssen. Quickly now."

George turned towards the kitchen door, his expression sullen. "Gute nacht Hartman."

"Gute nacht vetter. I'll be up and about to see you off in the morning."

"You know, I've no wish to leave Germantown. Ich habe kein Verlangen, nach Virginia zu gehen."

Hartman Richter gave his cousin a sympathetic smile. "You'll be back," he said.

Three

FORTON, GOSPORT

JANUARY 1853

The three storey infirmary was sturdy and imposing when viewed from offshore and, on an overcast winter's afternoon, its dull brick exterior could appear austere and unwelcoming in the fading light. It was set back behind a stony foreshore, which, at this time of year, was darkened by ribbons of seawrack that passing gales had cast high upon the beach.

Before the cholera epidemics had ravaged the neighbouring towns of Portsmouth and Gosport, the hospital had been discreet in disposing of its dead. But then a new burial ground had to be found and this became available on the fringe of poor salt marsh out on the Alverstoke road and just beyond the little hamlet of Clayhall. For three quarters of a century, following the initial admission of patients, this least savoury aspect of the institution's affairs had never impinged upon the neighbouring settlement. Yet the last twenty years had seen the hospital constantly spew its dead out into the village street, out towards the new cemetery. Clayhall, a homely cluster of flint and brick cottages, a single tavern and a coastguard station that rose out of the bleak, open landscape, had thus become accustomed to black, melancholy processions and witness to more than its fair share of sorrow.

It was on a winter's day, early in the year 1853, that the body of John Reynolds, a victim of consumption, five years certified, was brought out of the hospital gate, bound for the Clayhall cemetery. It was a fittingly dark afternoon to match the occasion. A few stark, leafless trees loomed the more sombre against the leaden sky and a stiff breeze off the sea was sufficient to set them swaying. They cast down a low wailing sound that suited the mournful state of things.

The gathering turbulence tossed the soft, flaxen curls of the young William Reynolds as he walked behind his father's coffin. The boy showed remarkable composure for a ten year old, yet it was hard. His small frame trembled with emotion in the chill, salty air. Once or twice he let his gaze dwell too long on the coffin ahead. Then, feeling the tears rise and finding the pretence all too harsh, he reached out for his uncle's hand, clutching it tightly. To William it felt secure. It provided the reassurance the moment demanded and quelled the youngster's burgeoning tearfulness.

It had been ten days since William had last set eyes upon his father. Consumption left its calling card shortly after the family's return to England but when the phithisis took its ugly grip upon him, when it stole his flesh and withered his frame, they admitted him to the naval hospital. William and his mother, Charlotte, had waited in a draughty, flag stoned concourse until an orderly wheeled John Reynolds out to them on a rickety hand-cart of sorts. They wouldn't let women and children be exposed to the sights and smells of the wards; for there were some pickled and crusty old salts who roamed and laid there, and cussed, and who, in their suffering and disinterest, were often devoid of propriety in how they behaved and presented themselves.

The concourse on which the family meeting took place was inset and set apart from the hospital's quadrangle which was open to the elements and flanked by towering inner brick walls that belonged to some of the wards. Even in the most clement of conditions, female visitors and children were discouraged from seeing their loved-ones here, for some of the more disturbed inmates and exhibitionists were prone to display themselves lewdly at the windows. The concourse, on the other hand, was out of sight of such coarseness, for here a glazed overhang, caked with and rendered opaque by algae and gull droppings, effectively obscured any view of the offending windows. Yet the meeting was short-lived. Although the consumptive inmates were encouraged to take fresh air, it was the draughtiness of the place on that last occasion which prompted Charlotte Reynolds to curtail the visit; for she was in fear of her husband contracting a chill that would compromise his already fragile state. It had been at this juncture, therefore, in the time taken for his wife to enter the hospital and beckon an attendant, that John Reynolds took the opportunity to address his young son with some words of advice. In so doing, and because of his affliction, his words were laboured and scarcely audible. His advice was phrased in a manner that had the stamp of being a shade abstruse for the average child some six months short of his eleventh birthday, but, despite this, William seemed to grasp the nub of it.

"Take care of your mother, Willie, and in the way you lead your life, always remember that its duration is fleeting. The hour flies, so use your time well and show goodwill to others. Trust in the Lord, my boy, and show fortitude in all you do and…" The poor fellow was forced to halt awhile, the sheer effort of uttering these words having triggered the need to give vent to a rasping cough. Once he had cleared his throat, John Reynolds proceeded to spit the product into a metal receptacle that nestled on his lap beneath a piece of muslin. That done, he composed himself and apologised to the boy before continuing. "I was about to say that if it's not too high an ideal, Willie, as you rest your tired head upon your pillow at the close of day, strive to avoid having cause to rebuke yourself for that day's conduct. God Bless you, my wee lad."

Sadly, little did William realise that this would be the last time he would see his father and hear that familiar Edinburgh accent, for the man had never lost the vernacular of his long abandoned birthplace. William had said nothing in reply to his father's words. During visits to the hospital he recalled feeling awkward in the elder's presence, supposedly because of his affliction, since, ordinarily, he had always been at ease with his father and they enjoyed a close relationship. But on that last day, Charlotte Reynolds had returned promptly with the orderly, whereupon – without undue delay – her husband was wheeled away to the promise of a further visit later in the week. John Reynolds had laid a hand on his son's head, they had exchanged smiles and that was it. There was to be no return visit. News had been brought to the family home in nearby Forton that their loved one had died in his sleep. Now they had come to bury him. He was forty-three years of age.

William had asked if he might accompany his Uncle James in following the hearse on foot and to this request his mother had consented, leaving the following carriage to the womenfolk – who were in the majority – and to the officiating clergyman. Parson Veck's troublesome gout and his advancing years had compelled him to take the comfort of a seat with the ladies as the mourners set forth from the portals of the infirmary's chapel.

William looked up at his uncle with a dolefulness that ill-suited his callow features and creased his brow. "Was my father held in esteem, uncle?" he enquired.

James Black smiled wanly and hesitated before replying. He knew from where that word had come. "Yes, Willie, he was loved and respected by all who were close to him and all who had made his acquaintance. You can be sure of that."

"Just like grandfather," said the boy.

"Yes, just like your grandfather."

"Mother and I will be able to visit father frequently." William said this with conviction, then reflected. "And one day, when I'm a man, I will go again to visit the grave of my esteemed grandfather. I will go to Chambray."

In truth William was not inclined to regard James Black as his favourite uncle. He had three uncles, all being his mother's younger siblings. They had all been born on the island of Gibraltar while William's esteemed grandfather had been garrisoned there with his regiment. The eldest, Uncle John, he had never seen and there was no immediate prospect of him doing so since he was away soldiering in the East Indies. Next came Uncle James, a naval man in his late twenties, who, when home from sea, was in the habit of lodging with the family in the house at Forton. He followed the same trade as John Reynolds, namely that of ship's steward, except it was the boy's understanding that his father had been a purser's steward while his uncle attended upon a captain. He was a tallish man, thick set with a fair complexion, stern grey eyes and light brown hair. He also had a great liking for poetry. Perhaps it was his bearing and rather serious demeanour that made William wary, almost frightened, of his Uncle James. Lastly there was Uncle Charley, the youngest of the brothers by two years. His was a lighter, more jaunty approach to life, and, like James, he had spent time with the family at Forton. Indeed, when William and his parents, together with Grandma Black, had come home from the island of Malta, Charley had eagerly awaited their arrival, being already numbered among the crew of the dear old *Victory*. The veteran of Trafalgar, her days of conflict behind her, lay moored in semi-retirement on the Gosport side of Portsmouth harbour where she fulfilled the role of flagship to the Port Admiral. Yet the old first rate, having been initially laid down almost a century before and having long since been paid off into the Ordinary, was ill-suited to accommodating her musicians who were quartered ashore in naval barracks. Here Charles Black and his fellow bandsmen would parade and practice their ceremonials, but, when not called upon by work commitments, William's youngest uncle would gravitate to the family home at 5 St. John's Place.

William recalled those days with affection, having spent much time in the company of his cheerful Uncle Charley. And when the bluejacket band was set to play on Grand Parade or Governor's Green, the family might take the Floating Bridge ferry to Portsmouth and proudly watch their musical rating demonstrate his skills with tuba or cornet. Yet to William's regret the curtain had come down on that close association all too soon. It had now been two years since dear Uncle Charley had been posted to a ship of the line and those happy times had become a distant memory.

Looking up at Uncle James, William saw his favourite uncle mirrored there. Although so different in temperament, the two seafaring brothers were markedly alike in their strong features and colouring. That aside, the elder stood three inches taller and a scar over the younger man's left eye was testament to a childhood accident. "Is it much further to walk, uncle?" As he looked up William felt his cheeks tingle with the salt spray drawn off the sea.

"We'll be there in a trice, my lad," came the reply.

"Does Uncle Charley know that father has died?"

"My information, William, is that his ship is presently lying at Valletta. I've sent word, but calculating that it's ten days sailing to Malta, then, even with favourable conditions, the mail-boat won't make Grand Harbour until early next week. But he'll know soon enough, Willie, and when he does you can be sure he'll write."

As Uncle James spoke of favourable conditions, William was aware that the stiff breeze continued to gather pace. A hundred yards off-shore he glimpsed an English lugger ploughing a boisterous path along the land, its sails close-hauled to the wind. It reminded the boy how precarious was life at sea and of his own susceptibility to sea-sickness. More significantly, it reminded him that his was a predominantly seafaring family and he would be expected to follow in those naval footsteps.

"It's a hard life at sea, Willie, but it's the making of you. And you soon find your sea-legs." He recalled the words that were uttered by his dear, departed father.

"Uncle James, why did Uncle Charley choose to play in the band and not become a steward like you and father?"

There was a lull before a reply fell upon the boy's ears. The modest cortege had now passed through the hamlet of Clayhall and, with its emergence, James Black was fleetingly distracted by the respectful good manners of the village innkeeper. The *Fighting Cocks* tavern stood back from the lane and the landlord, a gaunt, clean shaven fellow, was busying himself in the front yard. Noticing the approaching hearse he had proceeded to untie his apron and remove his cap. Clutching both, he now stood as if a soldier to attention, a gesture of respect that James Black acknowledged with a slight nod of the head in the innkeeper's direction.

"Sorry, William, what did you say?" came the belated reply.

"I was wondering why Uncle Charley became a bandsman yet you and father…"

"I'll tell you later, Willie." The elder's reluctance to launch into a lengthy discourse upon that subject was prompted by his realisation that their destination was close at hand.

The undertaker's vehicle that carried the deceased's coffin was a kind of extended and covered wagonette, elegant in its black lustre and flanked by the several pallbearers who proceeded on foot. As the receding lane now wavered in its alignment ahead of the vehicle, James Black and his nephew caught sight of the cemetery gate. To either side of them tracts of inferior and horse-sick pasture lay behind stunted hawthorn that in its profile had evidently been forced to cower before the prevailing wind. And soon a brackish drainage ditch came into view as it kept company with Clayhall Lane and served to carry the eye westwards to the line of stark alder that marked the cemetery bounds.

Inside the stuffy interior of the carriage that followed in the footsteps of uncle and nephew, the womenfolk and the officiating clergyman were insulated from their wintry surroundings behind heavy, velvet curtains. Here, amid heaped bombasine and crape, they clutched their *Books of Common Prayer* and made polite conversation about it being a blessed release. The widow and her mother apart, they looked forward to the prospect of a fine table that awaited them back at Forton. More especially, Parson Veck's thoughts were for the widow's strong tea and the celebrated sherry trifle for which the undertaker's caterer had a reputation.

As soon as the conveyances were pulled up at the cemetery gate the four pallbearers hastily set about their task. Men of few words and all, remarkably, of dejected and cadaverous appearance, they seemed eminently suited to their chosen employment. William ran to his mother as the parson and his company were helped into the grey daylight, yet Charlotte Reynolds, an upright and rather matronly looking woman for one in her early thirties, delayed a moment before taking the boy's hand. She adjusted her bonnet as the stiff breeze tugged at its ribbons, then, devoid of expression, acceded to the undertaker's silent and faintly simpering invitation to take her place in the wake of the pallbearers.

"Come, William, let us follow close behind your father's coffin." Charlotte's voice trembled as she dabbed her moist eyes and beckoned to her brother. "James, take Mother's arm will you. Let us put my dear husband to rest."

The Reverend Henry Aubrey Veck proceeded to take his time over formalities once those in attendance had picked their way across the burial ground. His white surplice and the little crimson prayer book he clutched to his breast contrasted with the black, amorphous form of the mourners, who, stooping together in their grief, faced the parson across the opened ground.

"Man that is born of a woman hath but a short time to live and is full of misery. He cometh up and is cut down, like a flower; he fleeth as it were a shadow and never…" As the pallbearers made ready to release their burden into the cold earth the clergyman's words faltered and flew in the wind and were gone. Nearby, the gravediggers' abandoned spades tilted in their loose anchorage of newly piled soil, their crooked pitch reflecting the rakish angles which settlement had already begun to impose upon the headstones to many a departed soul. Men of the sea were laid to rest here within the sound and salty reek of the element to which they had been so accustomed in life. Time would pass, little would change. There would always be the passage of the bereaved, a fleeting presence when tears were shed and elegies offered. Mourners would depart with mud on their boots and great sorrow and detachment in their hearts. As to the early crispness of the stonemasons' chiselled adornments, these would surely fade as salt and grey lichen exacted their toll upon lapidary inscription. And as years passed, tended headstones would cease to be tended. Visitors would come by, crouch and peer at faded memorials and wonder upon them, but the inevitable passage of time would have robbed those that lay in the consecrated ground of a caring presence.

As he continued with the formalities, a signal from Parson Veck prompted the widow and her brother to step forward.

"For as much as it hath pleased Almighty God…"

Charlotte Reynolds removed the glove she wore upon her right hand. Together the grieving siblings gathered up some crumbs of the freshly turned soil and cast these down upon the coffin as the parson's voice poured forth.

"…earth to earth, ashes to ashes, dust to dust…"

The little ceremony was viewed at a distance by the two gravediggers.

They watched with poker-faced indifference, accustomed as they were to observing these unhappy events. Patiently they crouched in the lee of the end wall bounding a quaint row of ivy-clad cottages which stood by the road on the Alverstoke side of the cemetery. They chatted, the two of them, nonchalantly drawing upon their pipes. Inwardly they were keen to set to work again, to return the damp, naked soil from whence it had come and to so conclude their day's toil. For all their apparent forbearance, they would hastily descend upon the graveside as soon as decency permitted.

Raising his eyes from the lid of the coffin, James Black observed the labourers with equal indifference. For a while he continued to listen attentively to the utterances of Parson Veck but, standing at the head of the open grave between his mother and his widowed sister, the comparatively generous height with which nature had bestowed him presented a clear line of vision beyond the melancholy foreground. His eye followed the course of the narrow creek which cut deep into the flat landscape, the upper reaches of an inlet that meandered its way out of the belly of Portsmouth's bustling harbour. It skirted the northern edge of the hospital cemetery as it pushed westwards towards the stumpy tower of Alverstoke's parish church which rose, straight ahead, a dark sentinel upon the land that loomed stern against the cheerless sky. James Black's thoughts began to drift as he scanned the creek's shimmering mudflats, freshly exposed by an ebbing tide. Beyond lay the bleak saltmarsh of Ewer Common, itself a fitting apron to the forbidding workhouse which stood behind. The sight of that place reminded him of the fragility and lottery of making one's way in life and how, at a stroke, one's circumstances might be thrown into a spiral of decline. His thoughts, in turn, came to dwell upon his brother-in-law's passing and how life might change for his Forton relatives. Not that he envisaged them falling upon particularly hard times, in a pecuniary sense, for he believed the deceased had been sufficiently prudent in recent years in the management of the family's affairs. Furthermore, James's mother, Margaret Black, was the recipient of a modest annuity and he believed that his sister had intentions to engage in teaching children at the village church school. That apart, James Black had already resolved that the now fatherless family at 5 St John's Place, being numbered among his nearest kith and kin, should benefit from some financial provision of his making. He was still a single man, devoid as yet of family responsibilities, but prone, when not at sea, to fall upon the family's hospitality, for which he would always pay his way. Yet with the demise of John Reynolds his soul had become infused with some greater sense of obligation, a feeling that it was incumbent upon him to do more; and accordingly he had decided that some regular allotment be deducted from his pay and directed to the family's account in the National Provincial Bank. Such thoughts aside, James Black's solicitous pondering – in his distraction at the graveside – was more particularly centred upon his young nephew and what the future would hold for a boy deprived of fatherly guidance and example. As his uncle he would strive to fill that void as best he could but his living took him away and shortly his ship was due to be hauled out of the Dockyard Basin. Soon enough she would put to sea.

James Black determined that he would speak to Veck. That was the answer. He would approach the parson that very day and seek an audience with him before he was required to report back onboard. The old clergyman was a constant in the boy's life and, with the parsonage just across the road from the family home, he would surely be happy to keep a close eye on William and counsel him when necessary.

The proceedings at the graveside had drawn to a close and, with that closure, the mourners composed themselves and together bandied a few hushed words. They took stock of the surroundings to which they had become insensible while immersed in the museful detachment that accompanied the formalities; and soon they began to trudge their way back to the cemetery gate, taking care to find safe foothold amid the dank and slippery grass. James Black provided a supportive arm for his mother as they returned to the lane, the afternoon light having markedly decreased since they had first entered the burial ground. Ahead they could see the hearse carriage pulled in beyond the entrance gate, its sheen now enhanced by a multitude of clinging water droplets, the consequence of a slanting drizzle borne in from the sea. Only the stallion made any obvious movement, shifting from time to time and gently pulling at the shafts as if eager to be on the move again. The driver, as dark in his regalia as both horse and carriage, sat motionless aloft, the only movement being offered by a black, crape scarf that decorated his tall hat and streamed in the wind like the warm breath of the animal.

"Mother, I assume the parson is to come to the house or has he other pressing commitments?" James posed the question in the knowledge that the clergyman was comfortably out of earshot. They halted short of the cemetery gate, Margaret Black anxious to catch her breath.

"That is his intention, son, as far as I'm aware. He loves his afternoon cup of tea does the vicar and he is always ready to admit that missing it brings on irritability. He's a convivial sort but without his blessed cup of tea his natural good humour takes flight and gone is the twinkle in his eye. Yes, you can be sure he'll stay awhile and pay his respects and take tea with us."

Margaret Black's Irish roots were still discernible in the pitch and modulation of her voice, despite having left her native city some thirty years past on the arm of her soldiering husband. A Belfast girl, she had exchanged Hibernia's shores for barrack life in warmer climes, never to return to her place of birth. And while the union had yielded four children who, with the Lord's good grace and guidance, had each attained adulthood, it had been a union and joy all too brief, snuffed out by the Malta fever in this same first month of the year. Now, on this bleaker January day, exactly twenty years later, Margaret Black grieved the passing of her son-in-law. It inevitably stirred sad memories that cut her the more as she recalled laying her own dear husband to rest under a Gozitan sky, flanked by her infant children and the scarlet tunics of the Colour Sergeant's comrades.

The mourners' eight-seater transport was pulled up in the lane behind the hearse, its animal temporarily unattended yet well behaved, with head lowered as if in deference to the occasion. As for the coachman, he had moved to the cemetery gate where, hat in hand, and now with damp and glistening pate, he waited to assist his charges back into the waiting carriage.

Having placed Grandma Black in the safe hands of the coachman to return to the shelter of the conveyance, James Black beckoned to his nephew who had accompanied his own mother back across the burial ground and was now in the throes of being made a fuss of by a number of the ladies.

"Come, Willie, you and I can share the box seat with the driver again for the journey home."

"Yes, uncle. I'd like that. Does the driver mind?"

"Not at all young fellow," interjected the coachman as he now assisted Charlotte Reynolds into the carriage. "It won't be as comfy a ride this time but at least the rain will be on our backs."

And thus, once all were seated inside, and the coachman had replaced the now sodden box-seat cushion with a dry pad drawn from beneath one of the inner side-seats, William and his uncle took their cramped place aloft. It was the manner by which they had made the outward journey to Haslar shortly after midday. As for the pallbearers, they also chose to take the weight off their feet, one riding on the box-seat of the hearse carriage, the others crouching within the now vacated chamber which, being curtained, enabled their unseemly and irreverent posture to be shielded from without.

The journey home was by way of Bury, taking the Annshill Lane bridge over the railway to thereby meet the Forton Road at Camdentown. Not a word was exchanged between the outside travellers on the mourners' carriage until they had passed beyond the Bury crossroads with half the full distance behind them. Until then the coachman's eye seemed reluctant to waver from the road ahead yet it was he who, in time, felt disposed to break the silence.

"I didn't like to ask before, sir, but I take it you were close relatives of the deceased?"

"Close, indeed my good fellow. He was my brother-in-law, but this young man was closer," came the reply. "John Reynolds was his father. It's a sad business when a boy loses his father. I was only seven when it happened to me, so I know only too well."

"Sailor was he, sir?" enquired the driver.

"Yes, but he'd spent a good many uninterrupted years in foreign parts. Been back here a few years now, but I can't help thinking that coasting in paddle steamers under a Mediterranean sun is poor preparation to face the rigours of these climes. Perhaps it was a weakness…bronchial, you know… and back in wet old England, what with this weather…well, I suppose it was his undoing. Consumption it was…wretched affliction."

James Black welcomed the break in silence, drawing him, as it did, from the introversion of solitary thoughts. Yet it also made him more aware of his own discomfort. For the replacement box-seat cushion was sparse, the better part of it already bolstering the rump of the coachman who, not unnaturally, saw himself as first claimant and was loath to offer it up to a passenger. With William sandwiched between his uncle and the driver, the former held his nephew close to, cupping his small frame within the weather lee provided by the upper right quadrant of his overcoat. As they headed northwards, an increasing rainfall drove at their backs and, with the formalities over and spurred on by a following wind, the drivers of both vehicles saw fit to put their horses to a steady trot across the levels that fanned out towards the Forton Road. James Black flinched as the increased velocity caused the box-seat to reverberate, more particularly when the wheels fell upon hollows newly gouged by winter frosts. And so, in turn, he straightened his back and stretched his legs, setting his heels into the splashing board to afford calf muscles, if not his sorely tested buttocks, a modicum of beneficial exercise and relief. Above, the clouds had lowered and scuds of a darker grey now swept in from the Channel, casting down a heavier precipitation in squalls which rattled against the side of the vehicle and began to drench those that rode aloft. Yet before they had crossed the railway the comparative shelter offered by his uncle's embrace, and the motion of the vehicle, brought a drowsiness upon William who soon lapsed into sleep.

Shortly the carriages reached the Forton Road where they turned eastwards towards the town of Gosport. What remained of the journey back to Forton was played out without recourse to further conversation on the driver's seat of the mourners' conveyance, other than brief mutterings about the state of the weather. Other sounds came to the fore as the travellers ran out of the wind and fell in behind the comparative shelter of buildings that huddled together along the high road. Background sounds of inconsequence were there. The rhythm of horses' hooves, a not infrequent cough and mumbled apology from the parson, the raucous call of gulls on the wing – gulls that swiftly dipped and rose with a controlled grace and elegance that displayed contempt in its ability to manipulate the gale. Not so the spiralling emissions of Forton's hearths that boisterously caught the draught, only to be dispersed rapidly amid the sheets of rain which bore down across the Millpond. Then, in the distance, the roll of gunfire from the Saluting Battery became muffled in the call of the wind and against the wild sound emanating from the tops of sombre elms in the grounds of the Reverend Veck's parsonage.

Once the carriages had come to a halt outside the family home it was the driver who was first to alight, leaving James Black to gently rouse his nephew from homeward slumber.

"Pass me down the boy, sir," came the call from below.

"Coming down, but go careful with him. He's still drowsy." James eagerly released his charge into the safe pair of arms proffered by the coachman, then clambered down himself, pleased to be free of the box. Intent on assisting the driver, who was already lending an arm to the ladies, he first established that William was sufficiently recovered from his sleepy state and in adequate command of his faculties to be left alone by the garden gate. And so the womenfolk were ushered out of their stilted discomfort and towards the garden path, the vicar being the last to his feet and not before he had grown a little sour tempered with his lot. An onset of coughing and an increasing tenderness about his sinuses had caused the Reverend Veck almost as much irritation on the home run as had the cramped conditions and the motion of the vehicle. Furthermore, being the only gentleman among the inside travellers, he had been inwardly conscious – perhaps the product of shyness or sensibility – that to shift his lower limbs, tightly confined as they were between flanking skirts, might have met with his motives being wrongly construed by his female companions. So the poor parson suffered in silence. Now, with freedom of movement, he began to reap the reward of self-imposed inertia. His numbed legs – already afflicted with the gout and a touch of arthritis – threatened for the moment to buckle beneath him as he was tormented by a surge of that loathsome tingling which comes with restored circulation. In consequence, the outstretched arm of the coachman was met with a firm rebuff as the parson, in his anguish, slumped back in his seat.

"All in good time…all in good time," he barked, tightly clutching his left leg. "I'll make my own way and I'll thank you not to hurry me."

The front garden at Forton, fringed with a neat tapestry of house leeks, was now studded with the muddy impressions of footprints, evidence of those who had bedecked the lawn earlier in the day with their floral tributes. Now, cloaked in their heavy mourning apparel and with skirts gathered before them, the ladies were first to tread its gravelled path that terminated in a short flight of steps to the front door. And in their pursuit of the beckoning warmth and shelter that lay beyond, albeit a haven steeped in sadness – and having turned their backs upon the highway with that in mind – the ladies appeared, for the moment, detached and insulated in that endeavour. The senses of William and his uncle, on the other hand, remained acutely attuned to external occurrence as they stood by the garden gate in wind and rain, waiting for the clergyman to extricate himself from the undertaker's vehicle. Without a word between nephew and elder, they both came to realise that it was now five minutes past the hour as, muffled by the din of the weather – yet still discernible to the attentive ear – the oncoming sound of the regular afternoon coach could be heard as it passed the Forton Barracks.

The smartly painted four-in-hand drag, that would have left Gosport on the hour, approached at a steady canter through the puddled street, its well-built coachman perched snugly and squarely on the box. He was cosseted against the elements beneath a heavy, old travelling cape, which, like coaching itself, had seen better days and, no doubt, much excitement on the road to Old Sarum. Added comfort was supplied by the placing of a good, thick rug and oilcloth about his lap. William immediately recognised the coachman as being one of the regulars on the Salisbury run. To his acquaintances the fellow was renowned for his jovial character and good humour. In all likelihood, it was a quality instilled or at least, heightened, by some customary and generous intake of ale before departing the *Old Northumberland*, for his complexion was as high and florid as a butcher's apron.

On this occasion the coachman's joviality was not in evidence as the vehicle, its lights already lit and showing brightly in the drab afternoon, prepared to draw level with St. John's Place. Suddenly, as his attention was drawn to the undertaker's carriages, drawn up at the side of the road, the coachman pulled up the horses, reducing them to a slow trot. Then he removed his low-crowned hat and adopted a decidedly stern yet sincere expression. The outside passengers, all gentlemen, followed his example. It was an impulsive, unexpected gesture but one that was much appreciated by James Black who, in grateful acknowledgement, raised his own hat high. Then a crack of the coachman's whip and the rattling of harnesses saw the animals gather speed again, off towards the hamlet of Brockhurst and the promise of a steady gallop along the open road to Fareham.

"That was a kind and thoughtful gesture, vicar," exclaimed James Black, the clergyman having left the carriage and found his feet again in time to have witnessed the event.

"Yes, yes indeed. Commendable behaviour. God Bless them on their travels."

Looking back towards the house, James was pleased to see that both his mother and, more importantly, his sister, had also seen the incident. They had formed the rearguard of the phalanx of ladies to have negotiated the front steps. As it transpired, progress had been interrupted by the domestic help, who, on opening the door, was almost sent tumbling over Grandma Black's cat as it closely hugged the girl's ankles. It was a near mishap that had delayed the ladies' passage beyond the threshold, sufficient for the Salisbury coach to catch the attention of mother and daughter.

"James, please assist Parson Veck in managing these steps...and William, hurry in now and warm yourself by the fire." Charlotte Reynolds' words told of her breathlessness as she assisted Grandma Black in gaining safe foothold on the top step. "Now, my dear, we must attend to our guests," she declared, guiding her mother towards the trusty outstretched arm of Sarah Ballantyne. The youngster proceeded to help the two women divest themselves of their outdoor garments, a luxury to which they were normally unaccustomed since they lacked the means to employ servants of any kind. As for Sarah, a pale, willing and conscientious girl, she had been placed at the disposal of Charlotte Reynolds for the afternoon by her neighbour, Hannah Barnes. It was a kindness that had moved the widow when Missus Barnes first broached her intention to make the girl available, viewing it as a deed that would ensure all was ready for the return of the funeral party; and so it had proved. Missus Barnes had already entered the house, keen to establish that her charge had left nothing to chance and was not about to cause her acute embarrassment through some deficiency of effort. She had found no reason for alarm and thus became more relaxed in her bearing as she engaged in conversation with another close neighbour, Missus Williams.

The terraced house known as 5 St. John's Place was a tall and inherently dark house. The gloomy weather had already prompted Sarah to light the lamps early and to prepare, in the parlour, what was now a well-stoked fire that merrily crackled and hissed its song of warmth. Momentarily, as Charlotte Reynolds and her mother sought to regain some composure after the trials of what had gone before, Sarah's retreating frame appeared strangely silhouetted to both of them as, standing by the open parlour door, she was viewed against the flickering reflections from the hearth. It was a jaunty glow that pervaded the inner depths of the front passage with a presence as bold as the wafted smell of compressed meats from the table. Then, as the girl prepared to enter the parlour, to establish whether she could be of assistance to any of the ladies now gathered there, her progress was arrested by the sound of the widow's voice.

"Sarah, tell me, was everything well with the caterers?"

"Yes, m'm," said the girl. "They came and set the table and I put out the mustard and the condiments as you asked. Been gone, they have, an hour since. There's a freshly boiled kettle in the hearth and I've just warmed the pot. Will you excuse me, ma'am, and I'll get some tea organised?"

"Thank you. Yes, please do."

Both the kindly Missus Barnes and Missus Williams were fellow churchgoers, as well as neighbours of the widow, and both had displayed Christian fellowship and kindness towards the bereaved family in this time of sorrow. The support they offered had now culminated in attendance at the graveside although, in truth, both would have preferred their husbands to have fulfilled that duty had they not been so committed to the affairs of the workplace. Yet Mister Williams, at least, was expected a little later to pay his respects at the house. A senior clerk to a firm of accountants, he had promised his wife that he would close his ledgers and depart his Portsmouth office a little earlier than habit and his employer normally permitted. Thereby, he would reckon to reach the Floating Bridge ahead of the early evening bustle. Mister Williams was a man blessed of a hearty appetite which was always sharpened by his customary brisk walk from the Steam Packet Pier. With such credentials he could be relied upon to despatch a generous portion of whatever the widow's funeral table had to offer.

In comparison to the Reynolds' circumstances and, for that matter, those of Mister and Missus Williams, Missus Barnes was a lady of comfortable means, derived from and sustained by a good salary drawn by her husband, a Gosport lawyer. Mister Barnes was a specialist in the art and science of maritime law in which a reasonable living was to be made hereabouts, but invariably, in the diligent lawyer's case, at the expense of a late home-coming. Today, however, there was to be no return, for his business commitments had meant a temporary removal from his littoral existence, if not from his littoral affairs. He had taken his skills to London, nervously placing his trust in the London and South Western Railway and one of its fiery steam engines that had the temerity to speed him through rural England at a frightful velocity of twenty miles per hour. An arranged meeting with a Falmouth ship-broker was to rule out any prospect of the solicitor having to endure the trauma of an immediate return journey to the Gosport town terminus. Instead he would have to remain in the city overnight. Yet, for all the reward of his occupation, Mister William Barnes' home at St. John's Place was identical to that of the bereaved, excepting that he owned the freehold. Added to which, the quality of furnishings and other chattels and the employment of Miss Ballantyne and a regular gardener were clear signals of the couple's comparative affluence.

Several minutes had passed since she had entered the house and uppermost in Charlotte's mind was the need to place a strong and sweetened cup of tea before the parson. So she left her mother to venture into the parlour ahead of her and proceeded to take stock of what was happening outside. She was pleased to find that William, at least, was in the process of slowly ambling up the path towards the house.

"Hurry up, son, and get out of this weather. Where's your uncle and Parson Veck?" Charlotte's words came laced with irritation.

"The parson sends his apologies. He'll be here in a moment but he says to tell you he needs a minute or two to walk off some discomfort. Uncle's still at the gate talking to the driver."

"I suspect he's expressing our gratitude for the way the men went about their work. But he shouldn't tarry long in these conditions. Come along, Willie, step inside now and dry yourself by the fire. Give me your coat."

Down at the front gate, James Black was in the throes of offering the coachman a reviving tipple to see him on his way. It was an offer eagerly accepted.

"What will it be then, driver? A tankard of ale or a glass of mulled wine to warm you…or maybe a brandy and water?"

"Brandy will do fine, sir." The reply was delivered without hesitation. "That's most kind of you. God Bless you, sir. Nothing with it, if you'd be so good."

"And will your fellow driver and the others join you?"

"Oh no, sir. Old Jack who drives the hearse never touches it. He's inclined towards the temperance way of things and I swear it's made him the sad and dejected sort he is…that and the job. Old Jack's always a'moping and you'll find him a man of few words. To be honest, a drop of alcohol now and again would ease his sullenness but he'll snap at the suggestion and tell you it invites the devil."

"I think you've got to respect his feelings," said James Black.

"Right enough, sir. But it's not as if he's a religious sort. Truthfully, I think old Jack's problem is the job. Carting all those corpses to their cold graves. Not meaning to be disrespectful, sir, but at least my passengers have a bit of life in them, even though it's a sad business."

"I'd say he looked well-suited to his occupation, without wanting to be unkind," said James, for it struck him that the man's sickly appearance was, itself, verging on the cadaverous.

"Yes, but he hasn't the constitution, sir. It's turning his mind, I fear."

"So what of the other men. Those who carried the coffin?"

"No, no sir," came the swift and forceful reply that was delivered in a strained whisper. "They can't be relied upon to be discreet, on top of which they've got work to do inside. New dead 'uns to prepare and box up, if you see what I mean, sir, and the guv'nor will be roaming around and he'll smell it on their breath and then they'll be out on their ears. No guzzling booze when we do a job."

"Then far be it from me, my good fellow, to encourage you to put your own livelihood in jeopardy," said James.

"Ah, but Jack and I are bound for the coach-house and stables once we've taken the others to deal with the dead 'uns. There's only the 'orses there to smell my breath. I'll be toiling awhile with the animals, then my work's done and I'm away for my supper," insisted the driver, who by now had sauntered the length of the garden path behind James Black. They were joined by the clergyman who seemed more composed. Certainly his expression was less severe. It suggested to those who, minutes before, had felt the cut of his tetchiness, that, for the time being, the short walk had furnished some relief from the torment of his circulatory problem. The fact was, however, that with advancing years, the old gentleman was finding both gout and arthritis to be increasingly troublesome. He would usually walk unaided but, since alighting from the carriage, had steadied himself with an old thumb-stick that he had left secreted in the vehicle when the party left for the hospital. It had not emerged to assist his passage across the slippery burial ground but, then, in the conduct of his clerical duties, Parson Veck would steel himself against affliction and suffer in silence.

Standing aside, James Black ushered the incumbent towards the steps and assisted him in his ascent to the front door that had been left ajar.

"Do go in, sir...do enter and warm yourself through," said the younger man, who, pushing the door open before the parson, caught the eye of the borrowed domestic as she was carrying a jug of fresh milk into the parlour. "Young lady, ask Missus Reynolds where you could find the brandy bottle. Then kindly bring it here." James Black's instruction was clearly audible to Parson Veck who misinterpreted its purpose.

"No, no, none of that Mister Black, thank you," he exclaimed, "I'm not opposed to a little drop now and again...in company, you understand, but I regret to say it doesn't agree with me. It aggravates my ailment you see...this infernal gout."

There was a slight hint of mirth in the vicar's words but this went unnoticed. James Black felt acutely embarrassed over what, in hindsight, had proved an untimely instruction to the parlour maid. And so he proceeded to tender his apologies.

"I beg your pardon, Reverend, but believe me, I was not meaning to ply you with liquor." He felt the flush of blood about his face and, with it, his colour heighten. "Er...what I really mean to say, sir, is that you're welcome to it, of course, but the brandy's intended for the driver, here. I thought you'd be preferring a hot cup of tea, sir."

"Quite so, quite so," said the parson, "but there's no way I would decry a little firewater if it is taken in moderation and good company. Church ale has paid for many a prayer book!"

Having entered the house, the Reverend Veck put aside his walking stick and placed his prayer book upon a small shelf below the hat stand. Climbing the front steps had caused him to bend his frame, placing some uncommon inertia upon his ageing sinews; and so, before relieving himself of his outdoor apparel, he straightened himself by grasping the lapels of his topcoat and gently easing his back. It served to correct his exaggerated stoop and he felt better for it. Meanwhile, William's time by the fireside amid the ladies' chatter had been brief. Thus he had reappeared in the hallway in time to overhear the instruction and ensuing conversation that had been a source of embarrassment to his uncle. The parson now turned to address the boy. "You'll find it in a cupboard in the scullery, William…the brandy bottle, that is…middle shelf. That's if my memory doesn't deceive me." The clergyman's words were delivered with a wink in his eye and William's expression suggested that he shared his uncle's amazement over what he had just heard. James Black, nonplussed by this utterance, felt it wise to remain silent for fear of inviting further cause to feel ashamed.

"Thank you, sir," said William.

The look of astonishment that gripped the features of Uncle James gave Parson Veck some cause for amusement.

"Let me first explain myself, William, and more especially for your uncle's benefit," he chortled. "It was during Advent and on one of my evening visits to your father's bedside, before he was admitted to the hospital. We dwelt upon the parables and took time to rehearse the articles of faith. And before we had gone too far your dear father had remarked upon how he would feel better for a little brandy and water. Well, as I remember, there was no one to call upon to satisfy your father's need. It was past the hour of your own bedtime…not that I would have expected you to have been of assistance, of course…and Missus Black, bless her, had taken to her bed early with a chill. As for your mother, William, she had taken the opportunity, with me present in the house, to call upon a neighbour a few doors away. And so, it was left to me, with your father's guidance, to find my way to the scullery in search of brandy and water. So there you are, William…the scullery cupboard, middle shelf! But let's face facts, my boy. You will want to know of such things in future. Now that your dear father's gone from this World and found solace in Abraham's bosom you will need to begin wearing the mantel of increased responsibility." There came a twinkle in the parson's eye as he continued, reducing his voice to a whisper. "But promise me this, William. Don't tell your mother I've told you where to find the brandy bottle!" Parson Veck chuckled: from his demeanour he appeared to have forgotten about troublesome ills.

It was a funeral tea fettered by the usual propriety and sense of awkwardness that prevails on such occasions. The clergyman, his irritability dispelled and good humour restored, mingled with the widow and her neighbours, lurching sometimes from superficial engagement in general prattle to that greater sense of sobriety which accompanies the expression of kind and hushed tributes to the departed. Missus Reynolds' kettle was kept busy and, in turn, the teapot constantly replenished, as Miss Ballantyne found herself frequently answering the parson's call for "a further cup of your sweet bevers m'dear." True to form, the sweet-toothed vicar would set aside his teacup to despatch some generous helpings of the caterer's sherry trifle, which never failed to please. Yet, in the wider realm of greasing the gills, the vicar was no match for Mister Williams. With the undertakers' men long since despatched, one with the questionable assistance of some liberal intake of brandy, the late January nightfall came quickly and with it the emergence of the senior accounts clerk, hot foot from the Steam Packet Pier. And as those who had earlier gathered to pay their respects began to drift away, or at least felt that they should soon contemplate a return to their own hearths, Mister Williams directed his ravenous proclivity upon the widow's victuals with true trencher-man resolve.

"I must be on my way, dear people," said Parson Veck. "God Bless you all."

The hall clock chimed the hour of seven as Charlotte Reynolds poured words of appreciation at the departing clergyman and her brother gathered up the old gentleman's hat and overcoat and readied himself to assist the incumbent; and so, once equipped to brave the elements, the parson grasped his stick and prayer book and began to take his leave. James Black had found little opportunity to approach the old man hitherto, since he had been constantly preoccupied taking tea with the ladies and engaging in their small talk and tittle-tattle. Only now had he re-emerged from the parlour, with intent to depart, leaving the room to a now flustered Missus Williams who was encountering little success in trying to coax her husband away from the table. Her thanks conveyed to the clergyman, Charlotte Reynolds turned on her heels and took herself off to find Sarah Ballantyne who, being unfamiliar with the place, awaited further instruction as she sought to clear away. It was the opportunity for James to speak alone with Parson Veck.

"Sir, sir…I beg you, before you go…," said the younger man, simultaneously leaning forward and grasping the other's coat sleeve at the cuff as he made to advance beyond the threshold.

"Yes, my good fellow, what is it?"

"Well, it's just…if you'd be so kind, vicar…it's just that I require a small favour of you, sir." James took a deep breath before putting his request directly. "Would it be too bold of me to ask for a few words in private? Not now, sir, but at a time to suit you."

Parson Veck looked inquisitively at James beneath a furrowed brow. He raised his hand to the flaccid lobe of his left ear, still clutching his prayer book as he did so and pulled gently upon the flesh. His reply came in ponderous fashion, suggesting the request had perplexed him yet also stimulated sufficient interest and willingness to accede to it without further enquiry. "Yes, yes, my dear fellow. Yes, of course. Come across to the parsonage. Not this evening, for I have a Missionary Society meeting in an hour and tomorrow it's the churchwardens. So we'll need to leave it until Saturday." He hesitated. "No, come to think of it, on Saturday I am lunching with friends in Titchfield followed by an afternoon engagement in Fareham. It'll be a long day for me. No, on reflection, it will have to wait until Sunday if you don't mind… after Evening Prayers. Come to the parsonage at seven-thirty if you would and we can talk of what concerns you."

"Thank you, Reverend Veck, that is most kind of you."

"Goodnight to you, Mister Black."

"Goodnight, sir."

★ ★ ★

Above the neat tuck-pointed house front, the sailor peered out of the dormer window that rose neat and square from the tiled roof. Behind him, on a bleached pine shelf set against the far wall, a single lighted candle stood sentry beside his bible, a ready reckoner and his beloved poetry books. The light flickered gently and cast a shifting and eerie glow around his silhouetted bulk. It was five minutes past seven o'clock in the evening, the last Sunday in January, and since taking an early supper with the family, James Black had spent time alone in his room. It had been time he had devoted to putting his effects in order, in readiness for some prolonged absence, and for getting his bag packed. On the morrow he would leave the house early and, in all likelihood, would not be back for many months, if not years. Perhaps his brother, Charley Black, would return home first and thus have prior need to lay his head upon the truckle bed that stood below the pine shelf. That was the thought upon which he pondered as he looked out into the darkness, watching for signs that Evening Prayers had run their course.

James had earlier attended the Eucharist service at St John the Evangelist and had seized the opportunity to establish that the incumbent had not forgotten of their intended meeting and that it remained convenient. The rest of the family had taken themselves off to prayers after supper and their return would signal that Parson Veck's congregation had dispersed and James could soon make his way to the parsonage. For the moment, however, he looked out upon a starry evening that was dry and clear and kissed with sufficient moonlight to amply define the buildings that stood across the Forton Road. Directly ahead, a large and imposing house, 'The Grange', cowered behind a screen of pollarded beech, several of its windows punctuating the darkness by the glow of lamplight from within. Then, to the westward, a more oblique view revealed the rather squat form of St. John's Church. It occurred to James that it was an edifice better viewed in daylight, its elegance being lost to the nocturnal observer; for it boasted a slender spire and high lancet windows, architectural detailing that ranked it among the more stylish of local parish churches.

A low brick wall surmounted by railings enclosed that part of the graveyard that lay to the north side of the church. Between this and the Forton Road, was a grassed and extensive swathe of glebe land, best appreciated during springtime when its drifts of daffodils tossed their heads with impudence in the March winds. James Black felt instant regret that this year he would miss their resilience and audacity. And with the sight of that swaying army of flower-heads in his mind's eye, his love of poetry drew thoughts of the conjured words of the Lakeland poet and of others who had dwelt upon the delights of the Lent lily. Traversing this greensward that played host to the daffodils, an earthen footpath linked Forton Road to the church, schoolhouse and parsonage. It was, as one might imagine, a well-trodden path by young and old alike. Now, into the moonlit ground that fell close to the road and out of the inky shadow thrown down by the church steeple, an ambling procession of returning churchgoers came into view. One or two carried lamps to light the way and some had mufflers about their throats to ward off the cold. All appeared cheerful enough from the general hubbub of their chatter, their words borne on breath that readily vaporized in the frosty air.

James withdrew from the window and took his watch from his waistcoat pocket. It was twenty minutes past the hour. He donned his outdoor shoes, then, with the aid of the mirror that hung by his bed, made cursory adjustments to his neck-tie. He snuffed out his candle, lingered a moment to inhale and enjoy the smoky whiff of newly extinguished wax, then closed the door behind him. By the time he arrived downstairs it was to find the family returned and divesting themselves of their outdoor garments.

"Welcome back. How did you find church?"

"Chilly. Strange to say I felt better outdoors," said Grandma Black, rubbing her hands together briskly to generate a little warmth.

"I'll go and make up the fire. I gave it a stoking earlier but it'll need more coal," said James, rather guiltily, being now only too aware that he had shown scant regard in the family's absence for building up the fire.

"Have you packed your bag, James?" enquired his sister.

"Yes, my dear. All done."

"Would you like a drink? I'm going to make a hot drink for the three of us. How about you?"

"No thank you, Charlotte," came the reply, as James clambered to his feet from a squatting position in front of the fender. "Those coals should burn through in a moment. No, I don't need a drink. I'm off out for a while."

"Off where, son? It's biting cold out there and the grass is already frosted. It's your last evening at home and you could do with a good night's rest." There was genuine concern in Margaret Black's voice for her son's welfare and not a small hint of disappointment that he had chosen to take himself off somewhere on the eve of going to sea.

"I won't be long, mother. I haven't slept well of late so thought I'd take a walk. The fresh air will do me good and in all likelihood I'll round it off with a drop of porter at the *Battle of Trafalgar*. That'll make me sleep."

"I'll be off to my bed by nine o'clock, son," said the old lady, fishing for some commitment to an earlier return.

"If I'm not back by then I'll make sure to wake you in the morning, mother. I'll speak to you before I go."

"Will I see you uncle?" piped up William.

"Yes, lad. I'll see you in the morning. I need to be on board by eight."

And with that James Black gathered up his greatcoat and scarf and stepped out into the rimy air.

Any sense of guilt that James felt about lying to his mother he soon put aside. As he picked his way across the glebe land, he quickly persuaded himself that it was not in the family's interest to be privy to the subject of his imminent meeting with the clergyman. That apart, the bestowal of such knowledge upon them would undoubtedly cause him acute embarrassment. So he approached the parsonage with an easy mind. It loomed out of the night, itself steeped in darkness save for the glow of lamplight that marked out Veck's study. Through a front window the caller could see the old man seated at his desk, his wire-rimmed spectacles perched low upon the gradient of his aquiline nose. He noticed how the flicker of firelight played upon the lenses and created an unusual and eerie effect and how his shock of white hair seemed the whiter for being highlighted in the unnatural light that pervaded the room.

"Come in Mister Black, come in and sit yourself down," said the parson, cheerily, as the housekeeper ushered his visitor into the study. "I've just seen the family at prayers and I get the impression they're bearing up well enough after a very sad turn of events."

"On the surface, yes, but to come straight to the point, sir, I'm deeply worried about the boy. That's why I asked to see you."

"Fine lad…fine lad. I'm sure your nephew has it in him to become a young man of whom his father would have been proud," reflected the clergyman. "Mister Wicketts, the schoolmaster, tells me he's been subdued and at times tearful. Yet to be honest that is to be expected of any child deprived of a parent, let alone one as sensitive as William. He's not a robust boy, of course, yet Wicketts tells me that events have not affected his studies. No, the boy has done well. And, if I might say so, Mister Black, he is greatly advantaged in having you as his uncle. I'm confident you'll help to shape him in the manner of a father and ensure that he is a credit to his mother."

This last remark drew a nervous smile from the younger man. "Sir, I am grateful for the faith you have in my nephew. Children are so resilient. I'm also flattered, Reverend, for the belief you express in my ability to guide the boy and I thank you for the compliment. But therein lies the problem. You see, I have been recalled to my ship, the *Rodney*. She's been in the Dockyard Basin for repairs but now she's out, lashed alongside the *Blake* hulk and being prepared for sea. The Dockyard artificers have done their work and I'm due back on board in the morning."

"Time is a great healer, my good fellow," observed the clergyman. "I detect that William is very close to both his mother and his grandmother and I'm sure their unyielding affection for the lad will see him through his sadness soon enough. While your absence is to be regretted, the two ladies will have his best interests at heart and their love for the boy will ensure that he turns out well."

"Don't misunderstand me, sir, but it's not love that's needed…well, not love alone, you understand." James Black hesitated. He felt awkward that he may have overstepped the mark, that he may have injudiciously appeared to be offering opinion on that affection of the mind held dear in the realm of Christian edification – and to none less than a respected member of the clergy. Yet Parson Veck remained unmoved and attentive as he awaited his visitor's further commentary. "What I mean to say," continued the younger man, rather bashfully, "is that it is a father's hand…or, sadly now, in William's case, a surrogate father's hand…that is also required. And that falls to me, as I see it. I don't want the boy to fall into bad ways and, with his father gone, I feel responsible."

"To be frank, Mister Black, I sincerely believe your concern is without foundation. Admittedly you know your nephew better than I, yet I have no doubt Missus Reynolds will do a fine job with the boy. My impression is that William is not a lad to require too much in the way of fatherly discipline and I have no doubt your dear sister will have it in her to chastise him when the occasion demands."

"Well, in truth, Reverend, she's already at her wit's end. William can be quite wilful at times. A few days after the death of his father, Charlotte sent him on an errand, telling him to return promptly. Yet he defied her. He failed to return until after nightfall. Well, being acquainted with the gentleman who lives opposite, at 'The Grange', I prevailed upon him to lend me his chaise cart. I then took to the local highways and byways in search of the boy. When I returned, an hour or so later, it was to find him newly arrived home in the company of a young bugler from Forton Barracks."

"So where had he been?" enquired the vicar.

"Seems he had wandered off to a remote spot beyond the Mill Pond. Out to some dismal burial ground by all accounts. No thought for his mother and grandmother."

"That would have been the convicts' cemetery. A desolate place, indeed. It's where they bury the deceased off the prison hulks," said the parson.

"It appears a heavy mist drifted in from Forton Lake and William got lost."

"In all probability he needed time alone, Mister Black, for he had just lost his father."

"Yes, sir, but for all that there was no thought for his loved ones. Added to which, anything could have happened to him. There's no knowing what dangers lurk there. A wrong step and he could have been in the water or sucked into the mud. Needless to say I was furious, not for the trouble it had put me to, you understand, but for the anguish he caused his mother and grandmother. But what could I do? William deserved to be punished for his behaviour but I had to acknowledge he was newly bereaved. He received a scolding that evening but I had to temper my words. I simply waited until my fury had subsided. But I see trouble ahead. I detect a determined and wilful streak in the boy," said the visitor.

"So what do you think drew William to that isolated spot if it were not a desire to be alone with his thoughts?"

William's uncle had little doubt as to the reason. His reply was delivered without hesitation. "The buglers and drummer boys. The new recruits from Forton Barracks. To my nephew's credit he has admitted it was not the first time he had ventured beyond the Mill Pond. Earlier visits had been fleeting and in the company of friends but now, of course, he has been forbidden to go anywhere near the place."

"You say it was the buglers and..."

"Yes, sir, let me explain," James continued. "I'm told that some of the local people living close to the barracks, especially those in Mill Lane whose homes face the parade ground, had found cause for complaint. After Christmas they had asked to be spared the offerings of the young musicians who assembled on the parade ground to practise on their newly inherited instruments."

"Quite so," said the clergyman. "I was made aware of this by the Royal Marines Commandant after last Sunday's Eucharist service. It seems he felt obliged to direct his novice bandsmen to hone their musical skills out of public earshot."

"That's correct. It explains why they go onto the marshes," added James.

"I take it that the young bugler who brought William home was not blameworthy with regards to his disappearance?" enquired the incumbent.

"Not at all, not at all. The youth is to be commended for bringing him home. He stumbled across him as he picked his way back to barracks through the fog, William having become disorientated and lost. From what I gather, my nephew has befriended one or two of these young musicians and has been drawn to the marshes to see and hear them practice. It's the uniform he's smitten by. The red tunic. And although the Marines are seafaring men they wear the red tunic like the regular army. William has long had it in his mind to become a soldier."

"I suppose that's not unusual in a lad of William's age," suggested the elder man. "Now, would you care to share a pot of tea with me or perhaps you'd like something stronger?"

"Tea would be fine, sir, thank you."

The clergyman lent forward in his chair and pulled a bell-cord beside the hearth. He then rose to his feet and took to stoking the fire; and, with this, his thrust of the poker broke the subdued and crusted coals, causing them to spark and spit and then to flame merrily once again. As he watched the old gentleman, James Black's thoughts were of how highly his sister spoke of Parson Veck and of how he was revered by his parishioners. A kind, old-time village incumbent, Veck was a well read and educated man, a man with an alert mind whose study was crammed floor to ceiling with learned books of a classical and devout nature. Born in some distant year belonging to the previous century, to middle-class Hampshire folk, his ordainment had followed a university education and he had long since served his curacy in nearby Alverstoke. In his political leanings the parson was an old Tory who could be drawn to rail against cant and ritual and Catholic dogma, who took his clerical duties seriously and professed staunch and unrelenting commitment to his Protestant Christianity. On occasion he might bemoan the loss of protectionism and rightly blame it for the dwindling value of the clergyman's stipend, but when it came to money, or lack of it, it was the lot of the poor among his flock that was uppermost in the parson's mind. As the vicar of Forton for the past twelve years he had invigorated the life of the village and, in his quest to nurture parochial well-being, had always posted the promotion of education among his priorities.

As Parson Veck rose to his feet, his face ruddied by the heat of the fire and thrown into sharp contrast with the whiteness of his billowy head of hair, the housekeeper presented herself at the door of his study. She was despatched to bring forth a pot of tea and some biscuits as the clergyman regained his composure and settled back into his chair.

"Now then, Mister Black, where were we?" resumed the parson.

"I was just saying that William aspires to join the Colours when he grows up. His mother, quite naturally, wishes to see greater attainment on his part. She wants him to pursue a more sedentary occupation and so do I, sir, if it's within his grasp and ability." James paused in a moment's reflection, then continued. "If not, then his father would have much preferred him to go to sea and, to be honest, so would I."

"There is, of course, no shortage of opportunity hereabouts to take the Queen's shilling or pursue a seafaring life. Boys follow fathers and grandfathers into one or other of the services, probably without a great deal of deliberation. And to be fair, along with the Dockyard, it's a ready and plentiful source of employment for youngsters raised in the streets of Portsmouth and Gosport," observed the vicar.

"My experience is that it is a tough life on the lower deck," said James. "Yet, if you're going to serve Her Majesty in distant parts, better to feel the salt air and sea breezes about your face than to be cooped up in some disease-ridden barracks."

"Do I take it that you're from a seafaring family, Mister Black?"

"No sir, far from it. I was born in barracks in Gibraltar. My father was with the Colours."

"Which regiment?"

"Scots Brigade. 94th Foot. My father has been dead these past twenty years. He died on the island of Gozo from enteric fever. It came in the goats' milk."

"A remote place, I'm sure. Was your father garrisoned there?"

"We were in barracks in Valletta at the time…St. Elmo. My father was on detachment on the neighbouring island when he succumbed to the Malta fever. We stayed on in Valletta. That was where my sister met her husband and where William was born."

"I was aware that Mister and Missus Reynolds had returned home from Malta. I believe that…ah, here comes our tea Mister Black." The housekeeper's return with the tray of tea and biscuits served to interrupt the parson's commentary, leaving his visitor pause to continue.

"We used to journey to Gozo once a year, in spring, to see the grave. Then my two brothers and I left Malta to make our own way in the world, but my mother and sister continued to make the annual pilgrimage. On the last occasion they took William. He was little more than an infant but the fort and the soldiers made a lasting impression. Since then he has always vowed to become a soldier."

"Well, you may rest assured I will make it my business to keep an eye on the lad," promised the parson. "As I said before, the schoolmaster is happy enough that William is making steady progress with his studies and I know for sure that he is one of the better pupils as regards the neatness of his copybook. For my own part, I see him in the schoolroom first thing on a Friday morning when I take the children for prayers. As far as I recall, he has never failed to pay attention or, indeed, faltered when it comes to reciting a collect that all had been required to memorise. Also, as chairman of the school management committee, I make it my business to regularly inspect the punishment book and I can assure you that William doesn't appear as one of the perpetual offenders who have regular encounters with Wicketts' cane. So I conclude that the boy is well behaved."

"That's encouraging, Reverend Veck, and I thank you. I believe William also regularly attends Sunday school and long may that continue," said James Black.

"Yes and I am pleased to say it is a most well-attended Sunday school, in no short measure due to the efforts of the superintendent and the fine group of voluntary teachers, including, of course, Missus Reynolds. In fact William is currently one of my bun monitors, a bit like the ink monitors in day school. I've always insisted that the children attending the schoolroom on a Sunday be provided with a bun and a glass of water or a little wine. Their bodies need sustenance if they are to concentrate and benefit from instruction in the catechism and I regret that many arrive ill-prepared and with empty stomachs, especially those from the poorer homes. So until Ash Wednesday, when Lent will necessitate a temporary halt to the practice, William will continue to help with the distribution of the buns. Which prompts me to invite you to take another biscuit or two with your tea," chuckled the old man. "You'll need some sustenance of your own to face the night chill again."

"Thank you, sir. I don't mind if I do," said James, as he helped himself to more.

"Now," began the incumbent, in words that seemed to suggest he was keen to bring the meeting to an early conclusion, "let's just see how the boy fares. He may surprise us all and soar to great heights. As to his being smitten with the army, time is on his side and the fascination may pass. Only one thing I would say. I get the impression, Mister Black, that you look to me to dissuade William and to point him in the direction of the Royal Navy. That I cannot do, being in no sense qualified to draw comparison and make a judgement. Nor should I do so. I am a clergyman, sir, and have no wish to associate myself with extolling the merits of one fighting force above another." The parson appeared to hesitate to draw breath, then continued, reflectively, and on a lighter note. "And, into the bargain, I am chaplain to the Royal Marines here in Forton, so perhaps I can claim the excuse of having a foot in both camps!"

"My apologies. It is remiss of me, Reverend Veck, to have sought to solicit your assistance in that regard."

"No matter. Let's trust that the lad's recent misdemeanour of venturing alone into dangerous places will see no repetition. Oh, and tell him, if there's ever a problem he can't speak to his mother about, then to come to me." Parson Veck pulled the bell cord to summon the housekeeper as the sailor rose to his feet.

"Thank you, sir, that's much appreciated, except I haven't told my sister about our meeting. I don't want her to think I have doubts about her ability to bring up the boy. It's not that which troubles me…she's a good mother… it was just the matter of keeping the boy in check. Paternal guidance, no more. Yet, from what you tell me, perhaps I have read too much into Willie's recent behaviour and I have failed to fully realise how deeply his father's death has affected him. Otherwise, I get the impression from you that he is a well adjusted boy and perhaps this is just a passing phase."

"Quite so, and I can understand why you do not wish Missus Reynolds to be privy to the substance of our conversation. Just mention to the boy that he can always speak to me, if needs be. Just in passing. He'll read little into such a remark, I'm sure, and it'll go no further," assured the parson.

And with that, James Black's audience with the vicar of Forton was drawn to a close amid the sailor's expressions of gratitude, a few bandied pleasantries and the parson's proclamation that his visitor's imminent return to sea should be a safe one and that it went with the Lord's Blessing.

★ ★ ★

James was out of his bed the next morning within a whisker of the emergence of dawn's eerie light. He took time to make ready, being most deliberate when it came to polishing his shoes and applying the brush to his uniform. As Captain's steward aboard the *Rodney* he took extreme pride in his appearance, pride to the point of fastidiousness; and today, while he could expect to be swept up in the turmoil of a ninety-gun line-of-battleship being provisioned for sea, he could also expect to be at the beck and call of a captain requiring the attentions of his steward. James Black had set himself exacting standards, maintaining that an impeccable appearance should be second nature to a man required to wait upon a ship's captain and his guests; and given those high personal standards he would be mortified and unable to brook the humiliation of ever being reprimanded over the state of his uniform.

The family had already retired to their beds when James arrived back home, around a quarter past nine, the previous evening. Now, armed with bag and ditty box, he picked his way gingerly down the stairs, trusting that a stealthy descent would avoid any premature disturbance of the still slumbering household. He breakfasted on bread and salted porridge, often maintaining, in the company of his nephew – and much to the boy's amusement – that a plate of hot oatmeal would stick one's ribs together and was just the thing for a winter's morning. Yet, on this particular morning, and knowing the viscous nature of porridge, the sailor dispatched it warily for fear of soiling his uniform. And so he took to eating his breakfast from a standing position, tilting his head forward to meet his spoon at a point where spillage and gravity would combine to avoid catastrophe. Such was the sight that confronted William as he arrived, bleary-eyed, within the dining room.

"Good morning, Willie. Are the others up and about?"

William took time to answer his uncle. Being still half-asleep, he stretched and yawned, then drowsily slumped into a chair. "I think I heard mother moving around," he said, rubbing the sleep from his eyes. He waited for his uncle to finish breakfast before engaging him in any further conversation. In time his shrill voice broke the silence. "Uncle, you never did tell me why you and father became stewards while Uncle Charley joined the band."

"It was pure coincidence that your father and I had that in common and I must confess we never discussed the whys and wherefores. Suffice to say, for my own part, I never relished the toil and hurly-burly of life on deck or aloft; and so I suppose I gravitated to the more seemly pursuit of waiting upon the officers. Of course, Willie, it's work that requires a knowledge of good manners and a sense of bearing and decorum that is not…how shall I put it… that is not naturally present or easily instilled in the minds of the majority of a ship's crew." There was no hint of awkwardness in the sailor's words, for he firmly held the belief, and with some justification, that he was well read, well mannered and a cut above most of his shipmates who featured many loafers, drunkards and former gaol-birds among their number. They were words of a proud man, delivered with a glint of arrogance.

"And what of Uncle Charley?" enquired his nephew, sensing that Uncle James was set to dwell further upon his own circumstances.

"Yes, well as for me and my brothers, I suppose I was the exception. Charley and brother John both had an aptitude for music whereas poetry was always the music to my ears. Well, your grandmother, to her credit, encouraged it. We had got to know this retired old musician, a former trumpet-major. A jovial Scotsman he was, with bushy ginger whiskers...not a grey hair in his head, but he would have been all of seventy years. Well, the old fellow could still play a sweet tune and often gave his time teaching the boy bandsmen at Fort St Elmo...that was where your grandfather was garrisoned and where the family lived when we first arrived in Valletta. I suppose we struck up a friendship with the old campaigner as a frequent visitor to the barracks. I remember him telling us tales of his time in India with the late Duke of Wellington, before the Duke was ever a duke or took a liking to fighting the French. Anyway, he was only too glad to school my brothers in fife and bugle and thereby earn a few more pennies. His instruction increased the boys' confidence and he taught them well. It was inevitable that both became bandsmen. Yet, if I'm honest, John was the better musician. Took to it naturally."

"I do hope I get to meet Uncle John some day," William declared.

"Well, I'd love to see my brother again. We all pray for his early homecoming, especially your Grandma. Do you know, it's nearly sixteen years since he took himself to regimental headquarters and spun a yarn to the recruiting sergeant that he was fourteen years of age. Twelve he was, in truth, yet a big lad. Not much older than you are today, Willie. Well, he came home, grinning ear to ear, proud as anything that he had taken the King's shilling and been sworn in for unlimited service. All he could talk about was the two guineas bounty he was due and the prospect of being in the band."

"So what happened next, Uncle?"

"Needless to say we were all in shock, especially your grandmother." James paused for thought, then continued, choosing his words carefully and with manipulative intent. "Well, it was fine at first. He was quartered in the town, so we saw him frequently enough. He gave Mother his bounty money and although she found it difficult, credit to him, he insisted that she took it for the family's benefit. They were lean times, of course, and being the eldest son, I suppose he was proud to contribute handsomely to our sparse household budget. Anyway, after about eight months and a final evening of tears and farewells, the regiment was embarked aboard a ship called the *Jupiter*. I can see her now, moored at a buoy off the Custom House. Once the regiment had been on board a few days the ship set sail. I remember we gathered with a small crowd in the Upper Barracca Gardens and waved the *Jupiter* out of Grand Harbour. Sad to say it was the last any of us saw of my eldest brother, but that's the army for you. Since then he has seen some wretched places but he is a robust enough fellow and, so far, that, and God's mercy, has seen him through."

"Has he been fighting, then, Uncle James?"

"No, no, Willie. He spent years in the West Indies which is rife with disease. Yellow fever and such like. The last few years he's been in India. After they docked in Calcutta they were confined to cholera camp and half the regiment perished. Since then they've moved on up the Ganges. A letter was waiting for me on my last return home and, I must admit, it was a relief to hear from him. His regiment's at Cawnpore, a hot and uncomfortable place by all accounts. Cholera is still a problem. Anyway, as I say, that's soldiering for you. A precarious trade my boy."

William was unsure of the meaning of the word precarious but sensed its import. And so, not wishing to foster any further sermon upon the perils of a military life, he chose to remain silent. What his uncle had to say about his own brother's experience was certainly disconcerting. Yet, in his own mind, William quickly persuaded himself that Uncle John had simply encountered accidental bad fortune in his regimental postings.

It was at this point that Uncle James decided that he could hear his mother and sister in conversation on the first floor landing, as a precursor to their descent of the stairs. He therefore addressed his nephew quickly in regard to matters of behaviour, charging him trustingly to be helpful to his mother and grandmother and under no circumstances to absent himself without their knowledge of his whereabouts. The Mill Pond and the remote country beyond was to remain off-limits and, were James to learn of any departure from that understanding, then his nephew would have him to reckon with in due course. Otherwise, and dependent upon his mother's prior agreement, beating the bounds on Holy Thursday might involve an exception to that rule, since William would be one among other children and be closely supervised by the parish officers. And, in the earnest hope that his words might instil sufficient apprehension in his nephew's mind as to be acted upon if so required – yet be so cursorily expressed to avoid any suspicion of collaboration – the sailor voiced the gist of the parson's offer to counsel the boy as tactfully as he could.

"Finally, Willie, you must on all accounts go about your studies with eagerness and diligence. Being scholarly is the key to being a gentleman and let's trust that we can make a gentleman of you. With my return I hope to see the beginnings of it."

"I'll do my best, Uncle," said William, anxiously, as if burdened by the elder's expectation.

"I'm sure you will my boy. But don't fret, work hard and apply yourself, but try to enjoy the attainment of knowledge. With that, and a following wind, you've a fair chance of becoming a gentleman. It's only then can you expect to extract good pickings from this world, like pearls from an oyster, so to speak. Failing that, Willie, I suppose we'll have to think about getting you a good start in the Navy."

★ ★ ★

It was Candlemas Eve and reliable information had reached the house at St. John's Place during the morning which conveyed the news that the *Rodney* was to depart her moorings on the afternoon tide at about four o'clock. The consequence of this was to find Charlotte Reynolds presenting herself at the nearby schoolroom a few minutes after the school clock struck noon and just as the children were heading homewards after morning lessons and drill. Skittish was the mood of the majority as they tumbled out into the chill air, buoyed by the prospect of a two hour release from instruction. William Reynolds was one of the last to leave, only to be halted upon the school steps by his approaching mother and told to wait awhile as she spoke to Mister Wicketts.

The schoolmaster, a balding, bespectacled man in his forties, sat at his elevated desk at the far end of the room beneath a portrait of the Queen. His expression, as he readied himself to make an entry in the school log book, hinted at the calming effect that being relieved of his young charges had immediately wrought on his state of mind. Yet he was not alone. At the opposite end of the schoolroom several children congregated about the stove and quietly vied for positions of greatest warmth. This handful of pupils was among the poorest in Forton, some grimy in appearance and all shabbily clothed and shod. For one reason or another the prospect of a midday meal was so remote or non-existent for these children, were they to take themselves home, that they were discouraged to venture beyond the comparative warmth of the schoolroom. And so they stayed in the knowledge that their salvation would arrive at one-thirty precisely in the form of the parson's housekeeper. The woman would appear carrying a large pot of hot soup or gruel and a loaf lodged under her arm. She would proceed to dispense to Mister Wicketts whatever food he required, then attend to the youngsters' needs. For the moment, however, they remained quiet and subdued, aware that they needed to bear their appetites for a further five and twenty minutes and that any misbehaviour in the presence of their master could yet see them go hungry.

Charlotte Reynolds approached the schoolmaster's desk. "Mister Wicketts, if I might plead your forbearance for intruding upon your time but I wish to keep William away from lessons this afternoon," she said. "As you know it's been a difficult time for us this past fortnight and today my dear brother, who's helped see us through it all, is off to foreign parts. His ship is due out of harbour on the afternoon tide and we'd like to see her leave, especially as they say she's tied up close to the Gosport shore."

"Then I heartily agree that your son should accompany you," exclaimed the schoolmaster. "He's done well in his work, despite the bereavement and some light relief and fresh air down on the foreshore will be good for the boy. Just remember to wrap up well. This quiet sunshine is deceptive. There's a real chill in the air and it'll be keener down on the harbour."

And so Willie sauntered home for lunch across the glebe land, in the knowledge that he was not expected to return to lessons when the clock struck two. Yet he felt awkward about being seen by his peers in company with his mother. It was the fear of others forming the impression that she had considered it necessary to meet him and escort him home. He was, furthermore, not heartily overjoyed at the prospect of braving the cold that Tuesday afternoon. He had bade farewell to his uncle already and there was little prospect of him being sighted above the upper deck hatchways, for Uncle James was no prime seaman raised to hand, reef and steer. No, he would surely be attending to his duties in the Captain's after-cabin quarters, oblivious in all likelihood to activities above and beyond deck. The sailor's sister and mother, however, felt that it would bestow luck upon the *Rodney* were they to be present at her leaving. William saw it differently, viewing it – albeit not in such words and with quite such adult reasoning – as a ploy to instil in him a sensibility to all things naval, that in time might forge a familiarity and affection for the service. Such suspicion on the youngster's part was, nonetheless, wide of the mark, for his mother held no affinity for naval or military life. She had seen enough of both and wanted better for her son. Quite naturally she hoped he might prosper at his learning and in the end equip himself for what her brother termed 'a gentleman'; and in Charlotte Reynolds' assessment, when it came to the services, even the officers fell short of what she regarded as 'gentlemen.'

No, Charlotte and Grandma Black had genuinely thought the spectacle alone of seeing a mighty line-of-battleship leave harbour would prove a pleasing experience for William. The fact that his uncle was on board would no doubt heighten the event but they were realistic enough to appreciate they would be unlikely to catch sight of him; and so it was, with these thoughts that, after lunch, and with time in hand, they closed the front door behind them and slowly made their way into Gosport on foot, determined that they would treat themselves on the short return by way of Hyslop's omnibus.

The two women and the child entered the old town by way of the Forton Road arches, then found their way into Clarence Square, an irregular space that on its east side opened directly onto the harbour whose waters now lapped its walled defence. Here was a space defined by its cluttered charm, where chandlers' goods spilt onto the cobbles and where timber carts, lobster pots and piles of cordage appeared to have found random points of rest and threatened to impede free passage. The knowledge that *Rodney* was set to depart had already brought forth a moderate-sized crowd who gathered by the harbour wall. William noticed that in the course of their assembly these folk were often drawn to purchase the wares of a pastryman who had shown the sense to set up his stall and was reaping good reward from those enticed and hungered in the chill sea air. A pair of scruffy street urchins, bare-foot and doubtless bent on mischief, disappeared among those huddled by the quayside, like rabbits down a burrow. In contrast, two Royal Marine Artillerymen hurried by, resplendent in their blue coatees, and intent on making haste from the Floating Bridge after a day's battery practice on Southsea Common.

Charlotte Reynolds led the way and succeeded in finding a vantage point on the south side of Clarence Square, where it began to narrow, soon to become a mere alleyway along the harbour wall as buildings sought to hug the waterside. Here, with the steadying hand of his mother, William clambered upon an upturned rowing boat that lay upon the cobbled surface. It offered the boy a good view of the lower harbour and, in particular, clear sight of the *Rodney* that lay off the Gosport shore lashed alongside the old hulk they called the *Blake*. The foreground, unsightly mud at low water but now clothed by the high tide, bobbed with open rowing boats, all roped to slimy mooring posts that rose skeletal and like Excalibur from beneath. These boats appeared to jostle for position, amid a welter of floating dunnage and old baulks of well-seasoned timber while to the southward, tied up in the lee of the North Wharf, a lateen-rigged barge stood proud and erect as if contemptuous of this confusion. Out in the water William readily recognised the old *Victory*. Yet he was unable to identify an impressive ship beyond until he overheard a gentleman speak of it in glowing terms as the one hundred and twenty gun *Neptune*.

By a quarter to four o'clock the crowd that had converged upon Clarence Square had probably reached its maximum. Out in the harbour the signs of an imminent departure by the *Rodney* seemed to be in evidence. Open boats that minutes before had hovered about the ship had now fulfilled their purpose and drawn back, or, being ship's boats, had been hoisted aboard: numbered among them was a cutter that had conveyed two of *Rodney's* midshipmen from the Common Hard, a Dockyard long-boat that had taken off several carpenters and shipwrights and a barge from the Royal Clarence Victualling Yard that had managed to complete some late provisioning with fresh beef and vegetables. Now the sound of men's voices and a series of calls on the boatswain's pipe could be heard across the water, as men went to their stations and the steamship *Echo* manoeuvred out beyond the ship's bows, in readiness to make whatever preparations were necessary to take *Rodney* in tow. All of a sudden the strains of the ship's band could be heard playing *Heart of Oak*. In turn came a heightening of anticipation among the spectators in Clarence Square who, hitherto, had been a quiet lot as they huddled together patiently in the keen air. The northerly breeze had stiffened somewhat and now bore the waft of newly baked hard-tack thrown out by the steamy emissions of the Victualling Yard's biscuit factory. The crowd began to jostle as some sought to command a better view and gentle murmurings were raised to a more audible level. Then, above the chatter of expectation, the strident voice of a new arrival broke the tolerant and warm-hearted nature of the occasion.

Sorely the worse for cheap porter, a coarse and blowsy woman had emerged to rail a volley of slurred and sometimes incoherent words of abuse in the general direction of the *Rodney*. Her raw anguish, it appeared, was fired by the actions of an unscrupulous companion who had chosen to run off to sea and, at this moment, was going about his new-found duties as a landsman aboard the departing ship of the line. Yet, as *Rodney* cast off from her mooring and, with perceptible movement, the steamship took her in tow, the woman's scathing words were mercifully drowned out by a now cheering crowd.

As the menfolk among the spectators raised their hats in farewell and ladies used their handkerchiefs to dab teary eyes or wave their goodbyes, it occurred to William that the *Rodney* was in fine fettle and made for a striking sight, not least the black and white chequer pattern about her gunports that gleamed with a fresh coat of paint. As pilot and master attendant set about taking her out of harbour, as men clambered upon her ratlines and topmen, already aloft, began to loosen sails, it struck William that the dear old *Rodney* was doing him a favour. It was not that he disliked his Uncle James. He respected him. But he was not the fun loving and approachable Uncle Charley and, of late, William had started to resent the way he had begun to usurp the role of his dear departed father, especially in matters of discipline and how he conducted his life. Moreover, in William's assessment, his uncle had taken this stance without, he suspected, having broached the matter with his mother, knowing she would be loath to take issue with a brother in whose presence she was a touch intimidated.

No, let Uncle James be lost for a while to the beck and call of his Captain, thought William, with a sense of satisfaction, as he watched *Rodney*'s hull disappear from view behind the buildings that crowded the North Wharf. Not surprisingly, Grandma Black shed a tear or two and her grandson felt sorry for her. Yet, selfishly perhaps, William's was a feeling of relief. His last sight of the vessel was the white ensign that streamed from the driver gaff aft of the mizenmast. Soon she was past Portsmouth Point and was gone.

Four

FORTON, GOSPORT: WESTMORELAND CO.,
VIRGINIA:
THE WESTERN MEDITERRANEAN
FEBRUARY 1853

Ten days had passed since H.M.S. *Rodney* cast off from the *Blake* hulk and took up a mooring at Spithead where preparations to depart home waters proceeded apace. In the last few days powder cases had been loaded on board and the pay clerks had come calling to pay the ship's company. It had been a dreary, murky time, since the *Rodney* stood out of Portsmouth harbour, benign rather than boisterous in the weather sense. Ashore, in Forton village, the mounting gloom of successive days seemed to be a reflection of William Reynolds' worsening state of mind. He had become depressed and the root cause had been the loss of his father. His low-spirited and melancholy mood had only recently become apparent as if the shock of his father's decease had taken time to strike home. He had shed tears, he had borne a brave front at the funeral, but perhaps only now had the boy started to grieve properly and give vent to his emotions. And in truth he felt little comfort in the smothering attentions of the two women in his life. They were alert to his maudlin inclination and his tendency to withdraw into himself but he preferred not to be fussed about and would choose to go to his room of an evening and find a degree of solace in that retirement. He had initially become attuned to the absence of a stable, fatherly presence – John Reynolds having been away in the Haslar hospital for some while prior to his death – and perhaps naively he had expected his father to return. Then Uncle James had been in the house and, although

William had been glad enough to see him return to sea, his departure had perhaps been untimely, coming so swiftly in the wake of bereavement. In essence it was the very thing that had troubled the sailor himself and had prompted him to seek his audience with the parson. William now found his home strangely empty. Yes, he cherished the love of his dear mother and grandma but, at this particular time, he somehow placed greater value upon his own solitude and he was finding it especially difficult without the reassuring and steadying influence of his father.

William's moodiness had begun to show in his schoolwork. He became detached and indifferent. On the previous Sabbath he had annoyed the Sunday school superintendent. His distraction and carelessness caused him to knock over and spoil a tray of buns and, as a consequence, he had been suspended as monitor. Then, this very morning, at the start of day school, he had let himself down in front of his peers, as well as Mr. Wicketts and Parson Veck. It had fallen to William and two of his classmates to memorise the collect for Ash Wednesday's morning prayers. It was a task with which William had struggled, yet, on former occasions, when it had been his turn to recite a collect or short prayer he had always been word perfect. And so William had left the schoolroom at five o'clock, still shamed and crestfallen by his morning's experience. He shivered as he made his way past the churchyard and out towards the Forton Road, for the weather had turned noticeably colder since lunchtime and William regretted not having brought his gloves and muffler.

After supper Charlotte Reynolds took to sewing and darning. Grandma Black, who had been swift to feel the soporific effect of a good meal, was soon asleep by the fireside with an equally inactive cat upon her lap. Carrying a lighted candle, William took himself up to the sanctuary of his bedroom at the back of the house but on his way stopped by and entered the room recently vacated by his uncle. There, upon the pine shelf, he found a copy of Defoe's *Robinson Crusoe*. He recalled Uncle James' recommendation that, should William ever feel temporarily inclined to escape life's trials and tribulations, it was a good yarn in which to immerse himself.

Propped up on his bed, William had made some inroads into the book when he heard from below the clock strike nine. He determined that he would persevere with the adventure story, albeit that he found the old style of English a shade confusing and was puzzled by some of the words. However, the distraction of the chiming clock awoke him to the fact that his eyes were being unduly taxed in the poor candlelight and he would do well to set *Crusoe* aside; and by the time he had marked his spot and set the book down his mother's voice rose clear from the foot of the stairs.

"Willie, are you still awake?"

"Yes, Mother," said William, his voice a little strained in the effort to lift himself out of his recumbent position.

"Would you like a hot drink, son? I'm just about to make one for myself and your Grandma."

"Thank you, Mother. I'll be down."

As he descended the stairs the thought struck William that it was a little strange, a touch ironic perhaps, that his uncle had encouraged him to read this book. For the young Crusoe to be bent on going to sea was one thing but it was an undertaking pursued against the wise counsel of his parents and to their great distress.

His drink despatched and feeling tired from reading, William was quick to bid goodnight and return to his room. Having got himself ready for bed and snuffed out his candle, he took a few moments to peer out into the back garden before pulling closed his curtains. With the onset of the colder weather the sky had cleared during the afternoon and the starry moonlit heavens of early evening had emitted a radiance that rivalled lamplight in the strength of its luminosity. That had passed. Now little was discernible since a heavy cloud cover had pushed in from the north, casting an amorphous blackness upon the ground; and so William dallied no longer at the window. He lay his head upon his pillow and thought about sleep. He pondered upon the fact that the light in his own life had succumbed to darkness since his dear father's passing. And today had been a day to forget. His failure to recite the collect at morning prayers had upset him and it rankled that he had let himself down. Perhaps in the morning he would confide in his mother with regards to the way he felt. On subsequent reflection, however, William decided against this. If he were to engage in any frank discussion he would feel obliged to mention his forgetfulness at morning prayers, as well as the Sunday school episode, Charlotte Reynolds having been absent on the Sabbath due to illness. Instead he preferred that she might glean the information from others. This was, in part, for want of courage but William was also possessed of such maturity of thought to realise that his mother was burdened by her own grief, which, if his feelings were a yardstick, could still be in the ascendancy. He was therefore loath to trouble her. Fleetingly he thought of his uncle's parting recommendation, to always consider Parson Veck as approachable, a ready listener and the source of good counselling in matters of a confidential nature. But again, William dismissed this option, suspecting that the old man would be vexed by his recent behaviour. On the contrary, however, whilst precious little had escaped the eyes and ears of the good vicar in recent days, it was with sympathy in his heart for the boy's feelings that he had already resolved to take him aside for a consoling talk when circumstances permitted.

No further thoughts crossed William's mind that Friday evening as he lay upon his pillow. Within minutes he was asleep. Meanwhile, three or four miles to the south, at Spithead, H.M.S.Rodney rode easily at anchor, all shipshape and Bristol-fashion and now ready to get under way the following afternoon. As the evening grew late and the men of the middle-watch prepared to stand to, the officer of the watch had cause to record that the northerly breeze had veered north north easterly and that snow had started to fall. Throughout the night it fell intermittently, icing yards and rigging. On Saturday morning, the twelfth of February, William Reynolds woke to a Forton cloaked white under tumbling snowflakes. He looked again upon the garden from the comfort of his bed and then into the enveloping grey of the Hampshire sky. For a while he was mesmerised by the oncoming swirl of flakes, each so delicately crafted, yet all too soon bent on joining its kind and surrendering that charm. It cheered him, and, for the first time in a while, he thought he might enjoy the day and make himself a snowman.

At Spithead, the men of Rodney's forenoon watch busied themselves with snow and ice clearance, a task assisted in the latter stages as the precipitation eased and a slight rise in temperature began to release nature's icy grip upon shrouds and yards. Later in the day H.M.S. Rodney weighed anchor under double reefed topsails, set her jibs and proceeded out to sea. It began to snow heavily once more as she departed the Solent and took a westward course out into the English Channel.

★ ★ ★

"Fishing. All the boy ever thinks about is fishing," exclaimed Heinrich Atzerodt, his rasping, guttural delivery of English only seeming to emphasise his frustration. Victore Atzerodt was becoming accustomed to her husband's irritation and lack of patience with their younger son's slothful and indifferent behaviour. While she often shared his exasperation her motherly compassion seemed to colour her attitude and this was invariably reflected in comments that appeared protective, thus fuelling Heinrich's annoyance.

"Give the boy time, my dear. You can't change people. He'll get it out of his system soon enough. Look at Johann."

"Give him time! He's nearly eighteen! He just can't continue to shirk responsibility as he does. He needs to settle in a job and do an honest day's work like his brother," was Heinrich's response.

"It'll happen, my dear. Es wird schon klappen. Remember that Johann used to worry us by spending time in that wretched billiard parlour with those rough-necks. He got over it though," said Victore.

"Yes, he did, I accept that. But he was always home at an acceptable hour and promptly at his work across town the following morning. In George's case it's all about fishing and little else. He's work-shy, plain and simple. Der Junge ist arbeitsscheu. He drifts from job to job. Just look at his record, Victore. Grocer's assistant…carrier…farmhand…the list is endless. He doesn't put his heart and soul into it and soon enough they part company with him or he walks out on them. Back to his fishing. And it's beginning to reflect on us, my dear. Folk talk."

"Then you must speak to the boy. Mit ihm sprechen. Impress upon him the need to knuckle down and do an honest day's work," implored Victore.

"Huh. You know I've been meaning to do just that, but I never see the boy. I get in for supper and he's gone off fishing with the horse dealer's son, whatever his name is…"

"Seth. Seth Morrison."

"That's right. The Morrison boy. Bad influence. Him and the youth from the nigger shanty who first taught him to fish. You've said you smell liquor on George's breath. Well that's the Morrison boy. I'm told he gets drunk on home-made whisky and if George is in his company then I'm sure he's plying him with it. If our boy takes a liking to it then he'll end up the same way and never hold down a job."

The blacksmith's words were heavy with indignation and resentment for a man of a naturally equable disposition. He was a big fellow, not in stature, but in his heavily muscled arms and shoulders, the product of arduous work that had forged both brawn and iron. Yet Heinrich was an inherently gentle character, a man of regular habits and a disciple of hard work and commitment. He eschewed liquor, although not to the point of abstinence, for he would turn to a little brandy occasionally when he saw it as having medicinal benefit. But he was alive to the evils of drink and since coming to these shores had witnessed only too well the ravages of cheap whisky. He was a man who was proud of his accomplishments, and rightly so, for he was good at his trade and his business had grown and enjoyed some moderate success; and, as a consequence, Heinrich Atzerodt had built a solid reputation in the little town of Montross since the family put down its roots in Westmoreland County back in the spring of '47.

"It puzzles me..." said Heinrich, as Victore placed his supper in front of him and interrupted his train of thought. "Thank you my dear," he continued. "It puzzles me why George chooses to sit out half the night at this time of year in the wet and cold with only a hurricane lamp to keep him company. I can think of nothing worse than sitting beside a dark lake in some soggy, ice-chilled thicket when he could be tucked up in the warmth of his bed."

"I agree. I've said as much to George but he says the black crappie and bluegill show little interest during the day. He tells me they take the bait better at night," explained Victore.

"So is that where he is now...fishing Morrison's lake?"

"No. Ethan, the miller's son, came by earlier and invited him to join him casting for yellow perch. He told George that since the winter ice and floods had cleaned out the millstream the perch had become active in the pools below the grist-mill. According to Ethan the fish have been feeding well after midnight. Well, George, needless to say, didn't have to be asked twice."

"Well I trust he has had the sense to wrap up well. There's a clear and cold night ahead. Seems to me that he'd do better to wait until the peeper frogs hail the onset of warmer nights. Better still he should get over this obsession with nocturnal fishing and daytime slumber. He needs to be out looking for a job, not confined to his bed," said the blacksmith.

"I'll tell him to come round to the smithy tomorrow, so you can talk to him, Heinrich," suggested Victore.

"I think that would be as well. He can't go on like this. It does rile me that he never made a go of working with me, but he said he didn't have the strength for smithing. Well, I wasn't born with these sinewy hands and muscular arms. My strength came from years of putting heart and soul into my work. It's all about pride and commitment and George seems to be devoid of both. No self-respect. It hurts me to say it, but the boy is a shirker and a drifter. He just doesn't like hard work."

"You shouldn't be too harsh on him," said Victore, words that her husband chose to ignore. "Remember he is your son, Heinrich. Du solltest nicht so streng sein."

"Do you know that if George had seen out his apprenticeship with me and done well he could have become my assistant. Then he could have taken on the forge when I finally decide to put my feet up or if the Good Lord first decides he has some shoeing to be done and I'm the man to do it. Do you know, Victore, the blacksmith from Stratford Hall came by recently to borrow a fuller and swage. He told me he needed a new assistant in the plantation smithy. I was only thinking that if George had seen his training through it would have been an ideal opportunity and an alternative to working with me should he have preferred it. Oh well, it was not to be…" Heinrich's words tailed off in a tone of exasperation and as if resigned to the fact that his younger son lacked the perseverance and self respect to ever make something of himself.

"Then you must surely have a good heart to heart talk with George tomorrow, my dear. Hopefully he'll take heed of what you have to say. I'll send him straight round to the forge as soon as he comes home from his night's fishing."

"Thank you, Victore. I'll talk to him tomorrow. Ich spreche morgen früh mit ihm. Now I'm off to my bed. I've got a lot of work on and will need to get the hearth fired up early on the morrow. Goodnight, my dear."

"Gute nacht, Heinrich."

★ ★ ★

"Tea cups…two, saucers…one, egg cups…one, three pie plates, two covered plates, milk pot…one…" They were James Black's words. Alone in the commanding officer's quarters, he was in the final throes of preparing an inventory of broken items from the captain's crockery. It had been a few minutes since he experienced some difficulty steadying himself when struggling to his feet, his sense of balance having been compromised by the inertia of time spent on all-fours. Now, with all shards gathered in by the diligent steward, his normally neat hand was far from precise. It was a reflection of the heavy roll of the ship that, with earlier onset, had cleared the captain's breakfast table.

Leaving wintry England in her wake, H.M.S. *Rodney* had made excellent passage as she ran before favourable winds and passed the Straits of Gibraltar in very good time. Now, in the forenoon of the twelfth day, as she ploughed a course towards the Maltese islands, the strong westerlies were becoming increasingly more troublesome. James Black had chosen a pencil with which to record the broken crockery, fearing that the conditions might cause ink to be cast upon the captain's carpet. All in all, a wise move, he reflected, as the motion of the vessel grew more violent and his writing implement made a habit of rolling off the table each time he laid it aside. The steward was alarmed that the mercury in the captain's glass had continued to fall sharply since he first attended the officer at his breakfast and he couldn't resist peering astern before taking his leave of the day cabin. Little was discernible, however, through the grey foaming opacity beyond the window glass that now rattled beneath sheets of driving rain and a maelstrom of foam and spindrift whipped off the cresting sea.

Once outside the captain's quarters, James Black was immediately aware of the clamorous nature of increased activity that now gripped the ship. The shrill modulations of the boatswain's pipe, the sound of barked orders from the quarterdeck and the footfall of seamen scurrying to their duties could be barely heard above the noise of wind and water. Topmen were already performing their agile and dangerous work aloft as they hurriedly fought to tame yards of straining canvas and to close-reef and furl the ship's sails before they were ripped to pieces. It was a hubbub that told of how conditions had deteriorated in the past half hour or so, since James was ordered to the day cabin.

The storm force winds peaked throughout the early afternoon, mercifully without injury, save for cuts and bruises, or any notable collateral damage. The dog watch saw welcome respite as the winds abated, enabling main and mizen topsails to be set and storm staysails to be lowered. Men composed themselves once more, whether at work or play, and the captain's steward, with time to relax, took to reading his poetry beneath a bulkhead lamp. All seemed relatively benign after the earlier turmoil as the ship ran before a stiff breeze. Yet not all on board allowed themselves to be lulled into thoughts of an improving and placid conclusion to what remained of the passage to Valletta. Those privy to the barometer's revelation were inclined at this stage to suspect otherwise. And so it was to prove. Worse was to befall the *Rodney*. As the evening progressed, so the wind rose again, and, with the approach of midnight, it blew a whole gale, then storm force eleven. Soon came an order to clear the lower deck and a call for more hands to be set to work as, once more, men struggled aloft to reduce sail now drenched with blinding rain and sea spray cast high by the wind's fury. Storm canvas was again hoisted to at least maintain some steerage way. Below, as James Black tumbled out of his hammock, the tumult that engulfed the ship seemed more intense this time, the dead of night perhaps serving to heighten men's senses to the ferocity of the elements that tossed and beat upon the ship. The worsening conditions had long since drawn him from sleep. Now, amid the gloom and noise of the lower mess deck, as men struggled to stow their hammocks, the captain's steward was acutely aware of the fear and agitation that seized many of his newly roused shipmates – landsmen and hardened salts alike. The violence with which the *Rodney* lurched and pitched, the unrelenting howl of the wind and the groan of ship's timbers under stress, left him in no doubt that he had never before felt the likes of such a frightful storm. Steeling himself to keep emotions in check, yet inwardly shaken, James made effort to reassure several of his terrified fellow ratings, that, as a consequence of recent trials, there was no better vessel than the *Rodney* when it came to steadiness and speed in rough weather. Alas, this was a rash commentary upon the merits of the ship's seaworthiness, for, within minutes, the main topsail split and blew away from the yard. Then, as the *Rodney* continued to scud before the tempest, at a fast pace of twelve knots – and through a sea that boiled and foamed eerily in the darkness – her starboard hawse buckler was stove in by the force of oncoming water. The result was potentially catastrophic. Immediately huge masses of water cascaded through the hawsehole, only to stream down the hatchways into the cockpit and holds. In the path of the surging body of water men were swept off their feet, one poor fellow sustaining a smashed shoulder, his screams lost in the howling gale. Others, distraught with terror, swore and cursed providence. Some gaped and froze in their panic. Some spewed vomit. Cries of doom were caught in the wind. Men fought for their lives. Those detailed to plug the hawse – stout, trusty fellows – battled their way forward to stem the torrent. Drenched through, frozen and stung with sea-spray, they wrestled with wet hammocks, their progress hampered all the while because of the ship's speed through the water. Finally, destination reached, with lungs gasping and knuckles red-raw, they set about taming the freezing and oncoming seawater. Steadying themselves as best they could, they threw all effort into cramming yards of sodden hemp cloth into the hawsehole, knowing their lives and those of the entire crew depended upon it. They toiled fervently for minutes that seemed endless, their wet, bleeding hands numbed and chafed as they thrust the hammocks into the watery void. In time their commitment brought dividends. The flow of water began to reduce through the makeshift buckler, then fell to a trickle, allowing the stout-hearted participants – exhausted to the point of collapse – to slump to their haunches.

Before the gushing ingress of seawater was stemmed the lower deck had already flooded and the chain pumps put to work. Men cussed as they worked assiduously in the teeth of the storm. Nonetheless, many a heart was to be lifted in realisation of a supreme success, the heroes being cheered as they stumbled aft to the promise of an extra rum ration. Yet, no sooner had hopes been raised, than word went about that the dear old *Rodney*, all but waterlogged, was in the neighbourhood of the perilous Sorelli rocks, which, if come upon, would dash her to pieces. Again men and boys were seized with terror, some drawn to blaspheme their Maker for their misfortune, convinced that they were now destined to be cast upon rocks and drowned. Grown men whimpered, cried and railed at their lot, their utterances lost or muffled by the unrelenting scream of the wind through shrouds and ratlines. The more reverent and God-fearing among the crew muttered prayers for deliverance then went about their appointed tasks with renewed vigour and in the earnest hope that their devotions would be answered. Daylight broke to the accompaniment of torrential rain and although the storm continued to rage around a foaming, high running sea, there were signs of increased optimism amongst the exhausted crew. The *Rodney* had not come to grief by being driven aground and, indeed, there was talk of her having passed to the south of the dreaded rocks just before dawn. The storm did abate, thank God, as the day progressed, and with it, canvas was restored and burgeoning optimism turned to joy.

The *Rodney* proceeded to limp her way to Malta, where, under the harbourmaster's supervision, she was taken in tow by the steam vessel *Triton* and brought to her moorings in Grand Harbour. To have survived the perils that were faced in the early hours, two days previously, was to the entire crew's great relief and men went about their work with a new zest for life, buoyed by their good fortune. And at sunset, on that first evening in Valletta, the customary lowering of *Rodney*'s royal and topgallant yards seemed to hold a poignant significance in bringing the curtain down upon a most frightful episode.

The following day the captain's steward chose to pen a letter to his relatives in Forton. He wrote of his safe arrival in Grand Harbour where his ship had joined the squadron of Vice Admiral Sir James Dundas. He also wrote of his eagerness, when on shore leave, to look up old haunts. Not surprisingly, he made no mention of the circumstances that had brought a close shave with death. There was no need to trouble the family with such particulars and he certainly had no wish to indulge his nephew in a true tale of grave danger and of churning stomachs upon the high seas. The motion of the Floating Bridge ferry across to Portsmouth, in the most clement of weather, had the ability to turn the boy a sickly-hue. Furthermore, knowing William's opinions and disinterest in nautical matters, James Black was already chiding himself for encouraging his nephew to read the adventures of the castaway, Crusoe. It had been a well-intentioned recommendation at the time but one which, in retrospect, lacked wisdom.

Five

FORTON, GOSPORT: PORTSMOUTH
EARLY 1854

The dawning of 1854 was viewed with foreboding by Charlotte Reynolds. She would normally embrace the Christmas season as a joyful time but now, as the old year drew to a close, she for once saw it through different eyes. Christmas 1853, unlike every Christmas in her living memory, brought the widow scant comfort. Missing was the delight and sparkle she would normally derive from the goodwill, warmth and spirituality of the season. Even the festive ministrations at St. John's, save for the Eucharist, which she cherished for the sake of regular communion, were shunned by Charlotte Reynolds, such was her state of mind. This particular Christmastide was to Charlotte an unwelcome harbinger of the New Year that was about to unfold; and she had begun to regard January with a sense of trepidation. It had been the month when her father had succumbed to the Malta fever and consumption had claimed her dear husband. Yet, as she approached the first anniversary of her later loss, they were the raw, benighted thoughts of delayed grief, rather than coincidence, which blighted her mind with melancholy. In the same way that the full shock and pain of John Reynolds' passing had tarried awhile before afflicting her son with profound sorrow and dejection, so that same dark prospect had lingered not weeks, but months, before casting its shadow upon her. To Charlotte, therefore, this Christmas was a mere shell of what it normally meant to her, its kernel devoured by her own grief.

William, on the other hand, had emerged from the nadir of his own sorrow and despondency, as spring turned to summer, and had become his old-self once again. And so, Margaret Black, mindful of the need for her grandson to derive some enjoyment from his Christmas and not to stray from regular worship, took to being more assertive and sought to relieve her daughter of certain responsibilities where she appeared to be failing. In so doing she hoped to offer some balm to Charlotte in her predicament, trusting that this might help to lift her from sad lethargy and indifference. As far as William was concerned, there was no dereliction of attendance at the services conducted beneath the roof of St. John the Evangelist. Grandma Black saw to that as she and her grandson took to their pews, offered up prayers, relished the warmth of fellowship and gave hearty voice to those much-loved hymns of Christmastide.

For Margaret Black the distractions of the festive season were welcome ones, deflecting her from thoughts that carried their own burden. Like her daughter, she knew only too well that, before long, things would have to change, except in Charlotte's case she was in no state of health to dwell and deliberate on such issues. The fact was, that, with the breadwinner having been dead nigh on twelve months, it was becoming increasingly more difficult for the two women to shoulder the upkeep of the Forton property. Margaret Black's annuity and the pension that had come Charlotte's way after the death of her husband were relatively meagre. James Black's allotment that he had put in place was a welcome addition to the family finances but Charlotte's good intention to become a day teacher in the village school had failed to materialise. That would have held the key to keeping heads above water. Instead the promise of employment a year ago had been dashed when the school budget prevented the management committee from engaging an additional member of staff after all. Furthermore, Charlotte was led to believe that circumstances would be unlikely to prove more favourable in the next financial year and, on the strength of this information, had effectively given up all hope of the teaching post to which she aspired. Not surprisingly, therefore, as the old year had unfolded, mother and daughter began to scrimp somewhat in matters of expenditure; and, as they started to feel the pinch of comparatively hard times, came the growing realisation that, not too far ahead, there loomed the prospect of having to vacate the Forton house in favour of something more modest and, thus, more affordable.

In addition, Margaret Black had cause to be uneasy about the European politics of the time, for it was beginning to appear that her two sailoring sons would soon be sucked into conflict. Since news had been received of the Russian fleet's destruction of Turkish ships at the end of November, public opinion had hardened towards the Russian Bear and the land was gripped with a truculent clamour for war against the aggressor. From early summer the British ships in the Mediterranean had assembled in the vicinity of the Dardanelles, their number including the *Rodney* as well as the *Vengeance,* a vessel that numbered among its crew the bandsman, Charley Black. Both battleships now comprised part of a combined Anglo-French fleet that was about to be ordered into the Black Sea where, in all probability, it would engage with the navy of Tsar Nicholas. And so Margaret Black had cause to have her whole family in the forefront of her Christmas prayers, not least James and Charley. She brought great strength of character to bear in rising above her preoccupations and especially in the face of her daughter's capitulation. Importantly, it was because of her doughty and stoical resolve not to allow life's troubles to dampen the occasion, that William enjoyed his Christmas Day. This was no more apparent than when Grandma Black brought her customary plum pudding to the table. It was in William's assessment a Christmas pudding that surpassed all others that had gone before and, like Oliver Twist, he asked for more.

Grandma Black reacted with a chuckle. "It's the same recipe I've always used my lad," she exclaimed. "Well, almost. You see, when I was mixing it I spilt a little too much brandy into the bowl and I must confess it's given it an edge. But I gather it's an edge to your liking Master Reynolds!" It was an incident that sparked a few spurious titters of disapproval from the elder woman and even Willie's mother was drawn to raise a smile or two as the amusement seemed to raise her from indifference. In turn, Margaret Black seized the moment of collective merriment to pour her daughter and herself a small glass of sherry, both for the sake of the occasion and as if the administration of a little alcohol might prolong Charlotte's newly-risen hint of enjoyment. In Willie's case there was lemonade. Then, a little teary-eyed, Grandma proceeded to toast and wish her three absent sons the compliments and best wishes of the season and, above all, she prayed for their safe-keeping in the year ahead. She resumed her seat and dabbed her eyes. It was time to spoon extra helpings of her plum pudding.

★ ★ ★

January was a harsh month with swirling snowstorms and plummeting temperatures. It was cold enough for those so inclined to don their skates and derive great joy and hilarity from testing their mastery of the ice – this being with notable success and celerity, or, as in the case of the vast majority, at the cost of innumerable tumbles and until bruised parts demanded submission. Charlotte Reynolds' state of health remained in turmoil but, by the middle of February, her dark, grief-ridden thoughts began to lift and gradually her old-self shone through. By early March, that progress, buoyed by a restorative tonic, seemed complete and, before the first week was spent, she had called upon a Gosport letting agent to explore the availability of alternative accommodation to rent.

As she suspected, Forton offered nothing to ease the family's finances. A move into town would be necessary where a greater abundance of more modest dwellings might be found with rents to match. That was the agent's advice. It was advice that Charlotte took back to St. John's Place to think upon and discuss with her mother. For her part, she disliked Gosport intensely. Hemmed in behind its ramparts, it was, in Charlotte's assessment, a meagre little town, over-populated with dark tenements and equally dark alleyways. When she had occasion to venture there it had struck her that it was a place possessed of more than its fair share of unwholesome exhalations that she found offensive. Furthermore, she recalled talk of Gosport having been rife with cholera shortly before the family came to Forton and she was fearful that its conditions might cause a further visitation. No, in Charlotte's opinion, it was not for them.

Margaret Black, on the other hand, was more ambivalent in her attitude and saw advantages in not venturing too far from St. John's Place.

"What of Willie's schooling, my dear? He's settled and seems to be making steady progress and Gosport would be in walking distance. He'd have to stay for lunch, mind you," observed the elder woman. "And then there's the Evangelist. It'd be a great shame if we have to find another church. I'd miss Parson Veck."

"Well, the only realistic alternative, Mother, would be to move to Portsmouth. The letting agent said as much and from my perusal of the *Hampshire Telegraph* it seems accommodation is more plentiful there and we're far more likely to find something to suit our purses."

"I wouldn't argue with that, but, as I say, what of Willie's schooling and the church? You've got to think of that, Charlotte."

"I have Mother. There are plenty of schools in Portsea according to Missus Williams. Her sister lives there and her young nephews seem to be doing well enough. I can find out more. There are National Society schools everywhere these days. Children are very adaptable."

"That's true, my dear. They so often have to be."

"As for St. John's," added Charlotte, with a hint of churlishness, "I'm not too bothered, myself. I'd sooner find a grander place with a church organ and a decent choir. Like you I'd miss Veck. He's a good man. But it's time to move on."

"Of course the parson loves his sacred music and he was telling me at Christmas that it is with great anticipation they await delivery of a harmonium. It's coming from Salisbury and is expected to have arrived before Easter week. That will help raise voices," said Grandma Black, knowing full well that her observation would do little to deflect her daughter from her stance. She was shrewd enough to appreciate that Charlotte's apparent indifference towards the church was fuelled by a touch of pique, of pride still wounded by the Managers' failure to engage her in the schoolroom. And so she continued with that thought in mind. "You know, my dear, you shouldn't continue to hold umbrage towards the church because of the school business. It wasn't any reflection upon your abilities. From what I gather it came down to shillings and pence. They wanted you, you know that, but they didn't get the grant they were expecting."

"I am aware of that, Mother, but it hurt all the same. And look where it's left us."

"You know, Charlotte, I think you've got more of your dear father's stubborn pride ingrained in you than in all your brothers put together." Pondering a moment, for reflection, she continued. "Well, perhaps we should exclude James from the calculation. I daresay his inclusion would shift the pendulum!"

It was a comment that drew a smile to Charlotte's face and, of course, she hadn't smiled much of late. "No, my dear," her mother continued, refreshed that her remark had drawn amusement and buoyed by the belief that her daughter's gloom was now well and truly extinguished. "But you would miss St. John's. Of that I am convinced."

And so these initial exchanges upon the move were somewhat inconclusive excepting that the women agreed that it would be prudent to take a look at Portsea to see what was to be had there in the way of suitable living quarters. Charlotte, therefore, returned to the letting agent, who, in turn, said he would contact his counterpart in the firm's Portsmouth office. The outcome was that within a few days mother and daughter found themselves taking the ferry to Portsmouth Point. It was Friday the tenth of March and, before they had closed the front door behind them, both women had developed misgivings over the wisdom of crossing to Portsmouth on this particular morning. For one thing, the weather had turned wet and boisterous overnight and, since daylight, a stiff March wind had continued to drive steady rain beneath a gun-metal sky. Furthermore, the prospect of being jostled and hampered by milling crowds was another cause for unease. For the Queen was coming to town and Charlotte reproached herself for having overlooked the fact when accepting the arrangements proposed by the letting agent. Instead, it fell to William's lips to jog her memory when, excitedly, he tumbled home from school the previous afternoon. "Mother, Grandma, guess what!" the boy had exclaimed, leaving too brief a split-second, before continuing, for either to proffer a reply. "Tomorrow I'm going to the end of the parsonage garden to see the Queen go by."

"What are you talking about, Willie?" his mother had said. "You're at school tomorrow. It's Friday."

"Yes, Mother, but the Queen is coming to view the ships. Mister Wicketts says morning school will end early and we are to be allowed to watch the Royal train go by and wave to Her Majesty."

Charlotte had had to admit that she had totally forgotten the Queen was due to review the Baltic Fleet at Spithead. She had read about Saturday's forthcoming event in the *Hampshire Telegraph* but it had since slipped her mind; and it was the realisation of her own forgetfulness that prompted her to remind William of Friday's arrangements, fearful that acute excitement might cloud his mind to matters of a more routine and mundane nature.

"Now don't forget, son, that Grandma and I are off to Portsmouth in the morning and I have arranged with Mister Wicketts for you to remain in the schoolroom and have your lunch there. If, when you return home later there is no reply to your knock, then you are to go along to Missus Barnes. She will get Sarah, her maid, to make you a hot drink and toast you a muffin. You can stay in the warm at Missus Barnes' until we get back. Now, don't forget Willie." It was a reminder that his mother had chosen to repeat the next morning, when bidding farewell to the boy as he set off to school. His exuberance undiminished, despite the threat posed by the weather, she was anxiously left to wonder whether it had fallen on deaf ears.

"Oh, and I hope you get a sight of the Queen, Willie," had been his mother's parting comment as she waved him off and he made to cross the Forton Road.

In the circumstances the journey into Gosport proved tolerable enough aboard the horse drawn omnibus. At least it offered a dry haven, and, although the inclement weather appeared to have generated more passengers, seats were to be had on the short trip into town. Charlotte Reynolds began to suspect that the Royal Family's imminent arrival might not, after all, draw many crowds on this side of the harbour. The weather was foul. Foul enough, she fancied, to deter most from departing their own firesides and, of course, tomorrow was meant to be the big day – the day Her Majesty would review the assembled ships.

"I wonder whether Willie and his classmates will get to see the Queen go by," uttered Charlotte, as mother and daughter crouched beneath their dripping umbrellas in the queue for the floating bridge. "If this weather does not relent then I seriously doubt that they will. He'll be mightily disappointed, poor lad."

"Ah, well, disappointment's to be preferred to getting your death of cold," exclaimed her mother, her voice raised to defy the combined noise of wind and ferry chains as metal now ground on shingle and took up the strain of the approaching conveyance.

The Forton day-trippers had encountered the need to wait longer than usual for the ferry. Folk who might have opted for one of the watermen's boats in less choppy conditions had decided otherwise. In such weather only the foolhardy would choose to be drenched for their pennies and have their innards turned topsy-turvy in an open wherry; and, consequently, the chain-ferry was busier than usual. Added to which, the increased water traffic to be expected on the eve of a Spithead review, with newly fitted out men-of-war leaving harbour to take up their moorings in the lines, had caused inevitable delays throughout the morning.

Eventually the Forton ladies were ushered forward with other foot passengers to board the floating bridge.

"Come, Mother," cried Charlotte, as she hurried to furl both umbrellas, only to realise that the rain had all but ceased; and, with that surrender, the leaden grey of morning was dispersing to a procession of broken clouds which, in their animation, threw down faint glimmers of brightness that promised a better afternoon. Clutching the wet cotton gamps and gathering her skirts, Charlotte seemed to pivot awkwardly and was pleased to feel the steadying hand of one of the ferrymen take her free arm and guide her aboard. Margaret Black followed with the benefit of similar assistance.

"Are you alright, Mother?" enquired Charlotte, once they had settled themselves in the comparative comfort of the passenger compartment.

"I am now, my dear. At least the weather seems to be picking up and the boy may get his sight of the Queen after all," came the reply, as Charlotte rummaged in her bag, momentarily preoccupied in finding her late husband's pocket-watch. The watch, which had always kept good time, revealed that midday was fast approaching – twelve minutes away to be precise – and, if the Royal train was at all punctual, it was due to run by Forton parsonage just short of the hour.

"Well, morning school should have finished by now. Quite a treat for them all…and Willie was so full of it. I'm pleased the weather's looked upon them so kindly after all and in such timely fashion." As Charlotte spoke and returned the watch to her bag the raising of the ramps on the landward side of the floating bridge caused a tremor throughout the vessel and signified that all wheeled traffic was loaded and secured. Then, without undue delay, the conveyance sprang into motion as the notched, steam-driven wheels on either side took their grip upon the chains, to a mixed tune of mechanical straining and groaning and a churning of water.

The seats they had taken in the passenger compartment afforded Charlotte and her mother an occasional view up the harbour once the floating bridge was clear of the Gosport shore. It was, nonetheless, only that – an occasional and fleeting prospect – on account of passengers moving about.

"Look, Mother," cried Charlotte, when they were barely half way across the harbour mouth. "Do you see the *Victory* there? She's making ready for the Queen's arrival. The sailors have gone aloft to man the yards. Oh, what a grand sight. And the ship next to her…I think it's the one Willie said was the *Neptune*. That's the same."

By the time her mother had reacted, it was, in fact, the capricious nature of the weather that contrived to impede the view. The rain's cessation had done nothing to cause any abatement of the accompanying high winds. Now, perhaps through some quirkish, eddying effect, those winds induced such a down-draught as to drive the smoky, steamy emissions from the vessel's twin-stacks almost to water level on the lee-side. And, for the few seconds that these emissions took to kissing the harbour brine, only to dissipate in the direction of the Royal Dockyard, they cast a misty opacity across the line of sight. When, ultimately, Margaret Black was presented with a clear prospect of the inner harbour, it was to tell her daughter, "My dear, I can barely see the ships, let alone the sailors."

"Well, Mother, it takes me back to Valletta. Do you remember, on the Queen's birthday, the ships were dressed and at noon they manned the yards, fired a salute and gave three cheers?"

"I do, Charlotte. It was a fine view looking down upon the ships from the ramparts. I always fancied that the men on the yards and ratlines looked a bit like little black aphids in a vegetable plot."

The recollection brought a smile to both faces as the floating bridge approached its docking point at the end of Broad Street.

"We'll be off in a moment," said Charlotte. "Don't forget your umbrella."

★ ★ ★

Back at Forton the school children had spent the best part of the morning in sombre mood. As usual, before drill and learning got under way, they had said their Friday prayers in the presence of Parson Veck. But they were prayers uttered half-heartedly and with distraction. Here and there young eyes were drawn from prayer sheets to the schoolroom's high windows in the earnest hope of seeing some evidence of the overnight rain having ceased. Then, for fear of being upbraided for inattentiveness, those eyes would nervously revert to the script or to the parson, himself, who stood below the schoolmaster's portrait of the Queen.

It was to prove a long morning, one to test the most optimistic of pupils, when many a young face adopted a forlorn expression. Concentration waned as time progressed, yet the schoolmaster understood and made allowance. And then, a few minutes before the reduced school morning had run its course, Mister Clarke, the parson's gardener, came knocking on the schoolroom door with a message for Mister Wicketts. The short conversation that ensued between gardener and schoolmaster was pitched at a whisper, giving nothing away to those who had pricked up their ears and who feared the worst, this being that the former bore news of their excursion's cancellation.

Once Clarke had left, the schoolmaster rose to his feet, and, with a dexterity and swiftness that comes with cultivation and routine, extracted, consulted and returned his pocket watch in a manner that had always struck his charges as being nothing short of impressive.

"Now, boys, listen to me carefully," said the master. It's nearly a quarter to twelve and you'll be pleased to hear that the rain seems to have stopped. We can therefore proceed with our plans."

This news, being sweet to the children's ears, was immediately greeted with a resounding cheer that was accepted by Mister Wicketts as being a natural expression of joy and relief. But to some of the more disruptive boys it was the signal to engage in a hubbub of unruly and over-excitable behaviour, the participants seemingly oblivious to the delay this would engender when there was no time to waste. A stern expression fell across the master's face as silently he waited for the several culprits to calm down. His patience, however, wore thin within the space of a few seconds. In what seemed a single movement, that rivalled in its subtlety his manipulative skills with the pocket watch, Mister Wicketts stooped to grasp his trusty cane, rose again to full height and brought the slender birch crashing down upon his desk. The swishing noise of the cane as it rent the air, the deafening thwack as it met the desk-top and the bellowing voice of the schoolmaster brought the whole class to a state of paralysis. "Silence! Silence!" barked Wicketts as birch met oak and quelled all commotion in a trice. The master hesitated before again addressing those that now sat cowed before him; time enough to permit his steely eye to fall upon each and every pupil, a moment to allow Wicketts to regain his composure and to leave each boy in no doubt that any further aberration in behaviour could have disastrous consequences. "You will appreciate," he continued, "that if we are to keep to our intentions there is no time to squander." They were words uttered in the self-satisfaction of knowing that his outburst had proved entirely effective and that, without exception, his charges were now as putty in his hands. And as renewed silence fell upon the schoolroom, in the wake of the master's words, their truth was immediately underlined by the sounds of outside activity: the noise of girlish chatter, the clunk of the schoolroom annex door being shut and the turn of the key in its lock. Miss Tillard, the mistress in charge of the girls' class, was already hastily preparing to lead her pupils across the gravelled yard in the direction of the parsonage.

"I'm told," resumed the schoolmaster, in due course, and as the sound of the departing girls diminished, "that on Parson Veck's instruction, Mister Clarke has erected a trestle-table at this end of the parsonage garden. You are to go there and receive a glass of lemonade and a cake from Missus Greaves, the housekeeper. Remember to be polite and express your thanks. Then you will follow me through the garden. Keep to the path at all times. Now, to enable us to be on our way you will quietly gather your coats, one row at a time, then line up outside and wait for me. Oh, and any boy who misbehaves will have my cane to reckon with later. Finally, when the train has gone you are to retrace your steps to the rectory gate and make your way home for lunch. Excepting, that is, the boys who remain behind and have bread and soup in the schoolroom. As I recall, that includes you today, William Reynolds."

"Yes, sir," said William, a hint of nervousness in his voice. He had not forgotten and, after recent events, was not relishing the prospect of spending the lunch break under the watchful eye of the vexed Mister Wicketts.

"Right, first row, gather your coats," said the schoolmaster as he simultaneously, once again, displayed his skill with the pocket-watch. "The Royal train is due to pass Forton in seven minutes."

★ ★ ★

It was five minutes to twelve when mother and daughter took their leave of the chain ferry. Broad Street was host to activities of a multifarious nature, but hereabouts, at the Point's extremity, sailors' beer-houses held a monopoly. The street's cobbles and flagged paving gleamed dark and wet, the smell of the morning's rain hanging fresh upon a lingering odour of stale porter, beefsteak and fried onions that otherwise pervaded the locality.

Charlotte Reynolds was patently aware that she was late for the appointment as she and her mother stumbled between the oyster boxes and draymen's barrels that littered the entrance to Bath Square. The arrangement with the Gosport office had been to present herself outside the *Roving Sailor* tavern at half past eleven. There she would be met by one of the Portsea-based agents, a Mister Walter Grimes, who would conduct her upon an excursion around several Portsea homes available for rent and considered to meet her stipulations.

A weasel-faced little man of indeterminate age, Grimes, to his credit, had arrived before the appointed time. The milling crowd and queuing horse-drawn vehicles that pressed towards the ferry's departure point, were testimony to the delays being encountered on the Gosport crossing. They were also encouragement enough to persuade the bedraggled letting agent to submit to the hostility of the elements and withdraw to the comparative comfort of the *Roving Sailor*. Dripping heavily from slouch hat and cape, he surrendered his bay horse and carriage to the safe keeping of the hotel's ostler. He then retired to the warmth of the tap room but not before placing a tuppenny tip in the hand of a grateful pot-boy. It was a monetary present which came with the instruction to keep an eye open for a lady enquiring as to the whereabouts of a Mister Grimes and to summon him accordingly.

Forty minutes elapsed before the pot-boy could consider himself released from that command as Walter Grimes re-emerged into Bath Square, drier and warmer and a shade better-humoured than when he had left it.

"Mister Grimes, I imagine?" enquired the woman who waited expectantly beyond the doorstep.

"Quite so, madam," came the reply. "I must be talking to Missus Reynolds."

"You are. Please accept my apologies for our lateness, Mister Grimes. The inclement weather and the little matter of the impending Review conspired to delay our crossing. Oh, and may I introduce my Mother... Missus Margaret Black."

Grimes had initially failed to register the presence of the elder woman. His Gosport counterpart had made no mention of Missus Reynolds being accompanied and, in practice, this presented him with a problem. Unfortunately for Grimes, he neglected to outwardly conceal his feelings in the wake of the introduction. His impassive visage was transformed by a sudden tic of facial muscle, his brow then creasing to a lingering frown that told, at best, of the man's confusion and, at worst, of his irritation.

If physiognomy ranked prominently among Charlotte Reynolds' intuitive skills, then it served her poorly on this occasion. The fact is she read the man's change of countenance as being manifestly indicative of the latter.

"I sense, perhaps, there is some difficulty," she said. "I sincerely regret our lateness, Mister Grimes, but I can assure you it was entirely beyond our control." There was a brusqueness in her voice, a reflection of being piqued on account of her own misinterpretation of the other's expression as an index to his thoughts.

"No, no, madam. I entirely understand and can vow there is no problem with the time," said Grimes. "My next appointment is not until four o'clock and if I appear troubled then let me explain," he added, his words tinged with awkwardness. "The rub is, Missus Reynolds, that I appear to have been dealt cause for embarrassment since the information I received from Gosport was that you would arrive here unaccompanied. In the circumstances I have travelled here in a two-seater conveyance and, therefore, find myself devoid of the necessary means to transport you two ladies about the town."

"Well, do not feel encumbered on account of that. I have to admit that it was not a matter I had raised with the gentleman from your Gosport branch, so there was no dereliction on his part. He was not to know that I was bringing my Mother, so the fault lies entirely at my door and it falls to me to apologise. You have no reason to feel embarrassed, Mister Grimes," said Charlotte, her words noticeably modulated and now delivered in a more conciliatory tone.

"Well, madam, we clearly agree we have a problem and must decide what to do about it." As he spoke the letting agent fiddled with his collar, an upright collar already soaked by the earlier rain and now further dampened by perspiration born of his recent unease. "I do have a suggestion and trust it will meet with your approval and that of Missus Black. It occurs to me that the several properties on our books most likely to meet with your interest are all within walking distance of my Portsea office." At this juncture Grimes chose to incline his sight towards the elder woman before continuing. "Perhaps, therefore, Missus Black, you would permit me to suggest that you let me convey you to my firm's office in Queen Street. My colleague will ensure that you are kept warm and comfortable while I return to Bath Square for the purpose of repeating the exercise, but this time, with your daughter, Missus Reynolds, as my travelling companion."

"That sounds a most sensible arrangement, Mister Grimes," said Charlotte, before her mother had time to offer an opinion. "So when do you anticipate returning for me?"

"At a gentle trot, ten minutes on the outward journey and ten minutes on the return, not forgetting five minutes to settle Missus Black comfortably before the office hearth. In addition, two minutes to stoke and make up the fire if my colleague is indisposed at the time. In summary, madam, seven and twenty minutes at the outside." It was with chirpier demeanour that Grimes now addressed his clients, buoyed by the impression that his suggestion had been well received.

"Then I will occupy the time at my disposal by walking round to the High Street where I know of a good draper and haberdasher. I need a few yards of taffeta cloth and, Mother, I can get you the cotton threads you need."

"Thank you, my dear," said Margaret Black. "White, two reels…and one of midnight blue."

"Once I've finished I will make my way back into Broad Street, Mister Grimes. If some of your seven and twenty minutes has still to run its course, I'll be biding the time looking at the shops between St. James Gate and the *Blue Posts*."

"Then I will look for you there, madam," observed the letting agent.

★ ★ ★

Midday had barely passed and, for upwards of ten minutes, the children had waited patiently for the first sign of the Royal train's approach. Then a shrill whistle drew forth an undercurrent of ebullience for it suggested the steam engine was wending its way between the drenched stubble-fields which bordered the vicinal settlement of Camdentown.

"Here she comes," exclaimed a large boy in knee breeches, who, in his excitement, lost his footing on the slippery bank. With domino effect several other boys, William Reynolds included, were carried off balance, only to accompany the large boy in his backward tumble on the falling ground. Fortuitously, equilibrium was restored at the cost of muddied hands and knees. The greater misfortune would have been to end up in a pile of wet soot that stood heaped below, in the corner of the clergyman's vegetable plot.

Looking down from above, Parson Veck addressed these boys, seemingly with little sympathy for their predicament. "Come now," said the parson, "that was a close shave. Best clamber back here...quickly now, before Mister Wicketts sees you." Then, directing his attention to the large boy who started the commotion, he added, "And I trust, young man, that your remark was levelled at the approaching steam engine and not Her Majesty the Queen. It does not behove the children of Forton to show disrespect for their sovereign."

The schoolchildren's vantage point lay beyond the parson's lawned garden – now brightly studded here and there with knots of young primroses – and his vegetable plot. It amounted to an elongated, raised bank that had been adapted by the incumbent from an old spoil heap placed there by the railway navvies when they built the Gosport line. Apart from providing some shelter to Veck's cherished vegetable garden, its crest could afford a line of sight into passing railway carriages, the track being more or less at grade as it ran towards the town terminus. Even the arthritic clergyman found the energy and determination to conquer the acclivity, he and his trusty gardener having assessed it prudent to claim their positions ahead of the tread of younger feet. Clarke stood beneath an old Union flag which he had found in the potting shed and now held high on an improvised flagstaff that had seen better days as a besom-stick. And thus, a phalanx of children was strung out along the top of the former spoil heap, between, at one end, the flag-flying gardener and his employer and, at the other, Wicketts and Miss Tillard. The housekeeper, Missus Greaves, was a late arrival, emerging hot-foot and breathless from her duties, anxious as any not to miss the spectacle.

"The signal is at go," shouted the gardener. As he spoke, a column of billowing smoke and steam, bent in the wind, was the first visible sign of the Royal train.

The noise of the children's excitement was now of sufficient volume to drown out the sound of cawing rooks that wheeled in the tops of the parsonage elms. Then, all of a sudden the front of the engine burst into view as it ran under the lofty footbridge known as Jacob's Ladder. Suppressed and laterally dispersed beneath the bridge's iron structure, the locomotive's streaming emissions were thrown into a foggy turbulence that framed its emergence with dramatic and ethereal effect.

For the young onlookers it took their very breath away. Out of the smoky maelstrom came a finely lustred engine, its Lincoln-green livery, its sparkling dome, the copper-topped stack, all burnished to perfection. Yet, for all the action and drama, the Royal train was already slowing perceptibly as it closed upon the terminus ahead. The engine driver – to his credit – seeing the assembled children, was the more nimble in the application of his brakes than would normally be the case. The first of four carriages drew level. Swirling wisps of smoke and vapour rose and fell but dissipated before threatening to cloud the inward view. Optimistic eyes strained and searched anxiously. The plush interiors of the first three coaches offered glimpses of the Royal party's entourage – an equerry, a valet perhaps, a lady-in-waiting – yet no one to conjure recognition upon the peering, expectant faces. Then, all of a sudden, two of the Royal princesses, seated at a window in the last coach, caught the eye. The Royal children – in Miss Tillard's later assessment, the Princesses Alice and Louise – spotted the Forton children, smiled, and returned their frantic waves. A moment later, fleetingly revealed with her back to the engine and seated opposite the princesses, was their mother. Queen Victoria in person, not the iconic, yellowing semblance that constantly looked down upon Wicketts' class from behind the master's desk. Here was the paper Queen metamorphosed. Here she was cast in the children's own likeness, happy to follow her daughters' example by raising her hand and smiling serenely at her young subjects. In a trice she was gone, the children transfixed in their disbelief as they watched the train recede. Within two or three minutes it would run onto the Clarence Yard jetty where the Royal yacht was already waiting with steam up.

★ ★ ★

Portsmouth harbour constantly reverberated to the sound of the big guns, often in salute of elegant ships-of-the-line arriving and departing the haven.

As Charlotte Reynolds watched her mother and Grimes take their leave of Bath Square, setting her own tread in the direction of the High Street, it was the noise of *Victory*'s guns that resounded across the harbour behind her: a volley of gunfire that told those in the know of the imminent arrival of the Royal family at the Clarence Yard jetty.

Charlotte was swift to complete her transaction at the High Street drapers although the walk proved uncomfortable enough in a wind reluctant to abate. Indeed, it now blew with a greater gustiness and, on more than one occasion, had the temerity to force a way beneath her mantle and administer a cold draught about the nape of her neck. And all the while she had good cause to hold on to her bonnet for fear of it being unseated and ruined upon the muddied thoroughfare. Broad and High Streets now teemed with an eclectic mix of characters from the well-to-do to ragged street urchins. With the rain's cessation it was as if all had been unshackled and committed to the streets, only to be hurried along with the March gale at their backs, or, conversely, forced to lean into it with determined gait. Military men, colourful and finely accoutred, strode out of Point Barracks, while naval officers and green midshipmen hastened to the nearby Sallyport to suffer perilous and choppy transfers to their awaiting ships. Outside the *Blue Posts* and *George* hotels, well attired ladies and gentlemen were being helped down from their coaches and carriages. In their wake came cumbrous portmanteaux, destined to be seized upon by scurrying, tip-conscious porters. Other newcomers, doubtless intent on soaking up the atmosphere on the eve of the Review, sauntered along the drying pavements, or exchanged them for accessible corners of the old fortifications from where some prospect might be had of the assembling ships at Spithead.

Charlotte Reynolds had retraced her steps to that part of Broad Street where she expected to encounter the returning letting agent. Being ten minutes short of the fellow's conjectural estimate of the duration of his round trip – and given her own assessment that this was all too brief a timescale – Charlotte permitted herself to be distracted and chose to cross the street, back in the direction of the Point. A surge of people had caught her eye as they hurried out of Broad Street towards the foreshore. Yielding to the thought that she had time to spare, Charlotte allowed her inquisitiveness to get the better of her. It was into Capstan Square that she followed the crowd, a small space that opened alongside the sea defences, just beside the Round Tower – itself an integral part of the old fortifications.

Here could be found a view of the harbour mouth, as good as any that might be had, although the object of the spectators' keen attention was not immediately obvious to the widow from Forton. Then, no sooner had she succeeded in finding a gap through the cordon of excited onlookers ahead of her, than she caught sight of the steam yacht, *Fairy*, running out of harbour, bearing the Royal couple and their children to Osborne. The vessel appeared to shift well enough in the turbulent conditions, her screw propeller evidently generating a good forward thrust from her engine as she ran into a strong headwind and scythed through the swiftly-running currents about the harbour entrance.

A full half hour had elapsed since Charlotte Reynolds left Bath Square and, with curiosity satisfied, she began to take her leave of the multitude into which she had descended. Simultaneously, a fulminous roar of gunfire rent the salty air as the Saluting Battery showed its respect with a twenty-one gun salute. *Fairy*, now standing out of harbour, set her course for East Cowes.

"Ah, Missus Reynolds, there you are. I was beginning to think you were lost," said Grimes. The intonation in his voice carried a hint of nonchalance and conceit, for he had correctly sensed that his client had doubted the accuracy of his predicted return. He had kept to his word, yet in truth, only at the expense of putting his ageing horse to an excessively brisk trot that fell little short of a gallop. The animal now stood forlorn with head bowed, the effect of its return sprint evident from the vapours of exertion that rose from loins and withers.

Charlotte Reynolds chose to ignore the letting agent's comment but proceeded to enquire of her mother.

"Missus Black is comfortably seated by a cosy fire as we speak and, I imagine, as warm as toast, madam. I believe she found the short ride to Portsea an exhilarating one," added Grimes as he assisted his client into the two-seater.

Taking stock of the vehicle as she clambered aboard, Charlotte gravely doubted whether her mother had ventured to express any enjoyment of the journey she was now about to experience. The carriage was an old, open tilbury, which, with cursory inspection, told of better and distant days, its sparse upholstery shabby and uncomfortable, its black lacquered body now lustreless and bruised.

"Did you manage to secure the goods you were wanting Missus Reynolds?" enquired Grimes as he took the reins and coaxed his weary horse into a gentle trot. "Not quite the cloth I needed, but otherwise, yes, I had a modicum of success. I was surprised to see such crowds emerge once the rain had ceased and there seemed to be no shortage of guests at the *George* and *Blue Posts*."

"Oh, not just at the better establishments, ma'am. For days now they say it's been hard to find lodgings anywhere in town because of the Review. Some visitors are having to settle for damp lodgings and stables to lay their heads. And no doubt at a price!" The agent was forced to raise his voice as the apron of granite setts which spanned the Town Quay rang to the unremitting clatter of iron shoes. To Charlotte Reynolds, however, it was the shock waves of discomfort from being jolted about on the uneven road that proved the greater affliction.

As soon as Grimes' tilbury had travelled beyond the Quay Gate and Custom House, the grating sound mercifully ceased. Thereafter, once within the lee of the Old Gun Wharf's encircling wall, the vertiginous feelings that had beset the lady passenger – and were born of the uneasy motion across the Town Quay – themselves began to recede.

"Tell me," said Charlotte, as soon as she had composed herself and felt confident that there remained no reason to shout. "Is Portsea as busy as the Point?"

"Bursting at the seams, Missus Reynolds, bursting at the seams," declared the driver, as they reached the outskirts of Portsea and came upon Ordnance Row with its attractive jumble of two and three storey houses. "Here in Portsea , it's not just the Review. It's the constant tramp of soldiers through the town on their way to the Dockyard. Then there are the newly recruited sailors who keep arriving to crew all the ships that are being fitted out. Most, no doubt, bound for conflict in this war they're all talking about."

"No war has been declared yet, Mister Grimes, but admittedly, it now looks inevitable," said Charlotte. "Our politicians seem to be truculently disposed to take the Russian Tsar to task. What with that and there appearing to be plenty of clamour in the land for a fight. They say the crux of the matter is that the Country hasn't exercised its muscles since Napoleon's day. With many hungering for a fight it appears the time is nigh."

"Well, the regiments keep coming, day after day. That must say something. All spruced up and accoutred with their bands a'playing and all given a capital send-off as they make to embark on the steam-transports. God Bless the dear fellows and let's hope their enthusiasm has cause to stay the fight," said Grimes, who clearly had misgivings about the whole affair.

Within a few minutes they were beyond the Old Gun Wharf and Charlotte was soon struck by the lively bustle that gripped the Common Hard. It seemed that all the world and his wife had been set loose with the onset of the improving weather. Civilians, be they at work or play, mingled with a diverse multitude of naval and military men – ratings and midshipmen, dragoons in braided tunics, middle-ranking naval officers and kilted soldiers from the Highlands. Bunting and Union flags fluttered and streamed from the higher sash windows of the many taverns and sailors' beer-houses; also, from the lesser number of retail establishments and slop-shops that looked out across the water. Glints of early afternoon sunlight sparkled on the harbour. With the wind now easing, unscrupulous watermen, their boats pulled up beyond the grassy foreshore, beckoned to passers-by to hire them, hopeful that they might prise some extortionate fee for a promised viewing of the Baltic Fleet. Naval cadets and sightseers thronged the Royal Albert steamboat pier. In the distance Charlotte caught sight of the *Victory* again, her yards now divested of the diminutive figures who had gone aloft to cheer Her Majesty down the harbour.

On the approach to the Dockyard Gate, a meagre, forlorn-looking gathering was in the throes of pitiful dispersal; mainly women and children, some looking bewildered, many red-eyed and tearful. They had recently said their farewells to soldiering loved-ones from the ranks of several departing companies of fusiliers, now gone from view, swallowed up in the bowels of the teeming Dockyard. Yet to the attuned ear the distant strains of the regimental band could still be heard from the Main Gate. On the Pitch House jetty, rousing tunes helped to lift the spirits of the fusiliers who waited for clearance to board the screw transport and be allocated their placements on the berth-decks. Meanwhile, a group of obdurate old tars and old soldiers sat against upturned rowing boats that lay upon the green swathe outside the Dockyard Gate. Here they jawed and smoked and chewed upon tobacco quids, a social intercourse cocooned around times past that dwelt upon the old campaigns. Wrapped up against the wind, they seemed indifferent, perhaps oblivious, to the excitement, joys and sorrow, being played out nearby.

"Tell those old fellows," said Grimes, pointing his horse-whip in their direction. "Tell them we're about to fight at the shoulders of Frenchmen and they'll scoff and swear they've never heard the likes of it in all their days. There's a Peninsular and Waterloo medal or two pinned to their breasts, you see, and I recognise two of them as old salts who will insist they fought alongside his Lordship off Cape Trafalgar. They'll quote the Admiral as having proclaimed that you hate a Frenchman as you hate the Devil. Truly, they'll find it incredulous."

Shortly, having negotiated passage through the swelling crowd, the letting agent and his passenger ran close by the Dockyard Gate and turned into Queen Street, Portsea's principal thoroughfare.

"I suspect you will be relieved to see the back of this poorly sprung contraption, for which condition, Missus Reynolds, I tender my firm's sincere apologies. Fortunately we can dispense with the vehicle shortly, for we are now in sight of my offices," said Grimes, as they passed the Sailors' Home and turned into a side street. "All the houses we are to view are located close by, just to the north of here…between the Dockyard and Anglesey Barracks."

Charlotte's rudimentary knowledge of the geography of the area was sufficient to make sense of her companion's points of reference and to provide reassurance that the properties were in easy walking distance.

"Come now," added Grimes, as the horse and carriage pulled up in the office yard. "Let us find Missus Black, have a hot drink and be on our way."

★ ★ ★

"I heard a cuckoo this morning when I ventured into the garden and, bless my soul, the weather has brought forth its namesake." As Charlotte Reynolds spoke she pointed to the delicate lilac-pink petals that mingled with the damp grasses below the churchyard wall.

Charlotte, her mother and William had just made their way across the well-trodden path that cut through the glebe land in the direction of the church. It was Palm Sunday and the open ground was strewn with its customary daffodils, now largely spent.

"What do you mean, Mother, the cuckoo's namesake?"

"Lady's smock, Willie. Some call it the cuckoo flower, saying it arrives with the cuckoo."

"I can't say I like the cuckoo. It's a lazy bird. So why name a poor flower after it?"

"Oh, don't be so harsh towards the poor bird, Willie," said his grandmother. "He's only like that because the Good Lord made him so."

"Isn't there an old saying about the cuckoo, Mother…one that talks of bringing good fortune?" asked Charlotte.

"Indeed there is, my dear. Something to do with turning your coins over when hearing a cuckoo and there'll be money in your purse until he returns."

"Perhaps we'd better empty our purses, turn over what little we have and hope for better times," reflected Charlotte with a chuckle. "Which reminds me, I must make a point of talking to the parson today about our decision."

It was one of those bright, confident, fresh spring mornings, when budding new growth rises from all quarters and promises much more to come – like a mighty river in its infancy. Whilst generous in its brilliance, the weak April sun had struggled to show its warmth. Just lately, however, a perceptible rise in temperature began to combine with the soft zephyrs off the Channel to dispel dawn's loitering dew. Yet, in shaded corners, watery gossamer webs still sparkled and seemed to defy the drying process. It was an invigorating kind of morning, with ingredients to quicken the senses, as the churchgoers wended their separate ways to church off the Forton Road.

As Charlotte Reynolds and her family reached the gravelled forecourt, which gave access to church, schoolroom and parsonage alike, it was to promptly mingle with others making their way to the morning service. Most seemed in good heart as hats were raised and pleasantries exchanged and there was a perceptible reduction in the progress of couples, families and individuals as they fell in together and engaged in conversation. In consequence, and because of such preoccupation, the church path was invariably reached at a mere gentle saunter, with new arrivals then forced to tarry awhile as they encountered a bottleneck of fellow parishioners milling about the church door. It seemed it was a reticence to put away tongues that regulated the seepage of worshippers across the threshold. As William lent an ear to snatches of conversation he detected some shared excitement about the arrival of the new harmonium. Yet it was the long anticipated and recent declaration of war that seemed to be on most lips.

The fact that it was Palm Sunday, and the weather clemently inclined, combined to offer an explanation for what promised to be a good attendance. From outward appearances many a Forton trunk and linen-press had been divested of its owner's Sunday best. For the womenfolk, caution had been the watchword, it being too early to abandon heavier winter frocks and mantles. Some clasped their tiny editions of the *Book of Common Prayer* and of *Hymns Ancient and Modern* squeezed into equally diminutive carrying cases, corded about their wrists; and they were devoid of head-wear. It was the Sabbath and, with church their destination, they had forsaken their bonnets, it being unseemly and unfashionable to do otherwise. Now, when it came to uncovered heads, one of the most striking belonged to a girl from Lees Lane who approached the church gate on the arm of her intended – a corporal from one of the Foot Regiments. Possessed of a blithe and cheerful disposition, her complexion was as smooth and delicately tinted as porcelain, her auburn tresses drawn together in a neatly coiled chignon that lay upon the nape of her neck. Across her corsage fell a crispin mantle, partly obscuring the grey dress which contrasted well with her lover's uniform. They made a handsome pair, so much so that William was mildly captivated by their appearance and undoubted compatibility and closely observed their approach as he waited to enter church. As they passed through the gate behind him, it was to become immediately aware of William's rapt gaze, both choosing to grant him a smile in return. There was no suggestion of being irked by the boy's attention which might have been construed as rudeness. Instead their smiles reflected a mutual happiness and joy. In the soldier – who was, perhaps, two and twenty – William had seen a reflection of how he might imagine himself, ten years hence. The young man's hair was flaxen, with a touch of curl, and he wore a moustache that was sleek and devilish. There was a twinkle in his bright eyes and he looked all the part a soldier, in his high collared, blood-scarlet tunic, with its gold trim and blue facings and its burnished string of brass buttons. The young lady was scarcely out of her teens, her pretty features and gay demeanour blending with a physical maturity to conjure an intriguing mix of girlish vulnerability and sophistication. William read these traits, these peculiarities, well enough, only for his fascination to be extinguished by those smiles. He swiftly turned away, anxious to hide his blushes. Meanwhile, his mother and grandmother had moved into church and William lost no time in squeezing his way ahead of others to secure lost ground. As he did so, his underlying thoughts were at loggerheads over which of the young lovers had attracted the greater part of his attentions. Ordinarily, little could challenge a fine military uniform, for therein lay William's aspirations. However, he was now approaching his twelfth birthday, his young loins on the cusp of an awakening interest in the opposite sex. Yet far be it from William to admit – excepting to inwardly concede – that perhaps the auburn-haired daughter of Forton had out-ranked her corporal. Now, clutching his cap and hymn book and straightening his green, velveteen jacket, William slipped into the pew seat beside his grandmother.

"Look William," whispered his mother, pointing to a group of music stands and ornate library chairs that had been placed to the south side of the nave. "Today we have some music at long last," she murmured, as a motley band of musicians seized upon the chairs and began rearranging them to their liking. Since the old cabinet organ had finally expired, on the first Sunday in advent, the choir had been bereft of music. Recently, it had also shown signs of languidness, the product of the choirmaster having been indisposed at some length through illness. Today, however, he was back in harness and, after several stints of putting his choristers through evening practice, the rejuvenated choir came to church with the added benefit of musical accompaniment.

It being Palm Sunday, and the new harmonium due to be pressed into use on Easter Day, Parson Veck had decided to enlist the services of a quintet of travelling musicians. They were known to the incumbent on account of hailing from the district of his birth, this being the ancient little market town of Bishops Waltham that lay beyond the Forest of Bere. That knowledge embraced an awareness of their proficiency – at least by rural standards – for they had gained a good reputation playing their instruments in many a country church. Questioned closely, however, they would always express a preference for performing at country square dances, since ale and cider would flow freely between quadrilles. When it came to hymnal renditions on the Sabbath, sobriety and a more circumspect behaviour was the order of the day, excepting that, on this Palm Sunday morning, they had the promise of some refreshment on conclusion of the service.

The appearance of the players, as they stumbled noisily into church, came as a new experience for William and the vast majority of the worshippers who waited patiently in their pews. St. John's had seen nothing like it in recent times. Quaint, middle-aged folk, they were, oddly rustic and possessed of an eccentricity in both conduct and attire. To a man they wore bright cravats, most were bespectacled and all had bushy, greying side-whiskers that aged them beyond their years. Men with garters and buckled shoes, knee-length corduroy breeches and faded waistcoats. Their coats were of a fustian type, excepting the treble fiddler who wore an old calico smock. They looked, altogether, incapable of telling a crochet from a quaver; yet, having emptied their moth-eaten, coarse woollen bags, to reveal three fiddles, a clarinet and violoncello, they proceeded to pluck and tune them with a nonchalance that strangely exuded confidence.

It was a confidence that proved to be justified, for, as the service got under way and the parson announced the first hymn, it was a harmonious sound that fell upon the people's ears: and with it came an inclination to open their mouths the wider and sing with a greater conviction than had been the case in recent times. Similarly, the choristers went about their business with a renewed enthusiasm and self-assurance, it being later claimed that the morning's melodious emissions could be heard as far afield as Forton Barracks.

When the service was concluded, Charlotte and her mother were in no hurry to leave church since Charlotte wished to speak to the parson. Those children in earlier attendance, William included, had long since departed, the receipt of their palm crosses from Parson Veck having been the precursor to making their way to the schoolroom where Sunday school was in progress.

Being of a particular age, and by natural course of events, William had lately progressed to accompanying the two women in his life to morning service. He had also embarked upon a weekly attendance at the parsonage to secure such spiritual counselling and instruction as was destined to culminate in his early confirmation. Also, at Sunday school, he had been endowed, by the superintendent, with some increased responsibility, this being to assist the teachers in a kind of monitorial capacity. His mother, on the other hand, had ceased her involvement on Sundays when taken ill some months before, only to subsequently refrain from advertising her availability once recovered; and, by dint of not broaching the matter again, the church body had, quite naturally – and by default – put two and two together and assumed she was still troubled by her ailment.

Margaret Black knew better. She was aware that her daughter admired Parson Veck. However, he was Chairman of the School Managers and there had been the thorny issue of shelving the creation of a new class. Charlotte continued to remain irked, a chagrin born of personal and selfish considerations that had soured her view of the parish church and fuelled a reticence to resume her work in the Sunday school.

"Good morning Missus Black…Missus Reynolds," said the clergyman, as mother and daughter emerged from the cool shadows of the church interior, only to be dazzled by the bright, midday sunbeams.

Momentarily disorientated by the sudden transition, the women were drawn to squint and frown before they could focus properly upon the hoary-headed old gentleman who stood upon the church steps.

"I trust you are both well and you found the music uplifting," said Veck, cheerily, his demeanour the very antithesis of what one normally expects from a lugubrious village rector of advancing years.

"It was a delight, Parson Veck, to hear music, once again, filling the church…and such accomplished musicians," exclaimed the elder woman. "And their eccentricity was charming in a rustic sort of way."

"Yes…they are good countryfolk, a miller and a maltster among them, the remainder farm labourers. They all show a love and commitment towards music-making that has marked out their families for generations. I suppose it's in their blood, and well-respected they are in the county. Anyway, I'm so glad you enjoyed it. It's been such a dull time without music and, having now taken delivery of the new harmonium, I thought it apt and wholesome to signal the approaching closure of that barren spell with a touch of tradition."

"It's arrived then, vicar?" enquired Charlotte. "The harmonium."

"Yes, dear lady. It arrived in good shape from Wiltshire on Friday and a fine piece of furniture it looks. I've had the instrument placed in the vestry for now, while we consider the best place for it…somewhere on the south side of the nave, I expect. Miss Tillard, bless her, being musically gifted, has agreed to play it. She needs to become accustomed to the harmonium, of course, but given time for practice, she hopes to introduce it to us on Easter Day. Good Friday is too solemn in the occasion to celebrate the instrument's arrival and use it to best effect."

"Then we shall look forward to Easter Day with even greater anticipation," said Margaret Black, a broad smile upon her face. In contrast her daughter chose to remain tight-lipped as inwardly she pondered upon the wisdom of opting for a church harmonium ahead of funding a new class. In truth, however, the instrument had been financed largely by public subscription.

"Now, tell me, ladies, how is your dear son and brother…Mister James Black…the gentleman on the *Rodney*? Have you heard from him lately? It must be almost a year since he returned to sea."

"A year and more, Reverend. It was Candlemas Eve, the one before last, when we waved the *Rodney* out of harbour," said the sailor's mother, her smile now displaced by a more wistful expression.

"Well, well," exclaimed Parson Veck, with a genuine hint of surprise in his voice. "Tempus fugit, I suppose. Quite remarkable."

"We did receive a letter from James earlier in the year," Margaret continued. "He was well enough, if not a trifle bored. His ship is with the British Fleet in the Black Sea, but his brother is with him…well, not with him, exactly, but he's also out there with the squadron. Charles is on the *Vengeance*. He's a naval bandsman. A letter arrived from him only last month…in fact it was addressed to William, much to the boy's delight. His ship was moored in the Bosphorus. He mentioned that the British and French ships were being joined by Turkish steamers."

"Then rest assured, madam, both your sons will be in my prayers," promised the clergyman. "With war actually declared, a fortnight ago, we are now, sadly, in a downward spiral towards conflict. It was inevitable, I suppose, for like Joshua, have we not heard a noise of war in the camp for several months now? A widely voiced appetite for the fight seems to have gripped the land and I suppose we must face up to the Russian foe. But who would have thought we would stand with the French!" Parson Veck's words were uttered with disbelief, his expression incredulous. "You know, ladies, I drove out towards Gilkicker Point, yesterday…in the gig…and took a walk along the foreshore. It's something I do from time to time, when I need a little inspiration. I wanted to clear my mind and think about my Easter Day sermon. Well, I couldn't help but notice the several large troopships sailing out of Southampton Water. I know Portsmouth is busy but many of the troops seem to be embarking at Southampton. God Bless them all! I pray it's not a protracted business but is done in the flicker of a candle," said Veck, solemnly.

"Let us, indeed, hope so," agreed Margaret Black. "And thank you for keeping our loved ones in your prayers. In that regard, however, might I make one request?"

"And what would that be, Missus Black? I'm sure it's a request we can accommodate," said Veck, light-heartedly.

"Just that you might kindly consider including my eldest son, John, in your prayers. He's a soldier in the East Indies. He's been there close on five years, the last three in the Cawnpore military station where his regiment spent a good part of last year in cholera camp. He survived that and the last we heard the regiment was moving up country to the Punjab. To be honest, I think John is in greater danger than his brothers."

"Then we must surely include John in those prayers," said the clergyman. "Now…if you'll excuse me, I'd better be on my way. Otherwise Missus Greaves will conclude that I have no interest in luncheon and nothing is further from the truth! However, before I take my leave," he added, reflectively, "it would be remiss of me not to enquire of young William. I try to keep as close an eye as possible on the boy when he's over here at school." Veck was careful to refrain from any suggestion that this was at the particular request of his Uncle James. "He seems committed in his confirmation classes and doubtless he's told you he should be confirmed in a few weeks?"

"Well, we have to be encouraged. William seems well adjusted and, in this respect, exceeds expectations, given that he lost his dear father only last year," observed Charlotte. "He went through a difficult time in the latter stages of my husband's illness and, but for a subsequent setback when his mind was troubled, I am pleased to say that Willie is now of a more robust and settled disposition. You implied, Parson Veck, that his confirmation was imminent. Can you be more precise about the date?"

"If my memory serves me well…and that I can far from guarantee… then the appointed day falls in the week preceding Whitsun. So that will be around the end of May. I regret that I can add no more without reference to the church calendar. However, I will let you know soon enough, since I am aware that you will both wish to attend." The parson proceeded to look quizzical, since he detected some unease in Charlotte's reaction. "Do I gather there is some…"

"Er…yes, Reverend Veck," interrupted the younger woman, "but I've no wish to delay your luncheon. It's just that…"

"Well, please go on. Tell me what is troubling you, Missus Reynolds," insisted the incumbent.

"To be honest, we are delighted Willie's confirmation is imminent and the date, hopefully, should not present a problem. However, the fact is, Reverend, my mother and I have decided to take our leave of Forton."

The clergyman looked perplexed. Gone was his cheerful expression, gone, in all probability, was the thought of his luncheon. As a man not normally inclined to be lost for words, he suddenly appeared to freeze. His jaw sagged, visibly, and he raised a hand to meet it, as if to tender some support. A few seconds elapsed before he spoke. "Tell me, dear lady, what has brought this about? Are you tired of the place? What has befallen you to bring you both to this decision?"

"Well, we are taking a lease on a house in Portsmouth…in Portsea, to be precise. We are due to vacate St. John's Place at the end of May and take up residence in King Street, Portsea, from the first of June," explained Charlotte.

"But why, ladies?" enquired Veck with an earnestness in his voice that suggested he was quite taken aback, quite saddened, by the announcement.

There was little to be gained in vacillation when it came to providing Parson Veck with an answer. In any event, Charlotte, buoyed by her enduring irritation, wished the clergyman to know the truth and this was apparent in her reply. "To put it bluntly, Reverend, it is simply a matter of making ends meet. It comes down to shillings and pence. Since my poor husband passed away it's been an increasing struggle and our means, though not meagre, are insufficient to maintain the upkeep of a house in St. John's Place. We have been slaves to frugality these past six months or so as funds have dwindled. By the turn of the year it became increasingly clear there was a need for some radical shift in circumstance. In consequence, we reached the decision to depart Forton, for there is nothing here, in the way of accommodation, to suit our pockets…or should I say, our purses. I suppose I could have taken Willie out of school later this year and sent him off to earn a wage, but I promised his dying father that the boy would not want for education. I promised he would get the best start in life and stay in school as long as possible."

"That in itself is commendable, Missus Reynolds. Commendable," observed the parson. "I have to say I had no idea that things were proving so difficult."

The message that Charlotte intended had surely registered in Veck's mind, but he was not prepared to doubt the corporate decision of the School Managers, to which he had been party. They had simply embraced what Charlotte's own family had been forced to do through circumstance – to cut their coat according to their cloth. And since the cloth in the school coffer had been effectively threadbare, there was simply no question of appointing an additional teacher.

The incumbent's clear-sighted view of the matter was reflected in his further remarks. "As Chairman of the School Managers, my dear Missus Reynolds, I have to say, in all sincerity, that it is a great pity we were unable to appoint you to the staff of Forton School. It is befitting to say as much, since, from what you tell me, it would have proved your family's salvation had it come to pass. But, like you, dear lady, we have no alternative but to live within our means. Si non possis quod velis, velis id quod possis. All I can promise is that the issue will be reviewed again next year and, if there is a real prospect of achieving our aim, then, rest assured, we are committed to seize it. But I suspect this is of little comfort to you now, given your expressed intentions. I have to admit I am truly sorry to hear of your impending departure, ladies. It has quite taken me aback. Now… if you will excuse me. Although your tidings have probably lessened my appetite, I must be on my way. Good day to you both."

It was thus with some sadness in his breast that the old gentleman turned upon his heels and uneasily made his way down the church path and across the intervening ground to the parsonage. His arthritis and gout continued to make increasing demands upon him, as was only too evident from his laboured gait and ungainly posture. Meanwhile, he persisted in snubbing all well-intentioned suggestions that occasionally spilled from the lips of Missus Greaves, the housekeeper, and one of the senior churchwardens – to set vanity aside and make regular use of a walking stick.

Mother and daughter had moved to the church gate where they halted awhile and watched the diminishing figure advance upon the parsonage. Charlotte felt better for having heard the preacher's words. She could not deny they were heartfelt. Importantly, they served to exorcise the self-delusional notion that she had been passed by, as if the Managers' action denoted an indifference towards her.

Opposite the church, the sounds that emanated from the schoolroom suggested the Sunday school was still well immersed in its activity. Furthermore, the hour was insufficiently advanced to warrant Charlotte and her mother remaining awhile, until William's emergence at one o'clock. Alongside the school building the musicians' four-wheeled cart had been left to await the afternoon return up-country, the two horses patiently tethered and still harnessed between the shafts. Their gentle whinnying perhaps reflected a satisfaction from being recently plied with hay and water by Clarke the gardener.

Veck, meanwhile, had reached his destination and was stooping to close the garden gate behind him. Missus Greaves was already in the front garden and proceeded to usher her employer into the house, in a manner which implied she was about to set his luncheon upon the table. For the moment, however, she was directing her attentions to victualling the musicians. She unfolded a white-linen tablecloth and spread it out upon the front lawn, the morning sunshine and warm April air having combined to drink up the heavy, limpid dew of daybreak. As she did so, those same country fellows tumbled out of the church with their bagged instruments, their exuberance only too obvious. Beyond the inherent mirth that derived from close fellowship, their high spirits were fired by the immediate prospect of filling their stomachs. In contrast, pocketing their modest earnings from the morning's music-making was the lesser consideration. Then, catching sight of the ladies by the church gate served to quickly stem the group's enthusiasm, prompting all to show good sense and trade jollity for due deference. It was to the countrymen's undoubted credit, yet their obsequious mutterings ran fast off the tongue and in such a broad Hampshire accent that their words all but fell on deaf ears.

Soon the two women turned away to tread a homeward path through the fading daffodils. No words passed between them but their silent thoughts were of a like kind. They would both miss Forton. So would Willie. He had not reacted well to being told of the planned move to Portsea. Behind them the faint murmur of distant laughter and genial prattle came drifting on the breeze. Stretched out on the parson's lawn, the men from Bishops Waltham had set about feasting themselves upon the housekeeper's fare: bread, cheese and cold mutton chops and a jug of sweet, freshly made frumenty.

★ ★ ★

Pinks and crimsons painted the western sky as twilight fell across Forton and brought a chill in the house more reminiscent of a late autumn evening. At No. 5 St. John's Place a fire was lit to warm what remained of Maundy Thursday. William took to his bed first that evening, soon to be followed by his grandmother. Before his mother retired she took time to shovel coal dust and slack across the hearth's smouldering embers. Her hope was that this scuttle dross would demonstrate some worth and keep the fire in for the night.

By eight the next morning, purveyors of freshly baked cross buns would be abroad in Forton Road with their laden trays and customary cries. Charlotte, however, had already attended to her family's needs with an afternoon visit to the village baker, selecting and purchasing seven of his best buns. On Friday morning she would look to revive the fire at an early hour. Then, once Willie and her mother had seen fit to abandon their beds – and the newly raised flames had subsided – she would turn her attention to toasting those buns upon the hot coals. Six would be sliced open, forked and brindled amid the glow, then enticingly smothered with rich butter for prompt consumption.

In its unfolding, Good Friday morning yielded to this envisaged pattern of events, leaving the breakfasted family to think about dressing for church.

"Do you remember the rhyme we used to say, Willie?" asked Grandma Black as the breakfast plates were put aside and the old lady applied a napkin to her buttery fingers. It was a rhyme the boy had always been pressed to recite at Eastertide, ever since his grandmother first chose to bounce the infant William upon her knee. With repetition came such an inculcation upon his young mind that it all but defied forgetfulness. Yet now Grandma Black wondered whether – being that much older – her grandson would deign to repeat it. Oblige, however, he did, and to the tune of his mother pouring a final cup of tea.

"Good Friday comes this month; the old woman runs
With one a penny, two a penny, 'hot cross buns'
Where virtue is, if you believe what's said
They'll not grow mouldy like the common bread."

"Well done, Willie," exclaimed both women in unison.

"Now, son, I've left you a bun on the table. Go and attach it to the hook above the bread steen and don't forget to discard last year's," said Charlotte.

"But Mother, we're going to be leaving soon. Should we bother this year? I could eat it instead."

"Don't be ridiculous, Willie. It's sure to be unlucky to abandon the old tradition. Host dough won't go mouldy in the twelvemonth, so they say, and will guard against evil. We simply have to remember to take it with us to Portsea."

William rose to his feet and gathered up the seventh bun on his way to the kitchen.

"Oh, and once you've attended to that, Willie, go and smarten yourself and put on your Sunday clothes," insisted his mother. "We must leave for church in forty minutes."

In contrast to the early sparkle that accompanied Palm Sunday's walk to church, Good Friday was slow to show its face, choosing to shy away beneath a pall of heavy mist. Stubborn to lift, it caused such a wetness upon the ground that all but the foolhardy elected to avoid a discomforting brush with grass and spent daffodils that hung thick and watery across the glebe path; and, with such avoidance, the vast majority who normally approached church from that direction arrived in their pews spared of sopping boots and petticoats.

The Reynolds family placed themselves in that majority as they, too, resolved to take a more circuitous route. Their chosen path saw them strike west along the Forton Road. In due course they were drawn southwards between dapper, weather-boarded cottages clustered about a newly gritted passageway. Here the crisp and wetted surface resounded to the crunch of churchgoing feet with such repetition as to suggest that a goodly congregation was in prospect. It was after all, Good Friday. Apart from

Christmas Day, this was the one day in the year when working men were afforded a holiday and those God-fearing folk in the parish knew the first call upon their time – on this given day of rest – was a visit to church. If commitment was inclined to falter among those who wished to remain confident about looking Parson Veck in the eye this side of Christmas, then that commitment would surely strengthen at the eleventh hour; and, in the knowledge of his implacable stance on the issue, they would forsake their beds, gather up their prayer books and be out of their homes in time for morning service. Added to which, war had been declared. For some, loved ones were being mustered and transported to the East. If loved ones were spared that call, there could be others – close acquaintances, perhaps – who were becoming entangled with it all. And with acquaintance unfolded a wish to offer up prayers.

In turning out of Forton Road, William caught a fleeting glimpse of the girl from Lees Lane. She approached, straight ahead, but absent was the handsome soldier whose arm she had taken on Palm Sunday. Gone, too, was the bright smile and her gay and carefree manner. Instead she walked with another girl…a sister, perchance…maybe a friend. William fancied that her soldier had gone away, his furlough having run its course, thus necessitating a return to barracks. Perhaps the explanation was as shallow as that, although William suspected there was more to the girl's doleful expression than the mere temporary forfeiture of her suitor. The war. Perhaps the war had summoned the soldier's regiment, condemning his love to trade joy for a heavy heart.

William put such conjecture to the back of his mind, yet sight of the soldier's girl had stirred recollections of his attendance at church the previous Sunday. He could not remember such a joyous service and the novelty of witnessing and hearing the travelling musicians. Sadly it would be the last Palm Sunday service he would attend at the Church of St. John the Evangelist.

"Mother, since we are to leave Forton I must take care of the palm cross given me by Parson Veck. It will forever be a reminder of Forton," said William, his words forged by mature and reflective thought and delivered with some conviction.

"That is a wholly laudable and sensible idea, Willie, but you'll need to keep it in a safe place. It's a fragile thing that will brook no mistreatment," advised his mother.

The way ahead now broadened to provide a more spacious approach to church, school and parsonage. Like the narrow thoroughfare which continued to siphon churchgoers between the receding timbered cottages, its surface was generously gritted. Its colour and texture had always reminded William of the Forton Barracks parade ground that would sonorously ring to the wholesome and melodic tread of leather boots at drill. He had often indulged in capricious thoughts of pulling on his old ankle-jacks and putting himself and his peers through those military routines upon the church approach. Then the real world would draw him from such whimsical notions and he would resolve to be patient and continue to harbour the ambition of eventually becoming a soldier.

Now any further thought and discussion upon the destiny of his Palm Sunday token was put aside as it occurred to William that he might hurry down to the parade ground after church. Normally, on the Sabbath, it was customary for the corps of Royal Marines – in the wake of its own morning service – to engage in drill routines, then to march out of barracks behind the Divisional Band, a formation guaranteed to cut a dash down the Forton Road. Much to William's regret, his Sunday school commitments would always prevent him from witnessing this little cameo of local pageantry but today, being Good Friday, he felt sure a similar spectacle would be in the offing. Only twice before had he found time to gawp at the serried ranks of red and white as, with impressive precision, they wheeled out of the main gate in the direction of Gosport town. On both occasions, a jaunty tune in quick four-four time had put an extra touch of zeal and crispness into the tramp of marching feet and, just perhaps, an extra flutter into the highly-held regimental flag. William recalled the emblem's splash of blue and the bright gold tassels that bobbed and dangled from the colour pike. Ahead marched the bandmaster, an incongruous sight in his black hat and plume, his red and gold trousers, and his white coat, cut long at the back.

"I very much doubt that the Marines will see fit to march out on Good Friday," opined Charlotte as she closed the front door and laid her prayer book upon the hall table. "However, Willie, I say that with no certainty and, to save you disappointment, I'm happy for you to take yourself down to the barracks. But you must return within the half hour when we'll sit down to eat."

"I suspect your mother's right, Willie," added Grandma Black as she divested herself of her outdoor garments, her voice betraying a weariness from the excursion to church. "Good Friday's not a day for pomp and pageantry, my boy."

Undiscouraged, William set forth with a promise to return within the prescribed half hour. A few minutes brisk walk brought him to within sight of West House, the Marine officers' quarters, then, almost immediately, came a glimpse of the parade ground beyond. The signs were not good. William was already conscious of there being no audible strains of military music as he hurried along the Forton Road. By the time he approached the main gate and obtained a clear prospect of the parade ground, it was to find it quiet and deserted. He might have known his mother and grandmother would be right. Yet he was convinced, in his own mind, that Good Friday was lumped with the Sabbath as occasions when the Royal Marines were put through their paces with a march through town. He was mistaken and felt frustration in being unable to counsel the immutably faced sentry for an explanation. Furthermore, to give vent to that frustration, William lashed out by kicking the parade ground's enclosing brick wall and, in consequence, incurred a badly scuffed right boot as testimony to this outburst.

As he quietly retraced his steps home, William was drawn from the introversion into which he had tumbled by the sight of a distant figure approaching from the opposite direction. It was a familiar figure, recognisable as much from its trundling, uneasy gait, as from its apparel. The Reverend Henry Aubrey Veck seemed to be toiling across rough cobbles rather than smooth, well-worn flagstones, such was his rolling manner. His shovel hat lay broad-brimmed and squat upon his head, as black as a witch's cat and as intense in its blackness as was his protruding shock of hair and whiskers contrastingly white.

For the moment William looked away. He was distracted by the hail of a school friend from across the street and, in returning his gaze, was surprised to find the parson had vanished from sight. Then he caught a glimpse of the old man making his way through the front garden of one of the houses in St. John's Place. William suspected it might be his own, although why the clergyman should choose to pay the family a call at this hour, and so soon after morning service, he found a trifle baffling.

The boy's suspicion proved to be justified as he reached his front gate. The parson had already ascended the entrance steps to number five, but had yet to lay his hand upon the brass knocker. Instead he was attempting to unfurl and ease a stiffened frame and took time to mop his creased and dampened brow with a square of linen handkerchief.

The noise of the gate's closure alerted the old gentleman, a discomforting half-turn of his body serving to satisfy his curiosity. "Why, hello, William.

From where have you suddenly appeared?" asked the parson, as he promptly recognised the boy on the path below.

"I've been down to the barracks, sir, in the hope of seeing the Royal Marines on parade. But nothing's happening."

"Well, that's because it's Good Friday. There's no more solemn a day in the Christian calendar and none more ill-suited to gaily marching to and fro," explained the clergyman. As he watched William approach the steps he couldn't help but notice the condition of his footwear. The superficial scuffing of his right boot against the boundary wall had evidently become the lesser problem to spring from the discharge of William's recent irritation, the sole having become detached below the toecap. It was a sight that got Veck thinking. He recalled Charlotte Reynolds' honesty after church the previous Sunday. Her words had come as a shock to him. She had told of the family's struggle to make ends meet, of being slaves to frugality and the fact that the reason for impending departure from Forton came down to shillings and pence. Was this a measure of the widow's problem? Was this how frugality was now manifesting itself? Many a street urchin in Gosport, or nearby Portsmouth, might be seen scampering around without a pair of boots to his name. However, from the parson's knowledge of Charlotte Reynolds and her mother, they were the kind of people who would spend their last farthing to prevent William going about with his boots in tatters.

The Reverend Veck's thoughts drifted back to the candid discussion he had had with William's uncle, before his return to sea. He recalled his uncle's concern that, without fatherly guidance, the boy's behaviour could take a wayward turn in the wake of his father's passing. He had felt at the time that James Black's fears were unfounded – and so it had proved – but he had given his word that he would keep an eye on the boy and be there to counsel him should he need a ready listener beyond the family hearth. As it transpired, there had been little cause for Veck to bring his influence to bear or to simply be available, but nevertheless, the clergyman felt a mild twinge of conscience as he observed the state of William's boots. He knew, full well, that the elusive additional teaching post would have proved the family's salvation but, equally, he remained steadfast and confident in the knowledge, that, because of the budgetary limitations, he could not have influenced the matter in the least. Nonetheless, perhaps it was simply the fact it was a decision from which he could not dissociate himself – that it had his hand upon it, so to speak – that now served to prick the man's conscience.

Without more ado, the Reverend Henry Aubrey Veck dipped his right hand into the far recesses of his frock coat pocket and extracted a clasped leather purse. He flicked open the tiny receptacle and fumbled within one of its compartments. A moment later he drew forth a coin and, as he did so, what appeared to be a keepsake accidentally fell out of the purse and spun down to land at William's feet. William, in turn, stooped to recover the little piece of blue card. A well-thumbed object, its extent ran to little more than two postage stamps laid side by side and upon it was inscribed verse 27 from Chapter 10 of St. Luke's Gospel.

And he answering, said, Thou shall love the Lord thy God with all thy heart, and with all thy soul, and with all thy strength, and with all thy mind, and thy neighbour as thyself.

Parson Veck was unaware that his diminutive token had fallen to ground and expressed surprise when William handed it to him. "Well, thank you, my boy," he exclaimed. "Now, put this in your pocket." The clergyman proceeded to hand William a bright silver shilling. "Perhaps you have a purse, William, for its safe-keeping?"

"No, sir, I have no purse...but thank you, sir," said William, his expression suggesting he was totally bewildered by the old gentleman's kindly gesture.

"Well, no matter, William, it's just that I'm a firm believer in having a purse. It helps one to be orderly. There's a little maxim I've been known to recite and it goes like this: 'may your pockets never be without a purse, nor your purse without a shilling.' Anyway, as far as this shilling is concerned it is intended for a purpose. I can't help noticing the state of your boots. One of your soles is hanging off and that won't do. Now, Missus Greaves happens to be arranging a second-hand clothing sale that will take place in the school annex next Tuesday evening. I know for a fact, William, that she has assembled a good selection of sturdy boots and shoes and that shilling will enable you to purchase a pair. Just be sure to come to the parsonage before Tuesday. Call at the tradesmen's entrance and see Missus Greaves. I'll tell her to expect you."

"Yes, sir," said William, meekly, not quite knowing how he should react to the parson's generosity and feeling a touch overpowered by his discourse. Furthermore, he found it strange that the verse from St. Luke's Gospel should fall at his feet at the very moment Parson Veck was drawn to show kindness towards him. William recognised it as the preamble to

Jesus' parable upon the good neighbour, the journeying Samaritan who showed compassion and kindness towards the man who had been set upon and abandoned by thieves; and was not Parson Veck, pondered William, demonstrating that same good Samaritan spirit by giving him money to purchase another pair of shoes?

The clergyman had now turned his attention to delivering a knock upon the door This prompted a quick response from William's mother who arrived hot-foot from the kitchen, seemingly startled and a little flustered. She had assumed the knock merely signalled her son's expected return and was more than a trifle surprised to see who accompanied him beyond the threshold.

"Good afternoon, Reverend. What brings you here so soon after church?" she enquired, simultaneously ushering William into the house.

"Good afternoon to you, Missus Reynolds. Well, put it this way. I am in the throes of fulfilling a long standing engagement. It was during church parade on the first Sunday before Lent that the Commandant invited me to lunch with him and his good lady. We settled upon Good Friday and hence I am on my way right now to his quarters in the barracks. However, it's a little while yet before they're expecting me. I therefore decided to call upon you briefly, in passing, dear lady, and present myself with a plea for your forbearance. I trust this is not inconvenient and that what I have to say will take but a few minutes. Then I'll be on my way."

"Why, yes, Reverend Veck, but…would you not care to come in?" asked Charlotte.

"No, no, Missus Reynolds. As I say, it won't take long. It's just that I saw you all in church this morning and intended to speak to you afterwards. But somehow I missed your leaving. Now, there are two matters I wish to broach with you. The first concerns William. I promised you last week I would establish the date of the boy's confirmation. Well, this is to be expected before the Bishop…here at St. John's…on the Tuesday evening in the week preceding Whitsunday. I imagine, from what you were saying of your impending move, that this should not prove a difficulty."

Charlotte looked pensive for a while as she took a moment to reflect upon the timing. "Oh, I'm so pleased," she then exclaimed. "No, that's not a problem. By my calculation we will take our leave of Forton on the Wednesday or Thursday. So, yes, by a hair's breadth, William will still be here to present himself before the Bishop. His grandmother and I will look forward to being there. Thank you."

"Good," replied the incumbent. "Now, madam, the second matter comes in the form of a request."

Charlotte regarded her visitor with attentiveness as he chose to hesitate a moment to draw breath. "And what would that be, Reverend Veck?" she asked, before the clergyman had the chance to elaborate.

"Well, I do recall you being of great assistance on a number of Easter Eves, when you kindly placed yourself among the ladies who so graciously gave of their time to decorate the church."

"Why, of course, that is always a joy…dressing the church in readiness for Easter Day," observed Charlotte. "If you require my assistance tomorrow, then you may certainly count upon it. Of course, with Easter being late this year, we have lost the daffodils," she added, reflectively. "I remember, last year, Missus Greaves placed jugs of wild daffodils in the baptistery. It was such a picture!"

"Yes, I remember," said Veck. "A copious riot of yellow. The daffodil's beauty is a veritable delight that has the power to intoxicate the mind with the joy of spring. To many, I suppose…myself included…it's the essence of Eastertide…but not this year," he added, ruefully. "But no matter, dear lady, the Good Lord is bounteous in his provision of woodland and wayside flowers and Miss Tillard has recruited some of her charges to gather baskets of them in the morning. Now, enough of my ramblings, since it behoves me, Missus Reynolds, to thank you for your willingness to assist. Your neighbour, Missus Williams, has offered to help, along with two ladies from the other end of the village. Miss Tillard tells me her pupils are under instruction to gather primroses, sweet violets and periwinkles. There were some other species she mentioned but the names escape me," said the parson, with a chuckle designed to acknowledge his forgetfulness.

"We'll need something white," said Charlotte. "Wood anemones are good and perhaps some sorrel and wild garlic if they have deigned to flower yet. Oh…and we'll require some moss and sprigs of ivy," she added, ardently, her enthusiasm beginning to burgeon.

Poor old Veck looked a shade bewildered, choosing to draw an ivory tablet and pencil from his coat pocket. Placing his spectacles astride his nose, he proceeded to ask his new recruit to repeat the names of the additional species she considered necessary to complete the floral ornament. "I shall make sure I speak to Miss Tillard later and that she talks to her gatherers before they venture forth in the morning," said the visitor, as he completed his jottings. "Perhaps you would kindly come to the parsonage at three o'clock, as the other ladies intend, and I'll accompany you to church and agree what needs doing."

"I imagine you'll want the pulpit decorated, as usual…and perhaps something to adorn the font?" prompted Charlotte.

"Yes, and I was thinking of a garland around the base of the paschal candle…oh, and maybe, this year, some prim little nosegays for the pew ends. But let's reflect further, tomorrow, dear lady. For now I'd better be on my way to see the Commandant. I bid you good day, Missus Reynolds." And with that and a courteous touch to the brim of his hat, the caller turned away and gingerly made his descent of the steps.

"A shilling! The Reverend Veck has given you a shilling! For what purpose William? I want an explanation," demanded his mother, her voice laced with anger and disbelief. Having closed the front door and begun retracing her steps towards the kitchen, it was to be confronted in the inner passage by William who was contenting himself by tossing high, and then catching, a bright silver coin. On asking her son how he came by the shilling she had been more than a little incensed by the reply.

"It was a present, Mother. I suppose the parson was in a kindly mood." William's words were very matter-of-fact.

"A present? A kindly mood? Am I to assume that Parson Veck is going round the village handing out shillings?" scoffed Charlotte. "That'll soon put pay to his benefice."

"He told me to see his housekeeper before the clothing sale on Tuesday. He said the shilling will buy me a good pair of second-hand boots."

"What!! Since when have I had to rely upon church charity to equip my son with boots?!"

The sound of her daughter's raised voice soon drew Margaret Black away from her chores. Suddenly she was there in the passageway, her colour high from busying herself in the heat of the kitchen, her forearms and apron dusted with flour. "Is everything alright, my dear?" she enquired.

"Well, it's all a bit odd, Mother. Parson Veck has given William a shilling, allegedly to buy a second-hand pair of boots. We have never had cause to accept church charity. We never have and, by Jove, we never will. I've never heard the likes of it!"

"I'm sure it wasn't church money, Mother. The parson took the shilling from his own purse," said William.

"Then that's even worse to my way of thinking," grumbled Charlotte.

"It's certainly out of character," suggested Grandma Black. "He's a parsimonious old fellow at the best of times, although, to his credit, his deeds show him to be a man with a social conscience and a much respected one at that."

"But why pick on William to give a shilling? And what's this ridiculous thing about a second-hand pair of boots? I don't need such charity and it hurts my pride to think the village parson considers I require assistance. William has a perfectly fine pair of boots in any event," said Charlotte, as she cast a glance in her son's direction and more specifically at his feet.

William felt himself blush as he became aware of his mother's prying eyes. He had not appreciated, until Parson Veck had mentioned his detached sole, that his boots had been reduced to such a parlous state. What distressed him was the realisation that this was his own doing and he saw little alternative to being less than honest, should his mother choose to interrogate him on the matter. Suddenly he knew what was coming. Incredulity was etched in his mother's features.

"I am clearly mistaken, William. I only purchased those boots for you in January. What has happened to them for goodness sake?"

William had to think quickly. "I…er…I stumbled, Mother…when I went down to the barracks. I tripped over an upstanding flagstone. I really jarred my boot against it and this happened. I'm sorry, Mother, but there was nothing I could do about it."

"Well you seem to have emerged from the experience otherwise unscathed," said Charlotte, as if to cast doubt on the boy's explanation.

"I somehow managed to steady myself and just kept my footing," replied William, somewhat more convincingly.

"You're still wearing your Sunday clothes. Best go to your room and change before we sit down to eat and before we have any more mishaps."

"I suspect I know how this all came about, Charlotte," interposed the elder woman as her grandson took his leave.

"How do you mean, Mother?" asked Charlotte, the tone of her voice suggesting she was becoming a shade more composed.

"Well put it this way. You know after church the other day you spoke to Parson Veck about our leaving Forton?"

"Yes."

"Well, my dear, you did choose to be frank about why we were moving. Perhaps you gave the parson the impression that our problems are greater than they are in actuality. Either that or, when he saw Willie in those boots, he drew much the same conclusion. He wasn't to know you were oblivious to the condition of the boy's footwear. In those circumstances you cannot condemn the man for showing a little compassion, a little kindness."

"Yes, but it is so galling, Mother, so infuriating, to think that Parson Veck might be drawn to conclude…whatever our situation…that I would permit my son to walk about the village with his feet hanging out. The fact is, it's charity, pure and simple…and I will not accept it. I would need to fall into the most dire state of wretchedness and destitution before acquiescing to anything purporting to be charity. Even then my own self-respect would surely intervene. Let any charitable distribution be restricted to the parish's poor and needy and if the parson so regards us, then I view it as an affront, an unjustified slight."

"You know, my dear, if my assessment of what transpired is close to the truth, then I can't help thinking you may be over-reacting. You know I've said it before…you and your brother, James, seem to have inherited your father's stubborn pride. Not that I am reproaching you for that, my dear…on the contrary…but there are times when pride can make you so unyielding."

"Well, I've a good mind to retract from decorating the church tomorrow. I'm not sure I wish to be in the parson's company. I think I might be inclined to say something."

"There you go, you see, and I think that would be churlish. We shall soon be taking our leave of the village. Better, in my opinion, to forget about this. Pretend it never happened or that Willie never mentioned the shilling. We don't want to be leaving Forton with any bad feeling, do we?" I somehow doubt whether Veck would necessarily mention the matter if you don't."

"He may well mention it to William if and when Missus Greaves reports there has been no sign of the boy. He'll surely want to know what's become of his shilling."

"That's true, my dear."

"Well, in that event, I will simply instruct William to tell the truth. I will ask him to inform his benefactor," said Charlotte, with a hint of sarcasm, "that I would not countenance him spending money that was not his own…that, after all is my prerogative…and that he placed the shilling in the Easter Day offertory on my instruction. If the parson has cause to quibble about that, then no doubt he will confront me. But take comfort, Mother, I cannot see that happening."

"I sense that is a good way forward, my dear," remarked Grandma Black, just as William reappeared.

"Now, Willie," said his mother, "listen here. I'm a proud person, sometimes too proud for my own good, if you listen to your Grandma. Not surprisingly, therefore, I abhor any form of charity that is placed at our door. Stand on your own two feet, I say. I do, of course, acknowledge, that I have never...but for the grace of God...been placed in the position of needing any form of kind-hearted benevolence; and, in all honesty, I am intelligent enough to realise that...if put to the test...if cast into straitened circumstances and facing the workhouse, a proud person might begin to think differently. As for our own circumstances, Willie, we are simply feeling the pinch but are actively going about resolving the situation with our intended move to Portsea. Grandma and I suspect the Reverend Veck has misjudged our situation and, in the unfounded belief that we are worse off than we are, chose to give you the shilling for another pair of shoes. Now, where is the shilling, Willie?"

"There, on the hall table, Mother."

"Right, fetch it for me please. I will look after it until Sunday. At church on Easter Day I will return it to you and you will place it in the offertory when the time comes. Next week I will pay a call on the village cobbler and see whether there is anything he can do to repair your boot. In the meantime you still have your last pair of shoes. They may be a little tight for you now, but they'll keep out the water. And it they're too uncomfortable you can always wear your old ankle-jacks which still fit."

"I somehow doubt whether the cobbler can do much with that boot," opined Grandma Black.

"In which case, Mother, we can doubtless rustle up the money to purchase Willie another pair of boots. Now, I'm feeling hungry. It is a long time since we had our hot cross buns and this unfortunate issue has already delayed us. Let us eat."

Six

WESTMORELAND COUNTY, VIRGINIA
JUNE 1854

"G'morning Mister Atzerodt," shouted the stranger as he proceeded to secure his chestnut mount to the tethering rail that stood beyond the smithy.

There came no reply from within the bowels of the forge despite the greeting being audible to the blacksmith. The caller realised this, but on no account appeared to take umbrage. On the contrary, he could see the blacksmith was engrossed in whatever preoccupied him. It was an overcast day that served to accentuate the glow of the hearth's embers, eerily silhouetting the smith's sinewy profile, as, bent to his task, he laboured amid rapt concentration. A minute passed. Then he set aside his hammer and tongs and stoked the fire. As he rose to full height, sparks flew from the ruffled embers, only to be extinguished against his thick leather apron.

Released from his concentration, Heinrich Atzerodt turned towards the wagon door that lay open to the road. "Why, it's good to see you, Mister Clough. What brings you into Montross today?" he enquired.

"I was in need of some oil and candles from the town chandler. I'd also been crabbing and had a barrel of the fresh critters for the fishmonger. It brings me in a few dollars which is always useful," came the reply.

Nathan Clough was a man in his mid-sixties, his tanned, weather-beaten features topped with a good head of hair with little hint of grey. He was a Connecticut man by birth, an oysterman by trade. His early days had been spent as a shucker in a New Haven packing house, this perhaps accounting for his gnarled and calloused hands. Out of season he would eke out a living by digging round-clam. But then the oyster industry turned its attentions to the Chesapeake, and with that southward shift came Nathan who took to

148

crewing sharpies, the Bay's oyster dredgers. Now, in his later years, Nathan Clough had built a waterside home on a brackish inlet upstream of Coles Point on the Virginia side of the Potomac. It was here that he and his wife spent a simple life, harvesting whatever fruits might be plucked from this plentiful waterland: good vegetables nurtured in their rich, alluvial backyard; crab, oyster and estuarine fish raised in the river.

"So is your horse in need of hot-shoeing?" asked the blacksmith, thinking it was most likely his farriery skills that had prompted Nathan Clough to call by the forge.

"No, my dear fellow, but now you mention it, I'm set to return three weeks today. By my reckoning the old mare could be close to requiring new shoes by then."

"In which case I'll expect to see you in three weeks," said Atzerodt, as, without further discussion on the subject, he scrawled the necessary reminder upon a large slate that listed forthcoming appointments.

"Actually, Mister Atzerodt, I've called by to ask a small favour. I was hoping you might allow me to nail this notice upon your entrance door, knowing that many folk are inclined to pass your smithy." The visitor proceeded to draw forth a rolled-up notice from his coat pocket. As he unfurled the document he was joined at the smithy door by the blacksmith, who, momentarily, and until better accustomed to the natural light, was forced to squint and strain his eyes in an effort to read the paper's content.

"A rowing boat, then. You're selling a rowing boat," declared the blacksmith.

"Yes, indeed. It's a twelve footer, surplus to my requirements. A good little boat it's been, of lap-strake construction and ideal for crabbing. Two pairs of oars and all original timbers, excepting that I had cause to replace one of the thwart planks a year or two back. I've got it hauled up in a boathouse in a far corner of my place. Whoever has it can keep it there if he so wishes and rent the boathouse on good terms. Anyway, perhaps you could pass the word around, Mister Atzerodt, and, if it's no trouble, spare me a nail and the use of a hammer to fix the notice to your door."

"Far be it from me to refuse a customer a favour," said the blacksmith, cheerfully.

"Then I've done well, I reckon, for I've got a notice here and in the chandlery. Thank you, Mister Atzerodt, I'm much obliged," beamed Clough, as, with proffered hammer and a cut nail, he secured his notice.

Then, setting the tool aside, he bade farewell, untethered and mounted his horse and was gone.

★ ★ ★

"Good evening, father. Mother tells me she's prepared my favourite stew for dinner."

"Yes, so I believe, son. I think it's an old Bohemian recipe. How's your day been Johann?"

"Not so bad, father. But with the weather having turned hot it's been uncomfortable pouring over bookwork in the absence of fresh air. It's given me a headache."

Heinrich Atzerodt chuckled. "Not so hot, I warrant you, as slaving over my hearth."

"Well, at least the forge is open to the street. And there's no reason you can't turn the bellows on yourself, father, if you're feeling the heat," joked the blacksmith's elder son. "Is George joining us for supper?"

"No, your brother's not home yet. Your mother will have to save him some."

"Is he working for Mr. Summers again?" enquired Johann, who had left home that morning before his brother had deigned to stir.

"I'm delighted to say he is, my boy. He at last seems to have knuckled down to an honest day's work. Trouble is, it's sporadic, but that suits George, of course, because he still has time enough for his wretched fishing. But old Elmer is pleased with him…says he shows both aptitude and commitment, so that's promising. I've never known it before, so long may it last," exclaimed the blacksmith.

Elmer Summers had become a close friend of Heinrich Atzerodt. An affable man, born and bred in Westmoreland County, he had spent more years at his trade than he cared to remember. He had served his apprenticeship by the time the war of 1812 had run its time and, over the years, had become a much respected country wheelwright. And, of course, the very nature of his work, cart and wagon making, often required him to call upon the blacksmith's craft, and thus Heinrich Atzerodt would be drawn to Elmer's yard to administer his skills in a variety of ways. Spring tended to be a busy time for Elmer. Farmers' carts and wagons were drawn out of barns and dusted down, only to reveal a need for prompt repair before they could be put to use. And although he had a fourth year apprentice, who by now was accomplished in his work, the recent spring season had begun to prove particularly trying for the wheelwright. For the first time in his life he had had cause to fret about his work. Customers had started to grumble about the time taken to effect repairs, since, in truth, he had overstretched himself.

Elmer had mentioned this one April morning to his friend Heinrich, as they and the apprentice toiled together over the wheelwright's tyring plate. In particular, he spoke of wishing to recruit some part time help, to see him through the spring and summer months and into quieter times. Someone, he said, who might lend a hand to cart and wagon painting, leaving him and his apprentice to concentrate upon the craft of wheelwrighting. Heinrich, being desperate to see his younger son knuckle down to regular work, instinctively volunteered George. Yet, on the way home, he wondered whether he had been too hasty. Knowing George's reputation for lacking commitment – except when it came to his beloved fishing – Heinrich began to question whether he would live to regret suggesting the boy and whether, ultimately, it might cause some souring of his relationship with old Elmer Summers. But that didn't happen. Now, at nineteen, and not before time, he suddenly began to show some responsibility, some application. Elmer was delighted with him and George, for his part, seemed to enjoy the work. There was, of course, no fancy stuff, no decorative scrolling or lettering, for that required a particular expertise. No, simple painting and varnishing was put George Atzerodt's way and he responded in a manner that far exceeded his father's expectations. Weaned initially on two of Elmer's newly built wagons, he was but a month into his new job when George was entrusted with a customer's side sprung buggy, only for its fresh lustre to promptly pass muster in the eyes of the smiling wheelwright.

"Supper's ready, my dears," said Victore Atzerodt, as she breezed into the room clutching a steaming pan of beef stew. "Please take your places." It was an invitation that need not have been tendered since, in eager anticipation, the two men were already bringing their hearty appetites to the table.

"So at what time, Mother, are you expecting George home this evening?" asked Johann, once his meal had been placed before him and his father had finished saying grace in his native tongue.

"Around eight o'clock I shouldn't wonder. It's not like George is it? Still, we shouldn't complain, eh?" chortled Victore.

"Indeed we shouldn't my dear," interjected Heinrich. "I was only saying to Johann that…er…my word…this stew is truly tasty, my dear…most nourishing. Sorry…I digress. I was about to remark that I was only saying to Johann that it's a pity the work is part time, and, of course, it'll become more so once the summer's flown."

"Yes, that's a shame because he seems to be doing so well," remarked Victore. I saw Missus Summers in the baker's shop yesterday and she says her husband is delighted with George. And last week the boy was so excited. He'd been asked to repaint old Doctor Thurston's close rockaway and by all accounts made a grand job of it, for the physician had been mighty pleased."

"Well, from what I hear, our George could have slapped on the paint with gay abandon. Old Doc Thurston's as blind as a buzzard so they say. I doubt he could distinguish his rockaway from a Cincinnati buggy, let alone notice any change in the condition of its paintwork," trumpeted Johann.

"That's not very kind, dear. Gar nicht nett. I think it wrong of you to be so flippant and so disrespectful towards an esteemed physician." Victore was swift to rebuke her elder son for what she deemed to be waspish humour, or, at the very least, humour in poor taste. As for her husband, he was not drawn to upbraid Johann, on the contrary, he found his son's words appealingly droll and, not surprisingly, therefore, chose to remain silent.

"I'm sorry, Mother. I did not intend to sound offensive," said Johann, apologetically.

"Well it doesn't behove you to speak ill or facetiously of your betters, my boy."

"Anyway, I was saying," piped up Heinrich. "Ich schon gesagt habe, Liebes. It's just a pity, knowing the work clearly appeals to George, that it's only part time. Sadly, once it tails off he'll find more time for his night fishing."

"You're probably right, Heinrich. But a part time job is surely better than none at all and, as you say, he goes to it willingly. Half a loaf is better than no bread and George will doubtless always find time for his fishing," suggested Victore.

"Quite, my dear. Then, I suppose, he'll be back to seeing more of that profligate Morrison boy, helping him to drain his bottles of cheap whisky and damaging his liver."

"I don't think there's any danger of that, father," remarked Johann, with an air of confidence about what he was saying. "I'd heard that Seth had recently gone south to work for his father's cousin. He's a cotton planter below Richmond and I'm told the Morrison boy, as you call him, has been taken on as assistant to the estate manager."

"Well, bless my soul, that's the best news I've heard in a long time," exclaimed the blacksmith. "But…mark my words…if concord and good grace prevails between master and slave today, then I fear for the poor niggers tomorrow. He's got a nasty streak in him, has that Morrison boy. He's a bully. I've seen how he treats animals and if he's placed in a position of authority on the plantation and can't learn to curb his drink, then pity the wretched negroes under his charge."

"It could otherwise be the making of the young man. He may take to it like George has taken to painting wagons and emerge as a very competent manager," suggested Victore.

"I somehow doubt that my dear," scoffed her husband. Ich halte das für äußerst unwahrscheinlich. Anyway, that is no concern of ours. What concerns us…no, delights us…is that we have hopefully seen the back of Seth Morrison. I always maintained he was a very bad influence upon George. Wirklich ein sehr schlechter Einfluß."

"These days I believe George sees more of the miller's boy when it comes to his fishing," said Johann.

"Ethan, you mean?"

"Yes, Mother. Ethan. They enjoy fishing the millpond together."

"I know. And I don't disapprove of Ethan. Do you, Heinrich? After all, he's been raised in a respectable family and always strikes me as being well-mannered."

"Quite so, my dear."

"Well, don't you think that now is perhaps the time to encourage George to pursue his fishing more seriously?" propounded Johann.

"What are you implying, my boy? It's a distraction. I'd sooner he think about making a more meaningful contribution towards society than hooking a few fish," insisted the blacksmith.

"He has begun to make a more meaningful contribution, father. That's just my point and in your presence I couldn't hope to draw upon a better metaphor than to suggest we should strike while the iron is hot. It's just that, when I called by the forge yesterday, I happened to see that Mister Clough had attached a notice of sale to the smithy door," said Johann.

"Yes, Nathan Clough came by two weeks ago. He has a rowing boat for sale. But what's the relevance of that?"

"Well, you and Mother are pleased that George has shown enthusiasm towards his work for Mister Summers but you say you are concerned it is part time and will tail off into the fall. It just seems to me that his painting and varnishing needs to be dovetailed with some other work, along with that same enthusiasm. And, the one thing to fire George's enthusiasm is his fishing."

"But Johann, that's not work, that's a mere pastime," contended his father.

"Yes, but if it is directed into something profitable, something that can earn him money when not working for the wheelwright and something that will quench his thirst for what is currently an amusement, then..."

"Sea fishing, you mean?" interrupted the blacksmith.

"Yes, father, precisely that. It struck me that Mister Clough was asking a very fair price for the rowing boat and the lower Potomac is highly regarded as a rich fishing ground. I think George would revel in the idea of possessing a boat. The bad influence that was Seth Morrison is away in the cotton fields and I suspect the miller's boy would be happy to assist George out on the water."

Johann's words made a lot of sense to his father but there remained in the blacksmith's mind a real obstacle to furtherance of his elder son's proposition. "All well and good," he proclaimed, "but however fair Clough's price, I have not got that sort of money to spend on a rowing boat for George's benefit. I was about to say 'dubious benefit' but, on reflection, I'm sure there's a good deal of truth in what you say, my boy. I'm sure George would rise to the challenge."

"Then I think I have the answer, father. Over the last three years I have managed to put a little money aside in the town bank. It is not a large sum, obviously, but it has accumulated to the point of being sufficient to cover Mister Clough's asking price. In consequence, with your concurrence and, of course, mother's agreement too, I am prepared...no, eager, father...yes, I vow that I am, indeed, eager...to purchase the boat. Clearly its acquisition would need to be dependent upon prior scrutiny of the vessel and if the purchase were to come to fruition then I would retain ownership of it. George would have exclusive use of the boat for fishing in the estuary and would need to keep it well maintained and in good condition. What do you say to that?" enquired Johann.

There followed a short pause as Heinrich and Victore sought to inwardly absorb and ponder upon their elder son's enterprise. Heinrich broke the brief silence. "Your words, my boy, embody a thoughtfulness of no mean generosity. Therein is a selflessness that touches the soul. And I am sure that were your strategy to come about then it could indeed be the making of your brother. What do you think, Victore. Was hältst du von Johanns Plan?"

"A wonderful idea. A kind and most brotherly gesture, Johann. I cannot envisage that George would not warm to the idea and show other than immense enthusiasm. He so loves his fishing. But what of the interest you would lose, my dear, in withdrawing your money from the bank?" queried Victore, a hint of anxiety upon her features.

"I can assure you, Mother, that my account draws little in the way of interest. George will find he can fish more intensively off-shore. He will need to find a market for his catch. In exchange for exclusive use of the boat we can come to an arrangement whereby I secure a proportion of George's profit. So both of us benefit; both of us have cause for satisfaction. I suspect no great effort on George's part should be sufficient to bestow me with proceeds that markedly eclipse anything the bank would have furnished me in interest."

"Then, let us talk to George about this once he's had his supper. If he is interested, and I am sure he will be, then I'll speak to Nathan Clough next week. He's bringing me his horse to hot-shoe. Of course, it all depends on whether he's had any offers for the boat already. Nobody has remarked on the notice displayed at the forge. Let's hope the same can be said for that left at the chandlery and, for that matter, let's hope Clough hasn't since agreed a sale by word of mouth. I sense it could be a long week," uttered the blacksmith, somewhat reflectively.

"What will be will be. No point worrying about it," said Victore, philosophically. "Now, who would like some freshly baked hoe-cake?"

There was a knock at the door.

"That'll be George, Mother. I'll let him in. And, yes, some hoe-cake for me," pleaded Johann. "Und für mich, mein Liebes. You know I love your hoe-cake!"

"Need I have asked," chuckled Victore. "Da brauche ich gar nicht fragen!"

★ ★ ★

In the heat of Heinrich Atzerodt's forge the lingering acrid smell of burnt hoof told of an earlier hot-shoeing as Nathan Clough dismounted his chestnut mare and led it to the smithy door. The blacksmith, hearing the approach of the whinnying horse and her master, looked up from rummaging in his farrier's box.

"Ah, Mister Clough, there you are. Good to see you," exclaimed Heinrich. "Now, before I turn my attention to your animal, there's something I wanted to ask you."

"What might that be, my dear fellow?" said the visitor.

"It's just that I'm anxious to know whether your rowing boat is still available for sale."

"Why…have you had some enquiries?"

"Not exactly, Mister Clough."

"Then, I suppose, I still crave a buyer…unless of course the chandler has anything to report. I'll wander over there in a while and see what he has to say."

"Well, unless you have cause to purchase some of his wares, I believe I can save you the trouble," beamed the blacksmith. "My elder boy, Johann, is very interested. He would like to come over and view the boat with his brother."

"Excellent. Is your son interested in fishing or does he simply enjoy splashing around in boats?"

"To be honest, Johann has not the slightest interest in boating. It's his brother, George, who loves to fish. Johann has kindly offered to purchase your boat in the hope that his brother could put it to profitable use. At present George's fishing extends to lakes and ponds, hooking the occasional perch or black crappie in the dead of night when he'd do better to have his head down. But he's supposedly good with rod and line and we feel he could make a reasonable living were he to turn to sea-fishing and take it seriously," maintained Heinrich.

"Well, who knows, your boy may well have the makings of a good waterman. There's very good fishing to be had in the river. As with any watercourse, I suppose, success depends upon becoming accustomed to the place and the ways of particular fish. But the estuary here is so rich in fish, like the Bay itself, that you've got a fine start. And you don't need to venture far offshore. My neighbour tells me there's good fishing for croaker in some of the shallows at present with some sizeable fellers taking bait of an evening. Personally, I've always enjoyed trolling for Spanish mackerel. There's plenty to be had this side of Coles Point. Mind you, if you're serious about fishing you'll need a friend to assist…unless it's placid enough to ship oars and play with rod and line."

"When it comes to fishing I think my son has a keen perception for that sort of thing…knowing just where to fish."

"Then he should do well," said Clough. "Is he excited at the prospect of taking a boat out on the river?"

"Since we broached the matter with him, a week ago, it's no exaggeration to say that he has been in raptures, so you can appreciate I've been on tenter-hooks ever since, hoping you'd not already agreed a sale. Oh, yes... George is excited alright. With a boat beneath him he'll be in his element... if you'll excuse the pun," laughed Heinrich, suddenly conscious of his choice of words.

"So when will your sons wish to look over the boat?"

"I've already asked them about that and they're wondering about next Saturday, around midday. Would that suit you, Mister Clough?"

"It surely would," confirmed the vendor, without hesitation. "I'll ask my good lady to prepare some fresh crab for your boys. Then, after they've eaten, they can take a look at the boat and, if they wish, go out for an afternoon's row to get a feel for it. If they want the boat then we can take it from there and, that being so, I'll be pleased to give your younger boy plenty of useful advice when it comes to fishing this bit of coast. Come to that, I'll teach him how to make and set crab pots. Oh, yes...and for a small monthly consideration they can retain use of the boathouse."

"That's sounds very fair," observed the blacksmith as he crouched on his haunches and resumed sifting through his farrier's box. When he stood up he was clutching a buffer, pincers and paring knife which he laid beside the anvil block. Then, in readiness to remove the waiting mare's old shoes, he took the horse by the bridle and led it to a corner already littered with hoof shavings. "Those sons of mine will be delighted to hear your boat remains unsold and will see you at the stroke of noon on Saturday next, Mister Clough. You can be sure of that."

"Good. I'll look forward to seeing them. For now, however, I'll get out of your way, Mister Atzerodt, and leave you to your work. I'll see you later."

The customer's departing words were largely lost to the blacksmith. Already bracing his bent frame against the animal, his pincers released a discarded shoe which noisily clattered and rang upon the smithy floor.

Seven

Portsea, Portsmouth
1854/55

H.M.S. Vengeance
Balchik. 16th June 1854.

My dear Sister,

No doubt you will wonder at receiving this message from me, being the first in a long while, but, believe me, it was not for want of affection. It was that I have been so boxed about the World, sometime in this part and, at another time, elsewhere, but now I find myself up to my stockings in war and that with Russia. You will see by the frontispiece what we have been doing and, strange to say, Brother James, in the Rodney, was quite near enough. But our steamers did the work, and that right cleverly, for we remained quiet spectators of the scene. We are next to attack Sebastopol which is the strongest place the Russians have. If we do it will be hot work and he'll be a lucky fellow that comes off wounded. 'Tis reported it is almost impregnable, but, if we have to do it, there's no fear but we will. The French and us number forty ships and the Turks number ninety others, so I will leave you to guess who or what Power could withstand us. In bombarding Odessa we only lost...

"Ah, Charlotte, my dear, there you are," exclaimed her mother in a shrill voice that instantly disturbed the younger woman's solitude and preoccupation.

"Oh, Mother, you quite gave me a shock," said Charlotte. An observer might have commended her for showing such composure after being startled in this abrupt manner. She remained momentarily unmoved, beyond what was demanded of voicing her reply, her back to her mother, her eyes directed towards her sibling's penned words, their clarity heightened in the light of the parlour window. Yet in reality Charlotte's inertia was but fleeting; and to her credit, in the second or two she was prepared to expend between expressing her shock and turning away from the front window, the newly arrived missive was deftly secreted about her person.

"I'm so sorry, Charlotte, to have taken you by surprise. My apologies, my dear. It was just to tell you that I'm going out…to the confectioner's shop." It was evident from her demeanour that Margaret Black had witnessed nothing irregular in the manner of her daughter's reaction.

"In Queen Street?"

"No, the one that stocks those candy twists that Willie likes…the one near the Trinity Church, in Lennox Row."

"On which evidence I surmise you are intent on treating the boy," said Charlotte.

"Well, yes," confessed her mother. "Well, actually, yes and no, my dear. You see, I am partial to their boiled sweets and thought of buying myself a quarter. Is there some little comfit or fondant I can bring you back?"

"No, Mother, dear. You know I haven't been blessed with your sweet-tooth. But thank you all the same."

"I take it, Charlotte, that you have no objection to my treating Willie?" enquired the boy's grandmother.

"No, not in the least, Mother. I was only thinking a few days ago that he is deserving of a treat. He has had a lot to contend with since the move and has shouldered it well…what with adapting to new surroundings and a new school and such like. By all means get Willie his candy twist and I'll think about treating him to something in a week or two. I had in mind a tiny booklet I recently spotted in a local bookseller's. It was published by the Religious Tract Society and contained daily texts for the young; one for each day of the year. A charming little thing…and quite apt, I thought, given that Willie is newly confirmed. Yet, on reflection, given that he has your liking for sweetmeats, Mother dear, I doubt he would favour it alongside some bonne-bouche of sorts."

"You're probably right, my dear," chuckled Grandma Black. "I'll be on my way, then," she added, as she made for the front door. "I'll see you later, Charlotte."

Charlotte was not sorry to see her mother depart. She fumbled to retrieve the letter sequestered up her left sleeve, displaying a lesser dexterity in its recovery than in its earlier confiscation. There was little more to it in content beyond the point of interruption. Dwelling briefly upon the minor losses suffered at Odessa, brother Charles asked to be remembered affectionately to family and enquiring friends and, most particularly, to his beloved mother. Charlotte turned her attention to the frontispiece which her brother mentioned, a neat lithograph showing the Anglo-French steamers bombarding Odessa. How it resembled the view from Southsea, out towards Spithead, thought Charlotte. Odessa, set against its shallow hillside, its church spire rising sentinel above the rooftops, so reminded her of Ryde. And there was a postscript, this proving to be extensive, for it comprised a melodic composition entitled *La Corvetta Polka*. Whether the composer was her own dear brother, he did not say, but Bandsman Black asked if his sister would send the tune to brother John in distant India, thinking he might wish to adapt it for his regimental band.

Charlotte returned the letter to its envelope. She would write to her soldiering brother shortly and send him the polka, but, otherwise, she made the decision not to mention the letter within the confines of 31 King Street. Not even to William. Her purpose was well-meaning and, in her own assessment, for her mother's good. Yes, she would feel a sharp tinge of guilt in not conveying Charley's expressed love and affection, and in not imparting the knowledge to her mother, that, at the time of his writing, no ill had befallen her youngest son. But if the letter were mentioned, Margaret Black would naturally expect to see it. Nothing was to be gained by her reading of a planned attack on the Russian garrison at Sebastopol in which two of her sons would be participants. And to learn of the prospect of it being hot work and of him being a lucky fellow who comes off wounded would most certainly prove the cause of unnecessary anxiety.

The family had retired to their respective beds at sunset, just as the evening gun boomed forth from its placement on the Duke of York's Battery. It had been a balmy, late July day and Charlotte Reynolds found sleep hard to achieve. In contrast, her mother slumbered contentedly, spared of her son's pronouncement upon impending danger and buoyed by the satisfaction she had derived from her grandson's delight at receiving his bag of candy twists. In her restlessness Charlotte's night thoughts began to unleash a modicum of apprehension, which, as time passed, only served to heighten. She had begun to miss Forton and her several friends there...

even Parson Veck. The cacophony of bell ringing and musket fire that customarily drifted over Portsea in the wake of the evening gun was far removed from the relative quietude of Forton village. During the day it was the constant hubbub of the Dockyard going about its business…from the porter's first muster bell until the last bell at six, when all fell silent. And here in town the seedier aspects of life were to be found in abundance, not least because this was a seafaring and garrison place where deprivation, uncertainty and the transient nature of a shifting population were spurs to profligacy and licentious behaviour. Poverty abounded and with it dirt and grime and bare-footed street urchins. Charlotte and her mother had not been entirely immune to these conditions when, in March, they had been escorted by Walter Grimes between prospective properties to rent. At the time it had been imperative to obtain suitable accommodation, and, with eyes so jaundiced by that overriding need, they were perhaps inclined to neglect such considerations. Added to which, they had seen Portsea dressed up in its finery, all of a bustle and colourfully decked out with bunting on the eve of the Baltic Fleet Review; dressed up sufficient to seduce the prospective tenants with all the acquired guile of a destitute young woman bewhored and lured into a life of harlotry in its dingy backwaters. And now the family had received its first letter from the Black Sea since the move to King Street and Charlotte had chosen to squirrel it away. That, she determined, was the right course, yet now, amid the doubt which stalked her in the dark hours – her mind emptied of the day's distractions – it was a resolve that threatened to buckle. Eventually, however, she succumbed to a shallow sleep. But it was short-lived. Before the stroke of midnight, Charlotte was roused from her half-sleep by an altercation outside the nearby *King's Arms*, a tavern which sat just across the street. The ruction was enough to prompt the casting aside of her bedclothes. She then made her way gingerly across the room towards the window drapes which seemed to hang limp and menacing in the gloom. A convenient chink between the curtaining presented Charlotte with enough scope to peer out upon the scene without further adjustment and thus avoided any cause to draw attention to her observation.

In the dim light that fell out of the taproom on to the opposite footpath, a soldier appeared to be jostled by two seamen. One of the tars was notably the worse for drink. His body rolled and swayed between gesticulations. Then his frame suddenly heaved as he proceeded to violently spew his evening's intake across the flagstones. The other two men continued to exchange gruff and accusing words. Charlotte sensed that they both strove hard to keep their feet, as if, ironically, it was not too late to preserve a mite of dignity and that perhaps, by steeling themselves, they might avoid the ignominy of the other fellow. Standing apart, a young woman, herself clearly inebriated, seemed to be slumped against the tavern wall. Her clothing dishevelled, she occasionally lurched forward to trade slurred expletives with her male counterparts. Then, amid the futility of it all, she fell silent. Suddenly Charlotte was aware of two other men upon the tavern threshold. She recognised one as the landlord, the other – a burly fellow – she believed to be one of his lodgers. The crapulent sailor, meanwhile, had ceased his retching, wiped his mouth upon his sleeve and staggered away into the night, as if he had totally forgotten what he had been arguing about.

Charlotte felt unnerved and dismayed by what she had witnessed upon the street below. The landlord and his companion, meanwhile, encountered little resistance in dispersing the remaining quarrelsome sots who went meekly into the night. As the sailor made off in pursuit of his mess-mate, the trollop and her soldier took unsteady, wavering steps in the opposite direction, the soldier having to muster sufficient strength and self-control to steady both himself and his stupefied friend. Charlotte made to return to her bed as the landlord of the *King's Arms* cast a pail of water across the footpath, so committing the sailor's vomit to the gutter. She hoped earnestly for a good night's sleep as she pulled the sheets about her, but, on earlier evidence, unwisely convinced herself that this was unlikely… and so it proved.

Charlotte's assumption, prior to the move and with March's first impression, was that King Street lay in a comparatively respectable neighbourhood, notwithstanding its proximity to the Dockyard. Unsavoury black spots of squalor, overcrowding and licentiousness lurked nearby; but Charlotte believed she was bringing William to live in a locality where outside influences were unlikely to prove too troublesome as childhood waned and he approached the cusp of his youth. And to a large extent this was true. King Street lay in the midst of the many terraced thoroughfares that huddled in the lee of the old Dockyard wall. By Portsea standards, the homes at the west end of the street, No. 31 included, were of sound enough construction, and, for that matter, were not bereft of charm, their homely red brick fronts attractively diaper-patterned with grey headers, all neatly set and mortared. And when it came to space these houses were deceptive. It was said that the previous tenant of No.31 was a clerk in the

Dockyard who numbered in his household, three sons and two daughters – one married and with a child – together with two servants. Grimes' talk of it being commodious accommodation had been no distortion of actuality but a fair enough assessment. Beneath its red-tiled mansard roof lay three bedrooms, one set high in the loft space – Charlotte's midnight-hour vantage spot – the others confined to the first floor. Below was a roomy parlour backed by a cosy dining room, a dark, narrow passage stepping down to kitchen and scullery and thence to a small back garden and outside privy. Underneath the house was a spacious cellar. This was sparsely lit by a grimy and meagre fixed light, set at street level, and showed signs of having seen better days. It was the place where the former tenant's servants had once laid their heads. Yet now, discarded as living space and what little heat might have been kindled in its tiny hearth, it had been left – at best – to the mercy of an imperceptible and insidious seepage of Portsea's groundwater and – at worst – to the ingress of more malodorous solutions. Not surprisingly, a heavy mustiness pervaded the gloom; and any glint of light off the pavement revealed the little window's lower architrave as having submitted to wet rot and with it, the incursion of street water, which, in its trickling, had stained the front wall.

There was, in summary – cellar aside – enough space in which the Reynolds family might be caused to rattle and, if the property fell short of St. John's Place, in both its appointments and its surroundings, it had nonetheless come up trumps for the family, in the pecuniary sense. Furthermore, within the short time since the new arrivals had assumed occupancy, Charlotte and her mother had busied themselves with some gusto, as they set about disposing to put their mark upon the place. And, in consequence, it probably now ranked as cosy as any home that was to be found in King Street. As for the neighbours, they had struck Charlotte, on the whole, as being a cheerful, affable lot, with a firm sense of community spirit, and, of course, strong seafaring connections. Most, quite naturally, were of local stock, but West Country accents were well represented. Many of the menfolk – shipwrights, riggers, iron moulders and the like – worked close by, in the Dockyard. Either that, or as guards or warders in the newly opened convict prison that had replaced the old floating hulks and lay three or four streets away, near the Anchor Gate. Womenfolk were in the majority in these modest streets, not especially on account of a greater longevity, but because so many were wed to sailormen; and with husbands cast far and wide about the globe many would occupy themselves as needlewomen, dressmakers or staymakers or by simply taking in laundry. Then there were the homes of old sailors who had long since swallowed the anchor and who, during their seafaring days, had brought home exotic mementoes from their travels, proudly displaying them in their street windows. William, in particular, had befriended one of these old salts who lived out his retirement just along the street, the attraction being his old and garrulous parrot. Having the bird placed upon his arm had reminded William of the time, five years before, in the house at Forton, when he had stood for a Southsea portrait painter. He told his mother that it caused him to recall the little brown velveteen jacket he wore and the artist's green parrot that sat patiently, for an hour or so, upon his left forearm. But the similarity stopped there; and when Charlotte learned, from another neighbour, that the old man's bird was possessed of a most ribald nautical vocabulary, she was swift to bring the curtain down upon that burgeoning friendship.

Since she had returned to her bed, all these thoughts and more had coursed through Charlotte's still active mind. Life had experienced a sea change, and, although Portsea was a far cry from Forton, it was a lifestyle that surpassed any she had experienced as a child. For a moment she remembered the cramped, insanitary and bug infested barrack quarters that were home beneath the heat of the Mediterranean sun. William would not be subjected to such unwholesome living conditions, yet here, in Portsea, he needed to be steered clear of venturing into the more unsavoury reaches of the town. Charlotte had spoken to a neighbour whose children had flown the nest, but who had formerly been alert to this same consideration. "Don't let the boy wander into…," and the neighbour had reeled off the names of the more notorious slum and vice ravaged courts and alleys. Squalid places they were, according to the neighbour, where some kept pigs and even more lived like pigs; where the stench of open middens, of stagnant mud and water and piles of uncollected, fetid refuse and dung, was so offensive as to encourage any vaguely discerning passer-by to take a very wide berth; where poor wretches shared a dearth of privies and some families were forced to lay their heads upon straw and rags in dank, black slum-cellars.

William was duly instructed neither to seek out nor simply chance upon these places but, in his perambulations, to stay well away, stick to the principal thoroughfares and, under no circumstances, talk to strangers. As she tossed and turned, Charlotte felt little cause to fret upon this particular issue, since, in the weeks that followed that stipulation, William had given his mother no reason to think he would defy her. Instead, the events that

164

had earlier drawn her to the window, kept looming in her mind. Seven weeks had elapsed since the family came to Portsea and this was the first occasion, in Charlotte's experience, that a rowdy disturbance had rent King Street's nocturnal tranquillity. She had noticed that the *King's Arms* and, for that matter, the *King's Head* four doors away, were both well kept, orderly premises. In the main, their custom was drawn from the working families who lived hereabouts, men who had a job of work to do, who had to be up with the lark and who usually knew when they had had enough. In contrast, it was in Queen Street and on the Common Hard that sailors' beerhouses were numerous and where simple-minded jack tars and their soldiering counterparts were snared and fleeced by scheming, shameless females; the places where such drunkenness and disorder, as Charlotte had witnessed, was sadly commonplace.

As Charlotte remained restless, deep into the small hours, it was concern over the *King's Arms* altercation that served to keep sleep at bay. Had she, after all, done wrong to bring the family to King Street or, indeed, to Portsea? She and her mother were broad-minded enough not to be troubled by Portsea life, excepting that it was always upsetting to witness the ravages of poverty, especially where children were concerned. And Portsea had more than its fair share of bare-footed street urchins and an alarmingly high rate of infant mortality. No, it was the impact upon William that worried Charlotte and she began to wish she had taken the boy out of school at Forton and found him some employment over there. At his age he could have been set to work in naval munitions, at Priddy's Hard, or in some capacity in victualling, in the Clarence Yard. That might have brought sufficient income to have tied the family over in St. John's Place, but then Charlotte dismissed the thought, remembering what she had promised her late husband. It was at this juncture that she eventually fell into the land of nod.

The following morning, Charlotte sat alone with her mother in the dining room, William having long departed for school. Mother and daughter had breakfasted late, after an early start toiling with wash tub and mangle, for this was their regular wash day and the weather had deigned to cooperate, with no little alacrity and good timing. For the moment they sat quiet – still flushed and newly tired by their exertions – as they sipped a well earned cup of strong tea. And, as they did so, it was with a firm sense of satisfaction that the two women looked out onto a modest rear garden, now largely obscured from view by white drifts of clean linen that bloused and fell in the summery breeze; sheets that in their billowy flight appeared to mock and mingle with the puffy white clouds that raced overhead.

"I'll fetch us another cup of tea, Mother," said Charlotte. "I think we need it."

"That will be lovely, dear. Thank you. By the way, Charlotte, are you feeling in low spirits today? You don't seem your usual self."

"Tired, Mother. Tired. I had a dreadful night."

"The warm weather can make it difficult to settle. I had to discard my blanket."

"Maybe that was the initial cause, Mother," opined Charlotte, in the full knowledge that it was nothing of the sort, but a disposition to doubt the decision she had reached regarding her brother's letter. "The fact is, I did get off to sleep, only to be woken by a disturbance in the street."

"Outside the *King's Arms*?"

"Oh, so you heard it too?"

"No, my dear, but when I was out in the backyard pegging out the washing I spoke to old Missus Powell, next door. She had ventured into the garden to instruct her housemaid in the matter of beating a carpet. She asked me whether we had been troubled by the disturbance but I had to profess to having no knowledge of it."

"Well, Mother, it was a most unseemly falling out, the likes of which would have not gone unnoticed on the Common Hard. Two drunken sailors, a military fellow and a vulgar, tawdry woman, equally besotted and a disgrace to her kind. It was an altogether sordid spectacle which I would never have expected to witness here in King Street. I only hope we see no repetition," remarked Charlotte, adamantly. "After that I just couldn't get back to sleep."

"Well, if it's any comfort, Missus Powell says the landlord is a respectable and neighbourly sort who has always kept a good house and usually brooks no nonsense from his regular customers. She is inclined to suggest, however, that last night's altercation is only a sign of the times," said Margaret Black, somewhat reassuringly.

"But what does she mean by that, Mother?"

"Well, as you know, my dear, since the onset of war the town has been bursting at the seams, with so many soldiers and sailors coming and going. Missus Powell's son tells her that the usual drinking establishments are so full of an evening that many of the men are looking further afield for other places to down their beer. And last night it seems some found their way into

King Street. I'm only too pleased that I slept through the consequences."

"Then let us hope, Mother, that the landlord of the *King's Arms* takes steps to avoid any repeat of such behaviour. It's not the sort of thing I'd wish Willie to see."

"Quite so, Charlotte. But don't rebuke yourself. I sense perhaps you've been having doubts lately about our moving to Portsea. It's William, isn't it? You're worried about William."

"Why, yes, Mother," admitted Charlotte, somewhat curtly. "I suppose it's a mother's prerogative to worry."

"Of course it is. But you've forbidden Willie from wandering off into unsavoury places and we've no reason to believe he has done otherwise. At the end of the day you can't shield him from the ways of the world forever. Another few years or so and I suspect he'll be gone from us and will have to cope with the deceits of the world as he and the Good Lord see fit," said the boy's grandmother, rather profoundly and with echoes of the Litany. "Anyway, enough of that. I said that linen should be dry in a twinkling. Let's see if it's time to gather it in."

★ ★ ★

The night's cleansing rain, hurried on by a stiff south westerly breeze off the sea, had ensured the day was blessed with a visibility to indulge the long-sighted eye.

"Look, Grandma…a lofty church spire, in the far distance," said William, his finger following the crest of the hill as it receded to the eastward and then fell away to the coastal plain.

"It's no good me trying to pick it out, Willie," chuckled his grandmother. "My eyesight's not what it was but I reckon from the direction you're pointing it'll be the cathedral at Chichester."

Margaret Black and her grandson had waited for the Portsdown conveyance amid the early morning turmoil of Queen Street, just as its many shopkeepers busied themselves in readiness for their day's trading. The excitement among the many children who queued with their elders was palpable. Only the sight of two companies of fusiliers had appeared to fleetingly distract them from their restlessness, as, accoutred for war, the soldiers marched by to join their awaiting troopship. The journey that followed had terminated at the *George Inn* which nestled in a fold beside the London Road where the highway spilled over the crest of Portsdown Hill. Here the passengers had alighted, as if there was not a minute to

167

spare, and set their collective gait in the direction of the many tents, colourful sideshow paraphernalia and other trappings that spilled across the neighbouring hillside.

This was the Portsdown Fair. In its hilltop location it aped many of the fairs of the South Country, downland fairs like Winchester and Weyhill, but there the similarity stopped. For they were ancient fairs and sheep fairs while Portsdown was bent on amusement and had yet to count a single decade in its annual repetition. And for that matter, unlike Portsmouth's Free Mart Fair of old – which it had latterly replaced – and those ancient downland fairs, Portsdown occupied an unrivalled and most singular vantage point that looked out over Portsea Island and beyond to the Isle of Wight.

William pondered a good while, soaking up the view and occasionally imploring his myopic grandmother to confirm that, what he perceived far below, was Portchester Castle, or the *Victory* at anchor, or Portsmouth Point, or some other landmark of note. Yet, needless to say, his requests were to no avail, his grandmother's constant retort being to the effect that she was sure he had got it right. In due course her boredom in delivering this utterance got the better of her, ahead of William allowing frustration to get the better of him. It prompted her to see about moving things on. That, and an oncoming headache, which she attributed to a touch of dehydration.

"Come, Willie, let's dawdle no longer if you've seen all you wish to see. Let's make haste to one of the refreshment tents. I don't know about you, my boy, but I'm feeling a little peckish, as well as needing something to drink," insisted Grandma Black. "Once we've eaten, you'll still have an hour or two to spend your remaining pennies before we seek out the homeward bound omnibus."

Having repaired to the nearest tent that proclaimed to purvey wholesome, cooked viands, William and his grandmother set themselves down upon some rickety seats beside an equally unsteady deal table. In truth, it was the uneven ground, rather than any lack in symmetry or quality of furniture, that was the cause of discomfort. Yet everyone complained good-heartedly about the furniture. To the company present, this was a wonderful day's outing, and, in consequence, it was a good natured, jovial crowd. Folk from Portsmouth and Fareham, on their day's excursion, sat and mingled with villagers from beyond the hill. Peripatetic entertainers, pedlars and itinerant musicians set time aside from their exertions to satisfy their hunger. All appeared intent on being convivial, the diners' good humour often spilling into a lively and friendly banter, as each came

168

and went and cleared their plates with enthusiasm: for the fare on offer was good and was despatched to the constant sound of the hurdy-gurdy man's music and the cranking of the merry-go-round just beyond the tent canvas. Grandma Black enjoyed a plate of pickled salmon, followed by fried oyster and sausage. William, being blessed with a youngster's more conservative palate, opted for a succulent and freshly roasted pork chop amid generous helpings of boiled cabbage and potato. Both meals were washed down with large glasses of a tasty cordial.

"So, Willie, you appear to have enjoyed your meal as much as I did mine," exclaimed Grandma Black, as she surrendered her knife and fork to an empty plate.

"It was good, Grandma. Now I'm ready to see more of the fair," said William, as he finished divesting his chop bone of whatever morsels of meat remained.

"Not quite yet, my lad. We'll go outside and sit awhile, otherwise you'll get indigestion. But first take this napkin. Your fingers look greasy and there's gravy on your chin."

Once outside, Margaret Black and her grandson joined a number of other fair goers who had chosen to sit and relax upon some makeshift seating, rudely fashioned from baulks of rough hewn timber.

"Well, are you pleased with your day so far?" enquired Grandma Black, as she shifted awkwardly in an effort to render herself more comfortable.

"It's a wonderful day and thank you for bringing me. I think this is our first day's outing since Parson Veck organised the parish excursion to the Great Exhibition. Then, of course, it was the four of us. It's a pity Mother couldn't come today," said William, reflectively.

"Well, your mother had other commitments and then she had to be in this afternoon to pay the rent collector. But you're right, Willie. It would have been four years ago that we set off to see Mister Paxton's glass palace. How exciting it was to ride aboard the railway train!"

"Indeed it was Grandma, but I almost preferred being perched up on the knifeboard with Father when we rode on the London omnibuses."

"That looked most dangerous to me and your mother…you two sitting precariously on the roof."

"I felt safe enough. It was great fun, if not a little uncomfortable. I think Father was giddy at first, after clambering up top."

"Talking of things being uncomfortable, I'm sure this log I'm sat upon is a good deal more uncomfortable than those parliamentary carriage seats.

They were bad enough and an enduring memory of our railway excursion to London. I think it calls for curtailment of our little relaxation, Willie." It was a remark tinged with resignation and terminated with a sigh. "Time to move on, Willie. Time to move on and see more of the fair."

"I'd like to see the organ-grinder and his monkeys...and the dancing bear...and, oh yes, I must take a turn at the coconut shy."

"What about the *Punch and Judy* show, Willie? I do so enjoy *Punch and Judy*," said Grandma Black, with excitement in her voice to rival that of her grandson.

"Yes, of course. And I'd like to visit the gingerbread stall and see a few more sideshows if we've time. And what is a freak show?" asked William, pointing to a nearby tent that gaudily advertised the attraction.

"Not something we need bother ourselves with, Willie. Full of unfortunates, no doubt, to be gawked at for a penny or two. Poor wretches with disabilities and afflictions the Good Lord never intended. There's enough sadness and wretchedness in the world to endure without that."

"There are two or three farthing peepshows over yonder I might look at."

"I think not, Willie. By the look of the queuing children they are of tender years. I see nobody such as yourself, fast approaching their thirteenth birthday!"

"Yes, you're right, you're absolutely right. Anyway, there's plenty to see."

"Yes, indeed, and we must begin to head home by mid-afternoon," insisted Grandma Black. "So let's make a start."

The early afternoon at Portsdown Fair unfolded quickly for William – and somewhat less so for his grandmother – as with frenetic enthusiasm he managed to squeeze in as many of the attractions as possible within the limited time available.

"It's five minutes past three o'clock, Willie," said the boy's grandmother, eventually. "We need to be making our way back to the inn at five and twenty minutes past the hour. There's a coach at a quarter to four and we ought to be there in good time ahead of the late afternoon rush."

The couple had gravitated to a largely open site towards the fair ground's point of exit. A large crowd mingled around the outer half of this open area where a fiddler sat high upon a large barrel. With his whiskery face raised in smile and reddened by drink, he appeared to relish his delivery of jaunty tunes for the benefit of a troupe of country dancers: young men all waistcoated and gaitered, who reeled and jigged with straw hatted girls, their headwear bedecked with flowers and braided with bright ribbons.

"Before we leave I'll take a ten minute rest watching the dancers, Willie. Now, don't wander off too far," insisted his grandmother.

"No," said William, his attention already distracted by the noise of three large pigs. High pitched squeals rose from the neighbouring piece of ground, as if to compete with the exuberant sounds of the dancers and that of the violin. William's further investigation revealed this other ground to be ringed with spile fencing, and, within its confines – to the great amusement of the many onlookers – several youths were rowdily engaged in pig-running as they strove to grasp the well-greased hogs. William was entranced by these antics, some of the spectators choosing to lay their private bets upon the ability of the black Berkshire, or the Tamworth, or the Old Spot, to prove the most evasive animal.

"Pst...pst...young'un. Hey, you there...young feller."

William's failure to respond to such utterances resulted in a firm poke in the ribs. The desired effect was achieved, since he was immediately drawn from his fascination with the pig-running. He turned abruptly, only to be confronted by a swarthy, fustian-clothed youth who towered above him.

"Would you care for your life's path to be rolled out before you, young man? You look like you could benefit from a tuppenny reading. What's that you're holding?"

"Just a fairing," said William, warily. "Won it at one of the stalls throwing hoops."

"A young gentleman like you don't want to bother wasting his money on fairings.

No, no, young sir. Better to spend it on something...constructive, as they say. Now tuppence will get you a reading that will doubtless reveal you're a young gentleman with high expectations. Have you got tuppence by chance?"

"For a reading? What do you mean?" asked William, as he struggled to conceal any hint of appearing nervous.

"Fortune telling. The ancient art of reading your palm to tell your fortune. My grandmother is the best around, the best Romany fortune-teller, so they say, throughout the length and breadth of the County. She'll read your palm lines for tuppence and look into your future. A very fair price...a very fair price, indeed. That I can assure you, young sir," said the youth, "and you can count on not being disappointed."

With his persuasive guile and patter, the young gypsy could doubtless be relied upon to solicit plenty of custom for his supposedly clairvoyant grandmother. As he spoke he pointed in the direction of his clan. The gypsies had established a pitch for themselves in the lee of their two horse-drawn carts that were gaily festooned with tin and basket ware and ribbons. Two or three young men and a girl busied themselves with the cutting, shaving and assembly of wooden pegs. And there was a tent set up beside the further placed cart. At its entrance William noticed an old woman, her features gnarled and deeply wrinkled, her skin the colour of mahogany. In front of her sat a well-attired young woman who was evidently in course of having a reading. She had removed her bonnet and William couldn't help notice how the nape of her neck rose white and elegant above the collar of her tan-coloured bodice; and how it lent support to a neatly pinned twist of golden hair. The contrast in the appearance of the two women was remarkable, the younger's fair complexion and light-coloured hair only serving to emphasise the old woman's swarthiness. The reading appeared to draw to a close, and, with its conclusion, the crone's face broke into a broad, toothless grin. William thought her facial distortion was something many would find disturbing, yet, from a distance, he also detected a kindness in the old woman's demeanour. Certainly her young customer turned away and took her leave without appearing to have suffered any disquiet. And perhaps she was buoyed by having been told of matters that heartened her.

"There you are, young man," resumed the gypsy as the pale young woman replaced her bonnet and vanished. "Hand me your tuppence, now, and you can go next."

William was sorely tempted to have his fortune told since, out of the silver florin and sixpenny piece, with which he had started the day, he still had three copper pennies jangling in his pocket. Yet he was aware his grandmother would be expecting him back very soon. He took a deep breath before he replied, then his lip appeared to quiver, for he felt intimidated by the gypsy youth. "I'd like to have my palm read and I've got the money but my grandmother will be looking for me any minute now. We've got to leave shortly so as not to miss the Portsea omnibus at a quarter to four."

"Portsea, you say? You live in Portsea? Well, before you scarper, listen here, young feller. We're not far away, encamped out on the Southsea Common, not far from where the soldiers practice and beyond the firebarn. If you ever want to learn whether you're shaping up to be a man with expectations then you can't miss our tents out there in the gorse. And if

I'm not to be found, then just say Ned told you to come. Say you spoke to me at the fair. Remember, it'll only cost you tuppence."

The youth took no issue with William's excuse of having to be on his way. William, for his part, inwardly relieved that he had not suffered any verbal abuse, or worse, at the hands of the gypsy, purchased some clothes pegs for his mother – as a kind of tacit apology for not agreeing to a reading – before taking his leave.

Once back with his grandmother, William told of his contact with Ned the gypsy.

"No need for any of that poppycock, Willie dear," was the dismissive response as they began to saunter back towards the *George Inn* to await their homeward conveyance "It's all a mite dangerous if you ask me…fortune telling and the like…best left to the heathens who peddle it. Be God fearing, my boy…be God fearing and you won't go far wrong."

William was not minded to heed his grandmother's advice. He had already set his heart upon seeking out the bender tents that nestled in the furze.

★ ★ ★

Uncles James and Charley had both returned home from the war long before William and his grandmother had spent their day at Portsdown. Uncle James' arrival, being unexpected, had taken everybody by surprise. He had presented himself at the house in King Street, much to everyone's great joy, one cold evening in January. There he had stood, on the threshold, all of a smile and wide-eyed, clutching his bag and a bottle of London particular; for he knew his mother liked nothing better than a glass of good madeira and a sailor's homecoming, after a precarious year at sea, was a worthy enough cause for celebration.

The spontaneity of the occasion, and the excitement of it all, made it a memorable one. Grandma Black appeared to cast discretion aside for once as she chose to indulge her liking for her favourite drink by downing more than a single glass full. And, as a consequence, she became what her son jokingly termed 'a little swipey', and had to retire early, before falling victim to sleep in her fireside chair. James had explained that the cause of his premature and unexpected return home was on account of the *Rodney's* Captain having been invalided and transferred to the flagship, *Britannia*, to await passage to England. As Captain Graham's steward, he, together with a man called Wilson, the Captain's cook, had been ordered to accompany the officer on his journey home. From *Britannia* they had later been discharged to the troopship *Simoom* for onward passage to Constantinople and thence to England.

"So here I am," he had declared, "looking for a warm niche to lay my weary head."

"Well, James, we are delighted to have you home. You can see the excitement's proved too much for Mother already...that and the drink," said Charlotte.

"I'm sure the drink is to blame ahead of any excitement. I think Mother's supped more than you and I put together," James had exclaimed with a hearty chuckle. "But I knew full well she'd enjoy it."

"Bless her. I suppose it's the sheer relief, as much as the surprise or the madeira, that has proved soporific. We should not underestimate the worry it brings, having two sons at war...that, and the added burden of not knowing what dangers brother John is facing. It's bad enough for me, as your sister, but for Mother...and she's not getting any younger, James."

"Well, nothing ill has befallen Charley. He was usually close by and we used to exchange messages by ship's cutter when, for some reason, one was required to ply between our vessels. I sensed he was always in good spirits, letting his music be his comfort and a soothing distraction...much like me and my poetry, I suppose. In his last message to me...in late October, it was...after we'd finished bombarding Sebastopol...Charley was talking of giving up the sea and turning his hand to becoming a publican."

William recalled that his uncle had seemed averse to talking of his recent experiences in the Crimea on that eventful January evening in Portsea. There was scant mention of 'something of a storm', that caused *Rodney* a few problems on the outward passage to Malta. But, beyond that, he seemed disinclined to speak of conflict.

"Now, we'll need to find you that place to lay your head, dear James. Had I known earlier of your intended return you could have had my room and I would have shared with Mother. But I couldn't disturb her now and..."

"Of course not, Charlotte, I wouldn't expect you to," James had replied. I'll sleep here in the chair."

"No, I won't hear of it. You can have the truckle bed you had in your room at Forton."

William recalled that his mother's mention of bed, had, at this juncture, triggered in her mind the thought that her son's continued presence had been overlooked. Normally, spared of such excitement, he would have long since retired to his own bed. And so, for a moment, Charlotte's conversation changed tack.

"Off you go to bed, now, Willie, otherwise you won't be fit for the schoolroom. Say goodnight to your uncle before you go."

"Goodnight, Uncle James. It's good to see you back."

"Goodnight, William, my boy. You've grown in stature since I saw you last and, I trust, also in wisdom and good sense. I expect to hear good reports of you from your Mother's lips."

At which point William had taken a lamp to the kitchen and, by its light, lit his candle. Returning the paraffin lamp to its rightful place in the parlour, he had dallied a moment to tender a final 'goodnight' before making his ascent of the stairs.

His mother had been gathering the empty wine glasses and William's half-consumed tumbler of lemonade. "Look," she suddenly exclaimed, "there's a measure of how your Grandma was affected by the sight of Uncle James! I don't recall having seen it before," said Charlotte, picking up the book that lay beneath her Mother's empty glass. The volume, a copy of Emily Bronte's *Wuthering Heights,* lay closed, devoid of its crocheted bookmark. "She is always so meticulous about marking her place. She'll probably blame one of us in the morning."

Charlotte's comments had caused a ripple of amusement, her son and brother expelling a restrained titter or two that had hardly subsided before she continued. "Willie, once you're upstairs please go to my room and look beneath my bed. You'll see Uncle James' truckle bed. Wheel it out, will you and leave it on the landing for your uncle to collect."

"Will you be happy with the truckle set up here before the hearth?" Charlotte had enquired of her brother.

"That'll be just fine, my dear," had been the reply. "You have to remember that I've been tossed around in a hammock for months now. I doubt I'll find the absence of roll and pitch easy to adapt to just yet. So forgive me if the comfort of a bed with fresh, sweet smelling home linen, fails to deliver me a good night's slumber."

Uncle James Black's presence at the house in Portsea had proved to be short-lived. In the few days that he came and went, William fully expected his uncle to take him aside in regard to matters he had deemed predictable: namely, to admonish him in respect of his behaviour or to ardently promote the notion of a career in the Royal Navy. Yet this expectation, much to the boy's delight, did not arise, and, in consequence, he was at least inclined to assume that his mother's report had been favourable. And so, before the month of February had truly got underway, James Black had gone to sea again, this time as Admiral's steward aboard the *Hannibal*.

A full three months and more had then elapsed before the affable Uncle Charley eventually returned from the Russian war, a letter to the family having preceded the event and acted as a most welcome harbinger. And when the homecoming occurred, one bright early evening, as spring turned to summer, William recalled how his heart leapt for joy on hearing the determined clonk, clonk, of the door-knocker and then his favourite uncle's voice in the passage. At the time he had been in the garden, sent there on the dictates of his mother. His mission had been to gather a posy of lily-of-the-valley for his grandmother; and, there and then, the sight and scent of those little white blooms became etched in William's senses as redolent of that joyous moment in the middle of May – the moment when dear Uncle Charley had crossed the threshold. And there was another floral essence, which, in time to come, would prove equally reminiscent. Earlier in the day William had detected a sweet scent drawn off the sulphurous wild wallflowers that sat high upon the Dockyard Wall. He had been standing in the school-yard and considered the fragrance remarkable in its intensity as it was borne off the crusty red-brick wall by a skittish onshore breeze.

"Well, bless my soul, Mother dear...Sister dear...wonderful to see you." Charley Black's words had been delivered with great glee and to the accompaniment of hugs and a brimming of tears on all sides. "And as for you, young man," he had begun, in culmination of William's hurried approach from the garden, "well, by Jove, you've grown into a grand fellow, Willie. I would hardly have recognised you, my boy." Uncle Charley had continued in demonstrative vein by wrapping his uniformed arms about his nephew and ruffling his hair with affection. Fleetingly, William had thought how different this was from his reunion with Uncle James who had tendered an outstretched arm to shake his nephew's hand. Instead he had found himself drowning in a loving embrace, immediate contact with his uncle's uniform imparting a musty concoction of seafaring smells – hints of cordage and canvas, of rum and the mess-deck.

"How grand and what a blessing to be back in dear old Portsmouth," boomed Charley Black once he had released the bear hug, leaving William to peel away from a grasp that, in its warmth and fleeting suffocation, had cast an erubescence upon his cheeks. And then, looking down, William had realised he was still holding his grandmother's freshly picked bunch of flowers, the tiny, tremulent blooms now bruised and crushed under the weight of Uncle Charley's embrace. Apologetically he had handed them to Grandma Black.

"You'll need to gather a further bunch, Willie," said his mother, dismissively.

"No, no," insisted Grandma Black who knew her flowers well and would often dwell upon the significance of particular species. "They may be a little damaged but thank you Willie, I'll find a vase for them. You see, in my mind it would be foolhardy to discard them because their picking has coincided with a joyous event and lily-of-the-valley has always been emblematic of the return of happiness. And you see, by coincidence, my happiness has just this moment returned…it is complete. First James, now Charley. My sons are safely home from the war and I could not be happier."

"It's a great pleasure to see you back safe and well, Uncle, after so long a time," William had said, his sincerity palpable, his feelings devoid of the ambivalence which had permeated his welcome home of Uncle James. "I hope you gave those old Russians a good hiding."

"We did our best Willie, but I fear it was not good enough. There's still hot work to be done before we tame the Russian bear. I'll tell you all about it, but that's for another time. Now, more importantly, how did you all find brother James?"

"Oh, his usual self I suppose," Charlotte had responded with a sigh. "He's not a man of many words and not one to talk glibly. In truth I always consider James the thoughtful type, rather like the poets he reveres."

"Now, now, you almost talk ill of your brother, Charlotte," Grandma Black had exclaimed, a touch of resentment in her voice.

"Well, I can assure you, Mother, no ill was intended. But in the few days he was here before joining the *Hannibal* we learnt precious little of what had befallen him this last twelve month. He was rather detached at times and seemed to be more interested in spending time in that literary society's rooms down in Bishop Street…"

"The Athenaeum," William had interjected.

"Thank you Willie…yes, the Athenaeum. Poring over the latest poetry books, no doubt. He's always been a bit of a bookworm, has James, and, to his credit, he's usually taken a keen interest in Willie's schooling. Trouble is he seems to wrestle with a contradiction. All of us, James included, want to see Willie do well at school and become a gentleman…but I sense James

would prefer him to follow in his own footsteps and those of his father…
into ship's stewarding."

"Choose the band, my lad, if you go in the Navy," Uncle Charley had
chortled. "You don't want to be at the beck and call of Captain this or
Admiral that and be minding your 'p's and 'q's all the time. Better still,
don't go to sea."

"Well, I must say, Charley, it's about time you and James settled down
and each found yourselves a good wife." Margaret Black's emphatically
delivered pronouncement had proved a shock to all and not least to her
youngest son.

"Dash my timbers, Mother, you've no sooner got me home from the
war than you propose me trading lower deck orders for those of a wife,"
Charley had spluttered, good-heartedly and amid ripples of laughter. "But,
I tell you this…you won't get our James to swallow the anchor. He's wed
to the sea is brother James, no mistaking."

"I think you're right, son…regrettably I think you're right."

"But then having broached the matter, Mother dear, and not wanting
to disappoint you entirely, I have a snippet of news for you right here and
now. In short, I am to comply forthwith with your wish that I should settle
down. Not in the sense of marriage, but more in the sense of divorce. For
I have already parted company with the sea. I am discharged to shore and
now intent on a civilian life at home."

"Well what a turn up to be sure, son. Goodness gracious." The beam
across Margaret Black's face had been a reflection of the delight and joy
that had gripped her in the wake of her son's announcement. "I'll say
this…," she had continued, "it's got to be a step in the right direction for
finding a wife."

Once the tittering had subsided, Charlotte's voice had cut a more solemn
tone. "What will you do for a living, Charley?"

"Well, Sister dear, that's something I've been considering long and
hard. And I've made my decision. I've set my mind on becoming a licensed
victualler."

"James said you had thoughts of giving up the sea and becoming a
publican."

"Did he now! Well, I don't recall that I had mentioned it."

"In your last letter by all accounts. I think he said it was after the sea
assault on Sebastopol."

"I must have forgotten, Charlotte. It was a hectic time, helping to effect repairs and assisting with Naval Brigade casualties being brought aboard from the trenches. We all had to set to and I've lost all recollection of writing to my brother. But, clearly, I must have done."

"So where do you intend engaging in licensed victualling?" Charlotte had enquired, before immediately proceeding to advance her own opinion. "You ought to go up country and find yourself a neat little village establishment with honeysuckle and roses over the doorway and a nice plot of ground to grow fresh vegetables. And we could stay over from time to time and while you dispense ale and cider to the village folk and such passing carriers and hauliers as might be in need of a quencher, Mother and I could help with the chores and ease you into the art of becoming domesticated."

"Becoming domesticated! Why, Sister, I'm quite taken aback to think… to think my own flesh and blood believes me ill-accustomed to fending for myself and keeping my own home in order. Well, well, 'pon my soul… whatever next," the home-comer had spluttered, feigning irritation beneath an impish smile.

"Well, the fact is, Charley, I could have believed it of James but…"

"But…but…and you could have believed what?…come now, Charlotte…believed what exactly?" the sailor had said, imploringly, yet with more earnest inclination to deliver a devilish wink in the direction of his nephew.

"Believed it of James had he taken up being an innkeeper. It's just that employment as a ship's steward would seem to render him better suited to a shore-based trade associated with matters of victualling."

"I can't deny you have a point, Charlotte. I'm sure my brother would keep a good cellar and would go about the work with aplomb and efficiency. But running a good tavern takes more than that and…well, don't misunderstand me…for I love my brother dearly…but I can't see him…well, creating the right atmosphere, so's to speak. To put it in a nutshell, James is a trifle too starchy, too aloof. It's been the excessive truckling to high ranking officers that I fear has dulled his spirits. Music, on the other hand, has nourished my spirits through good times and bad and I feel I have retained my inherent geniality sufficient to serve me well as a landlord. That's not to blow my own trumpet…if you'll excuse the pun, my dears!"

The retiring bandsman's last words had caused Charlotte great amusement, so much so that her laughter subsumed prior thoughts she had had of saying more on her absent sibling's behalf.

It had been at this juncture that William remembered Uncle Charley fumbling in his pocket, then extracting his hand and shouting, "Catch this, young fellow...a present for you."

The object launched towards William was a tiny drawstring bag of a coarse brown cloth, the type much used by sailors to store their dice and bone counters; excepting the little bag's content had felt heavy and boney and, in misjudging its flight, William had succeeded in jarring the middle finger of his right hand.

"Sorry Willie," had been his uncle's reaction, once he had realised his nephew had stubbed his finger. "But you seem to have as much dexterity with your catching ability as a Royal Marine has with a piece of rope in his hand."

William had chosen not to be drawn by his uncle's wit, but, loosening the leather thong that secured the bag, had proceeded, with eager anticipation, to empty its content into the palm of his left hand.

"So what do you make of that, Willie?"

William had been perplexed, his bewilderment mirrored in a grimace. "I don't know, Uncle...a blackened scrap of metal...I don't know..." His words had tailed to a murmur, as if his thought processes were stretched to the point of subjugating verbal intercourse.

"Well, it's a fragment of Russian shot, Willie...from Sebastopol. A keepsake from the war."

William's eyes had sparkled with joy, his expression of thanks profuse. "So how did you come by this fragment?"

"One of our upper deck wads...I mean gunners, Willie...one of our gunners gave it me. He'd been ashore in the naval battery. He was one of the lucky ones, for the sailors in the Naval Brigade took hell of a battering in the earthworks and suffered some heavy losses. Anyway, that's another story. I just thought you'd like the piece of shot as a memento."

"I will prize it, Uncle Charley. Thank you again. I'll put it away safely with Parson Veck's palm cross."

"Getting back to my earlier question, Charley...before you took issue with me regarding your domestic skills...where do you envisage embarking upon your new life as a landlord?"

"Right here in Portsea, of course."

"Portsea! A Portsea ale-house? Are you sure, Charley? Are you really sure?" His sister's voice had been tinged with both surprise and disapprobation.

"Sure as eggs is eggs, my dear. How else will I secure the promise of seeing you all with regularity unless I settle myself nearby? And apart from that I reckon a man would struggle to earn a pittance out in the country…I mean agricultural wages are poor and a man's first call is keeping a roof over his head and putting bread upon his table. Supping tankards of ale comes secondary, so to speak, unless one enjoys a squire's income or is bent on ruination. Besides, Mother is encouraging me to find a wife. I scarcely think I could foster notions of embarking upon matrimony and perhaps raising a family on the proceeds of running a village inn. In town, on the other hand, there will be good money to be made. When ships are paid off, poor old Jack comes tumbling ashore with sovereigns in his pocket and a thirst in his throat. And what with the war and all the comings and goings with the military and their transports…well, there's a good wage to be had locally just now for a licensed victualler with his wits about him."

From his sister's initial reaction to his plans to become a local publican, Charley Black had sensed he was about to be harangued and chastised on the subject. It had consequently been some relief to him to hear a knock at the front door.

"That should be for me my dears. It'll be a friend of mine from the *Vengeance*. A fellow musician by the name of George Cork. We messed together during the last four years and knowing you were a shade lacking in the accommodation you enjoyed in Forton, and that he had a room to spare, I prevailed upon him to take a short term lodger, which he was more than happy to do. He lives quite close, just round the corner…in Daniel Street. But since his wife hasn't seen him for nigh on eighteen months or whatever…well, I thought it right and proper that George went ahead to renew acquaintance while I came here to see you all."

Charley Black had placed a nuance upon his utterance of the words *renew acquaintance*, such as to hint of indelicacy and had simultaneously directed a mischievous smile towards his sister. This, in turn, received prompt rebuke, with the kind of feminine expression of disdain and haughtiness to infer such insinuations were better left for the lower deck and not bandied hereabouts in front of an impressionable nephew. Yet, unbeknown to Charlotte, the Portsea school-yard had already done its best to render her son amply versed in the ways of the world and sufficiently fly to grasp the subtlety upon his uncle's lips.

"Will you not stay for a bite to eat, son? We've long since had supper but I can rustle something together for you…and for your ship-mate, come to that." Grandma Black had fully expected her youngest son to linger awhile, this being his first evening ashore after so long an absence, and all in the house having been eager to hear more of the war from his own perspective. And so, as Charlotte had turned her attention to answering the knock on the door, disappointment had hung upon her mother's words. It was a disappointment William had shared, tempered by his delight over the piece of Russian shot from Sebastopol.

"Thank you, Mother, but George said he would call round once his good lady had got supper underway. So unless she's thrown him out, rather than welcomed him back, then I can only assume I'm already being summoned to his table. As his newly enlisted lodger I'd better not get off on the wrong foot. But now I'm back, I'll be seeing you frequently...starting tomorrow... and perhaps we can have an evening together shortly and I'll tell you all the ins and outs of my being afloat on the Black Sea."

And with that and the briefest exchange of introductions and niceties between his family and his newly acquired landlord, Charley Black, erstwhile bandsman aboard Her Majesty's Ship *Vengeance*, had taken his leave.

★ ★ ★

As the summer of 1855 ran its course, Charley Black was true to his word, for he became a regular caller at the house in King Street. Yet the overwhelming majority of such visits were none other than fleeting in their duration, a trait his mother and sister found sometimes irritating and, more often than not, maddening.

"We can never seem to pin your Uncle down, he's never got a moment to spare, Willie," would come the vexed call as, yet again, the visitor made his apologies leaving each and all to ponder when they might be afforded the luxury of engaging their loved-one in anything approaching a meaningful conversation.

Being a gregarious and convivial sort, Charley Black was always in a hurry to be meeting somebody or other, leaving his family to wonder how he could ever have endured the confinements of a sailing ship. If his visits were during the course of a working day, then he was invariably off to see about some temporary employment. If they came in the wake of despatching the supper his landlady had placed before him, then he was usually hurrying away to see an old shipmate, which euphemistically pointed to every intention of passing a bibulous evening – swaying the main and talking of old times as Charley would put it. Yet an exception to this galling routine – the prospect of sharing a supper together – presented itself one evening in early August. It was during the course of a summer downpour that William found himself answering a knock on the front door. Standing before him, dripping from head to toe, yet singularly unperturbed by his plight, was Uncle Charley.

"Room for a drowned rat, my lad?" boomed the visitor, his voice loud enough to rival the fulminations of the storm.

"Come on in out of that torrent son," gasped Grandma Black ahead of any reply from her flummoxed grandson; for she had followed closely in his footsteps, her curiosity whetted by the thought of who might be foolhardy enough to venture forth in such weather.

"Thank you Mother. I could do with a piece of towelling please…so that I can dry my hair before its watery content fully runs away beneath my collar." In the circumstances of his drenching, the chirpy and mellifluent sound of the newcomer's voice didn't go unnoticed.

"Then come with me to the scullery, son, and you can dry yourself down. Do I detect that you are in good spirits this evening Charley?"

"Not simply in good spirits, Mother, but soon to be purveying the likes of them!" exclaimed Charley as he followed his mother and nephew down the passage. Reaching their destination, Margaret Black handed her son a towel, then proceeded to watch him dry his hair. She observed him quizzically. "You know son, you do talk in riddles at times," she said, eventually catching his eye beneath the loftily propelled towel and his tousled locks. "I'm none the wiser as to why you are in good heart."

"Well, Mother, it has been a good day. The best since I returned to England. For I can report that the retiring landlord of the *Sheer Hulk* tavern has today successfully applied for a transfer of his license to one Mister Charles Black, currently resident in Daniel Street, Portsea! So you see, that is what I meant by purveying spirits."

"What wonderful news, son. So when do you replace the incumbent landlord?" said Margaret Black as she struggled to locate the hostelry in her mind's eye.

"On the first of September…which brings me to ask a favour of you and Charlotte, Mother. By the way, where is Charlotte?"

"She's taken to her bed, son. Thunder and lightning permitting, she is hopefully fast asleep."

"She's ill then?"

"No, son, not exactly. She spent the afternoon cross-stitching while I sat and darned. Well, I dozed off and must have slept for close on an hour and a half. When I woke, Charlotte was still toiling with her embroidery silks and she shortly began to complain of a headache. Perhaps it was too long straining her eyes with the intricacy of it all, perhaps it was the onset of this oppressive weather. Anyway, the headache became quite severe and she decided it wise to repair to her bed."

"I see. Do say I called by and that I wished her well. What I wanted to ask you both was whether I might prevail upon you to stay a few days... well, for a week to be precise...immediately before I embark upon my new venture."

"Of course you can, Charley."

"Are you sure Charlotte won't mind, Mother?"

"Not in the least, I can assure you. And you won't have any objection, will you, Willie?" exclaimed the boy's grandmother, knowing full well that he would be overjoyed at the prospect of having his dear Uncle Charley under the same roof. William said nothing, as it transpired, his beaming face surpassing the power of words to fully convey the strength of his assent.

"You can probably have my room, Charley, and I'll share with your sister. When James came home he had the truckle bed in the parlour, but his arrival was unannounced and it was only for a few days. If you're here for a week it wouldn't be very satisfactory to do the same."

"Thank you, Mother, if that's not too much trouble. The problem is that George is off to sea again and, although he's not said as much, I don't see that it would be right and proper to remain lodging in Daniel Street with only his wife in the house."

"Quite so, son. To do otherwise would be...well, it would appear most inappropriate and lacking in prudence. Besides, people are inclined to gossip and indulge in idle talk. It is wise to err on the side of discretion, so, yes...you must stay the week here," said Margaret Black. The final clause was delivered with an emphasis that left the recipient in no doubt that his mother's advice had turned to instruction. "So where is this public house you talk of...the *Sheer Hulk*? I can't place it."

"It's lies on The Hard, Mother. Just beyond Clock Street, but this side of the *Nag's Head*."

"Is that near the Royal Albert Pier, Uncle?" enquired William.

"More or less opposite the pier entrance my boy."

"Then I believe I can picture it."

At first Charley's mother remained silent. She had hoped her son might have found a public house in a quiet residential backstreet, or in one of the better parts of Portsea. It was not that she had personal cause to be concerned but knew full well that it would give her daughter reason to gripe. Charlotte had already reacted with disdain to the notion of her brother running a Portsea establishment and Grandma Black recollected how she had been appalled by the altercation at the *King's Arms*, castigating the participants and likening it to something that might have only gone unnoticed on The Common Hard. For her part, however, Margaret Black had every confidence her son would make a success of his new-found business venture, would preside over orderly premises and brook no nonsense, least of all, encourage, any overt acts of impropriety. And so, buoyed by such optimism, her voice struck a cheery tone when eventually it came to breaking that silence.

"Well, congratulations, son," she proclaimed, "we have every reason to rejoice in your good fortune. Now, you may or may not have overlooked the fact that, in barely a week's time, young Willie here is due to celebrate his thirteenth birthday. Might I suggest that you come here for supper, Charley…we'll do something special…in recognition of your own success and Willie's birthday. A double cause for celebration, no less. And, come to that, we never did have a special supper to mark your safe homecoming."

"Yes, and you never told me how you got on fighting those Russians, Uncle, and you've been home nearly three months now," added William, imploringly.

"Quite so my boy…most remiss of me. In consequence I fear I have little choice but to accept your grandmother's kind invitation. I'm prepared to overlook many things, but I'll not miss celebrating your birthday, Willie." Charley Black paused and looked pensive, as if to conjure an afterthought. Then, with a mischievous twinkle in his eye and an impudent glance in his mother's direction, he resumed with teasing intent. "So when is your birthday, Willie?…I didn't think it was yet awhile."

"The fifteenth. Next Wednesday," insisted William, his feelings clearly nettled by his uncle's apparent forgetfulness. Then eyes met and, with their engagement, Uncle Charley's pretence fell away and laughter filled the house.

★ ★ ★

In William Reynolds' assessment, attaining the age of thirteen was no bar to the possession of lead soldiers. In consequence, when asked by his mother and grandmother what he might cherish as a birthday gift, he had shown little hesitation in requesting a box of toy soldiers. It was to be a box of red-coated infantryman. Then came a change of heart as he decided upon the kilted variety, recalling the Highland regiments which had featured prominently and with distinction during the previous autumn's conflicts. He remembered reading avidly about the exploits of the Highland Brigade, usually in past copies of the *London Illustrated News*, kindly supplied by Mister and Missus Barnes, who were still resident at Forton. As regular subscribers to the publication they had got into the habit of passing on their discarded copies by way of that other former neighbour, Missus Williams, when she had occasion to visit her sister in Portsea. And once a batch of old copies found their way to King Street, William would be first to seize upon them, keenly scrutinising the woodcut depictions of the latest battle scenes and repeatedly poring over the accompanying letterpress accounts.

In the several days prior to his birthday, seemingly confident that his Scottish soldiers would materialise, William spent time fashioning a wired framework to which he applied layers of glued newspaper. His purpose was to create a papier mache representation of a section of ground upon one of the Crimean battlefields. At first it was to be on the Plain of Balaclava. In the end, since his inclination was to sculpture a section of rather dramatic terrain, he opted for the Alma Heights and, on the eve of his birthday, William's craggy little model was ready for painting. By the following morning it was ready to receive his promised scarlet-coated and kilted soldiery.

In the early evening of the fifteenth, at six o'clock precisely, Uncle Charley arrived in brisk and convivial mood. With the two ladies preoccupied in the kitchen, preparing supper, William was swift to respond to his uncle's knock. But in truth it was not so much an eagerness to greet the awaited guest; it was more the case of being excited by the prospect of Uncle Charley arriving with a birthday gift.

"Hearty congratulations, young fellow! Happy birthday to you," bellowed the visitor whose appearance bore little resemblance to the drenched apparition that had stood upon the threshold scarcely a week before. In sharp contrast, dry, and in no sense dishevelled, it was evident to his nephew that Charley Black had taken trouble with his attire. He wore a brown frock jacket, smart in its cut – if a little dated – and fawn, well-tailored trousers and waistcoat. His neck-tie was the colour of his jacket and his elastic-sided boots shone with a brilliance that told of dedicated polishing. In one hand

Uncle Charley carried his tall hat. In the other he held two brown-paper parcels, one neatly adorned with blue ribbon.

Divesting his uncle of his hat and, indeed, his jacket – since it was a warm evening – William proceeded to usher him into the parlour.

"Well, my lad, what's this I see?" asked the visitor, with enthusiasm, having spotted the product of his nephew's labours upon an occasional table by the window.

"It's a model I've made," said the boy, proudly. "The lead soldiers were a present from Mother and Grandma. It's a scene I've created from a real battle. I only finished it an hour ago."

"So which battle Willie?"

"Well, it was to be part of the Ninety Third's line at Balaclava as the Highlanders prepared to repel the Russian cavalry."

"Ah, yes, Sir Colin Campbell's men. What a brave stand that was. Death seemed inevitable to them all but they resolutely held their ground and saw off the enemy. I hear they've come to call it the thin red line after what the *Times* correspondent had to report."

"Well, I then changed my mind. I wanted to make the model more interesting…to give it more height. I thought of the account I'd read about the part played by the Highland Brigade at the Alma. So what I've shown is a bit of the Royal Highlanders' charge up towards the Russian guns."

"Bravo, Willie. Yes, the Ninety Sec…no, no, that's the Gordons. It's the Forty Second, if I'm not mistaken…the old Black Watch, my boy. Well it looks grand…a proper spectacle if I may say so. Not just red tunics, but kilts and bearskin caps and all. Quite a sight! Do you know, Willie, I remember we were anchored off the Alma last September. You could actually see the Russian army on the Heights and our upper yardmen got a good view of the battle from the mastheads." It was a nonchalant remark that awed William to the point of causing his lower jaw to sag open.

"Hello Charley." It was a greeting simultaneously delivered by mother and daughter that broke the abstracted discourse between uncle and nephew. Still clutching their discarded aprons and with the bulk of their preparations complete, they had seized the opportunity to leave simmering pans to look after themselves.

"Good evening to you both. I was just admiring the product of Willie's artistry and inventiveness. For the moment we were lost on the Heights of Alma. Now…Mother, Charlotte…a little gift for you, as a reflection of my appreciation for being invited to supper," said Charley, as he handed his mother the blue-ribboned parcel. "As for you, Willie, here's a birthday present I hope you will find interesting." In adding these words, Uncle Charley proceeded to release the second brown-paper parcel into his nephew's hand.

"Thank you, Charley," exclaimed Grandma Black, her thanks being immediately reiterated by Charlotte who had already turned her attentions to untying the ribbons. "I assume this is not the product of your own endeavours, son," she chuckled, eyeing the rich decorative ties that quickly fell away beneath her daughter's relatively nimble fingers.

"No Mother. Not my forte. That was down to the shopkeeper's assistant."

"Thank you, Uncle," cried William as he finished unwrapping his own parcel and extracted a book, full bound in red leather, its cover neatly tooled and impressed with gold decoration. It was a book with a good feel about it. Its title page carried the words *Uncle Tom's Cabin...or Life Among the Lowly* by Harriet Beecher Stowe and Uncle Charley had added his own words on the fly leaf...*To William Reynolds. Given to him with affection, as a memento of his thirteenth birthday, by his uncle, Charles Black. 15th August 1855.*

Having removed the ribbons on their own package, the two ladies had made little progress in divesting the content of its wrapping. Instead they allowed themselves to be distracted by the emergence of the birthday present.

"I've heard people speak highly of Missus Stowe's book," remarked Charlotte. "Apparently it's a wonderful story with a message that ridicules slavery in the United States and the book has proved very popular over here. Don't you remember, Mother, that not so long after its publication, the Women of Great Britain and Ireland despatched an address to their counterparts in the United States on the subject of slavery?" I think it involved some half-a-million signatures."

"Yes, I do recall that, Charlotte," said her mother. "I think it a good choice of present, Charley. From what I hear it's a story which takes a strong moral stance against the injustice of slavery."

"To be honest, Mother, that was not in my mind when I purchased the book. I just understood it to be a good yarn. Given the prejudice that seems to prevail against women writers, it says much for the quality of the story that Missus Stowe's book has sold so well."

"Absolutely, son. Anyway, that's humbug, all that irrational preference for male writers. Have people not heard of the Misses Bronte or read Missus Gaskell's *Cranford*? I must confess I applaud Missus Stowe for breaking through such bigotry. I only hope she can similarly succeed with her message and prove a beacon of hope for the downtrodden American negro." Grandma Black paused to regain her composure that was on the cusp of becoming a trifle ruffled. The matter of bias against women writers was one upon which she held firm views and, in the face of its advocacy, was inclined to take it in bad part; and this was never the time, place or company in which to hold forth and defend her own stance to any purpose. "I think I must make a point of reading Missus Stowe's tale myself sometime soon," she concluded, calmly.

Charlotte had resumed her unwrapping while her mother was having her say, revealing a box of fine candied fruits, figs and almonds impressed with the name of Queen Street's leading confectioner. It was thus in the wake of copious expressions of thanks for the same that the two ladies left to resume their culinary endeavours.

"Thank you again for the book, Uncle, said William, the two finding themselves alone once more. "I'll look forward to reading it...except...well, to be honest, I thought slavery had been done away with...I remember a lesson at school...we were told about eman..."

"Emancipation."

"That's right, Uncle."

"Well, that was in the British Empire, my boy, and down to the efforts of Mister Wilberforce and others. Slavery was outlawed here in the early years of the century and then ultimately abolished...and that would have been over twenty years ago. But, you see, it is still prevalent and widespread in the American South...in the so-called Slave States. Indeed, slave labour is the mainstay of all those cotton plantations which supply the Lancashire mills."

When Charlotte and her mother reappeared, it was to announce the imminence of the evening meal, there being sufficient time to partake of a pre-prandial sherry and, in William's case, a glass of ginger-beer. Uncle Charley raised his glass to toast his nephew's birthday, while Grandma Black added a few words which included wishing her son all good fortune as he prepared to embark upon his new venture. Several days earlier she had acquainted her daughter with Charley's news, including the pivotal fact that he was intent on exercising his newly acquired license along The Common Hard. Her reaction had been surprisingly muted, so much so that her mother wondered whether it was the product of a conscious attempt to hide her true feelings. Now, as glasses were raised a second time, to the accompaniment of Grandma Black's toast, Charlotte's silence was palpable.

In her mother's perception it was if her daughter was in denial of her own brother achieving his aspirations. This was sad; for Margaret Black saw it differently. Far sooner her son be running a local beerhouse than continuing to be at the mercy of his recent life at sea with its many perils, not least the dreaded cholera and such other afflictions and, of course, the Russian guns.

Once the sherry and ginger-beer had been despatched, Charley and William were invited to repair to the dining room and to take their seats at table; and there, as soon as all were gathered together, Uncle Charley recited an unfamiliar little prayer that served as grace and which – according to its deliverer – was something of a favourite among the more reverentially-minded sailors who messed between the guns. Out in the passage the hall clock chimed the half-hour. It was six-thirty, an hour beyond the customary time when, as a threesome, the family would sit down to eat. Yet this was a special supper where preparations had been more exacting, the extra hour, in a sense, merely setting it apart from routine, but additionally ensuring that whatever needed to be done could be executed without undue haste.

An entrée of shrimps, accompanied by thinly-sliced bread and butter was followed by boiled brisket of beef stuffed with Poole oysters, parsley and bacon and served with vegetables, boiled potatoes and piping hot gravy.

"My taste buds have not been feted by such delectableness in ages, Mother and Sister, dears," sighed Uncle Charley, as, contentedly, he surrendered his cutlery to an empty plate. "A most succulent and well-seasoned piece of beef if I might say so. What do you say, Willie?"

"I agree, Uncle. I enjoyed it immensely but I've left some of my vegetables so there's space for dessert."

"You and your sweet tooth, Willie. What if I said we've no dessert, on account of deciding we'd cooked more than enough meat and vegetables to fill you to overflowing ?" said Charlotte, in jest.

"I wouldn't believe you, Mother."

"No, I don't suppose you would, my lad. Just as well it's your birthday, otherwise I'd insist you cleared your plate, seeing you've still room for dessert. There are enough starving folk in this world, you know."

"Well, perhaps we could bide our time before I bring dessert to the table," suggested Grandma Black. "Better for the digestion if we pause awhile. We'll then feel better able to cope with it. What do you think, Charley?"

"Capital idea, Mother. I'm not the trencherman I was, I must confess… not after so long on the *Vengeance*. The opportunities, during the conflict, to take on board fresh meat and vegetables of any quality, were limited to say the least. I think your stomach shrinks in such circumstances, having to survive on meagre rations…dried goods, salt meat, hardtack and the like. So I think a break would be beneficial and prevent me from having to call upon the bicarbonate of soda before I turn in."

"Then why don't you two guests of honour return to the parlour while we attend to the dishes?"

"Sounds a good idea, Grandma. Perhaps Uncle Charley can occupy the time telling me about the Russian war," insisted William.

"Well I'm sure, like me, Willie, your grandmother doesn't want to hear about all that distress and suffering," interjected the boy's mother. Then, turning to her brother, she added, "It's more important to us, Charley, that you're safely returned from the Crimea. Far be it from us to want to dwell upon it." They were words that came reassuringly to Margaret Black. Hitherto she had viewed her daughter's reluctance to embrace Charley's new venture as being tantamount to wishing her sibling back in the theatre of war.

"It was good to receive your letters from the war Uncle Charley," said William, once they had retired to the parlour.

"You couldn't have received many, my boy. I was never a great letter writer. But I reckoned on your Uncle James writing home as well, so between us you had a bit of news."

"Mother did hide one until after Sebastopol. It had a fine frontispiece showing the steamers bombarding Odessa and you'd included a piece of music. She showed it to us once your next letter had arrived in November… one I think you wrote on the anniversary of Trafalgar. Anyway, it was after the bombardment, so we knew you were safe."

"So what was all that about, Willie…your mother hiding a letter?" enquired a baffled Uncle Charley.

"You wrote about the plan to attack Sebastopol, that it was such a strong fortification and he would be a lucky man to come away wounded. Mother didn't like to worry Grandma, so she decided not to show us the letter until the assault was over and we had heard you were safe."

"That, I must say, was very thoughtful of your mother, Willie, but I regret it says little for my tact. On reflection, it was wrong of me to spread alarm. I should not have mentioned Sebastopol."

"Maybe not, Uncle, but you can tell me now," said William, earnestly.

"Very well, Willie. Now then…as far as I can remember we were anchored in Balchik Bay when I wrote the letter your mother confiscated.

We had yet to go to the Crimea. In between putting to sea last summer we spent quite a bit of time in Balchik Bay. You see, it was off the Bulgarian coast, close to Varna, where the British Army …and, for that matter, the French…had rested, as they awaited embarkation for the Crimea. By late August there was a massive flotilla assembled there…not just the British and French warships but the many transports and steamers. Well, the regiments had suffered dreadfully throughout the summer months. Cholera you see. Deadly business. Thousands dead before the poor souls saw any action. And the French and Turks suffered worse than us. Trouble is…when the soldiers embarked, early in September, they brought the cholera to the fleet and it was really rife in the crowded transports. Our flagship, *Britannia*, lost a lot of her crew. Few of the ships escaped. Poor fellows could be in robust condition one minute, only to die a wretched death several hours later. No exaggeration, Willie, but lying in your hammock at night you could hear the plop and splash of corpses being cast into the Bay and if some were not properly weighted you'd see them floating around you during the day. A ghastly business it was. Right turned my stomach. You'd see this bloated cadaver…body, Willie…this bloated body…and you'd think to yourself that was someone's husband, someone's father, someone's son. And you always wondered whether it would be your turn next."

William listened intently, his expression immutable, his attention gripped, almost mesmerized, by his uncle's every word.

"I'm not so sure, young Willie, that your mother would be too pleased with me being so candid about all this, even though you're now thirteen," pondered Uncle Charley. Yet in the absence of any confirmation or denial upon the lips of his rapt nephew, he was quickly dismissive of his expressed misgivings and continued his discourse. "Anyway, we were pleased to get away from Balchik once all the troops had been taken off. I remember we weighed anchor in the eerie light of dawn. The seventh of September it was, lovely morning and a sight to behold…believe me, Willie, there were literally hundreds of ships. They were all lined up, as far as the eye could see, just like a grand review at Spithead with the steamers towing out the sailing ships…and all the while we in the band were on the upper deck playing our hearts out…plenty of stirring old tunes to buoy up the ship's crew as we got under way. Most of the sailing ships seemed to have their bands a'playing, while, naturally enough, the transports called on the regimental bands. There was a right old dawn chorus drifting over Balchik Bay that morning, I can tell you!"

The irritating buzz and tap of a bluebottle, as it flirted with a discarded sherry glass and then the parlour mirror, was sufficient to distract William, drawing him from his mused listening; and, with the break in concentration, came an accompanying proclivity to start asking questions.

"So where were you heading, Uncle?"

"We were now, at long last, on our way to the Crimea. Not Sebastopol, but a piece of coastline further north. Near a place known as Eupatoria. Calamita Bay it was called…a desolate stretch of sand and shingle beach backed by low cliffs."

"Were the Ruskies nearby, then…the Russian Army?"

"No, no, lad. We saw a few Cossacks in the distance…but, no, it was just a suitable spot to get the troops landed. From there they could advance on Sebastopol, poor devils."

"Why poor devils?"

"Well, there was sickness enough on the sailing ships but things generally improved for us once we had put to sea. But those poor soldiers…many were in a wretched condition. It didn't help, I suppose, being crammed aboard some of the smaller troopships for days on end. Well, we worked hard in the gigs and cutters, disembarking and towing the men in from the steamers and transports. But you know, some of those fellows could hardly manage on the rope ladders, what with all their stiff uniform and heavy, cumbersome equipment. Many were racked with pain and weakness. Some could hardly stand up, getting in the boats. You had to feel sorry for them, Willie. They actually adapted one of the vessels offshore as a hospital ship and brought back some of the soldiers who had collapsed once they'd been landed. But some of them just died on the beach and had to be buried there. And then it came on to rain in the after…"

"Was it the cholera then, Uncle?" interrupted William.

"Mostly. But there was all manner of ailment in the regiments…cholera, scurvy, colic, diarrhoea…but cholera was the main killer. And it was so quick. A poor fellow could be hale and hearty at breakfast only to be suddenly gripped with the agonies of cholera…then he would choke on his own vomit and be dead before he was due his midday rations. Wretched business, Willie…wretched. It was bad enough for us in the Fleet, but based on my own impressions of the campaign and from things I heard …well, it opened my eyes to what it was like to be a soldier."

"What do you mean…what it was like?"

"Well, son, I know you've got it in your mind…this romantic notion, as it were…to be a soldier. But it's not just colour and pageantry you know, not just those smart shakos and puffed out chests beneath scarlet coats, the likes of which you'd see on the Forton parade ground or marching down Queen Street to the Dockyard Gate. Oh, no, my boy, I've seen the common soldier at first hand, in the thick of fighting for Queen and Country. Treated little better than dogs they were. Thousands, they say, died at Varna and then, of course, on the transports, before they ever got close to any conflict…and they were so ill-equipped when it came to having the right clothing and stores and victuals and all…poor fellows. Nobody had given a thought to the climate, which could be intolerably hot during the day…much as we've had here lately…yet bitterly cold at night. At least with us, the day's heat would be tempered out at sea. Anyway, I was about to say, that having got the infantry and artillery ashore that first day, we had to delay landing the cavalry because the rain came and that night it fell in torrents. The poor soldiers ashore had no tents, would you believe, and got drenched to the skin. And by morning there were more deaths and interments. The bluejackets would get the cavalry and horses on to the beach, only to return to the transports towing men with whom they'd exchanged friendly banter the day before. Except then they had been helping them out of the boats and onto the shingle. Now some of those same fellows were slumped in the returning tenders…having succumbed to the cholera scourge or some other affliction overnight…as they were towed back from whence they'd come. Such a bad business, Willie…they might have preferred the bullet or the bayonet, such was the suffering of some of those men." Uncle Charley chose to pause a moment, being now quite animated, in his ongoing observations and narration of events. "Tell me if I'm boring you," he continued, "but what I do vividly recall is the morning when the Allied Armies began their advance on Sebastopol."

William had fallen quiet again, being clearly saddened and troubled by his uncle's testimony upon the dire and perilous lot of the British soldier he had accompanied to the Crimea. Yet he had waited long to hear of his uncle's experiences and, in that knowledge, Charley Black was not deflected by his nephew's silence.

"It was a glorious morning, Willie. The azure sky was cloudless and the sea, well…it looked as calm as Forton Millpond, excepting it was a comely shade of blue. I remember that long before dawn, many of us had been woken by the sounding of reveille on shore, the clarion call resounding eerily across the water in the clear air. Yet it was nine in the forenoon, after the soldiers had dug and filled the last graves, before the military got under way and we heard their bands strike up. A good many of us crowded about the port gunwale to take a look. Somebody said the French and us numbered sixty thousand men. Well, they all marched off in two double columns and what a spectacle it was to be sure. The French took a line on the right, closer to the shore and were thus well protected by us and the sea. The British troops were on their left, led, so it was said, by Lord Cardigan with regiments of Hussars and Light Dragoons. In the bright sunshine it was a grand sight, Willie. All those things you like about finely attired soldiery. Regimental colours and guidons fluttering and streaming away on high, the glint and sparkle of burnished metal in the sunlight... bayonets, lances, polished breastplates and brass-studded headgear...and all manner of fine red, blue and green tunics, plumes and shakos and black bearskins and blazing splashes of white. Well, it was a sight to raise the hairs on the back of your neck and to plant a lump in your throat and we gave three cheers because of it and we heard other ships' crews do likewise. But I suspect they were oblivious to that, Willie, for the regimental bands made a rousing sound, playing the old marching tunes, and you could hear the soldiers singing along with it, no doubt pleased to get going. Yet I don't expect that early cheerfulness lasted too long because so many of those fellows were racked with weakness and suffering and, according to the bluejackets in the landing parties, thirst had become a real problem owing to a lack of fresh water. It must have been a parched hell for many in the heat of that march towards the Alma."

Uncle Charley broke off from his discourse as he inwardly dwelt upon the very thought of those ailing souls, weak, heavily accoutred and craving water. William, for his part, looked thoughtful and a trifle sullen, for his uncle had doubtless given him cause to think upon the lot of the regular soldier in times of conflict.

"Speaking of thirst, Willie, it's a warm evening and right now I could do justice to a glass of that ginger-beer you were swigging before supper," remarked Charley Black. As he spoke he loosened his neck-tie and collar, then nimbly whisked a handkerchief from his trouser pocket. William, meanwhile, rose to his feet and quietly departed with his thoughts. Uncle Charley sighed and dabbed at the moistness that clung to his brow. It was not easy, talking about such events, for they stirred memories of the suffering and futility of what he had witnessed. He had seen death at first hand. Not the bloody gore of the battlefield but the pitiful agonies of those beset with cholera and dysentery in the last throes of life; and then, in the immediate wake of those death throes, there were the poor wretches reduced to rotting, fish-nibbled, bloated corpses that would suddenly bob out of the water in Balchik Bay because they hadn't been weighted sufficiently. They would appear upright, as if wanting to say a last farewell…yet, it never was, because they would constantly revisit him in his dreams…his nightmares…and he would wake, his nightshirt clammy from the ordeal. Sometimes, over breakfast, and before they became used to it, George Cork and his wife would recall him crying out at night. And although all that had stopped, after a month or so back in Portsmouth, Charley was loath to dwell too much upon his experiences, for fear of resurrecting those Crimean nightmares. Suddenly he wondered about the wisdom of going over it again…but it couldn't be helped…he could not deny his nephew knowledge of his encounters. He could not refrain from imparting information for which the boy had hankered these past three months. Now, however, he was mentally stronger and was on the cusp of a challenging new life; and, unbeknown to Charley Black, it was upon his nephew, that this fresh recitation of events was destined to have a profound, hapless and lasting impact. In contrast, and given his own, improved disposition, it would now fall short of triggering the stimuli to re-visit and taunt an unconscious, slumbering mind.

"Mother and Grandma asked me to tell you, Uncle, that they will be ready to return to the dining room in ten minutes," said William, as he re-emerged, clutching two glasses brimming with ginger-beer.

"Then we must have the good sense and good grace to join them," observed Charley, as he took a moment to consult his pocket watch, then hurriedly unfastened the shiny gold chain that adorned his waistcoat. "Thank you, Willie," he said, as, with one hand, he eagerly grasped his glass of chilled beverage and, with the other, placed both watch and albert upon a nearby side table.

"That's a fine watch-chain, Uncle Charley," said his nephew, in an enquiring tone of voice that clearly hinted at a desire to learn of its provenance.

"Bought it from a Turkish bumboat trader who was peddling trinkets of all sorts. The bumboats used to put out from Constantinople and Scutari when we were at anchor in the Bosphorus. It looks the part, Willie, but I doubt it's worth more than a shilling or two. Anyway, I must keep an eye on the time. We don't want to miss out on that pudding. Now, my boy, where were we?"

"The soldiers had begun their march south towards Sebastopol," replied William, the break having served to reignite his earlier interest.

"Yes, well, we shifted berth that same day to accompany the Armies south. We anchored off the River Alma. A lovely spot it was, that river valley, with its orchards and vineyards, but we could see the Russians... waiting upon the Allied advance they were, way up on the heights beyond the Alma. We could see them clearly, either side of the road to Sebastopol, menacingly barring the way south. By night I remember seeing the flicker of their distant camp fires and thinking you could hear the silence out there on the water. But it was a silence soon to be lost. You see, Willie, a great battle seemed inevitable...and so it proved. It came in the heat of the following day. For us, just off the coast, the twentieth of September began quietly...yes, a fine day it was...I remember being on the upper deck and hearing the soft lap of water against the ship as she rode at anchor and the gentle soughing of a breeze in the shrouds and rigging. But by early afternoon all hell was let loose. You could hear the distant roar of what proved to be the Russian artillery opening up on those heights beyond the river. Some of our topmen who went aloft said they had a masthead view of the Russian batteries. But actually they saw little beyond the constantly shifting wreaths of smoke and clouds of whatever fell to be pulverised beneath the hail of shell and roundshot. And one of those lofty spectators later told me how the anger of it all was constantly emphasised by the vermilion spew and spurt of flame. Well, from your model making, Willie, you seem to know all about the battle. Our boys showed great courage in storming those formidable Russian guns, you know...but I tell you, it was a victory that bore a huge cost in loss of life and suffering. Those of our sailors who spent several days getting the wounded off into the hospital transports became hardened to some of the carnage's aftermath, Willie, and had some gruesome tales to tell. One of them, a friend of mine, told me how very sad it was that some of those young fellows ever ventured to take the Queen's shilling and shoulder walnut."

Uncle Charley paused a moment to peer at his watch. "We must repair to the dining table shortly," he said, distractedly, as the bothersome fly that had earlier broken his nephew's concentration suddenly buzzed about his head. Seconds later it came again...then again. The fly's persistence began to irritate Charley. Spotting a nearby newspaper, he grasped and folded it, then petulantly launched into a frenzied pursuit of the ever-moving intruder, arm and newspaper flailing to no avail. Finally he returned to his seat, as if to accept that he had been outwitted.

"It's settled against the window now, Uncle," said William coolly, and seemingly unmoved by the irony of the insect's chosen time to trade flight for repose. Jumping to his feet, Charley recovered the discarded paper, then advanced gingerly towards the stationary blowfly. Fleetingly, he noticed a slight tic, a minute twitch, as if the fly was conscious of being stalked and on the brink of resuming its travels. Charley readied himself to wield his armament. His hope was that he had witnessed the irritant's last movement. He had. He brought the folded newspaper down swiftly and soundly, crushing the life out of the creature in that split-second, its gore, its life juices, spattered and drawn across the glass.

Charley Black had barely settled back into his chair when the creak of floorboards in the passage signalled that the kitchen chores had been concluded and dessert was being carried to the table.

"Ready, my dears when you are," came the beckoning call from Grandma Black.

"We'll be with you in a minute or two, Mother," said Charley. "Right," he added, quickly turning his attention to his nephew and now raising the pace of his conversation. "I'm just thinking how strange we are my boy... human beings, that is. To think I've just murdered that fly because it deigned to annoy me. It didn't know it was annoying me. It was merely doing what came naturally to a fly. But I killed it and perhaps I should be reproached for my deed. One of God's creatures you see and I squashed it on an impulse. It was a life we hold in no value. An irritating insect, no less. And when I come to think of it, Willie, that's what it was like in the Crimea. We and the Ruskies were reduced to viewing our respective lives as having little or no value. And that, I suppose, was down to the whims, the vagaries, the pride and convictions of far removed politicians. Yet, unlike me, they didn't hit out with a newspaper, an inanimate thing. In their detachment they sent young men, in their prime, to do their killing. I'm not saying it wasn't a just campaign, Willie. Someone had to curb the Russian foe and there were plenty enough clamouring for war back here. But they sent out those poor soldiers with such a shameful lack of care and thought for their welfare. It was so evident after the Alma, Willie. Men with dreadful injuries, cut to pieces by shot and shell and canister, were left too long in their agony on the battlefield. They say there were too few field hospitals and no properly trained and equipped people to tend and nurse the wounded. There were no stretcher bearers, few surgeons with the right equipment, no bandages or medicine or chloroform for those poor wretches who were put to the knife when they couldn't repair shattered limbs. And, in truth, for the few sawbones who worked tirelessly through the night, arms slippery with gore, I suppose it was the easier task, just to amputate. In short, it was a disgraceful shambles...and we heard some dreadful stories, Willie, from the bluejackets who went ashore and ferried many of the wounded out to the hospital transports. One I knew had spoken to a young drummer boy who had spent hours helping to gather in the casualties. Awful, sickening things that poor lad had witnessed...unrecognisable, seared lumps of flesh, arms and legs strewn about the field, clotted gore and more gore. The sailor said the boy was lucid one moment but would then descend into confused ramblings. It seems the poor young chap was bewildered by what he had seen and it appeared it was all threatening to turn his mind. And there were others, including some of our bandsmen, who were detailed to lift inboard some of the wounded, brought alongside one of the hospital ships. There was no room, they said, to lay the wounded, other than directly on deck timbers, already crowded with men in the same predicament. Worse still, there were men already lying there who were stricken with the likes of cholera and dysentery and diarrhoea on decks awash with vomit and loose excrement. The stench, they said, was unbelievable...and the flies, well...the flies...perhaps, Willie, that's why I appeared to be intolerant of that bluebottle just now...filthy things."

"Charley...William...are you going to join us?" called Charlotte, her words bearing a hint of irritation.

"Sorry, we're coming now, my dear," said Charley, raising his voice in reassurance. Then, rising quickly from his chair, he purposefully moved close to his nephew and chose to speak to him in a hurried whisper. "Now, Willie, hear me out before we go to the table. That little drummer boy I mentioned. Well, my shipmate said he had the most angelic face, poor boy, and when he told me about him I naturally thought of you...knowing you aspired to become a soldier and having formed the impression he was not a good deal older than you. Well, a short time later, I had a dream and, bless my soul, the drummer boy appeared on the battlefield. Turned away from me he was, sifting through the carnage, looking for signs of life. It right shocked me when he turned round, for his face was your face, Willie. So what I say to you, dear boy, is cast out of your mind any thoughts about taking the Queen's shilling. I wouldn't want you to witness what the drummer boy witnessed. Think about getting yourself an apprenticeship in Her Majesty's Dockyard if you want to serve the Queen and forsake all thought of the wretched Army…and the Navy, for that matter. Failing that, you could always come and work for your uncle as a potboy. That would be a good grounding if you, too, were ever minded to make a living out of licensed victualling but, to be honest, I can't see my dear sister letting you anywhere near the taproom of the *Sheer Hulk*! Anyway, let's speak no more of war but dwell on nicer things…and talking of victualling, be it licensed or otherwise, I think this break we've enjoyed has given my own victualling department greater cause to go in search of that pudding. As for the bombardment of Sebastopol, that will need to be left for another time. Tarry any longer and we'll be in hot water with your Mother and Grandma…if we're not already!"

William looked quizzically at Uncle Charley. "Victualling department, Uncle? What do you mean by your victualling department?"

"Stomach, my lad. It's what some of us seafaring types call their stomach…as in the supply of victuals or food to Her Majesty's Ships. Come," said Charley, hurriedly ushering William out of the parlour. "Pudding. I believe both our departments are ready for pudding."

Eight

BALTIMORE, MARYLAND
AUGUST 1855

The bell rang out to announce the imminent resumption of the performance. As he stood upon the theatre's entrance steps, George Atzerodt was in no great hurry to return to his seat. It was his first experience of seeing actors upon a stage, of being among theatregoers. If he was at all captivated by what he had witnessed before the intermission, then it was more about being absorbed by the whole atmosphere of the place – the rich drapes and ornament, the general hubbub before the lights went down, the whiff of grease-paint and, of course, the medieval costumes – than with the intricacies of the drama being played out. Will Shakespeare's plays might be revered but George was not the brightest of fellows. English was, after all, his second language and the old style penned by the Bard of Avon did little to assist his understanding of the plot.

Atzerodt cast the remnants of his cheroot onto the wet sidewalk. He followed its descent and promptly extinguished its faint glow beneath his boot. Beyond the building's canopy he now felt the cooling fall of soft rain. He lingered a moment and drew in a few more breaths of evening air. It had been a clammy day. Baltimore in the heat of August. Now it was cooler out on the street, or, at least, that is how it appeared to George, having recently removed himself from the discomfort of an over-heated auditorium. He reached for his hip flask and took a swig of what little remained of the Kentucky bourbon his cousin had given him before they left Germantown. Then he turned on his heels and ascended the steps into the entrance foyer. As he did so he could hear the distant rumble of thunder out on the Chesapeake.

George slipped into his seat in the stalls with the minimum of fuss, only having to disturb in the process, his cousin Hartman, who occupied the adjoining aisle seat. To George's right sat his brother, Johann, and beyond, his mother, Victore Atzerodt. George hesitated fleetingly as he lowered himself into his seat for, in that moment, he caught his mother's eye and, with a nod and a smirk, beckoned towards his father who sat beyond Aunt and Uncle Richter. The play had barely resumed and Heinrich Atzerodt's head had slumped to one side as the dialogue's pace and rhythm combined with warmth and fatigue to soporific effect.

It had been a tiring two weeks for the Atzerodts from Westmoreland County. They had made the long journey back to the family home they had once shared with their relatives in the rolling Maryland countryside. In part it was to be a family vacation. However, it was as much a matter of assisting the Richters with a backlog of maintenance work on the farm. In essence, they had got well behind with much needed repair work to a number of outbuildings and, in addition, a new barn required cladding and roofing before leaf fall. It was work that called for manpower. Johann Atzerodt was long overdue a vacation from his deskwork and was happy to oblige. As for George, it was a year since he turned his hand to sea fishing and crabbing, thanks to his brother's willingness to invest in Nathan Clough's boat; and to his family's delight he had taken to his work with relish, had found a market for his fish and was beginning to make a modest contribution to the family budget. As for setting this all aside for a couple of weeks and travelling north, George needed precious little persuasion; for it meant a much valued opportunity to renew acquaintance with Hartman Richter, the cousin he held in great affection. And so the two Atzerodt boys duly accompanied their parents back to Germantown; and with supper despatched and the toils of the day behind them, the three young men would sit upon the side porch, smoke and talk endlessly upon all manner of subjects. Sometimes they would dwell upon childhood memories of the annual vacation in Germany's Thuringer Wald. It was always in the same red-roofed village that nestled among fields and orchards between wide tracts of forest. Idyllic days at the end of summer, where the sun perpetually shone and where, as the time came to return home to Dorna, the leaves were turning gold and red among the hills.

By ten-thirty Johann Atzerodt would be ready for his bed and would bid good-night. George and Hartman would remain and, in due course, they would indulge in their liking for whisky. Soon they would become eerily conscious of the distant feelings that had beset them both when they sat together on that very porch the night before George's family took the road to Virginia. Eight years had passed. The bats still made their twilight appearance, entertaining the onlookers with their dexterous flight until the intensity of nightfall hampered the full appreciation of their antics. The moths had not tired of engaging the sulphurous glow of the paraffin lamp that still hung, a shade more rustily, beside the kitchen door. But the old tobacco shed, against which George had despairingly showered stones, had gone, its site an overgrown cabbage patch, host to the tympanic and ever-intensifying sound of cicada. Although mindful of them, gone also were those past feelings of despair. Instead, weary contentment reigned in the hearts and minds of the two cousins – now the hearts and minds of men – a contentment that only deepened and mellowed with their intake of liquor. That had been the nature of the cousins' cherished August evenings together – or at least, the majority of them – balmy evenings that fell into balmy night. And with nocturnal progression into the early hours, whisky and fatigue would call time on these episodes and the participants would ultimately drag themselves away to find their respective pillows.

Yet now, as the working vacation drew to a close, that nightly repetition had been broken. To show their appreciation for the family's willingness to journey from Montross and for the blacksmith's and his sons' contributions in helping put the farm in better shape, the Richters had decided to reward their relations. They had brought them to the city of Baltimore, knowing full well that Victore Atzerodt would be thrilled at the prospect of visiting some of the inner city stores – retail establishments where she could purchase goods for her family that she could never hope to find back in Westmoreland County. The travellers had booked into a modest lodging house for two nights and now, on the eve of returning to Germantown, the Richters had treated the Atzerodts to a night at the theatre on Charles Street. The entertainment on offer was Shakespeare's *Richard 111*. Tomorrow, after the return journey through Maryland, there would be the chance of a last reflective evening on the side porch. Yet George would need to be less reckless in whiling away the night hours downing whisky. The following morning it would be up with the lark and an early start on the road to Virginia.

"You should've come outside with me away from this sweaty place. I feel better for it." George's words were meant for the ears of both brother and cousin. In the comparative hush of the auditorium, however, with the play having already resumed, they carried further afield.

"Shhhh. Keep quiet, George. You'll disturb people." His mother's rebuke came swiftly and in a strained whisper. Yet it was audible enough to hopefully allay fears of any repetition and thus prevent others from expressing displeasure with her son's conduct; and it had the desired effect, nipping in the bud any prospect of that behaviour leading to greater embarrassment.

The play unfolded before an attentive audience. As the penultimate Act 1V drew to its close came the announcement that the exiled Henry Tudor, Earl of Richmond and pretender to the Plantagenet throne, had landed in Pembrokeshire. Once into Act V, Richmond made his entrance, appearing with his followers in camp, after advancing as far as the Midlands town of Tamworth. George Atzerodt began to take a keener interest as the play approached its climax with the prospect of battle between the opposing armies of Richmond and King Richard. In particular, he was impressed by the persuasive manner of the young actor who had just come on stage, cast in the role of the Earl of Richmond. In truth he was the very antithesis of the indolent and slovenly Atzerodt, although whether George, in his subconscious, might have registered this, one can only imagine. Certainly he did not fail to notice the confidence with which Richmond delivered his lines as he rallied his army to advance upon the King's position. Added to which, this dashing young thespian with his dark hair and rakish, downy moustache, was a handsome fellow indeed and of a more tender age than George's twenty years. For a moment George regarded the young actor with a sense of admiration, for he doubtless possessed charisma. But then, paradoxically, there occurred a sudden turnabout in fortune for the young man. As he engaged in conversation with the Earl of Derby, in his tent on Bosworth Field, Richmond forgot some of his lines. The audience was unforgiving to a point that surprised George. Boos and heckles rang out, notably from people in the gallery. Something was thrown onto the stage. Someone prompted the youth from the wings and got the dialogue moving again, only for further lines to be forgotten. More heckling and catcalls ensued. Yet in the face of this ridicule Richmond proceeded to show great composure. In his lengthy oration, rallying his soldiers, he, himself, rallied and delivered his lines, once again, with precision and confidence. Seemingly undeterred by the aberration, he went from strength to strength, convincingly proclaiming the slaying of Richard… "The day is ours, the bloody dog is dead…," before bringing the final act to its close with commanding, tragedian panache…

"...Abate the edge of traitors, gracious Lord,
That would reduce these bloody days again,
And make poor England weep in streams of blood!
Let them not live to taste this land's increase
That would with treason wound this fair land's peace!
Now civil wounds are stopp'd, peace lives again:
That she may live here, God say amen!

George Atzerodt had not exactly enjoyed his evening at the theatre. Being in the heart of a city, a few hours in a local hotel bar might have suited him better. Yet he had found it an interesting experience and was left in awe of the dark haired young thespian, seemingly for the qualities that eluded his own being...his good looks, his swagger, his supreme confidence and, of course, the remarkable power of recovery he had displayed. As the curtain came down, and the lights went up, George called for the programme that his mother had clutched throughout the performance. He cast his eye through the dramatis personae. "The Earl of Richmond," he muttered to himself... "Wilkes...John Wilkes." He read the short profile which disclosed little, excepting to say that Wilkes was a young man from Maryland who was making his acting debut in this production. George returned the programme to his mother as the extended family prepared to join the throng that shuffled its way towards the exit. The name of John Wilkes, actor, probably nestled somewhere in the labyrinth of his mind. Otherwise, and for the time being, the name passed into oblivion as far as George was concerned.

Across the theatre, in a dress circle box, a middle-aged woman and her daughter hesitated awhile to allow the crowd to disperse. Besides which they were in no great hurry. It was to be another fifteen minutes before their carriage would draw up outside the front entrance on Charles Street. Mary Ann Booth would need to speak to her son as a matter of urgency and long before the following day's matinee. He had work to do. The theatre owners would be displeased. The critics would probably write spitefully in the *Sun* and *Clipper*. The fact was the boy was too laid back. She would make sure he was up early the next morning going over his lines. His beloved sister, Asia, who had accompanied her mother to the performance, had already volunteered to assist her brother in this regard. The theatre would probably insist that he report back early on the morrow for more rehearsal, but Mary Ann and Asia would want John word perfect before he left his hotel room; and since they had booked rooms for the night in the same establishment, they were well placed to ensure that he refrained from sleeping-in or spending his time unwisely.

Mary Ann and Asia Booth left their theatre box with mixed thoughts. They were proud of young John. They were first to acknowledge that, at seventeen years of age, he showed great promise with his acting ability and they had no doubt he was destined to follow in the illustrious footsteps of his late father, the celebrated tragedian, Junius Brutus Booth. But perhaps the boy was over-confident. He needed to sharpen-up. He needed to take his craft more seriously and ensure he was always word-perfect. Mary Ann was certain that had his late father been here to witness the evening's performance he would have been infuriated by John's lack of preparation. His acting was in many ways perfection and he might be commended for his ability to shrug-off the audience's response to forgetting his lines. Yet Junius Brutus would have been incensed that a son of his had let himself down in such an unprofessional way. There was no excuse for not learning one's lines.

"You know it's as well, Asia, my dear, that your brother was happy to bill himself as John Wilkes in launching his acting career," said Mary Ann, reflectively, the coachman having just ushered the two ladies beneath enveloping umbrellas into the comfort of their carriage. "Your father's reputation would not have been dealt a lot of good by what happened tonight had he been using the family name."

"Quite so, Mother. But I'm sure he'll know when to bill himself differently and then he'll be proud to do so. I'm sure John will go far but, of course, he has to fully learn his chosen profession and that will come with time and experience." Asia's reply was emphatically delivered and to the sound of heavy rain that now beat upon the roof of the brougham. "Perhaps it may take ten years or so, but I'm prepared to wager that, by then, Mother, everyone will be talking of the famous actor, John Wilkes Booth."

Nine

PORTSEA, PORTSMOUTH
1855/57

The brothers shook hands. They stopped short of hugging each other, yet the joy of reunion was palpable in their demeanour.

"Well, it's been best part of a year, brother, since we last had any contact," exclaimed a beaming Charley Black. "That was a close shave for you and the dear old *Rodney*. We could see you were in trouble once we'd hauled off."

"You're damn right, Charley," said his brother with a smile and in a scoffed tone of voice. "It was certainly hot work. And, of course, we were sitting ducks. Trouble was our stern cable was shot away and we couldn't help but run aground. That wouldn't have been a particular problem had we been further away from the enemy forts. One of the steamers could have pulled us off. But, as you know, we were stuck there in the range of the Russian guns and they gave us a good shelling. The frustration was in knowing we couldn't throw much back at them. The after part of the ship had swung round to face the shore so we could only reply with our stern guns."

"Yes, James, I heard all about it from *Rodney*'s bandsmen. They said you received a pounding for the best part of three hours but got away lightly with only two men injured."

"Quite so, Charley, but that was on account of the Ruskies' guns having too much elevation. The ship itself was really knocked about, especially our masts and yards. And some of the shot was red hot so we had our work cut out to deal with a few fires. Fortunately, a smart gun vessel... the *Lynx* she was called...came to our assistance. It was well after nightfall and she came under our bows and took the only remaining hawser. The trusty little steamer, *Spiteful*, that had earlier towed us into position, was lashed alongside and both vessels managed to get us floated by going full speed ahead. Anyway, Charley, how come you were talking to our bandsmen?"

"You may well ask," sniggered Charley. "While you were as snug as a duck in a ditch, sailing home to dear old England with your Captain, *Rodney* and *Vengeance* were moored head and stern in some God forsaken creek to pass the winter. Quite often we in the band used to get together with your bandsmen and put some cheer into the men with a spot of music. They needed some light relief from the daily monotony. And, of course, stuck in some icy inlet that only drew down the cold…and some cold it was, James, I can tell you…seeped into your bones it did…well, we all needed our spirits lifting."

"So how did you pass your day, Charley, stuck in a creek?"

"Much of the time, brother, in open boat…certainly early on. There was no shortage of work, you see…ferrying despatches out to the Admiral who was lying off Sebastopol, towing animal carcasses out to sea, clearing some of the transports. And there was some salvaging work to be done what with the vessels that had been driven ashore in that vicious November storm. The fourteenth of the month as I remember …never known the likes of such a tempest."

"It certainly was a real sneezer, Charley. It was just prior to my transference to *Britannia*. We rode it out alright but it was a frightful business. Never felt so ill. I recall thinking I preferred the onslaught from the Russian guns!"

"Anyway, enough of the wretched Crimea, James. That, thank God, is behind us. How have you been doing lately?"

"Well, I've done six months on a fifth-rate as Admiral's steward. She's just paid off so I'm at a loose end for a while. But it's always grand to be back in Portsmouth and to see the family…"

Outside, a boy's face pressed against the taproom window. Judging by the state of the glazing, the landlord of the *Coal Exchange* was none too particular about reducing the gloom that pervaded his premises, prompting William Reynolds to spit into the palm of his left hand; and, primed with the spittle, he applied his fingers to scour an aperture upon the dirty pane, sufficient to permit him misty vision into the tavern's dim interior. It served its purpose, sating William's need for assurance that his Uncle Charley's former mess-mate, George Cork, had delivered the message. The two brothers were sitting across the taproom, absorbed in conversation and oblivious to their nephew's prying eyes.

Uncle James had returned, once again, to the house in King Street during the course of the previous evening. He had been at sea since February. The homecoming occurred the day after William's birthday and immediately prompted Charlotte and Grandma Black into utterances of regret that James had missed his nephew's birthday supper by a whisker. William, on the other hand, did not share that regret and was thankful for having spent some time alone with his Uncle Charley, listening to his reminiscences upon the war. Suddenly, Uncle James was back, a return that did little to cheer him: for William felt a sense of intimidation in his imposing presence. Once more he expected the constant scrutiny of his behaviour and irksome talk of a beckoning life afloat 'for the boy' as if 'the boy' was in need of naval discipline. Yet at least William was inclined to reflect on being spared his uncle's criticism on the occasion of the January homecoming. That was partly on account of it proving short-lived. But William suspected it had been largely attributable to his mother's timely comments upon the good report she had received from his schoolmaster. It rather served to pull the carpet from beneath her brother's feet and stifled any appetite he might have shown for picking upon his nephew.

As he retired to bed and bade goodnight to his elders, William hoped for some repetition, having at least gleaned something to the good. Uncle James had already organised temporary accommodation for himself, admitting that he had felt guilty about suddenly descending on the family when returning from the war. In future, unless able to give advance notice, he would always seek temporary lodgings so as to avoid unnecessary disruption.

William was heartened by this news. However, with the coming of morning, he fully expected to see his Uncle James seated at the breakfast table. It was an expectation fuelled by the protestations of the womenfolk that had accompanied his departure to bed: assertions aimed at condoning the right of one of their own to present himself without prior announcement and still expect a place to rest his head. Yet Uncle James had remained true to his expressed intention. He was not at breakfast, having passed the night elsewhere. The only trace of him was in the form of a neatly-folded message he had written and addressed to his brother Charles and left with Grandma Black.

"Be a good lad, Willie, and take this note round to your Uncle Charley once you've finished your breakfast," said Grandma Black, as they took their seats at the dining table. "And make sure you hand him the message since your Uncle James is making arrangements to meet him at five o'clock this afternoon, round at the *Coal Exchange*.

William had proceeded to take the message to his uncle's lodgings in Daniel Street where he was faced with no alternative but to leave it in the keeping of the owner. Mister Cork had explained that his lodger had recently gone out but he expected him back shortly and assured William he would hand it to Uncle Charley on his return. Yet having been unable to deliver the note into his uncle's hand – and knowing nothing of Cork's reliability – William had been left to fret upon the possibility of his favourite uncle never receiving the message. That would upset Uncle James. He didn't feel confident about returning to Daniel Street: it might seem odd or cause affront to George Cork were he to correctly interpret its intent. And so, in consequence, it was to allay unease upon the matter that brought William to the taproom window a shade after five in the afternoon. Now, his curiosity satisfied and anxiety dispelled, he continued on his way into Queen Street. There were errands to run.

"So what of yourself, Charley?" enquired James, hesitating a moment to wipe the beer froth from his lips. "What have you been up to since you came back from the fighting?"

"Well, in a nutshell, dear brother, I've left the service. But then I expect you heard all about that last evening, from Mother and Charlotte."

"No, no, Charley. They hinted, admittedly, that life had changed for you but stopped short of giving particulars. I gather they assumed you would want to be first to tell me. But I put two and two together and assumed you'd swallowed the anchor. You see, I recall that last message from you… just before the cannonade upon Sebastopol. It seemed you'd had enough of life afloat and were thinking about becoming a publican."

"You know, Charlotte said I'd mentioned that to you. To be honest, I can't even recall writing to you at the time." As he spoke, Charley's fixed and frowned expression told of intense endeavour to call to mind. He remained thoughtful for a few seconds before eventually yielding to his inability to remember. "Anyway, James, the fact is I've made the break. I've put the Navy behind me and obtained my publican's license."

"Bless my soul. So you've actually turned up being a sea-crab for a life ashore." James had suspected as much but his reaction rang with surprise. Briefly he looked pensive, reflecting upon – as he saw it – the wisdom of his brother's decision. Yet, whatever his judgement, his words were supportive.

210

"If it's what you want, Charley, then it was meant to happen. Well done, brother. Let me wish you every success in your forthcoming enterprise." And, as if to seal those words, James gave his brother a firm handshake, almost, in the process, sending his glass of ale plummeting to the floor.

"Thanks, James. You know, it wouldn't have been so much a case of letting me be the first to tell you...certainly as far as Charlotte's concerned."

"What do you mean my dear fellow?"

"Well, she has many fine qualities, has our dear sister...and I cherish her dearly, as I'm sure you do, James. But she has this annoying habit of shirking reality at times. Mother appears to have had no qualms about me becoming a licensed victualler and, in all fairness, neither did Charlotte at first. But she immediately conjured up this notion of me running a country inn festooned with roses and the like. When I tried to explain that I needed to stay here in town to make anything like a tidy penny she seemed contemptuous of what I was proposing. Well, I shrugged it off at the time but when I secured the license of the *Sheer Hulk* I was not relishing..."

"The *Sheer Hulk*?," interjected James.

"That's right. It's along The Hard."

"Of course. I can picture it, Charley. Sorry...do continue."

"Well, I was about to say I was not relishing the prospect of telling our dear sister that I was about to take over the reins of an establishment along The Hard. Anyway, fortuitously, when I went round to King Street, Charlotte had taken to her bed. According to Mother, she'd felt a touch queer and..."

"Ha, ha," laughed James. "You know, old chap, I've an inkling you're a touch intimidated by our dear sister."

"Not at all," insisted Charley with a smile. "Whatever gave you that idea?"

"Well, after all, Charlotte is the eldest of us siblings. The big sister. And you're the youngest of her brothers...her little brother, so to speak. So perhaps you've reason to be a mite fearful when she's inclined to be haughty," remarked James, playfully, and somewhat uncharacteristically, since he was not noted for his jest.

Charley continued his discourse, choosing to ignore his brother's banter. "So, in the end, it fell to Mother to inform Charlotte about the *Sheer Hulk* and..."

"And she didn't approve?" asked James, his words laced with a hint of derision.

"Well, not exactly, James, but she's since made no mention of my new venture. She's had every opportunity. On Wednesday evening I went to supper at King Street. Mother had invited me and for what was meant to be a double celebration...Willie's birthday and the fact I'd obtained my victualler's license. Well, in truth, my little enterprise didn't get a mention, which was not a problem since it was Willie's day after all. But I sensed Mother chose not to bring it up because she knew it would irk Charlotte and threaten to mar the evening."

"There you are then, Charley. Accept the fact. Charlotte doesn't approve. But don't let it bother you, old chap. It's really none of her business. Anyway...what good reason has the dear girl to show displeasure? She ought to be pleased for you."

"It's young Willie, without a doubt. I think she feels that a Portsea ale-house...as she puts it...is not the place to take a youngster."

"Well, no self-respecting woman would venture anywhere near a Portsmouth tavern, that's for sure, whatever the nature of its reputation," observed James. "Yet surely Charlotte should have no cause to prevent William from visiting his uncle when the public house is closed."

"No reason at all. After all, the private rooms are separately accessed from the back...from Havant Street. There'd be no call to stray into the public areas," said Charley.

"Not wishing to be critical...for like you, Charley...I love her dearly... but Charlotte has always been over-protective of the boy, in my opinion. *See yon blithe child......Fond mother, whence these fears?*" said James, abstractedly, recalling at that instant some obscure lines of relevance. "Discipline is what the boy needs...and a father figure. I don't know about you, brother, but I feel obliged to bring some influence to bear when at home. Great pity he lost his father. A good man was Reynolds. I fear our Charlotte has cosseted the boy since he's been gone."

"That's only to be expected, I suppose," reflected Charley.

"Well, I'll be damned, brother. Do I detect you're becoming a bit of a softy? Look at poor Mother. Left with all four of us back in Malta, she didn't indulge us in any way. Affectionate but firm. I don't think any of us suffered through lack of guidance or discipline. They were hard times and Mother was equal to them. She had her hands full and, to a large degree, we had to fend for ourselves. In comparison it seems to me that young William has something of a coddled existence."

"I have to say, James, I don't entirely agree with you. I wouldn't advocate too much discipline for discipline's sake. As far as Willie's concerned there's no call for being harsh with him. He's a good lad and well behaved compared with most boys of his age here in Portsea. Many of them are right little thieves and ruffians."

"I accept what you say about not being harsh on him. It's more a matter of giving firm guidance. A mother's love is one thing but there's no substitute for fatherly advice. A boy needs that constant to ensure he embraces manhood imbued with good moral force. I've always believed the Navy would be good for him and I'm sure that is what his father would have wanted," opined the elder brother. "What is he now, Charley… thirteen did you say? Well the time is nigh when he needs to be away from his mother's apron…and his grandmother's for that matter."

"I'm sure Charlotte continues to have aspirations of Willie wearing a suit of civilian clothes…of being in mufti, so to speak…rather than having to pull on a sailor's rig or a soldier's tunic," observed Charley. "And were you to obtain the boy's opinion on the matter, I warrant he'd display indifference to a life in clerking or whatever and express a preference for soldiering. I'm not so sure he's taken much with the Navy, James."

"Well, we'll just have to see," said James, with a presumption and confidence that suggested he harboured no qualms about wielding the kind of interference normally considered beyond the purview of a boy's uncle.

"Now, getting back to the *Sheer Hulk*," said Charley, "I suppose it doesn't quite fit the bill as far as Charlotte's concerned. For one thing, it's not nestling out there in the Meon valley under a neat, thatched roof."

"Indeed," spluttered the sailor, seeing the funny side of what he was about to say, "a hostelry on The Common Hard could not, one might argue, be further removed from Charlotte's ideal. I mean, well…to be honest, you couldn't have got it more wrong." James' laughter was infectious, his inherently good-humoured sibling being swift to share his amusement. "After all," he continued, having first composed himself, "The Hard has something of an unwholesome reputation. Not quite the notoriety of Portsmouth Point of old, but Jack does like his little diversions and you may find you've got your work cut out to keep good order."

"In my understanding the retiring landlord has kept an orderly enough house and I intend to keep it that way," remarked Charley.

"I'm sure your winning ways and good-humour will see you do well as a Portsea innkeeper, though I doubt you'll have the clout to influence the habits of The Common Hard, Charley m'lad," said James.

"Well I'll brook no nonsense, no licentious carry-on. In any event, things are a lot more stringent than in the old days. The lodging house registration laws must have queered the pitch for many an alehouse brothel keeper."

"I'm not so sure we see much evidence of that in Portsea," quipped James. "I suspect a few blind eyes are turned! Now, seeing as you use the words 'lodging house', it's got me thinking that you'll have a few rooms to let...especially since you're adamant they won't be set aside for the gratification of Jack Tar," said the elder, jokingly, and with a mischievous twinkle in his eye. "No, seriously, Charley, perhaps you'll consider allowing your brother to be your first lodger...'tween ships and at times of shore leave, you understand...and I'll pay you a retainer," he continued, raising his voice in false pomposity as if to suggest he was a man of substance. "Modest, mind you...a very modest retainer!"

"Far be it from me to turn a brother away from my door," said Charley.

"My worldly goods and chattels are simple enough and meagre. There's no reason they couldn't be stowed away and locked in a cupboard...then you could let the room on a weekly basis in my absence. Not for any unseemly purpose, mind you. Dash my timbers, Charley, I wouldn't want you further offending my sister!" It was a remark that prompted both men to laugh heartily together as they revelled in a brotherly companionship which had been long in coming.

Once their laughter had subsided, it was Charley Black who took up the conversation. "So did you spend last night round at King Street?"

"No, no...I didn't want to impose, considering they weren't expecting me. In truth, I secured myself a berth in the Royal Sailors' Home, just round the corner in Queen Street."

"Any good, James...your room?"

"Clean and comfortable enough if not bleak in its decoration."

"And what of you, Charley? I hear you've got lodgings in Daniel Street?"

"Yes, in a former shipmate's home...messed together on the *Vengeance*. Turns out he had a spare room, so I took it and it's worked out well. Quite the Fiddler's Green after all those months at sea and not least on account of his wife's cooking. She always places a hearty, nourishing supper in front of me and I think it shows...I've put on a lot of weight in the three months since returning home. It's sad in a way that, in a week's time, I'm having to take my leave."

"To take up residency on The Hard," said James with presumptive rather than questioning intonation.

"No, that's in a fortnight. My new enterprise begins on the first of next month," declared the prospective landlord with a beaming smile that told of pride and expectation. "No, I'm parting company with Daniel Street next week. Mother's agreed that I might stay with her and Charlotte since my old mess-mate, George, is off to sea again. He's not asked me to leave, but it would make it awkward…you understand, James…being alone in the house with his wife."

"Not so sure I do understand. Seems to me he's either very trusting or very naïve. No disrespect to you, brother. He clearly regards you as a good friend…but, being a naval fellow, one can but assume he is perceptive enough, when it comes to the ways of the world. He'll know how temptation can get the better of a man, by jiminy, so, to my mind, his silence has to raise suspicion. No, I'm inclined to wonder whether he's happy for you to hang around so as he might simply off-load his missus, fine cook or not."

Charley Black scoffed at his brother's reasoning, dismissing his final comment with a chuckle and a shake of his head that told of his amusement and incredulity. "Good God, James, they're smitten with each other… believe me."

"Then he's surely trusting or green…which takes some accepting…or both. Anyway, from what you tell me I'll make arrangements to extend my stay at the Sailors' Home until the end of August. That shouldn't prove a problem. Otherwise it would be too much for Mother and Charlotte were we both to impose upon their hospitality."

"You're right, of course, James, but I feel bad having caused you some inconvenience."

"Then don't. I said it wouldn't be a problem. I appreciate that you, on the other hand, Charley, are faced with a predicament and unquestionably have first call upon King Street. After all, a promise is a promise and if Mother has pledged to help you out of that pickle then far be it from me to upset the arrangement."

"Thank you, brother. But let me know if there's a problem at the Sailors' Home," said Charley.

"There won't be. And seeing I'm going to be at a loose end, you can rely on me to help you move into the *Sheer Hulk*…and I'll be on hand to choose my room!"

"Capital, James! Capital!"

"Now, Charley. My turn to buy you a drink…so finish downing that beer. Do you fancy a gin twist?"

"Why not!"

"Then two brandy and gins it'll be and we'll toast your new venture!"

★ ★ ★

From William's point of view the brothers' reunion had been advantageous. During the latter days of August, once Charley had parted company with his Daniel Street lodgings, it transpired that both ended up having supper with the family. James had been true to his word, having succeeded in extending his sojourn at the Royal Sailors' Home. Yet, in the final analysis, he pulled up a little short when it came to fulfilling his expressed commitment to avoid imposing upon the kindness of his mother and sister.

The stumbling block was James' fastidiousness when it came to comestibles. He soon tired of what was on offer in the Sailors' Home mess, succumbing, with little prompting, to the lure of home cooking. In essence, Grandma Black and Charlotte felt a shade awkward about excluding James from the supper table, especially once Charley had come to stay. "If we are cooking for four we'd just as well cook for five," came the call. But the women's gentle wheedling was more a matter of dispelling their unease, the root cause of which was James' continued generosity in contributing towards the family budget. Charley, for his part, would joke about his brother being difficult to please and his aversion to the food on offer in Queen Street.

"All this good fellowship at the tables of sea officers with their particular likes and dislikes has rubbed off on poor James," he would chortle when the other was out of earshot. "He would never have been that fussy on the *Rodney*. He'd have swallowed his wretched oat gruel like the rest of the lower deck or have gone hungry."

In truth there was common satisfaction with the arrangement; and, of course, it was a satisfaction felt keenest by Margaret Black who had two of her sons seated together at the dining table for the first time in years. Even William came to accept that his uncles' reunion and, more particularly, their presence at supper during that last week in August, had its good side.

Throughout each evening the two men revelled in each other's company, monopolising the conversation as they earnestly compared and weighed their Crimean experiences. After supper they would retire to the parlour with a bottle of port or Madeira. The two women, meanwhile, would tidy up before returning to the sanctuary of the dining room, there to occupy themselves with their sewing and darning. William, on the other hand, would follow his uncles and listen to their yarns about life below deck. It was not a topic which promised to entrance him, yet it was a subject matter devoid of the sadder and more brutal aspects of the war that had befallen the Army. William was happy to soak up the many anecdotal accounts concerning life aboard Her Majesty's warships and to hear his uncles' reflections upon the sea-going capabilities, limitations and idiosyncrasies of their respective ships. In truth he had tired of hearing about the wretched state of the common soldier. He had been discouraged by Uncle Charley's recent comments upon the soldiers' sufferings in the Crimea. Discouraged and nauseated. He was ready to be regaled with stories of a gentler and less sanguine nature.

After supper, on the eve of Charley Black collecting the keys to the *Sheer Hulk*, the brothers retired to the parlour in the usual manner, closely followed by their nephew.

"That was a fine dessert your Mother brought to the table, young fellow," stated Charley as William watched him pour an amber-coloured madeira that swirled and gurgled its way into the awaiting glasses.

"Cossack's pudding, she called it and a fine plum pudding it was to be sure," interjected Uncle James.

"I think Grandma found the recipe in the *Family Economist*, chirped William.

"I'll say this," quipped Charley. "As a sweet the Cossack is a mite more savoury than the real thing."

"The real thing? What do you mean, brother?"

"Didn't you find time enough between duties, James, to take a look at those Cossacks when we went inshore…the day after the hurricane struck?" enquired Charley, as he handed his brother a glass of the madeira. "By the way, Willie, my boy, you'd better go and get yourself a glass of something. You need to drink plenty in this hot weather."

"I seem to recall being busy below hatches…in the bread room…when somebody mentioned we were being fired at by Cossacks. But I didn't get to see the fellows myself," said James with an air of disinterest.

"Strange characters, they were. We'd gone inshore to attempt to assist several transports that had been grounded and wrecked by that fearsome wind," explained Charley. "The best we could do was to bring off what crew members were still holed up in some of the beached vessels. Difficult work for the landing parties and made the more difficult by those damn Cossacks. They'd appear on the cliff tops and fire at the parties of bluejackets who'd taken the cutters inshore. Our small arms men and marines had the devil's own job trying to pin them down. It was important, you see, to give cover to our boys in the open boats."

"Now you mention it, I recall the commotion at the time," said James. "But I didn't get a look at any Cossacks."

"Scruffy, uncouth-looking ruffians in heavy coats…which, in truth, probably made them look thicker-set than they really were…and, yes, they wore sheepskin caps and sat astride these high-saddled little nags that looked hard pushed to shoulder the weight. They each carried a lance and a sabre and fortunately appeared less accustomed to handling rifles…but they were nuisance enough at the time."

"What's a nag exactly, Uncle?," asked William, as he sought to conjure up a mental picture of a Russian Cossack.

"Well…a riding horse a bit on the small side…a pony, maybe. Which reminds me, Willie, m'lad…something I've been meaning to mention," replied Uncle Charley. "There's a small group of stables in the yard behind the *Sheer Hulk* and the retiring tenant tells me he used to keep a couple of naggies there in the past when his children were young. From time to time he and his missus would lead the children on their mounts out towards Ballards windmill, on Southsea Common…"

"The mill by the pond?"

"No, Willie, not that far. You're thinking of the old Lumps mill. Ballards is this end of the Common, near the troops' firebarn. Anyway, that was where the youngsters would perfect their riding skills under their father's close guidance. And by all accounts the two children grew up to be accomplished riders. Well, this got me thinking that when I get straight I could perhaps stretch to getting a riding horse. You see, to my mind, Willie, it befits a gentleman to be proficient in the saddle so you could…"

"But not exactly a skill for a sailor to turn to account," interrupted Uncle James rather pointedly.

William's initial reaction was to ignore the observation. Yet in a headstrong and impetuous moment, emboldened by the presence of his Uncle Charley, he permitted himself the liberty of a spirited reply. For once he refrained from allowing natural reticence and the intimidatory impact of so many of Uncle James' pronouncements from holding sway. "It would be good for a chap wanting to join the cavalry, though, Uncle," he claimed, in an unfaltering voice. It was the kind of enterprising reply that even amazed its young deliverer. In Uncle Charley's estimation it fell well short of being impudent or disrespectful but he wondered, with inward amusement, whether his brother would see it that way.

Uncle James at first remained silent. He rose to his feet, sighed, made a beeline for the bottle of madeira and poured himself another drink. "Another for you, brother?," he said in a bland sort of way that spoke of pre-occupation.

"No, no…you polish it off."

James let the bottle release its remaining content until the last vestiges trickled into his glass to the point of brimming. As he turned to face his brother and his nephew, he accidentally tilted the glass, causing a few drops of the fortified wine to spill against his trousers. At another time the sailor would have laughed it off, but now, its effect compounded by the simmering irritation generated by William's utterance, he quickly lost his temper.

"Drat and damnation!" he grumbled, doing his level best in the circumstances not to overstep the mark when it came to expletives.

It was an outburst that brought the ladies scurrying to the room. "Is everything alright, James?" said a flustered Grandma Black.

"Perfectly, Mother. I'll just finish this drink and be going. By the way, look at the hour…the boy, here, should be in his bed by now." Uncle James hesitated for an instant before directing a steely gaze towards his nephew. "Do you read your bible, William?"

"Yes, Uncle, at Sunday school. I've been a voluntary teacher this past six months."

"Teacher, indeed…'pon my soul. But that's as it may be, my boy, but not what I meant. Have you read the Good Book cover to cover?"

"Not exactly, Uncle."

"Then you should. Try to read a few verses every night…but not at the expense of saying your prayers. Read them before you snuff out your candle. I read my bible, cover to cover, before I ever opened a poetry book. I found that a proper acquaintance with the teachings of the Good Book is a great comfort when one is driven into the teeth of a howling tempest on the high seas."

To William, Uncle James' words and his customary, curt reference to his nephew as 'the boy', were testimony to the irritation he had caused his least favourite relative. Trust his uncle to have the last word and for that word to focus upon preparation for life at sea. For the moment, William derived more than a crumb of satisfaction from riling Uncle James. His thoughts strayed back to Uncle Charley's commentary upon the lot of the British soldier during those Crimean encounters and to Tennyson's new poem that he had recited in the schoolroom. What gave the sailor monopoly when deriving comfort from Christ's teachings? What of our gallant soldiers, what of Tennyson's noble six hundred? Had not those brave Hussars, Dragoons and Lancers of the Light Cavalry Brigade drawn upon the same comfort as they boldly rode their steeds into the jaws of death?

Yet William would let his uncle have the last word. He would not further antagonise him. To put those thoughts into words and to use one of Uncle James' favourite poets for the purpose of arguing a case for the common soldier would be beyond the pale. He would desist from testing the bounds of social and familial convention that prevailed in the King Street front parlour for fear of enraging his uncle to the point of apoplexy.

James Black downed his madeira. When he next spoke he had put away his authoritative and condescending voice. He thanked his mother and sister, made something of an issue of shunning his nephew and agreed to meet his brother outside the *Sheer Hulk* at ten o'clock the following morning. Then he promptly took his leave.

★ ★ ★

As England's hot summer drew to a close, the Russian war did likewise. September brought news of the fall of Sebastopol following the allied assaults on the Redan and Malakoff. The war had rumbled on and victory was now to hand: but all at great cost. The Redan had run red with British blood. The press echoed the words of Uncle Charley when it came to levelling criticism at the authorities, the Army having let down its servants like never before. And so William began to realise that were he, in due course, to take the Queen's shilling, he might well encounter a similar fate to the many disease-afflicted young fellows who perished in vain, their bones picked clean by carrion. In the British Army sent to the Crimea, over four-fifths of the deaths were attributable to cholera, dysentery, typhus and such like, a sad reflection upon the heedlessness of the authorities when it came to discharging their responsibilities and caring for their charges. Not surprisingly, therefore, William started to see beyond the scarlet tunics and the anaesthetised children's tales of derring-do upon the now distant fields of Waterloo and the Peninsula. All that had been swept away by what had now happened on the shores of the Black Sea...by the reality of war. It had tainted William's idealised view of the life of the regular soldier. Death, not life, held sway. Death was pre-eminent...inexcusable death, fostered by an incompetence that only nourished disease. For the time being it caused William to abandon the keen appetite he felt for depicting battle scenes with his lead soldiers; and so, in a corner of his room, the Highlanders' advance upon the Alma Heights quietly gathered dust as autumn came and went.

Meanwhile, Uncle Charley's occupancy of the *Sheer Hulk* proved uneventful enough and he quickly adapted to the ways of a landlord, hard work and his inherent geniality combining to good effect. As for Uncle James, he stayed with his brother for nigh on three months. Then, towards the end of November, the call of the sea saw him vacate his room on The Common Hard in favour of a berth aboard a Portsmouth-based screw steamship. Back in uniform, he was a ship's steward once again – more particularly a military steward – assigned to the troopship *Perseverance*.

★ ★ ★

In the house at King Street, little was seen of Charley Black as Christmas passed and the New Year began to unfold. His visits to the family home were both very occasional and fleeting, as he strove to build on the early success of his new venture: and they were unrequited visits as far as his sister and nephew were concerned. Charlotte had forbidden William to go anywhere near the *Sheer Hulk* and this she was beginning to regret. Grandma Black, on the other hand, had become accustomed to visiting the inn, always happy to discreetly enter the private quarters via the Havant Street entrance and the stable yard. She would return home and tell her daughter how well Charley was doing and how presentable he had made the place. She would talk of his having let two rooms beyond that previously occupied by James and dwelt upon the pleasant nature of the lodgers and of the local girl Charley had recruited as a general servant. More importantly, she would hint at the fact that she had found no occasion, indeed, no need, to venture into any of the establishment's public areas, such as might cause a woman a degree of embarrassment. And similarly, out of earshot of her grandson – so as to prevent any unnecessary ill-feeling between mother and son – she would insist that there was really nothing to fear in allowing William to visit his uncle.

All this, quite naturally, whetted Charlotte's curiosity. She secretly began to wish she had reacted differently in the first place, that she had shown at least some enthusiasm towards her brother's newly envisaged career, even mere acknowledgement of his intent. Instead, through her latent, unresponsive criticism she had adopted a somewhat aloof moral high ground. Inwardly she was humble enough to acknowledge she had been wrong. She had been too hasty formulating her opinion and, shackled by her own sense of pride, realised it would be difficult to retract her stance without considerable loss of face. As for William, he remained oblivious to his mother's introspection and regrets. But he had become increasingly disgruntled by her unwillingness to allow him to visit his uncle and this was beginning to reflect in his behaviour.

William's state of mind was not assisted by the conclusion of the Paris peace negotiations, since this signalled the withdrawal of British troops from the Crimea. Suddenly Portsmouth awoke to the spring of 1856 and began to welcome back its ailing and wounded soldiers. But it was a muted homecoming, one too often tinged with tears and sadness, and frequently played out in the streets of Portsea for all to see. Gone were all the bands, the flag waving citizens and the jingoistic enthusiasm that had once cheered the soldiers onto the awaiting transports. Now, throughout the length of Queen Street, shouts of "Clear the way please" and such like would often resound above the general hubbub of people going about their business. Horse drawn traffic would slow or pull up, invariably as much in deference to the oncoming convoy as to any particular need to ensure it clear passage. The abstracted minds of shoppers and of others treading the narrow footpaths would be suddenly alerted to what was happening; and again, these folk would be inclined to halt awhile out of both respect and curiosity. Soon came the crunch of determined feet with further calls to clear the way. The first stretcher bearers would come into view – four sailors to a stretcher – as stretcher after stretcher was borne eastwards, each carrying a casualty bound for the new military hospital. Short of the occasional noise of a whinnying horse, a deferential silence would usually prevail, allowing the brittle rasp of the bluejackets' boots to eerily predominate – at least until one of the leading bearers saw the need, once more, to shout ahead to clear the way. Just occasionally a shrill, anonymous cry would ring out from an overhead window or from a bystander moved to say "Well done, lads" or "God Bless you fine fellows" or some such approbative remark. And then, as soon as the last stretcher had passed by, the resumed activity of traffic and pedestrians would promptly bring the curtain down upon the cameo, obscuring the convoy's progress towards the Lion Gate.

William began to tire of witnessing such episodes. He would often find himself in Portsea's principal thoroughfare, usually by dint of a circuitous walk home from school or in the normal course of running shopping errands. It was a desire to clear his head of a day in the schoolroom that had him sauntering southwards in the lee of the old Dockyard Wall on an uncharacteristically, muggy April afternoon. Emerging from the umbral confinement of Bonfire Corner, where dark, meagre hovels stood but an alleyway's width from the towering old Admiralty enclosure, William was at once sensible to the way the light played upon the fronts of the little Chapel Row homes that fell enticingly out of reach of the high wall's grasping shadow. Yet it was a vivid contrast that fell away as, overhead, a gathering gloominess suddenly raised the prospect of unexpected precipitation. The heavily budded tracery of the great elms that rose out of the lawns of Admiralty House and the Royal Naval College now looked stark against the presaging gloom. The trees' inhabitants, the rooks, called and squabbled vigorously as they busied themselves above the industry of the Dockyard, their noise vying with the yard's usual cacophony: the incessant whirring of all manner of machinery, the tapping of the caulkers' mallets, the shriller sound of the boilermakers' hammers, the occasional thud and vibration of the big, steam hammer.

As William approached and entered Queen Street, the sounds of the Dockyard receded beneath the general hubbub of townsfolk going about their daily routine and the ring and clatter of hoof and wheel plate upon cobbles. He felt a spot or two of rain. Shortly a heavy squall caused him to scurry for the shelter of a cantilevered overhang that was a feature of the London Provincial Bank. The street emptied as others made for a variety of dry havens. Menfolk sought out welcoming taverns, ladies opted for such shops and modest emporia that were to hand, rascally street urchins made a commotion and ducked and dived in a manner that only served to hinder the progress of adults bent on avoiding a drenching.

As William sheltered in the lee of the bank's façade and the rain's intensity showed little sign of abating, his senses were momentarily pricked by the whiff of smells – indiscernible ones but with a freshness of sorts – newly drawn from the cobbles and flagstones by the soft, spring rain. It was a piquancy that seemed to jostle uneasily with the earthy pungency of fruit and vegetables from a neighbouring greengrocer's stall, with the street's coarse smell of effluvia and poor drainage, of old ale and beerhouse victuals and of warm and wetted horse droppings that steamed upon the cobblestones.

There was little to challenge William's presence or to usurp his chosen place of shelter as he lingered out of the rain. A swarthy, grimy, young fellow had followed him there but to William's relief his proximity was fleeting. Within a minute or so he had abandoned the refuge in favour of the greater comfort of the *Fighting Cocks* taproom across the street, leaving in his wake a malodorous waft to define a lost presence: a waft that quickly became immersed in those other street smells and was gone. A gentleman was next to appear, immaculately dressed in a finely-tailored frock coat and tall, silk hat. He strode out of the Bank with his wife on his arm, his business complete. Then a coachman, who had been waiting with the gentleman's carriage in nearby Hanover Street, caught his employer's eye and set his animal at a gentle trot. William had noticed the fellow – moments earlier as the rain intensified – trying to struggle into a waterproof cape whilst showing little inclination to remove himself from the box seat. Now, as he pulled up outside the London Provincial, in front of his master, he showed a greater proclivity to set himself in motion – and with impressive effect. Jumping down, he grasped hold of a gamp from beneath the box and proceeded to brandish and unfurl it with the dexterity of someone better accomplished at swordsmanship than with hoisting umbrellas. He then swiftly ushered the gentleman and his lady into the shelter of their conveyance, hurriedly retrieved his seat and, with a crack of his whip, took the carriage clattering away across the wet cobbles.

William peered out from the refuge in which he now found himself alone. Through the slanting rain and murk he began to behold the rolling approach of a stretcher party, the exertions of the bluejackets only too apparent from their misty exhalations. Three stretchers in all, they bore on towards Queen Street, hugging the Dockyard Wall as they came; and as the spectre approached and gained definition, so the sound of twelve pairs of boots on granite rang out with ever growing resonance. In William's estimation, the bearers set a determined pace, being anxious to secure a dry haven for their charges, yet cautious enough to avoid a fearful mishap in the slippery conditions. And, as the party strode within reach of the London Provincial, its beckoning refuge drew a barked order from the Leading Rate who ran postilion on the front stretcher.

"Let's halt here and shelter awhile. We don't want these military fellows whingeing to the ward orderlies that we'd got 'em wet and they were all sickening for a chill." The killick remained straight-faced as he spoke. But they were words delivered with ironic intent and all part of an ongoing banter between the leading casualty and his bearers.

"Wet, indeed. I'm already as wet as a shag, damn you," exclaimed the soldier as he caught sight of the nearby *Fighting Cocks* tavern. "Now, if you scaly fish were to indulge me with a glass of six-and-tips from across the street I won't make it an issue with the hospital about you lot giving us a drenching."

"You've got to be joking, soldier," roared the Leading Rate. "If I were to deliver you into the hospital in a state of three-sheets, then, sure as eggs is eggs, I would receive the rough side of the orderlies' tongues"

"Three-sheets? It mightn't take more than a single downing of whisky and small beer to get you bluejackets tipsy but we military men are made of sterner stuff. I just fancy a livener, no more."

"You heard me soldier. No drink."

"Why you stiff-ars…"

"Heh…hold your tongue," screamed the Leading Seaman, suddenly realising that young company was to hand. The sailors had failed to notice William when they thundered to a halt beneath the Bank's welcoming canopy. In their defence this was attributable to the lad having retreated into the entrance door cavity, ostensibly for fear of being tumbled over by the rush of the oncoming convoy. Now he had re-emerged.

"Hello, young feller," said the talkative soldier as William's sudden appearance served to distract him from his irreverent yet good-humoured banter with the Leading Rate. "Have you just been in there to bank your riches? Or perhaps you haven't earned any yet but have grand thoughts of how you might!"

"No, sir," said William in all innocence. "But I've had thoughts of one day taking the Queen's shilling."

The soldier chuckled loudly. "Hey, lads," he boomed to his soldiering colleagues on the following stretchers. "This young'un says he wants to join the Army!"

William looked towards the two other prostrated men but there was little reaction. The fellow on the second stretcher wearily raised his hand as if to merely acknowledge the boy's presence. The other man looked pale and drawn, his breathing laboured. He reminded William of his father, when he had lain in the Haslar hospital…it was the same pallor, the same haunted look.

"There's no money in the Army m'lad," continued the soldier. "Unless, of course, you come from a privileged background and buy a commission. Then you can draw an officer's pay. Trouble is," he added, with a cynical sneer, "it also helps to be incompetent…and I'm pretty sure you don't meet that requirement by the looks of yer. Now…if you want my advice young feller, don't take that shilling…not unless you want to end up like this."

The rain continued to fall from a leaden sky. For their part the twelve sailors seemed pre-occupied, chatting among themselves and occasionally looking intently at the cloud cover, eager to spot any hint of unfolding brightness beyond the rooftops Being curious to learn more of the Crimean veteran's circumstances, William chose to continue their discourse.

"So what happened to you, sir?"

"No need to 'sir' me, lad. Just a common private, you see," came the humble reply. "Well, I suppose I ran out of luck at Inkerman. Have you heard of the place?"

"Certainly have, si…er…mister. I've read about it."

"A bad business…Inkerman. Fought in swirling fog it was. I remember we were in this damn gully on the slopes above the Tchernaya valley when we came upon a party of Russians. We put each other to the bayonet, cutting and thrusting, hampered all the while by deep brushwood. It was a fearsome struggle I can tell you. Anyway, this Russian blade opened up my left thigh…a deep cut it was…lost a lot of blood and…"

"Not too lurid, now," barked the Leading Rate who had overheard the mention of blood and was heedful of the responsibility he bore for the actions and behaviour of his charges. "He's too young to frighten with your gory yarns, soldier."

"I'll be fourteen this summer," was the indignant retort that spilled from William's lips.

"Fourteen, eh?…do yer hear that Mister Killick? The boy's nearly fourteen. Old enough to be a seasoned drummer-boy I reckon." The invalid's words had the effect of silencing the other man who simply adopted a scornful expression, then looked away.

"Well, as I was about to say before I was interrupted," continued the soldier, "a fellow in my company saw me fall and when things quietened down he came back and applied a good tourniquet. Saved my life I suppose. Well, they later took me by mule to the hospital in Balaklava…a real shit-hole that was…rats everywhere. I'd wake at night to feel the wretched vermin scurrying across m' blanket." The soldier stopped and looked thoughtful. He shuddered as, in his mind's eye, he vividly recalled the experience. "I hate rats," he said, as if to explain his hesitancy. "Yet all credit to the place, it was a deep wound and I got over it. Knitted together well enough, it did, and I was soon back in active service."

The man then proceeded to withdraw his right arm from beneath the stretcher blanket which William noticed was covered with a good oilskin: for all the badinage about being exposed to the elements, it was evident that only the bearers were delivered a copious soaking and had any cause for complaint. It was the sight of the soldier's arm, heavily bandaged and devoid of a hand that made William's blood run cold.

"This happened in the trenches just before the fall of Sebastopol. Taken clean off by a gunner's piece. Sadly I never saw it again...and strange to say it's not so much the hand I miss as the signet ring I had on the little finger. It was my grandfather's you see...wore it fighting in the Peninsula and now it's gone in the Russian mud...crying shame, young 'un." William's jaw had dropped, the consequence of being touched by the foot soldier's words and the wistful expression that told of the man's sadness. A few moments passed before the fellow resumed his story. "Well, they patched me up, then shipped me off to the Barrack Hospital at Scutari...but it didn't heal so well as the leg wound...it would weep and look a bit angry at times. All the same, they saw fit to send me back to dear old England but I tell you this...I'm glad to be off the leaky old tub and get shot of that sling tail and hardtack. The wound's continued to be troublesome while at sea...probably got infected because of the poor victualling. It's no wonder these sea-crabs always look so under-nourished." The last sentence was delivered more lustily and with a smirk upon the soldier's face. It drew the sought-after response.

"Nothing to do with ship's eats...not that I'm defending them," said the killick. "The sick bay attendants told me you'd been suffering from a fever... got quite delirious by all accounts...in addition to that oozing of matter from your stump. You weren't steady enough on your feet to be sent to the hospital in the omnibus but had to be stretchered. Which, of course, is another good reason, soldier, for not allowing you alcohol."

"Poppycock, Mister Killick. What harm's a glass of six-and-tips to an old campaigner like me?"

"Well, I'll tell you this...it would make the hospital's milky gruel curdle in your gullet. Yes, I understand the dormitory gruel is something quite particular...quite distinctive in its way, so as to speak. Indeed, I wouldn't mind wagering, soldier, that once you've sampled it you'll be hankering to be back onboard with the pickled pork and hardtack!"

Not surprisingly the soldier chose to ignore the Leading Rate's reflections upon hospital gruel and resumed talking to William.

"So what I say young'un, is that if I were you right now, I wouldn't touch the Army with a pair of tongs. I've seen too many brave young men perish...too many coffined long before their time and many not much older than yourself. I've seen 'em sitting around in camp, drilling and polishing... drilling and polishing...and by the time we were under orders to move out the cholera had put 'em in their coffins. Poor souls never even got sight of a Ruskie. Dreadful waste! Dreadful waste of young lives. I suppose, when I think about it, I was one of the lucky ones. I've got knocked about, yet I've lived to tell the tale. But what..."

"He'll be a lucky man that comes off wounded," murmured William, reflectively.

"What's that, lad?"

"Oh, it was just something my uncle wrote home from the *Vengeance*... before the fleet attacked Sebastopol. Your words reminded me."

"Well, I think it rings true in my case...by jove, yes...couldn't have wished for greater luck than when this got shot away," said the infantryman, pointing to his left ear. William noticed that the lobe was missing. "Taken off by a Russian minie ball. An inch or two nearer and I'd have been done for. I think the Good Lord was looking down on me...but you can't always trust in that. So get the soldiering life right out of your mind, boy...and don't let others persuade you otherwise."

"Let's go, lads," shouted the Leading Rate, putting an end to the soldier's homily. The rain had been slowly easing and now the brightening skies off the Solent carried promise of a dry evening. "Let's get these fellows tucked up in their hospital beds."

"Cheerio, young 'un," said the soldier, replacing his bandaged stump beneath his blanket. "Don't forget what I told you."

"No, mister. Thank you...and good luck."

With that William stood and watched the stretcher convoy recede in its passage along the still thinly peopled thoroughfare. He lingered until the stretchers disappeared from sight just short of the town fortifications and, as he lingered, he began to ruminate upon the soldier's insistence that he should not don the scarlet tunic. Uncle Charley had said as much after he returned from the war. Now he had heard it straight from the horse's mouth. At the close of the day it was in a disillusioned frame of mind that William Reynolds snuffed out his candle and placed a thoughtful head upon his pillow.

★ ★ ★

"We'll try to get a horse omnibus to Clarence Esplanade later, Willie. It would be a shame not to get a sight of the ships. Enjoy the day with your friend."

His mother's words continued to ring in William's ears as he made his way towards the main Dockyard Gate. It was soon after nine in the morning and, as he rounded the corner out of Halfmoon Street, into The Common Hard, William couldn't help being amazed by the crowds that already thronged the foreshore. The majority seemed to be drifting in the same direction as himself: along The Hard, past the Old Gun Wharf, then down through the old town and past the Clarence Barracks, thenceforward to emerge upon the broad swathe of Southsea Common.

The morning had broken to blue skies and brilliant sunshine. Throughout The Hard, and back along Queen Street, the commercial and retail premises were festooned with bunting and Union flags. It was altogether reminiscent of that early March day, two years before, when Charlotte and her mother had ventured to Portsea in search of accommodation. Reminiscent in all but the weather which today promised to look kindly upon the residents of Portsmouth and the many others who flocked to the town to see the ships. For today Her Majesty was again to review her fleet and, as before, the town and its hostelries were bursting at the seams. Uncle Charley, among others, would be doing well from it. All his available rooms, including Uncle James', had long since been rented out for the extended Review weekend and no doubt at a good tariff, for any accommodation that could be had in Portsea was said to be at a premium. William reflected on this as he sauntered past the *Sheer Hulk* – itself emblazoned with a huge Union flag – wondering whether the family who paid well to spend the night in his uncle's hay-loft, had also passed a restful night. Across the street, on the modest stretches of greensward and shingle that lay either side of the Royal Albert Pier, hardier and more impoverished visitors set about brushing themselves down after a night in the open air.

"Good morning, Missus Downer," said William to the mousy little woman who opened the front door in Rosemary Lane. It was a tiny cottage that stood just across the street from the gun carriage stores, its dowdiness somehow complementing the diffidence of the widow who lived within. "Is John ready?"

The woman didn't answer her caller directly but sniffed and turned away, wiping her nose on a grimy piece of muslin as she did so. "John!...John!" the woman shrieked, in a manner raucous enough to conflict with her normally retiring nature, yet effective enough to penetrate the far reaches of her modest home.

The shrill call brought the boy hurrying from the scullery, his ablutions curtailed by the imperative tone of his mother's voice. "Hello, Willie," he panted as he tumbled into the front passage, his momentum threatening to carry him beyond the threshold. "Good to see you," he muttered, as, clutching the front door jamb, he exhaled audibly then greeted his friend with a broad grin.

"Calm down, John," said Missus Downer as she thrust a comb into her son's hand, the suggestion being that he was too dishevelled to take to the streets of Portsea. "Don't be late. There'll be a nice hot bowl of tripe and onions on the table at seven," she continued, watching John's cursory attempt to tidy his hair, "but at eight it will only be fit to put out for the cat."

"Yes, Ma." The boy's concise reply gave little hint of whether he grasped the import of his mother's remark.

"Goodbye, Missus Downer," said William. Again they were words that failed to summon a response, the mousy mother of John Downer having closed her door upon the world before they had fully faded.

Instead of turning right out of Rosemary Lane – past the old town stocks that had shackled many a miscreant over the years – the two friends decided to opt for a quieter route. Mingling with the crowds intent on following the course of the Gun Wharf's boundary wall into the old town, did not appeal to them. In preference they took off in the opposite direction, snaking and meandering through a myriad of poor little courts and backwaters which lay in the direction of the southern extremities of Portsea's landward fortifications. They were, according to John Downer, byways with which he was well acquainted. Soon, emerging from a dank alley, they came upon the Free Ragged School that cowered beneath the lofty edifice of an old brewery which must have cast the schoolrooms in perpetual gloom, even in high summer. The towering building rose cheek by jowl with the school but it struck William that it was the sickly sweet smell of mash and yeast that must have been the greater irritant.

"I don't think we'll complain of tarred hemp in future, Johnnie," observed William, having already remarked upon the relative acceptability of the Dockyard smells that often pervaded the school at Bonfire Corner.

For the moment William had entirely overlooked the fact that his friend's schooling had drawn to a close. A classmate of William for the past two years, circumstances had conspired to cause him to leave school the previous month – at Easter. His father had died. Found on the beach with his throat cut before the year was a month old. It was said, but not generally bandied about, that he had been drinking heavily and would have been too stupefied to have known much about it. But the police had yet to verify whether it was murder or suicide and it was beginning to appear that they never would. Anyway, the upshot was that John the elder's demise meant that John the younger had to assume the role of breadwinner. He had left school and been working until recently as an errand-boy for a Queen Street fruiterer…until the dealer discovered that, from the middle of May, John was to take up an apprenticeship in the Dockyard's block manufactory and he wanted an errand boy longer term.

"I can't say I dislike any of those Dockyard smells, Willie. Which is just as well, seeing I'll be in the midst of them soon."

"It's good that we can spend the day together, what with you no longer running errands and the schools being closed for the Review," said William.

"I don't miss the errands 'cos he paid a pittance and his fruit was rotten."

"Rotten?"

"Yes. Since he was so tight I thought I'd pinch some of his fruit when I made deliveries. Not so much that customers would notice, Willie…but most of it wasn't worth filching."

William said nothing. He knew that thieving and all manner of dishonesty was rife in Portsea. The place was awash with street arabs who'd rob their grandmothers of their last farthing, excepting that most of the little vagabonds were orphans with no grandmothers to plunder. But, for all that, he harboured a kind of frivolous admiration for the sheer brazenness, the brass-faced impudence, of the Portsea street urchins. Even some of his classmates had shamelessly admitted to nefarious deeds. One in particular would regularly regale his peers, on a Monday morning, with an account of how much coin he had drawn from the pockets of weekend shoppers. William, on the other hand, had been raised not simply to know right from wrong but, more importantly, to know, respect and cherish that distinction within the context of moral excellence and the dictum of the Ten Commandments. He had not seen this side of John Downer before, having never had cause to regard him as a dishonest boy. It shocked him mildly but, for all that, did not let it sully or threaten to undermine the friendship. William would not himself entertain stealing but he was prepared to turn a blind eye to such turpitude – at least when mildly engaged in – for the sake of preserving a good friendship. And, in William's simple judgement, the appropriation of poor fruit from an altogether niggardly employer, bent on foisting his inferior produce upon the unsuspecting, did not rank highly in the call for penance.

Nevertheless, for all his level-headedness and integrity there were powers at work which had begun to influence William's sense of conformity. To an extent this was attributable to external factors. Portsea was no Forton. For all his mother's attempts at cosseting him, William had spent the last two years growing up among youngsters who were generally more street-wise than him: invariably rough-and-ready types with greater freedom to roam and engage in unfettered, boyish pursuits. In contrast, William had been constrained in a female world where bourgeois values, propriety and intolerance held sway. He had never recovered from the loss of his dear father. A self-appointed substitute would periodically appear, always intent, it seemed – through assertive manipulation – to persuade William that a life afloat would be the making of him. In truth he loathed the thought. Then there was Uncle Charley – dear Uncle Charley. Granted, he saw more of him now, but the frustration of his mother's prohibition upon his visiting the *Sheer Hulk* cut William deep. Even his yearning to take the Queen's shilling had been rocked by Uncle Charley's stories and by what he had been told by the soldier from Inkerman who now reclined in the hospital in Lion Terrace. Added to which, William was on the cusp of his youth. In four months he would be fourteen. Physiologically there were changes afoot and, with those bodily changes, the parameters of William's ingrained sense of conformity were subconsciously being put to the test.

Emerging into the open beyond the Ragged School, the two friends turned south into a flagged concourse that fell between the Milldam Barracks – home to the Royal Engineers – and the towering right demi-bastion which defined the southern extremity of the landward fortifications.

"Race you to the top, Willie," cried John as he eyed the high terreplein.

"Not today, Johnnie," replied William who had already reached the short iron bridge which led to the Milldam Road. "We could do that any day," he continued, contemplating the sluicegate which fed the water ditches beyond the earthworks. The water that flowed through the sluice from the tidal millpond gurgled a tune, as freshly redolent of a bright spring morning as the vibrant daffodils that graced the turfed fortifications.

"We've time enough, Willie. The ships will be there to see all day."

"I'm not too bothered about the ships, Johnnie. The troops are turning out of Clarence Barracks this morning and they'll be parading on the Common. Should be a fine sight."

"In which case, Willie, I'll race you across the Mill Pond."

It was a challenge promptly taken up. A count of three triggered a hasty sprint down the Milldam Road which cut straight across the broad sheet of tidal water. Minutes later John Downer proclaimed himself the clear winner, as, gasping noisily, the contestants stumbled to a halt at the Landport Gate. There followed a gentle amble through the old town. Shortly the young companions found themselves amid a clamouring throng of exuberant sightseers who converged upon the Crooked Arch, the narrow, tunnelled footway that stood beside King William Gate. It was a time that called for patience, a time to ease and inch forward, until, released from constriction and temporary gloom, the expanse of Southsea Common unfolded beneath an azure sky.

"Look at the crowds, John," said William once they had ventured beyond the dispersing press of people who surged around the Gate's approach. In the middle ground, a detachment of soldiers was undergoing inspection, having attracted a significant body of onlookers. Further back, away from the foreshore, people strode determinedly from the direction of the Landport terraces and from Southsea homes and hostelries, clearly bent on joining those observers or on reaching the Clarence Esplanade beyond.

The friends agreed to take a look at the military parade before it returned to barracks, which was as well, for that return was not long in coming. Nonetheless, for ten minutes or more, they marvelled at the resplendent ranks of swallow-tailed red tunics that marched and wheeled across the turf. Occasionally, they were almost drawn to squint, such was the intense effect of metal accoutrements set sparkling in the sun; and then they would catch the whiff of pipe clay – freshly applied to belts and straps – borne on a delightfully invigorating breeze off the Solent. Once this spectacle had concluded, William and John set a course towards the Esplanade, first stumbling their way through a profusion of tents and equipages that hugged the edge of the greensward. Then, having cut and jostled a passage through the slow-moving crowds that thronged the seafront, they came upon the shingled beach where little space was to be had between reclining and high-spirited sightseers. Piemen and vendors of oranges, together with sellers of flags and all manner of trinkets, seemed to enjoy brisk business, such was the crowd they could trawl: and as a tray of oranges was thrust at the two companions, it prompted John Downer to jokingly quip that he hoped the fruit had been nowhere near his erstwhile employer.

Far out on the water, at Spithead, in a tender, blue haze, the fleet lay dressed at the anchorage, awaiting the scrutiny of its Sovereign. Closer in, and throughout the morning, the dimpling, jasper-blue water off the beach teemed with all manner of vessels that came and went: activity which climaxed, in the early forenoon, with the passing of the Royal family aboard the *Victoria & Albert*. It was in the immediate wake of this event, as the Royal Yacht receded in the distance, that William – and to a lesser extent, John – became increasingly restless and bored. In the late afternoon there was to be a sham attack by the ships on Southsea Castle but that was a few hours away and neither boy felt particularly inclined to tarry longer on their uncomfortable patch of shingle. And so instead they decided to stretch their legs by retreating to the comparative tranquillity of the Common, the intention being to take a walk eastwards, out towards Lumps Mill pond, before returning home.

As the companions moved away from the Esplanade and drew clear of the motley array of white tents which fringed the seaward edge of the Common, the boom of Royal salutes – initiated by the flagship, the *Duke of Wellington* – began to sound over the water. It suggested that Her Majesty was about to begin her inspection by moving through the lines and William – who had no particular head for heights – held a fleeting, sympathetic thought for the numerous bluejackets who were now manning the yards. Many, he reasoned, would consider it an honour. Others, with little stomach for it, and not being hardened topmen, could find the experience unnerving. It was fortuitous, thought William, that this St.George's Day had seen fit to bless the Hampshire coast with the most clement of weather.

Twenty minutes or so brought the strollers in sight of the windmill. Its home, the old Lumps area, boasted origins which long pre-dated the work of the convict gangs who had been brought here from the rotting hulks to transform the Great Morass. Now the Lumps Mill pond was the sole relic of that ancient, brackish marsh. A greensward, as fine as that upon which the troops paraded by the firebarn, lay before it; yet this was a more remote piece of ground, the noisy bustle of the crowds back on the foreshore – far less populous hereabouts – having fallen to a murmur at best. Instead, a more distinctive sound, the rich, sturdy thud of bat striking ball interspersed with shouts of 'howzat', 'well driven' or 'good ball' became increasingly audible to the boys from Portsea.

Clonk. It was the sound of a ball heartily struck in the middle of the bat. A ball administered such a thump as to carry it high into the blue…high enough that, when viewed from William's and John's approach, it rose well above the Lumps Mill backdrop on a trajectory that looped menacingly towards them. John Downer seemed transfixed. William, on the other hand, took the decision to try for a catch. Having reached its zenith the cricket ball seemed to slow, as if bent on deceiving the onlooker over its true path. William hesitated, unsure whether he would need to retreat or advance. As it fell to earth, and appeared to gather pace once again, he decided to move forward a few paces and braced himself…the cricket ball loomed threateningly…too far…he had committed himself too far forward…he fell back a step…the ground he needed to recover was not fully retrieved. In desperation William launched himself upwards and backwards, fearing he had misjudged the ball's flight and that it would fall to ground behind him. His feet parted company with the turf beneath, his right arm fully outstretched. Smack. It was the sound of leather upon sweaty flesh. Then, in the split-second it took William to complete his soaring movement and clatter spread-eagled upon the grass, he was gripped by a surging sense of achievement. Yes, the ball remained tightly cupped in his right palm. Silence seemed to accompany William's immediate thoughts, as he reflected upon his moment of triumph, but it was merely fleeting. Distant cheers and shouts of congratulation were soon to ring in the catcher's ears as just reward for his endeavour. Nearby, John Downer stood rooted to the spot, his gaping mouth testimony to his admiration for William's newly revealed prowess as a fielder of cricket balls and to his own astonishment.

"Brilliant catch, Willie," exclaimed John once he had collected his wits and William had set about standing up and dusting himself down. Before William had a chance to reply the two boys were distracted by the trample of approaching feet.

"Damn good effort, matey. Fine enough catch to grace the East Hants Cricket Ground," said the tallest of the three boys who had hurriedly made their way from their makeshift cricket pitch. "We've just started a game, two against two with the spare man in the outfield. Do you fancy making it three against three? We could do with your fielding, matey."

William noticed that the fourth boy had stayed away…the boy William had effectively dismissed with his fine catch. He had chosen to prostrate himself in front of his wicket, his pride decidedly wounded by having such a well-middled ball caught in the deep.

"Take no notice of him," said the tall boy, having realised William was peering into the distance at the procumbent batsman. "He'll be sulking but he won't be given out since you weren't playing at the time. But you will play, won't you?"

William caught the eye of John Downer in anticipation that the strength of his friend's willingness – or otherwise – to participate in a cricket match, would manifest itself. For his part William found the tall boy a shade intimidating. This was partly attributable to his height but also to his scruffy, unsavoury appearance. Up close he exuded a disagreeable smell that told of poor hygiene, the grime that clung to his threadbare garments suggesting that a visit to a wash-tub was long overdue. Yet, for all his resemblance of a street urchin, he spoke well enough and was of a friendly disposition. And as for his fellow cricketers…absent batsman aside…William detected similarities in terms of poor bodily hygiene, although both boys were better attired than the tall boy: and again, despite a rough appearance, affability seemed a strong point from the way they had enthused over William's catch and been quick to pat him on the back. The fact was that William seemed to warm to the company. As for his friend from Rosemary Lane, he said nothing, but his expression left William in no doubt that he was game for a contest. He had beaten William in the run across the Mill Pond but had been left in the shadow by this recent event. Perhaps he felt the need to put the record straight.

"We'll play," said William after some deliberation. It was the signal for the tall boy and his companions to collectively express their delight as the liberal application of further back patting was extended to both the newcomers.

"Come now," insisted the tall boy who cursorily introduced himself as Joshua Smith but expressed a preference for Felix. "These here friends of mine are Tim and John, but you can call them Mynn and Pilch."

"I'm William Reynolds and this is my friend, John Downer."

"Then come and meet another William…William Larkin. He's the one sulking at the crease. Also answers to the name of Parr as it happens," said Joshua, without further explanation.

"What's all this business with other names?" asked William Reynolds.

"Well the four of us enjoy our cricket…particularly me," explained Joshua, who had quickly shown himself, in the eyes of the new arrivals, as being the leader of the band of friends. "I got that love from my father, bless him. When Ma died of the cholera he gave up his job afloat to look after me and m'sister. Tried scraping something of a living at home, he did, by turning his hand to whipcording. It was then he used to tell me of how, when he was a boy, a carter would be hired to take his own father, himself, his uncles and cousins to the cricket matches on Broadhalfpenny Down. Apparently, after an evening's musical jollity in the *Bat and Ball* inn, the company would roll home as happy as anything and a shade over the mark…well, except the carter, I imagine…and hopefully my father and his cousins. Then, in his youth, he would go to see games at the East Hants Ground. And he would speak highly of the old Kent players…he was a Chatham man by birth you see. He loved Alfred Mynn, the fast bowler and Fuller Pilch, who he rated as England's finest batsman of his day. But he always said his favourite bat was Felix, the left-hander with his fine cover drives…and a good fielder at point by all accounts. Well they all played for Kent and he got to watch them a few times in matches against Hampshire… but after Ma died, and we fell on harder times, he couldn't afford to go to any more cricket matches…" Joshua's words tailed off as he became a touch reflective and a hint of sadness clung to them. "Anyway those old players had begun to get past their best."

"Mynn still plays, doesn't he?" piped up John Downer, suggesting he knew a little about the game.

"I think he does," declared Joshua, as the little group reached the bowling strip, such as it was. "Meet Willie Larkin…also known as Parr. C'mon Willie, get yerself up y' little beggar. Show some pluck and stop sulking. You're still in, courtesy of Willie Reynolds here not being one of us players when he caught you. But he is now…and this is Johnnie Downer."

The newcomers caught the eye of the recumbent bat who nodded in acknowledgement and began to clamber to his feet, his look of disgruntlement beginning to wane.

"So anyway," continued Joshua Smith, "we come out here on the Common and call ourselves by our cricketing nicknames. We used my old man's favourites and, with me being left-handed and lofty, it seemed right and proper that I adopted the name of his true favourite…Nicholas Felix. Larkin here was last to join the group and he chose the name of George Parr, the Nottinghamshire cricketer, on account of his mother coming from up that way."

"I've heard of him," said young Downer. "A very good batsman, I believe."

"Absolutely, hits the ball all round the ground. A good choice of name really, 'cos, as you've seen, Willie Larkin can strike a ball well enough."

The newly formed friendship was not put to the test there and then, Felix acknowledging that, in all fairness, the two against two in progress warranted a meaningful conclusion, unfettered by a further influx of players. And so the fresh recruits were asked to bide their time as the surly Parr renewed the dogged defence of his wicket, a defence not unduly threatened by some indifferent round-arm bowling from Messrs. Mynn and Felix. The 'Kent pair' had, by all accounts, amassed a good haul of runs before Parr's partner, Pilch, was dismissed cheaply, caught out by a snorter of a short-pitched ball from Mynn.

The afternoon drifted on. An hour and more elapsed and throughout, Willie Larkin – the surly Parr – stood resolutely, bails and stumps intact. Gone was any suggestion of gay abandon, gone the savage hitter. Indeed, William Reynolds might have been excused the thought that this batsman – still irked by having been caught by some upstart – had drawn upon such inner resources and powers of concentration to cause the new arrivals a lengthy wait before they could take to the field. Were this the lad's intent, then he succeeded. Runs were slowly garnered, by judicious running between the wickets, as Larkin whiled away the afternoon with an innings more notable for its forward defensive strokes than for any flamboyant wielding of his bat. And so it was mid-afternoon before the match was concluded, the immovable Parr eventually deceived and dislodged by a Felix spinner that found middle and off. It was a timely dismissal for the 'Kent pair' since the scores were tied with Pilch and Parr on the cusp of claiming victory.

There was no appetite for further competition, especially as far as Felix, Mynn, Pilch and the indomitable Parr were concerned. Their exertions and the warmth of the day had taken their toll. Thirst desperately required quenching, a need also shared by the two spectators.

"There were sellers of lemonade and ginger beer over on the Clarence Esplanade," remarked John Downer. "I expect they'll also be mingling with the crowds near Southsea Castle."

"Then let's go," said Felix, whereupon, without any argument or hesitation, all ambled off in the direction of the foreshore. As they approached the beach and set their tread westwards, towards the Castle, the crowds about them seemed to swell with every step. William, looking back from an elevated position where the high mark of the tide-tossed shingle crested against the salty turf, thought he could detect a distant blaze of yellow beyond Lumps Mill. Suddenly, memories of his day out with Grandma Black at Portsdown Fair came flooding back. It was April and the common gorse flower, being in its prime, reminded William of his late encounter with Ned, the gypsy youth…just before they left to catch the Portsea omnibus. For it was out there, somewhere amid the thorny whin, that Ned said his family pitched their tents. William remembered the youth imploring him to let his gnarled, toothless grandmother give him a tuppenny reading of his palm…and for this purpose to sometime seek her out in the furze. There and then he had promised himself that one day he would do so and, in this regard, his resolve had not diminished. But today was not the time. He would need to be heading homeward in the opposite direction before too long and, in all likelihood, the Romanies would now be away on their itinerant travels.

As the six approached Southsea Castle progress slowed. Myriads of sightseers were encountered, such that, behind the beach, the path became virtually impassable, the crowd seemingly loath to give ground. Attention had been drawn seaward as guns began to roar. Strollers upon the near parts of the Common interrupted their perambulations and hurried to the foreshore, there to vie for good vantage points amid the already milling throng of spectators. The sham fight had commenced. A flotilla of gunboats poured mock fire towards the old Tudor castle, much to the delight and amusement of the jostling onlookers.

"Do you have a few coppers?" asked Joshua Smith of his two new friends.

"I've tuppence ha'penny," said William, delving deep into his trouser pocket.

"That'll do, shaver," replied Joshua. "You'll have it back…just wait here." And with that he beckoned to his three cricketing chums who huddled close to their leader. Whispered words were exchanged. A split-second later and the four had gone, swallowed up in the midst of an assemblage of colourfully adorned tents and wagons which stood upon the near greensward, behind the pressing crowd.

Five or ten minutes elapsed during which time William and John became absorbed in the activity that surrounded them. The gunboat fire continued to reverberate briskly and repetitively across the water, the watching crowd itself infused with self-generated murmurings of expectancy and excitement. Veils of smoke drifted, wreath-like towards the beach. The whiff of powder hung in the air. Suddenly, Pilch, Mynn and Parr reappeared from the direction in which they had so quickly vanished. As they re-emerged William tried to banish thoughts of pseudonyms in favour of putting real names to the cricketing friends but could only recall that of his namesake whose pretence was that of Parr. The threesome panted heavily, each clutching a glass of fruit cordial.

"Share this," gasped Mynn as he thrust his glass towards William. "Drink it down and when Felix gets back we'll be out of here." It was a glass in which the liquid swirled about well below its brim, the deduction being that a gulp had already been extracted or a spillage incurred.

"Where is Joshu…er, Felix?" enquired William as he despatched a modest swig of the fruity drink before handing the glass to John Downer.

"I'm here," beamed Felix as he popped out of the crowd from the most unlikely direction, suggesting that he had forged his way through from the beach. Grasping Pilch's glass, he quickly drained whatever thirst quenching nectar remained.

"Did you have enough money?" chirped William.

"More than enough mate," chuckled Felix. "Hold out your hand." William tendered his right hand whereupon the smirking Joshua Smith dropped tuppence ha'penny into the outstretched palm. "Said you'd have it back, Willie."

"But…"

"Ask no questions, shaver," insisted Felix, who appeared pre-occupied, furtively casting glances all around. "Let's be on our way." His words were scarcely audible beneath a deafening finale of naval firepower: and as Her Majesty returned to harbour aboard the Royal Yacht, the six boys from Portsea hurriedly set a homeward course across the Common.

"Sorry you didn't get to play cricket this afternoon but we were down on our beam-ends and thirst-ridden by the time young Willie Larkin's wicket fell," said Joshua Smith as he walked with William ahead of the others. "Anyway, if you want to join us you're both welcome. We all live in Portsea and usually meet on a Saturday in St. George's Square…behind the church, at two o'clock. Since we already have a William and a John then it's important you each choose a cricketer's name…if you can't think of any it might help to find a copy of *Lillywhite's Guide*. Oh, and don't worry… we don't go all the way out to Lumps. We usually play near *The Cricketers* tavern and Ballards Mill, only today the area was swarming with people and the military got their shirts out when we tried to set up near the firebarn."

In William's estimation his new found cricketing friends would not be the sort of fellows his Mother would wish him to befriend: but then, she needn't be privy to the Saturday company he might choose to keep.

To simply be told he was engaged in the healthy pursuit of cricket, with chaps of his own age, would doubtless cheer her. As William saw it, they were typical Portsea lads…impoverished, rough diamonds, of dubious habit, yet likeable and good-hearted if he had judged Master Smith – alias Nicholas Felix – correctly. He had yet to strike up a relationship with the others. Yet William had been impressed by the way Felix had returned his tuppence ha'penny when he might have plausibly proclaimed it spent, albeit six thirsts had been slaked and suspicions raised. He chose not to dwell on that thought but to close his mind to it. He would grasp the weekly opportunity to break away from the constraints and shackles of the family home and play cricket.

William stopped and turned on his heels. They had entered Green Row, which, earlier in the day, had thronged with people freshly spilled through the tight tunnelled access that carried them expectantly beyond King William Gate. Now it was the haunt of a modest sprinkling of sightseers bent on an early evening homecoming. John Downer, in earnest conversation with the other fellows, sauntered along thirty yards behind Felix and William.

"John, do you fancy a game of cricket on Saturday afternoon?," shouted William.

"Count me in," came the reply.

Minutes later six young fellows tumbled through the Crooked Arch, their chatter resounding off the tunnel's walls. "Howzat!," someone screamed. Laughter followed. The utterance and ensuing noise of merriment reverberated eerily, then died.

★ ★ ★

A year passed. It was a year during which, on the surface at least, William's irritations and frustrations with life were held in check. He knuckled down to his studies when he had shown signs of indifference, the spark to arresting apathy having most certainly been his elevation to the role of pupil teacher in the schoolroom. An able enough scholar, William's fading aptitude had not gone unnoticed by his perceptive schoolteacher who saw fit to charge him – along with two other boys – to help in matters of class control. It was a masterstroke in the sense that it restored commitment. Furthermore, with that responsibility came the added inducement of receiving a certificate from the School Board, were William to acquit himself well. This cheered Charlotte since she was swift to appreciate that a pupil teacher certificate was a sure milestone upon the path to becoming a school teacher should her son have a calling for the profession.

On the domestic front, nothing extraordinary happened to impact upon or unduly stir the lives of those residing beneath the roof of 31 King Street, Portsea. Another birthday came and went – William's fourteenth – and, as before, a birthday supper was convened with Uncle Charley and John Downer the guests of honour. Young John had appeared on the doorstep in the wake of the sounding of the Dockyard's final bell, having decided it was too much of an effort, after a day lugging balks of timber for the machinists, to make his way home to change. And so he took his meal in his workaday clothes that seemed long overdue for the wash tub, so deeply imbrued were they with the smell of the block mills. Sweetly scented, however, and in sharp contrast, Uncle Charley arrived immaculately dressed in a light, summer-weight jacket which he promptly discarded in favour of sitting at table in billowing white shirt sleeves. His head seemed larger, an impression merely conjured by his cultivation of bushy side-whiskers that nestled into his upright collar – a blend of starched whiteness and wiry facial hair that set off his velutinous, burgundy waistcoat and the matching silk fogle in a manner that marked Uncle Charley out as something of a gentleman. Aside from acknowledging William's fourteenth birthday, it was a celebration memorable for two reasons for the family members present. Firstly, there was the overwhelming smell of stale perspiration and the block manufactory of which – presumably on account of familiarity – young Downer seemed oblivious and in no sense moved to feel uneasy. Secondly, it proved a watershed in the restoration of good relations between Charlotte and her brother. Charlotte, of course, remained bent on effecting reparation over the thorny issue of refusing to visit the *Sheer Hulk*. Yet she was bereft of any good reason to effect a climb-down without losing face. That good reason presented itself once the remnants of the birthday supper had been cleared away and the two friends had retired to the back garden to sit and jaw and sup ginger beer in the fast receding twilight. Indoors, meanwhile, the three adults had withdrawn to the parlour.

Charley had intended broaching the matter discreetly, out of earshot of his sister, for fear of her bridling somewhat. He was only too aware that she continued to hold reservations about his establishment, knowing full well that although he had held the licence for nigh on twelve months, Charlotte had yet to cross the threshold; and, of course, on her own instruction, neither had Willie. But as it happened, Grandma Black inadvertently paved the way for Charley to ask his favour since she had no qualms about quizzing her son over the state of his business in front of his sister, being somewhat contemptuous of her daughter's contrariness as she saw it. As Charlotte poured tea for the three of them Margaret chatted away to her son about his work. Yet the younger woman seemed unmoved as she listened to her brother elaborate about plans to refurbish the stable yard and to her mother's commiserations over the fact that liquor sales had gone into decline once the war had ended and the town's activity subsided. And so, with talk of the public house having seemingly failed to raise his sister's hackles, Charley was confident enough to ask the favour of his mother there and then, a favour which he hoped would not be viewed as too much of an imposition.

"Mother, dear," began Charley, "talk of the business reminds me of a little difficulty I seem to be facing. It only came to light last week and involves the servant girl, Rachel Ellis. Well…"

"Not in need of confinement, is she?"

"No, no, Mother. No, she's a good, responsible child…well, young woman…is Rachel. No, she needs to go to Alresford, out Winchester way, in three weeks' time and will be gone two or three days. Her sister is to be wed and Rachel tells me she's to be a bridesmaid."

"Not some yarn, son…to get time off?"

"No, Mother. I believe her and anyway she's due some time off. And apart from that she presented me with a letter from the clergyman who is conducting the marriage ceremony. Her widowed mother and the sister are unable to write but the village sexton – a family friend by all accounts – said he would ask the rector if he would kindly write to confirm and so he did and…well, it's all above-board."

"And so how does this concern me and what of this favour? They don't need another bridesmaid do they? If so I'm a bit up in the tooth and too full in the waist, son, to be donning white muslin, coronet and rose-buds!" It was a hearty retort, bolstered by an ensuing burst of laughter from the speaker that Charley attributed to a little excess sherry. He glanced at Charlotte. As their eyes met Charley realised that his sister was not shirking from the fact that she had been genuinely amused by their mother's witty remark, notwithstanding its association with goings-on at the *Sheer Hulk*. It had set her chuckling which, in turn, disturbed her composure and set the cup of tea she was handing to her mother rattling precariously in its saucer. Once equanimity was restored Charley continued.

"As a matter of fact, Mother, Rachel's absence…and it would be heartless of me to deny the girl…will coincide with a function I am committed to on the Friday evening…the day of the wedding.

"What sort of function, son?"

"Well, it's to do with a Friendly Society. They were wanting a room for a meeting, then a cold supper. They've said the large first floor room at the back of the building is ideal for their meeting…but I was relying upon young Rachel to prepare and lay out the food…in the oak-panelled anteroom that overlooks the stable-yard, if you can picture it."

"So is this where I come in, son? That you're wanting someone in your servant girl's stead to prepare the victuals?"

"Well…yes, Mother…if you'd consider it…and I'd recompense you well for the time and trouble, 'cos they're paying well, you see," said Charley, apologetically, and in a faltering tone.

"How many son?"

"Upwards of two dozen I think."

"Well, it sounds a tall order, Charley. I'm not getting any younger you know."

"I'd cart all the food upstairs, Mother…before I have to busy myself in the taproom."

"That's as may be, but it does sound a lot of work, son…although I'd dearly like to assist you with your difficulty."

"I'll help…you can't be doing it on your own, Mother," piped up Charlotte. The silence that had momentarily filled the room on the heels of Charlotte's interjection was palpable as mother and son inwardly dwelt upon her words in disbelief. Charlotte, for her part, had been listening intently to the course of the conversation and had made her move as the hoped-for opportunity presented itself. Here was good enough reason to retract from her previous stance through a commendable offer of assistance designed to benefit all three. Yet what Charley failed to appreciate was that the sense of relief it offered him was, in truth, outweighed by the greater degree of assuagement that played upon his sister's own sensibilities.

Margaret Black, on the other hand, was more attuned to her daughter's guile, be it on account of astuteness or womanly intuition. "Thank you, my dear," she had said in return, earnestly and secretly hopeful that this heralded an end to her daughter's contrariness and her obsession with acting out of pique to nobody's particular disadvantage save her own – and, of course, William's.

Not surprisingly, however, the last word had fallen to Charlotte. It was

244

as if to underline that her willingness to assist her Mother was in no way to be seen as her having come to terms with Charley running 'a sailors' beer-house', as she was prone to call her sibling's establishment.

"I have to say, brother, that I will not entertain venturing within sight or sound of any drinking den. Indeed, while I am favourably inclined to assist, this is entirely dependent upon my understanding that your private rooms can be separately accessed. Separately accessed that is from any areas which...what shall we say...well...any that may give a responsible and respectable woman due cause for embarrassment."

When the day arrived for the Friendly Society gathering, Charlotte and her mother had been greeted on the rear entrance steps by a beaming landlord, anxious to usher them inside and demonstrate to his sister that his own assurances held true; assertions which, after all, had received the constant affirmation of Grandma Black, already familiar with the nature of her son's hostelry. With that demonstration promptly effected by a tour of Charley's private rooms, the trio descended to the distempered cellar kitchen where Rachel had earlier lit the range and tidied up before setting off to catch the Friday coach to Winchester. And so the necessary preparations had been set about with ardour and, come the afternoon, Charley Black was flitting in and out as he ferried the component parts of a cold buffet supper to the first floor table.

In essence the day had proved a resounding success. By late afternoon Margaret Black and her daughter had completed their culinary preparations and made their way home. The Friendly Society had been delighted with what had been placed before it and said it would like to repeat the exercise when the need arose. More importantly, as far as brother and sister were concerned, the ice had been broken. Charlotte had not encountered any drunken sailors, although in truth she had not imagined she would. It was simply a concern she had manufactured in the course of maintaining her erstwhile intractability as far as the *Sheer Hulk* was concerned.

With cordiality fully restored between brother and sister, Christmas 1856 had been a joyous affair. On Christmas Day the family had answered the peal of church bells but on the conclusion of morning service it was not in the direction of hearth and home that they hurried away through the cold Portsea streets. Charley had insisted on providing Christmas dinner and, as the little group picked its way across a stable yard puddled with ice, it had been his cheerful cry of "Merry Christmas" from the threshold that enticed eyes away from the glistening cobbles. There followed a most convivial afternoon and evening for the landlord had gone to a lot of trouble. Downstairs the public house was open for business but Charley had left this in the capable hands of his senior potman, for he wished to devote his time and attention to playing host to the family in his upper rooms. There, in the front parlour – which doubled as a dining room – the spirit of the season had been there to behold. The room was festooned with holly, heavily berried and newly purchased from the holly cart, while, high on a corner drum table, a potted Christmas tree was gaily hung with sugar plums, walnuts and real and imitation fruits. And as the new arrivals sipped a little mulled wine, to ward off the street chill, Uncle Charley had coaxed William towards the window. Down below, close to the Royal Albert Pier entrance, a group of hardy carollers were working their way through some favourite hymns, ably supported by a waits band. Their breath billowed mistily in the still air but it was not the gentle strains of *Silent Night* that caught William's attention. A goodish crowd had assembled in a crescent about the singers, all stock still in their engagement: save, that is, for the subtle drift of new arrivals and of others now charged with such a sufficiency of listening – or so deterred by the cold – as to yield to more pressing interests elsewhere. The exception was a lanky youth who continued to weave his way among the spectators, a movement which promptly drew William's eye. The lad wore a grimy cap and muffler and draped over his left shoulder were strings of brightly painted wooden and tin trinkets: baubles that would grace a Christmas tree or thrill a young child if brought home by a returning parent, chilled yet with spirits lifted by the joyous hymns of the season. The muffled youth had doubtless been swift to realise this, and, as he meandered through the targeted throng, many onlookers had appeared only too willing to trade their pennies for his gaudy trifles.

Beckoned by a potential customer, the young pedlar had momentarily emerged at the back of the crowd and faced the buildings across the street. It had been then that William recognised his swarthy features…the same fustian jacket…the same dark complexion…in no sense paled by midwinter's clime. It was Ned, the Romany youth, Ned, the gypsy.

"So they must be back in the furze," William had whispered to himself, not intending that his murmuring should carry: yet Uncle Charley was blessed with an acute sense of hearing.

"Who must be back where, my lad?"

"Er…nothing, Uncle," muttered William. "I was just talking to myself."

"Well, you know what they say about people who do that."

William smiled and made a face as Uncle Charley wheeled around in reaction to a rat-a-tat-tat upon the door. "Come," he had bellowed, startling his mother and sister in the process.

The general servant, Rachel Ellis, opened the door. William had seen the girl before, on his several visits to his Uncle's abode since his mother had – without any particular explanation, it has to be said – lifted the prohibition. But she had not commanded his attention. Now, however, William had settled a watchful eye upon the girl, allowing his gaze to survey her from head to toe – from starched cap to peeping shoe – and back again. She had struck him as pretty, in the sense that her features were simple; a well proportioned, symmetrical face, framed gently between sweeps of chestnut hair, drawn back into a tight chignon. Her cheeks bore the most subtle of blushes, falling to pertly shaped lips that resembled a taut young rosebud. Her lashes were long and belonged to blue-grey eyes redolent of the colour of watery, distant hills, emergent through autumn mist. Yet it had been the air of confidence the girl exuded that William had found most appealing...that, and the crisp sweep of her dark dress and the fringed stiff apron bib that lay starkly white across her bodice.

"Dinner is ready to serve, sir," said the girl, as she simultaneously made a double curtsy towards the two female guests and followed her announcement with a polite "Compliments of the season ma'am...and to you ma'am."

With such formalities having been well received by Charlotte and her mother, Charley had responded with a cheery, "Well, bring the meal forth my dear without further ado." And so she did.

The fetching and carrying of what appeared to William, an endless assortment of covered dishes and a gravy boat, had heralded the arrival of a fine spit-roasted goose with an accompanying choice of apple or goose-stuffing sauce. The host had proceeded to roll up his sleeves before setting about dismembering the poor bird, and then, with this ritual despatched, little time was lost in setting about the meal with relish. Second helpings had followed, only to be hurriedly consigned, like the first, to the custody of digestive juices. Uncle Charley had then rung a bell to beckon the servant girl, who promptly arrived to clear away the dinner plates, only to re-emerge moments later bearing a rich plum pudding. Another ritual had followed. Charley doused the pudding with brandy from a silver hip flask, then ignited the liquor to the delight of his nephew, a joy swiftly followed by William having had the good fortune to bite upon a silver threepenny piece. No, he had not stirred the pudding mixture, but in his uncle's assessment, this did not disqualify the lad from making a wish; and so he had proceeded to do so in all seriousness and with a commitment to secrecy, for fear that his wish might otherwise remain unfulfilled. Sadly, for all its delectability, the bulk of the plum pudding had been destined for a return to the kitchen. There it was banished to the larder stillage to await cold eating, all having feasted a little too lavishly upon goose and vegetables.

At eight in the evening, following a lengthy interlude of post prandial slumber, tea and mince pies and the dispensing of sugared almond bon bons by Uncle Charley, it was deemed time to return to King Street. This was not least because Grandma Black had been feeling a shade liverish. And so, in William's estimation, a most delightful Christmas Day had begun to wind down. It was a day when he had carried home thoughts of a secret wish and of having seen Ned the gypsy, underlining the fact that the travellers were encamped, yet again, in the furze and of the need to venture there for his fortune-telling before they resumed their travels. It had also been a day when a girl of nineteen – five years his senior – had made something of an impression upon him, and, in the days and weeks to come, reflections upon wishes and fortune-telling were to become subordinated by infatuation.

In a social sense, the year since the Fleet Review had seen friendship blossom between William, John Downer and the four cricketers. Early on, one of the cricketers had confided in William and John what they already suspected. At Southsea Castle, Joshua Smith had distracted the vendor by proffering William's coppers, only for the others to snatch the drinks from under the poor fellow's nose and make off. It was an admission that amused young Downer, and, while such wrongdoing failed to impress William, he was still minded to turn a blind eye, since he had begun to cherish the cricket matches the new fellowship had brought forth. Downer, meanwhile, had found an article upon the heyday of the Hambledon club in which the two friends became absorbed. The outcome was that, from those pages, they each plucked the name of a celebrated old cricketer who had honed his craft on Broadhalfpenny Down in the last century, and these became their epithets when they played the game on a Saturday afternoon. William chose the name of 'Silver Billy' Beldham, reputed to have been the most elegant of batsman and a fine slip fielder, although it was not so much these attributes that influenced his choice but the fact that his Christian name was William. As for young John, he had quickly opted for the fiddle-playing batsman, John Small, again, no doubt, on account of his first name. And thus, as Beldham and Small, the two friends had enjoyed that first summer playing cricket upon the sweep of Southsea Common. And come September, when bat and ball were put away for another year, William could look back on matches when he had received repeated plaudits for his slip-fielding. He had not excelled with the bat, but, through his fielding alone, was able to derive a modicum of justification for having chosen the nimble 'Silver Billy' for his cricketing sobriquet.

In the wake of Christmas, as the New Year unfolded, William's thoughts of Miss Ellis had most certainly intensified. They became obsessive and he took to visiting his Uncle Charley with far greater frequency, in the earnest hope that he would, at the very least, catch a glimpse of the girl. At best he had wished to engage her in conversation although, had he done so, he had no idea what he might have said. In all likelihood nervousness would have thrust him into foolish prattle, so in awe was he of Rachel, but in actuality William's visits brought little contact with the self-assured young maid. And so, on those dark January and February nights, when he had retired to bed and extinguished his light, it was with pensive feelings of malcontent and frustration that he wrestled. Adolescence, of course, had brought him to this, for William was encountering its early stages, being in his fifteenth year. Physiological changes were in progress, changes that confused, changes that in the seclusion of his room transposed the reverence he felt for Miss Ellis into lustful cravings for the girl. They were yearnings that were destined to be unfulfilled, to be dashed and reduced to wreckage like an unmanned galleon adrift upon a turbulent ocean.

It was often in the turmoil of such yearnings that William found himself drawn into self-abuse, heightening and translating them, fleetingly, into something more tangible. His young loins would convulse, then subside in relief, confusing his sensibilities, perhaps offending them, in its wake. Then slumber would embrace him. Subsequently, on a March day, William had overheard two boys talking candidly upon the practice to which he had succumbed. One said he did it when taken with thoughts of a neighbour's daughter for whom he had a real liking. The second boy likewise appeared familiar with such gratification, claiming that on a recent occasion he had been horrified when his mother came in the room. Later he had been chastised by his step-father who told him it would turn him blind if he persisted and there was even a chance he would end up an imbecile. When William heard this it piled fear upon bewilderment. And so he had resolved to desist from any further activity that could precipitate the impairment of his sight or set him on course for the asylum.

★ ★ ★

It was April once again. The uplifting effect of vernal days was failing to impact upon William. Instead, the antithesis – despondency – seemed to invade his mind. For one thing the novelty of being elevated to a pupil teacher had lost its gloss; additional schoolroom responsibilities had become burdensome as the year progressed and now William saw little purpose, little incentive, in gaining a certificate for his labours. After all, he knew full well that teaching was not for him. And so apathy began to return and there was little place for it to hide. The perceptive schoolmaster, who had shown faith in his pupil and bestowed on him additional responsibility, was understandably irked to realise his judgement had been left wanting, that he had seriously overestimated William Reynolds. Indeed, it so raised his bile that he showed little compunction in swiftly demoting him for his lack of commitment. Charlotte was gravely disappointed by her son's behaviour. William became increasingly sullen and the relationship between mother and son so strained that an atmosphere pervaded the house in King Street.

Once the weather improved the prospect of playing Saturday cricket again would offer a welcome diversion from routine and no doubt help lift William's malaise. But for now the lighter April evenings promised some relief for William in getting him out of the house and meeting up with his cricketing friends, albeit with insufficient time to venture far and apply bat to ball. And there was no Johnnie Downer, for during the week he worked long and wearisome hours in the Dockyard and took to retiring early to his bed. There was, of course, the alternative allure of visiting dear Uncle Charley. It was a strong one, and in William's mind influenced more by the beguiling thought of seeing Rachel Ellis than spending time with his uncle. Yet he knew it would be futile. It was the worst time of day. Uncle Charley would be heavily involved in the taproom while the object of William's unrequited captivation would be busily occupied with her evening chores below stairs. And so William chose to engage himself in what he regarded as the next best thing. With supper finished and cleared away by half past six, he would usually depart the house for a couple of hours, ostensibly to meet up with his friends. It was a practice Charlotte considered prohibiting at first, because of continuing resentment over William's recent failings in the schoolroom. Grandma Black intervened, however, and she didn't mince her words. On the contrary, she was at pains to remind her daughter that a hasty action based upon wounded pride could prove a baneful one, citing the ill-feeling over her sibling's enterprise as a case in point and one entirely attributable to her own unreasonable behaviour.

"It is time to pour oil on troubled waters, my dear...time for reconciliation. The boy is at a difficult age and finding his feet. Why create cause for further bad feeling between you both? You will surely antagonise Willie by imposing a curfew upon him, Charlotte, and it will do you both some good not to be cooped up together all evening."

They were words forcefully delivered one afternoon before William returned home from school...words with which Charlotte resolved not to quibble. Instead she relented on the issue and William was not, after all, precluded from evening meetings with his friends...friends who Charlotte assumed to mean John Downer and others of his peers from the schoolroom, the same boys with whom she had believed he played cricket. Had she known otherwise...that her son was mixing with young rapscallions of doubtful parentage, products of the Portsea Union Workhouse and the Seamen and Marines' Orphans Home, she would have been mortified and doubtless have forbidden such intercourse.

William, for his part, saw his early evening excursions as a release. Perhaps, in his sub-conscious, he saw them as something of a panacea to his ills and frustrations. They offered welcome liberation from painful hours in school, where, not surprisingly, his relationship with the master – a weasel-faced little man by the name of Jenkins – had fallen into irreversible decline. In practice that meant being picked upon and ridiculed in front of his classmates, of being hauled out in full view of his peers for the slightest of perceived misdemeanours and of standing stock-still with a book balanced on his head while making a recitation. It was altogether a hard cross to bear for one who had previously shouldered responsibility as a pupil teacher. And in quiet moments William's thoughts would sometimes drift back wistfully to those halcyon days in the schoolroom at Forton...and, in his mind's eye, he would picture Mister Wicketts and old Parson Veck.

Furthermore William found release from the tensions of home life in those evening excursions. He would refrain from talking about his school torment for he knew full well that his vexed mother would show little sympathy. She had taken to calling him William – a sure sign she remained irked – and were he to confide in her he could imagine her delivering one of her favourite sayings from the Good Book... "Whatever a man soweth,

William, that shall he also reap." For her part, Grandma Black showed greater understanding. On any matter of disagreement surrounding her grandson's recent behaviour she would not openly contradict or upbraid her daughter in front of him on account of it being unseemly. Yet, unbeknown to William, he had reason to be grateful to his grandmother for the forcefulness which secured his mother's acquiescence to those early evening jaunts.

It was shortly after half past six o'clock, on a Friday in late April, when William closed the door on the family home, supper having been taken early. He would return no later than nine o'clock, the hour when Portsea's chiming timepieces found a rival in the Port Admiral's gun as its noise reverberated over the water. That was the substance of the promise to his mother and grandmother as William took his leave, a promise he had repeatedly made – and religiously kept – since he began venturing out in the fortnight following Easter. It was fine and the probing long shadows of approaching twilight appeared to point his way eastward towards the town fortifications. It was there he had arranged to meet Joshua Smith and friends – Felix, Pilch, Mynn and Parr – at the Lion Gate, the old entrance which pierced the fortifications at the far end of Queen Street. On arrival there were no familiar faces to be seen but the strains of band music drew William beneath the high arch with its distinctive, heavy tapered quoins and keystones, stained and pitted by years of weathering. Emerging beyond the earthwork, past the duty sentry – striking in his plumed, black shako – William halted awhile on the bridged road over the moat. In front of him, beyond the bridge, a Scottish military band was playing hearty strathspeys and reels to the delight of an attentive and appreciative crowd. The musicians had taken up position upon the turfed ravelin that comprised part of the outer earthworks and offered a suitably levelled greensward through which the Lion Gate Road ran out onto the glacis. William whiled away some time listening to the music and for ten minutes became so absorbed in the sight and sound of the band that his preoccupation banished all thought of why he was there. The light was beginning to fade quite perceptively now as the Scottish tunes gave way to a concluding medley of old hornpipes, in courteous regard to Portsea and its citizens.

The crowd's applause had barely subsided when the boom of the sunset gun from the neighbouring Duke of York's Bastion seemed to give emphasis to the conclusion of the band's public performance. William, drawn from his captivation, went to turn and scurry back into the town ahead of the departing crowd, minded that his friends may have arrived but since given up on him. But as he did so a familiar face – that of Pilch – lurched out of the milling crowd before him, only for the other boys to follow on behind.

"Hello, Silver Billy," shouted Pilch. "Have we kept you waiting?"

"Not at all," said William, surprised to see his friends emerging from the direction of the ravelin. "You weren't by the guard house when I arrived at the Gate so I wandered through to listen to the band. You obviously did likewise."

"Well, not exactly," retorted Parr, a comment that prompted smirks and stealthy exchanges between him and the other new arrivals.

William thought he detected a whispered "How did you do?" and an ensuing "Pretty good, mate" as, nearby, Mynn engaged in huddled conferral with Felix. Yet he gave scant thought to what they might have been alluding and soon Felix, being the most influential in the group, was quick to hold sway.

"Let's clamber up on the ramparts," he said as he rattled a bag of clay marbles in his pocket, the friends having now retraced their steps through the Lion Gate.

From William's recent experience that meant racing each other up the steep slope to the nearest elm on the terreplein. The dubious reward, for being last to reach and touch the bole of the tree, was having to squeeze through an embrasure above the Townsend Bastion where clear sight could be had of the sentry on the moated side of the guard-house. Armed with a few of Felix's marbles the hapless loser would be required to launch these clay missiles at the sentry, only to scramble back from whence he'd come and beat a very hasty retreat. William's heart fell. It was not his idea of fun. When recently called upon to participate in this same pursuit, it had been his sheer determination to avoid performing such a despicable act that saw him arrive, gasping heavily, ahead of the last man. Another time he might not prove so fleet of foot or he might stumble or slip. It called for diversionary tactics.

"Felix, are we going to start playing cricket tomorrow? After all, the weather seems set fair, don't you think?" enquired William.

"Sounds a grand idea. But we'd need to let your friend Downer know… sorry, Johnnie Small."

"Absolutely."

"Then what say the rest of you fellers?" asked Felix, a question that drew a collective and affirmative response.

"Then we'll need to go and call upon Johnnie," exclaimed William. "He lives in Rosemary Lane, down near the Gun Wharf."

William's digression had served its purpose and the suggestion of getting up to tricks on the ramparts was all but forgotten as the five friends set off in the direction of Rosemary Lane. Yet latent devilment was all too inherent in the sinews of Felix and his orphaned associates and to William's discomfort this was evinced as soon as they were sauntering past the elegant homes in Lion Terrace.

"Time for a little gingerbread," exclaimed Parr.

"Good idea," came Mynn's retort.

William knew immediately to what Parr was intimating, for it was a favourite sport among the Portsea urchins to knock upon the doors of respectable homes, only to then hastily cut and run.

"Let's take these few in a row," beckoned Felix, whereupon William stood transfixed upon the footpath as the others quickly departed to their respective stations. With each grasping a door knocker, a hand signal from Felix prompted the simultaneously thud of hammers upon plates whereupon the miscreants spun on their heels and collectively fled in the direction of the Mill Dam. For the moment William stood mesmerised by their actions.

"Get moving, Silver Billy," screamed Felix as he led the retreat.

"Not so fast you young rascals. What's the meaning of this?" The voice belonged to a rotund old man who seemed to have emerged from nowhere but who had evidently witnessed what had transpired. Brandishing a gnarled walking-stick, he attempted to bar the way of the fleeing culprits but, being fleet of foot, they simply side-footed him, cheeked him in the process and were gone. William meanwhile stood lead-footed on the pavement as the bushy-whiskered old man, his eyes bulging, his face florid with indignation, advanced towards him.

"What manner of behaviour is that?" he shouted stridently. "The likes of you m'lad deserve a good beating. You're lucky there's not a constable around." The old fellow continued to advance towards William and was still wielding his stick, as if intent on giving him a hearty swipe. Coming to his senses and aware that front doors were being opened by domestic servants with cause to vent their own ire on a suspected culprit, William turned about and ran back to Queen Street as if pursued by the devil himself.

Ten minutes later, by circuitous means, William found himself in the shadow of St George's Church which stands close to the end of Rosemary Lane. As he emerged beyond the front of the building, a shrill whistle pierced the air. He looked back. In a murky recess, set beneath the church's dignified front façade, he detected some shadowy figures. His four friends were lurking there in expectation of his appearance.

"What kept you?" said one of them as the four emerged from their gloomy niche.

"I took off back towards Queen Street to avoid that angry old chap. He seemed ready to clout me with his stick."

"You should've dodged past him and followed us. You'd have soon enough given that silly old grampus the slip. Too old and fat to get any speed up," trumpeted Felix. His words were proclaimed to the accompanying laughter of the others who seemed tickled by the irony of their innocent friend having come closest to receiving a thrashing. "I've seen the old feller before to tell you the truth. He gets quite excited. Someone told me he was one to be reckoned with in his day…he was one of the Johnnies, you see…one of the old watchmen who would patrol the fortifications and give you a good hiding if he caught you up to any mischief. I suppose it's in his blood but now he's too old and too blubber-bellied to outrun a snail."

"Right, let's look in on Johnnie Downer," suggested William, having tired of witnessing and fleeing from the gingerbread episode and of hearing reflections upon the old gentleman who saw fit to intervene.

"Why not? After all, that's why we're here," said Felix. "Let's look in on the fiddling batsman Johnnie Small and see if he'd like to play cricket tomorrow."

"Fiddling batsman?" enquired Pilch.

"Fiddling. Precisely that, matey. Young Downer told me that Small was a batsman who fiddled. Played the fiddle, that is," said Felix, reflectively. "In the manner of making music. Well, I'm assuming that's what he meant and not that he was a cheat." As he spoke, Felix caught the eye of all but William, before sardonically adding, "only we've got enough of that sort of fiddler hereabouts, haven't we lads?" It was a remark which prompted an exchange of wry grins.

The afternoon cricket match was played out under a halcyon sky and to the accompaniment of warm zephyrs off the Solent, more evocative of midsummer days than of springtime. John Downer was among the participants, who, at around five o'clock, collectively trundled back into Portsea, tired from their exertions yet unanimously intent upon meeting up later by the Lion Gate. At the end of Rosemary Lane, John and William parted company with the others who went their own way. Their origins, amid the myriad of Portsea's thoroughfares, had never been declared and, as far as William was concerned, he had not felt disposed to enquire. This was perhaps due to an indifference thrown up by an intuitive wariness about needing to retain a degree of detachment, of not letting himself become too close to youths whose behaviour was inclined to operate beyond the limits of social convention: indeed, behaviour that passed into the realm of criminality. It was that same indifference that caused him to refrain from showing any interest in their real names. He knew that Felix was called Joshua Smith but he had either forgotten or not been told the names of the other fellows. In truth he didn't want to know. He was content to call them all by their cricketing pseudonyms. It helped preserve that sense of detachment.

At about seven-thirty, as the sunset gun boomed from the fortifications, William shuffled his way down Portsea's main thoroughfare. It was already strewn with the detritus of a street market, the many passers-by only serving to impede free passage as they dallied and peered and pressed upon the many carts and barrows and their colourful awnings which lined the street. William was accompanied by John Downer, who had called for his friend after both had taken their suppers in their respective homes. Now, among the usual street smells, a strong whiff of frying onions and of beefsteaks, sausage and faggots hung in the air as they sizzled and steamed in blackened pans, the braziers' coals glowing vigorously in the twilight. To the friends it was an unwelcome smell in the immediate wake of having recently finished their suppers. Their preference was for the waft of molten tallow that occasionally came to the fore. Its distinctive fragrance would rise on soft coils of dark smoke from the barrow-men's newly-lit candles which flamed and flickered beneath shielding membranes of oily paper.

The bustle of the street going about its business and the distraction of the traders' wares conspired to slow the friends' progress towards the town gate. By the time they were in sight of their destination twilight had become dusk, which, in its advance, had furtively drained the street's colour to its very edges. Now it resided under the awnings, in the spread of soft candle-light eerily diffused by those unctuous membranes – there, and in the multitude of shop windows where merchandise of all kinds seemed the more enticing beneath the blush of lamplight.

As William and John neared the Lion Gate their attention was drawn to an altercation just across the street. The disturbance was outside the *Royal Oak Hotel* where the vehement clamour of raised voices, laced with obscenities, rose out of a fracas between two sailors and a brace of their military counterparts. It was evident that all four were afflicted with drink, an early evening intake of tap-house liquor having been sufficient to unleash tempers, doubtless over some trivial matter. But it was not so much the affray that grabbed William and John's attention. Instead it was the sight of the four lads they were due to meet elsewhere, further down the street by the guard house. On the near side of the *Royal Oak* an alley ran back towards the Anglesey Barracks, separating the public house from a brightly-lit sweet shop. It was on the shop steps, beneath the flare of an entrance lamp, that the raggedly-dressed quartet stood talking to three old men who sat below, slouched on upturned boxes. The old fellows happily drew upon their clay pipes while the youngsters each clutched what seemed to be newly acquired bags of confectionery. Young and old alike looked as if they'd lost a farthing and found a florin, such was their apparent contentment. And, in their collective introversion and cordiality, all seemed oblivious to the ongoing commotion, soon to be snuffed out by two truncheon-wielding policemen.

William and John wandered down the street towards the sweet shop as the burly constables set about prising the assailants apart and calming them with words of warning.

"Just as well we caught sight of you, Felix," shouted William, as they approached the shop. "It was only because of the brawl that we noticed you here."

"We've been busy this past half hour…earning a copper or two. Here… have a sweet," said Felix, proffering his bag of crystalline delights. "We were just about ready to go down to the guard house to meet you."

"So how have you been earning your coppers?" asked John, as he helped himself to a sugary morsel, realising this was how they had come by their confections and suspecting earning was a mere euphemism for stealing.

"Courtesy of these three gentlemen, Mister Small…courtesy of these gentlemen," proclaimed a blithesome Felix, who, with a sweep of his arm, bowed towards the pipe-smoking trio. In response and acknowledgement of this obsequious pleasantry the old men grinned and made garbled remarks.

"You're good lads," mumbled the most lucid of the three as his colleagues nodded in agreement, the one-legged fellow adding a confirmative double tap of his stump upon the cobbles.

"Same again next week m'lads if you can manage it," he continued, screwing his nose up and revealing a toothless grin that would have graced a witches' coven.

As the six youngsters took their leave of the old smokers, William pressed Felix for an explanation.

"So what was that all about? What did you do to persuade those old fellows to part with their money? They don't look like they've got many ha'pennies between them," suggested William.

"Don't you believe it young shaver," said Felix, his use of the word young having a patronising ring to it: for being tall, roughened and streetwise, his was an aura that belied the fact that he was some months younger than William Reynolds. "They're old seafarers turned beggars and seem to do well enough out of Portsea pockets. But they're too old to shin up walls and that's where we come in."

William and John looked at the others in bewilderment.

Fuller Pilch took up the story. "There's a tobacco manufactory around the corner and Parr here has a cousin who works there and twists the leaf into ropes ready for steaming. Well, there's a bit of wastage in the job and cousin Jane makes sure that, when she puts the sweepings out in the yard, any bits of tobaccy are left under cover in a particular bin…out of the rain you see. So on a Saturday evening, when all's quiet, we get over the wall and help ourselves to it. And those old fellers are our customers, you see, and if they're not around we know of others who'll buy the…"

"Tell 'em about the dog," interrupted Mynn, almost choking on a boiled sweet as he did so.

"Ah, yes, the hound," continued Pilch. "The manufactory has a guard dog chained up in the yard. It's a vicious looking beast with a bark to match. The thing is they keep it hungry and we found that if you throw it a tasty bone it'll not bother you. So we go to the butcher's shop before we climb over the wall and…"

"I could do with something tasty right now," observed Mynn, as he chose to interrupt Pilch yet again. "All that exercise on the Common this afternoon has left me gut-foundered. I could eat like a horse."

"I'm sure we all could," exclaimed Felix, "excepting Beldham and Small. I bet they've just scoffed their suppers." He looked reflective for a moment. "So let's see what we can do about it."

Rather than continue to the Lion Gate the six pals set off in the opposite direction, towards the Dockyard. This was at Felix's instigation and it was Felix who called their perambulation to a halt once they had advanced a hundred yards or so. It was in this middle section of Queen Street that the milling crowd was at its most dense, perhaps on account of the seductive lure of a wide variety of cooked foods and sweetmeats tendered by nearby vendors.

"Wait here," insisted Felix as he carefully took stock of the surroundings, using his height to observe what lay ahead and what tempting foodstuffs were to be had on local stalls and barrows. His scrutiny and assessment almost complete, Felix caught sight of two street Arabs scavenging beneath a fruiterer's barrow. The grimy orphans, both ragged and barefooted and perhaps no older than seven or eight, were busily targeting a few wormy russets that had been discarded in the gutter. As they re-emerged, clutching their rotten apples, Felix shouted a harsh command.

"Hey, young 'uns! Get over here!" In their abruptness and stridency, his words successfully carried to their intended recipients, yet caused several startled passers-by to mutter words of complaint.

William detected that the urchins recognised Felix. Either that or they were intimidated. Certainly they lost no time in complying with his command.

"Do you want to earn a nice bag of sweets?" asked Felix of the two street children, who stood wide-eyed and meekly expectant at the elder boy's feet. Being clearly excited by the prospect of such a treat, they took little time to nod in affirmation, whereupon Felix pulled them close and quickly proceeded to talk to them in earnest. In doing so his voice fell to a whisper; and hence William and the others ceased to be privy to what was being said as they held back, clear of the crowd, in the vestibule of a pawnbroker's shop. "Only when I give the signal, now…and remember, each go for one leg and both together." As the street Arabs scurried off, only to be swallowed up in the crowd, William's acute sense of hearing caught these parting words of Felix, but they made little sense.

Felix, standing ten feet away, now beckoned to his friends, who collectively moved towards him. "No, not you two," he declared, looking pointedly at William and John. "Stay there will you …oh, and here…look after our bags of sweets," added Felix as he led Mynn, Parr and Pilch in decanting his confectionery into William's safe keeping. His final words were then delivered in a hushed tone. "Let's meet up again in half an hour shall we?…down in Mitre Alley, bottom of Union Street."

With that, Felix turned his attention to the other three, losing no time encouraging them to stoop in a huddle and receive furtively whispered instructions. Then, as William and John looked on in some bewilderment, their friends rose out of their hunched communion and melted into the crowd.

A minute passed, perhaps two. William and John continued to linger in the pawnbroker's entrance way, puzzled by their friends' antics and wondering what – if anything at all – might happen next. They had but a short time to wait. Suddenly, perhaps thirty feet away, yet largely hidden from view by the crowd, a great commotion seemed to erupt. At first a shocked cry pierced the air, immediately followed by a clattering noise upon the cobbled street. Women's high pitched shrieks mingled with gruffer sounds of censure as those close to the disturbance gave vent to their sense of shock and outrage. And, within seconds, like the parting of the sea waters in the second book of Moses, the encircling crowd fell away to reveal a disconsolate muffin-man on his knees, his nose blooded, his tray upturned. Scampering away, and showing a great deal of nimbleness in avoiding the lunging efforts of two men to bring them down, were Felix and Parr. Both clutched handfuls of the street seller's toasted bread cakes, while, across the street and taking advantage of the diversionary effect of the rumpus, William caught a fleeting glimpse of Pilch and Mynn plundering a baker's stall.

As the former school friends tried to comprehend what they were witnessing, another cry rent the air. It was much nearer…too near…and was accompanied by the firm grip of a heavy hand upon the nape of William's neck. It froze him to the spot.

"So wot have we got 'ere?" the voice roared sadistically.

It was so hearty a bellow as to rise above the general hubbub and fall upon the ears of the swiftly fleeing Pilch and Mynn as they concluded their business to the ignorance of the distracted baker.

"By jove," shouted the scarpering Mynn, as his eye briefly registered what was happening across the street, "that fat old guts and garbage has got hold of Silver Billy…the old Johnnie who tried to stop us last evening."

"Well, well, m'lad. No chance of escaping my grasp this time, eh?" exclaimed the old watchman. "Just unlucky for you that I was on the spot to hear the commotion and see your accomplices running away." The old man continued to hold William in an iron grip and with his other hand had placed his trusty walking stick hard to his throat. At first he had probably taken little notice of John Downer, least of all associated him with William. Yet, to the boy's credit, rather than skulk away, he timorously piped up in his friend's defence.

"Accomplice, sir? My friend, William, here, is nobody's accomplice."

"And so who, boy, might you be?" enquired the watchman, as he gloweringly cast an eye upon young Downer. "Another of this gang of thieves and irritants?"

"No, sir…we've done nothing, sir," came the emphatic, yet nervous, reply.

"Done nothing, eh? Well…let's see what a policeman makes of it," said the watchman, an oblique reference to the fact that a constable had now appeared on the scene. At this moment he was busily engaged talking to a number of witnesses, as well as the astounded muffin-man who had got to his feet and was dabbing his nose in an effort to stem the bleeding.

"Constable!" boomed the old watchman. "This rascally fellow will interest you. I can vouch for his being one of the pilferers' accomplices. Caught red-handed, no less."

Frightened rigid, William was nonetheless incensed by the old man's words and chose to break his silence. "I'm innocent, sir," he shouted, "I've done nothing wrong." His voice trembled and quivered with fear and indignation.

"He's right, sir," implored John Downer.

The constable reacted to the watchman's call and strolled across to the pawnbroker's vestibule, but not before the baker had accosted him to tell of his loss. "Good evening, Mister Norris, sir," said the policeman, being familiar with the old man's past reputation and his propensity to exert continuing vigilance upon the streets of Portsea.

"I wasn't privy to all that happened, constable," began the watchman, "for I was idling my time, looking in the jeweller's window next door. But then I heard the hullabaloo and saw the culprits running away and…"

"It seems," interrupted the policeman, as if wishing to immediately dispel any doubt as to what had actually transpired, "that the upheaval was started by a couple of young urchins, perhaps on the instigation of others. The youngsters kicked the muffin-man behind the knees, taking him unawares and sending him sprawling. They then fled like the wind. Looked like any other street urchins according to witnesses. Anyway, no sooner had they fled than two older boys swept in, bagged plenty of the muffins, and again, before you could say Jack Robinson, they were gone. And the baker over there told me that, amid this turmoil, he had thieves stealing his Banbury cakes and penny tarts…obviously confederates of the other two."

"As is this young scoundrel, constable," said Norris, who finally saw fit to release his grip on William. "And possibly this stripling as well," he added, pointing to John Downer.

"Hmm. What's your name young man?" asked the policeman of William.

"Reynolds, sir...William Reynolds." His voice continued to waver with emotion.

"Do you have a family and a home to go to?"

"Yes, sir. I live in King Street."

"Well, I must say you don't look the part of a prowling young street thief. But this gentleman, Mister Norris, seems to think otherwise."

"Indeed I do, constable, although admittedly he didn't appear to play an active role in this particular deception...but an accomplice, most certainly."

"And how, sir, may I respectfully enquire, have you come to that conclusion?"

"I encountered this boy only last evening...in Lion Terrace...along with four other impudent ruffians who were making a flagrant nuisance of themselves and gave me plenty of lip when I confronted them. This one wasn't lippish, I'll admit, but he bolted like the rest of 'em and now, here he is, in place to oversee his friends' contemptible deed. And I wouldn't mind wagering, constable, he was on hand to signal to his friends had that proved necessary. I would also suggest to you that it is somewhat odd to find a lad clutching four bags of sweets, other than in circumstances where he was minding them for associates who were otherwise engaged. A large amount of sweets, indeed, which I also suspect, were not come by honestly." A smug, supercilious grin spread across Norris's fat, ruddy features as if to suggest he had demonstrated William's guilt beyond any shadow of a doubt.

"And you are sure, I take it, sir, that the perpetrators of this assault and act of thieving are the same ruffians you saw along with young Reynolds in Lion Terrace?"

"Indisputably, constable...indisputably. I only caught a rear glimpse of those fleeing the muffin-man but got a clearer sight of those seizing the baker's cakes. They were the same insolent rogues I encountered yesterday, believe me constable."

"Hmm," interjected the policeman with such lack of expression as to furnish no clue to his thoughts upon the watchman's allegations. He turned his attention to John Downer. "Tell me, lad, what have you to say for yourself?"

"Nothing, sir...only that I've done nothing, sir. Neither has William.

We know those boys…we've played cricket with them and just happened to meet them this evening," said John, being careful not to disclose that the cricket had become an established and regular summer pursuit or that their evening encounter had been anything other than a chance one. Cognisant of being in a tight corner, it was to his credit that he continued to be judicious with his words and disclosures, in essence being economical with the truth. "And the gentleman here is right about the sweets. They already had them when we met earlier but didn't say how they obtained them. We were wandering down the street and they suddenly made off after handing William the sweets and…"

"So they left their sweets with your friend, eh…and supposedly they'll be seeing you some time soon to retrieve them, son?"

John Downer thought quickly and, in the interest of self-preservation, now considered it prudent to trade guarded candour for fabrication. "Oh no, sir. They said we could have them …didn't they Willie?" The boy's words were ostensibly delivered with confidence but it was as if he doubted his ability to ward off further questioning with lies that saw him attempt to deflect attention back on William, if only for want of moral support. William, still trembling from the trauma of his apprehension, simply mumbled a grunt of affirmation whereupon the constable stuck to questioning his friend.

"Tell me, son, don't I know you?" asked the policeman, somewhat belatedly. "Your face looks familiar." He gazed fixedly at John. "You're not the Downer boy are you…from Rosemary Lane?"

"Yes, sir…John Downer, sir."

"Well now…I thought as much. Not very good with faces, but I suppose, with you living close to the police station, I must have encountered yours from time to time." The constable looked thoughtful for a few moments before continuing. "Right, more to the point, young Downer, I'm presuming that as you and your friend know these scoundrels you'll also be acquainted with their names and perhaps where they live?"

"Not exactly, sir. We only know them by their cricketing names," said John. He knew Felix's real name but felt disinclined to mention it for fear of reprisal. Conversely, few, by his reckoning, would associate those sobriquets with any particular local youths. In consequence, he felt he was in a sense removed from incriminating his nefarious friends by simply supplying the constable, and the lingering Norris, with a list of famous cricketers. This he did. And no, he didn't know where they were to be found, and neither did William; they were believed to be orphan and workhouse boys who probably lived by their wits and had no claim to a roof over their heads.

The policeman listened patiently to what John Downer had to say. In contrast, old Mister Norris reacted with incredulity, no doubt irked at the thought that the four ruffians, who had been disrespectful towards him, might evade their just desserts, despite this latest outrage. Yet, for all his derisive mocking and overt contempt for young Downer's words, this in no way influenced the constable's open-mindedness. Calmly completing his notes, he then looked the boy in the eye.

"Now, John Downer, I suggest you make your way home. I know where you live and may have to question you again." He then turned to William. "As for you, William Reynolds, you have already upset this gentleman, here, through your involvement with those street thieves..."

"Excuse me constable, but did I hear you correctly?" It was a familiar voice, one that William knew only too well. The sound of it filled him with foreboding, and, for the second time in ten minutes, he was gripped and frozen with fear. As the policeman stepped aside, it was to reveal the sharp-featured Jenkins, the dreaded schoolmaster who now had a greater dislike of William than even the blustering Norris. The master was taking an evening stroll with his wife, his choice of direction and the timing conspiring to further blacken William's name in the judgement of one who had already branded it black enough.

"Begging your pardon, sir...but do I take it you know this boy?" enquired the constable.

"I suppose I can claim to have that dubious privilege. I teach him. But, tell me, constable, did I hear you speak of him consorting with *thieves*? He is a boy who has done himself no favours of late, but I never once imagined he would stoop so low." Jenkins adopted a snarling expression as he spoke, yet there was a vestige of self satisfaction in his tone and demeanour which hardly augured well for William.

"Well, suffice to say," said the policeman, "that I am merely pursuing enquiries regarding an unfortunate incident that occurred a short while ago. It involved assault and stealing from local vendors and while it has become clear that this boy has been *consorting* with thieves, as you choose to put it, I have no evidence to suggest he's a thief himself...far from it, sir. That said, I have yet to conclude my investigations."

"If he's not a thief then I suspect he's one in the making," opined old Mister Norris, his words laced with sarcasm and aimed at the schoolmaster.

"Only last evening he was with the same vagrants who committed the crime. Up to no good they were, causing mischief banging on the doors of respectable folk...then making off. So he's hardly a credit to your school, good sir, and I'll wager, better suited to the reformatory. Take it from me...I've seen Portsmouth Magistrates sentence youngsters to hard labour and whippings for less."

William was glad to see the odious Jenkins depart with his simperingly imperious wife on his arm. How they deserved each other, he thought...a thought which immediately paled into insignificance. Instead, contemplation upon the likely repercussions of Jenkins' untimely appearance came to the fore. Its portentous significance caused him to shudder. His blood ran cold.

William had no doubt Norris had come to despise him and that he would dearly love to see him hauled before the justices. Of course, the old man's overriding wish would be for the four Portsea vagrants to be apprehended and handed down a stiff custodial sentence; but failing that William suspected the punishment of an *accomplice* – as Norris chose to regard him – would go some way to sating that aspiration. And if that wish fell by the wayside...well, fate had furnished him an ally in the shape of the weasel-faced Jenkins. Norris felt his words had been employed to good effect, confident they had helped intensify and hone the obvious dislike the schoolmaster already felt for his charge. And thus there was some good reason to suppose that, as a long-stop, William's school might exact its own retribution.

"Now, as I recall, I was in the processing of saying to you, William Reynolds, that you have already upset Mister Norris, who has positively identified you as recently keeping company with these thieves. The extent of your involvement, therefore, in this evening's most distasteful episode is well...what can I say...well, it's a moot point. In consequence, and for the time being, I am retaining an open mind."

Overhearing these words drew a sigh of exasperation from Norris. "Culpable, constable, the little wretch is culpable beyond a shadow of a doubt," he exclaimed in a suppliant tone of voice.

The policeman chose not to react to the old man's plea but displayed the kind of inexorable and laconic approach that marked him out as one well suited to being a constable on the beat. He knew Norris of old and of his tendency to quickly condemn. Ever since he had retired as a watchman the old fellow had been a fish out of water and his insatiable desire to show vigilance and exert authority upon the streets of Portsea had invariably proved more of an encumbrance than a benefit; and down at the police station it was jokingly said he fancied himself as one of the new breed of plain-clothes detective police with an attitude to match.

In due course the constable continued. "Now it may be, Master Reynolds, that if we apprehend these friends of yours it will help clarify what transpired. I have also taken the names and addresses of several persons who claim to have witnessed what happened and I intend to interview them shortly. However, as things stand, I am not going to arrest you...but don't think you are yet off the hook. And before any further ado I intend to accompany you home if only to verify what you tell me...that you are who you say you are and that you live in King Street."

William's sense of foreboding continued to intensify. He was mortified. He felt crushed. He despaired. It was one thing being traduced by Mister Norris in front of the repugnant Jenkins but now his mother and grandmother's tranquil, uneventful evening was to be torn asunder. He knew full well he had done little to warrant being punished. He had merely been naïve, to have kept company with undesirables and for that he was now to be shamed in front of his dearest kith and kin. At best, through gullibility alone, he would be seen as having abused the fundamental values of a good and godly upbringing and, for the first time in his life, he felt an overwhelming urge to cut and run. He would drown himself in the Mill Pond or cast himself off the ramparts...

"Can you hear me, boy?" said the policeman, having just tried and failed to obtain a response to a question. Being so distressed, so gripped with fear, William's mind had been momentarily afflicted by a kind of hiatus in rational thought that somehow dulled his sense of hearing. "William!" The constable's voice was distant. It came again, louder this time. "William Reynolds!"

William gently stirred from his state of abstraction. He looked at the policeman, his expression vacuous, his eyes brimming with tears.

"Are you sure you're alright, lad?"

"Yes, sir," came the mumbled reply.

"So what number?"

"Number, sir?"

"King Street...what number King Street?"

"Oh...thirty-one, sir." The intonation in William's reply told of his being resigned to the inevitability of what now awaited him; of the shame and distress soon to be felt on both sides of the threshold.

The policeman turned towards Norris, his courteous intent to express some thanks for the old fellow's interest and involvement. However, the retired watchman had already vanished, doubtless irked and frustrated by his own apparent lack of persuasiveness, coupled with his perceived intractability of Portsea's police force.

The constable shrugged. "Come," he said, grasping William by the shoulder.

A few minutes later they arrived at the house in King Street. The police officer laid a heavy hand upon the knocker and delivered it with a firm thud on the door plate. It was the signal for William's tears to well again. As he heard the familiar footfall in the passage, his frame seemed to convulse with emotion. He sobbed openly, wetting cheeks drawn white with fear and anguish.

Ten

Port Tobacco, Maryland

1857

The young man had tired of his ramble as the early evening showed signs of becoming chill. He had set out across the fields that fell close upon the town, while the low shafts of late afternoon sunlight still played orangey warmth on the high stands of corn. Leaving that cultivation behind him, he had chosen a dirt path that held promise of a route through the marsh grass and in the general direction of the river. Yet it renaged on that promise, condemning the young man to rather circuitous wanderings. Sometimes he would happen upon gloomy thickets of laurel wherein the feathered denizens of equally sombre backwaters would take flight and cause the walker to be greatly startled. He had been constantly minded not to stray far from the sight of the old tobacco warehousing which rose to the north. That was his point of reference, the buildings hugging the wharves on the opposite side of the creek, a waterway that drew the Port Tobacco River out into the wide Potomac. Frustratingly, those edifices were inclined to recede along with the forest of masts and yards that marked out the traders' vessels, transiently lying in the anchorage; frustratingly, because the young man's purpose had been to seek out shallow inlets on the remoter side of the creek where an open rowing boat might be drawn up and safely secured. Yet his efforts had been fruitless where a trampling had first offered hope of progress. Impenetrable clumps of reed and bulrush would invariably bar his way or water would suddenly well up beneath his feet.

In consequence, the young man had sought to recover the dirt path that would take him back to town. What vestige of sunlight remained was now but a soft reddening in the western sky against which he turned his back and made for firmer ground. When he came once again upon the farmer's fields, and followed the way through the high corn, his senses seemed the more acute, pricked by the hush that pervaded the countryside as dusk succumbed to darkness. An owl hooted shrilly in a neighbouring pine thicket. Waders called to each across some distant mudflat while the salty scent of the river, of estuarine decay and exposed sediment, suddenly acquired a greater piquancy. Nearby, a disturbed feral creature caused such a precipitous rustling in the corn as to freeze the walker's blood, encouraging him to lengthen his stride. His quest was a bite to eat and a comforting drink at Brawner's. Thereafter, and as pre-arranged, eight o'clock would see one of the house slaves arrive in a curricle to convey him back to the plantation.

The distant sound of music fell upon the young man's ears as he trudged on, yet paradoxically, as he neared its source, he became insensible to its increased volume. He fell instead into the most introspective cogitation upon the way his life had changed, not least in the sense he had been drawn apart from his nearest and dearest. His thoughts strayed to his beloved mother in far away Baltimore and to his brother, George, who continued to bide his time out there, beyond the Potomac. He thought of his father, Heinrich the blacksmith, lying beneath freshly turned soil in Westmoreland County and had fallen into a melancholic and sentimental state of mind by the time he reached the town square. Distractedly, and a few minutes later, he found his way onto the hotel's gravelled approach, the wavering light from several house lanterns conspiring to warm the red brickwork and cloak the porch in a radiance that seemed enticing. At a higher level, the tracery of an old oak, its tired leaves now browning, lay stark against the white shingles. Beneath it and within the spillage of porch light, rested a small group of negroes. One of them, a banjo player, leant his scraggy frame against the tree trunk, while he busily picked at his instrument. The young man realised this had been the source of the distant strains of melody which had reached him in the stillness of the cornfields, although at the time he fancied a fiddler having been at work, as well as a banjoist. And he was right, for squatting on a rooted knoll was a negro of more rounded proportions who appeared to be somewhat enervated. His violin and bow upon his lap, he had elected to take a break from the exertions of fiddling and occupied his time counting the money that had already been cast into his upturned straw hat.

The banjo picker played on, his rendition of *Oh! Susanna* being promptly followed by another Christy's Minstrels' favourite and one that did nothing to mollify the young man's sad and sentimental drift of mind. *Old Folks at Home* had been one of the blacksmith's best-loved songs and, in that knowledge, the sound of it caused the young man to fight tears and chew upon his lip. He halted to listen, at the same time ridding his ears of the crunching sound beneath his tread. Then, once the tune had been played out, the listener approached the musicians and dropped a few coins in the straw hat.

"Dat real gen'rus of you, mas'r," said the fiddler, excitedly, as the banjoist took up playing another tune. "It ain't fer us but for the young 'uns, suh...to keep the chillen's bellies full, you see. Bless you, mas'r, the Lord bless you."

To the fiddler's left, two barefooted negro women sat upon a grimy old bolster placed across a pile of white-oak logs. One drew nonchalantly on a corncob pipe, the other chewed a plug of tobacco, occasionally extracting it from her mouth to wipe it in a bowl of molasses that lay at her feet. Both were sensible of the visitor's kindness, the tinkling sound of his contribution being sufficient to distract them from their recreations and to nod and mumble their own signs of gratitude.

As the young man went to ascend the porch by way of a flight of side steps he stopped to draw his boots across the scraper, thereby divested them of caked river silt. He avoided being drawn beneath the overhang to the side of the steps, where an open door led to a long flight of well-worn stairs that descended to the cellar bar. It was an aperture through which the visible reek of cigar smoke rose to quickly dissipate in the evening air and where the hovering odour of stale liquor showed it to be the haunt of those accustomed to hard drinking, hard smoking and other dubious pursuits.

Once settled in the comparative comfort of the main body of Brawner's Hotel, in a nook where refreshments might be taken, Johann Atzerodt ordered a plate of griddled oysters with potatoes and toasted corn-bread. He applied honey to his last slice of toast and finally washed his meal down with a glass of golden Charles County cider.

Atzerodt had parted company with Montross a few months earlier, in the wake of the death of his father. The blacksmith's passing had been sudden and unexpected and it had been a shock to all, his mother, Victore, quickly deciding to remove herself to Baltimore to live close to her two married daughters. It meant that if her two sons were not of a mind to follow they would need to make their own way in life, shorn of the comfort, love and stability of their family home. Neither relished the prospect of city life. George, the younger brother, was the more distressed, at least outwardly, the grief of bereavement being compounded beyond measure by his mother feeling the need to move away. Johann, on the other hand, felt at ease about making a fresh start, having long since become bored with his clerking job in Montross. Indeed, a month before his father's death, he had applied to a south Maryland tobacco plantation that had advertised quite widely for a right-hand man to assist its overseer of slaves. It was something he had entirely forgotten about amid the upset of the blacksmith's passing, so it came as something of a surprise, a week after the funeral, to receive a letter from the estate owner. This had invited him for interview. Well, Johann made a good impression, his experience in clerking and book-keeping serving to tip the balance in his favour, vis-à-vis other candidates.

As for brother George, he was unwilling to uproot himself from his fishing haunts along the Potomac and in the neighbouring countryside of Westmoreland County. Added to which, he continued to do intermittent carriage painting for the old wheelwright, Elmer Summers, and at this he had become most proficient. And, when it came to finding a roof over his head, he was kindly offered lodgings at the gristmill by the parents of his fishing companion, Ethan Sharp.

Out in the entrance hall the grandfather clock struck eight. Johann Atzerodt pushed aside his empty plates and cutlery, arched his back and stretched his legs beneath the table. Rising to his feet, he straightened his neck-tie and pulled taut his polished cotton vest. Then, extracting his pocket watch with a flourish, he checked its timekeeping before the rapidly fading reverberations from the hall clock had quite died. He returned to the Windsor chair he had occupied for the previous fifty minutes and waited a further five until the crunch of carriage wheels were heard upon the gravelled front yard. Johann stood again and wandered across to the front window. Below he could see the distorted light of the curricle's lamps as the conveyance drew to a halt, one serving to illuminate the profile of the cheerful old mulatto coachman, Jeremiah, as he alighted from his perch and made to secure the two horses to the tethering rail. Johann Atzerodt gathered up his hat. It was time to take his leave.

Outside the darkness had intensified to leave a starry eventide. There was little noise. A slight breeze off the river gently rustled the crisp, withering leaves of the overhanging oak and, as Johann passed the cellar bar steps, he detected a few raised voices now mingling with the foggy waftage of tobacco smoke. As for the musicians, they had gone, doubtless having retired to their shanties. And so Jeremiah's shrill greeting seemed to possess a strident edge to it in the relative quietude and caused his emerging passenger to be momentarily startled.

"G'd evenin' mas'r!"

"Good evening to you, Jeremiah."

"Hop aboard if you will, suh. We've got a fine moon to light our way, mas'r and you'll have no cause to be long out of your bed."

★ ★ ★

Two days had passed, two days of clement weather that saw the field work proceed apace, a large quantity of leaf having been pulled and got up and hung in the curing barns. On the afternoon of the second day, this being a Wednesday and October Eve, Johann Atzerodt was summoned to talk with the plantation owner in his office in the big house. The master, as he was generally known by all in his employ – whites and negroes alike – had been away with his lady since Sunday, visiting folks down in Leonardtown. Freshly returned, he was now eager to be acquainted with the outcome of Atzerodt's meeting with an English trader. The ensuing discussion was conducted in a most convivial manner, one of the house slaves being called upon to serve brandy and water, another to proffer the finest of Connecticut cigars. The former was graciously accepted by the young man, finding himself in need of a reviver after a busy day. The cigar, however, he deferentially declined, appearing distinctly nervous in so doing, for fear of giving affront to his employer. Yet the master recognised his discomfort, gave a sympathetic smile and waved his abstention aside as if to rank it a matter of no consequence. A beam of satisfaction soon displaced that understanding smile when young Atzerodt told of the trader's imminent intent to place a substantial order for tobacco leaf, the cargo of hogshead to be ready for shipment at a date to be decided late in November. It was news which prompted the master to express his appreciation and ply his employee with further refills of brandy and water until the latter made his excuses and repaired to his cabin. As he ambled the few hundred yards to his door, Johann felt uplifted, flushed with the intake of alcohol and with the pride of having acquitted himself well, in the eyes of his employer. If only, he pondered, he might feel at ease about the whole experience of working at the plantation. He prepared and enjoyed a leisurely supper, cleared away, then attended to a few chores. At eight o'clock he sat himself down to read a book, his sisters having made him a present of several on the occasion of settling his widowed mother in Baltimore. His meal, the brandy, the strain of reading small print in unnatural light, combined to soporific effect. Before he succumbed Johann drew himself out of his chair and took himself into the night air, taking a few minutes to inhale some deep breaths. For the past two weeks he had intended writing to his brother, George, on a matter of some importance. He had constantly put it off until tomorrow. He suddenly felt it ill became him to delay further, to allow laziness and fatigue to triumph. He returned across the threshold and closed the front door behind him.

Junior Overseer's Lodge,
The Land of Canaan Plantation, near Port Tobacco, Wednesday,
September 30, 1857.

My Dear Brother,

It's nine o'clock in the evening, my hot supper was eagerly despatched long 'ere now and I've taken a candle into the little niche I grandly call my study. My quest is twofold. Firstly, to pen you a quick letter. Secondly, and in so doing, to occupy my mind with purpose. The alternative, dare I say, would be to yield to dull sloth and, in the wake of my meal, allow the day's fatigue to get the better of me, for I would surely fade into slumber in the comfort of my battered old wing chair. My excuse, George, I hasten to add, is finding it a necessity to be at my duties at an untimely hour – five o'clock, alas – and this with the intent of ensuring the field slaves are fed and assembled, and ready to go to their stations. So you see, I'm not long for my bed as I steal a half hour to write you this letter.

Our harvesting time is getting into full swing and consequently all, excepting those, perhaps, in the big house, seem to be swept up in spiralling activity. For the moment it's all about cropping the tobacco before the frosts come and getting the leaves hung for curing. Speaking personally, I had occasion to venture into town two days ago on the estate owner's instruction, to attend to a business matter with an English trader (I felt quite privileged to have been asked). Well, the meeting proved to be of shorter duration than I expected and, in consequence, I had time of my own to while away between leaving the port and partaking of my evening meal at Brawner's Hotel (at my employer's invitation and expense I might add – privileged again!!).

Well, I resolved to put that time to good use – at least, that is how I saw it. Two weeks ago I had taken a couple of negroes down to the public road from which a long, meandering approach leads up through the tobacco fields to the plantation house. We had had two days of a heavy and persistent rain and the waters had brought down debris that had clogged some drainage ditches. This, in turn, had led to a serious spillage of flood water on to our lower field. While lingering at the gate and directing the negroes as they set about the necessary clearance work, a gentleman of some standing in the town came by in a gig. He was heading for home but I sensed he was in no great hurry, for he chose to pull up for ten minutes to pass some time in conversation. He explained that he had been out to the nearby village of Bryantown where he was in the habit of taking his wheeled conveyances to a long established painter of carriages and wagons. He said he presently had an old spider phaeton in need of fresh coats of paint and seemed more than a trifle irked that the fellow had appeared to have packed up and gone. To make matters worse, he knew of nobody in the neighbourhood who could be trusted with the work and expressed a dire wish to see a carriage painter set up business in Port Tobacco. When he said this I hurriedly mentioned that my own brother was accomplished – as, indeed, you are, George – in the trade of carriage painting. This, in turn, prompted the gentleman to enquire of your whereabouts. Well, I had to explain that you lived in Old Virginny, albeit just across the Potomac, but, with the necessary incentive in the way of opportunity, you might be persuaded to move across the water. Now, kindly accept my apologies, George, if I was too presumptuous but the gentleman seemed more than a little interested in your skill. He suggested that were you to consider the pursuit of such work in Port Tobacco you would surely be blessed with a surfeit of employment. More importantly, he is prepared, for a modest rent, to permit a responsible craftsman to use land to the side of his property, including a coach house that's warm enough to fire-cure tobacco (his words). The warmth, by all accounts, emanates from large adjoining chimneys (he has the need to heat a substantial home which I fancy I can picture just off the town square).

Well, George, we parted company with the gentleman telling me to acquaint you with his proposition and to give him an answer as soon as practicable. So I leave that with you to cogitate upon. I merely ask that you give it earnest thought and not tarry long in giving me your answer. All I would say, brother, is that surely here is a God's sent opportunity to bid farewell to Montross and engage upon a fresh start. Oh, and by the way, I'm reliably informed the shad fishing is good on this side of the river – which brings me back to the spare time I encountered after Monday's meeting with the tobacco trader. Well, I had indulged my mind with the notion of you being immediately taken with the aforementioned proposition. That being so I thought of our boat, for in all honesty I could not envisage you wishing to abandon your beloved fishing and what quicker means of getting here than putting your hands to the oars and rowing across. With that in mind, we would need a place to beach the vessel and to leave it where we might feel confident of freedom from any malevolent interference. So I took a ramble down the remoter side of the town inlet, to explore what opportunities might lie in that direction. Yet my wanderings drew a blank, it was a bleak, impenetrable landscape where reed beds and rising water barred my way at every turn. Yet, no matter, I intend exploring other opportunities further south, towards Pope's Creek, where there is the added advantage of a significant narrowing of the Potomac. I am, you see, eagerly jumping to conclusions, dearly hoping, no less, that you will feel inclined to try your hand in Port Tobacco.

That is a prospect which excites me, the more I contemplate it, yet I have to openly admit, George, there is an element of personal interest, which, in a moment such as this – as I pen these words – causes me to feel a mite self-reproachful. I will explain. I entered upon this job of mine in order to fully occupy my mind at a time when moping over bookwork in Montross would not have been good for me. I think you already appreciate that. I still think deeply about Father and miss him dearly. I fret about Mother, but am comforted in the knowledge that she is near our sisters and will want of nothing. I even think of you, dear brother, believe it or not. But, after sedentary duties back home, I find my work here physically tiring (God knows how the field negroes manage) and, once my head is set down upon my pillow, there is no time for dwelling upon sorrows and solicitude, for I am immediately transported to the land of Nod. Yet not all is rosy. The alluvial soils here are good for tilling and yield a fine crop, yet, despite its name, this place is no Canaan, no promised land. I cannot speak too highly of the master and his good lady, both kind and God fearing people who treat the house slaves as if they were part of their own family no less. And equally they have been generous and amiably disposed towards me since the day of my arrival. Indeed, I feel heartened this very day, for my impression is that my considered value to the estate continues to rise in my employer's estimation. But the overseer, the man with whom I have most dealings, is not a fellow I would care to work with indefinitely. He is a brutal man, a laodicean, bereft of Christian virtues, who is prepared to lay his hickory switch across a slave's back for the most trifling of misdemeanours. Oh, yes, George, and I have seen him horse-whip a black youth for helping himself to a piece of blighted fruit in the peach orchard. Horse-whipped him until his shirt ran red.

Well, I have remained tight-lipped and not rebuked the man for the actions I've witnessed for I know it would be futile. After all, I am his subordinate and realise full well that I could be out on my ear were I to be candid about my feelings. Cowardly, perhaps, but suffice to say I have resolved to bide my time. Yet I know the brute has an intuitive awareness of my dislike for him and my disapproval of his methods. If a field slave annoys him he will frequently embark upon a rant about the untrustworthy nature of niggers, of how inherently dishonest they are and how their occasional flogging is necessary to get the best out of them. My ensuing silence and failure to offer any morsel of concurrence with such remarks has doubtless proved as powerful as any words and I am sure he regards me as soft.

But enough of that, other than to say that therein is the crux of my personal interest. I am simply thinking brother, that were you to come to Port Tobacco and make a good fist of carriage painting – which, on the strength of the gentleman's opinion, you surely would – then it might just prove a venture to which we could both put our shoulders and I could turn my back on this so-called land of Canaan. Yet let this not influence your judgement. Instead, you must make your decision based on a balanced weighing of your own personal considerations, knowing only too well of your continuing attachment to Montross and the wrench it would entail to abandon such familiarity. All I ask, George, is that you let me know of your resolution as soon as you are able, so I might acquaint the influential gentleman with the dowdy phaeton!
With warm regards from your affectionate brother,

Johann Atzerodt

P.S. Please remember me to Mr & Mrs Sharp and Ethan to whom I send my kindest and most cordial regards.

Eleven

Portsea, Portsmouth

1857

An overwhelming feeling of disgrace and desperation had gripped William Reynolds from the moment he realised he was to be led home by an officer of the law. The chastisement that might ensue had paled to insignificance when ranked with the ignominy of being leagued with vulgar street ruffians in the execution of some sordid act of assault and thieving. A feeling of hopelessness had pervaded his every sinew. A queasiness rose in his craw. He had felt close to retching. And, as he stood and sobbed on the doorstep, William had desperately hoped time might stand still. The thought of facing his mother and grandmother, as the constable explained what had happened, filled him with dread. It was unreal. He had wished he could vanish but, alas, sorcery was beyond his talents. He had wished he could flee. It was too late for that. For a brief moment his thoughts had dwelt upon the hapless Eliza, from the book Uncle Charley had given him as a thirteenth birthday gift; of how desperation had led her to flee the only home she had known, of leaving all things familiar and the scene of happy associations…the flight with her child to render him safe from the clutches of Haley, the obnoxious trader. How William had pitied that girl in the story and recoiled from reading of her plight. Yet now he felt the horror of his evening's experience had infused in him some measure of the enslaved girl's desperation such that he would have readily exchanged places. Indeed, in that wretched moment, he would have considered himself fortunate to have had the opportunity to hurl himself across the torrent, then to have leaped and stumbled and lurched from one slippery, pitching, heaving ice floe to the next. Oh, how he had craved his own Ohio River and of reaching its far bank…

But that was perhaps the worst of it. The front door had opened. William had stood, disconsolate, ashamed, wet-eyed, his line of sight downwardly inclined to avoid his mother's gaze. Instead, he had immediately focussed upon the swaying hem of her tan dress with its braided trim of dark brown ribbon. In that first second or two – which seemed to William an eternity as he stood there transfixed – it was the rustle of the garment, its brush and swish against the hall floor that fell solely upon his ears and became magnified by his taut and heightened sensibilities. It had been the constable who spoke first, William being blind to his mother's countenance as she strove to assimilate the incongruity of what confronted her beyond the threshold.

"Missus Reynolds?" enquired William's uniformed and burly companion.

"Why, yes, constable…but what…" Charlotte's voice had faltered for a moment, so taken was she with the surprise of seeing her son in the company of a policeman.

"Well, not wishing to be the bringer of bad tidings, madam, or to cause you any distress but I am simply wishing to verify that the young Master William Reynolds here is indeed who he says he is…"

"But, of course, constable," interjected Charlotte. "Why on earth might he claim otherwise? Has there been some unseemly business involving my son?" Her tone had stopped short of appearing at all patronising but William detected that his mother spoke firmly and with a calmness of manner that belied that female reputation for faint-heartedness.

"A troublesome episode, without doubt, Missus Reynolds, yet I'm reasonably confident your son William can be steered clear of the Magistrates Court."

"Troublesome? Magistrates Court? What, pray, is this all about, constable?" asked Charlotte, her words spoken with imploring modulation yet without loss of composure.

And so the policeman had proceeded to explain all that had taken place, being at pains to point out that he had not been privy to witnessing the attack upon the muffin-man and the plundering of his wares and was, in consequence, heavily dependent upon word of mouth. He broadly recounted the events involving the four Portsea ruffians, the peripheral presence and questionable involvement of William and the Downer boy, and the contributions – to the extent they be so described – of old Norris the watchman and Jenkins the schoolmaster.

Being aware that his mother had not been rendered apoplectic or placed on the brink of syncope by the events of the preceding few minutes, William had begun to feel a mite less sorry for himself and so deigned to unfurl his pitiful frame while the constable had his say. Having raised his eyes, he had caught sight of his grandmother, who, being intrigued by her daughter's failure to return to her chair in the parlour, had set aside her darning ball and ventured enquiringly into the passage. There, as she lingered at her daughter's shoulder, Grandma Black's knitted brows had shone spectrally in the comparative gloom, her features highlighted by the hall lamp.

"What is it my dear…what's the problem?" had muttered the elder woman, simultaneously prodding her daughter in the back.

"Hush, Mother dear, I'm listening to the constable." It had been a terse reply and with its utterance Charlotte had stepped aside and, placing a hand on her son's shoulder, ushered him across the front step and into the house. "Kindly take William indoors Mother. I'll be with you shortly." Charlotte had then immediately apologised to the police officer for her interruption and quickly became immersed again in his story.

She might have sounded composed when talking to the policeman but Charlotte had returned to the parlour, some ten minutes later, her face ashen and stern. She had found William squatting disconsolately by the hearth, his bottom planted firmly upon one of a pair of circular rosewood footstools, his chin firmly cupped in his hands. "Well I never," she had mumbled, "well I never."

Shuffling into the room in her immediate wake, Grandma Black had come clutching a small tray upon which steamed a cup of hot chocolate.

"So what was that all about, Charlotte? You look quite shaken, my dear." And, before waiting for her daughter's response, she had immediately addressed her grandson who remained unmoved upon the footstool. "Get this comforting beverage down you, my lad."

"Thank you Grandma," had been the scarcely audible reply.

"Would you like a hot drink Charlotte?"

"No, Mother, thank you, but kindly pass me that little bottle of smelling salts on the shelf in the alcove." Charlotte had taken a moment or two to inhale a few draughts of the stimulant before putting the little vinegarette aside. "What it's all about, Mother," she had continued, "is for William to disclose. I feel he has a good deal of explaining to do. I dread to think what shame he may have brought upon himself and upon our home." She had then addressed her dejected son, directly. "I suggest you finish your drink, William, then dry your eyes and blow your nose. That done, you'd better get yourself up and tell your grandmother and I what has been going on. It's not the time to be sitting on top of the hearth, snivelling to yourself."

William had felt most awkward getting to his feet and looking his mother in the eye. But, having done so, his discomfort had slowly waned, since Charlotte's questioning was of a dispassionate, collected kind. There was no hint of a readiness to condemn, despite her initial brusqueness in directing William to his feet. If anything this came as a surprise, taking him as much unawares as the impassiveness she had displayed when talking to the constable. Of course, it was a case where anticipation, heavily clouded with apprehension, had already distorted William's perception of how his mother might react. And so, refreshed by her attitude, any initial tendency to guardedness had soon yielded to candour as William proceeded to tell of how he and John Downer had first befriended *the four ruffians* – as his mother promptly came to call them – and of all that had since transpired. Most importantly, he had recounted the full events of the evening, not least the biased attitude of old Mister Norris and the supercilious, gloating manner adopted by Jenkins the schoolmaster.

A half hour and more passed. Grandma Black had said little throughout. Charlotte had listened intently to her son's account, only briefly interrupting him with the occasional question. Eventually William fell silent. Charlotte sighed. It had been a sigh that spoke of weariness, perhaps laced with relief – a relief born of the confidence of knowing that her son had been entirely candid about his associations with the four street thieves. He had been honest with her – she had seen it in his eyes.

"You know, William, you have been gullible to the point of recklessness, getting involved with those ruffians. You should have nipped your friendship in the bud on that very first day…when you came to believe they'd robbed the drinks vendor at Southsea Castle. And last evening, when you thought they'd been picking the pockets of those poor unsuspecting folks on the ravelin…well, you should have come straight home. I am dismayed that you were prepared to ignore such shameful goings-on…and look where it led you, William. Had you not been seen with the ruffians in Lion Terrace by this man, Norris, then your presence in Queen Street this evening would have gone unnoticed."

"Trouble is, I did so enjoy playing cricket with them all, Mother…but, yes, it was foolish of me to get involved with those fellows," had been William's meek response.

"I think we have to steel ourselves for the possibility that you might

280

be summoned before the Portsmouth Magistrates, William." Charlotte's words had caused her to shudder at the prospect and the thought of the humiliation this would inflict; and she was only too aware of the severity of punishments the Justices had meted out in the recent past to miscreant youngsters, including spells of hard labour. "The constable, in fairness, thought there was a reasonable chance no further action would be taken... except, of course, against those four ruffians, if apprehended. Certainly he felt there was nothing to suggest John Downer had played a part...said he vaguely knew the family, what with the business of John's father being found with his throat cut. Unfortunately, he felt it wasn't so straightforward in your case, William, on account of what this Mister Norris had to say... although he appeared to acknowledge there was little, as matters stand, to suggest you'd shown complicity...certainly in any active sense. I obtained the distinct impression that the constable had little time for this Norris man."

"I'm not surprised," Grandma Black had exclaimed, being sufficiently incensed to break her silence at the thought of others making defamatory accusations against her grandson.

"Well, yes, Mother. It seems to me this Norris has chosen to vent his spleen, to show spitefulness against William for the most puerile of reasons...for having been cheeked and side-stepped, one can only presume, by these elusive ruffians. If, as we are led to believe, he saw them making a nuisance of themselves in Lion Terrace, then it must have been obvious to the man that William was taking no part in it. Accomplice, indeed!...and as for claiming that William was abetting this evening's appalling episode..."

"Quite ridiculous. The man must have a vengeful streak in him...one who somehow derives a perverted delight, no less, by drawing credence from seeing an innocent condemned." It was as if the talk of William's accuser had now thrust Grandma Black beyond the cusp which separated engrossed silence – her having been content to listen, absorb and dissect the exchanges between mother and son – and the realm of verbal animation, the outcome being that she swiftly nailed her colours to the mast in firm defence of her grandson.

Balm to William had been his mother's own continued expressions of support and her unwillingness to even consider the notion that he was other than entirely innocent. Gullible...naïve...foolish...lacking in good sense...all of these, yes, but as to being at all blameworthy, when it came to the unfortunate events to befall the muffin vendor, most certainly not. Yet what cheered William more than anything had been the manner in which Charlotte chose to speak disparagingly of his schoolmaster, the weasel-faced Jenkins. Perhaps he had misjudged his mother. The ill-feeling between them over the preceding fortnight had been rooted in William's growing apathy in the schoolroom and his failure to discharge his duties as a pupil teacher. The fact that this had greatly irked Charlotte had led William to believe it futile to speak of the way the schoolmaster had chosen to repeatedly humiliate him in front of his peers. He had assumed, perhaps mistakenly, that she would have shown little sympathy in regard to that particular cross he was having to bear, viewing parent and teacher as potential allies in their common resentment of his behaviour. Yet disclosure of Jenkins' prying intervention outside the Queen Street pawnbroker's was met with a scathing reaction from Charlotte. It was the apparent delight he had supposedly derived from her son's predicament as well as from the calumnious balderdash peddled by the old watchman, Norris, which had proved the irritant. Of course, being contemptuous of the schoolmaster was one thing, but it did nothing to assuage the blunt fact that the wrongful impression he had gloatingly extracted from that evening's perambulation – that William was in the habit of actively consorting with thieves – was something he would undoubtedly use to advantage. For his part, William was already gripped with trepidation at the very thought of facing Jenkins once again, of what Monday morning would bring. Charlotte's thoughts had not been dissimilar in their tendency. In the context of the master's burgeoning dislike for her son, Jenkins had completed his walk armed with grist to his mill, something which did not bode well; yet for a schoolboy to be picked upon or to be dealt a warming corporal chastisement was comparatively small beer in Charlotte's assessment. Schoolroom discipline, after all, was good for a boy's moral welfare. Instead, as the hall clock chimed ten, a matter of greater consequence, concerning the machinations of school politics, had entered her head; and there it had been set to occupy her mind and stifle sleep during the forthcoming hours of darkness.

"I think, Willie, your eventful evening has run its course. Better get off to your bed. It's church in the morning and if ever it behoves you to be remorseful in the presence of your Maker then perhaps it is tomorrow." William had not balked at his mother's suggestion. He had been heartened beyond measure to hear his mother address him as Willie once again.

By the time William had turned out of his bed and quietly attended to such toilet as was necessary to render him smartly attired for Morning Service, mother and daughter had already breakfasted and retired to the front parlour; and as he came downstairs and passed the parlour door, which stood ajar, he had been aware of earnest, yet suppressed exchanges, which by their modulation and apparent gravity were clearly not intended for his ears. The conversation had abruptly ceased, furthermore, as William passed down the passage towards the dining room and, in the process, had caused ill-fitting floorboards to tell of his whereabouts.

"Go and get some breakfast, Willie. Hurry now…we must be on our way before the next quarter strikes," Charlotte had said, in a normal enough voice, which, in its artlessness, had merely served to underline the subdued nature of the women's erstwhile colloquy.

And in consequence William had breakfasted alone – swiftly on account of his mother's briefing and perfunctorily by reason of his thoughts being taken with abstraction. As he ate he had peered out into the neat, walled back garden where the morning sunlight was already at work, succouring and warming April's fresh, budding growth and hastening May's greater fecundity. But it had not been such overt signs of spring that drew his unshackled thoughts, rather a sparkling cobweb strung between twigs that almost grazed the window. Here the resident spider, hunched in its peripheral lair, eyed its newly snared prey that twitched helplessly amid the gossamer's mucilaginous grasp. The spider had readied itself to pounce, an unfolding drama that caused William's thoughts to enter the schoolroom which, on the morrow, would beckon once again. In his mind's eye William had pictured the spidery Jenkins, perched in his own lair, seated at his high desk at the front of the class. High on the wall behind him the words *Thou shalt not steal* had a sardonic ring to them as the schoolmaster surveyed his own prey – plentiful quarry, but none so tasty, none so sweetly seasoned with the taint of perceived wrongdoing – than his once favoured pupil teacher…

William had eventually been roused from this unpleasant abstraction by a call to be ready to leave in two minutes and not to forget his prayer book. And thus the ten minute walk to church had got underway. To William it proved an irksome perambulation. Charlotte had harked on to him about the importance of good resolve and of showing remorse when saying his prayers. Only through repentance could he hope to be cleansed of his transgressions.

"Look at St. John, son. See what he has to say about confessing our sins and forgiveness."

"The first epistle, mind you…not the gospel, Willie," Grandma Black had added.

"Quite so, Mother," said Charlotte. "I was about to say as much."

"I think I know the passage of scripture," had been William's retort.

"Then read it again and be guided by it," had been the gist of the women's rejoinders.

And so it had been to the considerable contentment of his close kin that William Reynolds took heed of their good advice and immersed himself in the Morning Service; and most particularly, with conviction previously unrivalled, he had knelt and determinedly repeated the parson's words as he read the general confession...

Almighty and most merciful Father; We have erred and strayed from thy ways like lost sheep. We have followed too much the devices and desires of our own hearts. We have offended against thy holy laws. We have left undone those things which we ought to have done; And we have done those things which we ought not to have done; And there is no health in us. But thou, O Lord, have mercy upon us, miserable offenders. Spare thou them, O God, which confess their faults. Restore thou them that are penitent; According to thy promises declared unto mankind in Christ Jesu our Lord. And grant, O most merciful father, for his sake; That we may hereafter live a godly, righteous, and sober life, To the glory of thy holy Name. Amen.

After the service's conclusion, and the exchange of parting pleasantries with the minister, it had been in William's absence that Charlotte and her mother retraced their steps to King Street. Without further prompting, their charge had remained seated in church where he proceeded to thumb through the Bible, re-acquainting himself with what the Apostle, John, had to say about sin and forgiveness; and, before exiting the church portals, he had entered into contrite communication with his Maker. As he sauntered home he had felt solaced from that spiritual union; yet, unexpectedly, that simple comfort was about to turn to joy once he had divested himself of his coat, put down his prayer book and answered his mother's call to join her in the parlour.

"Sit down, Willie," she had said as she busied herself arranging writing materials at her little roll-top bureau. "Last night I spent some sleepless hours thinking about your most unfortunate situation and where we go from here. I have concluded that we need to take some radical action. Waiting upon the outcome of the police investigations is one thing but your Mister Jenkins' judgement was all too easily coloured by his own prejudices and what he instantly gleaned from Norris. Knowing what I do now of the man, I have no doubt he will not shirk from making your life uncomfortable, Willie, whatever the police have to say."

"I'm dreading tomorrow, Mother," William had admitted with candour, his colour drained white with trepidation.

"Well dread no more, my boy. After breakfast this morning I talked over my thoughts with your Grandma and she agrees with me. As a consequence, I propose to write a letter to the School Board, informing them that, with immediate effect, you will no longer be attending the school. Out of courtesy...not that the man's attitude warrants it...I will also be penning a letter to Jenkins and I fancy it will forestall the fellow to the point of frustration."

At this juncture William's jaw had sagged, his mouth gaping open with disbelief. "I'm to leave school, Mother?" he had blurted, his incredulity soon displaced by an uplifting surge of delight as Charlotte had nodded affirmatively.

"Forthwith, my boy. You see, I sense your Mister Jenkins will not be satisfied picking upon you. No, from the distorted impression he obtained last evening, I fully expect him to try to oust you...to get you expelled on the strength of contravening school precepts. And when I think of the shame of that, especially when it is totally unjustified, then, yes, we must surely take action to pre-empt and head off the likelihood of such a ploy. Now, take yourself off to the kitchen and help your grandmother with the chores while I get these letters written. I intend to deliver them into the school letter-box before the day has run its course."

★ ★ ★

April had given way to May. Uncle Charley had understandably been incensed on hearing that his nephew might have cooperated in an act of aggression and thieving, dismissing the suggestion as ludicrous and 'sheer humbug.' And, within days of William parting company with his school, he had found the boy some temporary work to give him purpose while thought might be given to securing what his mother termed 'a proper job.' Some weeks had passed since the affable landlord had stolen a march on those other licensed victuallers who plied their trade within sight of the Dockyard Gate. He knew that many a 'yard employee would cut things fine, it being human nature to do so when the day ahead held only the promise of mundane routine. Many would tumble out of bed, peckish, yet with little inclination, or time in hand, to do much about it, the more immediate ambition being to get to the Gate ahead of the Porter's muster bell. The more conscientious of these bleary-eyed dockyard mateys – who realised that ambition with time to spare – would dally awhile to part with their pennies and avail themselves of hot meat pies, courtesy of several vendors who found the Main Gate a most profitable early morning pitch.

Yet Charley Black had asked himself whether a hot fried breakfast, taken in the *Sheer Hulk* taproom, might prove a greater attraction. Might just the prospect of a reasonably priced fry-up of beefsteak, onions and blood pudding – washed down with a modest drop of sweet porter – do more to coax a man to rise a little earlier from his night's slumber and so partake of his victuals in comparative comfort? What better start to prepare a man and sustain him through his day in the 'yard? In the landlord's assessment his idea had been worthy of being put to the test; and so it was and with more than a modicum of success.

Charley was now in the habit of opening up just short of half past five, by which time his preparations in the cellar kitchen were well placed to begin answering the call for his cooked breakfasts. The cooking was his domain, for he seemed to have an aptitude for such, he enjoyed the work and, most importantly, his meals soon proved to be popular. Yet, as to taking the orders, carrying the food to customers and gathering up and washing the dirty crockery, cutlery and utensils, he had been forced to reach some temporary accommodation: he had prevailed upon the services of one of his tenants in exchange for some concession over the cost of the fellow's lodgings. However, it was a mutual understanding that was far from ideal, with Charley soon sensing it was not the modest financial saving that motivated his lodger as much as a kindly preparedness to simply do him a favour. Yet with Rachel Ellis already heavily engaged with her early chores and the regular potmen not long since returned to their respective abodes – after lengthy stints in taproom and cellar – Charley had been left with little alternative as he swiftly embarked on his new venture.

Suddenly William was done with his schooldays and Uncle Charley most content to use him in this capacity, knowing that – with predicament resolved – his obliging lodger would be more than happy to stand aside.

"Ask your Mother, Willie, my lad, whether she'd let you be my 'breakfast boy' on weekday mornings," Charley had declared. "Tell her it will help us both and give you a few shillings in your pocket until you land a job to your liking."

Charlotte had not railed at the proposition but then Charley hardly expected vehement opposition. After all, circumstances had changed. His sister's responsiveness was more taken with the worrying matter of whether her son could soon end up appearing before the Portsmouth Magistrates. Now she was far more relaxed about him visiting the public house which she'd cease to call a sailor's beerhouse. Added to which, William was no longer a schoolboy and even Charlotte recognised that he could not remain tied to her apron strings. She was keen that his good reason to get up out of bed of a morning should not be extinguished and if she still harboured any lingering residue of doubt about her boy being exposed to the dubious influences of a public taproom, then it was in the allaying knowledge that it was to be exposure at an acceptable time of day. There was only one stipulation as far as Charlotte was concerned: that at a lonely hour, William should not have to wander through the gloomy Portsea streets which lay between his home and the house on The Common Hard. And so he duly became his uncle's 'breakfast boy' and, to this end, beginning on Sunday evenings and ending on Thursdays, he became accustomed to sleeping in a rickety truckle bed in Uncle Charley's first floor quarters.

William had rarely been happier. His joy at being rid of school and beginning his day in the company of his favourite uncle was only tempered by the gnawing anxiety that he could yet be called upon to answer to criminal allegations. Only the occasional sight of or hurried exchange of words with that pretty object of his fantasy – the pert-lipped Rachel Ellis – as she went busily about her duties, would serve to briefly expunge such thoughts from his mind. That and those heightened, quiet moments in the truckle bed, when, in frustrated realisation that Rachel lay so near, William was sometimes drawn to close his mind to rumoured consequence and surrender to carnal thoughts in taut and joyous relief.

Yet that succession of mornings ferrying hot breakfasts from cellar kitchen to taproom and of jovial exchanges between uncle and nephew was destined to be short-lived. It was now the middle of May and William had spent two weeks working for his Uncle Charley. And, as he strolled home to King Street, late in the morning of the second Friday, contentedly jingling his second week's earnings in his trouser pocket, William was suddenly aware of a familiar sulphurous whiff that hung in the air. He hadn't noticed it on previous days. Perhaps the earlier showers had served to tease the scent from the bright array of flowers rooted in the crusty capping of the old Dockyard wall. The wallflowers were in bloom, exuding that same smell which pervaded the back garden when, on an earlier occasion, Uncle Charley had come home from the war. It must be that same time of year, thought William to himself. Two years. He could hardly believe that two years had flown by.

"Hello, son. Had a busy morning?" enquired his mother as she held open the front door.

"As busy as I've known it. I do believe Uncle Charley has hit upon a profitable idea serving breakfasts. I stayed on a while to help him tidy the back yard. I think he still intends getting the outbuildings in order so he might stable a couple of riding horses."

"Ah, there you are, Willie," said Grandma Black as she shuffled into view clutching a newspaper, her spectacles perched precariously on the end of her nose.

"Hello, Grandma," replied William cheerily. It was just then that his senses were strangely pricked by that same sulphurous smell he had encountered by the Dockyard wall, as if some lingering residual hint of the same had temporarily sequestered itself in the labyrinth of his nasal cavity. Its release prompted William to continue. "Do you know, it occurred to me while walking home that it is exactly two years since Uncle Charley returned from the Russian war. Can you believe it, two years!"

"Yes, lad," mumbled Grandma Black, "but don't talk to me of war. I've just been reading the newspaper…about recent events in India. It doesn't look good and I can't but wonder about your Uncle John."

"From what I glean from the reports, Mother, I'm not so sure we need worry too much as matters stand," said Charlotte, reassuringly. "I've taken a look at Willie's atlas. The last letter we received from brother John…it must be a month ago now…was from a place called Peshawar. That's way up near the Afghan border and hundreds of miles from Meerut and Delhi where the native infantry are said to have rebelled."

"I'll grant you that, my dear, but these things have a habit of spreading and getting out of hand."

"Well, yes, Mother. But if we can put the Russians to the sword I can't imagine we'll have much trouble quelling a bunch of sepoys," exclaimed Charlotte with a mix of flippancy and arrogance.

★ ★ ★

As the Sepoy Mutiny of 1857 spread like wildfire and hostilities intensified, the activity that had characterised Portsea during the Russian War was, to some extent, resurrected, not least within the confines of Her Majesty's Dockyard.

"You'd do well to enquire at the Porter's Lodge, Willie, to see what work is available," said his mother, insistently, once word was abroad that the 'yard was to take on more hands. "It's been good for you working with your Uncle Charley, but…"

"I enjoy it, Mother, I really do…and I've had some good tips lately."

"That's as may be, my boy, but I believe it's time to think about a proper job. When you're on your way home tomorrow morning, remember to call by the Main Gate. See what they're looking for. If there's something to which you can turn your hands to good effect and make the right impression, then who knows what it could lead to…you might be able to land yourself an apprenticeship in due course, like your friend John Downer. I'm told those apprenticeships are not something to be sneezed at, Willie, and you get to attend the Dockyard school some afternoons."

Not surprisingly, once spring had turned to summer, William found himself in the employ of the Royal Dockyard. He had sometimes caught sight of John Downer as his friend passed by the *Sheer Hulk* of a morning on his way to the 'yard. Now he would meet up with him at the Main Gate, just before six, and together they would briskly walk the greater part of the Dockyard's expanse until they caught sight of the Steam Basin. There the two youths would go their separate ways, John entering the Block Mills, William carrying on past No.7 Dock to his place of work in the Steam Factory at the far end of the 'yard. It was a formidable, modern edifice, a huge engineering workshop in red brick that ran the length of the Steam Basin and, in its grandeur, could be excused for appearing to derisively stand aloof from the old Dockyard. For herein lay mechanical and assembling devices that signified change and were to forge the new navy, the steam-powered navy; and blessed with such significance, the Steam Factory, along with the newer Steam Smithy and Iron Foundry, seemed to draw the greater part of what temporary additional recruitment was called forth by the Royal Dockyard.

William went with his uncle's blessing, despite the landlord having, once again, to rely upon the services of his good natured tenant – a fall-back now bolstered by Charley's ardent promise to find a new boy to serve breakfasts before the week was out. As for William, his apprehension over embarking upon a working life in the 'yard, albeit in all likelihood a temporary one, was greatly assuaged by the joy that gripped him on the last Friday he worked at the *Sheer Hulk*. He had completed serving breakfasts and tidying up and had returned home to King Street, only to reappear in the most agitated state within the half hour. Tearing into the stable yard, where Uncle Charley was in course of burning rubbish, William excitedly pulled up just short of the smoking brazier but not before he had inhaled some of its reeky emissions. This immediately threw him into a fit of coughing, stifling his dire wish to pour forth the cause of his delight.

"Well, shiver m'timbers, lad," exclaimed Charley with a sympathetic chuckle, concurrently administering his nephew a gentle back slapping. "I thought I'd seen the last of you for today. Let me fetch you a glass of water to stem that cough...and come this side of the fire to get away from the smoke."

"No, no, Uncle," spluttered William, his wetted eyes blinking from the smoke's lacrimatory effect, his face bearing a grin that told of joy having got the better of momentary discomfort. "No...I promise you, I'm alright." And, in confirmation, William cleared his throat with a final cough and wiped his eyes upon his shirt cuff, actions which promptly rendered him more composed and equipped to continue. "It's just that I had to tell you, Uncle Charley, that there's to be no Magistrates' Court. Mother and Grandma were overjoyed when I got home having just heard the news that..."

"You mean..." interjected Charley, his words quickly suppressed and drowned by the more resilient utterances spawned by his nephew's elation.

"Yes, Uncle. I mean there is to be no...I think Mother used the term summary offence, yes...no summary offence...no reason for me to appear before the Portsmouth Justices in connection with my friends'...well, my so-called friends'... robbery and assault upon the muffin seller."

"Well, I'm mighty pleased to hear your news, Willie. It'll be a great burden off everyone's mind to be sure," opined Charley, as cheery flames suddenly flared, engulfing the brazier's smouldering contents and setting all to hiss and crackle as if in coincident celebration.

"It seems the police caught two of them dipping into a few pockets in Camden Alley. Once in custody, and identified as being among those who robbed the muffin man, I suppose they couldn't tolerate seeing the others go free. So they promptly informed on their whereabouts."

"Hoping for a bit of leniency, as well, by squealing on their friends," suggested the landlord.

"Maybe," said William, pensively. "Anyway, Uncle, it seems the police never really believed I might have been an accomplice...or Johnnie Downer, for that matter. And although those caught pick-pocketing were prepared to shop the other two, it appears that, when questioned, all insisted I hadn't been involved."

"I should think not, my boy. I suspect the Magistrates will show them little mercy but, as far as you're concerned, it's a worry you can safely put to rest. I'm delighted. Now, in turn, there's some news you can take in the opposite direction," said Charley as he cast more scraps upon the fire. "Tell your Mother and Grandma that, after you left here this morning, the postman brought me a letter from your Uncle John. I'll bring it round for them to read on Sunday. It was written before the recent troubles broke out but he was still at Peshawar, about twenty miles from the Khyber Pass. They've been there several months now and, by all accounts, the regiment's health has been excellent. Apparently, the Seventieth is one of two infantry regiments in the garrison, along with two battalions of artillery and, as far as I can judge, the tone of brother John's writing suggests he remains in good spirits. Tell them that, Willie. It should provide further peace of mind to swell what the day has already bestowed upon a deserving family. Oh, and tell your Grandma that I'll bring my flute with me on Sunday and play her a few tunes. She keeps reminding me and I keep forgetting."

★ ★ ★

The summer of 1857 slipped by without anything remarkable happening in the Reynolds' household to mark it out as what Grandma Black might be tempted to call a grand spell or, conversely, a real stinger. Yes, there was an undercurrent of anxiety, where Charlotte and her mother were concerned, as they made sure to keep abreast of news of the rebellious events in India; and daily they would keep an eye for the approaching postman, flush with expectation that tidings from their loved-one were on the brink of delivery. William, for his part, was in a perpetual state of tiredness, the growing pains of youth according to his grandmother, yet, in truth, the product of long and busy days in the 'yard to which erstwhile schooldays had rendered him ill-prepared.

As to life in the Steam Factory, William would find himself pulled hither and thither at the whim of this smith, or that shipwright, to run errands and transport ships' fittings to all quarters of the 'yard. Otherwise he would be confined all day in the factory, machine minding and alley-dashing or detailed to undertake other menial tasks in the nearby engine smithy or the new foundry or in the boiler or anchor forges. He had begun to take a liking to working in the anchor forge, watching anchors of all types and description being fabricated. It suddenly furnished William with a totally new vocabulary...shanks and flukes, stocks, hoops and shackles, stream, kedge and bower anchors and mud-hooks, palms and blades, loops, pins and pellets, hawse-hole rollers and fish-buckles, toggles and throat-pieces, pee, crown and cable-stoppers – a vocabulary he was inclined to let loose over supper after a day in the forge, much to the well disguised anguish of his companions. Well disguised, since it was the ardent wish of both his mother and grandmother that William should not be deterred from doing his best and giving himself every chance of ultimately landing a good apprenticeship.

"Do you realise, Willie, it's six weeks since you began work in the Dockyard?" said Grandma Black, as she followed her grandson into the back garden one sultry July evening. "Do you enjoy the work or would you sooner be back at school?"

"It's usually hard work, Grandma, but more often than not it's monotonous. But I'd rather answer to an angry master shipwright than that awful Mister Jenkins."

"Ah, but remember, you've been exonerated…cleared of all suspicion over that Queen Street business. You could have held your head up high and…"

"Yes," interjected William, "but it would have irked him all the more."

It dawned on Margaret Black that there was substance to William's contention. She simply raised her eyebrows in silent concurrence. "So would you like to stay in the 'yard, my boy?" she continued.

"No, not really. You know, Grandma, for all the suffering in the Crimea that Uncle Charley mentioned, I'd still choose to take the Queen's shilling. I'd sooner be a soldier."

"There's something to be said for working in the Dockyard, son, or at any rate, near home. It's not as dangerous as going to sea or shouldering walnut."

"You may be right Grandma, but since I've been in the Dockyard a fellow was badly burnt and maimed in the tarring house and a rigger was killed by a falling yard."

For the second time inside a minute, William's grandmother chose not to take issue with the point he was making.

"There must be better jobs in the 'yard but I suppose working in the anchor forge isn't so bad. It's hot and noisy what with the steam hammer and furnace heat but I get on well with the anchorsmiths. They seem to be a cheerful lot…some say it's because of all the beer they drink. They work up such a thirst you see, Grandma, that they're plied with beer all day long. Mostly small beer, otherwise they'd be drunk on their feet…but it's probably that which makes 'em cheerful. And they let me go to work with a cold chisel, cleaning up some of the anchors in store. That's got to be better than sweeping floors. One of their senior shipwrights even gave me time off last week to watch a new ship going off the slip. It was grand to see a launching."

"But you wouldn't care to work with anchors? You'd prefer soldiering?"

"Yes, Grandma, without a doubt. It's hard work in the forge. You need to be a brawny fellow and I doubt I'd have the build. Besides, there's a lot of talk among the anchorsmiths as to whether there's a future for anchor work in Her Majesty's Dockyards. It's already been abandoned in some of the 'yards."

"But ships will always need anchors Willie," observed Grandma Black.

"I'll grant you that, but apparently, when the Baltic Fleet returned home, it brought back too many Admiralty mud-hooks that had been broken and were in need of repair. I'm told it meant a lot of bad publicity that questioned the uniformity and quality of 'yard forged anchors. And to an extent this is true, on account of there being too few smiths to the number of shipwrights. Well, the upshot, so they say, is the likely creation of a civilian factory to make all the anchors needed by the Royal Navy, leaving the manufacture of other shipwork to the Dockyard smitheries. So, you see, there's a lot of uncertainty at the moment."

Margaret Black was impressed by her grandson's apparent grasp of Dockyard politics, if his insight into matters influencing the manufacture of ships' anchors was any criterion. As she watched him return indoors she pondered upon whether it was right to expect him to go on and make a life-long career of working in the Dockyard. Perhaps her daughter would not agree but, as far as Grandma Black was concerned, she was not convinced of the wisdom of stifling the boy's firmly held view as to where his future might lie. He was, after all, a comparatively intelligent lad who would not – at least in his grandmother's opinion – enter into anything rashly or without due and deep consideration.

Putting her thoughts aside, Margaret called after her grandson. "Willie, dear, I've forgotten to feed the cat. Do it for me, will you, while I go and make us all a bedtime drink. There's some cold fish in that old chipped tureen on the stillage."

"Leave it to me, Grandma. I'm honoured to be allowed to feed your cat. Perhaps not only the anchorsmiths are inclined to give me a little responsibility," came the chuckled reply. "Oh, and by the way, it's too warm a night for one of your hot cocoas. A glass of chilled fruit cordial would suit me fine, thank you."

★ ★ ★

The sun had begun to adopt that full blown mellowness which often signals the approach of autumnal twilight; and with it those distinctively rich, orangey shafts of late September sunlight fell upon The Common Hard and began to cause a shimmer across the exposed mudflats that lay before. It was the close of the working day and William was part of the surging throng that spewed wearily out of the Main Gate. It had not been one of his better days but one in which he had been confined to the Steam Factory and constantly burdened by a surfeit of tiring, menial tasks that ultimately had rendered him both tired and a trifle downcast. Yet once released beyond the Dockyard confines his mood lightened, his interest pricked by the sight and sound of a yellow-whiskered fellow who had climbed upon an upturned box on that scant piece of greensward that stood behind the foreshore. A tall, well-built man, with a bellow to match, he rose high above the dispersing crowd, the vast majority of departing mateys oblivious to his presence, or simply disinterested in their single-mindedness and desire to look their suppers in the eye. Some, however – William included – loitered awhile, their purpose to catch the drift of the barrel-chested man's pronouncements. For his words flew forth with such stridency that their delivery alone was worthy of observation. Temperance was his message, abstinence from the affliction that is liquor, his denunciation pouring forth with such evangelical zeal and ardency as to contort his features. Yet the dog-eared bible he held aloft was no signpost to his profession. He was no man of the cloth, yet in his custom not far removed from the itinerant preacher with that propensity to deliver his oratories extempore. And although hungry stomachs held sway and kept the majority heading their way homewards, those who dallied a few minutes were captivated by his rhetoric, words which in their fervency would sometimes set the man's eyes bulging and his nostrils flaring.

Ten minutes elapsed. A scavenging herring gull suddenly distracted William as it swooped low and brushed his shoulder. It took his gaze away from the orator and, for the first time, his eyes fell upon the several characters to his seaward side, most notably a young man who, like most, appeared spellbound by the speaker's performance. He sat astride the stem of a skiff drawn up on the foreshore and William recognised him

294

immediately: the swarthy gypsy youth who had once accosted him at Portsdown Fair…Ned the gypsy of whom he had last caught sight on Christmas Day from the comfort of Uncle Charley's rooms…just along the way, near the pier entrance. He had filled out, thought William to himself, the wispy excuse for a moustache having become a stubbly affair, and the fustian jacket – that he had worn at Portsdown and was still on his back at Christmas – having finally been discarded in favour of a frock jacket. It was a dowdy and doubtless second-hand jacket but with a waistcoat, rigid-stand collar and narrow necktie, it marked him out as more of a man than a boy. William felt he should be making his way home but on a whim decided to approach the gypsy.

"You're Ned aren't you?" said William, jauntily, his boots shifting and grating upon the shingle as he neared the skiff.

"And who might you be young feller?" enquired the gypsy as he turned his attention from orator to questioner. "I can't say I recognise you."

"Portsdown Fair. Don't you remember?"

"Can't say I do…but then I wouldn't," said the gypsy, reflectively. "I was away up country during the Fair…harvesting and making wattles and hurdles from coppiced timber."

"I don't mean this year. It must have been, what…two…no, three years back."

"Three years!" scoffed Ned. "How the hell d'yer 'spect me to remember you after three years, young sir? Anyway, what did y'do to make me remember?"

"Nothing. You tried to get me to pay tuppence to have my fortune told but I was in a hurry to catch the Portsea omnibus."

Ned eyed William closely until a faint smile suggested recollection to be on the brink of confirmation. "I do remember young feller. Yes, I do remember. Told you to seek us out on the Common if you wanted your palm read by my grandmother. Did you ever do so?…can't say I ever recall seeing you over our place."

"No, no…I always meant to, but didn't get round to it. But I still intend to come over there when…" William hesitated. "I'm assuming your grandmother is still living, Ned?" he continued falteringly.

"Yes, oh yes. Strong as an ox, bless her. Lives on soups and gruels, for there's not a single tooth in her head. But she's got all her wits about her and there's not a better gypsy fortune-teller in all of Hampshire," said the swarthy youth, a hint of boastfulness rising in his voice. "Come over any time now. We've just returned from a spot of hop picking in Kent and have settled back in our usual place in the furze to see the winter out."

"One Saturday, soon. I'll wander out to you on a dry Saturday and make sure I've tuppence in my pocket," said William.

"Tuppence, indeed! Well, not wishing to disappoint you young feller," exclaimed Ned somewhat derisively, "but last year old Gran put her price up to a silver thrupence. Still dirt cheap, mind you."

"Then I'll just make sure I've a thrup'ny piece on me," remarked William.

"No...let's be fair," said the gypsy youth, light-heartedly. "Seeing that you're a mite overdue with your reading and you were offered it at tuppence, then tuppence it'll be."

It was at this point that an altercation brought an end to the discourse between William and Ned the gypsy and set both on a homeward course. A torrent of fatuous banter and jeering from a party of drunken bluejackets, high on cheap porter and newly emerged from the nearby *Waterman's Arms* had been the root cause. The sailors had perhaps prior knowledge of the orator for they quickly set about drawing a sharp and fiery reaction from one whose temperate inclinations, when it came to drink, were clearly not matched in matters of self-control. Impassioned perhaps, when it came to delivering his message, the yellow-whiskered speaker had nonetheless retained his composure until the sailors' badinage sorely put his dignity to the test. Perhaps it was just too much to be taunted by a group of heavy imbibers who, all too readily, had the capacity to stir contempt in his breast. The orator flew into an uncontrollable rage. Yet it was not his bellowing that distracted William and Ned, or took his more attentive listeners by surprise. Instead, it was the immoderate nature of his language. A string of vile oaths caused shock and embarrassment among the small crowd, momentarily prompting passers-by to stop and gawp in disbelief or to simply compel a good many of the assembled audience to tire of the man's deteriorating rhetoric and take their leave. William and the gypsy youth could be numbered among them.

On a Saturday afternoon, deep in October, William kept to his word. The preceding week had been fine with the drying effect of a prevailing and brisk south-easterly ensuring that a trudge across the Common could be set about without fear of miring one's boots. It was in consequence, aided by an unseasonably firm footing, that William made swift progress across the extensive greensward; and, within five and thirty minutes of departing King Street, he came upon the Lumps Mill stump and its huddle of weathered old buildings which seemed to turn their backs to the sea. Immediately ahead the firm ground gave way to soft, boggy terrain bordering the Lumps Mill pond. It was an obstacle reputed to be a remnant of the old morass, once extensive in these parts before convict reclamation gangs were put to work, an obstacle to be negotiated with discretion by those lacking an intimate knowledge of the area. William heeded the 'danger' signs by giving the pond a wide berth, whereupon the flat, unfolding landscape before him seemed gaunt and cheerless, terminating mistily in the distant Fort Cumberland and old Eastney Farm.

In the middle ground of this bleak, open prospect, in a clearing amid the furze, William could now make out his destination – the gypsy encampment. He halted awhile. He could see three black bender tents nestling in the whin, two spewing smoke from top openings in their tarred sailcloth. A fine salty spray seemed to account for the mistiness across this end of the Common, driven in from the sea before a stiff south easterly breeze that soon caught the tent emissions and sent them streaming inland. William resumed his walk, humming contentedly to himself all the while. Just occasionally he would be distracted by birdsong, sometimes sweet, mostly the raucous screech of gulls. Along the foreshore the constant watery drag of shingle across the beach played its own distant tune. And so, in time, William came upon a stationary farm cart piled high with furze-faggots, two freshly snared rabbits hanging limp from the tailboard. Another few strides across rutted turf and he reached a clearing where two chained horses quietly grazed. He could now see the bender tents, at close quarters, rising behind the animals, yet partly obscured by gorse thicket. Only the rasp of stone upon metal challenged nature's noises and told of a human presence.

"Hello, Ned," exclaimed the visitor, as he rounded the thicket and confronted the gypsy.

"Well...so y' kept to yer word, eh?" came the reply.

William smiled, almost apologetically, in confirmation.

"No, that's fine," said Ned, detecting that his visitor was a shade embarrassed. "Let me put m' tools aside and I'll have a word with m'grandmother."

"What tools have you been using?"

"Oh, just this hook, really," muttered the gypsy as he gingerly felt the newly sharpened blade, then set his whetstone down upon a pair of discarded gauntlets. "The Town Council's engaged me to clear a large swathe of the whin over towards Eastney Farm. They used to leave it to convict labour, but thankfully no more, for it earns me a few shillin's. I've been furze-cutting and making up faggots since dawn so I'm ready for a rest and a bite to eat." Ned fell silent for a minute or so while he bent down to unbuckle and remove his leather leggings. "Phew," he sighed, "that's better with them out the way. Now, young sir, what did y'call yerself?"

"I didn't...but it's William...William Reynolds."

"Right, stay here if y'will, William Reynolds, and I'll see about getting y'palm read." The gypsy spun on his heels, strode off and disappeared into the furthermost tent. In his absence two snotty-nosed children emerged from nowhere and proceeded to stand, gape and frown at the newcomer.

"My sister's children," explained Ned, as he reappeared clutching an earthenware jug and two glasses. "Always curious when strangers come to call. Now, m'grandmother will beckon you to her tent in a few minutes. In the meantime y'must be thirsty after that walk, so why not join me in a glass of nettle?"

"Nettle?" queried William, in a perplexed tone of voice.

"Nettle beer. Brewed by my aunt."

"Does it sting?"

"She might, but the beer's good," quipped Ned with a broad grin. "Here, see what y' think of it."

William grasped the proffered glass and sipped the bittersweet liquid. "It's good," came the eager retort.

"Then I'll leave the jug here with a cloth over," said Ned. "Y'may wish for another glass after the reading before y'set back. I'll have gone off for a nap by then but do help yerself."

At this juncture William hadn't noticed the beckoning from the furthermost tent, such was his preoccupation in supping the nettle beer.

"Old Gran's just signalled to me, William. Best get over to her tent young feller and learn y'fortune. I've told her it's tuppence and she's agreed. Just lift the tent flap and enter."

William's walk to the clairvoyant's tent was taken with tentative steps. He remembered the gnarled, swarthy features of the old lady as she had conducted her palmistry in the open air on Portsdown Hill. He also recalled he had detected a kindness in her demeanour but, at this moment, it did little to allay his sense of trepidation and, in any event, he may have been mistaken. He hesitated before lifting the tent flap, opting to cough or rather clear his throat as a way of announcing his arrival. It had the desired effect.

"Come in." It was a croaky, guttural voice that welcomed the newcomer.

William took a deep breath, raised the tent flap and entered, stopping to squint as his eyes sought to become accustomed to the reduced light.

"Careful with that flap, boy, or you'll spread the fire smoke and start us coughing." The instruction seemed to emanate from a distant part of the tent. It drew William's eyes past the fading embers of a central open hearth from which wisps of wood smoke spiralled upwards towards a beckoning aperture in the sailcloth. It took a few moments before the old lady came into view, although, with William's eyes continuing to acclimatise to the relative gloom, her materialisation amounted to little more than a silhouette.

There was a distinctive smell inside the tent or rather a merging of smells. Lavender, a hint of musk, sage and rosemary…herbal and floral fragrances effused from bunches of leaves and garlands of faded dried flowers that hung about…odours that melded with the astringent whiff of spiralling wood smoke and freshly burnt ashes. And there was a pervading scent off the enveloping sailcloth that reminded William of the Dockyard, for it was redolent of the caulker's pitch bucket.

"Come hither, boy and join me at the cat," said the old woman, her features now more discernible, her face contorted by what she intended as a smile but which her deeply wrinkled features could only cast as a sneer.

William tensed, his trepidation still strongly felt.

"Come on boy, nothing to fear," said the old hag, her arm beckoning. "Come sit at the cat. I think you've got tuppence to give me, then we'll see what the future holds for you."

William appeared to freeze but then slowly moved forward, fearing that to disobey his host might irk her sufficiently to turn him into a toad or something equally repellent. "The cat, ma'am? What cat?" There was a noticeable tremble in William's voice.

"Ma'am? No need for that sort of talk. Call me Gran. Ned calls me Gran, you know…calls me his darling old Gran. Yes, you can call me that."

William did not react to the gypsy's words. She was closer now. Another smile, a leer that revealed toothless gums as her right arm cupped her young visitor about the shoulders and ushered him into a rickety chair that faced a small, oval table.

"You asked about my cat, dear. Well, this is it…you're sitting at it," she exclaimed with a guttural cackle that suggested she was greatly amused. Meanwhile her guest raised a timid excuse for a smile to politely suggest he shared her amusement. In truth, however, he remained beset with anxiety.

"They call it a gypsy's cat, my dear," said the old woman as she tapped her middle finger upon the little table that lay adorned with a beaded and fringed scarlet cover. "Goodness knows why, but there we are."

Right in front of William, on the cat, stood a small pudding bowl. He eased himself forward to take a closer look, assuming that whatever lay within might be called upon in conducting the palm reading.

"Hedgehog fat," exclaimed the gypsy woman as she became aware of her customer's inquisitiveness. William recoiled in horror.

"Ned caught me a plump little fellow yesterday evening. Well fed and chubby, he was, as if well prepared for his winter hibernation. Anyway, into the pot he went and now I've got a goodly amount of fat to make up some ointment."

Inwardly, William sighed with relief as the old woman removed the bowl, then proceeded to take her place opposite him.

"You look a little anxious, boy. Relax now, no need to be frightened of Gran," said the old crone. "Just hand me your pennies and we'll get underway."

William proceeded to do as he was told, then, once his coins had been grasped and secreted in Gran's apron pocket, she withdrew a candle and holder from a pine box beneath the cat.

"The light's poor now and my eyesight's not what it was," she muttered. "I need a good light to read your lines and bumps."

The old woman impaled the wax column on the spike of the candleholder, then, rising from her chair, took a taper to the hearth embers and returned a moment later to light the candle.

Having resumed her seat, William was struck how the candle light played upon and sharpened the gypsy woman's chiselled, weather-beaten features. Yet, as before, on that occasion at Portsdown, he detected a kindness therein.

"With which hand do you write, boy? Give it here, then we can begin." The old woman took hold of William's tendered right hand and began to study it closely. All quarters she examined, not simply his palm but the back of the hand, his fingers, his nails. She turned to the other hand and set about a similar scrutiny, returning again to the dominant one and a closer perusal of the configuration of its lines and patterns. The old lady looked up and smiled occasionally in reassurance. William began to feel less aversion towards the contortive nature of those smiles, sensing that appearances and the throaty nature of the old gypsy's voice were not to be feared. He began to relax and, as he did so, his host began to tell him a little of his background, of his immediate family and of naval and military connections.

As to William's life path, the old woman's pronouncements did little to raise the spirits of her listener. In matters of the heart she told him he would marry but could not say whether children would flow from the marriage. She told him he would fulfil an ambition…it was a uniform, she saw a uniform.

"A scarlet tunic?"

"No boy, I see no scarlet." The gypsy fell silent a moment, her eyes tightly closed. "I see the colour blue."

William's heart sank. "The navy?"

The old woman's eyes glared fixedly at William's right palm. It seemed an eternity before she spoke again. "No…I see a row of soldier's buttons."

William relaxed once more, a deep breath telling of his relief.

"Oh, and I see a man…a man keeps coming into my mind's eye. He seems nervous and all the while is looking back, looking over his shoulder."

"So why should this man keep appearing? What is he to do with me?" It was not an issue of such import to William as the uniform, but it intrigued him nonetheless.

"Let's say, boy, that as you tread life's path he's someone you will encounter on the way."

"Should I be afraid?"

"No, not at all. In my picture of him it is he who is afraid. It's in his demeanour you see…a furtive man if ever there was."

"Then what more can you tell me about this mysterious man?" said William, his interest intensifying.

"Very little…except for one thing."

William said nothing but looked intently at the old woman as if expecting some clarification. Yet its delivery was checked by a young kitten that jumped out of the shadows and leapt into its keeper's lap. Its mewling provoked the old crone to get up and wander off, the kitten in close attendance. It was a few minutes before she returned.

"Fed it with what was left of the hedgehog," she chuckled. "A rare treat. Now, I think we were about finished with the reading."

"You were about to tell me about the furtive man," said William.

"The furtive man…ah, yes. All the signs suggest he's a foreigner. A German…yes, I'm sure you'll find he's a German."

It was late in the afternoon when William set about retracing his steps back home. He had thanked and bade farewell to the old gypsy woman, tarrying awhile to rid himself of the dry mouth that was the legacy of his earlier apprehension; for Ned had been true to his word in leaving behind the jug of his aunt's nettle beer.

The walk across the Common proved a languorous one, William's lassitude perhaps attributable to an imprudent intake of the traveller's brew. He was glad his long held wish to have a gypsy palm reading had been fulfilled and, as he sauntered on, his thoughts returned to what the old woman had told him. He had been impressed and baffled by her knowledge of his family, not least what she had said of his uncles and their chosen occupations; and, swayed by the gypsy's apparent competence in her craft, William was inclined to attach credence to her insistence that one day he would wear a soldier's tunic. That said, the blue uniform was puzzling. He struggled to call to mind a regiment that wore blue. The Royal Marine Artillerymen he saw about town always looked resplendent in their blue coatees but they were sea soldiers. Perhaps the old woman was confused. Perhaps she meant a regiment with blue facings.

In the rapidly waning light of dusk, by the time William turned the corner into King Street, he felt sure he was destined to wear those blue facings. As for the furtive German, whose path he would sometime cross, the information did not rank at all highly in the youth's judgement; and, in consequence, and with no further cause for forethought, it was committed to some distant niche in the labyrinthine depths of his mind, there to be consigned to oblivion or some future awakening.

★ ★ ★

The dank, autumnal mistiness that daybreak had ushered in off the Solent drained the very colour from King Street's bricks and mortar, casting an amorphous greyness about the place and transforming the night's gossamer to sparkling filigree. It was a thin fog that was slow to dissipate as the morning progressed, a veil that to any observer quickly swallowed up passing traffic, wheeled or pedestrian, into its drab and neutral clutches. The one exception was the postman as he picked his way down the street, for his distinctive scarlet coat stood out like a beacon, colouring the gloom. His timing was perhaps a shade on the early side of what the observer might regard as commonplace, his gait a mite more hurried than usual for there was little need to tarry, his mailbag haven to a mere three missives for the residents of King Street. The last of these he handed to Charlotte

Reynolds as she busied herself cleaning her front step and blacking the foot scraper.

"Good morning, Missus Reynolds, ma'am," said the postman, cheerily, raising his beaver hat in courteous respect. "A correspondence which I trust will brighten your day!"

Charlotte accepted the letter with a smile. "Thank you, Mister Postman." On seeing and recognising her sibling's hand she had no cause to disbelieve the other's assumption. It was not often she received a letter from brother James.

Brushes and blacking were put aside as Charlotte interrupted her chores and re-entered the house, a more pressing interest being to coax her mother from her scullery attentions and to sit her down in the front parlour. There she would read the letter to Grandma Black as mother and daughter enjoyed the amusing anecdotes that James invariably recounted, be they of life between the guns or from the after-cabin. As Charlotte closed the front door behind her and beckoned her mother to the parlour, vapid, eerie rays began to pierce Portsea's overhanging gloom; yet it was a fleeting incandescence which flattered to deceive, for the enveloping murk came again, closing out the watery sun and leaving the parlour still bereft of sufficient natural light by which to read. Charlotte trimmed and lit a lamp. Margaret Black arrived hotfoot from the scullery having excitedly put her pot cleaning aside.

"Well, let's hear what he has to say, dear," said the elder woman, impatiently, as she handed her daughter a paring knife to slit open the envelope.

The incision was duly made, the letter extracted. Charlotte stooped to bathe her brother's missive within the lamplight and began to read out loud. The content was, to say the least, unexpected, precipitating feelings of complete surprise, of consternation, but above all, of conflicting emotions in reader and listener alike. And for once there were no little anecdotes to raise a smile, none of those touching snippets of poetry that were customarily the hallmark of James' letters home. Numbed and thus, for the moment, devoid of quite knowing her true feelings upon its impartation, Charlotte quietly folded the document and returned it to its envelope. Her mother looked bemused. Half an hour later, the two women, heavily cloaked and bonneted against the damp chill, stepped out into the street and proceeded to make their way purposefully towards The Common Hard.

Charley Black frowned, sighed, pulled at his side-whiskers and slumped back into his favourite, rumpled armchair. Before him, his mother and sister had chosen to seat themselves on dining chairs, either side of the mahogany table on which they had cast their bonnets. Charley fidgeted for a moment, regretting that he had not first taken time to untie and discard his inhibiting leather apron. He had hastened from below when Rachel announced his visitors' arrival and had not given it a thought. Once in their presence the excitement and agitation had been all consuming and his brother's letter thrust under his nose.

"I know James said he had hopes of Willie becoming a gentleman…much like the rest of us," said Charley as he continued to stare at the letter. "Told me so, he did…and said he'd always encouraged the boy to be diligent and hard-working when it came to his lessons. But when talking to that brother of mine I always got the feeling he thought the Navy would be the making of Willie. Too much of a dyed in the wool sailor, that's his trouble."

"Like you, Charley, I always felt James shared our hopes for Willie," added Charlotte, "although I know Willie was always uneasy in his presence because of his constant harping on about the Navy and implying that he should become a ship's steward."

"Never much liked the sea and ships, my young nephew," observed Charley. "Partial to the military, yes, but knowing your own feelings on the matter of him soldiering I thought I'd given him enough to think about and to shy away from that."

"Don't you believe it, Charley," said Grandma Black. "He had his fortune told a couple of weeks ago, much to my dismay, and says he's destined to become a soldier. It's all he talks about at the moment."

"Well, the fortune-teller got that wrong, for sure," muttered Charley.

"In truth it irks me greatly that James has been so interfering…after all, it's hardly his place to exert such influence and…"

"In fairness, Charlotte, my dear, I am sure he has Willie's interests at heart…by no means is he intent on distressing the lad," suggested Grandma Black, being always minded to see the positive aspects of her children's actions. "But, yes, I know what you mean. He's acted beyond his compass has James, as if he had been the boy's own father. The fact is, Charlotte, I was quite encouraged the way Willie had settled down to work in the Dockyard and hoped for that to continue."

"I've probably got myself to blame," remarked Charlotte, downheartedly. "As you recall, I did write to James. I told him of the problems that had arisen, what with Willie getting involved with those street urchins and having to take him out of school. I can see now he took it to mean that any prospect of Willie becoming a gentleman had gone forever. It must have been his signal to act. It was foolish of me."

"Don't blame yourself, Charlotte. I'll grant you the boy won't like it but…"

"Won't like it! I'm sure Willie will be devastated," scoffed Charlotte. "And he'll blame me, of course."

"I was about to say, Charlotte" continued her brother, "that there are at least some encouraging aspects to what James has set in motion. I think what we have to appreciate is that, while our brother messes between the guns, in the officers' eyes, he's an efficient and hence, esteemed and very popular, steward. In consequence, he invariably has the Captain's ear, so to speak, and it's evident, in this instance, he's used it to advantage…in his assessment at least. Now, what does he say?" pondered Charley, as he studiously combed James' text until he found again what he was seeking. "Here we are

…William has been assigned to join the gunnery school ship Excellent, moored at Portsmouth, wherein he will be graded Ship's Steward's Boy and receive pay amounting to eighteen shillings and a penny per month. I am informed that he will be required to report on board the training ship before the year is out in accordance with instructions to be forwarded to him directly, in due course, from H M S Excellent. I am delighted to be able to bring you this news, Charlotte, in the wake of all the worry to which you and Mother have been subjected over that unfortunate incident in Queen Street and the distress occasioned by having to take William out of school. Anyway, all's well that ends well, as they say and I trust you will share my indebtedness to the Captain with whom I had a candid talk about the boy. I have to say he was sufficiently moved by what I had to say to use his good offices and influence to bring this about. It is a good and prized placing for William. It will provide him with a sound platform for life…good training and firm discipline…and I am sure I can rely upon you, dear sister, to ensure he sees it through, reports punctually to wherever he is required to report on his first day, keeps up to the collar and is dutiful at all times. What I am saying, of course, is that it behoves me to ensure the boy does not let us down, since I can contemplate no greater ignominy after the Captain's kind efforts than my having to tell him that William has spurned, for whatever reason, the opportunity to become a Boy RN. That would inevitably annoy the Captain although I am sure the magnitude of

305

his irritation would be trifling compared with my own indignation over the shame I would feel...'

Charlotte bristled at her brother's words. "And what of our feelings? Indignation, indeed! James should have thought of that before soliciting his Captain's assistance. He should have first consulted us instead of taking matters into his own hands. Now, I fear, we are presented with a fait accompli."

Charley could see his sister was vexed that James had gone beyond the pale by usurping her right as a parent. Of course, it would never have happened had John Reynolds been alive but he could empathise with his sister's sentiments: brother James had, undoubtedly, overstepped the mark. He tried to defuse the situation.

"I was on the brink of saying, Charlotte, that although all three of us recognise there is cause to be critical of James' action, insofar as he should have first consulted you, there are nonetheless some crumbs of comfort to draw from it all."

"And what, pray, are they Charley?" said Charlotte in a tone that seemed to evince dispiritedness above annoyance.

"Well, the Navy has changed. It's not the Navy of old. Long gone are those resentful old salts who were the product of impressment, long gone the days when the only youngsters to be schooled were the well-shod sons of gentlemen they turned out as midshipmen...you know, those sawney cadets from the Royal Naval College you see about town. No, Charlotte, even since my day afloat, things are much better organised and more professional. I know, for one thing, that boy entrants are now engaged for ten years continuous service, effective from the age of eighteen, and there seem to be more of these training ships being established for the proper development of boys destined for the Lower Deck. The *Illustrious*, out in the harbour, is a fine example, while the likes of the *Excellent* gunnery school clearly has its own intake of boys. And with the ship permanently moored up in Fountains Lake there will always be good, fresh victualling available. Bear in mind, Charlotte, that it's not like Willie will be going off to sea. I suspect he'll be attached to the *Excellent* until he's rated at eighteen and he'll get plenty of shore leave. A couple of the gunnery instructors are my taproom regulars. I'll ask them what leave the boys get...as far as I'm aware they're allowed ashore after Divine Service on the Sabbath...so we should see Willie regularly enough."

Charlotte remained tight-lipped in the wake of her brother's discourse but Charley sensed from the telling silence that he had probably succeeded in smoothing a few ruffled feathers.

"It is, I fear, an impossible situation," continued the innkeeper with a sigh, "but I feel we must use our best endeavours to persuade young William that to enter the *Excellent* is for his own good. The alternative…to spurn the opportunity…would undoubtedly prove ill-considered, for it would surely embarrass and infuriate our Captain's steward to the point of risking the most calamitous of family rifts. If I know James at all well then I regret it would be a massive affront to his pride and render him apoplectic."

"I wouldn't disagree, Charley, but seeing as you know much more of naval matters than your sister and me, I think it will rest with you, son, to largely exercise those best endeavours. Added to which," continued the elder woman, "Willie attaches considerable importance to what you have to tell him."

"Trouble is, Mother, I've said some discouraging words to the boy about joining the Navy. I've never laboured the matter, mind you, but I daresay he'll think it strange I've changed my tune…not that I have, you understand, but, yes…I'll try to make the best of it."

★ ★ ★

William felt betrayed and bewildered. He would usually spend the allotted spell to despatch the contents of his sandwich tin in the company of whatever work-mates were at liberty to do likewise. Today, a Monday, was different. For one thing, the weather had taken an exceedingly clement upturn by November's standards. Secondly, William was in a maudlin frame of mind, maudlin to the point of being close to tears; and so his inclination had been to steal away from the Steam Factory, to sit alone with his bread and ham and to ruminate alone upon his situation. He could be found, perched on a pile of dunnage beside the timber shed, which lay between the Steam Factory and a group of three slips. Here, as he ate his sandwiches, he appeared to gaze vacuously at the looming oak hull of a newly emerging frigate that rose high on her timber shores above the middle slip. His thoughts were distracted thoughts, played out against the noises that emanated from behind and beyond the oak walls: the whirr of the shipwrights' augurs, the constant tapping and ringing of the caulkers' mallets and irons, the hammering of trenails to tightly secure the vessel's planking. They were sounds that in their constancy and repetition were quite melodious and certainly familiar to those working nearby. In a sense, therefore, they were commonplace enough not to distract an idle thinker accustomed to earning his keep in these surroundings and drawn to leisurely dwell awhile upon what he might consider matters of more solemn import.

The fragrant aroma of fresh sawdust hung in the still midday air. William finished his bread and ham and closed his tin, allowing his gaze to drift northwards, beyond the slips, where a lofty ship of the line had been floated into number 8 dock on the last high tide. The sight of this vessel in her new home drew him out of his abstraction, since, for some weeks, William's attentions had often been attracted to her presence. Moored off the dockhead, she was an impressive spectacle until sailors and Dockyard labourers began the methodical advance to divest her of anything weighty. Ballast by the ton had been removed, before the great guns, anchors and cabling were craned into some decrepit old hulk that served as a floating store. Then the proud warship, her draught greatly reduced, had been shifted alongside one of the sheer hulks only to be deprived of her masts and bowsprit. The transformation complete, it saddened William that the now dismasted vessel looked a poor shadow of her former self. Grasping his tin, he clambered down from his timber perch and sauntered towards the edge of the dry dock. Below, a gang of men had commenced a close inspection of the ship's copper plating. It then struck William that this grand old lady seemed like a huge beached whale as, forlornly, she lay slumped behind the dock gates, awaiting her overhaul. The wetted keel blocks and the residual puddling of water were the product of her tears, the inspecting shipwrights with their copper scrapers, resembling the whale fishermen with their blubber hooks. It occurred to William that her mood perhaps mirrored his own and for similar reasons. She had been dragged from her natural home and shackled within close confines, only for others to impose their will on her. William understood. Against his own wishes he was being forced into the Navy, forced to leave his Portsea home and live and work out there on the cold, grey water, confined in some damp hulk to be trained and bullied into following a lifestyle for which he had no appetite. In the corner of his eye he became aware of some offshore movement, and, following the line of the docked vessel's stern windows, caught sight of a ship's boat pulling for the Gosport shore. In its wake was H.M.S. *Excellent*, lying in the Fountain Lake channel…the floating gunnery school which promised, within a month, to be his home.

William shuddered, his eyes brimmed with tears. He felt in his jacket pocket and, fingering a small object, drew out a silver coin. It was the threepenny piece from Uncle Charley's plum pudding on which he had bitten on Christmas Day. He had stumbled across it the previous evening, when sorting through some knick-knacks and trifles, and had clearly failed to return it to its usual place of repose. He regarded it wistfully, his thoughts returning to the secret wish its discovery had prompted. He lifted the little coin from his palm and, raising it to eye level between thumb and index finger, addressed it in the spoken word as if it were truly capable of understanding.

"Wished on you, I did, that I would thwart any intentions of my Uncle James to get me to go to sea. A fat lot of good, you were…seems it's time to part company."

With a look of disdain, William appeared ready to toss the coin into the harbour, then thought better of it and returned the thrupence to his pocket. "Seems that if we're set to say farewell, then I'd do better to spend you."

At six o'clock, at the end of the working day and despite all the madding press of departing mateys through the main gate, William briefly caught sight of his Uncle Charley…just across the road, on the corner of Halfmoon Street.

"Ah, there you are Willie, my lad. I was worried I'd miss you. After we all talked to you on Saturday about the *Excellent* I was concerned you might have been moping to yourself."

William omitted a gentle grunt which, having a disconsolate edge to it, served to confirm to the landlord of the *Sheer Hulk* that he was right to think that way.

"Consider it a gentle way to join the Navy. After all, most new entrants end up going straight to sea, particularly in my day. And look at your Uncle John. Went to sea at the age of twelve, he did. Straight on to the ship and a long voyage out to the West Indies. Now, you, Willie, are going nowhere until you're eighteen. Just out in the harbour, you'll be…within a stone's throw of home, with plenty of shore leave and only Irish hurricanes to worry about."

"Yes, but Uncle John joined the Army, which I wanted to do. I don't like being tossed about on boats. And what's that about hurricanes?" said William, indignantly.

"Irish hurricanes. In the upper reaches of the harbour you'll get little more than that to worry about. Irish hurricanes…flat calm and soft drizzle," replied Charley Black with a hearty chuckle, to which his nephew offered no discernible reaction; and so the landlord reverted to a more sober tone. "I think that if to begin with you can put a bold face on the matter, my boy, then you just may, in time, find you have a liking for it."

"I think not," opined William. "I've convinced myself recently that I would take the Queen's Shilling…ever since I had my fortune told by some fiddle-faced old gypsy woman across the Common."

"I heard about that from your Grandma, Willie. You can't trust these pikey folk, you know. I'll warrant you half of them are witches."

"I don't know about that, Uncle, but she said I'd satisfy an ambition by wearing a blue uniform with soldier's buttons."

"H'mm…well, seems she got a part of it right, m'lad. You'd have seen the ratings about town in the new uniforms they've just brought in…blue cloth jacket and trousers, black silk scarves and a ribbon on the hat bearing their ship's name. The boy sailors have something similar."

"She didn't get it right at all, Uncle. I asked whether she meant the Navy and she said no. And that's when she mentioned the soldier's buttons. I think she meant blue facings."

"Then it's got to be a lot of rot, my boy," said Uncle Charley, emphatically. "Now, I'd better not delay you further or your Mother will be fretting her guts upon your supper getting cold. Let me know, now, when you hear anything from the *Excellent*…and Willie…keep your pecker up, my boy." And with that and a prompting gesture to his nephew to be on his way, Charley Black bade farewell, turned on his heels and made his way back to the *Sheer Hulk*.

★ ★ ★

It was a time of heavy-heartedness in the house in King Street. The year was edging towards its conclusion, with Christmas Day but three weeks hence; and although Charley Black had again offered to host a goose dinner, there was some doubting on all sides whether it would be anything like as enjoyable as last year. William had received his call to present himself for entering the *Excellent*, and any setting one's hope upon his being granted shore leave to spend the holy day with his family was, for the most part, vanquished, for fear of tempting providence. It had been during the last few days that the heavy-heartedness had descended, ever since the reality of William finishing at the Dockyard had struck home. Now it had reached its nadir, for today was the eve of William joining his ship. Charlotte and her mother had striven to maintain an air of normality throughout the day but both found difficulty in casting aside the shackle of despondency. At supper they made every effort to appear cheerful and brought to the table a tureen of Irish stew and then one of Grandma Black's celebrated plum duffs, two particular favourites of their charge. Yet, for once, Willie's appetite was left wanting and, before the hall clock had chimed the hour of nine, he had crept away with a sullen 'goodnight' and a promise to finish packing ahead of snuffing his candle.

"Go aboard looking smart, my boy," urged Uncle Charley as, earlier in the day, he had called by to make arrangements to witness his nephew's departure. "Don't look like some waif but always remember, Willie…first impressions. Most important my lad, most important. Once you've had a medical you'll have to stow your civilian clothes and put on your new uniform. Yes, there should be one of those fancy new uniforms waiting for you, my boy, and if it doesn't quite fit it will be made to fit soon enough," Uncle Charley had said. "It's not like in my day when we had to make do with slop clothing out of the purser's chest. Anyway, with your new togs on, I warrant you, Willie, you'll feel so neatly rigged as you'll want to be back home soon enough to show them off."

William didn't reply. He secretly wished that when it came to the customary medical he would be promptly declared unfit and his presence aboard the *Excellent* summarily curtailed. He was realistic enough to appreciate, however, that the chance of that happening was indeed remote.

"You can use my old canvas ditty bag, Willie," Uncle Charley had continued. "It's seen better days and journeyed a bit but it'll do you a turn."

But Willie had thought better of accepting this kind gesture for he knew his uncle held some nostalgic feeling for the receptacle. It was no coincidence that it hung behind the bar and carried the names of the various ships and naval barracks in which Charley Black had served. The thought of it being taken down and used again, with the risk of being mislaid or stolen, was something his nephew could not contemplate. Instead, William's mother had found a small black leather case, hinged and top opening, but suited well enough for a young man to carry the minimum supply of civilian clothes beyond those he stood up in: which, in essence amounted to a few handkerchiefs and an ample supply of clean underclothing. Added to which, Charlotte had placed upon the said garments a fresh tin of tooth powder and a boar hair brush, a bar of soap and a comb, for fear that such necessities might not be readily available to her son on the *Excellent*. Grandma Black, bless her, had contributed an assortment of sweets, including some of William's favourite candy twists from the confectioner in Lennox Row.

With a pat on the back and a promise to see William off at the Dockyard Gate at half past eight on the morrow, Uncle Charley had departed, leaving his nephew to return to the melancholic polishing of his boots. And now, as the clock chimed the quarter after nine, William stood by his bed adding a few personal belongings and keepsakes to his bag...his prayer book and his bible with the palm cross tucked inside...the cross given him by Parson Veck at that last Palm Sunday service at Forton. Finally, he tucked away an ambrotype image of his Mother and Grandma Black, a prized item that nestled in its casing of red leather and pinchbeck. It had been presented to him after the family's recent excursion to Portsea's new photographic studio and, being a cherished and fragile item, he took care to pack it in a piece of old muslin for fear of the glass plate becoming cracked. Then, snapping closed the leather case, William tried to steel his heart and mind against burgeoning thoughts of how his life was on the very brink of change. Gone tomorrow would be the solitude of his room, replaced by the pell-mell of the Lower Deck and the inevitable loneliness of being cast among strange new workmates with a fair peppering of those surely bent on making his life a misery. Gone would be his soft pillow and the airy warmth of home, traded for a slung hammock amid the draughty and malodorous smells of an overcrowded gun-deck. He wondered when he might again enjoy the comfort of his own bed, as, in his usual way, he knelt beside it to say his prayers and vowed that never again would he take Home, Sweet Home for granted. As William applied his candle snuffer, and surrendered to the dark, he was in two minds about sleep. It was a welcome release from troublesome thoughts, yet it hastened the unwelcome dawn. As it happened, William's slumber was disturbed as anxiety and fraught anticipation triumphed over sleepiness. In truth it was a night when none slept well beneath the roof of number 31 King Street.

The following morning, a Saturday, broke fine and clear, the dawn temperature a whisker away from frosting Portsea's lawns. Bleary-eyed and feeling capable of sleeping for a week – were circumstances and somniferous tendencies to conspire – William dragged himself out of his warm bed as the hall clock struck seven. Then, in preparing and dressing himself, he made sure to adhere to Uncle Charley's maxim relating to his attire and accordingly gave considerable attention to the arrangements of his toilet. This, needless to say, was something of an achievement given the poor night he had spent and his altogether lack of enthusiasm, but achieve it he did. Then he proceeded downstairs, where, in the dining room, a cheery fire hissed and crackled in the grate, thanks to the diligent attentions of Grandma Black.

"Good morning Grandma," said William in a rather flat, downbeat kind of tone, that reflected his mood.

"Good morning, Willie," came the reply in a contrastingly cheerful manner, as his grandmother, poker in hand, struggled to her feet. "Sit yourself down, boy. Your Mother will have your breakfast here in a trice."

William had barely settled himself down at the table before his mother's approaching footfall heralded the arrival of a hearty cooked breakfast and thickly buttered toast.

"Get this down you, Willie," insisted Charlotte. "A good meal to fortify you and set you up for the day. After all, it's an important one and I must say, you look right as ninepence."

"Uncle Charley insisted that I should be smartly turned out even though I'll soon be given a uniform," replied William, blandly. "First impressions, he said."

"Charley's right, of course," added Grandma Black. "You need to begin as you intend to carry on. No room for slovenly types in the military."

"I'm not joining the military, Grandma. I'm joining the Navy," insisted William, sullenly.

"Sorry, Willie, a slip of the tongue…yet all wear a uniform in the name of Her Majesty the Queen and all have an obligation to be fastidious in their appearance."

"I'm not aware that I've tended to be found wanting when it comes to being neat and tidy," observed William, with a hint of indignation that prompted his mother to interject.

"William! Don't speak to your grandmother in such a churlish manner. I know it's a big day for you and you're obviously apprehensive, but that's no reason to show anything other than unmistakable respect for your dear Grandma."

"Yes, Mother," said William, clearly shamefaced by such chastisement. "Sorry Grandma."

"Apology accepted, my boy. It was just that I wanted to reinforce what your Uncle had said. I wasn't implying that you were inclined to be untidy. Good heavens, no…why, just look at you today, as smart as a carrot, indeed, and destined to be the best looking boy to enter the Royal Navy this side of Christmas."

"Thank you Grandma," added William, his manner now markedly more affable.

"And as for what your Mother has just said, always bear that in mind. Try not to be churlish but at all times polite. It is a policy which marks one out as being of a refined nature...like honesty and punctuality...all good principles with which to adhere, Willie. Just listen to your dear old Grandma as you go forth in the world."

"Now, finish up your breakfast, William," insisted Charlotte, "for you'll need to be on your way soon. You dare not be late. Punctuality, remember..." Suddenly Charlotte's voice faltered as she began to grasp the import of the hour. It was not simply a significant day in William's life. It was the realisation that this was the hour when she would relinquish, not motherly love, but certainly the maternal nurturing role that had shaped her life for more than fifteen years. Now the Royal Navy was to be entrusted, in a surrogate sense, with fulfilling that same function. Inwardly Charlotte Reynolds cursed her seafaring brother for his meddling.

It was now a quarter to nine. On such a raw Saturday morning, William Reynolds would normally expect to be still tucked up in the warmth of his bed, his week's work in the 'yard behind him. Instead he was back in the Dockyard sitting anxiously upon a cold bollard above the Kings Stairs, his own nervousness and trepidation and the low temperature conspiring to set him trembling. The harbour's water shimmered and dimpled beneath a wintry sky, the overhanging blueness of which was softly dulled by a faint mistiness and the tinge of high cirrus. Already the day seemed peerless in its calm tranquillity.

William's departure from King Street had witnessed, not tears, but emotions firmly bridled, neither woman being inclined to appear outwardly mawkish. Nevertheless, the composure of both had been keenly tested as they bade farewell to their charge, their sorrow at least tempered in the knowledge that he would soon return and all the while be just across the water. Uncle Charley had put in his appearance at the Dockyard Gate to wish William well and to give him a lift with some good-natured chaff; and in turn the landlord's nephew had responded favourably and managed to raise a smile.

"I've been so grumpy these past few days, Uncle. Apologise for me, if you will, to Mother and Grandma," had been William's parting words.

"I will my boy…but I'll warrant you they'll understand, don't you fret," shouted Charley towards the receding figure of his nephew.

Now, as he sat perched by the Kings Stairs waiting for a ship's boat to convey him to the *Excellent*, William listened and gazed about him with vacuous expression, yet with senses heightened by things of inconsequence: the lapping and sucking sounds of water as it played beneath two open boats secured alongside the lower steps; the overhead beat and sight of a skein of geese; wintry morning light playing upon the highly varnished bowsprit and gilded figurehead of a brig tied up alongside the adjacent South Jetty; the green and glutinous strands of algae hanging limp from rope painters. A few minutes elapsed while William, in his abstraction, contemplated such trifles. Then the crunch of approaching feet upon gravel startled him. A glance to his left revealed the arrival of three men who had just come to a halt perhaps thirty feet away. From his uniform William recognised one as a Private, Royal Marines. Yet as to appearance, his was a far cry from the resplendent fellows he used to see and admire about Forton. Grubby and dishevelled he was, with several days' stubble darkening his swarthy countenance. In contrast, the two bluejackets, one wearing what William recognised as the new petty officer's rig, were as grand in their attire as the other man was grimy.

Five minutes to nine. The three men broke their silence and, as they did so, a youth sauntered past them and approached William.

"Wager you'll get the cells on half rations for your troubles, young Joey." The petty officer's words were clearly discernible to William in the still air.

"Ten days I wouldn't mind betting," said the other man, a leading rate. "Either that or they'll open up your back. Fifteen to twenty lashes might seem about right for five days ashore." The rating's words were delivered in a taunting manner, designed to prompt a reaction.

"Damn the lot of you," slurred the private – clearly worse for drink – as he jostled with the leading rate.

The Marine's riposte caused the other two to laugh mockingly.

"Save your energy, Joey," exclaimed the leading rate as he made short work of restraining his charge. "After all, you'll need it in reserve if they put you on bread and water!"

"Are you joining *Excellent* as well?" enquired the new arrival as he sauntered up to William. He was a lanky fellow for his fifteen years who had his possessions rolled up in a piece of old pigskin beneath his arm. From his appearance, he had clearly not been instilled with the likes of Uncle Charley's advice about first impressions. William nodded in affirmation.

"Me too. Looks like them sailors are part of the Master-at-Arms' crew, only they've got the other fellow's 'ands in snitchers and going on about him getting lashed. I suppose the likes of us will need to quickly learn to play our cards right," exclaimed the newcomer, as if he was in the habit of doing quite the opposite. "I wouldn't fancy a towelling with the cat-o'-nine-tails."

William remained silent. To hear such tough-minded, matter-of-fact words out of the mouth of another boy entrant did nothing to bolster William's state of mind. On the contrary, it underlined his own lack of self assurance, his mental frailty, his absence of any enthusiasm for the gunnery school. He felt sick to the pit of his stomach.

Suddenly the rhythmic thwack and splash of oar blades breaking water heralded the appearance of the *Excellent*'s boat as she rounded the South Jetty brig and ran under her bows. In a trice the vessel had come alongside the Kings Stairs whereupon the rowers shipped oars. It was nine o'clock: precisely the time William had been instructed to present himself at this place for conveyance to his new home. With the boat secured, the stroke-oar – a ruddy-faced leading seaman with a thick beard nestling into his broad silk cravat – stepped ashore and addressed the two youths on the quayside.

"By what names are you young gentlemen known?"

The two new entrants gave their names as the stroke-oar withdrew a fragment of paper tucked into his trouser top. The names clearly tallied with those he had scrawled down earlier.

"That being the case," he continued, "get down and settle yourselves into the sternsheets. We'll have you introduced to our dear old lady of a gunnery ship in no time. Now, move over to the starboard side," came the instruction, as William and the lanky youth cleared the port gunwale and stepped into the boat. "Only we need room to accommodate these other gentlemen, one of whom looks ever so anxious to get back on board." They were words uttered with a chuckle and a quick wink in William's direction as the leading rate proceeded to gesture in the direction of his counterpart and the petty officer. His shipmates had already loomed into sight with the errant Marine and commenced their descent of the Kings Stairs.

With the several passengers settled into the sternsheets, the bowman unhitched the painter from the securing bollard and the boat was cast off. William was struck by the crew's precision as the dripping oars rose and fell in unison, causing the Kings Stairs and the adjacent South Camber entrance to recede at a startling pace. Soon, as the rowers stuck unrelentingly to their task, the Dockyard's jetties and its many slips and dry docks came into view, with all manner of moored vessels and ships in varying states of repair and construction towering to starboard. In the *Excellent's* boat nobody spoke. The lanky youth fidgeted alongside William and amused himself by letting his arm dangle outside the vessel, so allowing his fingers to caress the water. Opposite, the two sailors sat impassively. Between them the captive Marine had closed his eyes, his unshaven chin having dropped and become cradled in the unbuttoned top of his tunic. Just occasionally the low morning sun glinted on the prisoner's handcuffs and caused William to squint.

Here then was rapidly closing the civilian chapter of William's life: life as he had always known it. Within minutes he would enter upon a new life…not a life perhaps, more an existence, on the Lower Deck of Her Majesty's Navy, something to which he had never aspired. He felt at this moment, entirely lonely, the feeling of sickness in the pit of his stomach in no sense relieved by being afloat. He pulled his jacket and muffler tightly about him as the chill conditions seemed to intensify out here on the water, notwithstanding that all was clock-calm. His thoughts quickened. They were much as before, thoughts he had rehearsed many times since hearing he had been recruited for the Navy. It was his Uncle James' fault, pure and simply, the uncle he had respected but never got close to in the way he had taken to Uncle Charley. He still respected him but now he also despised him. Yet, as he rapidly approached the floating gunnery school, William's thoughts took on another dimension. He would not shirk from the challenge. As much as he detested the prospect of going to sea, he would, as his Uncle Charley insisted, keep his pecker up. Suddenly, that old pride his Mother possessed welled in his breast. The way she had not doubted him over the episode with the Portsea vagabonds and remained steadfast…the way she had reacted to Parson Veck's gift of a shilling on that Forton Good Friday. As the open boat came alongside and the bowman reached for the boarding ladder, it was William's realisation that, instilled within him, was no mean slice of that motherly pride. There and then he hoped it would steel him…that in the face of his total lack of fervour for a life afloat it would give him the fortitude not to succumb to the rigours that undoubtedly lay ahead.

Twelve

Port Tobacco, Maryland
October 1859

"Old Mister Gibbons was mightily pleased with that recent job you did for him, George. I ran into him outside the Courthouse on Saturday. Says his buggy looks better than new and that those German carriage makers up in Cleveland would find your skills a great acquisition in their paint shops."

The sound of his brother's voice caused George Atzerodt to push aside his tin of copal varnish and to ease his frame sideways. Clambering up from beside a newly painted depot wagon and with brush in hand, George looked enquiringly at his brother who was busily occupied donning his working garments.

"Cleveland?"

"Ohio."

"Good God, Johann, I know where it is. What possessed old man Gibbons to think I'd want to move to Ohio?" remarked George in an incredulous tone of voice.

"He didn't think you'd want to move. He was merely suggesting that you were so accomplished in your work that they'd welcome you with open arms in a carriage and wagon manufactory. I thought it was a grand and rare compliment coming from such a fussy old devil."

"Hmm...I suppose I should feel honoured then," said George, reflectively, and with apparent lack of enthusiasm as he ducked behind the wagon and resumed his application of varnish.

"You know George you shouldn't be so dour. Lighten up, man. It should be a tonic to learn that your work is held in high regard. Anyway, I'm going to start ridding Doc Simpson's rockaway of that flaking paint. He's banking upon it being ready for him next week."

The brothers fell silent as they became engrossed in their respective tasks. It had been close on two years since Johann Atzerodt had succeeded in encouraging his younger brother to leave Montross and join him in Port Tobacco where prospects were good for one accomplished in carriage painting. It was a venture in which Johann had been happy to join his sibling, for he had misgivings about his former post as a junior overseer of slaves. George, of course, being already proficient in the trade, had soon acquired a fine reputation in the neighbourhood and with it the business had flourished. For his part, Johann had begun to display increasing aptitude in the job but he would readily admit that, inherently, he was more of a book person, more clerkish, and would always play second fiddle to his brother when it came to working with carriages. He was nonetheless happy in his work and was quite prepared to turn his hand to its more menial aspects. As for the gentleman of some standing in the town, Mister Barton, who Johann had chanced upon meeting at the plantation entrance as he passed by in his gig, he had been true to his word. He lived in a grand, white, clapboarded residence, 'The Chimney House', that had stood for a century facing the town square. Here, independently accessed from the adjacent Marsh road, Mister Barton had made available to the brothers – for a most reasonable consideration – a sizeable area to the side of his dwelling. In addition there was a coach house at their disposal, which, being integral to the property and nestling between stout brick chimney flues of monumental proportion, was inclined to be as warm as toast; a facility that proved invaluable to the Atzerodts during inclement weather and, especially, in aiding the drying process.

Johann's thoughts had moved on as he became increasingly absorbed in his task. Several minutes elapsed before George's voice cut through the abrasive rubbing noise of his brother's assault upon the rockaway's ailing paintwork.

"I could never live up North," said George, his thoughts still immersed in what old man Gibbons had said.

"Well, you'd be hard pushed to make a better living in a carriage manufactory. If we keep on as we are we should do well for ourselves right here in Port Tobacco."

"I wasn't thinking of my livelihood."

"What then?" enquired Johann. "The winter weather's harsher up there, if that's what you mean."

"No, it's just that ...well, I don't like what I hear of Northern attitudes to our way of life. Yesterday I picked up a copy of the *Baltimore Sun* in Brawner's. There was an article about that fellow Brown who recently led the raid on the Federal arsenal at Harper's Ferry. Tried to cause a slave uprising in Virginia, by all accounts, but his plans were thwarted. But it dominated the talk in Brawner's and there was much anger in evidence. We seem to hear more and more about these damn abolitionists. All they seem to want is to drive a wedge between North and South. I truly fear for the old Southern traditions the way things are going."

"Well, well, brother...are you sure we're permitted to defend those traditions? After all, we're Prussian by birth and parentage," remarked Johann.

"I'm a German-American for God's sake, but primarily an American with an allegiance firmly rooted south of the Mason-Dixon Line. I'll have no truck with those insolent Northerners. As for our homeland...that's gone...it's in the past brother."

"Strong stuff, George, but to be honest I share your fear. Not any demise of slavery, for I have worked with it and seen its evils at close quarters... but I do fear that the way things are shaping up any overthrow of the old Southern traditions will only be achieved with bloodshed. All the while two directly opposing attitudes are becoming increasingly entrenched. But you know I cannot, in all honesty, champion the cause of slavery, however much of a cornerstone it is to the Southern way of life. If I'm true to myself then I would always champion the cause of liberty. The alternative is fundamentally contrary to the ethics and principles of Christianity."

"You'd do well to keep your mouth buttoned up, brother, if you're going to spout those sort of sentiments. You'll find few to agree with you in Port Tobacco."

"I'm aware of that, George. Rest assured, I will tread carefully and keep my own counsel. But when I've witnessed what I have and when I hear of deeds the like of which came to my ears only last week, then I can understand why..."

"What was that Johann?"

"It was hearsay, I'll admit, but I can believe it. It was across the Patuxent, in Calvert County, by all accounts. A planter became incensed that one of his house-slaves, a young quadroon girl, overcooked and burnt a joint of meat. He dragged her screaming out onto the stoop, ripped down the back of her dress and, despite the hysterical protestations of his wife, lashed the poor girl repeatedly with his horse-whip. Now how can such actions be those of Christian men? What does the Bible say? Wrath is cruel and anger outrageous. It is no wonder such brutality is denounced by radical abolitionists. They quite understandably see it as immoral and fiercely at odds with Christianity, especially those hard-headed Puritan families from New England. I truly think it inevitable that the system of free labour will replace the Southern bondage of blacks and I sense the time is almost nigh, especially if the Republican party are victorious in next year's presidential election."

George did not challenge his brother's contentions as he continued to apply varnish to the depot wagon. A minute or so elapsed before he spoke again.

"Rose would not leave Maryland," he said, emphatically.

★ ★ ★

Rose Wheeler was a young widow from Baltimore. She had come to town with her late husband when he was offered work in the tobacco warehouses but tragedy befell the couple within a month of their arrival. Rose's husband had been bludgeoned to death, his body discovered in the nearby Zekiah Swamp. Yet no one had been held accountable for the poor fellow's murder. It was said that thirty-six hours before the body was stumbled upon, the unfortunate Wheeler, ill-accustomed to hard liquor yet geed on by others in Brawner's steamy cellar bar, had had the misfortune to imbibe a shade too much whisky than was good for him. He had taken to chewing a quid and, being in slack control of his faculties, had wildly directed a substantial gobbet of brown spittle well clear of the mark. What had been intended for the cuspidor slid glutinously down the trouser leg of a local wharfinger who was known to locals – but not to the newly arrived Wheeler – as a man of some influence and one who was not beyond exacting revenge where he deemed this appropriate. Embarrassed and enraged by the incident, the recipient confronted young Wheeler in a frenzy of incandescence, his eyes bulging, his face reddened as if on the brink of apoplexy. In turn, by all accounts, Wheeler had slurred some sort of apology but his demeanour gave no hint of contrition. And so there were subsequent whisperings abroad – fed by the tittle-tattle of some who had witnessed the incident in the crowded cellar bar – that pointed the finger at the wrathful wharfinger: whisperings to the effect that he had paid a ruffian or two to exact vengeance on his behalf.

It had been a few weeks after the body had been recovered, and laid to rest in an unmarked grave, that George Atzerodt made the acquaintance of the young widow from Baltimore. The brothers had acquired an old buggy on setting up business together and, for a very modest addition to their rent, came to an understanding with the owner of the 'Chimney House' to have ready access to one of his horses to draw their conveyance. George had availed himself of the animal after his day's work, one early June evening in the summer just past. His purpose was to head east out of town for a couple of miles as far as the crossroads where he would turn south, eventually terminating his journey north of the riverside settlement of Pope's Creek. Here stood the neat, shingle-clad home of a farrier he had met in Brawner's one market day, soon after his arrival in Port Tobacco. They had got talking, there being common ground, what with George's childhood familiarity with blacksmithing and shoeing. Well, one thing led to another and, hearing that George had a boat drawn up in Dent's Meadow, the farrier disclosed that this lay close to his property and on occasions he wished to fish the river he was welcome to leave horse and buggy in his safe keeping. In turn the grateful carriage painter had promised to reward him with a portion of his catch, an arrangement which had continued to work to the acquaintances' mutual satisfaction for the best part of two years.

However, on that particular evening in June 1859, George Atzerodt failed to dip his oars in a Potomac that glowed and shimmered beneath the compass of a Virginian sunset. Instead, as he approached the two mile crossroads, he saw a young woman approaching. Her gait was laboured and, as he neared her, it was clear she was close to exhaustion. George pulled up, enquired of her circumstances and destination and, establishing that she was heading all the way back to Port Tobacco, offered to turn about and take her home. Her name was Rose Wheeler. She gratefully accepted and tearfully explained to George that, having buried her husband, she had still wished to see the spot where her dearest had perhaps breathed his last. And so that morning, to the accompaniment of birdsong's dawn chorus, she had set out with directions upon how to reach the desolate spot that lay on the fringe of the Zekiah Swamp. As she trudged onwards between clumps of pinewood and open fields – where blacks hummed soulful melodies as they busied themselves with planting and tending – she gradually assembled a little posy of wayside flowers. These she placed on the spot where young Jed Wheeler's body had been dumped or where he had actually succumbed to brutality. She had lingered there some while to shed her tears and rest before retracing her steps, but eventually fatigue had taken its toll and, as George lifted her into the buggy, she had been on the verge of collapse.

That had been the start of the couple's friendship. Rose had called George her Good Samaritan, later maintaining that as she had slumped in the buggy, she felt like a child of Israel in the wilderness, whose needs had been answered with manna from heaven. Well, as summer ran its course the friendship gradually took a romantic turn. Then George announced he would be leaving the rooms he had shared with Johann in order to move into the widow's lodgings; and, by the end of September, he disclosed to his brother that Rose had had signs she was with child.

★ ★ ★

"Is that because she suspects she's in a gravid condition?" enquired Johann.

"What was that?" said George, distractedly, as he felt around to recover the brush he had just dropped.

"Rose not wishing to leave Maryland. Is that on account of her thinking she's expecting a child?"

"No…no. I'd like to think it's Port Tobacco she wouldn't leave because of me being here. Perhaps that's the case, especially as it seems her belly is about to swell on my account. Her late husband had the devil's own job persuading her to move here from Baltimore. She relented but what did it achieve? A dead spouse. Despite her interest in me, I know she's homesick for Baltimore. But I think with Rose her attitude is akin to mine. We only know the upper South. We've no call for the ways of the North. Granted, you've had the same upbringing as me, brother, but I reckon there's an urbane and more gregarious streak in you that would allow you to mix well enough with these townies and businessmen in the Northern States. Or do I sense it's increasingly a matter of politics? Do I detect our attitudes are diverging?"

"I suppose it centres on my conscience, my thoughts upon what is right and wrong…added to which, my experience of working on a plantation has shaped my outlook. I try to be pragmatic, to be realistic, and notwithstanding my affection for Maryland and Virginia, I fear I see no future for the old order…we cannot continue keeping blacks in bondage. It's not in tune with Christian ethics…it is morally wrong. But enough of this, for I can see, George, we are potentially at odds. Now, when did you say you wanted me to accompany you fishing?"

Thirteen

HALIFAX, NOVA SCOTIA
AUTUMN 1862

William Reynolds lay wide awake for all of two hours, pondering upon his lot and wondering how life would treat him in the coming weeks. His mood was not conducive to sleep. He was disconsolate. There were also feelings of remorse as well as resentment and anger. Furthermore, William had difficulty in coming to terms with his new surroundings. Gone was the eerie glow from bulkhead lanterns and the clean hammock with its soporific motion: instead nightfall meant enduring darkness, while a wooden board, topped with an old sweat-drenched straw mattress, served as the place to lay his head. There was an absence of sounds, which, on account of familiarity, might be considered comforting: no shipmates snoring, no creaking timbers of a ship riding at anchor. Gone was the malodorous night air which pervaded an overcrowded lower deck in a place where hearty intakes of fresh sea air at least offered a ready antidote. Instead, it was the foetid stuffiness of a confined space set within cold granite walls with only the most meagre of apertures; a mere slit through which an acute ear might detect the faint wash of seawater upon the rocky shore of the Northwest Arm. William found sleep hard to come by, yet fatigue eventually triumphed and he succumbed. As slumber deepened he began to dream. Almost five years melted away. Once again he was a fifteen year old readying himself to board the *Excellent* one chill December morning...

"Grasp the manropes properly," screamed the bowman as William temporarily lost his footing on the boarding ladder. The new entrant felt his wrist chafe against the white hemp as he struggled to regain his footing, unsure whether the shock of almost falling or the bellowed instruction from below was the more frightening. "New entrants, eh?" leered a bluejacket, once William and the other new arrival had found their footings on a deck ghostly white from constant holystoning. William recoiled from the smell of the man's breath. "See that petty officer over yonder? Quartermaster of the watch…best report to him now," he snapped.

"Please, sir," bleated the new entries in unison a few moments later.

The petty officer swiftly turned on his heels. "New boys I presume? Names?"

"William Reynolds, sir."

"George Engledene, sir."

"Follow me, then. Time to meet the First Lieutenant," whereupon the quartermaster took the boys below, their eyes struggling to accustom to the dingy conditions on the gun deck as they were led aft along an endless row of formidable smooth bore cannon. A moment later they had been left in the company of the first-luff.

"So you young shavers are wanting us to make sailors of you, eh?"

"Yes," mumbled William as he cowered beneath the cold scrutiny of the officer's piercing, steely-blue eyes.

"Yes, *sir!*" boomed the first-luff with a vehemence that shook William to the very core.

"Yes, sir. Begging your pardon, sir," spluttered William in a quavering voice that told of his fear.

"Then we shall," continued the First Lieutenant. "We shall make sailors of you…and gunners, by God. But you'll need to keep your noses clean and apply yourselves to the utmost in all your instructions. Above all, never be insubordinate or absent yourself from the ship without all proper authority. Punishments can be severe."

The first-luff shuffled a few papers in front of him, then fixed his cold eyes on William. "So you're to be schooled in stewarding, eh, Reynolds? Another young idler, b'gads."

"Pardon me, sir," mumbled William, "but I'm not idle, sir. I'll work hard, but yes, sir, I'm joining as ship steward's boy. I'm not intent on becoming a gunner, sir."

The officer roared like a bull, the strength of his cachinnation almost serving to unseat him. William and George Engledene froze. Regaining his composure, the first-luff turned his attention once again to the new entrants, first directing his gaze at young Engledene.

"Now Engledew…"

"Engledene, sir."

"Don't interrupt boy! If I choose to call you Engledew, then Engledew it is. Now… I'm sure we can knock the rough edges off you, boy, and make you into something resembling a naval gunner. As for you, Reynolds, I'm not suggesting you're idle and if you are, then that's a quirk we'll rid you of soon enough. It's simply that the nature of your work will exclude you from standing the normal watches once we've made a sailor of you. Other than that you'll undergo instruction in all aspects of seamanship with the emphasis on handling the big guns. After all, this is a damn gunnery school." The lieutenant now beckoned to his steward. "Take these new entrants to the breadroom and seek out the purser's steward. Tell the man I want them fed and watered. He can then take them down to the orlop… to the purser's office…and get them supplied with bedding. The usual procedure, steward…they can wait down there until they get a call to go to the dispensary. Once they've had their medicals and been measured for slops they can have their liberty and bed down in the orlop. Tomorrow will be soon enough to introduce the poor darlings to their new messmates and give them a first taste of life on the lower deck."

All these first day happenings aboard the *Excellent* flooded back into William Reynolds' troubled mind as he entered a spell of restlessness which broke his dream, yet failed to draw his consciousness from its suspended state; and this was despite the untimely and harsh ring of a passing guard's hobnail boots upon the corridor's stone flags. Perhaps the dream had been triggered by the similar routines which had just confronted him in this new place as had confronted him that day, nearly five years before, when entering the naval gunnery school. He slumbered on, his sleep deepened and, once again, he was aboard the *Excellent*.

"Show a leg! Rouse out and lash away," shouted the boatswain's mates as they piped up hammocks. "Let's see a purser's stocking!" It was six o'clock on a freezing November morning, the best part of a year having elapsed since William presented himself as a new entry. "You laggards had better show a leg at the double or risk feeling the weight of the corporal's cane," added one of the mates as he spotted a couple of dawdlers.

Bleary eyed, William nevertheless made haste in stowing his hammock and began to make his way to the main deck wash house. There he would take his turn at one of the battery of metal wash bowls, to sluice and soap himself into wakefulness.

"Hey, Willie. Bet you my breakfast cocoa you'd shirk away from taking that dip this morning," shouted one of the older Boys who spotted William making for the wash house. He was a lad who had been miffed on more than one occasion by William's competence when it came to firing at targets during rifle drill. Together with two of his mess-mates – who considered themselves stout-hearted and robust fellows – he had for some weeks been daring William to take a plunge out of one of the lower deck entry ports that was cut down near the water line. In fairness he had done it himself but knew it to be a daunting prospect to many of the other Boys.

"I'll do it," exclaimed William somewhat rashly, yet spurred by the thought that it might just be in his interests to take up the challenge. He reasoned that it was one thing to take a header in the height of summer but to do so on a freezing November morning would be seen to his credit and he'd be regarded as a good egg.

It was as if time stood still. Entering the intensely cold water prompted an immediate desire to bob back up and clamber onboard, yet William seemed to be held down, unable to release himself from the enwreathing and murky harbour water. He began to panic. Suddenly, a ghostly white face rose up inches in front of him. He recognised it as the face of a waterman who had had the misfortune, early the previous Sunday morning, to fall from his boat alongside. His corpse had been later recovered and brought on board and it had fallen to William and one of the ship steward's assistants, to help a sick berth attendant lay out the cadaver. This had been to ensure its readiness for the Admiralty Coroner's afternoon arrival on *Excellent* to perform an inquest. The man's features, a deep scar on one cheek, remained etched in William's memory and now they leered and grimaced at him, features as white and cold as marble, whiter than they had ever been that Sunday morning on the Surgeon's table. William stiffened with fear and screamed. The waterman's mouth gaped open, revealing a tongue partly nibbled away by fish. He screamed again and, as the second scream subsided, the face receded, quickly faded and was gone. There was still resistance as William struggled to wrest himself free, yet strangely his plight brought no sensation of being deprived of air or of gulping in water. He seemed immune to drowning, other than being drowned in terror. A face came again but this time it was a visage set amid swirling clouds of blood. As before, William recognised it. It was the face of a former shipmate, an able-seaman by the name of Francis Boney who, some nine months previously, had been fatally wounded. At the time, a party had been deployed on the lower deck – under the watchful eye of one of the Marine drill sergeant instructors – engaged in the experimental firing of diaphragm shells. The target had been the *Serpent*, an old brig sloop, anchored in one of the channels which dissected the mudflats in the direction of Portchester Castle. Unfortunately, one shell burst at the muzzle of the gun. Able Seaman Boney was in a boat outside the range posts and the poor fellow was hit by a flying fragment, severely wounding him. William had seen him brought aboard where the Assistant Surgeon did his best to stem the blood with a tourniquet before he was taken across the water to Haslar hospital. A day or so later poor Boney died.

There was no sign of distress in the face which now confronted William. There was a calmness about it. It was the Boney he remembered. He even wore his Scotch bonnet. Then, suddenly, the face buckled, the eyes bulged and out of the mouth spewed the most frightful haemorrhage that came in a torrent towards him. He smelt the blood and immediately felt nauseous at the taste of its sweetness. His own body flexed and strained and he screamed again, this time emitting more of a piercing cry. William woke with a jolt, his body clammy, beads of moisture clinging to his brow. The dampness of the lumpy straw mattress and meagre pillow beneath him was as if he had been feverish, such had been the effect of the torturous experience upon his sweat glands. He lay there for ten minutes in the pitch black absorbing reality, relieved to be released from his nightmare, yet fearful of what that reality held in store over the coming four weeks. He needed to urinate and felt around in the darkness for his tin bucket. He held the receptacle close for fear of misdirecting his emission and being admonished for such in the morning, although, in his assessment, the cell already smelt of piss. The sound of the rattle and splash William inflicted in the bucket seemed the louder on account of the pervading silence. He lay back on his bed and for an hour again found sleep difficult. Eventually, when it came, it was tranquil and undisturbed.

★ ★ ★

When William awoke he lacked any idea of the time. It was no longer pitch black, however, since he could now make out the bucket that served as his latrine. He could hear noises: the jangling of keys, the sliding open and closure of peep hole covers, keys in locks, the pulling of bolts, grumbled exchanges. They were all muffled sounds, on account of the thickness of the masonry, but William detected they were possessed of an increasing audibility and heading his way. He stood up and shuffled across to the tiny aperture that allowed his cell a modicum of light and air. He knew he was confined on the first floor but, looking out, the fall of the ground beneath a tumble of undergrowth sloping away to the foreshore, gave the impression of a higher vantage point. In the distance, beyond the inlet they called the Northwest Arm, the hilly, tree-clad land of west Nova Scotia – still dark and featureless in the early dawn – seemed to exude a moodiness in its misty solidity. To William's mind there was an ethereal quality in the way it rose starkly against a sky that began to steal a pinkish hue from the emerging daylight. On the opposite shore there appeared to be a stone quarry, the distant chink of a stoneworker's chisel being audible across the water at this quiet hour. William strained his neck to obtain a wider view but the extent of his lateral vision was greatly hindered by the restricted width of the little opening.

The prisoner did not consciously register the sound of approaching footsteps outside his cell, such was his preoccupation at that moment. Suddenly, the grating noise of the peephole cover being slid open startled him. It made him jump. A gruff voice rang out. It belonged to one of the guards or under-keepers.

"Rouse yourself number thirty-one!"

"I'm awake and out of my bed," said William.

"Then stow your bedding away on the high shelf on the other wall."

The man proceeded to insert the key in the lock. The bolt withdrew into the mechanism with a crisp and resounding thud. Then the door, an imposing slab of pine, heavily studded with ironwork, swung open. The man who had spoken, one of the under-keepers, filled the door opening with his corpulence. He eased his way into the cell, allowing a guard to pass him with a jug of cold water that he had drawn from a wheeled metal receptacle. This he proceeded to pour into a tin bowl that stood on a small deal table attached to the wall below the bedding storage shelf.

"Attend to your ablutions and get yourself dressed," declared the under-keeper. "You'll soon get to know the routines. Have you been given soap and a comb?"

William nodded to affirm that he had.

"Then get yourself sorted out. Your breakfast will be brought to you in due course." The under-keeper then turned and withdrew from the cell, promptly followed by the guard with the empty jug. As they left, William caught sight of a third fellow who had held back in the corridor. He was a huge, muscular man, armed with a cudgel, a presence to deter any inmate from thoughts of causing trouble.

Half an hour later came the promised second visitation when a surly, truncheon-wielding guard opened the cell door to briefly allow the cook's assistant, an unsavoury-looking individual, to dispense William's breakfast. Once the door had slammed closed the recipient surveyed his meal with dismay, the sight of it causing what little appetite he had to evaporate. He sat on his cell's single, rickety chair eyeing the dish of weak gruel that had replaced his wash bowl on the deal table. A chunk of stale bread lay to the side of it together with a mug of water. Suddenly naval scran and cocoa, Clarence Yard biscuit and one's customary grog seemed the height of luxury. As he sat and contemplated his dish of pallid oatmeal William thought how odd is was that an inmate was addressed, not by name, but by the number of his cell. Furthermore, it struck him as strange that his was number thirty-one, the number of the family home in King Street. It seemed an eternity since he was last there with his dear Mother and Grandma. For a moment he shuddered and went cold at the thought of what they and dear Uncle Charley would make of the way he had since disgraced himself and of how things had come to this. As for Uncle James, last known to be serving on the steamship *Urgent,* in the East Indian and China station, William could not bear to imagine the nature of his reaction.

In actuality, it had been no eternity, but less than eighteen months since William last saw his nearest and dearest…in early June of '61. It was during a spell of shore leave, after his discharge from the Channel Squadron flagship, the *Edgar,* on which he served seven months. He wondered when he would see them again and just how he could explain his behaviour. Perhaps he wouldn't have to explain it. No, he would keep it quiet. Why after all would he choose to reveal his failings, to give kith and kin reason to think ill of him? And why, in particular, would he want to enrage Uncle James, to give our respected Captain's steward – as William was inclined to irreverently think of him – cause to hold his nephew in true contempt?

Thoughts of home and family had crowded in on William these last few days, since his apprehension on the streets of Halifax by a party of marines from Vice Admiral Milnes' flagship, the *Nimble.* The thought of running had been festering in William's mind since his ship, the gun vessel *Cygnet,* had been at anchor in St John's harbour, Newfoundland. Two or three weeks later the *Cygnet* was lashed alongside Halifax Dockyard, about to undergo a refit. It was a Sunday and, following a ten o'clock muster, the ship's company was sent to Divine Service on board H.M.S. *Immortalite,* returning thereafter to partake of midday dinner. The opportunity then presented itself to William to rid himself of the naval life he had grown to detest. The ship's company was given shore leave and he decided not to return on board at the appointed time. He laid low until after dark, then, rashly and naively, after fortifying himself with several whiskies, took to roaming the streets of the town in search of a safe and quiet spot to lay his head. When seized and interrogated by *Nimble's* joeys, in the early hours of Monday morning, it brought back memories of the occasion the police officer accompanied him home to King Street, except now he had a good idea of the fate which awaited him. Desertion was a serious business. He had seen others attempt it and fail, only to receive a severe encounter with the lash or a lengthy incarceration in the cells on half rations. Yet, strangely, the terror that had gripped him as an innocent in Portsea was of far deeper intensity than the fear which seized him as a guilty party on the streets of Halifax. Perhaps the drink served to dull his senses but the greater likelihood was William's sheer dread of being held in disgrace by his beloved mother and grandmother. In comparison, being returned to the *Cygnet* in the middle of the night, having to explain his behaviour to the officer-of-the-watch and the gnawing prospect of harsh punishment, was altogether a less daunting prospect to the errant steward.

The deserter had been placed in irons and, on the Tuesday forenoon, the ship's company was turned up to hear the commanding officer read the warrant. For attempting to run, William Reynolds was to be sent to the Provincial Penitentiary for a period of twenty eight days, there being no room for cells on board a gun vessel. And the punishment was duly put into effect that same afternoon.

A ship's boat would normally be lowered to take a prisoner to a civilian prison on shore and the Halifax establishment's waterside proximity, to the south of the city, rendered it eminently reachable by this means. However, the *Cygnet's* boats were unavailable, having been hauled up on an adjacent slip where they were in course of being scraped and repainted. In consequence, arrangements were made, with the assistance of the Yard's Master Attendant, to requisition a carriage and pair for use by the Master-at-Arms to convey the manacled prisoner to gaol. Yet it had been well into the afternoon before they set off. This was on account of the Master-at-Arms having taken delivery of the mails from England shortly after midday, the mail steamer having arrived during the forenoon; and, as was customary, an expectant crew had gathered aft, around the Jonty's table, as he emptied the mail-box and distributed its contents to the lucky recipients.

As the carriage climbed out of the town through a grid-iron of streets hugged by a predominance of white, clapboarded buildings, William had felt apprehensive over what to expect. He was, however, ambivalent about his enforced absence from the gun vessel. He detested the ship, or rather, he detested several of his shipmates and was pleased to be free of it all for a while. Yet the Halifax Penitentiary was an unknown quantity. He knew some of these penitentiaries had fearsome reputations. In particular, he recalled one of the stokers, by the name of Sprake, having spent time in the Kingston Penitentiary for desertion when *Cygnet* was in Port Royal, earlier in the year. He described it as a filthy, rat infested shit-hole where one rarely caught a glimpse of the light of day. To make matters worse, the poor fellow had little option but to exceed his allotted time there, on account of *Cygnet* absenting herself with sailings to Navassa island and to Cartagena on the Colombian coast. Yet that was Jamaica and William convinced himself that the Nova Scotians were an altogether more civilised bunch.

No one had been inclined to engage in conversation as the journey unfolded. Once on the higher ground above the main body of the town, the man at the reins – a Dockyard employee familiar with the lie of the land – cracked his whip and set the horses at a gallop past the lofty Citadel. Behind him, William, his wrists shackled, had sat between the Master-at-Arms – a surly fellow who reeked of tobacco – and a Marine corporal whose uniform expelled a strong whiff of newly applied pipeclay. He recalled looking back across the rooftops which fell away to a harbour that sparkled beneath dappling sunlight. A jumble of wharves and jetties, which fringed the waterfront, drew the eye northwards towards the Naval Dockyard. The visibility had been good, with broken clouds speckling the blue, the smart white cupola which capped the sail loft's clock tower, marking out the approximate position of the *Cygnet*. Moored off the Dockyard, the newly arrived ship of the line, the *Nile*, waited clearance to proceed to the coaling wharf while the *Plover* steamed past the grassy knoll of George's Island and prepared to ease her engines.

Momentarily it had been a scene reminiscent of somewhat happier times, when, early in '61, and in the flush of being newly rated as a man – an Ordinary Seaman and ship steward's assistant – William had experienced his maiden sea voyage aboard the flagship, H.M.S. *Edgar*. Although he would have then readily traded his lot for a life back on terra firma, they were at least brighter times. He was still appreciative of being liberated from the close supervision and sometimes stifling atmosphere of the gunnery school.

It was good to be treated as a man and no longer as a Boy RN and William developed a liking for his newly acquired grog ration. More significantly, he had yet to encounter life aboard the *Cygnet*. That first voyage had taken him to the port of Lisbon where, on one occasion, he had taken himself up to the lofty Bairro Alto. Looking down on Halifax harbour, across to the Dartmouth shore, drew echoes in its grandeur of that earlier prospect of the Tagus when the *Edgar* and her moored consorts had seemed as toys from on high.

Such recollections had swiftly dissipated as the carriage began a descent beyond Citadel Hill through more sylvan, outlying districts. It was a treed character that intensified as, correspondingly, signs of habitation diminished until, eventually, the party neared the wooded and remote Point Pleasant. It was hereabouts that the inlet known as the Northwest Arm pushed its way out of Halifax harbour in the direction from which it derived its name. And it was to the granite portal of the three storey edifice which nestled close to the Arm's north east shore – a short distance from Point Pleasant – that William Reynolds had been delivered the previous afternoon.

A few minutes before the Dockyard carriage pulled up on the penitentiary's gravelled concourse, William had been taken aback by what appeared to be an uncustomary kindness shown by his curmudgeonly escort. The Master-at-Arms lowered his head towards the prisoner's ear and simultaneously dropped a small, white envelope in his lap.

"This, Reynolds, came to my attention earlier, when distributing the contents of today's mail box." The Jonty's voice had been strained as he sought to be heard above the clatter of cantering hooves and the harsh rattle of wheels on the coarse surface. "Letter posted in Portsmouth…guess it's from your folks, eh? Well, you'd do well to read it now for they're bound to confiscate it. Then you'll not retrieve it until you're discharged. Kind, aren't I?...trouble is, Reynolds, I'm getting soft...I'd normally let a scoundrel like you wait for his mail 'til he's back onboard."

"Thank you, sir...much obliged," mumbled William, as he had immediately recognised his mother's neat hand. He had then proceeded to make heavy weather of extracting the letter – to the warped satisfaction of the onlooking Master-at-Arms – for his dexterity was greatly hampered by the restraining effect of the handcuffs. In consequence, by the time he had succeeded in pulling the missive from its envelope the carriage had drawn up and, almost immediately – with a nod from the Jonty – the Marine corporal had alighted from the carriage, simultaneously grasping the prisoner's arm. Beckoned by a grunt from the Joey to follow, William had irritated the Master-at-Arms by hesitating a few moments to assimilate the greater part of his letter in advance of its confiscation.

"Out!" bellowed the disgruntled Jonty, a remark which had prompted the corporal to tug at William's sleeve; and so he had tumbled out of the conveyance, in the process relinquishing his hold on the letter. It had momentarily lain at his feet but, in a trice, was swept up and briskly taken in the breeze.

"How unfortunate," guffawed the Master-at-Arms as he had watched the several sheets of paper gather pace and disappear. "My intentions were good, Reynolds, but, by jove, I'll wager your letter took off with more speed than a deserting steward's assistant!"

William had appeared to ignore this derogatory remark but inwardly it hurt – the thought of being held in such contempt. But at least he had had a cursory glance through the letter before being brusquely cast out of the carriage. Certainly sight of his mother's handwriting had only served to heighten and reinforce those thoughts of home and family which his feelings of guilt had already brought to prominence. Charlotte Reynolds had begun by thanking her son for his last letter which William recalled penning on a hot evening in Bermuda. That would have been in late June, after a busy day taking in provisions and stowing them in *Cygnet's* holds. His mother had mentioned that both she and Grandma were in good health, although Uncle Charley had been suffering from a bout of bronchitis. They all looked forward to the day of William's homecoming, whenever that might be…and there had been mention of Parson Veck, now in his seventy-eighth year and still the incumbent at St John's. Missus Barnes had by all accounts drawn attention to the forthcoming presentation of a testimonial of esteem and respect to the ageing and much revered parson. It was shortly to be held in Forton and William's mother and grandmother had every intention of making a return to the village to pay homage to the old gentleman.

Dear old Veck. As the Marine corporal pounded a clenched fist upon the gaol's lofty, timber entrance door, William had recalled that he still retained the palm cross handed him by the doughty old parson at that last and memorable Palm Sunday service at St. John's. He had heeded his mother's advice at the time – that the keepsake would brook no mistreatment on account of its fragility; and, in consequence, it lay in almost pristine condition with other treasured mementos, back onboard the *Cygnet*, in his ditty box.

The corporal's rapping upon the door had been answered soon enough as a heavy bolt was noisily withdrawn on the inner side, allowing a hatchway to be swung open. Amid the thick timber, it lay recessed behind metal bars through which squinted a weather-beaten, heavily bearded face.

"Make yourself known and declare your business," the owner of the hirsute visage had snapped in irritable fashion.

The corporal had countered the remark in swift and equally curt tone as if contemptuous of the other's testiness. "I have to announce that this gentleman I accompany is the Master-at-Arms from Her Majesty's gun vessel *Cygnet*. We are escorting the prisoner, Mister Reynolds, of the said vessel, to place in your custody for twenty eight days."

"Papers?"

The Jonty thrust a document into the corporal's hand. In turn, the Marine passed it through the barred aperture into the clutches of the irascible guard, who had then proceeded to take his time scrutinising the paperwork. His silent perusal passed. Next, the jangling sound of a bunch of keys had been followed by the hearty clonk of a bolt springing back into its mortise. Then came the chink and clatter of hasps being freed from their toggles as, finally, the huge entrance door swung back on its well-oiled hinges and, in no time, William had been in the custody of the gatehouse guards.

Twenty eight days…twenty eight days. William pulled his thoughts back into the here and now as he continued to contemplate his first bowl of insipid gruel and wondered how he would manage on such fare for twenty eight days. He chewed on the lump of stale bread and took a sip of water. How he would give six months' wages to exchange twenty eight bowls of such distasteful swill for equivalent servings of his mother's wholesome milky oatmeal or rice pudding; and to trade the prison crusts for the fresh wedges of hot buttered bread Uncle Charley served up in the *Sheer Hulk*.

The loud ring of a bell was followed by a bellowed proclamation from afar.

"Ten minutes to slop out!"

In all probability the edict was barely audible to the majority. Yet William would quickly realise that the familiar chime of the bell was the signal to all to set about emptying their bowels and bladders before the opportunity was lost; lost to all until a mid-morning break in the day's labours would permit an escorted return to one's cell to make use of the customary bucket. An accident during morning toils, because of a failure to heed that signal, would not be looked upon kindly. Apart from the ignominy of it all, an untimely defecation of one's garments would herald a week on stale bread and water.

To William, the ten minutes seemed like twenty before his cell door was opened once more.

"On your feet, thirty-one," barked a one-eyed guard, who, seeing the new inmate had made little progress with his breakfast, was prompted to discharge a further curt volley of words. "Toss that food in the bucket. You'll learn soon enough to take your victuals for there's nothing else."

William did what he was told without comment. He was then ushered out into the corridor carrying his bucket and clutching the now emptied dish and the wooden spoon with which he was meant to eat his wretched gruel. Shortly he was joined by five neighbouring inmates. They were all similarly burdened and were collectively marched – one guard to each prisoner – some fifty yards. Here they came upon an outside wall within which was set a padlocked metal plate of sorts, except, being slop-out time, the padlock had been released and the door drawn back. A pine table stood to the side. William proceeded to watch the three prisoners in front of him. Each stepped forward when his number was called, placed his gruel dish and spoon on the table, then lifted up his bucket. Partly leaning into the dark void, now exposed by the opened metal plate, he stretched out his arms and emptied the bucket's contents down what William perceived as an enclosed metal chute. The man withdrew with his bucket, retrieved his dish and spoon and joined the back of the advancing line of inmates.

When it came to William's turn his accompanying guard, the one-eyed fellow, whispered in his ear as he went to move.

"You'd do well not to lean too far forward. Hold your bucket tight so as not drop it…otherwise it'll block the outlet or just end up out in the Arm. And if you see as much as a glimmer of light from above, pull back and wait awhile. It'll be the women on the top floor emptying their buckets. They're meant to call down a warning to stay clear but rarely seem too particular about abiding by the rule. Strikes me they take delight from showering you boys with their excrement."

Having discharged his bucket without incident, prisoner number thirty-one took up his dish and spoon and rejoined the line of inmates. The bath-house was next on the escorted itinerary. Here the six queued to swill out their buckets in an open bath of tepid water. The foetid smell of the bucket chute still hung in William's nostrils, as next, he waited his turn to cleanse dish and spoon in a second bath that stood against the opposite wall. Here the colour of the water and its glutinous sheen led him to wonder whether a previous batch of inmates had mistaken the purpose of each bath and done the unthinkable. He felt instantly queasy at the thought but kept his own counsel, considering it politic to do so. Yet it was unnerving. Then it was back to the cells to return the bucket, dish and utensil to their usual places of repose…in the case of the dish, to await the midday offering of what purported to be wholesome prison grub. At least that was how the Governor described the meals William might expect, when, shortly after admission, number thirty-one had been brought before him in the reception cell.

"Come with me, thirty-one," said the one-eyed guard, once William had returned the several chattels to his cell. "You're working in the shoemaker's shop today…and remember, the rules require silence, no communing with others. The Governor insists on all prisoners being industrious. Only speak if you're spoken to first by the shoemaker and if you have a question raise your arm. Above all be civil. Failure to observe these requirements can only mean sanctions."

"Sanctions?" queried William.

"Sanctions. Bread and water diet…solitary confinement…hard work in the treadmill house with a taste of the whip to keep you on your toes. What I'm saying, sailor, is don't try to be smart…just serve your time and do as they tell you."

★ ★ ★

Eight days gone…the second Wednesday, post meridiem. William Reynolds had spent a full week in the Provincial Penitentiary. It was time for reflection. He kicked a small pebble across the stone flags as he completed another circuit walking the exercise yard. He was not alone. One of the under-keepers patrolled a covered veranda that ran the extent of one side of the enclosed quadrangle, occasionally barking orders at the men to run or walk so many circuits or to stop and do particular exercises where they stood. Two guards, each with grim expressions and grimmer-looking cudgels, loitered at either end of the yard while nine inmates accompanied number thirty-one as they collectively engaged in the several exercise routines. Wednesday afternoon in the yard was a concession to remanded inmates – those awaiting trial – and to servicemen, such as William, who were held as short-term prisoners for serious misdemeanours, invariably attempted desertion. By contrast, convicted criminals were subject to greater dietary restrictions, to spells of hard labour – often the tedious and finger-chafing picking of oakum – and to exercising their under-nourished frames on the dreaded treadmill.

In William Reynolds' assessment, however, what he had to endure was bad enough. As he launched into a fresh routine and became reflective, he concluded he missed little about the *Cygnet,* bar the familiarity of his floating home and the victualling. There was no denying lower deck food had the beating of prison grub. Much of what was plied to him in his cell he found inedible or bland and far removed from the wholesome description bestowed upon it by the Governor. The occasional morsel of meat, such as it was – for the portions were small – and the boiled potatoes, could be palatable enough. The same could sometimes be said of the midday pint of soup. But generally speaking, William found the food, at best, unappetizing and, at worst, inedible and, in consequence, he continued to discard much of it into his bucket. It had begun to show. The previous day he had been taken to the barber for his weekly shave. It had been the first time since his admission that he had confronted his own image in a mirror and he felt he looked a shade gaunt, a mite shallow about the cheeks.

The silence he considered intolerable, having to speak only when spoken to by the staff. It was worse for the convicted men, however, including the common prisoners serving less than two years. At least here, in the exercise yard, it was permissible for the short term and remanded men to converse with fellow inmates during the two ten-minute rest periods: a concession largely influenced by such prisoners being considered less likely to engage in subversive collaboration. On his first full day in the penitentiary, after his morning in the shoemaker's shop, William had felt inclined to keep himself to himself, being then in low spirits and feeling a touch reclusive. However, on this second Wednesday, as he sat, quite exhausted, after a second half hour of rigorous exertion, he was in an altogether more talkative frame of mind.

"Drink?" The fellow who spoke was a swarthy-skinned individual, whose pock-marked face glistened beneath beads of sweat. He proffered a wooden ladle of enticingly cool water, newly scooped from a bucketful that the under-keeper had drawn from a nearby well.

William nodded, clasped the ladle by its bowl and downed the water. "Thank you, friend," he murmured, raising a smile.

"Do I detect from your voice that you're not a local man?" said the other.

"You're correct. I'm English. And what of you my friend?"

"Local…well, Bridgewater way…that's west of here. Saddle maker by trade…name of Jake. Or should I say, number twenty-four. Awaiting trial for horse stealing. That's what they call it. There were signs our next child was on its way and I had to alert the physician in town. Borrowed an old mare for the purpose…that's all. Then I get accused of larceny. What about you?"

"William Reynolds. They address me as number thirty-one. I'm in the Royal Navy. I ran."

"Deserter, eh? I'm told desertion's quite rife from ships that put into Halifax. Soldiering folk get itchy feet too. A private in one of Her Majesty's infantry regiments from the barracks on Melville Island only finished his term here last week."

"I always wanted to join the Army," said William, reflectively.

"So why didn't you?"

"My uncle, damn him, arranged for me to join a gunnery training ship. I didn't get a say in the matter."

"Well, if it's any comfort," said the saddler, "your foot soldier compatriot thought taking the Queen's Shilling was the worst thing he ever did. Said he was drunk as a besom at the time and knew nothing of what he'd done 'til the following day…and he could only speak ill of the Army, saying they treated common soldiers like dogs. What was your reason for trying to abscond from your ship?"

"I joined up with the wrong attitude if I'm honest. I was never good on the water but it was mainly a reaction to an overbearing uncle's insistence that I should go to sea and be a ship's steward. I'd convinced myself I wouldn't like it. Besides, I'd always had a fondness for the Army. I always wanted to become a soldier."

"Would you do it again after your time in here?"

"Jump ship you mean? Sure I would. It's made me all the more determined to rid myself of the Navy."

"So what would you do with yourself should you succeed? There's not much work in these parts save fishing, farming and stone cutting," remarked the swarthy saddle maker.

"Hadn't given much consideration to that, friend," said William. "My only fear is how to explain it to my family since I know they'd be shocked and think ill of me. They'd feel I had brought disgrace upon them. But, there again, I'm thinking positively. Perhaps I can avoid them finding out. And, if they do, then maybe I can atone for a tarnished reputation by making a real success of my life here in Canada. Then, in a few years time, I might return home as a gentleman."

"Grand expectations, indeed," chuckled number twenty-four who then proceeded to lower his voice such that it was little more than a whisper. "I wish you luck, thirty-one, and if you're that determined to get away then…" The saddler hesitated before completing what he had to say. "Then, for a modest financial consideration as it were, me and a friend or two could help you realise your wish. Now, having said that, would you be interested in hearing my little proposition?"

William eyed the saddler warily, as, without waiting for an answer, the latter strode back to the well, scooped up another bowl of cool water and proceeded to gulp it down. Then, with the ladle replenished, he sauntered back to William and again offered him a quenching drink. Number thirty-one took the ladle, held it high and tipped the contents upon his own head. For a moment he savoured the cooling effect of the drenching which saw tiny rills of water drain from his hairline and find passage down his features.

"Honest to God, my dear fellow," whispered the swarthy saddler, "I can help you for sure. Just listen to what I have to tell…"

"On your feet again," bellowed the under-keeper. "Time for another half hour to keep the blood flowing. Let's commence running. Quickly now or risk a flogging!"

As the prisoners scrambled to their feet, under the critical eyes of their several custodians, William glanced at the saddler and appeared to gently nod in affirmation of a willingness to hear him out.

"That was our second and last break…we'll speak again next Wednesday," came the mumbled reaction and with that the inmates resumed their exertions.

★ ★ ★

The week that followed was one of harsh routine, most of it spent in isolation within the cramped confines of a foul smelling cell. Daily labours were exacting and performed under the scrutiny of guards who, all too often, took delight in finding the slightest of excuses to be brutal and spiteful towards their charges. Yet, for all that, life beyond the uric reek of cell number thirty-one was a welcome respite from the stink, the incarceration and the attendant boredom. It was often to the shoemaker's shop that William Reynolds was directed. Here no sharp implements were entrusted to inmates, save the needles required to sew soles to uppers.

But sharper still were the eyes of the guards who brooked no nonsense and had no compunction about laying heavy canes across the knuckles of those stepping out of line or showing a tendency to be inactive. As for the shoemaker, a rather diffident little man, it was with some reticence that he seemed prepared to engage with the prisoners, such that he imparted precious little beyond the most rudimentary of instruction. Instead, he busily went about his own work, cutting welts, soles and uppers, leaving the sewing to the prisoners. William, for his part, was no seamster, but then this was no cordwaining of distinction. The final product, the likes of which had been issued to prisoner thirty-one on admission, was a shoddy form of footwear intended solely for inmates' use, including those housed in the city's Rockhead Prison.

A problem that emerged for William by having to work in the shoemaker's shop, sewing strips of leather, was the soreness it caused to the comparatively soft fingers and thumb of one accustomed to pursuing the trade of stewarding. It might have been a different matter for hardened yardmen, for those engaged in reefing and rigging, and going aloft but prisoner thirty-one, with his callous-free hands, was soon to realise that a product of sewing for the shoemaker was chafed and blistered hands. And so William's second Sunday in the penitentiary, after several consecutive days – morning and afternoon – making boots and shoes, provided a much needed break from what was becoming an uncomfortable routine; for Sunday meant Divine Service. There was no compulsion when it came to attending but most inmates chose to join the congregations – there being both Protestant and Catholic chapels on the first floor – since to do otherwise meant being confined to one's cell for the duration of the Sabbath, there being no labours to turn to on the day of rest. And so attendance at least guaranteed an hour's respite from the monotony of a full day's incarceration. As for William, he readily joined the Protestant majority, his natural desire to do so being bolstered by that further consideration.

The chapel itself was capacious yet sparse in its furnishing and decoration. A bland wooden pulpit immediately stirred in William fond recollection of the Forton schoolroom. Like Wickett's high desk, it was not offset but placed equidistant from the side walls and, in common with the schoolmaster's desk, stood below a very similar portrait of the Queen. As to its medial placing, this was clearly necessitated by the requirement that the officiating clergyman could both see and be seen by his entire congregation; for prison rules demanded that male and female inmates remain segregated during Divine Service, a plain timber screen having been erected for that purpose.

The women were first to be escorted into the chapel by their guards, there to be joined by the formidable matron and wife of the Governor, Missus Lucy Fish, whose presence all but guaranteed that others of her gender remained impeccably behaved. Once the female inmates were settled in their seats the men were led in and took their places under watchful eyes. All knew that the instigator of any disturbance would be summarily bundled back to his cell with worse to follow: the odious treadmill and a bread and water diet. And so a customary silence hung about the crowded chapel as the wayward congregation awaited the emergence of the Minister, closely followed, as always, by the institution's doddery and corpulent Governor, William Fish.

"All rise!" shouted under-keeper Munro who had been standing sentinel at the door vigilantly watching for the pair's approach. By the time the assemblage had obeyed the instruction, the bewhiskered clergyman, his bible clutched high beneath his chin, swept in ahead of the burly Fish. He immediately ascended the pulpit and called for all to be seated as the Governor took his place ahead of the men, as if to complement the station already occupied by his firebrand of a wife beyond the adjacent screen.

If ever a Wesleyan Methodist Minister was inaptly named it was the Reverend Henry Pope. The irony amused William, the thought that his name might far better equip him to officiate at the Roman Catholic service getting underway across the hall. But then how apposite a name might it be for a Catholic Priest? Might just the congruity seem anything but? William was soon drawn from such trivial thought as Pope began his discourse. And, as it progressed, his recollection was that the chaplain's theme was not dissimilar to that he'd delivered the previous Sabbath...and probably the Sabbath before that...and, in all likelihood, the one before that. Yet his evangelical message was ardently and rousingly put in a way that marked him out as a dedicated Wesleyan Methodist. The first hymn, which followed close on Pope's opening address, was an uplifting one, in the Wesleyan tradition, yet William considered it somewhat inappropriate, for all that, since he recognised it as Heber's fine hymn for Trinity Sunday...*Holy, Holy, Holy, Lord God Almighty*. The musical accompaniment was competently provided upon a small harmonium by a convicted West Picton man, who, despite at one point being afflicted with a fit of sneezing, kept the tune going well enough. Prisoner thirty-one had already been told by one of the more amiable and talkative guards that this man – the occupier of cell eighteen – had become something of a favourite with the Reverend Pope. Serving seven years for arson and attempted rape, the fellow had resolved to mend his ways and turn to Christ as a consequence of regular attendance at the clergyman's Sunday services. He had heeded the Minister's message and, possessed of musical ability, had eagerly offered his services when learning – earlier in the year – of the imminent loss of the regular harmonium player, an outsider. He had since enthusiastically embarked on playing the instrument, viewing it as an expression of his contrition and penitence as he strove for reconciliation with his Maker. And that was the essence of the Reverend's perpetual message…redemption…atonement for one's sins…the reconciliation of man with God…the importance of contrition being sincere and springing from the heart.

"Redirect your destiny, let today be the day you renounce evil, confess your sins unto the Lord and pray for His forgiveness for your past wickedness," implored a gesticulating Henry Pope. "Better to return to the Lord thy God than be cast into Hell, for surely, my friends, as transgressors you are already condemned to hellfire. Yet, the will of God can wrest you free from that great inevitability if you only turn to Him. Believe me, my friends, it is never too late to turn to God. Pray for His forgiveness and let it come from the heart. You need look no further for an example. Just follow the path taken by your fellow prisoner, the harmonium player, who has chosen the way I advocate, asking the Lord to be merciful and forgiving of his past wickedness." The harmonium player showed no reaction to the Minister's remark. His eyes remained fixed on the keyboard ahead of him, doubtless embarrassed by the words directed at him; for although he was inwardly at ease about the trust he had placed in Jesus, he was mindful that his actions were not of a kind to ingratiate himself with many of his fellow prisoners. To most, religion was anathema, or so they would have others believe, for credibility in such a community rested upon appearing hard…as hard as Nova Scotian grindstone. The pursuit of religion and hanging one's head in prayer did not fit that rugged image.

Two more uplifting hymns were intermingled with the chaplain's pronouncements, both by Charles Wesley and both introduced by Pope with words plucked from their texts…words chosen by the clergyman as if to underscore the crux of each hymn's central message and thereby, yet again, his own.

"From our fears and sins release us, let us find our rest in thee," cried Pope. "We will sing *Come, Thou Long-Expected Jesus.*"

All rose and the harmonium began to play. Governor Fish, being tone deaf, refrained from singing, but, in his habitual way, chose to mouth the words. From the pulpit, stentorian words flew from the mouth of the Reverend Henry Pope, closely matched by the shrill voice of Lucy Fish, their combined vocal expression rising above the somewhat reticent and subdued offering from the main body of inmates. Then, a few prayers later, and as if finally spent of words relevant to his particular congregation, Pope brought the service to its end.

"We will together sing *Love Divine, All Loves Excelling.* Raise up your voices, now…and take good heed of the words you utter…take away our bent to sinning, pure and spotless let us be."

Prisoner number eighteen pressed the keys and the music struck up…

And so it was back to labouring on Monday. Sewing leather had been bad enough for unaccustomed hands but William would have settled for that when his number was called to pick oakum. A dozen or more of the remand prisoners joined him, much to their displeasure, for this was work normally bestowed upon those convicted souls destined for hard labour. The explanation given was that some of the regular pickers had been singled out for stone cutting in one of the quarries above Purcell's Cove on the other side of the North West Arm. A consignment of granite was urgently required to construct an outbuilding for the penitentiary yet, equally, the caulkers in Halifax Dockyard were awaiting a promised shipment of three hundredweight of hemp fibre. A batch of oakum meant good Dockyard money for the penitentiary, but less in the way of it were an order delayed; and so more hands had to be drafted in to keep up to schedule.

By Tuesday evening, when prisoner thirty-one returned to his cell to sluice his tired face and rid it of a brown dusting of old hemp, his fingers were causing great discomfort. He lay on his lumpy mattress wondering what wretched fare would soon arrive under the misnomer of being termed supper. He held up and examined his poor fingers. Reddened and blistered they were, some cut and bleeding after two days of struggling to unravel bits of old rope. Beneath his fingernails was packed tar that had coated old pieces of running rigging. The nail beds throbbed from constant leverage.

Wednesday arrived. It was the last morning picking oakum for William had been told he was detailed next day for work in the prison laundry. Moreover, respite that afternoon would be found in the exercise yard.

They called it junk – short lengths of old rope piled up in front of each inmate as he took his place upon one of the open benches ranged across the room. William arrived feeling nauseous. In slopping out his bucket he had been careless in allowing the right sleeve of his jacket to brush against the wall of the chute. The foul stench emitted through the opened metal plate was, in William's limited experience, unsurpassed in its intensity. As he hurried to withdraw his bucket he had fleetingly felt his arm touch and slither against the inner wall. He realised, to his horror, that his sleeve was liberally coated in loose, glutinous faeces, which, having been cast from above, had clung to the chute wall. Recoiling from the sight and odour, William had torn off his jacket only for his guard – an irascible fellow on this occasion – to have taken great delight in castigating him for so doing.

"Replace your coat immediately thirty-one," the guard had screamed. "The fact you have got your sleeve soiled is your own fault. Carelessness, indeed. You'd have done better to have soiled your own trousers. At least you'd have found wallowing in your own shit less repulsive."

As the men were marched off to the bath-house, the quick-tempered guard spoke again.

"You can remove your coat shortly and wash your sleeve in the bucket bath," he had declared with a disdainful smirk, knowing full well his invitation left number thirty-one with something of a dilemma.

An inmate was only permitted to remove his jacket when exercising so the choice had been to leave the offending excrement coating his sleeve or to dip the garment in water already heavily tainted by slop buckets and to endure the repugnant task of removing the faeces by hand. The former would have doubtless left William retching throughout his morning toil, let alone the poor fellow at his shoulder; and so he had taken the latter course, cringing as he did so and finally vomiting up what little breakfast he had managed to stomach.

As he set about picking hemp with his chafed fingers there remained a faint smell of excrement. William's jacket, after all, could hardly be termed clean, the sleeve having been tentatively rubbed beneath tepid, contaminated water. Its dampness had wetted his shirt and both hung clammily against his arm. Perhaps its faint, yet continuing, presence was a quirk of memory. Perhaps, pondered William, the smell was ingrained on his right hand, with which he had reluctantly rubbed the soiled garment. Returning to his cell with bucket, dish and spoon he had done his best to wash his hands with the soap and cold water at his disposal. He lifted his right hand and sniffed it. All he could perceive was the smell of old tar, stubbornly packed beneath his fingernails. And so, throughout the morning, prisoner thirty-one continued to feel nauseous and the soreness in his fingers intensified.

The afternoon's exercise brought relief despite a chill breeze off the Atlantic. Casting aside the damp, fustian jacket, William was pleased to have seen the last of oakum picking, at least for the time being. At first he revelled in the intake of deep breaths of fresh, maritime air as he began a circuit of exercise routines under the close scrutiny of under-keeper and guards. Yet it was hard work after a full fortnight of scant nourishment from what penitentiary food William had deigned to pass his lips. His fingers throbbed as he went through the routines. He felt sorry for himself. It occurred to him that, with two weeks gone, the duration of his time in prison was now past the half-way mark. Yet this failed to cheer him. It didn't quell the misery. He would merely trade dislike of prison for dislike of life aboard the *Cygnet*. Certainly more palatable food and cleanliness and, perchance, companionship, were to be re-discovered, but this seemed small beer to one who considered the Navy the bane of his life.

William felt a hearty slap on the back. The first ten minute rest period had begun and he had wandered across to the well to slake his thirst with a good swig of water. He looked round. The clout had been dispensed by Jake, the pock marked saddler.

"We need to talk, my friend," he murmured.

William must have adopted a vacuous gaze, for the week's events and hardships had erased any recollection of the saddler's parting words the previous Wednesday. It was an expression which prompted the speaker to elaborate.

"Getting you off your ship and away, lad…that's what you want, ain't it?"

"Well…yes," murmured William. "But what can you do to help me?…I mean, seeing as you're awaiting trial for larceny and, in all likelihood, destined to remain here or be placed in Rockhead…"

"Contacts, my friend…and the means of getting word to those who matter on the outside." The saddler winked at William, then added, "but that's nothing which need concern you. If you're interested, it'll cost you, of course. Six pounds. Three between those who help spring you, the rest for us for making it possible…for facilitating it, shall I say. And when I say *us*, sailorman, I mean me and that darky sitting over yonder."

"Who's he then?" enquired William.

"Young man by the name of Reuben. I've known him perhaps a year now.

346

He was a field slave on a southern cotton plantation until he committed some misdemeanour and was due for a flogging…told me he managed to escape before being dragged to the whipping-shed. Said he concealed himself in a canebrake until nightfall, then began a long trek following the North Star until eventually he found his way to Ohio…but then having crossed Erie, to gain his freedom, he was not much smitten by the prospect of a Great Lakes winter. So he parted company with Ontario and worked a passage on vessels plying the lakes and St Lawrence. Ultimately he found his way to Halifax, which was when I met him. He was living hand to mouth but I got him some temporary work and accommodation and…"

"So how has this Reuben the means to help me? After all, here he is in clink with you. Not much use to me back on the *Cygnet*."

"Coincidentally, my good fellow, young Reuben was here when I was brought in. He's doing three months for a bit of minor pilfering…that's all…helped himself to a few shingles. Well, he's due for release a week Friday which I guess is before your time's up."

"I'm in for twenty-eight days, so…yes, I leave the following week."

"In which case everything falls into place. Reuben will do what's necessary," said Jake with an air of confidence.

"So what is your plan?" implored William in a strained whisper.

"If you're keen to proceed and you can pay your way, Reuben and I will go through the detail of it with you next Wednesday afternoon. Reuben lives not too far from me, in a town called Lunenburg. It's a fishing port and he makes himself busy there by helping the local fishermen…cleaning up after the catches…swabbing decks and such like. Sometimes he's required to repair nets, gut fish and shuck scallop. So he's well acquainted with the fishing community and is valued by it as one who can be called on to do a job. And he knows one or two boat owners who are only too happy to assist naval deserters in exchange for using them for unpaid work for a few weeks before they move on."

William looked uneasy. Jake immediately detected his discomfort.

"Something troubling you, sailor?"

William shrugged. "It's just that a few weeks ago we put into St. John's. We'd been up round the top end of Newfoundland, down the Strait of Belle Isle, most of the while trying to steer clear of icebergs, often in dense fog. Well, to cut a long story short, we were called to the assistance of a merchant ship, the *Dalhousie*, said to be in a sinking condition. We made her safe, brought her to an anchorage and landed her cargo. Then, in due course, we took her in tow and four days later dropped anchor in St John's harbour. After several days at St John's and late one evening, the Officer-of-the-Watch spotted an open boat with several on board, pulling rapidly for the shore. The party was intercepted and found to comprise several fishermen in the process of aiding and abetting the escape of William Spirit, one of our able-seamen. The fishermen were prosecuted by the Captain and, I believe, each fined three pounds."

"Hmm…not a sufficiently spirited enterprise, if you'll excuse the pun," chuckled the saddler. "I'm sure Reuben's plans will be better executed and if he takes to the escape boat he won't need to blacken his face. After all, they won't spot him in the dark! So don't worry yourself about failure, my friend."

"OK, time to resume exercises," shouted the under-keeper from across the yard, the ten minute rest period having evidently elapsed.

"Think about it during the next half hour, then we'll talk again," said the saddler, hurriedly, as the men scrambled to their feet.

William Reynolds had little doubt over the course of action he would follow. What trace of uncertainty pervaded his mind concerned the effect on his family, for were he to succeed it would be out in the open. There would be no concealment and, whereas others' hearts might soften in time and show forgiveness, he would no longer be able to look his Uncle James in the eye. Uncle James would carry contempt for his nephew to the grave. Nevertheless, as he trudged, exhausted, around the exercise yard, he resolved not to be deflected from the ambition that now consumed him. He would try once again to part company with the Navy. He would place his trust in Jake and Reuben.

"So have you decided whether you would welcome our assistance?" enquired Jake, as he and William resumed their conversation during the second break.

"Yes, I have," came the unwavering reply. "I have resolved to place my trust in you and your negro friend. I must be rid of the Navy."

"Good. I'm sure you won't regret it." The saddle-maker hesitated a moment to blow his nose on a grimy piece of old cambric. "Two things…I'm assuming the money's no problem and you'll have it to give Reuben before our little operation gets into full swing?"

William nodded in affirmation.

"Secondly, can you swim?"

"Yes…but not too far."

"That'll do," said Jake who promptly turned on his heels and shuffled across the yard. A few minutes elapsed before he returned. "I've spoken to Reuben, told him of your circumstances and alerted him to the need to devise a plan of escape. We'll go over it in detail next Wednesday. Now, enough of that. I'm sure intrigued to know why you're so anxious to part company with your current employer."

At first William appeared a little disconcerted by the manner in which the saddler perfunctorily brought the curtain down upon any further discussion to do with prising him from the *Cygnet*. However, the fact was that, until the negro's stratagem could be presented, there was little more to be said. Realising this, William re-directed his thoughts and embarked upon an account of such salient aspects of his naval career as might satisfy Jake's overt curiosity.

"I never wanted to go to sea. My father was a steward but in the comparatively short time I knew him I do not recollect him expressing a wish for me to follow in his footsteps. He died when I was ten."

"So, your mother...?"

"No, not at all. But it was always the wish of a maternal uncle that I join the Navy. God knows why, excepting he was a dyed-in-the-wool naval man and a steward himself...and somehow I always sensed, that for whatever reason, he held some antipathy towards me. Well, being his Captain's steward, he had the old man's ear and out of the blue he'd arranged for me to join the floating gunnery school at Portsmouth as a ship's steward's boy."

"So you were as good as pressed and a disgruntled recruit from the beginning," concluded Jake.

"Yes and no. I despised my uncle for what he'd done but, on the other hand, I didn't want to show him that I wasn't up to it...so, I resolved to brace myself for what lay ahead."

"Did you succeed?"

"I made quite a good fist of it. It wasn't easy for a fifteen year old used to the coddled and restricted compass of home life." William paused a moment and looked reflective. "Strange...when I first went onboard, I recall the smell of the place was somehow as intimidating as anything else...you know, damp canvas, paint and cordage, caulker's pitch. But yes, it was hard. Cocoa and what we knew as Clarence Yard biscuit was poor substitute for my mother's hot stews. But with time I warmed to the life and hoped to impress, striving always to be diligent and attentive when it came to my instructions."

"You were being trained as a steward?"

"Yes, but the *Excellent* was a gunnery school and without exception, all the ship's company had to be conversant with the big guns. We were expected to take up any station and be fully versed in their manual exercise."

"That must have been challenging," observed Jake.

"The noise and operation of the big guns was frightening enough when we fired them at targets across the adjacent mudflats. But I can assure you the guns themselves were not as intimidating as the gunner's mate and the drill sergeants barking their orders. I much preferred cutlass drill with the ship's corporals although most of those were bullies. They revelled in making a hapless learner look a fool. However, I suppose I was fortunate, since I enjoyed the drill. My enthusiasm was seemingly apparent and I was told I displayed proficiency with my cuts and guards. So cutlass and small arms drill caused me few problems, unlike some instructions. I hated knots and splices!"

"How long were you in this gunnery school?"

"I was there about three years," said William.

"And did your dislike of the Navy intensify because of the experience?"

"To be honest…no, I don't think it did…at least, not markedly. Yes, it was tough and hard work but there were good times. We would sometimes go ashore in the summer to play cricket on what was known as Southsea Common. It was a game with which I was well acquainted and it brought back fond memories. I have to say that I made few enemies, but I believe I can honestly claim to have forged some good friendships. Sadly, of course, pals were either left on board when I was discharged or went their separate ways in the world. Yet I'd be wrong to say that throughout my time on *Excellent* I wouldn't have traded my lot for hearth and home and a life ashore."

"So, when did it really turn sour? asked Jake, searchingly.

"Not until after I joined the *Cygnet*. Before that…I suppose two years ago, at the age of eighteen, I was discharged from the *Excellent* and joined the *Edgar*. She was a second rate of ninety-one guns and was flagship to our Channel Squadron. To be frank there was a strong sense of freedom about throwing off the shackles that beset a boy sailor aboard a training ship. A boy devoid of circumspection would soon become the target of bullying… not so much among his peers, you understand, but in the company of men and especially the instructors. Yet overnight, once I had become a ship's steward's assistant and rated as a man…an Ordinary Seaman…aboard the

350

Edgar, then gone was the stifling supervision of the *Excellent*. I got treated differently and became eligible for my grog." William winked at Jake and smiled wryly, suggesting that, if nothing else, that was something he still valued back on the lower deck.

"So it sounds as though life improved for a while?"

William appeared thoughtful. "Marginally, perhaps," he uttered, after some delay, the tone of his reply lacking any sense of conviction. "The greater freedom was good but I took time to adjust to life on a sea-going ship of the line. Portsmouth harbour had been a comparative millpond to what I encountered beating down the English Channel and across the Bay of Biscay…it took me time to even begin finding my sea-legs and to steady my innards in a heavy sea. But I got to see the fine city of Lisbon. And I once recall no grander sight than that of our consorts astern and in close company. The visibility was razor sharp and, with the breeze directly astern, each was under all plain sail and booming forward with her studdingsails set. It was a sunlit, truly dazzling spectacle with the three vessels resembling some huge birds, preening and puffing out their chests."

"But I gather your presence aboard the *Edgar* was short-lived?"

"Yes, I was discharged after seven months, at the end of May, last year. Yet I was greatly delighted with events a few days before my leaving. We had returned from Lisbon and come to at Spithead…off Portsmouth… around the middle of April. There we stayed for the remainder of my time and on the twenty-seventh of May – I distinctly recall the date – the ship was dressed with flags. Then, in the late afternoon, the yards were manned and we delivered a twenty-one gun salute."

"What was that all about?" asked Jake.

"Well, the salute signalled the approach of the Royal Yacht, *Fairy*, carrying the Prince Consort. He was accompanied by the King of the Belgians and the Count of Flanders. Their Royal Highnesses came onboard the *Edgar* for an hour's reception and I had the honour to assist waiting upon the esteemed gentlemen in the officers' mess." William looked as if the satisfaction derived from that incident would take some overhauling as the pinnacle of a naval career he would constantly deride; then, in a trice, his bearing became pensive. "Who could have imagined that, before the year was out, Prince Albert would have departed this life?"

"Goes to show we are but mortal and how fragile is our existence. Like the cresting wave, sailorman…there and gone. What sayeth the Good Book?…chaff, morning cloud, the early dew that passeth? We are, in the great realm of things, little different." The saddler hesitated a moment, as if to disengage his thoughts from such profundity, then changed his tack. "So what of the *Cygnet*?"

"An altogether different ship…a gun vessel carrying a mere sixty officers and men, launched a year before I joined her, in June of '61. We left Spithead one early afternoon in the middle of the month and set a westerly course down the Channel. I remember dear old England receding with our last sight of the Longships light late the following evening. And I think I eventually found my sea-legs on that voyage when, in mid-Atlantic, we encountered some strong running swells and a heavy head sea. The force of it all carried away the jib-boom and part of our figurehead. Four weeks after weighing anchor we came to in Halifax harbour and that's where I really had cause to become disenchanted with my lot."

"I'm all ears," uttered Jake. "What happened?"

"It was my own fault to be honest. A fateful mistake because of my own carelessness…fateful, I suppose, since it marked me out as one prone to negligence, one who couldn't be trusted. And after all, if a steward has to display one essential attribute it is that of being trustworthy if he is to merit the approbation of his superiors. Well, I failed in that regard…and how I failed. Being in port, we were in the regular habit of taking in fresh beef and vegetables and, on this particular occasion, I went and spoilt forty-nine pounds of fresh meat. I had no plausible excuse…it was sheer carelessness…and what I found galling and caused me to scold myself, time and again, was the fact that I had left the *Edgar* with my character intact and a good conduct rating. Now I had blundered in a manner that would mar my standing in the ship. Not surprisingly, perhaps, in the nights that followed and during spells of fitful slumber, I was caused to toss and turn in my hammock; for my mind was repeatedly assailed by images of my Uncle James, mockingly grinning and trotting out the same old maxim… 'competence, diligence, trustworthiness, my boy.'"

"I'm assuming you were punished for this unfortunate indiscretion?" said the saddler, as he pursued his questioning, intrigued to know what had fed William's appetite to break with the Navy.

"I escaped physical punishment, but the cost of the beef was charged to my wages. Trouble is, I found the episode so distressing that I believe it caused me to become depressed and I suppose, in turn, it perpetuated bad habits…I mean, drink. I enjoyed my grog when I joined the *Edgar*, for I considered it lifted my mood and made life below deck a shade more tolerable than it might otherwise have been. Well, with me being in the business of stewarding you might be excused for thinking I could help myself to a little extra of the dark stuff to stiffen my grog. But, no...the spirit room door is kept under lock and key and, when the day's keg is brought up on deck, both it and the rum tub remain under close supervision throughout the noon muster. And once each man has received his due, even the plushers...the liquor left in the tub... are tossed into the scuppers."

"So you're saying your intake of drink...or your liking for it...increased once things started to go wrong on the *Cygnet*?"

"Liking for it, certainly, so shore leave was blissful."

"Well at least you limeys still have your rum ration," remarked the inquisitive Jake. "I hear the United States Navy did away with theirs only recently."

"Trouble is, our grog's not even half-and-half but three to one."

"So did your drinking ashore get you into further trouble?"

"Well, I had angered the wardroom steward, to whom I'm answerable, because of the wasted beef. Also, I knew for sure the Paymaster and Captain held me in poor regard because of that incident. It sorely distressed me that I had marred my previous good character and I found solace in drink on the next occasion I went ashore. It was two or three weeks later. We had left Halifax and set course for Bermuda. No sooner had we arrived than we were transported alongside an American collier. It was hot and we were set to work coaling the ship, a filthy operation at the best of times. When coaling takes place it tends to involve most of the crew and this was no exception. Added to which we were re-provisioning the ship, taking on a ton of water, cleaning the holds and in the wake of coaling, scrubbing the grime off coal screens and windsails. As I say, it was hot...eighty five degrees on the lower deck so we needed to set up windsails to ventilate the ship. By the time we had been in Bermuda a few days the whole crew were pretty exhausted and ready for the shore leave which came our way."

"So let me guess. You went and got yourself drunk," said Jake.

"Not exactly...a little groggy, perhaps. I had a good few drinks, I'll admit, but it was sheer fatigue as much as the drink that got the better of me. That night, back on board, I tossed and turned because of the balmy conditions and those images again. I struggled to get much sleep. I remember being wide-awake come the sound of the boatswain's pipe and had little difficult turning out. But it caught up with me. After breakfast I was preparing an inventory in the starboard breadroom and must have fallen asleep. The next I knew, one of our petty officers was dragging me to my feet. By then I should have completed my inventory and been elsewhere cleaning the mess-traps. So I was in trouble again and beginning to get a bit of a bad reputation. More importantly, I was alienating the wrong people."

"I'm assuming you suffered some retribution?"

"Well, yes...but it could have been worse. I was severely reprimanded and the first lieutenant sent me to the masthead. It was scorching up there but at least there was a breeze. Well, they let me down after an hour or so before I baked and I was black-listed for three days."

"Black-listed?"

"Given extra duties. Like having to help get out the tanks and scraping them...and whitewashing the store room and chain cable lockers. Messy jobs. And then I was ordered by the first luff to go to the mainmast each evening and remain there at attention for two hours."

"I guess you were glad to leave Bermuda."

"It made little difference. My behaviour had already upset and alienated people. That wouldn't have been too bad on a big ship of the line but on a gunboat there's no hiding place. I've constantly felt, while on the *Cygnet*, that I've been persecuted... bullied...for the slightest thing. But let me assure you...my dislike of the Navy has nothing to do with any lack of allegiance to Queen and Country. No, if I could turn back the clock to my days in Portsmouth I would seek out a recruiting sergeant before my time came to join the gunnery school."

"But you've seen a bit of the world being on board ship," suggested the saddler, as if that was an ameliorating consideration.

"Yes, some faraway places, some delightful places. Sun-kissed islands like Navassa, the Port Royal Cays, Anguilla Island and Cay Sal...beautiful places strewn with white sand and palms...tranquil lagoons...sparkling water breaking over limestone and coral reefs...azure waters to rival the colour of the sky. Oh, yes, and Rum Cay, which was all of this. We were there back in January for a few days and took delivery of fresh pineapples from the island's plantations. I've never tasted such divine fruit."

"Rum Cay? Wasn't Rum Cay the place where that British ship foundered?"

"You mean the *Conqueror*...yes, a first rate carrying fourteen hundred men and not a soul was lost. That's why we were there. We had been with her at Jamaica, last December. Well, the *Conqueror* left Port Royal on Christmas Eve bound for Bermuda. Then, a week into the New Year, her pinnace suddenly turned up in Port Royal manned by some of her officers and crew and bearing news that their ship had run onto a reef at Rum Cay. We were immediately despatched to offer assistance, having taken on board the men from the pinnace and provisions for the rest of the *Conqueror's* crew who had gone ashore and made camp. The pinnace was taken in tow by securing her fast astern with hawsers and we made good passage under steam. We were able to offer some assistance but it was clear the stricken vessel was doomed, and seemingly because of a navigational mistake... but at least there were no fatalities. Anyway, I digress. Yes...I encountered some fine places but equally, some dreadful holes. On one occasion, we were anchored in Limon Bay on the coast of Panama for a few days. It was an awful, swampy area. Mosquitos and sandflies were a constant irritation and we limped back to Cartagena with a third of the ship's crew on the sick list. And while the weather was sometimes grand, the tropical climate in the Caribbean could be very oppressive, often wet and threatening with vivid lightning storms. I've known the heat so fierce as to cause pitch to melt and drip from the ship's rigging."

"So you're saying there was little to cheer your heart, nothing to help counter the persecution you began to feel?" enquired Jake.

For a moment William wore a wistful expression. "I made one or two close friends...from my home town...Portsmouth lads. They were men I felt I could trust and that means a lot." He paused to smile gently. "I remember them doing their utmost to raise my spirits earlier in the year. We were in Jamaica and, lo and behold, the *Edgar* came into harbour. That was in February and it made me feel especially downhearted, for her presence stirred my emotions. I suppose she had been my home in better days, a time before I blotted my copybook. Well, the *Edgar* remained there until May and all the while we were in and out of Port Royal. Each time we returned she was there and each time the sight of her seemed to trigger a desire to lay my head once more between her guns and rid myself of the wretched *Cygnet*. It was frustrating and I suppose, on reflection, the seeds of my wanting to run had already begun to germinate."

William had hardly finished his sentence when the under-keeper, hitherto lost in earnest conversation with one of the guards – and unaware that more than ten minutes had flown by – emerged from his digression to bellow a belated instruction.

"On your feet! Now...not tomorrow! Six circuits, marching speed, six again at the double, then six running. No shirking. Remember, physical exercise purifies and invigorates the body and mind…and if any wretches are in dire need of purifying then it's got to be you lot."

★ ★ ★

The following Saturday's work in the men's laundry-room had finished early. The amount of dirty clothes and linen assigned to be washed had been dispatched in good time. Furthermore, outside in the drying yard, fair conditions and a stiff breeze had enabled it to be quickly gathered in, folded and committed to a huge, pine storage cupboard that reeked of camphor. Otherwise, the nicety of ironing was solely reserved for the Governor's madras handkerchiefs and his Sunday shirt and cravat – a responsibility left to the more accomplished hands of the prison's chief washerwoman who had charge of the women's laundering.

Prisoner thirty-one had, in consequence, been returned early to the chill and lonely confines of his cell. He glanced at his reddened hands and took comfort from them being in a far better and less painful state than at the start of the week. He felt a draught. The stiff breeze which had earlier proved effective in the drying yard was seemingly out of the west and found easy penetration through the aperture in the outer cell wall. William Reynolds shivered. The draughty coldness of his cell was in contrast to the comparative warmth of the laundry-room. He saw merit in endeavouring to close the aperture. Alongside his latrine bucket lay sheets of old newspaper, sufficient that he might spare a few. Crumpled and stuffed into the aperture, they might prove an effective draught excluder, yet this would darken the little room prematurely when a mid-October afternoon would fall gloomy soon enough. And, once it had, the darkness would prevail until his miserable supper arrived and the guard lit him a candle by which to eat. So, instead of plugging the opening and hastening twilight, William cast an eye towards the tree clad slopes that rose up in the distance, beyond the North West Arm. The splashes of red maple leaf, which, until recently, stunningly peppered those slopes, had now surrendered to gravity, while predominant greens had turned to rusts and yellows and dowdy browns. As William pondered upon the beauty of nature's autumnal tints, his attention was drawn to the sudden appearance of an open boat close to and standing for the near shore. Oars were shipped as the small vessel came alongside a short wooden jetty that belonged to the penitentiary. The rickety structure, clearly visible from William's high vantage, snaked out into the water just beyond the dense thicket that fell away below.

One of the oarsmen, in naval uniform, promptly leapt out and secured the boat's painter to a timber bollard. He was immediately followed by two men clambering out of the sternsheets. William recognised both as Marines, although the manner in which the second to alight required some assistance – being somewhat unsteady – implied he was restrained. The appearance of the third man to disembark – by virtue of his bearing and his uniform – but principally the former, told William that this was a ship's boat hailing from the *Cygnet*; for this man was undoubtedly her repugnant Master-at-Arms. As for the other two passengers, William struggled to identify either as all three took to the path leading up to the prison from that seaward side. Soon they had disappeared from view – hidden by the intervening undergrowth – leaving the observer to ruminate upon just who from *Cygnet* might be about to join him.

Sunday...ante meridiem. A hushed congregation in the Protestant chapel sat awaiting the arrival of the Reverend Pope and the Governor. Several rows ahead of him, William Reynolds recognised a newcomer in a newly-issued plain fustian suit. It was a young fellow about his own age, a private by the name of Pryce, Royal Marines Light Infantry. He couldn't recall his Christian name. He looked so different, much younger, in his prison clothes, having, like William himself, signed over his uniform in the inmates' property register for onward fumigation and temporary storage. At the end of the service the seats were emptied from the front. As Pryce sidled along his emptying row and turned to shuffle back, he had a diffident look about him, mindful no doubt that he was a new arrival and hence the object of some curiosity. Then, fleetingly, he caught William's eye. Nods of recognition were quickly exchanged before the Marine and those in proximity to him were ushered out into the adjoining corridor by one of the guards. Recognition...yet seemingly little evidence of surprise on Pryce's part; but then William supposed the newcomer would have known of his presence in the penitentiary or, failing that, would have had someone remind him. After all, the *Cygnet* was a small vessel where news travelled fast.

★ ★ ★

Twenty-two days gone...William Reynolds' fourth Wednesday, post meridiem. The inmates of those cells facing the North West Arm – or, more specifically, those among them who were eligible to participate – were first to be led to the exercise yard. In total this numbered five, including

William and the negro who Jake had referred to as Reuben. And as prisoner thirty-one was first to enter the yard behind the escorting guard it was to find not only the duty guards and under-keeper in attendance but also the errant Royal Marine.

"Hello, Reynolds. Bet you were surprised to see me turn up on Sunday," said Pryce as he lingered rather awkwardly close to the building's entrance, having discretely placed himself well away from the three members of staff. He looked pale and sheepish.

"Not exactly, Pryce. You see, I saw you coming…well, not you exactly, but I recognised the damn Master-at-Arms with two joeys in tow. I couldn't identify either of you from the distance of my cell's aperture but I detected that one of you was manacled. You look as if you've seen a ghost by the way…or perhaps something's ailing you?"

"I've been on hospital duty since Monday with two other fellows. God only knows what their names are…I only know them by number. We were drafted in to help the physician since he's short of staff and there's some kind of germ going around. Four men and a woman came in yesterday, vomiting and throwing out diarrhoea like a fall in spate. I've been on the go all morning, emptying and swilling out shit buckets. The stench in that little ward is putrid. Then there's some poor wretch smothered in scrofulous ulcers, his skin livid and weeping. I was given mortar and pestle and asked to mix a dollop of lard with some iod…with some zinc concoction…"

"Ioduret?…I recall my…"

"Yes…that might have been it, Reynolds…anyway, I mixed up this so-called ointment and had to apply it to the poor fellow's ulcers. Quite turned my stomach, not being cut out for that sort of thing, you understand, and what with the pervading smell of liquid excrement it made me feel real queer. The surgeon saw me retching in one of the shit buckets…let me out early he did…told me to come out and take some gulps of fresh air. Good sort, really," said Pryce, reflectively. "You know, they say that poor chap's ulcers are down to an impoverished constitution. Seems he's a convicted man with plenty of time to serve, so what hope has he of putting that right, what with all the pigswill they serve up in here? Christ, Reynolds, it makes Navy grub seem grand."

William, while sympathetic, chose not to dwell on the plight of the ulcerated patient, being more interested in what was happening on the *Cygnet* to which he was soon to return. "Talking of the Navy, Pryce, when are you to go back to the ship?"

"Sooner than I first imagined. I've been given twenty-eight days, like yourself, but they'll have to retrieve me earlier, unless they'd prefer me to rot here. Word is that *Cygnet*'s due to leave Halifax for the Bahamas on the first of the month."

"So is her refit finished?"

"Pretty well. She was still lashed alongside the Dockyard on Saturday and early this week was due to be provisioned and have stores drawn. Today or tomorrow she's meant to haul off from the Dockyard and moor to a buoy out in the harbour."

"So why have they sent you to the peniten..." William's question was cut short by a shrill whistle sounded by the supervising under-keeper, the other inmates due to exercise having now gradually assembled in the yard.

"Attention you scum!" bawled the under-keeper. "Now, you'll commence with six circuits walking, just to get your blood moving. Off you go!"

As usual, conclusion of the first half-hour session would mark the start of a welcome ten-minute rest period. William, of course, was only too aware that he needed to talk to Jake as a matter of priority. He could not afford to resume conversation with Pryce because today he needed to fully understand the nature and timing of Reuben's stratagem and, more particularly, what his confederates required of him. As it transpired, he need not have worried. Jake's and Reuben's intentions were of similar ilk. The three needed to talk and the sooner the better and none wished to be sidetracked by others likely to engage any one of them in trite commentary. In consequence, all remained in close proximity throughout the first exercise session and swiftly came together upon its conclusion.

"Hello thirty-one. Let's wander over here, out of the way of any attentive ears." Such was Jake's opening comment. "Now remind me of your name, friend," he added. "I remember you telling me two weeks ago, but it's slipped my mind."

"William...William Reynolds."

"Then allow me, William, to introduce you to my friend Reuben."

Both men stifled any natural inclination to shake hands, not wishing to draw attention to themselves. Instead William nodded, an action which, in its reciprocation, provoked the most subtle of smiles from the negro.

"Reuben has given thought to how we might wrest you from the clutches of H.M.S. *Cygnet*," continued Jake. "Isn't that so, Reuben?"

"I'z sho' have Mister Jake an' I'z thinkin' we's can git Mister Willum off dat ship wid'out an'un knowin'. Yassuh!"

As William observed the negro he thought how handsome a man he was, as handsome and smooth-skinned and plump-cheeked as was his accomplice pock-marked and hard-featured.

"So what's the plan Reuben?" enquired the saddle-maker.

"Well, I'z 'sumin' dis *Zignit* is still 'longside de Dockyard?"

"Actually…no." It suddenly occurred to William just how fortuitous had been Pryce's timely appearance in the penitentiary; and even more so their earlier conversation. "Do you see that fellow over there," he continued, pointing out the figure of Pryce "Well, he's recently come off my ship. He tells me she's about to haul off from the 'yard and will moor to a buoy out in the harbour. She's to put to sea on the first of the month."

"Well, by jove, a touch of good providence with that information coming our way," exclaimed Jake. "Perhaps it augurs well for us, William Reynolds, except it'll put a different complexion on things, not least the timing of your run. What do you make of it, Reuben?"

"You didn't tell dis feller you'sa proposin' t'run ag'in, Mister Willum?"

"No, no, certainly not. He's a decent enough chap but me being a sailor… well, I wouldn't trust a joey with that sort of information."

"That's a blessing," interjected Jake.

"Well, you ask me what I'z think of it Mister Jake…I'z think it's good… de ship bein' out in de water, dat is. Arter all, des likely gonna be more 'quisitive folks on de quayside, dat's fo' sartin. O Lawd, yes, al'ays bet'r out in de harbour."

"So what is your plan, Reuben?" asked Jake.

"I'z git my release dis Friday thank Gawd. De followin' Friday, I'z figger, gonna be de last day o' de month. Dat gives l'il time befo' we's must act. I'z 'sumin', Mister Willum, dat by de followin' Friday you'z bin back on de *Zignit* fo' a few days?"

"Yes, Reuben. I get out on Monday."

"Dat Friday night, den, but berry late…mebbe two in de mornin' an we's hope fo' a night to match my'z 'plexion. Haw, haw…yes, mister, dark as a Ca'lina slave nigger, jes like me!"

"So, you're saying two o'clock on the Saturday morning, Reuben?" said the saddler, in order to underline the importance of agreeing a firm time.

"Yes, Mister Jake. Two o'clock…dead o'night when most 'spectable folks in thar beds."

"Well, yes," observed William, "but as you know, Her Majesty's ships never sleep. Two o'clock will be the middle of the graveyard watch but you're right, it has darkness in its favour. Whatever the hour I'll need to be alert, act shiftily and hope for a bit of luck. So, yes, let's stick with two o'clock."

"Okay, Reuben, what is planned to happen at two o'clock?" asked Jake in a hurried manner that reflected his growing impatience to get things tied up.

"I'z several friends over'n Lunenburg who sho' would help, Mister Jake. One in 'ticular has a yawl rowboat wid a sail rig. Single feller, named Tom, allers keen on night work dat will earn a pound or two. We'z sail up de coast, wid a small skiff in tow...wedder permittin' o'course...and anchor somewhere nawth of McNab island. Tom's cussin...feller called Henry... an' I will den row de skiff t'within a hunned yards of de *Zignit*. No closer y'understan' as I kinda 'speck dat we's be spotted."

"So what if you find, when you get out, that friend Tom and his cousin have other commitments that night?" asked the saddler, searchingly.

"I'z not 'zactly short of friends in Lunenburg town, Mister Jake. Jes' trust me. It'll be awright."

"And how will I know you're out there on the water and where?" enquired William with apprehension etched in his voice.

"No cause t'be afeard, Mister Willum," said the negro, reassuringly. "I'z intend we's bes' be in place off McNab berry early so's we's in de skiff a hunned yards off de *Zignit* well 'fore two. At two o'clock you's need t'be hidin' on de uppa deck and you's hear two shrill whistle blasts. Dat's de time t'lower yerself inta de water and git swimmin' de hunned yards."

"Yes," said William, in a tone of voice which clearly solicited further reassurance, "but we need to agree your position in relation to the *Cygnet*."

"I'z 'ware of dat, Mister Willum. On Friday, 'fore I head home I'z gonna 'stablish whar'de *Zignit* lies in de water."

"Well, I can tell you now, Reuben. She will have come off the Dockyard and be moored to a buoy south east of there, in the lee of George's Island... and she'll have her fore-and-aft line parallel with the shore. But yes, that's important...to establish precisely where she lies. God forbid, I wouldn't want you sat waiting beside the wrong vessel, especially since I'm not a particularly strong swimmer." William hesitated, time enough to release a stifled and nervous chuckle. "And I think it would be easier for me to slip off the ship up for'ard. If, for example, you placed yourself off the port bow then...sorry, it's remiss of me to assume you're familiar with nautical parlance but..."

"No reason t 'pologise Mister Willum. I'z sho''cquainted wit dat thar jargin 'cos workin' on tradin' ships led me t'settle in Nov' Scotier. An' since den I'z gittin' work wid de fishin' folks crost in Lunenburg. So I'z knowin' dat port is de lef' side awright. Yassuh!"

"So that's it then," exclaimed Jake, his scarred, pitted features breaking into a broad smile. "Now, don't forget the money, William Reynolds…hand it to Reuben…and remember, you'll be expected to contribute a few weeks free labour to the good folks in Lunenburg who facilitated your escape. Kind of a gentleman's agreement you'll need to honour and I'm thinking your enough of a gentleman to do just that."

"Yes, Jake, that's a fair enough assessment. I'll be delighted to pull my weight. After all, I'll be a free man with time on hand to consider my next move."

"A free man. Glory be t'Gawd! I'z knows wat bein' a free man is al' 'bout. Yassuh!"

"Then tell me, Reuben. I guess you must view freedom a little differently from us white folks," said William, laughingly.

"Well, yes, Mister Willum. Thing is, you's awready a free man, 'spite de 'straints dat bind you in servin' de Engleesh Maj'sty. Now, bein' a slave nigger is a fa' cry from…"

And at that point the triumvirate's exchange was hastily drawn to a conclusion as the under-keeper ordered a resumption of the afternoon's exercises.

They came together again a half-hour later, William, Jake and Reuben…a final ten-minute gathering.

"I'z 'bout t'say earlier, Mister Willum, dat you's be a reely free man soon as we's git y'out of Hal'fax…arter all, if de *Zignit's* gwine t'sail away den kinda o'vious thar's nobody lef' t'cotch ya. Now, ain't dat grand, 'cos let me tell ye dis…when I'z a slave nigger an' 'scaped I'z not free till I reeched Sandusky an' crost de big, wide lake to dis promised land. No suh! Sum'times dodgin' 'em pattyroller nigger cotchas, hidin' in de barns an' wood cellars of kin'ly 'bolitionists, afeard all de time…ev'ry minnit."

"I suppose to you, Reuben, my friend, that was your simple objective… to be free, an end in itself," muttered Jake, somewhat reflectively. "So what's your goal, William? You told me when we first spoke you once wanted to be a soldier."

"To be honest I haven't given much thought to what I will do," said William. "But one day, when the time is right, I would want to return home."

"Well, if y'still wanna be a soljer den git yerself south to help dat good

Mister Linc'n. Only dis summa he vowed t'bolish slavery in de 'cessionist States den called 'pon more men t'enlist fo' three years. Dey say de bounty money 'cruits git is kinda 'mazin.' Yassuh, dat good Mister Linc'n will sho'ly take ya fo' a soljer."

"So they're still fighting each other, eh? Word was that that brotherly conflict would be over long 'ere now," remarked William.

"No sign o'dat jes' yit," said Reuben. "My's latest unnerstandin' is dat, jes' recently, Army o' Nawth'n Virginny crost de river P'tomac an' 'gaged Yankee soljers in Marylan.'...place call'd Sharpsburg. A reel bloodlettin' it 'pears 'fore Gen'l Lee 'treated back crost de river. Oh, no, I'z afeard dat it's gonna be a long struggle yit. Jes'mark my words, Mister Willum."

William Reynolds did not react to the negro's remarks. His inner thoughts were already preoccupied with the more immediate issue of breaking clear of the *Cygnet*. He dwelt upon the fragility of the situation. Reuben appeared confident enough that his stratagem would succeed and that not bringing the rowing boat under the bows of the gun vessel would avoid the fate of the St John's fishermen and their nervous cargo. Yet William himself considered thought of success to be nothing short of foolhardy and a tempter of fate. The one major impediment was the weather, for rough conditions could put an end to the venture. But then it occurred to him it would be All Hallows' Eve, the night before All Saints' Day, the night in the ancients' calendar when witches and warlocks would roam. For a moment William indulged his thoughts in the fanciful notion that such sorcerers might be abroad in the neighbourhood of Halifax, Nova Scotia. That being so, they would presumably not countenance any mischievous and boisterous behaviour on the part of the elements, but surely command that clement conditions prevail. In the course of this contemplation William fell silent, then grunted to himself, amusingly and with gentle self-reproach for entertaining such whimsy. Instead, his thoughts strayed to dear old Uncle Charley. "Don't worry your head, lad, over matters you can never influence. It's futile." They were words he recalled his uncle saying more than once. He smiled and felt much better for the recollection.

Little else transpired during that final rest period. Jake reminded his friend Reuben to make sure he delivered to his wife those few pounds earned from charging him with the task of abetting William's flight; and in no uncertain terms he warned William that failure to hand over six pounds, as soon as he was pulled from the water, would see him tossed out of the skiff and swimming back to whence he'd come. Conversely, William was more gracious towards the saddler, wishing him good fortune at his forthcoming trial. And then the three men said their goodbyes in similarly restrained fashion to when they had earlier come together. Seconds later the day's final exercise session got under way.

★ ★ ★

Thursday daybreak and William woke with shivers; he felt nauseous, his head ached. He pulled about him his meagre, moth-eaten blanket, although he could hear the noisy activity of the approaching guards: their rousing shouts, the metallic ring of shifting peephole covers and jangling keys, the clonk of lock mechanisms, the squeaking wheels of the water-carrying conveyance. Very soon he would be verbally bullied to get himself out of bed and attend to his ablutions. He felt awful. He longed at that moment to be back in his little room in King Street. There any impending knock on the door would signal the arrival of his dear Mother with a soothing drink and a piece of muslin, wetted-warm, to smooth his throbbing brow. Then he realised it might be foolish to say he felt ill, for he remembered what Pryce had said. There was a germ going round the place and people were being taken to the hospital ward. Yet he didn't want to go there. Instead he hoped the nausea and shivering would pass. Perhaps it was something he had eaten. Although more discerning than most in what he allowed to pass his lips, he was prepared to believe that anything served up in this wretched place could be tainted and the cause of the most spiteful of digestive maladies. If not afflicted with the germ already, to be sent to the prison hospital, cooped up with those ailing patients, would more than likely cause him to succumb to whatever contagion had laid them low. And if what he had was a fleeting ailment he wouldn't wish to be unnecessarily confined to the hospital. He envisaged himself being detained there on surgeon's orders when he needed to be back on the *Cygnet* preparing for the risky undertaking which soon lay ahead. Pryce was confident that he, himself, would return prematurely to the ship because it was to put to sea, but would they want a sick man possessed of some virulent ailment brought on board? No, he needed to steel himself, to somehow override his feelings when the guards arrived.

In all likelihood, or rather, in William's opinion, it was over three weeks of meagre sustenance which had reduced him to a state of debilitation and was the root cause of his current malaise. He determined to shake it off, even to the point of despatching most of a breakfast he would normally commit to his bucket. And he did well when it came to pretence, giving no hint of how he felt when the guard came in with his jug of water and when the cook's assistant later appeared with his breakfast. Yet his success was short-lived. Having consumed a portion of doughy, undercooked bread and several tentative spoonfuls of watery gruel, William's chest was gripped by an involuntary muscular spasm, its product a violent surge of vomit. Its abruptness and forceful expulsion prevented him from directing it as he might have wished: into his bucket or tin wash bowl. Instead, as the slopping-out bell rang forth, William was cognisant of his stomach contents gushing forth across the cell floor. And what failed to go to ground ended up drenching a sizeable portion of his straw mattress.

The situation was desperate. William struggled in his discomfort to gather up what newspaper lay to hand to wipe up what he could of the slimy emission. In five to ten minutes the cell door would be flung open and he would be expected to join his short convoy of inmates bound for the shit chute and bath-house. He felt the urge to defecate. Removing his trousers, he cursed his misfortune. He squatted over his bucket and noisily emptied his bowels, then cleaned himself using a few sheets of what discarded newspaper was at his disposal. One thing that tempered his annoyance was the realisation that his stools were well formed, for he recalled Pryce saying the germ-affected patients were all stricken with bad diarrhoea. Readjusting his clothing, William resumed his efforts to mop up his vomit. It was not easy in the relative gloom of the cell, in addition to which the newspaper sheets lacked absorbency, a property not shared by his old straw mattress. In a futile effort to rid it of his unpleasant discharge, William reflected on the fact that the next occupant of cell thirty-one would have to lay his head upon a mattress newly permeated with vomit. Poor wretch!

The cell door creaked on its hinges, opening fully to reveal the one-eyed guard, William's customary escort to the chute and bath-house. The fellow recoiled, visibly. Here the usual dank, ammoniacal smell of each cell, often heavy with the stench of freshly expelled faeces at this hour, was noticeably different, augmented as it was with the reek of vomit. In the sparse light which filtered through the outer wall aperture, the wetted floor glistened while prisoner thirty-one continued to busy himself with his futile attempt to reduce the seepage into his mattress.

The guard gently rocked back and forth on his heels and looked at his charge with scornful intent.

"Are you ill, thirty-one?" he said, mockingly. "Are you pouring forth at both ends? If so we better get you to the hospital. Orders are to confine those stricken with sickness and watery excrement."

"It's just a passing thing and I've not got diarrhoea," said William.

"Not by the stench in here, man. No point lying to me. Remember, if you're at your morning labours and you get the shits there's no excusing you. You'll be in an unholy mess and end up on stale bread and water."

William bent down and gingerly eased sideways the soiled and crumpled pieces of newspaper that crowded the top of his bucket. He proceeded to lift and tilt the receptacle, then proffered it towards the one-eyed guard for his inspection.

The guard grimaced. "Hmm…solid enough, eh? Rescued by your own turds, thirty-one. Mind you, what's wrong with spending the day in a hospital bed? Better than knuckling down to work, I'd have thought, and now they've brought in some bowls of iodine the smell's a lot more tolerable than in here."

"What's the delay there, Murphy?" came an irritated voice from the corridor where several inmates had already assembled with their escorts, ready to depart for the chute and bath-house. It was a question which immediately prompted the guard to withdraw into the corridor, only for him to reappear a minute later.

"I've spoken to Under-keeper McDougall," said the returning guard. "He says that if you're not sick enough to go to the hospital then you're well enough to work. According to my information you were due back in the shoemaker's shop today. However, having soiled your cell in this manner you will instead be required to attend to its disinfection. Mister McDougall says you must repeat the task in the unoccupied cells and when you've finished you'll have to swab out the hospital ward…and, yes…for spewing your guts all over the place it'll be a bread and water diet for two days. Now, up on your feet and get in line with your bucket. We're holding everyone up."

Instead of being left in his cell, on returning from the bath-house, prisoner thirty-one was taken by the one-eyed Murphy to the penitentiary store-rooms, a huddle of austere outhouses which lay beyond the men's exercise yard. Out in the open, as the raw chill off the sea triggered an eruption of his involuntary shivering and further whitened his already puttied features, William felt an intense desire to be back on the *Cygnet*. Not, of course, for any want of affection for the wretched vessel or even for the sake of navy grub, since his condition had now rendered him quite devoid of appetite: but, paradoxically, because in order to be rid of the damned ship, he had first to be back on board her. He longed for Monday to dawn. To be cast asleep at this moment and to wake refreshed, spared of the tribulation promised by the next few days would be the ultimate, the sovereign remedy. If only consciousness…even life itself…could be switched on and off at a whim.

With little more than a grunt, the mittened storekeeper accepted a chit from Murphy, then turned away and stooped to decant vinegar from a huge barrel-shaped earthenware jar. The fellow's habits were as unsavoury as his appearance, but arguably not at odds with the general standards of behaviour and cleanliness which seemed to prevail within the penitentiary. Closing the tap, he snorted inwardly to loud and ripe effect, hesitating, as he unbent his frame, to direct his mouth's accumulation of phlegm into an imaginary spittoon. Then, corking the receiving bottle, he stood tall and belched violently before slamming it on the counter. There followed a row between the guard and storekeeper, the first accusing the other of unwarranted, uncouth behaviour, the second telling the other to go and do something unmentionable to himself. Feeling so ill, William felt he could scream in condemnation and for want of quiet as he listened to the two men berate each other. In frustration he lunged forward, grasped the corked demijohn and made for the door, thus prompting the immediate curtailment of the altercation. Although not shackled to their guards within the establishment's confines, prisoners were not allowed to wander off but to be accompanied at all times. And thus Guard Murphy was bound to follow his charge who, in turn, expected some severe reprimand as one followed the other out of the store-rooms. Yet it didn't materialise.

"Christ Almighty, what an ignorant bastard," roared Murphy. "As for you, thirty-one, well…I think I was on the brink of putting him on his back, so I reckon I've got to thank you for acting as you did. They let us get away with knocking you villains about but if I'd pulverised that arsehole I'd have doubtless lost my job. And I'd have done it alright. My blood was up…oh, yes, to be sure, my old Irish temper was about to explode."

William said nothing. Back in his cell two buckets full of steaming hot water awaited him together with a long-handled swab.

"Once you've disinfected your own cell, thirty-one, bang on your door with the swab handle. But look here," continued Murphy, "you're a spunky fellow to be sure, feeling as you do and rejecting the chance of a few days rest in preference to this." His voice carried an air of sympathy for he had no inkling of William's motive. "I'm thinking you're not a bad sort in the circumstances and I'm grateful for you hoofing-it just now, 'cos there's no doubt, I'd have found myself in trouble. So look here…I'm a duty guard on this floor until noon. Before you swab out take a couple of hours' rest. You'll feel better for it and I'll turn a blind eye…which isn't that difficult for me, you understand," chuckled Murphy, as he inclined his socket in William's direction and winked with his one good eye. "Lost it as a youth in a brawl in Galway town. Took a dislike to an agent's lackey 'cos he worked for a detested landlord and had too much lip. But my undoing was too much fire-water, too much poteen…fair dulled my senses, it did, and I came off worse."

"Thank you," said William in comparative disbelief.

"I'll look by to wake you just before I go. Then you can get scrubbing. I'll tell my replacement that you'll be done in an hour or so, then you'll need to move on to another cell in accordance with McDougall's instructions." And with that the one-eyed guard closed the door and was gone.

William immediately dipped his chilled hands into one of the buckets and savoured the warmth derived from their immersion. He cupped them to sluice his weary face and cleanse his still vomit-smeared chin stubble. Then he wrenched the cork from the demijohn and poured a liberal amount of its vinegar into the two buckets, stirring with the swab handle to produce more than enough acidulated water to give his cell a generous dousing. Once the water had cooled its efficacy would doubtless be reduced. Be that as it may, Murphy had presented William with some respite. He gathered up his blanket, turned his soiled mattress and in no time had fallen asleep.

★ ★ ★

Monday 27th October 1862. Its dawning had seemed so distant, so unattainable, such a hill to climb, when, stricken with sickness, William had fallen into a restful sleep and dreamt that he might magic its arrival with the assistance of his own genie of the lamp. His rude awakening, three hours later, by the helpful Murphy – as he prepared to go off duty – had brought him back to painful reality. Yet the unexpected slumber had done him good and he had gone on, that Thursday afternoon, to disinfect his cell. Then he had been put to work cleansing two others. He had felt dreadful, but in truth less dreadful than earlier in the day. On Friday the headache and nausea had lifted and William was called upon to direct his attentions to the hospital and with it the fear of contracting something worse than the germ already troubling him. Furthermore, it was a task which filled him with unease, given the experience of Pryce. But Murphy was right, for the appearance of several strategically placed bowls of iodine, each covered with a little muslin, had since rendered the malodorous atmosphere far more tolerable to the visitor. That, and Matron Fish's recent insistence that lavender water be sprinkled unstintingly about the ward at regular intervals. In consequence, although weakened by his afflictions and want of nutrition, prisoner thirty-one had laboured assiduously under the eagle eyes of the deputy matron. Thus his work had passed muster without cause for censure.

Feeling much better in himself and thus with spirits buoyed, William had found a return to the shoemaker's shop, on the Saturday, a comparatively facile business. The Sabbath had passed uneventfully. Now, with Monday's long-awaited arrival, prisoner thirty-one waited patiently in the reception cell pending whatever discharge procedures called for attention. He had already been shaved ready for release. The room had a chill familiarity about it for he recalled having sat here nervously on the day of his admission.

Suddenly the door was flung open revealing a portly and balding middle-aged fellow with bushy, grey mutton-chop whiskers and an unhealthy-looking, glazed countenance. He said nothing but took a key to a tall pine cupboard that stood in one corner of the room. From the cupboard he removed a large green-leather bound volume which he carried to a small table positioned below the light of a window, more generous in its proportions than the apertures of the prison cells. William recognised the volume as the prisoners' property book which he had signed against the recorded intake of his uniform.

"Thirty-one, eh?...Reynolds, William. Naval uniform...ordinary seaman's rig...one in number. Also one small brass key. Correct?"

"Yes, sir."

"Nothing else in locker thirty-one, according to the property book. Correct?"

"Yes, sir."

The bewhiskered man then disappeared from whence he'd come, closing the door in the process. Moments later he returned carrying a neat pile of clothes which he also placed on the table. He also handed the prisoner the said brass key. Then, returning to the cupboard, he brought forth pen, ink and footwear and beckoned William to the table to sign for the receipt of his items.

"Get out of your issued suit and into your uniform. While you're attending to that I'll go and notify the Chaplain that you're ready for discharge. He'll want to speak to you. My information is that you're due for collection at eleven o'clock. That's twenty minutes hence."

Donning his uniform again felt strange, for it was decidedly better fitting than the shapeless prison garments. And there was a distinctive smell about it, the product of fumigation applied to all clothes taken off new entrants' backs, with the exception of those considered better suited to the furnace. As William completed his transformation, by attending to his lacings, the door was again opened and in breezed the Reverend Henry Pope.

"Ah, yes...Reynolds, isn't it? Name back and number dropped, eh, young fellow? But you'll do well to remember this. Dropped but not forgotten. The ignominy still remains. Your misdemeanour will forever be a stain...a blemish...on your character. I always make a point of talking to those about to depart this bleak institution, for the vast majority go forth from here thinking they've wiped their slate clean...that they've served their punishment. But no, it is not as simple as that in the eyes of God. What was it Reynolds? Desertion?"

Thereafter Pope became highly agitated. His colour became raised, a spasmodic twitch afflicting the left side of his face. "Desertion, eh? Prepared to throw over your colleagues and your Queen and Country for your own selfish gain...'tis the kind of wicked business that angers the Lord God Almighty." He then ranted for a few minutes about wickedness, in the manner which characterised his regular Sunday sermons; and all the while William sat motionless as the clergyman proceeded to draw vividly upon the Psalms of David...of how transgressors risk being turned into hell and of encountering snares, tempest, fire and brimstone. "Your one salvation, Reynolds, is to banish any thoughts of repetition and to go from this place with the intent of immediately turning to God. Seek out your naval chaplain and be guided by him. And remember you will need to turn from darkness to light and henceforth live an exemplary Christian life. Only then might you hope for atonement and reconciliation with the Almighty."

At the conclusion of his discourse the Reverend Pope's face had stopped twitching and his florid colour had paled. It was as if his mention of the word desertion had sent him into a frenzy of condemnation which had spiralled to a crescendo, then subsided.

William remained impassive throughout. He didn't fear the Minister's admonition. He felt sorry for him, having to preach exclusively to the inmates of the Provincial Penitentiary. Here he suspected he needed to draw upon all his evangelical zeal and rhetoric to make any impression upon a majority who were hard, uncompromising and inherently bad types. Yes, William winced inwardly at his being labelled wicked, for, in his own mind, it was an adjective more aptly reserved for the likes of murderers, rapists and others of a depraved disposition: not a sailor who decides to part company with his ship. He thought of dear old Veck and felt in no doubt that the village parson would have more understanding of his predicament and not paint him so black as the zealous Pope. And so William's resolve for what lay ahead remained intact as he courteously thanked the clergyman for his attentions and bade farewell.

A couple of minutes later the custodian of the property book reappeared to announce that a ship's boat had just tied up down at the jetty and two gentlemen of Marines had commenced their ascent.

Fourteen

PORT TOBACCO, MARYLAND
OCTOBER 1862

"Whisky please bartender." It was market day and the stranger, a pale-skinned, thin-faced youth, had found his way into the cellar bar at Brawner's. He had been riding for some time and while he was attracted by the thought of a fortifying slug of liquor, the want of that was not the prime reason for his being here. Grasping his glass, he turned his back on the bar counter and appeared to make a few discrete enquiries among fellow drinkers who lounged close by. He had an air of self-assurance about him, a characteristic that seemed to belie a callowness which otherwise marked him out as a mere eighteen year old.

After a short time the youth meandered his way through the fug which hung about groups of the establishment's hard-drinkers. In the room's far extremity, at the end of the bar counter, a lone imbiber sat astride a high stool ruminating over what little remained of his corn whisky. The stranger sidled up to him, since he had been given to understand that this was the man he was seeking. He coughed to draw attention to himself. The seated fellow reacted immediately, directing a furtive and quizzical glance in the newcomer's direction.

"George Atzerodt?" enquired the stranger.

"You've found the very same," came the reply. "How can I be of service to you?"

"I was told by the gentleman at 'The Chimney House' that I'd probably find you here."

"Are you wanting a carriage painted?" George's interest in the stranger began to stir at the thought that he might be the bringer of work.

"No. What brings me here is…well, shall we say, it's a matter of some sensitivity," said the stranger, simultaneously lowering his voice.

The carriage painter eyed the youth with a searching look which portrayed his deep suspicion. "Who exactly are you and who directed you to 'The Chimney House'?"

"My name is Surratt…John Surratt. This morning I rode down from my home in Prince George's County for a meeting at Rich Hill Plantation."

"With the Captain?"

"Correct. With Captain Cox. I wished to introduce myself to him, to leave some important papers in his keeping and to discuss some matters I can only describe as being of a delicate nature. He suggested I should take the opportunity to meet you while in the neighbourhood. He directed me to Mister Barton's residence."

"Well, I've painted a carriage or two for Sam Cox and he seemed to be pleased with my work." George Atzerodt had a conception as to the stranger's particular interest, yet a strong sense of suspicion prevented him from speaking freely. He feared that it might be some sort of trap…that the stranger might be intent on lulling him into a false sense of certainty as a means of tricking him into disclosing details of his activities on the river. He needed to know more about young Mr Surratt.

"Pleased you say? Spoke highly of you, did Captain Cox, and told me if ever I needed a carriage or wagon put to rights then you were the fellow to seek out. He said you'd reupholstered and painted a vehicle for him back in July. A dowdy, lustreless old rockaway, by all accounts, but now a smart plum-coloured contraption that turns heads when he takes it for a spin. But he also told me you were as fine a boatman as a carriage painter."

It was a comment which provided George with the sort of reassurance he needed. How would Surratt have otherwise known about that particular job, its timing, the rich, plum finish. He began to feel more relaxed.

"I've no call for carriage painting but let me tell you a little about myself," continued the stranger, likewise sensing that he needed to fully convince George Atzerodt that he was friend, not foe. "Until recently I was attending seminary college near Baltimore but sadly, my father, a village postmaster in Prince George's County, passed away this summer. I had little choice but to curtail my studies and return home to take my father's place. I became the postmaster at Surrattsville, which, if you don't know it, lies the best part of thirty miles from here, and perhaps a dozen miles short of Washington. In addition, I was able to help my dear mother run the family tavern. To be honest, forsaking my studies came as no great loss but a significant advantage has flown from the situation in which I have found myself." John Surratt halted awhile, sensing that as a stranger in the place he was under the scrutiny of prying eyes, although it wasn't so much eyes as ears that troubled him. "I'm thinking we should go outside before I say much more," continued Surratt.

George pulled on his grimy, slouch hat and eased himself off his lofty perch. Moments later the two men emerged from the cellar bar and began to amble in the direction of the town square, well out of the earshot of Brawner's hard drinkers.

"Incidentally, where's your horse?" said George, noticing that only two old nags belonging to regulars were tethered outside the front of the hotel.

"I left it with the ostler's boy round the back," replied Surratt.

"That's as well," remarked George. "The place is full of thieves and it's a long walk back to Prince George's County."

Shortly, on the far side of the town square, the two men happened upon an unoccupied, rough-hewn bench set under an arching maple. As they approached it and set a striking, red carpet of newly fallen leaves rustling beneath their feet, John Surratt resumed his discourse.

"To put it bluntly, Mister Atzerodt, I suspect you will not be surprised when I describe myself as a good Confederate...nay, a fervent Confederate. And I'm led to believe by the good Captain Cox, another of that ilk and well respected as such in this county, that you are of the same persuasion...or at the very least, sympathetic to the Southern cause. Indeed, the Captain speaks highly of you as a valued ferryman, knowing as you do the topographical intricacies of the Virginia shore."

"I've done some night work for Sam Cox I'll not deny," said George, who was beginning to realise that he could safely lower his guard in the presence of his new acquaintance. "In fact he put a lot of work my way earlier this year, usually ferrying Southern agents with contraband mail bound for Richmond. I've also been across to Mathias Point with guns and brought couriers the other way on their journeys north. Yes...I know the river alright."

"So do I gather from what you say that work from the Captain has dried up?"

"He has a half-brother or foster brother named Jones who farms land along the Potomac shore, down at Pope's Creek. The fellow's got his own boat and is most energetic and committed when it comes to ferrying courier agents and such like across the river. Sam Cox holds him in high regard as a Confederate operative and tends to put a good deal of work his way. I can't argue with that but, as it happened, at the end of last year, Jones got into trouble with the authorities and did a spell in the Old Capitol Prison for seditious practices. Well, in truth that served me well because, with the Captain not having Jones at his disposal, he gave me a lot more assignments. It was just what I needed since the war has hit my business hard and the money I earn crossing the river is more than welcome…after all, I have a good woman and young daughter to support. I suppose, in these difficult times, folks are less inclined to worry about their carriages. Anyway, they say the Federal authorities got Thomas Jones to take an oath of allegiance before he left prison but I know for sure he's resumed his ferrying activities because my jobs have tailed off again."

"So how are you managing?" asked Surratt.

"With some difficulty," scoffed George. "We…that's my brother Johann and I, were crying out for work for much of this year. Since we couldn't make ends meet, Johann decided to seek work elsewhere. He landed a job with McPhail."

"McPhail?…James McPhail?"

"That's him. He's joined the staff of the provost marshal up in Baltimore."

"But surely…" began Surratt.

"Let me explain," interrupted the carriage painter, anxious to dispel in the other's mind any cause for concern. "My brother and I don't share the same politics. Johann knows I sympathise with the Confederate cause… with the Southern way of life…after all, we grew up in old Virginny. But bless him, he has no care for the ways of the Old South. He's a Union man. About five years ago he worked for a time as a junior overseer…not far from here, at The Land of Canaan Plantation. But he couldn't abide the brutal ways of the overseer, the way he spitefully horse-whipped the slaves and drew their blood for the most trivial of misdemeanours. It helped turn him against slavery."

"So what did your brother make of your clandestine river crossings and is there not a real danger that he might betray you?"

"No…none at all," said George with an air of confidence. "You see, he knew nothing of my secret ferrying. What he did know was that I love to fish the river at night. Indeed, in our early days in Port Tobacco, he would sometimes accompany me, until he quickly discovered he preferred to be tucked up at his lodgings with a good book. Anyway, whenever I went out at night, it was always Johann's belief that I'd gone fishing"

"So he had no knowledge of the likes of Captain Cox or Thomas Jones?"

"He knew Samuel Cox since he was one of our customers, but he walked away, back in the summer, when the Captain brought in that rockaway for painting. Wouldn't speak to him, although, thankfully, Cox was unaware that my brother had decided to make himself scarce when he saw him coming."

"What was all that about then?" enquired Surratt.

"Well, at the beginning of this year, one of the Captain's fugitive slaves was handed over to him by Union soldiers. Tied to a rope, the poor nigger was pulled back to Rich Hill behind the Captain's horse, then roped to a tree and whipped mercilessly for three hours under the wintry night sky. They say he was cut down before dawn and left to die. Johann couldn't come to terms with Cox's brutality. On reflection, I'm glad he walked away. Had he clashed with him that would have been an end to Sam Cox's custom, let alone the underground work he puts my way."

Surratt nodded. "I agree. From what I've heard of the Captain's reputation, and today gauged from first impressions, he wouldn't be a man to cross. But he is an influential man hereabouts and an impassioned Confederate, thank God. Now, what I want to say is that it is my earnest wish to help play a part in strengthening the underground route through Prince George's and Charles Counties. As far as I can see we have people with the will and capacity to do it. I for one, having succeeded to the job of postmaster at Surrattsville, feel I can use my position to good effect and my mother's tavern already serves as a safe haven. I also intend travelling to Richmond in the near future to make myself known to others with influence. Anyway, all being well, Mister Atzerodt, I anticipate they'll be a significant increase in the need for your services by the turn of the year. So pray keep that boat of yours in good order."

George Atzerodt's mood had changed since John Surratt came upon him in Brawner's bar. As he had come to realise that the stranger was genuine in what he had to say, his taciturnity had given way to a more animated and cheery demeanour.

"It's been my pleasure, Mister Postmaster, to have made your acquaintance and an honour to think you have gone out of your way to meet me," he exclaimed.

"Well, Mister Atzerodt," said Surratt. He hesitated. "May I call you George?"

"You may indeed and in return I'll call you John, my friend," said George, while proffering an outstretched arm. The gesture was reciprocated and hands firmly shaken.

"As I say, you have to thank your friend Captain Cox for suggesting I meet you. Of course, it helps for us servants of the Confederacy to be acquainted with others who play their part along the underground route. To be able to put faces to names, you understand. Now, I must be on my way but first will you join me in another whisky? An Old Bourbon perhaps?"

George Atzerodt raised his eyes and inclined his head in a manner which affirmed his interest in the proposition. And so the two men rose to their feet and began to amble back through the fallen leaves in the direction of Brawner's.

"Tell me, George, do you know a Doctor Samuel Mudd?"

George looked pensive as he allowed his right hand to ruffle his moustache and goatee, as if that were conducive to feeding the thought process. "Hmm...I know a George Mudd...worked on a buggy for him in what must have been the spring of sixty-one. He's a physician...lives over at Bryantown as I remember."

"No, this man's Samuel...definitely Samuel. And he lives about eight miles on the Washington side of Bryantown."

"Then the answer is no...I don't know him. Why do you ask, John?"

"It's just that he's another of our friends, another gentleman who shares our fervour. Again, on the Captain's recommendation, I'm going to call on him on my journey home to make his acquaintance. He's given me a letter of introduction."

John Surratt let his words tail away as the two men descended out of the afternoon light into the murky, frowsty, babbling lair that was Brawner's cellar bar.

Fifteen

HALIFAX AND BEYOND
LATE OCTOBER / NOVEMBER 1862

Friday 31st October 1862. For the past four days, since William Reynolds returned from the penitentiary, the crew of the *Cygnet* had busied themselves with final preparations and exercises to ready the gun-vessel for putting to sea. Dockyard artificers continued to work away assiduously, attending to a variety of defects. Parties of the ship's crew were variously engaged with the likes of shipping awning stanchions and reeving gear, staying topmasts, setting up rigging and backstays, making sail, reeving ropes and generally ensuring that all was in good order and Bristol-fashion. Others toiled at scraping masts and booms, while the stokers made preparations in the engine room or were employed yellow washing the ship's funnel.

William, meanwhile, had considered himself extremely fortunate when he stepped back on board and confronted the first lieutenant, late on the Monday forenoon. Indeed, the officer's instruction took him aback and gave him rare cause for belief in the goodness of people. This, bear in mind, was the same officer, the first luff, who had ensured William's black-listing after he was found asleep in the starboard breadroom; the same officer who, more recently, had been outraged by the actions which landed him in the Halifax Penitentiary. Nevertheless, it appears the first luff was so astounded by William's gaunt and lifeless appearance that he took pity on him. Despite the approach of midday, when the boatswain's mate would pipe the men to dinner, the first lieutenant immediately ordered William to the galley with a message for the ship's cook to provide him with some wholesome victualling forthwith. Added to which, the officer saw to it that he was excused duties for the remainder of the day, followed by two days of light duties. And so, come Thursday, when he was detailed to help stow the breadrooms and slop rooms, William had begun to feel more equal to the task.

The fateful day, Friday, had dawned calm and overcast with drizzle, clearing to a partially blue sky and opening clouds. It looked promising as the forenoon ran its course, with no sign of unsettled weather to wreck the forthcoming night's work. In the early afternoon the stewards' involvement in drawing and stowing spirits was completed ahead of schedule and William and others were detailed to assist in cleaning the upper deck. This was especially fortuitous since it gave William unhindered access to the ship's bow where he happened upon some coils of old rope that had been tucked away in a niche, just aft of the port hawsehole. These he gathered up for the purpose of disposal, with the exception of a seven feet length which was conveniently looped at one end. Conveniently, since William quickly realised it could be slipped over a brass cleat that was attached to the deck nearby and as such prove an invaluable aid to his escape plans. In essence, it would enable him to lower himself over the side, sufficient to access the water without causing an almighty splash which might alert others; and so he took particular care to secrete this now cherished accessory in a manner intended to avoid the later scrutiny of the inspecting petty officer.

And so the time grew closer. The day's frenetic activity began to wane, except in the engine room where the stokers busied themselves laying fires and getting up steam. Around his chest William set about strapping a waxed canvas wallet in which he placed the princely sum of seven sovereigns and a couple of florins. To these coins he added his palm cross, the Palm Sunday token given to him by Parson Veck in that last year at Forton; also his collection of family photographs...his Mother, Charlotte... Grandma Black...Uncle Charley. He dithered when he picked up the image of Uncle James. He decided it would unnerve him to look at that image if he succeeded in his imminent mission to part company with the Navy, knowing how unforgiving and enraged his uncle would become. And so he promptly returned it to his ditty box.

As to the money, itself, this had been locked away in William's ditty box where he had returned it for safe keeping after his abortive attempt to run a month previously. It had been its little brass key that he had taken with him to the penitentiary, the key which had been placed in his locker and entered in the property book. As to the money's accumulation, like many a single fellow he would lay aft each month to present himself to the paymaster and his clerk for the purpose of drawing compo. This was a not insubstantial proportion of his due wages. Yet, while not in the habit of leaving and saving his compo, in the manner of many a married shipmate, William was not profligate with his money when he went ashore. In consequence, what he had accrued in his ditty box was more than sufficient to serve him well in settling his forthcoming debts. Indeed, since resolving to run he had begun to wonder whether some intuitive process had been at work – or whether fate itself had intervened – to ensure he was equipped with such liquidity of ready money to facilitate his escape.

Eight bells…midnight…start of the middle watch. William Reynolds had found difficulty sleeping since his return from the penitentiary. Somehow he couldn't re-accustom himself to the roll of a hammock, the doleful ripple of water washing against the ship's side, the repetitive strike of its bells. But then, tonight, as eight strikes told of November succeeding October, sleep was the last thing William needed. He now had to stay awake until it became necessary to sneak onto the upper deck and there to keep himself well hidden until two o'clock showed its hand. He would lay in his hammock and wait for the half hours to be sounded, at least that is what he told himself. He daren't fall asleep. It therefore came as a shock, in what seemed a flicker in time, when he heard two bells, for it meant an hour had passed since midnight. He shuddered in realisation that he had succumbed to sleep. Thank God it was fleeting and he had woken. For the next half hour until a shade after three bells, he would talk to himself, perhaps silently reciting snippets of poetry that came to mind, like he was back in his childhood bed at Forton trying to memorise, parrot-fashion, the Friday collect.

Three bells…one thirty o'clock. William's heart was beginning to race. All seemed quiet on the lower deck save for the snoring of two of his messmates. Ten minutes or so went by. Time to go. William clambered out of his hammock and struggled into his uniform. Nobody stirred, not that it mattered too much as a good few broke their nightly slumber during the early hours to empty their bladders. William had resolved to make his way on deck but not in a skulking manner, since any observer on the graveyard watch, who spotted the likes of furtive behaviour, would consider it unnatural. No, he would move purposefully but seek to keep in the shadows, his intention being to avoid recognition. Donning his Scotch bonnet and making adjustments to the broad bow of his silk scarf, William could feel his heartbeat thumping in his chest cavity. He needed to go. He took a deep breath. The terror that gripped him as he made his ascent towards the night air was tangible. His brow was laden with beads of sweat. As he was about to emerge via the fore-hatchway onto the upper deck he was suddenly aware of footsteps scurrying aft: he hesitated until the sound of those steps receded, then rose up from below, in his anxiety almost drawing attention to himself by tripping on the hatch coaming. Correcting his stumble, he quickly moved further for'ard. There was no one in his forward line of sight. Glancing round, he noticed two men silhouetted in a location amidships, just aft of the ship's funnel on the port side. They were in earnest conversation and hadn't noticed him. He felt sure that one was the officer-of-the-watch doing his rounds. He continued to move forward with steadfast resolve, yet with his heart in his mouth, until a few yards short of the ship's prow. Up here in the bows William's luck held out: the area was deserted. He quickly slipped into the shadows beneath an overhanging wooden housing that mushroomed from the deck and marked the presence of a ventilation shaft and scuttle-hatch. He estimated that it was about five minutes short of two o'clock. He lay stock still. If anyone ventured by he reckoned on it being an even chance he would be discovered. All he could do would be to keep his head down and remain still.

Those next few minutes seemed endless, such was William's heightened state of anxiety and his longing to hear expected sounds: four bells to denote two o'clock, the middle of the graveyard watch, and two whistles to spring him into action. He yearned for both but in his own mind his preference was to first hear the ship's bells. They would be the precursor to Reuben's whistle and ready him for the task. On the other hand, were he to hear – or God forbid, imagine – whistles, without the comfort of first having heard the chiming of two o'clock, then he might be inclined to waver, to shrink from committing himself to the water. The thought of swimming a hundred yards was daunting. Yes, the Acadian witches had done well with the weather. The night was calm enough with just the hint of a light air, the heavens partly screened by broken cloud, the temperature in the mid-forties fahrenheit. Yet the waters of Halifax harbour would feel so much colder.

Four bells. Confirmation at last! Across the water the sail loft clock followed suit. Then quiet. Ten…twenty seconds passed. William waited, his emotions in suspense, his ears pricked up as if fearful of missing the signal. Then it came, two shrill blasts of a whistle. He removed his shoes and stripped to his undergarments amid feelings of fear and relief. He eased forward from his hiding place and looked aft. He could hear no sounds, no suggestion that the whistling had raised suspicions. Then he darted forward, retrieved the piece of rope he had squirreled away, looped it over the deck cleat, and fed the other end through the port scupper. It was a movement undertaken with a swiftness and dexterity impressive enough to have rivalled schoolmaster Wicketts' guile with his pocket watch. Then he hesitated for a split-second to glance behind him. All seemed quiet. He rolled his body up and over the ship's side, grasping the gunwale as he sought out the dangling rope below. His arms began to ache as they took his full weight. There was nothing further to grab hold of in edging his way down towards the rope that emerged at deck level below the bulwark. To the left he caught an oblique sight of the ship's figure-head, a young swan which seemed a ghostly white, nestling high in the shadows between stem and bowsprit. Seconds passed. William's arms and shoulders were at breaking point, his strength still compromised by having spent four weeks in the penitentiary. He didn't want to drop straight into the water for fear of the noise attracting attention. That is why the rope seemed a most helpful accessory. Yet he could see it dangling enticingly below. He needed to drop two or three feet and in so doing clasp hold of it firmly. If he missed then there would be an almighty splash, the louder for it being in the stillness of the night. He peered to right and left, urgently looking for an alternative hold…a ledge, an overhang in the blackness of the ship's side: that, or a foothold to ease the unbearable strain on arms and shoulders, something to carry him closer to that rope. It was an unavailing search. All seemed dark and shadowy. He could delay no longer. With eyes straining below, William released his grip on the gunwale. As he plummeted he snatched at the rope. He felt it brush the back of his left hand as contact with his lower body caused its vertical lie to ripple and thus evade his grasp. Almost simultaneously, he made to grab it with his other hand. He succeeded but in being pulled up short, his body weight caused a searing pain in already tortured shoulders. For a moment William clung motionless to his new station as he waited for that hurt to subside. Then, easing his legs about the rope he lent back, allowing his feet to contact the ship's side and in consequence assist his descent towards the beckoning brine. Yet it was a fleeting contact, given the receding curvature of the ship's bow, coupled with which William began to run out of rope. Suddenly he was dangling vertically, his feet brushing the water. He released his grasp on the rope and slipped quietly into the harbour.

The shock to his system was intense, such was the icy chill of the water, a shock which in other circumstances might have caused the recipient to cry out in horror. However, William managed to repress such a reaction as he struggled to cope with the jarring effect of the experience; and, while in an instant the initial shock eased, it was soon replaced by a burgeoning numbness, such was the freezing nature of the sea water. Minded that were he to dally the cold might cause his leg muscles to cramp, William quickly pushed off, choosing the breast-stroke ahead of the crawl on account of it offering the more surreptitious execution.

Perhaps a minute passed and William began to detect the shape of an open boat through the darkness. He adjusted his course, since the vessel stood a mite to starboard of the direction in which he was swimming. His hopes began to soar. As he drew ever nearer the boat his fear receded; conversely his excitement heightened, an emotion which somehow helped nullify, or at least render more bearable, the extreme cold permeating his body. Six or seven yards to go and suddenly a few whispered words carried over the water.

"Come on, Mister Willum." It was a familiar voice, a voice which spurred him on. William broke into a crawl and within seconds was being hauled into the bows of the skiff by two pairs of eager hands. For a short while he lay panting in the foresheets like a landed fish.

"You'z done reely well Mister Willum, dat's fo' sho.' I'z 'summin no folks seed y' leave de *Zignit*. Thar's fo' sartin no sounds, no c'motion coming from dat d'rection. Now, git hold of dis large piece o' linen an' dry yerself. An' thar's some dry clothes 'fore y' gits yer death o'cold."

"Thank you Reuben, my friend," gasped William quietly. "I think the plan worked well, thank God."

"'llow me t' intr'duce Mister Jackman," continued Reuben. "P'rhaps you'z hand him de 'scape fee fo' safe keepin'."

William looked up and nodded at the stranger who had already become seated, with oars shipped, their looms resting across his thighs. "Pleased to make your acquaintance, Mister Jackman."

"Henry's the name. Likewise, pleased to make yours Mister Reynolds."

"Give me a moment," said William in a tremulous voice as he set about divesting himself of his sodden undergarments. His teeth chattered because of the pervading chill gripping his body. "You'll have your money in a trice…just let me dry myself and don these other clothes. By the way, my name's William."

"Don' forgit t' keep 'em voices down," implored Reuben in a strained whisper. "I'z kinda thinkin' you'z berry happy t' be off de *Zignit*, Mister Willum."

"Yes," came the reply. "Yet, ironically, I've been treated well these past few days since returning from the penitentiary. I guess my disappearance won't be detected for the best part of two hours…until eight bells call the watch and idlers to muster, that is. I can't help thinking our first lieutenant will go mad when he finds out I've run, particularly after the leniency he's shown me."

The shivering that had beset William after tumbling into the foresheets soon ceased once he was clothed in the fisherman's jersey and old pantaloons thoughtfully supplied by Reuben. Then, from his canvas wallet, he extracted six sovereigns and placed them in the custody of Henry Jackman.

"Thank you," said the oarsman in a whisper. "Pleasure to do business with you William. Perhaps we should get under way now," he added, whereupon he cautiously put his shoulder to the oars and eased away, all the while building distance between skiff and gun-vessel.

"My cousin Tom's yawl is not too far away, out near the harbour mouth. It's looking as if there's little if any breeze to catch just here although I'm thinking conditions will be better once clear of the harbour. All being well, I'm inclined to believe that unless we run into Captain Semmes we'll be safe back in Lunenburg before the day's grown too old."

"Captain Semmes?" asked William, his interest aroused.

"Only jesting. The likes of him wouldn't be interested in a Nova Scotian fishing boat."

"Well who is he?" pressed William. "Some sort of pirate?"

"Yes, I suppose he is…well, I reckon the Yankees will see him as such. You see, Raphael Semmes commands a Confederate commerce raider and has built himself quite a reputation. They say this past month he's been using local waters as a cruising ground. He's caused mayhem, seizing and burning Federal merchant ships and whalers, and just south east of here, by all accounts."

As Henry Jackman put his back into rowing and Reuben took on the role of lookout, William – exhausted by the day's and night's exertions – took up the cloth he had been given to dry himself, screwed it up into a cushioning bundle and stuffed it under the breast hook against the bow apron. Then, seizing upon a piece of oilcloth, he pulled this about him for warmth, curled himself up in the foresheets and rested his head upon his makeshift pillow. Within no time he was asleep.

★ ★ ★

Lunenburg, Nova Scotia. Saturday 1st November 1862, post meridiem. A shaft of eerily mellow, late afternoon sunlight broke through the lumpy, yet broken cloud cover. Streaming out of the western sky that was the backdrop to the little fishing port, it lit up the dimpling harbour in mutable colour. From his vantage point on Tom Driscoll's returning fishing boat, William Reynolds thought how warm and welcoming was the scene ahead; and of how the colourful play of light on doughy grey water strangely complemented the hues of the timber buildings hugging the low ridge above the harbour. William felt heartened by what he saw.

The fore and aft rigged yawl had made steady, if not rapid, progress down the coast and then across Mahane Bay once the three occupants of the accompanying skiff had scrambled aboard. That had been just before three in the morning. William had exchanged opening pleasantries with its owner, Tom Driscoll, before falling again into the land of nod, a slumber that lasted until late in the forenoon. Thereafter it appeared to the Englishman that Driscoll was a man of few words as he and his cousin busied themselves with the demands of the sailing boat. As for William and Reuben, they sat in the sternsheets where the negro instructed the former in the rudiments of mending nets as they set about repairing a badly snagged seine net.

Approaching one of the many robust timber landing stages, Reuben made sure the boat's stuffed canvas fenders were suitably in place, then leapt onto the staging and secured the vessel.

"Get yourself off the boat, William, and taste your freedom…but I'll wager here in Lunenburg it'll taste like it smells. Fish, the smell of fish!" Tom Driscoll's deep bass voice was followed by a hearty chuckle. He had just uttered as many words as he had spoken since first setting eyes on William some twelve hours since. A large man with thick bushy side whiskers, a fleshy nose and a complexion turned ebony by the nature of his trade, he struck William as being as tough as local granite. Yet his eyes, the window to his soul, sparkled with a gentleness that hinted at there being a caring and softer side to him.

"It smells and tastes grand to me. A far cry from the smells of the lower deck and that wretched penitentiary," replied William. "In actual fact it's redolent of Portsmouth Town Quay. It reminds me of my childhood."

"Then be off with young Reuben here. You'll stay with him, for the time being, until you decide on your next move. And remember, part of the arrangement is that you put in some work for us over the next few weeks in exchange for which you'll get your meals and a bed in Reuben's loft. But tomorrow's the Sabbath and I'm guessing, William, that if you're a God-fearing man you'll want to join us at church...to thank the Lord for your liberty, your deliverance to Lunenburg and, like the rest of us, to seek forgiveness for your sinning. Undoubtedly all four of us have sinned this past night...we three for actively abetting your desertion."

It seemed to William that apart from the latent kindness he detected in Tom Driscoll, here was a man who thought deeply about his actions and was possessed of a strong sense of conscience. Yet while willingly engaged in clandestine deeds, assisting desertions such as his own, he clearly felt a dire need to appear remorseful before his Maker. Some of course would see it as a puzzling contradiction; some might consider him a hypocrite.

"I will surely wish to attend church," said William, "for it has always been my custom to do so on the Sabbath. But it is you, Mr Driscoll, and your cousin, Henry, I need..."

"Tom," interjected the fisherman. "Everyone calls me Tom except Reuben. I fear his deference has become ingrained by subjugation."

"What I am saying is that I remain indebted to you both...and to Reuben and his friend Jake. Right now, setting foot on this landing stage in the most delightful of places, freed of the wretched *Cygnet*, I for once feel truly liberated and cock-a-hoop with my lot. Most significantly, I'm ready to make my own choices in life."

"You sound like Bunyan's joyous pilgrims reaching the land of Beulah, in readiness to cross over the river to find the Celestial City," piped up Henry Jackman. It was a remark which spoke favourably of his being well-read but was lost on his three companions.

"All I would say, William Reynolds, is that a few days' hard work on the dock-side, starting Monday, should work wonders at assuaging your feelings of indebtedness," exclaimed Tom. It was a remark which set all four laughing. "By the way, William, is this yours by any chance?" continued Tom, as he bent down to gather up a little willow cross that had fallen onto the staging.

William nodded in affirmation as, recognising the little symbol Parson Veck had handed him on that distant Palm Sunday, he held out his hand to accept the keepsake. The photographs of his loved ones had become wet during his swim and he had laid them out to dry as the fishing boat plied its way across Mahane Bay. Minutes earlier, in following Reuben off the vessel, William had returned the items to the canvas wallet and, in so doing, must have failed to notice the little palm tumble out. As he looked at it in his outstretched hand he realised that time and brittleness had finally told on his flimsy memento, for it had broken in two. As long as it remained in his keeping that breakage would be a constant reminder of the day William secured his freedom.

Tom Driscoll smiled as he contemplated the broken little cross. "See you in church tomorrow William. Sleep well tonight."

"I will," came the reply. "And thank you."

★ ★ ★

Halifax, Nova Scotia. Saturday 1st November 1862, post meridiem. H.M.S *Cygnet*'s officer-of-the-watch picked up his pen and dipped it in his inkwell, simultaneously taking up a wad of blotting paper in his left hand. He lent over his desk where the ship's log lay open awaiting the first entry relevant to the afternoon The officer proceeded to record that the vessel remained moored to a buoy in Halifax harbour. There was blue sky overhead but strewn with detached, opening clouds, while a light to moderate breeze blew from a northerly direction. The air temperature was 52 degrees fahrenheit. He dipped his pen again and, on the right hand side of the page under the 'Remarks' column, he wrote *Mustered Ship's Company and found Wm. Reynolds (s.s. asst.) absent.*

In fact, evidence pertaining to the run man's flight had been discovered for'ard prior to the muster. During the forenoon, as final preparations were being made to put to sea, that discovery had been the cause of wrathful expression among some senior members of the ship's crew, not least the enraged First Lieutenant and the loathsome Master-at-Arms.

At 3.55pm the *Cygnet* loosed and made sail to topgallants and braced her yards abox. Fifteen minutes later she slipped from her buoy, filled on the port tack and proceeded out of harbour in company with H.M.S *Medea*. At 4.30pm she had passed George's Island and by 5.00pm, the Maugher Light. An hour later, with the breeze now north-easterly, gentle to moderate, the *Cygnet* was in two reefs of topsails. By 7.15pm she had altered course to south west by west. Trimmed and in gaff sails, her destination was Rum Cay.

★ ★ ★

William Reynolds wondered whether the smell of fish, which Tom Driscoll had jovially spoken of pervading Lunenburg, was anywhere to be found with such potency as prevailed in Reuben Miller's modest quarters: for they comprised the rather cramped loft space above a workshop where fish were regularly gutted, split and salted. Added to which, for over a century, the building had formerly been used for the smoking of fish. It meant that the heavily impregnated floor and roof timbers, between which the lodger laid his woolly head, were themselves an intense and constant reminder of the old smokehouse.

Reuben's place was at least dry and warm and William found he slept far sounder than he had managed in the penitentiary or during his brief return to the lower deck. Commencing that first Monday, he and Reuben would descend the rickety outside staircase that led from loft to rear yard, a descent closely accompanied by wheeling, squawking gulls breakfasting on fish offal that lay in open bins. Somehow the salty air had a greater piquancy than seemed the case in Halifax, sharpened perhaps by an awareness that life for the citizens of Lunenburg was at the very least, touched, and at the most, steeped, in the sea and ships. Very few trod an existence not inextricably affected by the ways of the sea, by Neptunian caprice; and hence most appeared possessed of an intuitive weather-eye. Sometimes, as in most seafaring communities, life could be hard, occasionally tragic. And so, maybe all of this explained why – to the outsider – a close fellowship was evident among these seafaring folk, an amity that fostered trust and of sharing and exchange beyond the norm: an attitude of give and take, of one good turn deserving another.

The strong sense of community became apparent to William almost immediately, not least in terms of the kind of work put his way by Tom Driscoll. As for Reuben he was not committed to work for any individual but was rarely without jobs since he was seen as trustworthy and hard-working. And so he was shared throughout the fishing community, any member in need of labour having to wait in line and defer to others who had registered an earlier claim to his own.

"I'z down on dis or dat stage dis morning, Mister Willum," he would say as, bleary-eyed, William would clamber out of his truckle bed. "Mister Langton, or Mister Zwicker or Mister Smith" – or whoever – "needs me to mend a scoop net or to repair and tar some lobster traps or to do a spot of caulkin'" – or whatever.

And so at first light they would go their different ways, William always taking the same route along the waterfront, Reuben to his particular calling along this jetty or that. Invariably it was a peaceful, if not eerie prospect, a forest of silhouetted masts and flaccid canvas rising sentinel from a softening, yet gunmetal-grey harbour, the stone dockside and timber staging littered with all manner of things nautical: crabbing nets, lobster buoys and pots, coils of rope, cork, blocks and fenders, boxes of empty scallop shells, old dunnage. Occasionally a feral cat would be disturbed while rapt in a fishy breakfast salvaged from yesterday's discarded waste. Depending on the state of the tide, a fishing boat might be seen departing the harbour. Tart smells quickened the olfactory senses: briny and fishy in the main, laced with that of kelp and exposed tidal mud. If the weather was clement and cloud cover sparse the emerging light of the new day would radiate from the watery far horizon, softly illuminating the Atlantic heavens and casting a tremulous shimmer upon the ocean. If inclement and wet, or if beset with the sea mist or fog that troubled this coast, then the forenoon's persisting grey garb could darken the mood of those unaccustomed to living one's life in such a remote fishing community: even for the likes of William Reynolds, himself long since divorced from the company of loved-ones and the hustle and bustle of town life. Conversely, when the sun shone and the day progressed there could be a vibrant charm about the picturesque little settlement.

"Good morning, William," would be Tom Driscoll's usual greeting from his customary perch. Assuming the weather was dry he would normally be seated upon the bollard to which he invariably secured his boat's painter. Here he would be whiling away a quiet half hour smoking an old meerschaum tobacco pipe, the yellowed appearance of the ecume de mer testimony to its antiquity. On William's approach Tom would draw the bit from his mouth, tamp the bowl's content then carefully set the pipe aside for a moment as he gave thought to how William might be best employed. In actuality there never seemed to be many chores that Tom wanted done: a few nets needing attention maybe, a few blocks oiled, a spot of varnishing, the boat's deck requiring a clean and then a scrubbing with vinegar. On two occasions, when Henry was indisposed, Tom required William to go out in the yawl to bait and re-set some of his lobster traps, which he found interesting enough. But on most occasions Tom would simply direct his new-found attendant elsewhere.

"Take yourself along the quay, William, and seek out the Johnson brothers," said Tom one morning. "They've got a little office room in that blue painted building with the lofty smoke stack. The elder brother, Theo, tells me they need someone to do a spot of painting and oiling on their winch barge over yonder." Another time it was "Well, William, I was partaking of a little spirituous beverage last evening with the fellow in charge of Slip No 2. He asked me whether I could point him in the way of any casual labour. His sawyers and carpenters are working all hours to keep up to schedule building that new schooner up on the chocks. I said I knew an ideal man, meaning yourself, William. Well, it seems there's more than a day's work by the sounds of it, clearing up masses of timber waste and such like, especially in and around the sawpit. Make yourself known, if you would, in the little green hut with the up-ended dory leaning against it. Tell the gentleman at the high desk that I sent you and for what purpose."

Having allocated his charge a day's work, Tom Driscoll would take up his pipe again until Henry Jackman showed up which was invariably a few minutes later.

It had occurred to William that this greater tendency for him to be despatched to labour for others pointed to a system of making mutual concessions – of sharing labour in this fashion – being prevalent in this close-knit community and, indeed, commonplace among the fishing folk and dockside trades. Nothing wrong with that, in principle, thought William. Perhaps Tom Driscoll, having insufficient work to put his way was simply leasing him out, leaving him scope to call in past favours. Or maybe he received straight payments from the likes of the Johnson brothers or the slipway proprietor: nothing wrong...indeed, it showed resourcefulness, it made sense. Yet in William's assessment it also appeared to reinforce the perception that, however outwardly idyllic, this was very much an inward-looking, insular sort of place in which he could never put down roots.

It was now the sixteenth of the month, a Sunday. In his short time here, William had become accustomed, on the Sabbath, to climb the hill up into town to attend morning service. His destination was St John's Anglican Church, an exquisite old building and former settlers' meeting house clad in white-painted clapboard. But for it possessing a tower, as opposed to a spire, it reminded William of Forton parish church and, of course, not least, because of its dedication to Saint John. Reuben would be at his side. On this particular Sunday it was no different, although the service was not one to which the negro had an affinity. It was at variance with the kind of Methodist persuasion that prevailed among the Southern slaves and their free negro counterparts yet, for all that, this was a house of God – the overriding consideration – and therefore enough to set that proclivity aside.

After the service, and with it being a bright and mild morning, William and Reuben lingered awhile outside the church portals to chat with the rector. Having exchanged a few pleasantries they took their leave, only to inadvertently stumble into the path of the approaching Tom Driscoll and a lady companion – themselves similarly delayed in their departure on account of neighbourly communion.

"Ah, William," exclaimed Tom as, simultaneously, he pulled on his decidedly crumpled felt hat, only to then remove and doff it towards the clergyman in a departing gesture. "Thank you, rector. Good day to you, sir." Then, returning his attentions to William, he proceeded to introduce his companion. "Let me introduce you, William, to my dear wife, Ruth." Then, before William had a chance to respond he turned to his spouse. "Ruth, my dear, this is William Reynolds, the young English gentleman from Halifax I told you about."

"Good morning, ma'am," said William, taking the lady's hand. "I'm very pleased to make your acquaintance." William considered the woman looked sickly, her complexion – beneath a shock of ginger hair – as pallid as her husband's was dark- hued, her delicate nose as bony and aquiline as was Tom's thick and bulbous.

"You know, Reuben, of course, my dear," added Tom, beckoning towards the negro. "Perhaps you would care to walk on with him for a minute or two while I speak to William."

Ruth Driscoll smiled meekly at the two younger men before deferring to her husband's bidding, Tom and William following on a few paces behind.

"Coming across you a moment ago made me think that it was opportune to speak with you, William. After all, we are at the start of your third week here," began Tom. "If you haven't already done so, you should be giving due consideration to how you intend spending the rest of your life. Of course, for all I know, you may wish to remain in Nova Scotia or venture far. It's a vast country. You may even care to stay longer here in Lunenburg. Not that I have any call on your time, my boy. You've worked well since you arrived and were you minded to remain, I would have no trouble finding you some permanent employment."

It seemed to William, as he and Tom descended the hill past cheerfully painted timber framed buildings, that the town's founding settlers must have considered it the location to put down their roots in perpetuity. Yet, however halcyon and quaint a place it might appear on a fine day, and notwithstanding Tom's pledge about work, William had already made up his mind to be on the move. He had been reflecting on the matter for some days. Perhaps it was because he was now widely travelled; he had seen a little of the world and what it had to offer. He had sampled a flavour and was enticed by the thought of seeing more. Above all, there came again and again into his mind the tormenting thought that he should sate his long standing wish to pull on a soldier's tunic.

"Thank you for broaching the matter, Tom," said William, "but to be honest, for all its charm, I could not envisage remaining here forever. I need to move on but I'm not sure where. They talk of America being a land of opportunity and I'm wondering whether I should try my luck there. I've no particular skills or talents but I can muster plenty of endeavour to do well…well enough to have no cause for self-reproach."

"I understand what you say about America and it's easily reached. But be warned, William, the United States are war-torn, brother fighting brother."

"I know, but strange to say it's that I find alluring."

"What…you mean you'd enlist?" said Tom with surprise.

"It was a boyhood dream of mine to join the army," came the reply.

"But fighting for a foreign country?.. and where do your sympathies lie? North or South? I'm told opinion in Great Britain is divided on the issue, but with support weighted towards the secessionist states. And, of course, your cotton industry is in hell of a pickle because of the Federal blockade of southern ports. There's no doubt sympathies around here are markedly secesh and Halifax offers a safe haven for Confederate ships."

William looked pensive. "As for taking up arms for another country I fear that if I seek to satisfy that old boyhood desire my circumstances leave me with little alternative at present. I cannot take the Queen's Shilling. As for allegiance, I've spoken at length to Reuben and, in view of the harrowing yarns he's told me, I'd be inclined to enlist in the Union Army. It's lamentable how many of the Southern planters treat their slaves. But first I want to get an impression of what life can offer, what opportunities are available, in one of the big cities. A civilian job could be the answer…I'd have to see… but from what Reuben tells me, enlisting in the Union Army comes with a fine bounty. They say time is a great healer and one day I intend to put my transgressions far behind me, return to England and look my folks in the eye. But first I need to make my way in the world, to redeem myself and to secure the means of paying my passage back across the ocean. I very much doubt I could make sufficient headway here in Lunenburg, yet the Union bounty would give me a good start."

"I like you, William, and, to be frank, I find it troubling that you might be prepared to place yourself in grave danger," said Tom. "No good having money in the bank and lying dead on some battlefield. But I can see you have made up your mind to move on and I respect your decision." At this point Tom stopped in his tracks and squinted into the distance. He then raised his right arm and pointed over the rooftops. "Do you see that steamer moored out in the harbour? Well, her skipper is a distant relative of Henry. The vessel arrived here on Friday evening from Ship Harbour with a cargo of sawn timber and laths bound for Boston. She's to lie here until Tuesday afternoon's high tide. Tomorrow a consignment of grindstones is to be winched on board. Now, as it happens, Henry tells me the *Snowgoose*...as she's called...is in desperate need of a cook, hers having been taken off at Halifax with some severe ailment and admitted to hospital. Well, I'm inclined to think your background as a naval steward could make you an attractive candidate."

William was for the moment speechless. Tom called ahead to his wife and Reuben to tarry awhile. The fisherman had suddenly presented a simple enough proposition to William but one that could have a profound effect on his future and see him whisked away from Lunenburg in little more than forty-eight hours. A proposition which, in a few days, would see him step ashore in the United States of America.

"Think about it, my boy," remarked Tom, simultaneously patting the younger man on the shoulder as, once again, he began ambling down the hill. "But don't take too long about it. You see, if you're interested, I'm seeing Henry later this afternoon and I'll need to get him to speak to his cousin as soon as possible. To delay might see the skipper of the *Snowgoose* enlist a new cook, assuming he's not done so already."

"Thank you but I don't need time," said William, impulsively, as he shuffled forward to catch up Tom. "I'm thinking the chance opportunity to sail to Boston may not present itself again for a while. I should grasp it...yes, please speak to Henry this afternoon, Tom. I may not be a cook but my stewarding put me in close contact with the galley and you can tell Henry that, in good naval tradition, I make a grand plum-duff."

Without further rumination and discussion upon the issue, the two men increased their gait and had soon caught up with Reuben and Tom's good lady who had reached the bottom of the hill, close to the waterfront.

"Leave it to me William," shouted Tom, resoundingly, in his deep voice, as, re-united with his wife and with a wave – coupled with a demure glance from Ruth – the couple went their separate way.

"So wot was dat 'bout?" enquired Reuben, as he and William began to retrace their steps towards the negro's modest lodgings.

"Well, it seems there may be a ready opportunity for me to leave for America," exclaimed William, elatedly, being unable to contain his excitement. He then proceeded to recount to Reuben what Tom had said about the *Snowgoose* and her need for a cook. "Tom's going to get Henry to speak to his relative about my suitability. I'm hoping he'll have some news for me in the morning."

"I'z ruther not see y'go, Mister Willum, dat's fer sho'. But I'z wish y'well an' you'z go wid my blessin' if you'z gwine inlist in dat Nawth'n army… de army o' dat kin'-hearted Mister Linc'n whose pr'claimed t' 'mancipate allers nigger slaves in de 'cessionist States. An' now we'z nearly done wid '62 an' mebbe dem better times they'z a'comin.' When de year o' '63 dawns bright, my brudders an' sisters in Car'lina an' elsewhere, po'things, will sho'ly be ready t'climb de steps o' de blessed Temple o' Freedom…climb de steps, dey will, wid thar po' l'il chillen! Oh, Lawd, yes…an' all thanks t' Mister Linc'n. Oh, yessuh…praise de Lawd! Oh, blessed Jehovah!"

"I don't know whether I'll join the army, Reuben, but what you have told me about the recruitment money whets my appetite. Yet, whatever happens, I have this feeling that America will hold opportunities for me to make good. Strange, in a way," said William, thoughtfully, "that you struggled to be free of the Country whereas I could be seeking it out. I'll know more tomorrow, my friend, with any luck."

"Jes don' go gittin' yerself kill'd, Mister Willum, if you'z gwine inlist in dat Mister Linc'n's army. I'z reely scairt you'z might git hurt."

"I'll do my best to keep out of harm's way, Reuben, whatever I choose to do."

Monday morning broke fine but misty. William was up with the lark, having spent a restless night, his wakefulness punctuated by thoughts that he might just be on the brink of yet another life-changing event. Tom, having yet to light his pipe, was seated, as usual, on the landing stage bollard, his feet resting on a coil of old sisal rope. An upturned oyster box lay beside him on which he had carefully spread a cotton handkerchief, with the exactness one might exercise in adorning a dining table with fine damask linen. Onto the 'kerchief he was paring slices of tobacco from a rope of navy cut, his implement a stout-looking clasp knife, its whalebone handle finely embossed with scrimshaw.

"You're a mite early this morning," said Tom, in a tone that caused his words to fall somewhere between a question and a statement of fact and which William took to be the former.

"I couldn't sleep," William replied, perfunctorily and without elaboration, his interest taken by the ornate appearance of Tom's knife handle.

"Carved it myself," said Tom, noticing William's curiosity. "Years ago, in idle moments. It's a banker…a Banks schooner, scudding before a gale. By the way, William, I did raise the matter of the *Snowgoose*'s cook with Henry. He promised to speak to his relative, the skipper, as a priority. Seems he's staying with Henry while his ship's in harbour, so I'm kind of expecting my cousin to have some news for you when he shows up. We're going out to do a spot of fishing once the visibility improves and I need to look at some of the lobster traps. You may like to join us," added Tom, as he drew upon his newly lit pipe.

Tom proceeded to explain the convoluted relationship between Henry Jackman and the master of the *Snowgoose*, his words interspersed with reeky, aromatic exhalations that spiralled lazily into the still, damp morning air. It transpired that Henry and Tom were first cousins on Henry's maternal side. As for Henry's relationship with the captain, William gathered it was an obscure cousinship on the Jackman side but in all truth he couldn't give a tinker's cuss about the intricacy of it all. Just as long as Henry brought some influence to bear upon his distant kinsman.

After fifteen minutes or so, the creaking of loose timbers preceded Henry Jackman's emergence through the mist. William looked at Henry intently as he approached, his face etched with expectation. Momentarily he thought how fit, how in rude health, he seemed to be. For Henry's frame was lean and muscular-looking, his face deeply bronzed like his cousin Tom's from unremitting exposure to a littoral and sea-faring existence.

"G'morning, cousin," said Tom. The inflection in his voice hinted that something beyond mere reciprocation of the greeting was expected. Indeed, Tom's supposition was that Henry would immediately report upon the outcome of his exchange with the master of the *Snowgoose*. And so it proved, without any overt prompting.

"Good morning Tom…and a good one to you, William, which I sure guess it promises to be if you're still bent on finding your way to America," remarked Henry, his set and well-chiselled features breaking into a broad smile.

"By crikey…it seems you're destined to follow your dream then," said Tom. His attention was directed at William, now momentarily struck motionless and lost for words by the shock of his supposed good fortune. "Tell us more, Henry…tell us more," implored Tom.

"Well, I'm assuming William is still sure about going to Boston?" replied Henry, expecting William to break his silence with confirmation or denial.

William hesitated, glancing from Henry to Tom as if in anticipation of the latter's further countenance upon his desire to leave Lunenburg. Tom rightly sensed from William's expression that he felt uneasy and sought reiteration of the sanction already expressed on the Sabbath.

"Remember what I told you, yesterday, William. You've worked well since being here and Henry and I have no further call on your labours. Follow your heart. Go make your way in the world. You are eager to redeem your reputation and let's be frank…you won't do that spending a lifetime in Lunenburg."

"Thank you, Tom," said William, immediately glancing across to Henry. "I haven't changed my mind. No, it is my earnest wish to make a fresh start in America, if you're both in agreement."

"Well, we are William, as cousin Tom has just confirmed," assured Henry.

"Good, well that's that settled," said Tom, somewhat impatiently, as he ceased smoking his pipe and proceeded to empty and clean the bowl with the aid of his clasp knife. "So, for God's sake, Henry, tell us what arrangements you've made with the master of the *Snowgoose*."

"Your journey to Boston in the *Snowgoose* is not a problem," began Henry, "and you have the choice of either travelling as a passenger or working your passage as the ship's cook. You'll doubtless gather from cousin Tom, here, that Jacob Burns, the master, is another relative of mine. Well, whenever he puts into Lunenburg, he tends to come ashore for a while and stays in my spare room. He says it's good from time to time to get off that old hulk he commands. He leaves it in the capable hands of the first mate and we spend time downing a few glasses of whisky and exchanging news. That was the case this past weekend. Anyway, Jacob was up long before I stirred this morning and back on board the *Snowgoose* but I took the opportunity to have a talk with him last evening…about you, William…before we turned in. I have to say I was quite candid about your circumstances…no shilly-shallying, you understand…but they raised no qualms as far as old Jacob was concerned. He said it wouldn't be the first time, or in all likelihood, the last, that he helped a deserter on his way. To be honest, I didn't think I'd have a problem with him, seeing how many times I've shown him hospitality…and, would you believe, I always seem to provide the whisky.

Strange how the old fellow is such a tight-fisted bastard when he holds a ticket to command a coastal trader and must draw a decent enough wage."

"So, what's this about William having a choice about the way he travels?" said Tom, with continuing fretfulness over his cousin's failure in getting to the crux of the matter.

"Well, it appears the *Snowgoose* is still in need of a ship's cook but Jacob is minded to draft one of his deck-hands into the job on account of the fellow having expressed a liking for cooking and for filling the vacancy. After all, he says the need is only temporary. The regular cook was due to finish his term aboard the vessel on reaching Boston. Once there the *Snowgoose* is due to take on a new cook. So, in those circumstances, the only option available to William would be to take a berth as a passenger, excepting that would cost two or three pounds and…"

"But I've no more than a few shillings to my name," interrupted William, with dejection in his voice.

"Ah, but hear me out, William. When I told Jacob of your previous career, as a ship's steward and of your apparent eagerness to fill the position of ship's cook, he seemed more than happy to dismiss the notion of appointing this deck-hand to his galley."

"Then he'll take me on as cook in exchange for free passage?"

"Yes, he will."

"But presumably he'll want to interview me?"

"No. The job is yours…on the strength of what I told him about you. Just call by this morning. I can't point out the *Snowgoose* because of this mist but she's now tied up at the end of the fourth pier beyond ours. Ask for Captain Burns, or, if he's busy, the first mate…fellow by the name of Hodges. Say that I sent you. Say that you lack the means to be a paying passenger but you'd be pleased to be taken on as ship's cook for the sailing to Boston."

"Thank you, Henry. I'm very appreciative. And thank you, Tom."

"Think nothing of it," said Henry, a comment which drew a murmur of concurrence from his cousin.

"Just one thing," said Tom. "You'll have to write us a few lines once you've settled down in Massachusetts or find yourself sitting around some distant army camp fire. Reuben, Henry and I will want to know how you're faring. Just be sure to think long and hard if you continue to harbour thoughts of fighting for the Union, young feller. There's sure to be easier and safer ways of earning a crust."

"That I'll promise," said William, being only too aware of Tom's sincerity and caring nature. "I'll certainly pen you all a letter when the time is right."

"Now, you'd best forget about coming out on the boat with us today," urged Tom. "It's more important that you pay a visit to the *Snowgoose* and introduce yourself to Captain Burns."

"Oh, there is another thing," piped up Henry. "The *Snowgoose's* presence at Boston will be short-lived. She's to discharge her cargo before taking on livestock for conveyance to Baltimore. Meat on the hoof bound for the quayside slaughterhouses…to help feed a hungry army and navy according to Jacob. Now," continued Henry, "Jacob says you're welcome to remain onboard until they reach Baltimore, excepting the *Snowgoose* will have taken on its new cook by then and he'll need to find you other work. But that's not a problem…as matters stand, Jacob lacks sufficient hands to tend and feed the bullocks."

"Baltimore might be a preferred destination to Boston. Too many bloody Irishmen for the liking of most Nova Scotians," said Tom with a chuckle.

William appeared bemused, prompting Tom to qualify his remark.

"Scottish heritage, you understand…we Nova Scotians have a predominantly Scottish heritage. But no, seriously, that's something to think about, William. Baltimore is more at the heart of things with Washington, Philadelphia…even New York, at no great distance."

"Conversely," said the well-read Henry, "the American philosopher and writer, Wendell Holmes, has described the State House in Boston as the hub of the solar system. It's a city with a fine historical and cultural reputation and I'm told plenty of jobs are to be had in its great wealth of manufactories."

"Well, that's as may be," was Tom's retort, "but I'm sure William will have time to ponder on what's better for him as he labours over his galley stove."

The *Snowgoose's* anchor cable was shackled to a mooring buoy some distance off the adjacent landing stage. As William sauntered along the staging, the outline of the steamboat loomed out of the mist and with his approach the cranking noise of an operating manual winch grew louder. At relatively close quarters, from the end of the jetty, the *Snowgoose* appeared a good-sized vessel, if a trifle down at heel. An old side-wheeler, the timbers of its port wheel housing – now largely grey and laid-bare – appeared to be in need of urgent attention. Dulled, salt-worn remnants of former colours sadly pointed to a time when the old tub might have ridden the waves gaily painted and peacock-proud from stem to stern.

William recognised the winch barge as that belonging to the Johnson brothers. He wondered if, without his recent oiling and greasing of its working parts, it might have made an even greater din than it was currently emitting. He beckoned to one of the winch crew and gestured that he wished to board the ship, even shouted conversation being all but impossible above the ongoing racket. The fellow whose attention he had attracted promptly grasped the meaning of his gesticulation and pointed to a dory tied up below the landing stage. Then he moved his arms in a fashion to imitate the act of rowing. The visitor descended the landing stage stairs, untied the dory's painter and clambered into the little open boat. Quickly engaging the oar shafts in their crutches, he began rowing across the short intervening distance separating the paddle-steamer from the end of the jetty. Within minutes he was alongside the vessel's port side ladder and hailing a seaman who seemed busily engaged overhead in some aspect of work to do with the port gunwale. Being unable to communicate above the noise of the labouring winch, the deck-hand grasped the manropes and descended the ladder to the point where conversation was possible and William could make himself understood.

"I've come to seek an audience with Captain Burns, assuming he's available," the visitor called out, stridently. "Could you tell him it's William Reynolds. I think he's expecting me, although, I confess, at no particular time. It's about passage to Boston."

The seaman nodded and scrambled back on board. Several minutes later a young lad appeared who William took to be the regular side-boy, for he made his descent into the dory, secured it and then assisted the visitor in finding his footing on the ship's ladder. Once beyond the entry port, William was immediately confronted by the deck-hand to whom he had already spoken.

"I've talked to the Master. He was up in the poop 'tween main and mizzen. Says he'll be pleased to make your acquaintance and will meet you in the chart room. So if you'd please accompany me aft."

As William followed in the wake of his escort he was astonished by the standard of cleanliness and the immaculate appearance of gleaming brasswork and of deck timbers whitened by constant holystoning. His incredulity stemmed from the marked contrast between the poor state of repair of the ship's hull and the apple-pie order which now confronted him. Then, on reaching the poop and, at its break, the vessel's uncovered wheel, a rotund middle-aged figure appeared ahead at the recessed chart room door. Here was further cause for disbelief, William being taken aback when this decidedly scruffy fellow ordered the deck-hand back to his duties and proceeded to introduce himself as Jacob Burns, Master of the *Snowgoose*. In terms of the figure he cut, Skipper Burns was not what his visitor had expected. He was a corpulent little man who probably stood no higher than five feet and three inches in his stockings. He wore an old fashioned benjamin overcoat that had seen plenty of better days and in its bulkiness did nothing to ameliorate his heavy appearance. Yet his demeanour seemed pleasant enough, his fleshy, weather-beaten cheeks creased in a smile and framed by bushy, brindled side-whiskers. Momentarily William thought his bearing had the feel of someone's favourite uncle. It was also his quick assessment that he had probably seen a decade more summers than his distant cousin, Henry. He thought he was probably about fifty.

"So you are interested in passage to Boston, young Reynolds?" said Captain Burns. "I told Henry Jackman that I could take you as a paying passenger…two pounds, seven shillings and sixpence all found would be the fare. Otherwise, I understand you might be interested in working your passage as ship's cook."

"I've little money, sir," said William, "and I'd need to…"

"Come in here," interjected the skipper, ushering William into the chart-room. "Out of this wretched chill and more importantly the noise of that machinery. We're a little short of ballast, having discharged some cargo in Halifax. It left the old girl crank, which puts the block on carrying sail in bad weather…too dangerous, you see…had no choice but to steam all the way from Halifax tho' I would have chosen otherwise. Anyway, we're putting that to right 'cos I've got a shipment of Scotian grinding-stones and crates of brownstone to take to Boston. That's what they're winching into the holds. You can't leave these old paddlers poorly laden. They don't like it. The floats can't get a good purchase on the water if the wheels aren't well immersed. Anyway, I digress…you were saying?"

"Yes, sir…well, it's my lack of money which prevents me from taking a passenger's berth. I'll need to work my passage if you're in agreement."

"That's alright by me. What with you being an acquaintance of Henry, if it were down to me I'd take you to Boston for ten shillings. But the owners insist I levy charges based on an agreed schedule of passenger tariffs. A niggardly bunch they are. I keep thinking I should tell them to go to hell and take my chances elsewhere for this old tub is decrepit. I swear she's close to bursting at her seams and all because the owners won't spend money on her…not even on paint to smarten the old girl's sides. I at least strive to keep things looking shipshape onboard."

It amused William to hear Captain Burns criticise the *Snowgoose*'s owners, on account of niggardliness, when Henry had bad-mouthed his collateral relation for the very same shortcoming.

"I'm allowing three days to reach Boston, departing tomorrow on the afternoon tide," continued Burns. "With favourable conditions we can be waiting in the roads for a pilot come Friday forenoon. Now, when it comes to the galley you'll need to be organised, making preparations for breakfast and firing up the stove by five o'clock. I'll get my steward to take you down there shortly to show you the ropes and introduce you to your pots and pans. Incidentally, we're well provisioned after calling at Halifax and we're taking in fresh bread this afternoon. Tomorrow I require you to be onboard at the beginning of the forenoon watch…eight o'clock…but for now will you join me in a tipple?" asked the skipper. Simultaneously he leant across the chart-room table and grasped a crystal decanter containing some dark, spirituous liquor. "Take it now, man, since the offer won't be there tomorrow. It's not a privilege I extend to members of my crew, though I swear my steward takes the odd, surreptitious glass." He chuckled. "I doubt the sun's over the foreyard yet, but how can a man be expected to tell, what with this wretched mist? We'll just assume it's meant to be." He chuckled again and whilst not waiting on his visitor's response, let the glutinous-looking liquor burble into two whisky glasses. "Get that down you, young Reynolds. It'll put hairs on your chest."

"What is it, sir?" mumbled the recipient as he sniffed at the liquor and caught the strength of it.

"Blackstrap, lad. None of that bad port wine, you understand. Oh, no… good North American blackstrap. Whisky, rum and treacle…what you call molasses. Get it down you…do you the world of good."

That evening William Reynolds began to say his good-byes. It was an emotional time, for although the duration of his acquaintance with Reuben and the two fishermen had been brief, all three had had a profound influence in wresting him away from Halifax and the clutches of H.M.S. *Cygnet*. With Tom and Henry, William downed an early evening farewell drink in the fishermen's regular quayside bar. Later, back in Reuben's lodgings, William had just finished packing his few possessions in a draw-string bag when his negro friend returned from a lengthy day's work, swabbing down fishing boats and mending nets. He brought with him a basket of freshly landed, shucked scallops which were fried and hungrily despatched by both men while William recounted the events of his day. Reuben, in turn, reiterated his feelings of sorrow in seeing someone he now regarded as a friend move on. Yet, as he had implied before, his feelings were tempered by thoughts that William might be enticed – by his own admission - to end up fighting for a just cause.

"I'z afeard I ain't gonna be 'bout t'see y'go, t'morrow, Mister Willum 'cos I'z leavin' early t' 'compn'y de Tanner boy t' Bridgewater," said Reuben, the Tanner boy being the son of the proprietor of a local ship's chandlery. "We'z gwine at six in de chand'ry wagon t' obtain supplies an' I'z be takin' de opportun'ty t' visit Jake's missis. I'z gwine pay her her husbin's share o' your desertin' money."

"Wake me when you're about to leave, my friend," said William, as both he and Reuben were in course of donning their nightshirts. "I need to be onboard the *Snowgoose* by eight o'clock." Moments later each bade the other goodnight. Reuben extinguished his little sperm oil lamp and all was black as ink.

Shortly before six the next morning, William was roused from his slumber by some rough tugging at his shoulder.

"Mister Willum…Mister Willum…I'z havin' to git gwine. Young Mas'r Tanner is ou'side fo' I'z seed de lamps o' de chand'ry wagon from de lof' winna. Remem'er t'write an' tell us zackly how you'z gitten on."

"I will, Reuben…and thank you for all you've done. Good-bye my friend."

They warmly shook hands. Reuben said no more but looked downcast. As he closed the door on his lodgings, William noticed there was a tear or two in the negro's eyes. Later, having attended to his ablutions and partaken of a bowl of oatmeal and some toasted hoe-cake, William prepared to take his leave. As he did so it occurred to him that he was no longer so aware of the reek of fish in Reuben's loft. He had already become accustomed to it. It triggered the thought in him that the time was indeed right to move on. Were he to stay much longer in Lunenburg he would soon become adapted to the place itself and familiarity would foster inertia and the prospect he would never venture far afield. Then, buoyed by that little sense of reassurance and approaching the door, William caught sight of a small envelope lying on the floor, close to the threshold. He bent to pick it up. It bore his name…*Mister William*. Realising that Reuben had left it there, where conspicuousness would ensure he noticed it, William slit open the envelope with his forefinger. It appeared more bulky and shifting than had its content been mere writing paper. He cupped his left hand and tipped it into his palm. Out of the envelope tumbled a collection of small whalebone buttons and a slip of paper on which were scrawled the following words :

Mister William,

Take good care of yourself. It has been a pleasure to make your acquaintance. Please accept these buttons. I thought that when you have made your way in the world and can afford to purchase a gentleman's fine silk vest...I think you call it a waistcoat... you might care to have these whalebone buttons sewn upon it to recall the very start of your new life, here in Lunenburg, in the fall of 1862.

With affectionate regard,

Reuben Miller

P.S. Being a slave nigger in my former life I was not afforded the privilege of being taught how to read or write. It was not permitted on the plantation and were you to defy the forbiddance, you and your teacher (sometimes an older house slave who had acquired the rudiments in more liberal times) could reckon on being sorely punished if caught. So, in anticipation of your imminent departure to Boston, I prevailed upon Mister Henry Jackman to pen this short missive for me. Whereas I apologise for this liberty, I can assure you that the words, with the help of Mister Jackman, fully reflect what I wished to say. – R.

William slipped the buttons and the little message into his bag. As he opened the door and cast a backward glance at the modest quarters that had briefly served as home, his eyes were brimming, much as Reuben's had welled up earlier.

The coastal mist had lifted, courtesy of light nocturnal airs, and on board the *Snowgoose* preparations were well advanced for putting to sea. On this occasion, the second mate, a Cape Breton man by the name of Jed McAllister, was alerted to William's arrival and, in no time, had broadly acquainted the newcomer with the layout of the vessel and some of its idiosyncrasies. Weary men from the morning watch made their way off duty as the next watch was sounded. On the upper deck, boxes of goods from a lighter, lying off the starboard side, had been in course of being passed aft, hand-to-hand. As he walked by in the wake of the second mate – and prior to resumption of this hand-to-hand progression by men of the forenoon watch – William noticed that a box of prayer books – blocks of sandstone scrubbing blocks, not the printed, spiritual kind – had been set down. These, together with two boxes of coir scrubbing brushes, spoke volumes for the Master's insistence upon an impeccable standard of inboard cleanliness. As for Captain Burns, himself, he was said to be ensconced in the chart-room with the first mate, conferring and poring over navigational charts and the *Snowgoose*'s earlier track charts covering the sweep of ocean she was again set to ply. After fifteen minutes or so in the company of Mister McAllister, the second officer received a message that Captain Burns had summoned him to the poop, leaving William in the hands of Will Sweeney, the skipper's steward. It was with Sweeney - who had been instructed to replace McAllister – that William had become acquainted the previous day.

"Now," said Sweeney, "has the officer shown you your sleeping berth?"

"No, not yet."

"Well, for whatever reason, the old man seems to have taken a shine to you. Come with me," whereupon the steward led William below to the berth deck. What confronted William there surprised him, for he was simply not accustomed to what he saw. There was scant sign of hammocks, but then he thought it strange that there was little hammock-netting around the ship's bulwarks and none at the break of the poop. And, of course, there were no great guns, no smooth bores or Armstrongs, those trusty, familiar old bedfellows that one messed and slept between and one immediately associated with the lower deck of a fighting ship. Likewise, that sense of orderliness and discipline rooted in the wearing of uniforms was patently missing. There was little colour about the place, no gold braid, no belted and collared marines with their pipe-clay and red tunics. Orderliness... yes, in the sense of cleanliness derived from the captain's obsession with impeccable appearance; and, of course, the inculcated knowledge that to be caught by the old man – or the first mate, Hodges – dropping litter, would risk a stiff flogging. Looking beneath the fo'c'sle, a sizeable colony of plywood bunks, ranged on either side, appeared to comprise the crew's quarters, whereas amidships, a better grade of bunk, each with a sliding mahogany door, neatly chamfered, was reserved for what Sweeney termed second class travelling passengers. According to the steward there was none of this category at the present time. Some distance aft of these bunks, beyond the paddle wheel housing, was a cluster of cabins.

"The accommodation back there is reserved for first class passengers," remarked Sweeney, "of which, again, there are none." He chuckled. "I suppose there are more sumptuous passenger steamboats in which to take to the ocean. I mean…who, in all honesty, would prefer a decaying and groaning old merchantman that hasn't seen a lick of paint in years? Now, step in here will you," he continued, opening a door on the port side that gave access to a cosy little cabin, like the kind of cuddy one might encounter aft, beneath the poop. "It's surplus to requirements and, while there's no bunk, you'll see there's a hammock hanging from the bulkhead. The old man said you could rest your head here, especially on account of your being accustomed to slinging a hammock. He says that seeing you're temporary you'd probably appreciate some privacy and not wish to take a berth with the men around the fo'c'sle. I think he's got your welfare in mind. You see, collectively they might goad you…what with being English and ex-navy. On the other hand, they might just see you as a bit of a hero…in view of your having taken a run, you understand."

William nodded and, without opening his mouth, murmured in appreciation. *Well done the old man*, he thought to himself, although, given his experience on the *Cygnet* and in the penitentiary, he felt he had served a good apprenticeship in coping with a bit of verbal bullying and repartee.

"Well," exclaimed the steward, "We best be off to the galley. There's no cook's assistant as such but, seeing as you're a bit of a novice in the cook-house, the old man has seen to it that one of the new young deckhands is kept on in the galley to give you help with chores. He's new on board…a youth from Prince Edward Island, by the name of Jim Sherrard. Since we lost the ship's cook in Halifax, he and one of my assistants have done well enough holding things together. As far as I know they gave no cause for complaint, but then this crew are none too particular and seem to eat anything. Oh, and by the way," continued Will Sweeney as an afterthought, simultaneously closing the little cabin door behind him…"in the corner you'll see a flock mattress you can toss in your hammock."

Down in the engine room, late in the forenoon, fires were lighted in the boilers. By the time steam was up, William and Jim Sherrard had finished cleaning the galley traps and were setting about making preparations for supper. The temporary cook even felt a sense of satisfaction that he had passed his first test by conjuring up a dinner for the crew – pea-soup with bread and butter, boiled beef, potatoes and pickles – that had not led to mass mutiny. At two thirty the fires were drawn forward and engines started. Then, unshackled and cast off from her mooring buoy, the *Snowgoose* began proceeding out of Lunenburg harbour under steam, the throb of her old reciprocating engines and the swishy sound of the paddle wheels being enough to entice William on to the upper deck. It was a vantage point that offered him a last look at the little fishing community. And as the jumble of colours that characterised Lunenburg's timber facades receded off the port quarter, there was a touch of sadness in his heart. But it was fleeting. Returning below to the galley, he was soon pre-occupied with his work again, having convinced himself he was doing the right thing. The city of Boston beckoned.

Having stood out of harbour under steam, the weather continued to offer little, if any, incentive to make sail, until, late in the afternoon, the prevailing soft airs picked up to a light to moderate breeze from the north east. By five o'clock, with topgallant sails set, the *Snowgoose* altered course to a south westerly direction; thus, running before a fair wind, trimmed and now in topmast studdingsails, she proceeded on a steady course down the coast. The following day, Wednesday, having passed Cape Sable Island, at the southern extremity of Nova Scotia – and still running before a fair breeze – the old steamship took a more westerly course and began her crossing of the Gulf of Maine.

Late on the Wednesday evening, with a fresh to strong breeze right astern, the *Snowgoose* was making far better speed than she had the previous afternoon under steam. Cleaning up in the galley, after a supper of meat and potato pie, had been time consuming, but William was eager to create a good impression in the eyes of Captain Burns, knowing the pedant he was when it came to cleanliness. He also remained undecided as to whether he might continue to Baltimore and, with that possibility in mind, was loath to upset the old man. It was, consequently, past eight o'clock before William finished hanging up his sparkling pots and pans. And, as he sent Jim away, he realised that without the diligent youth's assistance his lot would have been a good deal more burdensome.

After long hours in the warmth of the galley, the temporary cook was pleased to grab an hour's nap in the privacy of what he now termed his little cuddy. When he woke, he was for a moment disorientated in the pitch black, a moment when, being in a hammock, he was once again back on the *Cygnet*, yet a *Cygnet* devoid of the glow of ship's lanterns and of the sweaty smells and snores of neighbouring shipmates. He quickly came to his senses. The sounds and smells were different. A reek of oil and grease from the engine room pervaded his little space and, despite the weather being relatively calm, the old ship's ribs groaned and strained as if she were any normal vessel caused to heave-to in rough conditions. At least, with the engines closed down, the throb and chunter that otherwise reverberated in William's tiny cabin – on account of it lying close to the wheels' common driving shaft – was noticeably absent. It was between the repetitive creaking of timbers that William detected ripples of laughter. They emanated from up in the fo'c'sle as men at leisure amused themselves with dice, cards and tall stories. He suddenly felt hot and in need of fresh air and took himself up on deck. The heavens were clear and starlit, and the stiff breeze, now fine on the starboard quarter, caused the overhead canvas to crack and billow.

"Good evening. If I'm not mistaken I'm thinking you're the temporary man in the ship's galley. Guess it must be a blessed relief to get away from the heat of the cook-house fire and indulge yourself in a dose of fresh sea air."

Having clambered through the main hatchway, William had for a short spell been distracted by looking aloft at the magnificence of the night sky. He had assumed he was alone in his contemplation. Yes, there were the human sounds of a few duty deck-hands going about their work but, otherwise, William thought his was a solitary, unhurried presence. He looked towards the source of the spoken words. They had come from the mouth of a seaman of ostensibly advanced years, a man with deep-set, rheumy eyes, his countenance profoundly creased and strewn with snowy white stubble. He lent against the starboard gunwale, a lean, flickering cheroot pressed between his lips, his back to the wind. A woolly tam-o'-shanter nestled about his head, in its limpness affording his ears full shelter from the evening chill.

"Yes, that's me...temporary cook," remarked William, having taken a few moments to digest the fact that he had company.

"How far are you travelling, young feller? By the way, do I detect from that accent you're from England?"

"I'm undecided."

"Undecided? Well, you're a queer fish, my boy, if you'll forgive me saying so," remarked the old fellow. "Undecided?! You must come from somewhere...unless you're a male sea nymph that's spirited itself from the depths. Now tell me your skin is scaly."

William laughed when he realised the misunderstanding. "No, no...I'm English for sure. I was referring to my destination. I'm undecided whether I'm only going as far as Boston."

"You could do worse," said the old sailor, "but my understanding is we're then bound for Baltimore, so you might do better."

"Do better? How do you mean?"

"Depends what you're looking for. I'm assuming you're at a loose end, young feller, and I'm thinking you may just be intent on getting a bit of Yankee bounty safely tucked away in your coffers."

"Why would you think that, mister?"

"None of that mister business. Edwin Skelly is my name." He hesitated before continuing. "Intuition. A hunch...no more. You see, my boy, I've seen it all before. Irish...Scots...English fellers...young men going south, looking for something better than they've just tossed aside. I'm told the Yankee private draws one hundred and fifty six dollars a year, but the signing-on bounty can greatly exceed that and there's many an unscrupulous sort...Yankee sailors on the run included...who make a habit of being bounty jumpers. They enlist in one regiment, secure their bounty, then desert and join another unit. Now, I'm not saying that that's in your mind, my boy, for my intuition doesn't stretch that far. But from my limited knowledge, I'd say Baltimore's a better bet if you're looking to join the Union Army."

"Why would that be?" asked the listener, without denying that there might be substance to the other's intuitive conjecture.

"For one thing it's closer to where everything is happening."

"Now that's what a friend of mine told me back in Lunenburg."

"So you're not denying it," exclaimed Skelly with a hearty laugh.

William was not drawn by the old sailor's remark.

"Look, Mister temporary cook...tell me, what's your name for God's sake?"

"William Reynolds."

"Well, William, whether you join the army in one place, as opposed to another, will have little bearing on whether or not you'll see the elephant. Fate will decide that and..."

"See the elephant? What are you talking about?"

"Something big, I guess. It's what those soldier boys hope to encounter when they march off to war. But no...if it were my choice, I'd settle on Baltimore. Like Boston, it's a large port and commercial city but, unlike

Boston, it's one of the principal mustering and staging areas for Federal troops. Large numbers of soldiers are encamped there, waiting to move off with their regiments. And, of course, it's a city well served by the railroad… north, south and…by way of Harpers Ferry…west, to Ohio."

Old Edwin paused for a few seconds during which William listened once again to the noise of billowing canvas aloft and now, over the side, the running, foaming sound of water cast aside at the cutwater. When he resumed his discourse he had changed the subject.

"We're making good progress and by daybreak should be in sight of the Maine coast…Portland way," opined Skelly, as he took a moment to dab his watery eyes with the greasy, red sweat-cloth tied about his neck. "Then there'll be no shortage of landmarks, not least the stone lighthouses which pepper that coast. Usually the Monhegan Island light is first to be seen off the starboard bow, then that on Seguin Island, then the old conical lighthouse on Portland Head…and there are many more. Mind you, running up to Bar Harbor and beyond, it'd be a treacherous place to try and navigate without the blessed pharos."

"You sound as if you know this coast very well," observed William, in an awed tone of voice.

"For years I went to sea on a Yankee schooner out of Gloucester, Massachusetts," came the reply. "We plied this east coast with cargo from Savannah to St John's but I reckon the ports with which I became most familiar lay between Portland and the Chesapeake Bay. That's why I know a bit about places like Baltimore and Philadelphia, my boy. Now, I'm getting tired after working the two dog watches and still need to do a little mending and darning before I turn-in. I suppose I'm an early bird and would always choose the morning watch ahead of the dogs. In my younger days I could always stand a good fag but, since I turned fifty, I've lost my stamina. I guess the answer is not to get old, young feller…just don't get old, but be sure to wallow in youth," murmured Edwin, as he flicked the tail-end of his cheroot into the dark, oily brine. "I'll bid you goodnight, William, and leave you to your thoughts and the night sky."

The following morning, having attended to breakfast, cleaned up and replenished and stoked the galley fire, William felt a touch liverish.

"Jim," he said, addressing his young helper, "I need to take myself up on deck to get some fresh air. Perhaps you could start preparing the vegetables for dinner. You'll need to go below to fetch another sack of carrots. I won't be long."

"As you wish, Mister Reynolds," replied the callow youth with an eagerness as sharp as a barber's razor.

Up on deck, with the coast of Maine now clearly discernible to starboard, William was surprised to find that daylight had ushered in a marked fall in temperature. With the night's stiff breeze having fallen light, the rocky coast looked merciful enough, with no breaking spume or flying spindrift to hamper its visibility. Sailing along the land, the *Snowgoose* was now holding a south south westerly course with royals and flying jib having been hoisted and sheeted home to the breeze on her port quarter. William, for all his queasy feelings, seemed engrossed with his first sight of North America. Sandwiched between a gently lilting, jasper sea and a sky increasingly peppered with shower clouds, the Maine coast seemed possessed of a singular character, its sometimes rugged, sometimes glabrous, rocky outcrops interspersed with bluish-green drifts of pine, spruce and hemlock. A passing deckhand, noticing the rapt expression of interest that pervaded William's features, interrupted his own progression aft. Halting beside the spectator, he raised his right arm to direct his attention to a point fine on the starboard bow.

"We're approaching the Portland Head Light if you're interested. A grand old light. George Washington ordered it to be built and it's stood there for over seventy years." And with that the man was gone about his business with a word or two of thanks ringing in his wake.

William remained on deck inhaling the clear, bracing air. Looking about, it struck him that here, in the offing, there was a good deal more sail in evidence, mainly small vessels such as sloops and ketches and fishing boats, some leaving or putting in to Portland. There were also the ubiquitous schooners on far horizons, bound for more distant places and, way out on the port bow – in the outer offing – a U.S. naval frigate was standing to the northward. When William began feeling the benefit of the sea air and better equipped to return to the galley, the lighthouse was more openly visible, with Portland Head now broad on the starboard bow. He afforded himself a few minutes of dalliance admiring the white, conical tower standing sentinel upon its lumpy, rocky ledge. By the time it was directly abeam of the ship he had dutifully gone below.

Come mid-evening, with the colder weather producing showers of sleet, the *Snowgoose* had rounded Cape Ann and the pair of newly erected lights on Thatcher Island. She then set a steady course south westwards across Massachusetts Bay towards her initial destination, eventually shortening sail and coming to in the roads around dawn. In due course, having flagged for a pilot, the boilers were lighted and by the time steam was up the *Snowgoose* had her navigator on board. Then, with engines easy, and the pilot's cutter towed astern, the old vessel began her progress into Boston's inner harbour and, with some assistance from a couple of doughty steam tugs, was soon secured to a berth on Long Wharf. As William and Jim had toiled in the galley – while the *Snowgoose* waited for her pilot – a message arrived courtesy of Will Sweeney, who had dropped by to collect a pot of coffee for the Captain. It was a heartening missive from the old man himself, congratulating William for his efforts since leaving Lunenburg and requesting that he report to his cabin at ten o'clock.

By a quarter to ten William had ensured that, faced with any inspection, the galley was blessed with such immaculacy it couldn't fail to pass muster. He then re-heated some of the cocoa left over from breakfast and, both he and Jim Sherrard sat awhile over their steaming cups, jawing upon matters of inconsequence. Draining the last dregs from his mug, William thanked the young lad for what he termed his "invaluable assistance" but refrained from bidding him farewell; for he had already resolved to act upon old Edwin Skelly's advice. He would travel on to Baltimore, subject, of course, to the old man's agreement. And, bolstered by that resolve, he clambered out of the main hatchway, on his way aft, on to a deck darkened and wetted by passing showers of wet snow. William was taken aback, momentarily, by what he saw of the inner harbour but refrained from letting himself be distracted, as he pressed ahead for his audience with the Master.

When he reached the skipper's cabin it was Sam Hodges, the first mate, who answered his rap on the door.

"Captain Burns says he'll see you in half an hour," said Hodges. They were words delivered with a surliness that could have been mistaken as chastisement for William having the temerity to bother the old man. For his part, despite knowing the first mate to be a curmudgeonly sort, William felt miffed – after all, he was merely answering the Captain's call. And so he returned to the galley, prepared himself another mug of cocoa and went back on deck to take a look at Boston.

The port and quaysides bustled with activity below austere looking warehousing punctuated by rows of small-paned windows, variable height loading doors and cat-head hoists and pulleys. It was a liveliness derived from eclectic avocation: seamen, longshoremen, costers, officious-looking gentlemen in smart garb, fish-fags, oyster sellers and many others – a constantly changing picture alongside the forest of masts, rigging and limp canvas which crowded Long Wharf. Directly below, on the quayside, a vendor of hot chestnuts shuffled his charred wares over a flaming brazier and appeared to enjoy a brisk spell of business. Out on the water, a Union revenue cutter quietly made her way up the harbour towards the Charlestown Navy Yard. And all this activity was played out to the background noise of wheeling gulls, to the shouts of porters and hucksters and – from beneath an awning on a neighbouring wharf – the strains of military music. The source was the drum and fife band from a regiment encamped at Fort Meigs, its participants revelling in the delivery of stirring patriotic tunes as a welcome diversion from the routine and monotony of daily drills.

After half an hour of being absorbed by the rich tapestry of life upon Long Wharf – during which time the wintry precipitation eased and work got underway unloading *Snowgoose*'s cargo – William again made his way aft to the old man's quarters.

"Come in, William Reynolds," exclaimed the Master, now alone in his cabin. "My apologies for having to send you away earlier. Since tying up in port I seem to have been inundated with wretched bits of paper to fill in and today it seems to have taken forever. Anyway, enough of that. I was wanting to ask you whether you now intend to part company with the *Snowgoose* or whether you wish to accompany us to Baltimore."

"Without a shadow of a doubt, sir, I would dearly like to work my passage to Baltimore," said William. "That's assuming, Captain, you have no objection or, indeed, no misgivings regarding my suitability for the work with which I'd be entrusted."

"Good God, man…no qualms at all. Put it this way…if I can trust you filling the bellies of my crew…and you made a good enough fist of that… then I can surely assign you the task of feeding and watering a herd of animals."

"Thank you, sir."

"Right," said the Captain, determinedly, taking that to be settled. "We're to take onboard a hundred and fifty head of cattle tomorrow forenoon… young bullocks destined to provide fresh meat for Union troopships leaving the Chesapeake. I'm told they're ready for us to load, the cattle drovers from Haverhill having had them penned up on Boston Common for the past two days. I've just sent word that we'll be ready to bring them onboard tomorrow at ten."

"What would you like me to do in the meantime, sir?" said William.

"Nothing my dear fellow. If I could be sure of fair weather I've men enough to handle both ship and bullocks but insufficient were conditions to turn boisterous. Frankly, I can't take the risk, so I'm taking on a few more hands this afternoon. They'll have to set up the cattle pens and stalls and get things organised for feeding and watering the animals. But today you needn't trouble yourself with livestock. Tomorrow will be soon enough. I'd prefer you to get back to the galley and, with young Sherrard's help, rustle up some dinner for the crew. The new cook won't be reporting on time and will need to know the ropes. But once you're done with that, the rest of the day is yours. I'm sure you'd like to take a look at Boston."

★ ★ ★

The following morning dawned clear and frosty, a dusting of snow holding to the *Snowgoose*'s ice-encrusted yards and rigging. With preparations well advanced to receive the livestock on board, William had become cursorily acquainted with the several temporary hands – four in all – who had been signed on to assist with the animals. All were young Bostonians, yet three bore the names Quinn, O'Leary and Collins, leaving only Robert Kinder to lay claim to what might be deemed indigenous ancestry dating back to the time of the Revolutionary War. Conversely, the three-quarters majority, all in their teens, were first generation offspring of Irish immigrants who, in the forties, had been among the earliest to flee the potato famine. One, sixteen year old Collins, overhearing disparaging remarks from O'Leary about the incommodious nature and damp condition of his sleeping-bunk, let it be known that he had been born in steerage during heavy weather. It was a birth conducted in dank, rat-infested conditions to the tune of a howling gale, the violent rush of water through scuppers and hawse-holes, the scream of wind-lashed rigging and – in the blackness – the pitiful cries of hapless wretches afflicted with terror. Although his poor mother had succumbed, he had mercifully survived such dire parturition as well as the remaining journey to Boston. It had rendered him tough, he proudly proclaimed, cocking a chest with a smile and treating O'Leary's complaint with contempt; tough enough, he arrogantly contended, that he'd have taken a berth in the *Snowgoose*'s bilge were he required to do so, and hell to a damp mattress.

The bullocks were loaded without incident at ten o'clock. By midday a pilot had come onboard and, an hour later, the old steamship had cast off from Long Wharf and was proceeding out of harbour past Fort Independence. Once a path through the neighbouring islands had been navigated and the pilot discharged, the engines were shut down and, with a good breeze blowing from directly astern, the *Snowgoose* made what canvas might be drawn as she set a south easterly course towards Cape Cod. For the cattle men, William included, it proved a busy afternoon as they set to work feeding and watering the animals and replenishing the water barrels and scuttle-butts; and for the Englishman, at the tender age of twenty, he almost felt the father figure, labouring among the young Bostonians. At five o'clock, having finished ministering to the needs of the cattle, William and his fellow-helpers were served a welcome supper of Yankee hash and tea, a meal devoid of its expected ration of bread and butter. Instead, it came with Boston pilot bread, an eleventh hour cracker-like substitute mustered from hucksters' bumboats, when – with steam up and the *Snowgoose* about to leave Long Wharf – a steward discovered that dampness had invaded the breadroom. This had blighted most of the soft tack with mildew, a misfortune that proved a source of hilarity to Collins. As he dipped one of the hard tack chips into his bowl of stew, he waggishly quipped that O'Leary had better inspect his bunk linen for the dreaded mould.

Sometime after supper and with a chill, lingering sunset having seemingly prolonged crepuscular progression into night, a shrill cry went up of "light on the starboard bow." An Argus-eyed lookout had spotted the flashing Race Point lighthouse at the northern tip of Cape Cod, an early landmark in the journey south. A short while later William joined his new workmates in the crew's sleeping area below the fo'cs'le, it being the first time he had had the temerity to go for'ard and mix with the men at their evening leisure; for now, relieved of being ship's cook, he was no longer fearful of criticism, which, in any event and on account of his sterling efforts, would have been entirely unwarranted. Furthermore, having quickly gained the respect of the young Bostonians and having regaled them with stories of his time in the Royal Navy, his had become a popular presence among the young men from Massachusetts. He joined them in a hand or two of cards but couldn't concentrate. Tired, yet in the belief that he was on the brink of new adventure – which thought instilled in him a shivery sense of excitement –William retired to his little cuddy at ten o'clock. And, although tingling with that thrill of expectation, there was nevertheless a firm sense of calm and satisfaction in his loins. Pulling his blanket about him, he was soon in the depths of untroubled sleep.

Next morning it was up at five to find the dawn light playing eerily upon Nantucket Island off the starboard beam. The salty air seemed possessed of a greater piquancy here and, overnight, had lost its chill edge, the erstwhile north westerly breeze having fallen light, then variable in direction. By seven o'clock the cattle had been fed and watered whereupon William and the Bostonians partook of a breakfast of oatmeal, pilot bread and coffee before resuming their day's work, commencing with replenishment of the animals' water barrels. With the receding southern coast of Nantucket Island now well astern, the variable light breezes had, by mid-morning, fallen to light airs and, in consequence, the order was given to shorten all plain sail and proceed under steam. With a rising glass and the promise of continuing fine weather, there emerged the real prospect of life aboard the *Snowgoose* settling into a none too rigorous routine; and, in all likelihood, three days would elapse before the old paddle steamer would once again sight landfall, yet not until south of Delaware Bay.

★ ★ ★

It would have been the third day out of Boston. The forenoon had been occupied with the usual chores, relieved by an hour's nap after dinner, while the remainder of the afternoon had been spent giving hay to the cattle and sweeping up. Then, in the wake of supper, William joined young Sherrard and the Bostonians at cards, excepting that Bob Kinder declined and chose to write a letter. After a few hands of napoleon at a penny stake a trick, with whalebone counters masquerading as pennies, William tendered his apologies and retired early. Yet, fatigue and calm state of mind did not contrive to soporiferous effect as it had on that first night out of Boston. Instead, William tossed and turned repeatedly as sleep eluded him, a frustration not aided by the throb and incessant grumble of the steam engines and that still pervading smell of engine room grease and oil. In the end he threw off his blanket, donned his dirty rig and a pair of shoes and went up on deck to clear his head.

Surprisingly, there leaning against the starboard gunwale, in the same fashion as he had loitered late on that second evening out of Lunenburg, was the watery-eyed Edwin Skelly. No cheroot on this occasion. Instead he drew upon a briar pipe. As before, he wore his woolly bonnet and the bright red sweat-cloth about his neck.

"Well, hello, William Reynolds," exclaimed the elder man. "I've seen you around of late, so knew you'd decided to journey on to Baltimore…

and, by jove, I've remembered your name. So, you've decided to enlist after all, eh? I'd have done the same had I been a young man in your shoes."

"Quite probably I will," said William, proving far less guarded on the matter than hitherto. "Strange to meet you once again, Mr Skelly, in similar circumstances… excepting it's much later tonight."

"Funny thing is, I don't make a habit of it. It's the first time I've been up here for a smoke after dark since we last met. Like you, I expect…I just couldn't get to sleep …touch of indigestion. Perhaps we shouldn't have lost you as temporary cook." The old sailor's final sentence was delivered with a wry smile.

Old Edwin's mention of a smoke coincided with a noticeable downdraught. This had the effect, in the prevailing light airs, of lowering to deck level a strong reek of sooty emission from the ship's funnel: a reek that seemed slow to disperse.

"Phew," muttered William, as he unexpectedly felt the effect of being showered in coal smuts and sparks.

"Cheap coal, that's the problem, my lad," retorted Skelly. "At least when you coal in Baltimore you usually get a decent bit of Pennsylvanian anthracite. Shouldn't be too long now…"

"Too long?" queried William.

"Getting to Baltimore. Another day or so and we should be off the Virginia coast and entering the Chesapeake."

"Off the Virginia coast? But isn't Virginia one of the seceded states?"

"It certainly is," said Skelly.

"So aren't we likely to be stopped by the Confederate Navy and our cargo seized?" asked William with a touch of concern in his voice.

"I don't think there's any likelihood of that, my boy. The Union Navy control the Chesapeake. On the other hand, I suspect we'll be boarded by the Federal authorities to verify our credentials. And if you tell them you're bent on enlisting in the Army they might even escort us to Baltimore," said Edwin, jokingly.

★ ★ ★

Late in the afternoon of the fourth day, the *Snowgoose* was back in the offing and in sight of the low, marshy barrier island of Assateague which fringes the Atlantic coast of southern Maryland and Virginia. By daybreak, on the fifth, running past Cape Charles, she altered course to west south west and, by nine o'clock in the forenoon, was steaming very easy using ashes with coals. An hour later, having given her number, she had stopped, drawn her fires, and come to at single anchor in Hampton Roads.

"Since we sail under a foreign flag and circumstances being as they are, in this part of the world, we are to remain here until we receive clearance to proceed to Baltimore," bellowed Captain Burns, who, at eleven o'clock, had called for all hands to muster on deck. "For those of you who don't know, this is common practice. We've received a signal from Fort Monroe that a Federal boat will come alongside in due course. They'll want to see the ship's papers and inspect the cargo. In the meantime continue as normal about your business."

William Reynolds and the Bostonians had already fed and watered their charges, breakfasted and refilled the animals' water butts and, in consequence, were due a break from their toils. While the youngsters opted for a short rest in their bunks, William sauntered aft to get a feel for the lie of the land. It was an extensive, watery panorama. Immediately to the north, off the port quarter, on a promontory terminating in Old Point Comfort, the stone and moated Fort Monroe looked a formidable structure, proudly flying the stars and stripes, its embrasures bristling with armaments. But what seemed more impressive, here in the Roads, at the confluence of Bay and James River, was the multitude of vessels at anchor between the fortress and the little offshore island of Rip Raps. It was an eclectic armada...frigates, corvettes, brigs and schooners, barques, ketches and small lateen-rigged craft. There were naval ships and merchantmen of all types, while almost nonchalantly and undauntedly, a river steamboat ploughed a steady course through the massed flotilla, dark smoke streaming from its twin funnels.

At eleven thirty a Union cutter put out from one of the jetties on the Old Point Comfort side of the fort and came alongside the *Snowgoose*. The officer in charge – resplendent in his distinctive naval frock coat – grasped the manropes and hoisted himself up the boarding ladder, closely followed by two attendants from the lower deck. Once aboard the steamship he was welcomed by Samuel Hodges, the first mate, who led him and his escorts aft for an audience with Captain Burns. Ushered into the chart room, the naval officer politely introduced himself to Jacob Burns as Acting Lieutenant Dalrymple, United States Navy. He immediately began trotting out – parrot-fashion – certain pertinent regulations by which he was obliged to adhere in making his inspection. Yet he was quickly pulled up, in full flow, by the Master of the *Snowgoose*.

"With all due respect, Lieutenant, you can save yourself all that. Not wishing to be rude, you understand, but I'm accustomed to your regulations, having been through all this more than once in the past. Now, I have to hand, all necessary papers that I'm aware you'll need to see," said Burns, beckoning to the several documents laid out on the chart room table. In addition, should you wish to see my ticket and those of the first and second mates, then these can be produced."

"That won't be necessary, Captain," replied Dalrymple with a curt smile.

"Very well. Now…you'll see from the manifest that we're carrying one hundred and fifty bullocks…meat on the hoof, you understand, for the Union troopships departing the port of Baltimore. I'll shut up while you study the paperwork, then, Mister Hodges here, will be pleased to conduct you on your inspection."

"Thank you, Captain Burns. I'm much obliged." The Lieutenant sat himself down at the Captain's invitation and spent a few minutes poring through the several documents. Rising to his feet, he remarked that all appeared satisfactory. "But," he added, "I do appear to be missing the ship's sick list."

"Ah…remiss of me, Lieutenant," said Burns. "Probably because, to my knowledge, we're all hale and hearty," a remark of which Dalrymple didn't appear to see the funny side. "My apologies, Lieutenant. I'll get my steward to chase it up immediately. It'll be waiting for you on your return from inspecting ship and cargo."

By a quarter past midday Mister Dalrymple, his attendants in tow, had completed the inspection. Accompanied throughout by Sam Hodges, the three men were taken back to the chart room where a beaming Captain Burns handed the officer a sick return. It seemed to verify what he had suggested in jest: that there was little troubling the ship's crew where ailments were concerned. The Lieutenant thanked him, perused the paper and with a nod, yet no further comment, placed it on the table. There followed a few moments hesitation on the naval officer's part, during which time he coughed and sneezed and blew his nose, remarking that he had always had an aversion to hay and that, being in the company of such, when passing the animals, had caused his eyes to water. Jacob Burns viewed the episode as little more than a contrived one. In his opinion, Dalrymple's intention was to delay matters, as if to keep him in suspense over the conclusions drawn from his inspection and to underline where the authority lay. Yet, in fairness to Acting Lieutenant Dalrymple, the ability to simply conjure up such a rhinal performance seemed remote.

Once he had regained his composure, the Lieutenant addressed the Captain and his first mate.

"Gentlemen, I am pleased to inform you that, in my assessment, I have found no irregularities. None which might conflict with the regulations currently being enforced by the Federal authorities regarding the movement of merchant shipping and cargo in home waters. In the circumstances, you are cleared to proceed on your journey to Baltimore and I will file my report accordingly on my return to Fort Monroe. However, I will just add a word of warning. Although the United States Navy controls the Chesapeake Bay you should remain wary and alert at all times. Only a few weeks ago a merchantman bound from Baltimore to London was taken and fired by a Rebel boarding party in the Bay. The vessel had dropped anchor at the mouth of the Rappahannock which, with hindsight, appears to have been a foolish thing to do. So don't do anything similar. Make straight for Baltimore. I bid you farewell, Captain Burns."

"Thank you, Lieutenant."

And with that the naval officer spun on his heels and, facing his two subordinates, ushered them out of the chart room door ahead of him. Yet, before Dalrymple shut the door in his wake, he hesitated a moment to address the Captain with a passing comment.

"It's good, Captain, that you're to provide our departing troopships with the means of getting fresh meat. I'm well acquainted with Baltimore and, while I know it's not your concern beyond delivering your cargo, I just hope your bullocks don't get into the hands of those butchers on Hampstead Hill. They seem obsessed with supplying the army and navy with canned meat. All being well the victualling authorities won't let that happen and, where your animals are concerned, our boys will get the chance to stick their teeth into fresh beef." The Lieutenant smiled and was gone.

At two o'clock in the afternoon the *Snowgoose* weighed anchor and, with a favourable stiff breeze springing up, stood out of Hampton Roads and set a course northwards under sail. By late afternoon, with mainsail set and in first reef of topsails, a general air of contentment seemed to settle over the crew of the old steamship as they went about their work. After all, sometime the following day the *Snowgoose* was due to reach Baltimore. Thereafter there was the prospect of a few days elapsing before the old vessel would set sail again, her holds replenished. It meant the likelihood of some cherished shore leave once the bullocks had been disembarked, coaling completed and the upper deck holystoned to a sparkle and, more importantly, to the Master's entire satisfaction. Of course, William Reynolds, with no such obligations, would be first to leave the ship, having worked a free passage and to his fellow workers – the young Bostonians – his state of excitement was palpable. After supper he once again sat with his young friends under the fo'cs'le, where, too high-spirited to concentrate on cards, he channelled his ebullience into recounting more stories about his previous life afloat. As he did so he handed round a bag of sweets he had purchased in the marketplace near Boston's Fanueil Hall.

"Careful," said William, "they're hard enough to break your teeth."

"I know," said Quinn. "Salem Gibraltars. I suppose that's why they're so named." It was a remark which prompted William to talk about his grandfather's time on the Rock, his regiment's later posting to Malta and of his being laid to rest at an early age in the secluded little cemetery at Fort Chambray.

"What has given you the most satisfaction...stewarding, tending to a herd of cattle or cooking grub?" quipped Bob Kinder, as the gathering began to think about turning in.

"Well, not stewarding that's for sure," said William. "Being an Ordinary Seaman in Her Majesty's Navy I was truly under the thumb and I always felt things used to conspire against me when I was on the *Cygnet*. But you mention grub. It's a word which triggers the thought of yet another story...if you can take another before you retire...a story I heard of in my days as a ship's steward's boy on the *Excellent*. Well, the old vessel was moored head and stern in the upper reaches of Portsmouth harbour and we would practice with the big guns on the starboard side, firing over the water in the direction of the town of Fareham. There was never gunnery practice at low tide, since extensive mudflats were exposed across the target area and locals would wade out to recover our shot. They would return this to the ship and earn themselves a bit of money. Anyway, there was a Portsmouth family called Grubb who seemed to hold a monopoly when it came to mudlarking for shot...not that the Grubb family is the subject of the yarn but our shot has a key part in it. It was a well known story that was passed down in the ship's annals and dated from a time before I entered the *Excellent*. There was a grand old country house called Cams Hall that lay back from Fareham Creek. It stood in the direction of our general line of fire, but well outside its range. Well, the mansion was occupied by a cantankerous old man who had little faith in the *Excellent's* gunners. It seems he kept complaining to the Captain that our shot landed irksomely close to his house. Learning of this, three of the men from the Lower Deck appropriated one of the ship's boats and, under cover of darkness, rowed over to Fareham Creek. Carrying spade and shot, they furtively made their way to Cams Hall where they cut a furrow in the old man's lawn and, at the head of the rut, just short of the drawing room window, they placed the round metal shot. Well, you can imagine, there was a real hue and cry from the peppery old man and, while the miscreants confessed to their prank, I think the Captain saw the funny side of it. Barring a stern talking to, they were excused a much stiffer punishment."

The storyteller's final sentence was drowned in ripples of laughter and, seconds later, to goodnight exchanges, William and the Bostonians wearily repaired to their bunks, or, in the former's case, to his little cuddy. As William slung his hammock and donned his nightshirt, it was with the thought that he might never again have cause to sleep in canvas. Tomorrow he would begin to find his way in the city of Baltimore. The thought was enticing, tinged with a little trepidation for the unknown. Coming hot on the heels of that other defining moment in his life – his parting company with the *Cygnet* – this promised to be another momentous occasion, excepting now he was on his own. There would be no Reuben Miller, no Tom or Henry, no new-found friends from the *Snowgoose*. The attraction of Union bounty money loomed large in his thoughts. Equally, there came again that deep-seated, long-held notion of becoming a soldier.

Lightning Source UK Ltd.
Milton Keynes UK
UKOW06f0315131015

260413UK00004B/77/P

9 780993 336904